FOUR PAST MIDNIGHT

FOUR PAST

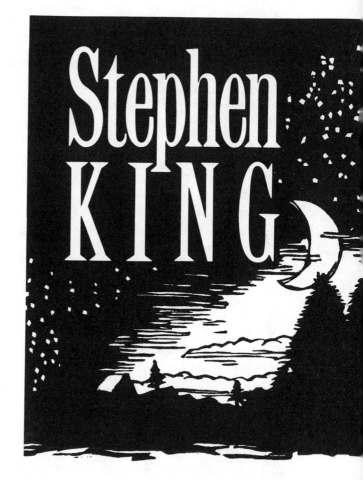

MIDNIGHT

VIKING

VIKING
Published by the Penguin Group
Viking Penguin, a division of Penguin Books USA Inc.,
375 Hudson Street, New York, New York 10014, U.S.A.
Penguin Books Ltd, 27 Wrights Lane,
London W8 5TZ, England
Penguin Books Australia Ltd, Ringwood,
Victoria, Australia
Penguin Books Canada Ltd, 2801 John Street,
Markham, Ontario, Canada L3R 1B4
Penguin Books (N.Z.) Ltd, 182–190 Wairau Road,
Auckland 10, New Zealand

Penguin Books Ltd, Registered Offices:
Harmondsworth, Middlesex, England

First published in 1990 by Viking Penguin,
a division of Penguin Books USA Inc.

10 9 8 7 6 5 4 3 2 1

Grateful acknowledgment is made for permission
to reprint an excerpt from "In the Midnight
Hour" by Wilson Pickett and Steve Cropper.
© 1966 Cotillion Music, Inc. & East/Memphis
Music Corp. All rights on behalf of Cotillion
Music, Inc. administered by
Warner-Tamerlane Publishing Corp.
All rights reserved. Used by permission.

Library of Congress catalog card number 90–50046
ISBN 0-670-83538-2

(CIP data available)

Printed in the United States of America
Composition by NK Graphics, Keene, New Hampshire
Set in Garamond No. 3 and Latin Bold Extra Condensed
Designed by Amy Hill
Illustrations by Lars Hokanson

I*n the desert*
I saw a creature, naked, bestial,
Who, squatting upon the ground,
Held his heart in his hands,
And ate of it.

I said, "Is it good, friend?"
"It is bitter—bitter," he answered;
"But I like it
Because it is bitter
And because it is my heart."
                              —*Stephen Crane*

I*'m gonna kiss you, girl, and hold ya,*
I'm gonna do all the things I told ya
In the midnight hour.
                              —*Wilson Pickett*

CONTENTS

STRAIGHT UP MIDNIGHT

A N

I N T R O D U C T O R Y

N O T E

Well, look at this—we're all here. We made it back again. I hope you're half as happy to be here as I am. Just saying that reminds me of a story, and since telling stories is what I do for a living (and to keep myself sane), I'll pass this one along.

Earlier this year—I'm writing this in late July of 1989—I was crashed out in front of the TV, watching the Boston Red Sox play the Milwaukee Brewers. Robin Yount of the Brewers stepped to the plate, and the Boston commentators began marvelling at the fact that Yount was still in his early thirties. "Sometimes it seems that Robin helped Abner Doubleday lay down the first set of foul lines," Ned Martin said as Yount stepped into the box to face Roger Clemens.

"Yep," Joe Castiglione agreed. "He came to the Brewers right out of high school, I think—he's been playing for them since 1974."

I sat up so fast I nearly spilled a can of Pepsi-Cola all over myself. *Wait a minute!* I was thinking. *Wait just a goddam minute! I published my first book in 1974! That wasn't so long ago! What's this shit about helping Abner Doubleday put down the first set of foul lines?*

Then it occurred to me that the perception of how time passes— a subject which comes up again and again in the stories which follow—is a highly individual thing. It's true that the publication of *Carrie* in the spring of 1974 (it was published, in fact, just two days before baseball season began and a teenager named Robin Yount played his first game for the Milwaukee Brewers) doesn't seem like a long time ago to me subjectively—just a quick glance back over the shoulder, in fact—but there are other ways to count the years, and some of them suggest that fifteen years can be a long time, indeed.

In 1974 Gerald Ford was President and the Shah was still running the show in Iran. John Lennon was alive, and so was Elvis Presley. Donny Osmond was singing with his brothers and sisters in a high, piping voice. Home video cassette recorders had been invented but could be purchased in only a few test markets. Insiders predicted that when they became widely available, Sony's Beta-format machines would quickly stomp the rival format, known as VHS, into the ground. The idea that people might soon be renting popular movies as they had once rented popular novels at lending libraries was still over the horizon. Gasoline prices had risen to unthinkable highs: forty-eight cents a gallon for regular, fifty-five cents for unleaded.

The first white hairs had yet to make their appearance on my head and in my beard. My daughter, now a college sophomore, was four. My older son, who is now taller than I am, plays the blues harp, and sports luxuriant shoulder-length Sammy Hagar locks, had just been promoted to training pants. And my younger son, who now pitches and plays first base for a championship Little League team, would not be born for another three years.

Time has this funny, plastic quality, and everything that goes around comes around. When you get on the bus, you think it won't be taking you far—across town, maybe, no further than that—and all at once, holy shit! You're halfway across the next continent. Do you find the metaphor a trifle naive? So do I, and the hell of it is just this: it doesn't matter. The essential conundrum of time is so perfect that even such jejune observations as the one I have just made retain an odd, plangent resonance.

One thing hasn't changed during those years—the major reason, I suppose, why it sometimes seems to me (and probably to Robin Yount as well) that no time has passed at all. I'm still doing the same thing: writing stories. And it is still a great deal more than what I know; it is still what I love. Oh, don't get me wrong—I love my wife and I love my children, but it's still a pleasure to find these peculiar side roads, to go down them, to see who lives there, to see what they're doing and who they're doing it to and maybe even why. I still love the strangeness of it, and those gorgeous moments when the pictures come clear and the events begin to make a pattern. There is always a tail to the tale. The beast is quick and I sometimes miss my grip, but when I *do* get it, I hang on tight . . . and it feels fine.

When this book is published, in 1990, I will have been sixteen years in the business of make-believe. Halfway through those years, long after I had become, by some process I still do not fully understand, America's literary boogeyman, I published a book called *Different Seasons.* It was a collection of four previously unpublished novellas, three of which were not horror stories. The publisher accepted this book in good heart but, I think, with some mental reservations as well. I know I had some. As it turned out, neither of us had to worry. Sometimes a writer will publish a book which is just naturally lucky, and *Different Seasons* was that way for me.

One of the stories, "The Body," became a movie (*Stand By Me*) which enjoyed a successful run . . . the first really successful film to be made from a work of mine since *Carrie* (a movie which came out back when Abner Doubleday and you-know-who were laying down those foul lines). Rob Reiner, who made *Stand By Me,* is one of the bravest, smartest filmmakers I have ever met, and I'm proud of my association with him. I am also amused to note that the company Mr. Reiner formed following the success of *Stand By Me* is Castle Rock Productions . . . a name with which many of my longtime readers will be familiar.

The critics, by and large, also liked *Different Seasons.* Almost all of them would napalm one particular novella, but since each of them picked a different story to scorch, I felt I could disregard them all with impunity . . . and I did. Such behavior is not always possible; when most of the reviews of *Christine* suggested it was a really dreadful piece of work, I came to the reluctant decision that it probably *wasn't* as good as I had hoped (that, however, did not stop me from cashing the royalty checks). I know writers who claim not to read their notices, or not to be hurt by the bad ones if they do, and I actually believe two of these individuals. I'm one of the other kind—I obsess over the possibility of bad reviews and brood over them when they come. But they don't get me down for long; I just kill a few children and old ladies, and then I'm right as a trivet again.

Most important, the *readers* liked *Different Seasons.* I don't remember a single correspondent from that time who scolded me for writing something that wasn't horror. Most readers, in fact, wanted to tell me that one of the stories roused their emotions in some way, made them think, made them *feel,* and those letters are the *real* payback for the days (and there are a lot of them) when the words come hard and inspiration seems thin or even nonexistent. God bless and keep Constant Reader; the mouth can speak, but there is no tale unless there is a sympathetic ear to listen.

1982, that was. The year the Milwaukee Brewers won their only American League pennant, led by—yes, you got it—Robin Yount. Yount hit .331 that year, bashed twenty-nine home runs, and was named the American League's Most Valuable Player.

It was a good year for both us old geezers.

Different Seasons was not a planned book; it just happened. The four long stories in it came out at odd intervals over a period of five years, stories which were too long to be published as short stories and just a little too short to be books on their own. Like pitching a no-hitter or batting for the cycle (getting a single, double, triple, and home run all in the same ball game), it was not so much a feat as a kind of statistical oddity. I took great pleasure in its success and acceptance, but I also felt a clear sense of regret when the manuscript was finally turned in to The Viking Press. I knew it was good; I also knew that I'd probably never publish another book exactly like it in my life.

If you're expecting me to say *Well, I was wrong,* I must disappoint you. The book you are holding is quite different from the earlier book. *Different Seasons* consisted of three "mainstream" stories and one tale of the supernatural; all four of the tales in this book are tales of horror. They are, by and large, a little longer than the stories in *Different Seasons,* and they were written for the most part during the two years when I was supposedly retired. Perhaps they are different because they came from a mind which found itself turning, at least temporarily, to darker subjects.

Time, for instance, and the corrosive effects it can have on the human heart. The past, and the shadows it throws upon the present—shadows where unpleasant things sometimes grow and even more unpleasant things hide . . . and grow fat.

Yet not all of my concerns have changed, and most of my convictions have only grown stronger. I still believe in the resilience of the human heart and the essential validity of love; I still believe that connections between people can be made and that the spirits which inhabit us sometimes touch. I still believe that the cost of those connections is horribly, outrageously high . . . and I still believe that the value received far outweighs the price which must be paid. I still believe, I suppose, in the coming of the White and in finding a place to make a stand . . . and defending that place to the death. They are old-fashioned concerns and beliefs, but I would be a liar if I did not admit I still own them. And that they still own me.

I still love a good story, too. I love hearing one, and I love telling one. You may or may not know (or care) that I was paid a great deal of money to publish this book and the two which will follow it, but if you do know or care, you should also know that I wasn't paid a cent for *writing* the stories in the book. Like anything else that happens on its own, the act of writing is beyond currency. Money is great stuff to have, but when it comes to the act of creation, the best thing is not to think of money too much. It constipates the whole process.

The way I tell my stories has also changed a little, I suppose (I hope I've gotten better at it, but of course that is something each reader should and will judge for himself), but that is only to be expected. When the Brewers won the pennant in 1982, Robin Yount was playing shortstop. Now he's in center field. I suppose that means he's slowed down a little . . . but he still catches almost everything that's hit in his direction.

That will do for me. That will do just fine.

Because a great many readers seem curious about where stories come from, or wonder if they fit into a wider scheme the writer may be pursuing, I have prefaced each of these with a little note about how it came to be written. You may be amused by these notes, but you needn't read them if you don't want to; this is not a school assignment, thank God, and there will be no pop quiz later.

Let me close by saying again how good it is to be here, alive and well and talking to you once more . . . and how good it is to know that *you* are still *there,* alive and well and waiting to go to some other place—a place where, perhaps, the walls have eyes and the trees have ears and something *really* unpleasant is trying to find its way out of the attic and downstairs, to where the people are. That thing still interests me . . . but I think these days that the people who may or may not be listening for it interest me more.

Before I go, I ought to tell you how that baseball game turned out. The Brewers ended up beating the Red Sox. Clemens struck Robin Yount out on Yount's first at-bat . . . but the second time up, Yount (who helped Abner Doubleday lay out the first foul lines, according to Ned Martin) banged a double high off the Green Monster in left field and drove home two runs.

Robin isn't done playing the game just yet, I guess.

Me, either.

Bangor, Maine
July, 1989

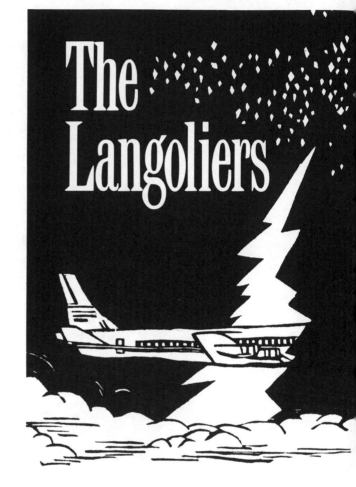

The Langoliers

THIS IS FOR JOE,
ANOTHER WHITE-
KNUCKLE FLIER.

ONE PAST MIDNIGHT

A NOTE ON "THE
LANGOLIERS"

Stories come at different times and places for me—in the car, in the shower, while walking, even while standing around at parties. On a couple of occasions, stories have come to me in dreams. But it's very rare for me to write one as soon as the idea comes, and I don't keep an "idea notebook." Not writing ideas down is an exercise in self-preservation. I get a lot of them, but only a small percentage are any good, so I tuck them all into a kind of mental file. The bad ones eventually self-destruct in there, like the tape from Control at the beginning of every *Mission: Impossible* episode. The good ones don't do that. Every now and then, when I open the file drawer to peek at what's left inside, this small handful of ideas looks up at me, each with its own bright central image.

With "The Langoliers," that image was of a woman pressing her hand over a crack in the wall of a commercial jetliner.

It did no good to tell myself I knew very little about commercial aircraft; I did exactly that, but the image was there every time I opened the file cabinet to dump in another idea, nevertheless. It got so I could even smell that woman's perfume (it was L'Envoi), see her green eyes, and hear her rapid, frightened breathing.

One night, while I was lying in bed, on the edge of sleep, I realized this woman was a ghost.

I remember sitting up, swinging my feet out onto the floor, and turning on the light. I sat that way for a little while, not thinking about much of anything . . . at least on top. Underneath, however, the guy who really runs this job for me was busy clearing his work-space and getting ready to start up all his machines again. The next day, I—or he—began writing this story. It took about a month, and it came the most easily of all the stories in this book, layering itself sweetly and naturally as it went along. Once in awhile both stories and babies arrive in the world almost without labor pains, and this story was like that. Because it had an apocalyptic feel similar to an earlier novella of mine called "The Mist," I headed each chapter in the same old-fashioned, rococo way. I came out of this one feeling almost as good about it as I did going in . . . a rare occurrence.

I'm a lazy researcher, but I tried very hard to do my home-work this time. Three pilots—Michael Russo, Frank Soares, and Douglas Damon—helped me to get my facts straight and keep them straight. They were real sports, once I promised not to break anything.

Have I gotten everything right? I doubt it. Not even the great Daniel Defoe did that; in *Robinson Crusoe,* our hero strips naked, swims out to the ship he has recently escaped . . . and then fills up his pockets with items he will need to stay alive on his desert island. And then there is the novel (title and author will be mercifully omitted here) about the New York subway system where the writer apparently mistook the motormen's cubicles for public toilets.

My standard *caveat* goes like this: for what I got right, thank Messrs. Russo, Soares, and Damon. For what I got wrong, blame me. Nor is the statement one of hollow politeness. Factual mistakes usually result from a failure to ask the right question and not from erroneous information. I *have* taken a liberty or two with the airplane you will shortly be entering; these liberties are small, and seemed necessary to the course of the tale.

Well, that's enough from me; step aboard.

Let's fly the unfriendly skies.

CHAPTER ONE

*BAD NEWS FOR CAPTAIN
ENGLE. THE LITTLE BLIND
GIRL. THE LADY'S SCENT.
THE DALTON GANG
ARRIVES IN TOMBSTONE.
THE STRANGE PLIGHT OF
FLIGHT 29.*

1

Brian Engle rolled the American Pride L1011 to a stop at Gate 22 and flicked off the FASTEN SEATBELT light at exactly 10:14 P.M. He let a long sigh hiss through his teeth and unfastened his shoulder harness.

He could not remember the last time he had been so relieved—and so tired—at the end of a flight. He had a nasty, pounding headache, and his plans for the evening were firmly set. No drink in the pilots' lounge, no dinner, not even a bath when he got back to Westwood. He intended to fall into bed and sleep for fourteen hours.

American Pride's Flight 7—Flagship Service from Tokyo to Los

Angeles—had been delayed first by strong headwinds and then by typical congestion at LAX . . . which was, Engle thought, arguably America's worst airport, if you left out Logan in Boston. To make matters worse, a pressurization problem had developed during the latter part of the flight. Minor at first, it had gradually worsened until it was scary. It had almost gotten to the point where a blowout and explosive decompression could have occurred . . . and had mercifully grown no worse. Sometimes such problems suddenly and mysteriously stabilized themselves, and that was what had happened this time. The passengers now disembarking just behind the control cabin had not the slightest idea how close they had come to being people *pâté* on tonight's flight from Tokyo, but Brian knew . . . and it had given him a whammer of a headache.

"This bitch goes right into diagnostic from here," he told his co-pilot. "They know it's coming and what the problem is, right?"

The co-pilot nodded. "They don't like it, but they know."

"I don't give a shit what they like and what they don't like, Danny. We came close tonight."

Danny Keene nodded. He knew they had.

Brian sighed and rubbed a hand up and down the back of his neck. His head ached like a bad tooth. "Maybe I'm getting too old for this business."

That was, of course, the sort of thing anyone said about his job from time to time, particularly at the end of a bad shift, and Brian knew damned well he wasn't too old for the job—at forty-three, he was just entering prime time for airline pilots. Nevertheless, tonight he almost believed it. God, he was tired.

There was a knock at the compartment door; Steve Searles, the navigator, turned in his seat and opened it without standing up. A man in a green American Pride blazer was standing there. He looked like a gate agent, but Brian knew he wasn't. It was John (or maybe it was James) Deegan, Deputy Chief of Operations for American Pride at LAX.

"Captain Engle?"

"Yes?" An internal set of defenses went up, and his headache flared. His first thought, born not of logic but of strain and weariness, was that they were going to try and pin responsibility for the leaky aircraft on him. Paranoid, of course, but he was in a paranoid frame of mind.

"I'm afraid I have some bad news for you, Captain."

"Is this about the leak?" Brian's voice was too sharp, and a few of the disembarking passengers glanced around, but it was too late to do anything about that now.

Deegan was shaking his head. "It's your wife, Captain Engle."

For a moment Brian didn't have the foggiest notion what the man was talking about and could only sit there, gaping at him and feeling exquisitely stupid. Then the penny dropped. He meant Anne, of course.

"She's my ex-wife. We were divorced eighteen months ago. What about her?"

"There's been an accident," Deegan said. "Perhaps you'd better come up to the office."

Brian looked at him curiously. After the last three long, tense hours, all of this seemed strangely unreal. He resisted an urge to tell Deegan that if this was some sort of *Candid Camera* bullshit, he could go fuck himself. But of course it wasn't. Airlines brass weren't into pranks and games, especially at the expense of pilots who had just come very close to having nasty midair mishaps.

"What about Anne?" Brian heard himself asking again, this time in a softer voice. He was aware that his co-pilot was looking at him with cautious sympathy. "Is she all right?"

Deegan looked down at his shiny shoes and Brian knew that the news was very bad indeed, that Anne was a lot more than not all right. Knew, but found it impossible to believe. Anne was only thirty-four, healthy, and careful in her habits. He had also thought on more than one occasion that she was the only completely sane driver in the city of Boston . . . perhaps in the whole state of Massachusetts.

Now he heard himself asking something else, and it was really like that—as if some stranger had stepped into his brain and was using his mouth as a loudspeaker. "Is she dead?"

John or James Deegan looked around, as if for support, but there was only a single flight attendant standing by the hatch, wishing the deplaning passengers a pleasant evening in Los Angeles and glancing anxiously toward the cockpit every now and then, probably worried about the same thing that had crossed Brian's mind—that the crew was for some reason to be blamed for the slow leak which had made the last few hours of the flight such a nightmare. Deegan was on his own. He looked at Brian again and nodded. "Yes—I'm afraid she is. Would you come with me, Captain Engle?"

2

At quarter past midnight, Brian Engle was settling into seat 5A of American Pride's Flight 29—Flagship Service from Los Angeles to Boston. In fifteen minutes or so, that flight known to transcontinental travelers as the red-eye would be airborne. He remembered thinking earlier that if LAX wasn't the most dangerous commercial airport in America, then Logan was. Through the most unpleasant of coincidences, he would now have a chance to experience both places within an eight-hour span of time: into LAX as the pilot, into Logan as a deadheading passenger.

His headache, now a good deal worse than it had been upon landing Flight 7, stepped up another notch.

A fire, he thought. *A goddamned fire. What happened to the smoke-detectors, for Christ's sake? It was a brand-new building!*

It occurred to him that he had hardly thought about Anne at all for the last four or five months. During the first year of the divorce, she was all he *had* thought about, it seemed—what she was doing, what she was wearing, and, of course, who she was seeing. When the healing finally began, it had happened very fast . . . as if he had been injected with some spirit-reviving antibiotic. He had read enough about divorce to know what that reviving agent usually was: not an antibiotic but another woman. The rebound effect, in other words.

There had been no other woman for Brian—at least not yet. A few dates and one cautious sexual encounter (he had come to believe that all sexual encounters outside of marriage in the Age of AIDS were cautious), but no other woman. He had simply . . . healed.

Brian watched his fellow passengers come aboard. A young woman with blonde hair was walking with a little girl in dark glasses. The little girl's hand was on the blonde's elbow. The woman murmured to her charge, the girl looked immediately toward the sound of her voice, and Brian understood she was blind—it was something in the gesture of the head. Funny, he thought, how such small gestures could tell so much.

Anne, he thought. *Shouldn't you be thinking about Anne?*

But his tired mind kept trying to slip away from the subject of Anne—Anne, who had been his wife, Anne, who was the only woman he had ever struck in anger, Anne who was now dead.

He supposed he could go on a lecture tour; he would talk to

groups of divorced men. Hell, divorced women as well, for that matter. His subject would be divorce and the art of forgetfulness.

Shortly after the fourth anniversary is the optimum time for divorce, he would tell them. *Take my case. I spent the following year in purgatory, wondering just how much of it was my fault and how much was hers, wondering how right or wrong it was to keep pushing her on the subject of kids—that was the big thing with us, nothing dramatic like drugs or adultery, just the old kids-versus-career thing—and then it was like there was an express elevator inside my head, and Anne was in it, and down it went.*

Yes. Down it had gone. And for the last several months, he hadn't really thought of Anne at all . . . not even when the monthly alimony check was due. It was a very reasonable, very civilized amount; Anne had been making eighty thousand a year on her own before taxes. His lawyer paid it, and it was just another item on the monthly statement Brian got, a little two-thousand-dollar item tucked between the electricity bill and the mortgage payment on the condo.

He watched a gangly teenaged boy with a violin case under his arm and a *yarmulke* on his head walk down the aisle. The boy looked both nervous and excited, his eyes full of the future. Brian envied him.

There had been a lot of bitterness and anger between the two of them during the last year of the marriage, and finally, about four months before the end, it had happened: his hand had said go before his brain could say no. He didn't like to remember that. She'd had too much to drink at a party, and she had really torn into him when they got home.

Leave me alone about it, Brian. Just leave me alone. No more talk about kids. If you want a sperm-test, go to a doctor. My job is advertising, not baby-making. I'm so tired of all your macho bullshit—

That was when he had slapped her, hard, across the mouth. The blow had clipped the last word off with brutal neatness. They had stood looking at each other in the apartment where she would later die, both of them more shocked and frightened than they would ever admit (except maybe now, sitting here in seat 5A and watching Flight 29's passengers come on board, he *was* admitting it, finally admitting it to himself). She had touched her mouth, which had started to bleed. She held out her fingers toward him.

You hit me, she said. It was not anger in her voice but wonder. He had an idea it might have been the first time anyone had ever laid an angry hand upon any part of Anne Quinlan Engle's body.

Yes, he had said. *You bet. And I'll do it again if you don't shut up. You're not going to whip me with that tongue of yours anymore, sweetheart. You better put a padlock on it. I'm telling you for your own good. Those days are over. If you want something to kick around the house, buy a dog.*

The marriage had crutched along for another few months, but it had really ended in that moment when Brian's palm made brisk contact with the side of Anne's mouth. He had been provoked—God knew he had been provoked—but he still would have given a great deal to take that one wretched second back.

As the last passengers began to trickle on board, he found himself also thinking, almost obsessively, about Anne's perfume. He could recall its fragrance exactly, but not the name. What had it been? Lissome? Lithesome? Lithium, for God's sake? It danced just beyond his grasp. It was maddening.

I miss her, he thought dully. *Now that she's gone forever, I miss her. Isn't that amazing?*

Lawnboy? Something stupid like that?

Oh stop it, he told his weary mind. *Put a cork in it.*

Okay, his mind agreed. *No problem; I can quit. I can quit anytime I want. Was it maybe Lifebuoy? No—that's soap. Sorry. Lovebite? Lovelorn?*

Brian snapped his seatbelt shut, leaned back, closed his eyes, and smelled a perfume he could not quite name.

That was when the flight attendant spoke to him. Of course: Brian Engle had a theory that they were taught—in a highly secret postgraduate course, perhaps called Teasing the Geese—to wait until the passenger closed his or her eyes before offering some not-quite-essential service. And, of course, they were to wait until they were reasonably sure the passenger was asleep before waking him to ask if he would like a blanket or a pillow.

"Pardon me . . ." she began, then stopped. Brian saw her eyes go from the epaulets on the shoulders of his black jacket to the hat, with its meaningless squiggle of scrambled eggs, on the empty seat beside him.

She rethought herself and started again.

"Pardon me, Captain, would you like coffee or orange juice?" Brian was faintly amused to see he had flustered her a little. She gestured toward the table at the front of the compartment, just below the small rectangular movie screen. There were two ice-buckets on the table. The slender green neck of a wine bottle poked out of each. "Of course, I also have champagne."

Engle considered

(Love Boy that's not it close but no cigar)

the champagne, but only briefly. "Nothing, thanks," he said. "And no in-flight service. I think I'll sleep all the way to Boston. How's the weather look?"

"Clouds at 20,000 feet from the Great Plains all the way to Boston, but no problem. We'll be at thirty-six. Oh, and we've had reports of the aurora borealis over the Mojave Desert. You might want to stay awake for that."

Brian raised his eyebrows. "You're kidding. The aurora borealis over California? And at this time of year?"

"That's what we've been told."

"Somebody's been taking too many cheap drugs," Brian said, and she laughed. "I think I'll just snooze, thanks."

"Very good, Captain." She hesitated a moment longer. "You're the captain who just lost his wife, aren't you?"

The headache pulsed and snarled, but he made himself smile. This woman—who was really no more than a girl—meant no harm. "She was my ex-wife, but otherwise, yes. I am."

"I'm awfully sorry for your loss."

"Thank you."

"Have I flown with you before, sir?"

His smile reappeared briefly. "I don't think so. I've been on overseas for the past four years or so." And because it seemed somehow necessary, he offered his hand. "Brian Engle."

She took it. "Melanie Trevor."

Engle smiled at her again, then leaned back and closed his eyes once more. He let himself drift, but not sleep—the pre-flight announcements, followed by the take-off roll, would only wake him up again. There would be time enough to sleep when they were in the air.

Flight 29, like most red-eye flights, left promptly—Brian reflected that was high on their meager list of attractions. The plane was a 767, a little over half full. There were half a dozen other passengers in first class. None of them looked drunk or rowdy to Brian. That was good. Maybe he really *would* sleep all the way to Boston.

He watched Melanie Trevor patiently as she pointed out the exit doors, demonstrated how to use the little gold cup if there was a pressure loss (a procedure Brian had been reviewing in his own mind, and with some urgency, not long ago), and how to inflate the life vest under the seat. When the plane was airborne, she came by his seat and asked him again if she could get him something to drink. Brian shook his head, thanked her, then pushed the button which caused his seat to recline. He closed his eyes and promptly fell asleep.

He never saw Melanie Trevor again.

3

About three hours after Flight 29 took off, a little girl named Dinah Bellman woke up and asked her Aunt Vicky if she could have a drink of water.

Aunt Vicky did not answer, so Dinah asked again. When there was still no answer, she reached over to touch her aunt's shoulder, but she was already quite sure that her hand would touch nothing but the back of an empty seat, and that was what happened. Dr. Feldman had told her that children who were blind from birth often developed a high sensitivity—almost a kind of radar—to the presence or absence of people in their immediate area, but Dinah hadn't really needed the information. She knew it was true. It didn't always work, but it usually did . . . especially if the person in question was her Sighted Person.

Well, she's gone to the bathroom and she'll be right back, Dinah thought, but she felt an odd, vague disquiet settle over her just the same. She hadn't come awake all at once; it had been a slow process, like a diver kicking her way to the surface of a lake. If Aunt Vicky, who had the window seat, had brushed by her to get to the aisle in the last two or three minutes, Dinah should have felt her.

So she went sooner, she told herself. *Probably she had to Number Two—it's really no big deal, Dinah. Or maybe she stopped to talk with somebody on her way back.*

Except Dinah couldn't hear *anyone* talking in the big airplane's main cabin; only the steady soft drone of the jet engines. Her feeling of disquiet grew.

The voice of Miss Lee, her therapist (except Dinah always thought of her as her blind teacher), spoke up in her head: *You mustn't be afraid to be afraid, Dinah—all children are afraid from time to time, especially in situations that are new to them. That goes double for children who are blind. Believe me, I know.* And Dinah did believe her, because, like Dinah herself, Miss Lee had been blind since birth. *Don't give up your fear . . . but don't give in to it, either. Sit still and try to reason things out. You'll be surprised how often it works.*

Especially in situations that are new to them.

Well, that certainly fit; this was the first time Dinah had ever flown in *anything,* let alone coast to coast in a huge transcontinental jetliner.

Try to reason it out.

Well, she had awakened in a strange place to find her Sighted Person gone. Of course that was scary, even if you knew the absence was only temporary—after all, your Sighted Person couldn't very well decide to pop off to the nearest Taco Bell because she had the munchies when she was shut up in an airplane flying at 37,000 feet. As for the strange silence in the cabin . . . well, this *was* the red-eye, after all. The other passengers were probably sleeping.

All of them? the worried part of her mind asked doubtfully. ALL *of them are sleeping? Can that be?*

Then the answer came to her: the movie. The ones who were awake were watching the in-flight movie. Of course.

A sense of almost palpable relief swept over her. Aunt Vicky had told her the movie was Billy Crystal and Meg Ryan in *When Harry Met Sally . . . ,* and said she planned to watch it herself . . . if she could stay awake, that was.

Dinah ran her hand lightly over her aunt's seat, feeling for her headphones, but they weren't there. Her fingers touched a paperback book instead. One of the romance novels Aunt Vicky liked to read, no doubt—tales of the days when men were men and women weren't, she called them.

Dinah's fingers went a little further and happened on something else—smooth, fine-grained leather. A moment later she felt a zipper, and a moment after that she felt the strap.

It was Aunt Vicky's purse.

Dinah's disquiet returned. The earphones weren't on Aunt Vicky's seat, but her purse was. All the traveller's checks, except for a twenty tucked deep into Dinah's own purse, were in there—Dinah knew, because she had heard Mom and Aunt Vicky discussing them before they left the house in Pasadena.

Would Aunt Vicky go off to the bathroom and leave her purse on the seat? Would she do that when her travelling companion was not only ten, not only asleep, but *blind*?

Dinah didn't think so.

Don't give up your fear . . . but don't give in to it, either. Sit still and try to reason things out.

But she didn't like that empty seat, and she didn't like the silence of the plane. It made perfect sense to her that most of the people would be asleep, and that the ones who were awake would be keeping as quiet as possible out of consideration for the rest, but she still didn't like it. An animal, one with extremely sharp teeth and claws, awakened and started to snarl inside of her head. She knew the name of that animal; it was panic, and if she didn't control it fast, she might do something which would embarrass both her and Aunt Vicky.

When I can see, when the doctors in Boston fix my eyes, I won't have to go through stupid stuff like this.

This was undoubtedly true, but it was absolutely no help to her right *now*.

Dinah suddenly remembered that, after they sat down, Aunt Vicky had taken her hand, folded all the fingers but the pointer under, and then guided that one finger to the side of her seat. The controls were there—only a few of them, simple, easy to remember. There were two little wheels you could use once you put on the headphones—one switched around to the different audio channels; the other controlled the volume. The small rectangular switch controlled the light over her seat. *You won't need that one,* Aunt Vicky said with a smile in her voice. *At least, not yet.* The last one was a square button—when you pushed that one, a flight attendant came.

Dinah's finger touched this button now, and skated over its slightly convex surface.

Do you really want to do this? she asked herself, and the answer came back at once. *Yeah, I do.*

She pushed the button and heard the soft chime. Then she waited.

No one came.

There was only the soft, seemingly eternal whisper of the jet engines. No one spoke. No one laughed (*Guess that movie isn't as funny as Aunt Vicky thought it would be,* Dinah thought). No one coughed. The seat beside her, Aunt Vicky's seat, was still empty, and no flight attendant bent over her in a comforting little envelope of perfume and shampoo and faint smells of make-up to ask Dinah if she could get her something—a snack, or maybe that drink of water.

Only the steady soft drone of the jet engines.

The panic animal was yammering louder than ever. To combat it, Dinah concentrated on focussing that radar gadget, making it into a kind of invisible cane she could jab out from her seat here in the middle of the main cabin. She was good at that; at times, when she concentrated *very* hard, she almost believed she could see through the eyes of others. If she thought about it hard enough, wanted to hard enough. Once she had told Miss Lee about this feeling, and Miss Lee's response had been uncharacteristically sharp. *Sight-sharing is a frequent fantasy of the blind,* she'd said. *Particularly of blind children. Don't ever make the mistake of relying on that feeling, Dinah, or you're apt to find yourself in traction after falling down a flight of stairs or stepping in front of a car.*

So she had put aside her efforts to "sight-share," as Miss Lee had called it, and on the few occasions when the sensation stole over her again—that she was seeing the world, shadowy, wavery, but *there*—through her mother's eyes or Aunt Vicky's eyes, she had tried to get rid of it . . . as a person who fears he is losing his mind will try to block out the murmur of phantom voices. But now she was afraid and so she felt for others, *sensed* for others, and did not find them.

Now the terror was very large in her, the yammering of the panic animal very loud. She felt a cry building up in her throat and clamped her teeth against it. Because it would not come out as a cry, or a yell; if she let it out, it would exit her mouth as a fireball scream.

I won't scream, she told herself fiercely. *I won't scream and embarrass Aunt Vicky. I won't scream and wake up all the ones who are asleep and scare all the ones who are awake and they'll all come running and say look at the scared little girl, look at the scared little blind girl.*

But now that radar sense—that part of her which evaluated all sorts of vague sensory input and which sometimes *did* seem to see through the eyes of others (no matter what Miss Lee said)—was adding to her fear rather than alleviating it.

Because that sense was telling her there was *nobody* within its circle of effectiveness.

Nobody at all.

4

Brian Engle was having a very bad dream. In it, he was once again piloting Flight 7 from Tokyo to L.A., but this time the leak was much worse. There was a palpable feeling of doom in the cockpit; Steve Searles was weeping as he ate a Danish pastry.

If you're so upset, how come you're eating? Brian asked. A shrill, teakettle whistling had begun to fill the cockpit—the sound of the pressure leak, he reckoned. This was silly, of course—leaks were almost always silent until the blowout occurred—but he supposed in dreams anything was possible.

Because I love these things, and I'm never going to get to eat another one, Steve said, sobbing harder than ever.

Then, suddenly, the shrill whistling sound stopped. A smiling, relieved flight attendant—it was, in fact, Melanie Trevor—appeared to tell him the leak had been found and plugged. Brian got up and followed her through the plane to the main cabin, where Anne Quinlan Engle, his ex-wife, was standing in a little alcove from which the seats had been removed. Written over the window beside her was the cryptic and somehow ominous phrase SHOOTING STARS ONLY. It was written in red, the color of danger.

Anne was dressed in the dark-green uniform of an American Pride flight attendant, which was strange—she was an advertising executive with a Boston agency, and had always looked down her narrow, aristocratic nose at the stews with whom her husband flew. Her hand was pressed against a crack in the fuselage.

See, darling? she said proudly. *It's all taken care of. It doesn't even matter that you hit me. I have forgiven you.*

Don't do that, Anne! he cried, but it was already too late. A fold appeared in the back of her hand, mimicking the shape of the crack in the fuselage. It grew deeper as the pressure differential sucked her hand relentlessly outward. Her middle finger went through first, then the ring finger, then the first finger and her pinky. There was a brisk popping sound, like a champagne cork being drawn by an overeager waiter, as her entire hand was pulled through the crack in the airplane.

Yet Anne went on smiling.

It's L'Envoi, darling, she said as her arm began to disappear. Her hair was escaping the clip which held it back and blowing around her face in a misty cloud. *It's what I've always worn, don't you remember?*

He did . . . now he did. But now it didn't matter.

Anne, come back! he screamed.

She went on smiling as her arm was sucked slowly into the emptiness outside the plane. *It doesn't hurt at all, Brian—believe me.*

The sleeve of her green American Pride blazer began to flutter, and Brian saw that her flesh was being pulled out through the crack in a thickish white ooze. It looked like Elmer's Glue.

L'Envoi, remember? Anne asked as she was sucked out through the crack, and now Brian could hear it again—that sound which the poet James Dickey once called "the vast beast-whistle of space." It grew steadily louder as the dream darkened, and at the same time it began to broaden. To become not the scream of wind but that of a human voice.

Brian's eyes snapped open. He was disoriented by the power of the dream for a moment, but only a moment—he was a professional in a high-risk, high-responsibility job, a job where one of the absolute prerequisites was fast reaction time. He was on Flight 29, not Flight 7, not Tokyo to Los Angeles but Los Angeles to Boston, where Anne was already dead—not the victim of a pressure leak but of a fire in her Atlantic Avenue condominium near the waterfront. But the sound was still there.

It was a little girl, screaming shrilly.

5

"Would somebody speak to me, please?" Dinah Bellman asked in a low, clear voice. "I'm sorry, but my aunt is gone and I'm blind."

No one answered her. Forty rows and two partitions forward, Captain Brian Engle was dreaming that his navigator was weeping and eating a Danish pastry.

There was only the continuing drone of the jet engines.

The panic overshadowed her mind again, and Dinah did the only thing she could think of to stave it off: she unbuckled her seatbelt, stood up, and edged into the aisle.

"Hello?" she asked in a louder voice. "Hello, *anybody!*"

There was still no answer. Dinah began to cry. She held onto herself grimly, nonetheless, and began walking forward slowly along the portside aisle. *Keep count, though,* part of her mind warned frantically. *Keep count of how many rows you pass, or you'll get lost and never find your way back again.*

She stopped at the row of portside seats just ahead of the row in which she and Aunt Vicky had been sitting and bent, arms outstretched, fingers splayed. She was steeled to touch the sleeping face of the man sitting there. She knew there *was* a man here, because Aunt Vicky had spoken to him only a minute or so before the plane took off. When he spoke back to her, his voice had come from the seat directly in front of Dinah's own. She knew that; marking the locations of voices was part of her life, an ordinary fact of existence like breathing. The sleeping man would jump when her outstretched fingers touched him, but Dinah was beyond caring.

Except the seat was empty.

Completely empty.

Dinah straightened up again, her cheeks wet, her head pounding with fright. They couldn't be in the bathroom *together,* could they? Of course not.

Perhaps there were two bathrooms. In a plane this big there *must* be two bathrooms.

Except that didn't matter, either.

Aunt Vicky wouldn't have left her purse, no matter what. Dinah was sure of it.

She began to walk slowly forward, stopping at each row of seats, reaching into the two closest her first on the port side and then on the starboard.

She felt another purse in one, what felt like a briefcase in another, a pen and a pad of paper in a third. In two others she felt headphones. She touched something sticky on an earpiece of the second set. She rubbed her fingers together, then grimaced and wiped them on the mat which covered the headrest of the seat. That had been earwax. She was sure of it. It had its own unmistakable, yucky texture.

Dinah Bellman felt her slow way up the aisle, no longer taking pains to be gentle in her investigations. It didn't matter. She poked no eye, pinched no cheek, pulled no hair.

Every seat she investigated was empty.

This can't be, she thought wildly. *It just can't be! They were all around us when we got on! I heard them! I felt them! I smelled them! Where have they all gone?*

She didn't know, but they *were* gone: she was becoming steadily more sure of that.

At some point, while she slept, her aunt and everyone else on Flight 29 had disappeared.

No! The rational part of her mind clamored in the voice of Miss Lee. *No, that's impossible, Dinah! If everyone's gone, who is flying the plane?*

She began to move forward faster now, hands gripping the edges of the seats, her blind eyes wide open behind her dark glasses, the hem of her pink travelling dress fluttering. She had lost count, but in her greater distress over the continuing silence, this did not matter much to her.

She stopped again, and reached her groping hands into the seat on her right. This time she touched hair . . . but its location was all wrong. The hair was on the seat—how could that be?

Her hands closed around it . . . and lifted it. Realization, sudden and terrible, came to her.

It's hair, but the man it belongs to is gone. It's a scalp. I'm holding a dead man's scalp.

That was when Dinah Bellman opened her mouth and began to give voice to the shrieks which pulled Brian Engle from his dream.

6

Albert Kaussner was belly up to the bar, drinking Branding Iron Whiskey. The Earp brothers, Wyatt and Virgil, were on his right, and Doc Holliday was on his left. He was just lifting his glass to offer a toast when a man with a peg leg ran-hopped into the Sergio Leone Saloon.

"*It's the Dalton Gang!*" he screamed. "*The Daltons have just rid into Dodge!*"

Wyatt turned to face him calmly. His face was narrow, tanned, and handsome. He looked a great deal like Hugh O'Brian. "This here is Tombstone, Muffin," he said. "You got to get yore stinky ole shit together."

"Well, they're ridin in, wherever we are!" Muffin exclaimed. "And they look *maaad*, Wyatt! They look *reeely reeely maaaaaaad*!"

As if to prove this, guns began to fire in the street outside—the heavy thunder of Army .44s (probably stolen) mixed in with the higher whipcrack explosions of Garand rifles.

"Don't get your panties all up in a bunch, Muffy," Doc Holliday said, and tipped his hat back. Albert was not terribly surprised to see that Doc looked like Robert De Niro. He had always believed that if anyone was absolutely right to play the consumptive dentist, De Niro was the one.

"What do you say, boys?" Virgil Earp asked, looking around. Virgil didn't look like much of anyone.

"Let's go," Wyatt said. "I've had enough of these damned Clantons to last me a lifetime."

"It's the Daltons, Wyatt," Albert said quietly.

"I don't care if it's John Dillinger and Pretty Boy Floyd!" Wyatt exclaimed. "Are you with us or not, Ace?"

"I'm with you," Albert Kaussner said, speaking in the soft but menacing tones of the born killer. He dropped one hand to the butt of his long-barrelled Buntline Special and put the other to his head for a moment to make sure his *yarmulke* was on solidly. It was.

"Okay, boys," Doc said. "Let's go cut some Dalton butt."

They strode out together, four abreast through the batwing doors, just as the bell in the Tombstone Baptist Church began to toll high noon.

The Daltons were coming down Main Street at a full gallop, shooting holes in plate-glass windows and false fronts. They turned the waterbarrel in front of Duke's Mercantile and Reliable Gun Repair into a fountain.

Ike Dalton was the first to see the four men standing in the dusty street, their frock coats pulled back to free the handles of their guns. Ike reined his horse in savagely and it rose on its rear legs, squealing, foam splattering in thick curds around the bit. Ike Dalton looked quite a bit like Rutger Hauer.

"Look what we have got here," he sneered. "It is Wyatt Earp and his pansy brother, Virgil."

Emmett Dalton (who looked like Donald Sutherland after a month of hard nights) pulled up beside Ike. "And their faggot dentist friend, too," he snarled. "Who else wants—" Then he looked at Albert and paled. The thin sneer faltered on his lips.

Paw Dalton pulled up beside his two sons. Paw bore a strong resemblance to Slim Pickens.

"Christ," Paw whispered. "It's Ace Kaussner!"

Now Frank James pulled *his* mount into line next to Paw. His face was the color of dirty parchment. "What the hell, boys!" Frank cried. "I don't mind hoorawin a town or two on a dull day, but nobody told me The Arizona Jew was gonna be here!"

Albert "Ace" Kaussner, known from Sedalia to Steamboat Springs as The Arizona Jew, took a step forward. His hand hovered over the butt of his Buntline. He spat a stream of tobacco to one side, never taking his chilly gray eyes from the hardcases mounted twenty feet in front of him.

"Go on and make your moves, boys," said The Arizona Jew. "By my count, hell ain't half full."

The Dalton Gang slapped leather just as the clock in the tower of the Tombstone Baptist Church beat the last stroke of noon into the hot desert air. Ace went for his own gun, his draw as fast as blue blazes, and as he began to fan the hammer with the flat of his left hand, sending a spray of .45-caliber death into the Dalton Gang, a little girl standing outside The Longhorn Hotel began to scream.

Somebody make that brat stop yowling, Ace thought. *What's the matter with her, anyway? I got this under control. They don't call me the fastest Hebrew west of the Mississippi for nothing.*

But the scream went on, ripping across the air, darkening it as it came, and everything began to break up.

For a moment Albert was nowhere at all—lost in a darkness through which fragments of his dream tumbled and spun in a whirl-pool. The only constant was that terrible scream; it sounded like the shriek of an overloaded teakettle.

He opened his eyes and looked around. He was in his seat toward the front of Flight 29's main cabin. Coming up the aisle from the rear of the plane was a girl of about ten or twelve, wearing a pink dress and a pair of ditty-bop shades.

What is she, a movie star or something? he thought, but he was badly frightened, all the same. It was a bad way to exit his favorite dream.

"Hey!" he cried—but softly, so as not to wake the other passengers. "Hey, kid! What's the deal?"

The little girl whiplashed her head toward the sound of his voice. Her body turned a moment later, and she collided with one of the seats which ran down the center of the cabin in four-across rows. She struck it with her thighs, rebounded, and tumbled backward over the armrest of a portside seat. She fell into it with her legs up.

"*Where is everybody?*" she was screaming. "*Help me! Help me!*"

"Hey, stewardess!" Albert yelled, concerned, and unbuckled his seatbelt. He stood up, slipped out of his seat, turned toward the screaming little girl . . . and stopped. He was now facing fully toward the back of the plane, and what he saw froze him in place.

The first thought to cross his mind was, *I guess I don't have to worry about waking up the other passengers, after all.*

To Albert it looked like the entire main cabin of the 767 was empty.

7

Brian Engle was almost to the partition separating Flight 29's first-class and business-class sections when he realized that first class was now entirely empty. He stopped for just a moment, then got moving again. The others had left their seats to see what all the screaming was about, perhaps.

Of course he knew this was not the case; he had been flying passengers long enough to know a good bit about their group psychology. When a passenger freaked out, few if any of the others ever moved. Most air travellers meekly surrendered their option to take individual action when they entered the bird, sat down, and buckled their seatbelts around them. Once those few simple things were accomplished, all problem-solving tasks became the crew's responsibility. Airline personnel called them geese, but they were really sheep . . . an attitude most flight crews liked just fine. It made the nervous ones easier to handle.

But, since it was the only thing that made even remote sense, Brian ignored what he knew and plunged on. The rags of his own dream were still wrapped around him, and a part of his mind was convinced that it was Anne who was screaming, that he would find

her halfway down the main cabin with her hand plastered against
a crack in the body of the airliner, a crack located beneath a sign
which read SHOOTING STARS ONLY.

There was only one passenger in the business section, an older
man in a brown three-piece suit. His bald head gleamed mellowly
in the glow thrown by his reading lamp. His arthritis-swollen hands
were folded neatly over the buckle of his seatbelt. He was fast
asleep and snoring loudly, ignoring the whole ruckus.

Brian burst through into the main cabin and there his forward motion was finally checked by utter stunned disbelief. He saw a teenaged boy standing near a little girl who had fallen into a seat on
the port side about a quarter of the way down the cabin. The boy
was not looking at her, however; he was staring toward the rear of
the plane, with his jaw hanging almost all the way to the round
collar of his Hard Rock Cafe tee-shirt.

Brian's first reaction was about the same as Albert Kaussner's:
My God, the whole plane is empty!

Then he saw a woman on the starboard side of the airplane stand
up and walk into the aisle to see what was happening. She had the
dazed, puffy look of someone who has just been jerked out of a
sound sleep. Halfway down, in the center aisle, a young man in a
crew-necked jersey was craning his neck toward the little girl and
staring with flat, incurious eyes. Another man, this one about sixty,
got up from a seat close to Brian and stood there indecisively. He
was dressed in a red flannel shirt and he looked utterly bewildered.
His hair was fluffed up around his head in untidy mad-scientist
corkscrews.

"Who's screaming?" he asked Brian. "Is the plane in trouble,
mister? You don't think we're goin down, do you?"

The little girl stopped screaming. She struggled up from the seat
she had fallen into, and then almost tumbled forward in the other
direction. The kid caught her just in time; he was moving with
dazed slowness.

Where have they gone? Brian thought. *My dear God, where have
they all gone?*

But his feet were moving toward the teenager and the little girl
now. As he went, he passed another passenger who was still sleeping, this one a girl of about seventeen. Her mouth was open in an
unlovely yawp and she was breathing in long, dry inhalations.

He reached the teenager and the girl with the pink dress.

"Where are they, man?" Albert Kaussner asked. He had an arm around the shoulders of the sobbing child, but he wasn't looking at her; his eyes slipped relentlessly back and forth across the almost deserted main cabin. "Did we land someplace while I was asleep and let them off?"

"My aunt's gone!" the little girl sobbed. "My Aunt Vicky! I thought the plane was empty! I thought I was the only one! Where's my aunt, please? I want my aunt!"

Brian knelt beside her for a moment, so they were at approximately the same level. He noticed the sunglasses and remembered seeing her get on with the blonde woman.

"You're all right," he said. "You're all right, young lady. What's your name?"

"Dinah," she sobbed. "I can't find my aunt. I'm blind and I can't see her. I woke up and the seat was empty—"

"What's going on?" the young man in the crew-neck jersey asked. He was talking over Brian's head, ignoring both Brian and Dinah, speaking to the boy in the Hard Rock tee-shirt and the older man in the flannel shirt. "Where's everybody else?"

"You're all right, Dinah," Brian repeated. "There are other people here. Can you hear them?"

"Y-yes. I can hear them. But where's Aunt Vicky? And who's been killed?"

"Killed?" a woman asked sharply. It was the one from the starboard side. Brian glanced up briefly and saw she was young, dark-haired, pretty. "*Has* someone been killed? Have we been hijacked?"

"No one's been killed," Brian said. It was, at least, something to say. His mind felt weird: like a boat which has slipped its moorings. "Calm down, honey."

"I felt his hair!" Dinah insisted. "Someone cut off his HAIR!"

This was just too odd to deal with on top of everything else, and Brian dismissed it. Dinah's earlier thought suddenly struck home to him with chilly intensity—who the fuck was flying the plane?

He stood up and turned to the older man in the red shirt. "I have to go forward," he said. "Stay with the little girl."

"All right," the man in the red shirt said. "But what's happening?"

They were joined by a man of about thirty-five who was wearing pressed blue-jeans and an oxford shirt. Unlike the others, he looked utterly calm. He took a pair of horn-rimmed spectacles from his pocket, shook them out by one bow, and put them on. "We seem a few passengers short, don't we?" he said. His British accent was almost as crisp as his shirt. "What about crew? Anybody know?"

"That's what I'm going to find out," Brian said, and started forward again. At the head of the main cabin he turned back and counted quickly. Two more passengers had joined the huddle around the girl in the dark glasses. One was the teenaged girl who had been sleeping so heavily; she swayed on her feet as if she were either drunk or stoned. The other was an elderly gent in a fraying sport-coat. Eight people in all. To those he added himself and the guy in business class, who was, at least so far, sleeping through it all.

Ten people.

For the love of God, where are the rest of them?

But this was not the time to worry about it—there were bigger problems at hand. Brian hurried forward, barely glancing at the old bald fellow snoozing in business class.

8

The service area squeezed behind the movie screen and between the two first-class heads was empty. So was the galley, but there Brian saw something which was extremely troubling: the beverage trolley was parked kitty-corner by the starboard bathroom. There were a number of used glasses on its bottom shelf.

They were just getting ready to serve drinks, he thought. *When it happened—whatever "it" was—they'd just taken out the trolley. Those used glasses are the ones that were collected before the roll-out. So whatever happened must have happened within half an hour of take-off, maybe a little longer—weren't there turbulence reports over the desert? I think so. And that weird shit about the aurora borealis—*

For a moment Brian was almost convinced that last was a part of his dream—it was certainly odd enough—but further reflection convinced him that Melanie Trevor, the flight attendant, had actually said it.

Never mind that; what did *happen? In God's name,* what?

He didn't know, but he *did* know that looking at the abandoned drinks trolley put an enormous feeling of terror and superstitious dread into his guts. For just a moment he thought that this was what the first boarders of the *Mary Celeste* must have felt like, coming upon a totally abandoned ship where all the sail was neatly laid on, where the captain's table had been set for dinner, where all ropes were neatly coiled and some sailor's pipe was still smoldering away the last of its tobacco on the foredeck . . .

Brian shook these paralyzing thoughts off with a tremendous effort and went to the door between the service area and the cockpit. He knocked. As he had feared, there was no response. And although he knew it was useless to do so, he curled his fist up and hammered on it.

Nothing.

He tried the doorknob. It didn't move. That was SOP in the age of unscheduled side-trips to Havana, Lebanon, and Tehran. Only the pilots could open it. Brian *could* fly this plane . . . but not from out here.

"Hey!" he shouted. "Hey, you guys! Open the door!"

Except he knew better. The flight attendants were gone; almost all the passengers were gone; Brian Engle was willing to bet the 767's two-man cockpit crew was also gone.

He believed Flight 29 was heading east on automatic pilot.

CHAPTER TWO

DARKNESS AND MOUNTAINS. THE TREASURE TROVE. CREW-NECK'S NOSE. THE SOUND OF NO DOGS BARKING. PANIC IS NOT ALLOWED. A CHANGE OF DESTINATION.

1

Brian had asked the older man in the red shirt to look after Dinah, but as soon as Dinah heard the woman from the starboard side— the one with the pretty young voice—she imprinted on her with scary intensity, crowding next to her and reaching with a timid sort of determination for her hand. After the years spent with Miss Lee, Dinah knew a teacher's voice when she heard one. The dark-haired woman took her hand willingly enough.

"Did you say your name was Dinah, honey?"

"Yes," Dinah said. "I'm blind, but after my operation in Boston, I'll be able to see again. *Probably* be able to see. The doctors say there's a seventy per cent chance I'll get some vision, and a forty per cent chance I'll get all of it. What's your name?"

"Laurel Stevenson," the dark-haired woman said. Her eyes were still conning the main cabin, and her face seemed unable to break out of its initial expression: dazed disbelief.

"Laurel, that's a flower, isn't it?" Dinah asked. She spoke with feverish vivacity.

"Uh-huh," Laurel said.

"Pardon me," the man with the horn-rimmed glasses and the British accent said. "I'm going forward to join our friend."

"I'll come along," the older man in the red shirt said.

"I want to know what's going on here!" the man in the crew-neck jersey exclaimed abruptly. His face was dead pale except for two spots of color, as bright as rouge, on his cheeks. "I want to know what's going on right *now*."

"Nor am I a bit surprised," the Brit said, and then began walking forward. The man in the red shirt trailed after him. The teenaged girl with the dopey look drifted along behind them for awhile and then stopped at the partition between the main cabin and the business section, as if unsure of where she was.

The elderly gent in the fraying sport-coat went to a portside window, leaned over, and peered out.

"What do you see?" Laurel Stevenson asked.

"Darkness and mountains," the man in the sport-coat said.

"The Rockies?" Albert asked.

The man in the frayed sport-coat nodded. "I believe so, young man."

Albert decided to go forward himself. He was seventeen, fiercely bright, and this evening's Bonus Mystery Question had also occurred to him: who was flying the plane?

Then he decided it didn't matter . . . at least for the moment. They were moving smoothly along, so presumably *someone* was, and even if some*one* turned out to be some*thing*—the autopilot, in other words—there wasn't a thing he could do about it. As Albert Kaussner he was a talented violinist—not quite a prodigy—on his way to study at The Berklee College of Music. As Ace Kaussner he was (in his dreams, at least) the fastest Hebrew west of the Mississippi, a bounty hunter who took it easy on Saturdays, was careful to keep his shoes off the bed, and always kept one eye out for the main chance and the other for a good kosher café somewhere along the dusty trail. Ace was, he supposed, his way of sheltering himself from loving parents who hadn't allowed him to play Little League baseball because he might damage his talented hands and who had believed, in their hearts, that every sniffle signalled the onset of pneumonia. He was a gunslinging violinist—an interesting combination—but he didn't know a thing about flying planes. And the little girl had said something which had simultaneously intrigued him and curdled his blood. *I felt his hair!* she had said. *Someone cut off his HAIR!*

He broke away from Dinah and Laurel (the man in the ratty sport-coat had moved to the starboard side of the plane to look out one of those windows, and the man in the crew-necked jersey was going forward to join the others, his eyes narrowed pugnaciously) and began to retrace Dinah's progress up the portside aisle.

Someone cut off his HAIR! she had said, and not too many rows down, Albert saw what she had been talking about.

2

"I am praying, sir," the Brit said, "that the pilot's cap I noticed in one of the first-class seats belongs to you."

Brian was standing in front of the locked door, head down, thinking furiously. When the Brit spoke up behind him, he jerked in surprise and whirled on his heels.

"Didn't mean to put your wind up," the Brit said mildly. "I'm Nick Hopewell." He stuck out his hand.

Brian shook it. As he did so, performing his half of the ancient ritual, it occurred to him that this must be a dream. The scary flight from Tokyo and finding out that Anne was dead had brought it on.

Part of his mind knew this was not so, just as part of his mind had known the little girl's scream had had nothing to do with the deserted first-class section, but he seized on this idea just as he had seized on that one. It helped, so why not? Everything else was nuts—so nutty that even attempting to think about it made his mind feel sick and feverish. Besides, there was really no time to think, simply no time, and he found that this was also something of a relief.

"Brian Engle," he said. "I'm pleased to meet you, although the circumstances are—" He shrugged helplessly. What *were* the circumstances, exactly? He could not think of an adjective which would adequately describe them.

"Bit bizarre, aren't they?" Hopewell agreed. "Best not to think of them right now, I suppose. Does the crew answer?"

"No," Brian said, and abruptly struck his fist against the door in frustration.

"Easy, easy," Hopewell soothed. "Tell me about the cap, Mr. Engle. You have no idea what satisfaction and relief it would give me to address you as Captain Engle."

Brian grinned in spite of himself. "I *am* Captain Engle," he said, "but under the circumstances, I guess you can call me Brian."

Nick Hopewell seized Brian's left hand and kissed it heartily. "I believe I'll call you Savior instead," he said. "Do you mind awfully?"

Brian threw his head back and began to laugh. Nick joined him. They were standing there in front of the locked door in the nearly empty plane, laughing wildly, when the man in the red shirt and the man in the crew-necked jersey arrived, looking at them as if they had both gone crazy.

3

Albert Kaussner held the hair in his right hand for several moments, looking at it thoughtfully. It was black and glossy in the overhead lights, a right proper pelt, and he wasn't at all surprised it had scared the hell out of the little girl. It would have scared Albert, too, if he hadn't been able to see it.

He tossed the wig back into the seat, glanced at the purse lying in the next seat, then looked more closely at what was lying next to the purse. It was a plain gold wedding ring. He picked it up, examined it, then put it back where it had been. He began walking slowly toward the back of the airplane. In less than a minute, Albert was so struck with wonder that he had forgotten all about who was flying the plane, or how the hell they were going to get down from here if it was the automatic pilot.

Flight 29's passengers were gone, but they had left a fabulous—

and sometimes perplexing—treasure trove behind. Albert found
jewelry on almost every seat: wedding rings, mostly, but there were
also diamonds, emeralds, and rubies. There were earrings, most of
them five-and-dime stuff but some which looked pretty expensive
to Albert's eyes. His mom had a few good pieces, and some of this
stuff made her best jewelry look like rummage-sale buys. There
were studs, necklaces, cufflinks, ID bracelets. And watches,
watches, watches. From Timex to Rolex, there seemed to be at least
two hundred of them, lying on seats, lying on the floor between
seats, lying in the aisles. They twinkled in the lights.

There were at least sixty pairs of spectacles. Wire-rimmed, horn-
rimmed, gold-rimmed. There were prim glasses, punky glasses, and
glasses with rhinestones set in the bows. There were Ray-Bans,
Polaroids, and Foster Grants.

There were belt buckles and service pins and piles of pocket-change.
No bills, but easily four hundred dollars in quarters, dimes, nickels,
and pennies. There were wallets—not as many wallets as purses,
but still a good dozen of them, from fine leather to plastic. There
were pocket knives. There were at least a dozen hand-held calculators.

And odder things, as well. He picked up a flesh-colored plastic
cylinder and examined it for almost thirty seconds before deciding
it really *was* a dildo and putting it down again in a hurry. There
was a small gold spoon on a fine gold chain. There were bright
speckles of metal here and there on the seats and the floor, mostly
silver but some gold. He picked up a couple of these to verify the
judgment of his own wondering mind: some were dental caps, but
most were fillings from human teeth. And, in one of the back rows,
he picked up two tiny steel rods. He looked at these for several
moments before realizing they were surgical pins, and that they
belonged not on the floor of a nearly deserted airliner but in some
passenger's knee or shoulder.

He discovered one more passenger, a young bearded man who
was sprawled over two seats in the very last row, snoring loudly
and smelling like a brewery.

Two seats away, he found a gadget that looked like a pacemaker
implant.

Albert stood at the rear of the plane and looked forward along
the large, empty tube of the fuselage.

"What in the fuck is going on here?" he asked in a soft, trembling
voice.

4

"I demand to know just what is going on here!" the man in the crew-neck jersey said in a loud voice. He strode into the service area at the head of first class like a corporate raider mounting a hostile takeover.

"Currently? We're just about to break the lock on this door," Nick Hopewell said, fixing Crew-Neck with a bright gaze. "The flight crew appears to have abdicated along with everyone else, but we're in luck, just the same. My new acquaintance here is a pilot who just happened to be deadheading, and—"

"*Someone* around here is a deadhead, all right," Crew-Neck said, "and I intend to find out who, believe me." He pushed past Nick without a glance and stuck his face into Brian's, as aggressive as a ballplayer disputing an umpire's call. "Do you work for American Pride, friend?"

"Yes," Brian said, "but why don't we put that off for now, sir? It's important that—"

"*I'll* tell you what's important!" Crew-Neck shouted. A fine mist of spit settled on Brian's cheeks and he had to sit on a sudden and amazingly strong impulse to clamp his hands around this twerp's neck and see how far he could twist his head before something inside cracked. "I've got a meeting at the Prudential Center with representatives of Bankers International at nine o'clock this morning! *Promptly* at nine o'clock! I booked a seat on this conveyance in good faith, and I have no intention of being late for my appointment! I want to know three things: *who* authorized an unscheduled stop for this airliner while I was asleep, *where* that stop was made, and *why it was done!*"

"Have you ever watched *Star Trek?*" Nick Hopewell asked suddenly.

Crew-Neck's face, suffused with angry blood, swung around. His expression said that he believed the Englishman was clearly mad. "What in the hell are you talking about?"

"Marvellous American program," Nick said. "Science fiction. Exploring strange new worlds, like the one which apparently exists inside your head. And if you don't shut your gob at once, you bloody idiot, I'll be happy to demonstrate Mr. Spock's famous Vulcan sleeper-hold for you."

"You can't talk to me like that!" Crew-Neck snarled. "Do you know who I am?"

"Of course," Nick said. "You're a bloody-minded little bugger who has mistaken his airline boarding pass for credentials proclaiming him to be the Grand High Pooh-Bah of Creation. You're also badly frightened. No harm in that, but you *are* in the way."

Crew-Neck's face was now so clogged with blood that Brian began to be afraid his entire head would explode. He had once seen a movie where that happened. He did not want to see it in real life. "You can't talk to me like that! You're not even an American citizen!"

Nick Hopewell moved so fast that Brian barely saw what was happening. At one moment the man in the crew-neck jersey was yelling into Nick's face while Nick stood at ease beside Brian, his hands on the hips of his pressed jeans. A moment later, Crew-Neck's nose was caught firmly between the first and second fingers of Nick's right hand.

Crew-Neck tried to pull away. Nick's fingers tightened . . . and then his hand turned slightly, in the gesture of a man tightening a screw or winding an alarm clock. Crew-Neck bellowed.

"I can break it," Nick said softly. "Easiest thing in the world, believe me."

Crew-Neck tried to jerk backward. His hands beat ineffectually at Nick's arm. Nick twisted again and Crew-Neck bellowed again.

"I don't think you heard me. I can break it. Do you understand? Signify if you have understanding."

He twisted Crew-Neck's nose a third time.

Crew-Neck did not just bellow this time; he screamed.

"Oh, wow," the stoned-looking girl said from behind them. "A nose-hold."

"I don't have time to discuss your business appointments," Nick said softly to Crew-Neck. "Nor do I have time to deal with hysteria masquerading as aggression. We have a nasty, perplexing situation here. You, sir, are clearly not part of the solution, and I have no intention whatever of allowing you to become part of the problem. Therefore, I am going to send you back into the main cabin. This gentleman in the red shirt—"

"Don Gaffney," the gentleman in the red shirt said. He looked as vastly surprised as Brian felt.

"Thank you," Nick said. He still held Crew-Neck's nose in that amazing clamp, and Brian could now see a thread of blood lining one of the man's pinched nostrils.

Nick pulled him closer and spoke in a warm, confidential voice.

"Mr. Gaffney here will be your escort. Once you arrive in the main cabin, my buggardly friend, you will take a seat with your safety belt fixed firmly around your middle. Later, when the captain here has assured himself we are not going to fly into a mountain, a building, or another plane, we may be able to discuss our current situation at greater length. For the present, however, your input is not necessary. Do you understand all these things I have told you?"

Crew-Neck uttered a pained, outraged bellow.

"If you understand, please favor me with a thumbs-up."

Crew-Neck raised one thumb. The nail, Brian saw, was neatly manicured.

"Fine," Nick said. "One more thing. When I let go of your nose, you may feel vengeful. To *feel* that way is fine. To give vent to the feeling would be a terrible mistake. I want you to remember that what I have done to your nose I can just as easily do to your testicles. In fact, I can wind them up so far that when I let go of them, you may actually fly about the cabin like a child's airplane. I expect you to leave with Mr.—"

He looked questioningly at the man in the red shirt.

"Gaffney," the man in the red shirt repeated.

"Gaffney, right. Sorry. I expect you to leave with Mr. Gaffney. You will not remonstrate. You will not indulge in rebuttal. In fact, if you say so much as a single word, you will find yourself investigating hitherto unexplored realms of pain. Give me a thumbs-up if you understand *this.*"

Crew-Neck waved his thumb so enthusiastically that for a moment he looked like a hitchhiker with diarrhea.

"Right, then!" Nick said, and let go of Crew-Neck's nose.

Crew-Neck stepped back, staring at Nick Hopewell with angry, perplexed eyes—he looked like a cat which had just been doused with a bucket of cold water. By itself, anger would have left Brian unmoved. It was the perplexity that made him feel a little sorry for Crew-Neck. He felt mightily perplexed himself.

Crew-Neck raised a hand to his nose, verifying that it was still there. A narrow ribbon of blood, no wider than the pull-strip on a pack of cigarettes, ran from each nostril. The tips of his fingers came away bloody, and he looked at them unbelievingly. He opened his mouth.

"I wouldn't, mister," Don Gaffney said. "Guy means it. You better come along with me."

He took Crew-Neck's arm. For a moment Crew-Neck resisted Gaffney's gentle tug. He opened his mouth again.

"Bad idea," the girl who looked stoned told him.

Crew-Neck closed his mouth and allowed Gaffney to lead him back toward the rear of first class. He looked over his shoulder once, his eyes wide and stunned, and then dabbed his fingers under his nose again.

Nick, meanwhile, had lost all interest in the man. He was peering out one of the windows. "We appear to be over the Rockies," he said, "and we seem to be at a safe enough altitude."

Brian looked out himself for a moment. It was the Rockies, all right, and near the center of the range, by the look. He put their altitude at about 35,000 feet. Just about what Melanie Trevor had told him. So they were fine . . . at least, so far.

"Come on," he said. "Help me break down this door."

Nick joined him in front of the door. "Shall I captain this part of the operation, Brian? I have some experience."

"Be my guest." Brian found himself wondering exactly how Nick Hopewell had come by his experience in twisting noses and breaking down doors. He had an idea it was probably a long story.

"It would be helpful to know how strong the lock is," Nick said. "If we hit it too hard, we're apt to go catapulting straight into the cockpit. I wouldn't want to run into something that won't bear running into."

"I don't know," Brian said truthfully. "I don't think it's tremendously strong, though."

"All right," Nick said. "Turn and face me—your right shoulder pointing at the door, my left."

Brian did.

"I'll count off. We're going to shoulder it together on three. Dip your legs as we go in; we're more apt to pop the lock if we hit the door lower down. *Don't* hit it as hard as you can. About half. If that isn't enough, we can always go again. Got it?"

"I've got it."

The girl, who looked a little more awake and with it now, said: "I don't suppose they leave a key under the doormat or anything, huh?"

Nick looked at her, startled, then back at Brian. "*Do* they by any chance leave a key someplace?"

Brian shook his head. "I'm afraid not. It's an anti-terrorist precaution."

"Of course," Nick said. "Of course it is." He glanced at the girl and winked. "But that's using your head, just the same."

The girl smiled at him uncertainly.

Nick turned back to Brian. "Ready, then?"

"Ready."

"Right, then. One . . . two . . . *three*!"

They drove forward into the door, dipping down in perfect synchronicity just before they hit it, and the door popped open with absurd ease. There was a small lip—too short by at least three inches to be considered a step—between the service area and the cockpit. Brian struck this with the edge of his shoe and would have fallen sideways into the cockpit if Nick hadn't grabbed him by the shoulder. The man was as quick as a cat.

"Right, then," he said, more to himself than to Brian. "Let's just see what we're dealing with here, shall we?"

5

The cockpit was empty. Looking into it made Brian's arms and neck prickle with gooseflesh. It was all well and good to know that a 767 could fly thousands of miles on autopilot, using information which had been programmed into its inertial navigation system—God knew he had flown enough miles that way himself—but it was another to see the two empty seats. *That* was what chilled him. He had never seen an empty in-flight cockpit during his entire career.

He was seeing one now. The pilot's controls moved by themselves, making the infinitesimal corrections necessary to keep the plane on its plotted course to Boston. The board was green. The two small wings on the plane's attitude indicator were steady above the artificial horizon. Beyond the two small, slanted-forward windows, a billion stars twinkled in an early-morning sky.

"Oh, wow," the teenaged girl said softly.

"Coo-*eee*," Nick said at the same moment. "Look there, matey."

Nick was pointing at a half-empty cup of coffee on the service console beside the left arm of the pilot's seat. Next to the coffee was a Danish pastry with two bites gone. This brought Brian's dream back in a rush, and he shivered violently.

"It happened fast, whatever it was," Brian said. "And look there. And there."

He pointed first to the seat of the pilot's chair and then to the floor by the co-pilot's seat. Two wristwatches glimmered in the lights of the controls, one a pressure-proof Rolex, the other a digital Pulsar.

"If you want watches, you can take your pick," a voice said from behind them. "There's tons of them back there." Brian looked over his shoulder and saw Albert Kaussner, looking neat and very young in his small black skull-cap and his Hard Rock Cafe tee-shirt. Standing beside him was the elderly gent in the fraying sport-coat.

"Are there indeed?" Nick asked. For the first time he seemed to have lost his self-possession.

"Watches, jewelry, and glasses," Albert said. "Also purses. But the weirdest thing is . . . there's stuff I'm pretty sure came from *inside* people. Things like surgical pins and pacemakers."

Nick looked at Brian Engle. The Englishman had paled noticeably. "I had been going on roughly the same assumption as our rude and loquacious friend," he said. "That the plane set down someplace, for some reason, while I was asleep. That most of the passengers—and the crew—were somehow offloaded."

"I would have woken the minute descent started," Brian said. "It's habit." He found he could not take his eyes off the empty seats, the half-drunk cup of coffee, the half-eaten Danish.

"Ordinarily, I'd say the same," Nick agreed, "so I decided my drink had been doped."

I don't know what this guy does for a living, Brian thought, *but he sure doesn't sell used cars.*

"No one doped my drink," Brian said, "because I didn't have one."

"Neither did I," Albert said.

"In any case, there *couldn't* have been a landing and take-off while we were sleeping," Brian told them. "You can *fly* a plane on autopilot, and the Concorde can *land* on autopilot, but you need a human being to take one up."

"We didn't land, then," Nick said.

"Nope."

"So where did they go, Brian?"

"I don't know," Brian said. He moved to the pilot's chair and sat down.

6

Flight 29 *was* flying at 36,000 feet, just as Melanie Trevor had told him, on heading 090. An hour or two from now that would change as the plane doglegged further north. Brian took the navigator's chart book, looked at the airspeed indicator, and made a series of rapid calculations. Then he put on the headset.

"Denver Center, this is American Pride Flight 29, over?"

He flicked the toggle . . . and heard nothing. Nothing at all. No static; no chatter; no ground control; no other planes. He checked the transponder setting: 7700, just as it should be. Then he flicked the toggle back to transmit again. "Denver Center, come in please, this is American Pride Flight 29, repeat, American Pride Heavy, and I have a problem, Denver, I have a problem."

Flicked back the toggle to receive. Listened.

Then Brian did something which made Albert "Ace" Kaussner's heart begin to bump faster with fear: he hit the control panel just below the radio equipment with the heel of his hand. The Boeing 767 was a high-tech, state-of-the-art passenger plane. One did not try to make the equipment on such a plane operate in such a fashion. What the pilot had just done was what you did when the old Philco radio you bought for a buck at the Kiwanis Auction wouldn't play after you got it home.

Brian tried Denver Center again. And got no response. No response at all.

7

To this moment, Brian had been dazed and terribly perplexed. Now he began to feel frightened—really frightened—as well. Up until now there had been no *time* to be scared. He wished that were still so . . . but it wasn't. He flicked the radio to the emergency band and tried again. There was no response. This was the equivalent of dialing 911 in Manhattan and getting a recording which said everyone had left for the weekend. When you called for help on the emergency band, you *always* got a prompt response.

Until now, at least, Brian thought.

He switched to UNICOM, where private pilots obtained landing advisories at small airports. No response. He listened . . . and heard nothing at all. Which just couldn't be. Private pilots chattered like grackles on a telephone line. The gal in the Piper wanted to know the weather. The guy in the Cessna would just flop back dead in his seat if he couldn't get someone to call his wife and tell her he was bringing home three extra for dinner. The guys in the Lear wanted the girl on the desk at the Arvada Airport to tell their charter passengers that they were going to be fifteen minutes late and to hold their water, they would still make the baseball game in Chicago on time.

But none of that was there. All the grackles had flown, it seemed, and the telephone lines were bare.

He flicked back to the FAA emergency band. "Denver come in! Come in right now! *This is AP Flight 29, you answer me, goddammit!*"

Nick touched his shoulder. "Easy, mate."

"The dog won't bark!" Brian said frantically. "That's impossible, but that's what's happening! Christ, what did they do, have a fucking nuclear war?"

"*Easy,*" Nick repeated. "Steady down, Brian, and tell me what you mean, the dog won't bark."

"I mean Denver Control!" Brian cried. "*That* dog! I mean FAA Emergency! *That* dog! UNICOM, that dog, too! I've never—"

He flicked another switch. "Here," he said, "this is the medium-shortwave band. They should be jumping all over each other like frogs on a hot sidewalk, but I can't pick up jack shit."

He flicked another switch, then looked up at Nick and Albert Kaussner, who had crowded in close. "There's no VOR beacon out of Denver," he said.

"Meaning?"

"Meaning I have no radio, I have no Denver navigation beacon, and my board says everything is just peachy keen. Which is crap. *Got* to be."

A terrible idea began to surface in his mind, coming up like a bloated corpse rising to the top of a river.

"Hey, kid—look out the window. Left side of the plane. Tell me what you see."

Albert Kaussner looked out. He looked out for a long time. "Nothing," he said. "Nothing at all. Just the last of the Rockies and the beginning of the plains."

"No lights?"

"No."

Brian got up on legs which felt weak and watery. He stood looking down for a long time.

At last Nick Hopewell said quietly, "Denver's gone, isn't it?"

Brian knew from the navigator's charts and his on-board navigational equipment that they should now be flying less than fifty miles south of Denver . . . but below them he saw only the dark, featureless landscape that marked the beginning of the Great Plains.

"Yes," he said. "Denver's gone."

8

There was a moment of utter silence in the cockpit, and then Nick Hopewell turned to the peanut gallery, currently consisting of Albert, the man in the ratty sport-coat, and the young girl. Nick clapped his hands together briskly, like a kindergarten teacher. He sounded like one, too, when he spoke. "All right, people! Back to your seats. I think we need a little quiet here."

"We *are* being quiet," the girl objected, and reasonably enough.

"I believe that what the gentleman actually means isn't quiet but a little privacy," the man in the ratty sport-coat said. He spoke in cultured tones, but his soft, worried eyes were fixed on Brian.

"That's *exactly* what I mean," Nick agreed. "Please?"

"Is he going to be all right?" the man in the ratty sport-coat asked in a low voice. "He looks rather upset."

Nick answered in the same confidential tone. "Yes," he said. "He'll be fine. I'll see to it."

"Come on, children," the man in the ratty sport-coat said. He put one arm around the girl's shoulders, the other around Albert's. "Let's go back and sit down. Our pilot has work to do."

They need not have lowered their voices even temporarily as far as Brian Engle was concerned. He might have been a fish feeding in a stream while a small flock of birds passes overhead. The sound may reach the fish, but he certainly attaches no significance to it. Brian was busy working his way through the radio bands and switching from one navigational touchpoint to another. It was useless. No Denver; no Colorado Springs; no Omaha. All gone.

He could feel sweat trickling down his cheeks like tears, could feel his shirt sticking to his back.

I must smell like a pig, he thought, *or a—*

Then inspiration struck. He switched to the military-aircraft band, although regulations expressly forbade his doing so. The Strategic Air Command practically owned Omaha. *They* would not be off the air. They might tell him to get the fuck off their frequency, would probably threaten to report him to the FAA, but Brian would accept all this cheerfully. Perhaps he would be the first to tell them that the city of Denver had apparently gone on vacation.

"Air Force Control, Air Force Control, this is American Pride Flight 29 and we have a problem here, a *big* problem here, do you read me? Over."

No dog barked there, either.

That was when Brian felt something—something like a bolt—starting to give way deep inside his mind. That was when he felt his entire structure of organized thought begin to slide slowly toward some dark abyss.

9

Nick Hopewell clamped a hand on him then, high up on his shoulder, near the neck. Brian jumped in his seat and almost cried out aloud. He turned his head and found Nick's face less than three inches from his own.

Now he'll grab my nose and start to twist it, Brian thought.

Nick did not grab his nose. He spoke with quiet intensity, his eyes fixed unflinchingly on Brian's. "I see a look in your eyes, my friend . . . but I didn't need to see your eyes to know it was there. I can hear it in your voice and see it in the way you're sitting in your seat. Now listen to me, and listen well: *panic is not allowed.*"

Brian stared at him, frozen by that blue gaze.

"Do you understand me?"

He spoke with great effort. "They don't let guys do what I do for a living if they panic, Nick."

"I know that," Nick said, "but this is a unique situation. You need to remember, however, that there are a dozen or more people on this plane, and your job is the same as it ever was: to bring them down in one piece."

"You don't need to tell me what my job is!" Brian snapped.

"I'm afraid I did," Nick said, "but you're looking a hundred per cent better now, I'm relieved to say."

Brian was doing more than looking better; he was starting to *feel* better again. Nick had stuck a pin into the most sensitive place—his sense of responsibility. *Just where he meant to stick me,* he thought.

"What do you do for a living, Nick?" he asked a trifle shakily.

Nick threw back his head and laughed. "Junior attaché, British embassy, old man."

"My aunt's hat."

Nick shrugged. "Well . . . that's what it says on my papers, and I reckon that's good enough. If they said anything else, I suppose it would be Her Majesty's Mechanic. I fix things that need fixing. Right now that means you."

"Thank you," Brian said touchily, "but I'm fixed."

"All right, then—what do you mean to do? Can you navigate without those ground-beam thingies? Can you avoid other planes?"

"I can navigate just fine with on-board equipment," Brian said. "As for other planes—" He pointed at the radar screen. "This bastard says there *aren't* any other planes."

"Could be there are, though," Nick said softly. "Could be that radio and radar conditions are snafued, at least for the time being. You mentioned nuclear war, Brian. I think if there had been a nuclear exchange, we'd know. But that doesn't mean there hasn't been some sort of accident. Are you familiar with the phenomenon called the electromagnetic pulse?"

Brian thought briefly of Melanie Trevor. *Oh, and we've had reports of the aurora borealis over the Mojave Desert. You might want to stay awake for that.*

Could that be it? Some freakish weather phenomenon?

He supposed it was just possible. But, if so, how come he heard no static on the radio? How come there was no wave interference across the radar screen? Why just this dead blankness? And he didn't think the aurora borealis had been responsible for the disappearance of a hundred and fifty to two hundred passengers.

"Well?" Nick asked.

"You're some mechanic, Nick," Brian said at last, "but I don't think it's EMP. All on-board equipment—including the directional gear—seems to be working just fine." He pointed to the digital compass readout. "If we'd experienced an electromagnetic pulse, that baby would be all over the place. But it's holding dead steady."

"So. Do you intend to continue on to Boston?"

Do you intend . . . ?

And with that, the last of Brian's panic drained away. *That's right,* he thought. *I'm the captain of this ship now . . . and in the end, that's all it comes down to. You should have reminded me of that in the first place, my friend, and saved us both a lot of trouble.*

"Logan at dawn, with no idea what's going on in the country below us, or the rest of the world? No way."

"Then what *is* our destination? Or do you need time to consider the matter?"

Brian didn't. And now the other things he needed to do began to click into place.

"I know," he said. "And I think it's time to talk to the passengers. The few that are left, anyway."

He picked up the microphone, and that was when the bald man who had been sleeping in the business section poked his head into the cockpit. "Would one of you gentlemen be so kind as to tell me what's happened to all the service personnel on this craft?" he asked querulously. "I've had a very nice nap . . . but now I'd like my dinner."

10

Dinah Bellman felt much better. It was good to have other people around her, to feel their comforting presence. She was sitting in a small group with Albert Kaussner, Laurel Stevenson, and the man in the ratty sport-coat, who had introduced himself as Robert Jenkins. He was, he said, the author of more than forty mystery novels, and had been on his way to Boston to address a convention of mystery fans.

"Now," he said, "I find myself involved in a mystery a good deal more extravagant than any I would ever have dared to write."

These four were sitting in the center section, near the head of the main cabin. The man in the crew-neck jersey sat in the starboard aisle, several rows down, holding a handkerchief to his nose (which had actually stopped bleeding several minutes ago) and fuming in solitary splendor. Don Gaffney sat nearby, keeping an uneasy watch on him. Gaffney had only spoken once, to ask Crew-Neck what his name was. Crew-Neck had not replied. He simply fixed Gaffney with a gaze of baleful intensity over the crumpled bouquet of his handkerchief.

Gaffney had not asked again.

"Does anyone have the *slightest* idea of what's going on here?" Laurel almost pleaded. "I'm supposed to be starting my first real vacation in ten years tomorrow, and now *this* happens."

Albert happened to be looking directly at Miss Stevenson as she spoke. As she dropped the line about this being her first real vacation in ten years, he saw her eyes suddenly shift to the right and blink rapidly three or four times, as if a particle of dust had landed in one of them. An idea so strong it was a certainty rose in his mind: the lady was lying. For some reason, the lady was lying. He looked at her more closely and saw nothing really remarkable—a woman with a species of fading prettiness, a woman falling rapidly out of her twenties and toward middle age (and to Albert, thirty was definitely where middle age began), a woman who would soon become colorless and invisible. But she had color now; her cheeks flamed with it. He didn't know what the lie meant, but he could see that it had momentarily refreshed her prettiness and made her nearly beautiful.

There's a lady who should lie more often, Albert thought. Then, before he or anyone else could reply to her, Brian's voice came from the overhead speakers.

"Ladies and gentlemen, this is the captain."

"Captain my ass," Crew-Neck snarled.

"Shut up!" Gaffney exclaimed from across the aisle.

Crew-Neck looked at him, startled, and subsided.

"As you undoubtedly know, we have an extremely odd situation on our hands here," Brian continued. "You don't need me to explain it; you only have to look around yourselves to understand."

"I don't understand anything," Albert muttered.

"I know a few other things, as well. They won't exactly make your day, I'm afraid, but since we're in this together, I want to be as frank as I possibly can. I have no cockpit-to-ground communication. And about five minutes ago we should have been able to see the lights of Denver clearly from the airplane. We couldn't. The only conclusion I'm willing to draw right now is that somebody down there forgot to pay the electricity bill. And until we know a little more, I think that's the only conclusion *any* of us should draw."

He paused. Laurel was holding Dinah's hand. Albert produced a low, awed whistle. Robert Jenkins, the mystery writer, was staring dreamily into space with his hands resting on his thighs.

"All of that is the bad news," Brian went on. "The good news is this: the plane is undamaged, we have plenty of fuel, and I'm qualified to fly this make and model. Also to land it. I think we'll all agree that landing safely is our first priority. There isn't a thing we can do until we accomplish that, and I want you to rest assured that it will be done.

"The last thing I want to pass on to you is that our destination will now be Bangor, Maine."

Crew-Neck sat up with a jerk. "*Whaaat?*" he bellowed.

"Our in-flight navigation equipment is in five-by-five working order, but I can't say the same for the navigational beams—VOR—which we also use. Under these circumstances, I have elected not to enter Logan airspace. I haven't been able to raise anyone, in air or on ground, by radio. The aircraft's radio equipment appears to be working, but I don't feel I can depend on appearances in the current circumstances. Bangor International Airport has the following advantages: the short approach is over land rather than water; air traffic at our ETA, about 8:30 A.M., will be much lighter—assuming there's any at all; and BIA, which used to be Dow Air Force Base, has the longest commercial runway on the East Coast of the United States. Our British and French friends land the Concorde there when they can't get into New York."

Crew-Neck bawled: "*I have an important business meeting at the Pru this morning at nine o'clock AND I FORBID YOU TO FLY INTO SOME DIPSHIT MAINE AIRPORT!*"

Dinah jumped and then cringed away from the sound of Crew-Neck's voice, pressing her cheek against the side of Laurel Stevenson's breast. She was not crying—not yet, anyway—but Laurel felt her chest began to hitch.

"*DO YOU HEAR ME?*" Crew-Neck was bellowing. "*I AM DUE IN BOSTON TO DISCUSS AN UNUSUALLY LARGE BOND TRANSACTION, AND I HAVE EVERY INTENTION OF ARRIVING AT THAT MEETING ON TIME!*" He unlatched his seatbelt and began to stand up. His cheeks were red, his brow waxy white. There was a blank look in his eyes which Laurel found extremely frightening. "*DO YOU UNDERSTA—*"

"Please," Laurel said. "Please, mister, you're scaring the little girl."

Crew-Neck turned his head and that unsettling blank gaze fell on her. Laurel could have waited. "*SCARING THE LITTLE GIRL? WE'RE DIVERTING TO SOME TINPOT, CHICKENSHIT AIRPORT IN THE MIDDLE OF NOWHERE, AND ALL YOU'VE GOT TO WORRY ABOUT IS—*"

"Sit down and shut up or I'll pop you one," Gaffney said, standing up. He had at least twenty years on Crew-Neck, but he was heavier and much broader through the chest. He had rolled the sleeves of his red flannel shirt to the elbows, and when he clenched his hands into fists, the muscles in his forearms bunched. He looked like a lumberjack just starting to soften into retirement.

Crew-Neck's upper lip pulled back from his teeth. This doglike grimace scared Laurel, because she didn't believe the man in the crew-neck jersey knew he was making a face. She was the first of them to wonder if this man might not be crazy.

"I don't think you could do it alone, pops," he said.

"He won't have to." It was the bald man from the business section. "I'll take a swing at you myself, if you don't shut up."

Albert Kaussner mustered all his courage and said, "So will I, you putz." Saying it was a great relief. He felt like one of the guys at the Alamo, stepping over the line Colonel Travis had drawn in the dirt.

Crew-Neck looked around. His lip rose and fell again in that queer, doglike snarl. "I see. I see. You're all against me. Fine." He sat down and stared at them truculently. "But if you knew anything about the market in South American bonds—" He didn't finish. There was a cocktail napkin sitting on the arm of the seat next to him. He picked it up, looked at it, and began to pluck at it.

"Doesn't have to be this way," Gaffney said. "I wasn't born a hardass, mister, and I ain't one by inclination, either." He was trying to sound pleasant, Laurel thought, but wariness showed through, perhaps anger as well. "You ought to just relax and take it easy. Look on the bright side! The airline'll probably refund your full ticket price on this trip."

Crew-Neck cut his eyes briefly in Don Gaffney's direction, then looked back at the cocktail napkin. He quit plucking it and began to tear it into long strips.

"Anyone here know how to run that little oven in the galley?" Baldy asked, as if nothing had happenend. "I want my dinner."

No one answered.

"I didn't think so," the bald man said sadly. "This is the era of specialization. A shameful time to be alive." With this philosophical pronouncement, Baldy retreated once more to business class.

Laurel looked down and saw that, below the rims of the dark glasses with their jaunty red plastic frames, Dinah Bellman's cheeks were wet with tears. Laurel forgot some of her own fear and perplexity, at least temporarily, and hugged the little girl. "Don't cry, honey—that man was just upset. He's better now."

If you call sitting here and looking hypnotized while you tear a paper napkin into teeny shreds better, she thought.

"I'm scared," Dinah whispered. "We all look like monsters to that man."

"No, I don't think so," Laurel said, surprised and a little taken aback. "Why would you think a thing like that?"

"I don't know," Dinah said. She liked this woman—had liked her from the instant she heard her voice—but she had no intention of telling Laurel that for just a moment she had seen them all, herself included, looking back at the man with the loud voice. She had been *inside* the man with the loud voice—his name was Mr. Tooms or Mr. Tunney or something like that—and to him they looked like a bunch of evil, selfish trolls.

If she told Miss Lee something like that, Miss Lee would think she was crazy. Why would this woman, whom Dinah had just met, think any different?

So Dinah said nothing.

Laurel kissed the girl's cheek. The skin was hot beneath her lips. "Don't be scared, honey. We're going along just as smooth as can be—can't you feel it?—and in just a few hours we'll be safe on the ground again."

"That's good. I want my Aunt Vicky, though. Where is she, do you think?"

"I don't know, hon," Laurel said. "I wish I did."

Dinah thought again of the faces the yelling man saw: evil faces, cruel faces. She thought of her own face as he perceived it, a piggish baby face with the eyes hidden behind huge black lenses. Her courage broke then, and she began to weep in hoarse racking sobs that hurt Laurel's heart. She held the girl, because it was the only thing she could think of to do, and soon she was crying herself. They cried together for nearly five minutes, and then Dinah began to calm again. Laurel looked over at the slim young boy, whose name was either Albert or Alvin, she could not remember which, and saw that his eyes were also wet. He caught her looking and glanced hastily down at his hands.

Dinah fetched one final gasping sob and then just lay with her head pillowed against Dinah's breast. "I guess crying won't help, huh?"

"No, I guess not," Laurel agreed. "Why don't you try going to sleep, Dinah?"

Dinah sighed—a watery, unhappy sound. "I don't think I can. I *was* asleep."

Tell me about it, Laurel thought. And Flight 29 continued east at 36,000 feet, flying at over five hundred miles an hour above the dark midsection of America.

CHAPTER THREE

THE DEDUCTIVE METHOD.
ACCIDENTS AND STATIS-
TICS. SPECULATIVE POSSI-
BILITIES. PRESSURE IN THE
TRENCHES. BETHANY'S
PROBLEM. THE DESCENT
BEGINS.

1

"That little girl said something interesting an hour or so ago," Robert Jenkins said suddenly.

The little girl in question had gone to sleep again in the meantime, despite her doubts about her ability to do so. Albert Kaussner had also been nodding, perchance to return once more to those mythic streets of Tombstone. He had taken his violin case down from the overhead compartment and was holding it across his lap.

"Huh!" he said, and straightened up.

"I'm sorry," Jenkins said. "Were you dozing?"

"Nope," Albert said. "Wide awake." He turned two large, blood-shot orbs on Jenkins to prove this. A darkish shadow lay under each. Jenkins thought he looked a little like a raccoon which has been startled while raiding garbage cans. "What did she say?"

"She told Miss Stevenson she didn't think she could get back to sleep because she *had* been sleeping. Earlier."

Albert gazed at Dinah for a moment. "Well, she's out now," he said.

"I see she is, but that is not the point, dear boy. Not the point at all."

Albert considered telling Mr. Jenkins that Ace Kaussner, the fastest Hebrew west of the Mississippi and the only Texan to survive the Battle of the Alamo, did not much cotton to being called dear boy, and decided to let it pass . . . at least for the time being. "Then what *is* the point?"

"I was also asleep. Corked off even before the captain—our *original* captain, I mean—turned off the NO SMOKING light. I've always been that way. Trains, busses, planes—I drift off like a baby the minute they turn on the motors. What about you, dear boy?"

"What about me what?"

"Were you asleep? You were, weren't you?"

"Well, yeah."

"We were *all* asleep. The people who disappeared were all awake."

Albert thought about this. "Well . . . maybe."

"Nonsense," Jenkins said almost jovially. "I write mysteries for a living. Deduction is my bread and butter, you might say. Don't you think that if someone had been awake when all those people were eliminated, that person would have screamed bloody murder, waking the rest of us?"

"I guess so," Albert agreed thoughtfully. "Except maybe for that guy all the way in the back. I don't think an air-raid siren would wake *that* guy up."

"All right; your exception is duly noted. But *no one* screamed, did they? And no one has offered to tell the rest of us what happened. So I deduce that only waking passengers were subtracted. Along with the flight crew, of course."

"Yeah. Maybe so."

"You look troubled, dear boy. Your expression says that, despite its charms, the idea does not scan perfectly for you. May I ask why not? Have I missed something?" Jenkins's expression said he didn't believe that was possible, but that his mother had raised him to be polite.

"I don't know," Albert said honestly. "How many of us are there? Eleven?"

"Yes. Counting the fellow in the back—the one who is comatose—we number eleven."

"If you're right, shouldn't there be more of us?"

"Why?"

But Albert fell silent, struck by a sudden, vivid image from his childhood. He had been raised in a theological twilight zone by parents who were not Orthodox but who were not agnostics, either. He and his brothers had grown up observing most of the dietary traditions (or laws, or whatever they were), they had had their Bar Mitzvahs, and they had been raised to know who they were, where they came from, and what that was supposed to mean. And the story Albert remembered most clearly from his childhood visits to temple was the story of the final plague which had been visited on Pharaoh—the gruesome tribute exacted by God's dark angel of the morning.

In his mind's eye he now saw that angel moving not over Egypt but through Flight 29, gathering most of the passengers to its terrible breast . . . not because they had neglected to daub their lintels (or their seat-backs, perhaps) with the blood of a lamb, but because . . .

Why? Because *why?*

Albert didn't know, but he shivered just the same. And wished that creepy old story had never occurred to him. *Let my Frequent Fliers go,* he thought. Except it wasn't funny.

"Albert?" Mr. Jenkins's voice seemed to come from a long way off. "Albert, are you all right?"

"Yes. Just thinking." He cleared his throat. "If *all* the sleeping passengers were, you know, passed over, there'd be at least sixty of us. Maybe more. I mean, this *is* the red-eye."

"Dear boy, have you ever . . ."

"Could you call me Albert, Mr. Jenkins? That's my name."

Jenkins patted Albert's shoulder. "I'm sorry. Really. I don't mean to be patronizing. I'm upset, and when I'm upset, I have a tendency to retreat . . . like a turtle pulling his head back into his shell. Only what I retreat into is fiction. I believe I was playing Philo Vance. He's a detective—a *great* detective—created by the late S. S. Van Dine. I suppose you've never read him. Hardly anyone does these days, which is a pity. At any rate, I apologize."

"It's okay," Albert said uncomfortably.

"Albert you are and Albert you shall be from now on," Robert Jenkins promised. "I started to ask you if you've ever taken the red-eye before."

"No. I've never even flown across the country before."

"Well, I have. Many times. On a few occasions I have even gone against my natural inclination and stayed awake for awhile. Mostly when I was a younger man and the flights were noisier. Having said that much, I may as well date myself outrageously by admitting that my first coast-to-coast trip was on a TWA prop-job that made two stops . . . to refuel.

"My observation is that very few people go to sleep on such flights during the first hour or so . . . and then just about *everyone* goes to sleep. During that first hour, people occupy themselves with looking at the scenery, talking with their spouses or their travelling companions, having a drink or two—"

"Settling in, you mean," Albert suggested. What Mr. Jenkins was saying made perfect sense to him, although he had done precious little settling in himself; he had been so excited about his coming journey and the new life which would be waiting for him that he had hardly slept at all during the last couple of nights. As a result, he had gone out like a light almost as soon as the 767 left the ground.

"Making little nests for themselves," Jenkins agreed. "Did you happen to notice the drinks trolley outside the cockpit, dea—Albert?"

"I saw it was there," Albert agreed.

Jenkins's eyes shone. "Yes indeed—it was either see it or fall over it. But did you really *notice* it?"

"I guess not, if you saw something I didn't."

"It's not the eye that notices, but the *mind*, Albert. The trained deductive mind. I'm no Sherlock Holmes, but I *did* notice that it had just been taken out of the small closet in which it is stored, and that the used glasses from the pre-flight service were still stacked on the bottom shelf. From this I deduce the following: the plane took off uneventfully, it climbed toward its cruising altitude, and the autopilot device was fortunately engaged. Then the captain turned off the seatbelt light. This would all be about thirty minutes into the flight, if I'm reading the signs correctly—about 1:00 A.M., PDT. When the seatbelt light was turned out, the stewardesses arose and began their first task—cocktails for about one hundred and fifty at about 24,000 feet and rising. The pilot, meanwhile, has programmed the autopilot to level the plane off at 36,000 feet and fly east on heading thus-and-such. A few passengers—eleven of us, in fact—have fallen asleep. Of the rest, some are dozing, perhaps (but not deeply enough to save them from whatever happened), and the rest are all wide awake."

"Building their nests," Albert said.

"Exactly! Building their nests!" Jenkins paused and then added, not without some melodrama: "And then it happened!"

"*What* happened, Mr. Jenkins?" Albert asked. "Do you have any ideas about that?"

Jenkins did not answer for a long time, and when he finally did, a lot of the fun had gone out of his voice. Listening to him, Albert understood for the first time that, beneath the slightly theatrical veneer, Robert Jenkins was as frightened as Albert was himself. He found he did not mind this; it made the elderly mystery writer in his running-to-seed sport-coat seem more real.

"The locked-room mystery is the tale of deduction at its most pure," Jenkins said. "I've written a few of them myself—more than a few, to be completely honest—but I never expected to be a part of one."

Albert looked at him and could think of no reply. He found himself remembering a Sherlock Holmes story called "The Speck-led Band." In that story a poisonous snake had gotten into the famous locked room through a ventilating duct. The immortal Sherlock hadn't even had to wake up all his brain-cells to solve that one.

But even if the overhead luggage compartments of Flight 29 had been filled with poisonous snakes—*stuffed* with them—where were the bodies? *Where were the bodies?* Fear began to creep into him again, seeming to flow up his legs toward his vitals. He reflected that he had never felt less like that famous gunslinger Ace Kaussner in his whole life.

"If it were just the plane," Jenkins went on softly, "I suppose I could come up with a scenario—it is, after all, how I have been earning my daily bread for the last twenty-five years or so. Would you like to hear one such scenario?"

"Sure," Albert said.

"Very well. Let us say that some shadowy government organization like The Shop has decided to carry out an experiment, and we are the test subjects. The purpose of such an experiment, given the circumstances, might be to document the effects of severe mental and emotional stress on a number of average Americans. They, the scientists running the experiment, load the airplane's oxygen system with some sort of odorless hypnotic drug—"

"Are there such things?" Albert asked, fascinated.

"There are indeed," Jenkins said. "Diazaline, for one. Methoprominol, for another. I remember when readers who liked to think of themselves as 'serious-minded' laughed at Sax Rohmer's Fu Manchu novels. They called them panting melodrama at its most shameful." Jenkins shook his head slowly. "Now, thanks to biological research and the paranoia of alphabet agencies like the CIA and the DIA, we're living in a world that could be Sax Rohmer's worst nightmare.

"Diazaline, which is actually a nerve gas, would be best. It's supposed to be very fast. After it is released into the air, *everyone* falls asleep, except for the pilot, who is breathing uncontaminated air through a mask."

"But—" Albert began.

Jenkins smiled and raised a hand. "I know what your objection is, Albert, and I can explain it. Allow me?"

Albert nodded.

"The pilot lands the plane—at a secret airstrip in Nevada, let us say. The passengers who were awake when the gas was released—and the stewardesses, of course—are offloaded by sinister men wearing white *Andromeda Strain* suits. The passengers who were asleep—you and I among them, my young friend—simply go on sleeping, only a little more deeply than before. The pilot then returns Flight 29 to its proper altitude and heading. He engages the autopilot. As the plane reaches the Rockies, the effects of the gas begin to wear off. Diazaline is a so-called clear drug, one that leaves no appreciable after-effects. No hangover, in other words. Over his intercom, the pilot can hear the little blind girl crying out for her aunt. He knows she will wake the others. The experiment is about to commence. So he gets up and leaves the cockpit, closing the door behind him."

"How could he do that? There's no knob on the outside."

Jenkins waved a dismissive hand. "Simplest thing in the world, Albert. He uses a strip of adhesive tape, sticky side out. Once the door latches from the inside, it's locked."

A smile of admiration began to overspread Albert's face—and then it froze. "In that case, the pilot would be one of us," he said.

"Yes and no. In my scenario, Albert, the pilot is the pilot. The pilot who just happened to be on board, supposedly deadheading to Boston. The pilot who was sitting in first class, less than thirty feet from the cockpit door, when the manure hit the fan."

"Captain Engle," Albert said in a low, horrified voice.

Jenkins replied in the pleased but complacent tone of a geometry professor who has just written QED below the proof of a particularly difficult theorem. "Captain Engle," he agreed.

Neither of them noticed Crew-Neck looking at them with glittering, feverish eyes. Now Crew-Neck took the in-flight magazine from the seat-pocket in front of him, pulled off the cover, and began to tear it in long, slow strips. He let them flutter to the floor, where they joined the shreds of the cocktail napkin around his brown loafers.

His lips were moving soundlessly.

2

Had Albert been a student of the New Testament, he would have understood how Saul, that most zealous persecutor of the early Christians, must have felt when the scales fell from his eyes on the road to Damascus. He stared at Robert Jenkins with shining enthusiasm, every vestige of sleepiness banished from his brain.

Of course, when you thought about it—or when somebody like Mr. Jenkins, who was clearly a real head, ratty sport-coat or no ratty sport-coat, thought about it for you—it was just too big and too obvious to miss. Almost the entire cast and crew of American

Pride's Flight 29 had disappeared between the Mojave Desert and the Great Divide . . . but one of the few survivors just happened to be—surprise, surprise!—*another* American Pride pilot who was, in his own words, "qualified to fly this make and model—also to land it."

Jenkins had been watching Albert closely, and now he smiled. There wasn't much humor in that smile. "It's a tempting scenario," he said, "isn't it?"

"We'll have to capture him as soon as we land," Albert said, scraping one hand feverishly up the side of his face. "You, me, Mr. Gaffney, and that British guy. He looks tough. Only . . . what if the Brit's in on it, too? He could be Captain Engle's, you know, bodyguard. Just in case someone figured things out the way you did."

Jenkins opened his mouth to reply, but Albert rushed on before he could.

"We'll just have to put the arm on them both. Somehow." He offered Mr. Jenkins a narrow smile—an Ace Kaussner smile. Cool, tight, dangerous. The smile of a man who is faster than blue blazes, and knows it. "I may not be the world's smartest guy, Mr. Jenkins, but I'm nobody's lab rat."

"But it doesn't stand up, you know," Jenkins said mildly.

Albert blinked. "What?"

"The scenario I just outlined for you. It doesn't stand up."

"But—you said—"

"I said *if it were just the plane,* I could come up with a scenario. And I did. A good one. If it was a book idea, I'll bet my agent could sell it. Unfortunately, it *isn't* just the plane. Denver might still have been down there, but all the lights were off if it was. I have been coordinating our route of travel with my wristwatch, and I can tell you now that it's not just Denver, either. Omaha, Des Moines—no sign of them down there in the dark, my boy. I have seen no lights at all, in fact. No farmhouses, no grain storage and shipping locations, no interstate turnpikes. Those things show up at night, you know—with the new high-intensity lighting, they show up very well, even when one is almost six miles up. The land is utterly dark. Now, I can believe that there *might* be a government agency unethical enough to drug us all in order to observe our reactions. Hypothetically, at least. What I cannot believe is that even The Shop could have persuaded everyone over our flight-path to turn off their lights in order to reinforce the illusion that we are all alone."

"Well . . . maybe it's all a fake," Albert suggested. "Maybe we're really still on the ground and everything we can see outside the windows is, you know, projected. I saw a movie something like that once."

Jenkins shook his head slowly, regretfully. "I'm sure it was an interesting film, but I don't believe it would work in real life. Unless our theoretical secret agency has perfected some sort of ultra-wide-screen 3-D projection, I think not. Whatever is happening is not just going on inside the plane, Albert, and that is where deduction breaks down."

"But the pilot!" Albert said wildly. "What about him just happening to be here at the right place and time?"

"Are you a baseball fan, Albert?"

"Huh? No. I mean, sometimes I watch the Dodgers on TV, but not really."

"Well, let me tell you what may be the most amazing statistic ever recorded in a game which thrives on statistics. In 1957, Ted Williams reached base on sixteen consecutive at-bats. This streak encompassed six baseball games. In 1941, Joe DiMaggio batted safely in fifty-six straight games, but the odds against what DiMaggio did pale next to the odds against Williams's accomplishment, which have been put somewhere in the neighborhood of two *billion* to one. Baseball fans like to say DiMaggio's streak will never be equaled. I disagree. But I'd be willing to bet that, if they're still playing baseball a thousand years from now, Williams's sixteen on-bases in a row will still stand."

"All of which means what?"

"It means that I believe Captain Engle's presence on board tonight is nothing more or less than an accident, like Ted Williams's sixteen consecutive on-bases. And, considering our circumstances, I'd say it's a very lucky accident indeed. If life was like a mystery novel, Albert, where coincidence is not allowed and the odds are never beaten for long, it would be a much tidier business. I've found, though, that in real life coincidence is not the exception but the rule."

"Then what *is* happening?" Albert whispered.

Jenkins uttered a long, uneasy sigh. "I'm the wrong person to ask, I'm afraid. It's too bad Larry Niven or John Varley isn't on board."

"Who are those guys?"

"Science-fiction writers," Jenkins said.

3

"I don't suppose you read science fiction, do you?" Nick Hopewell asked suddenly. Brian turned around to look at him. Nick had been sitting quietly in the navigator's seat since Brian had taken control of Flight 29, almost two hours ago now. He had listened wordlessly as Brian continued trying to reach someone—*anyone*—on the ground or in the air.

"I was crazy about it as a kid," Brian said. "You?"

Nick smiled. "Until I was eighteen or so, I firmly believed that the Holy Trinity consisted of Robert Heinlein, John Christopher, and John Wyndham. I've been sitting here and running all those old stories through my head, matey. And thinking about such exotic things as time-warps and space-warps and alien raiding parties."

Brian nodded. He felt relieved; it was good to know he wasn't the only one who was thinking crazy thoughts.

"I mean, we don't really have any way of knowing if *anything* is left down there, do we?"

"No," Brian said. "We don't."

Over Illinois, low-lying clouds had blotted out the dark bulk of the earth far below the plane. He was sure it still *was* the earth—the Rockies had looked reassuringly familiar, even from 36,000 feet—but beyond that he was sure of nothing. And the cloud cover might hold all the way to Bangor. With Air Traffic Control out of commission, he had no real way of knowing. Brian had been playing with a number of scenarios, and the most unpleasant of the lot was this: that they would come out of the clouds and discover that every sign of human life—including the airport where he hoped to land—was gone. Where would he put this bird down then?

"I've always found waiting the hardest part," Nick said.

The hardest part of what? Brian wondered, but he did not ask.

"Suppose you took us down to 5,000 feet or so?" Nick proposed suddenly. "Just for a quick look-see. Perhaps the sight of a few small towns and interstate highways will set our minds at rest."

Brian had already considered this idea. Had considered it with great longing. "It's tempting," he said, "but I can't do it."

"Why not?"

"The passengers are still my first responsibility, Nick. They'd probably panic, even if I explained what I was going to do in advance. I'm thinking of our loudmouth friend with the pressing appointment at the Pru in particular. The one whose nose you twisted."

"I can handle him," Nick replied. "Any others who cut up rough, as well."

"I'm sure you can," Brian said, "but I still see no need of scaring them unnecessarily. And we will find out, eventually. We can't stay up here forever, you know."

"Too true, matey," Nick said dryly.

"I might do it anyway, if I could be sure I could get under the cloud cover at 4,000 or 5,000 feet, but with no ATC and no other planes to talk to, I can't be sure. I don't even know for sure what the weather's like down there, and I'm not talking about normal stuff, either. You can laugh at me if you want to—"

"I'm not laughing, matey. I'm not even *close* to laughing. Believe me."

"Well, suppose we *have* gone through a time-warp, like in a science-fiction story? What if I took us down through the clouds and we got one quick look at a bunch of brontosauruses grazing in some Farmer John's field before we were torn apart by a cyclone or fried in an electrical storm?"

"Do you really think that's possible?" Nick asked. Brian looked at him closely to see if the question was sarcastic. It didn't appear to be, but it was hard to tell. The British were famous for their dry sense of humor, weren't they?

Brian started to tell him he had once seen something just like that on an old *Twilight Zone* episode and then decided it wouldn't help his credibility at all. "It's pretty unlikely, I suppose, but you get the idea—we just don't know what we're dealing with. We might hit a brand-new mountain in what used to be upstate New York. Or another plane. Hell—maybe even a rocket-shuttle. After all, if it's a time-warp, we could as easily be in the future as in the past."

Nick looked out through the window. "We seem to have the sky pretty much to ourselves."

"Up here, that's true. Down there, who knows? And who knows

is a very dicey situation for an airline pilot. I intend to overfly
Bangor when we get there, if these clouds still hold. I'll take us out
over the Atlantic and drop under the ceiling as we head back. Our
odds will be better if we make our initial descent over water."

"So for now, we just go on."

"Right."

"And wait."

"Right again."

Nick sighed. "Well, you're the captain."

Brian smiled. "That's three in a row."

4

Deep in the trenches carved into the floors of the Pacific and the
Indian Oceans, there are fish which live and die without ever seeing
or sensing the sun. These fabulous creatures cruise the depths like
ghostly balloons, lit from within by their own radiance. Although
they look delicate, they are actually marvels of biological design,
built to withstand pressures that would squash a man as flat as a
windowpane in the blink of an eye. Their great strength, however,
is also their great weakness. Prisoners of their own alien bodies,
they are locked forever in their dark depths. If they are captured
and drawn toward the surface, toward the sun, they simply explode.
It is not external pressure that destroys them, but its absence.

Craig Toomy had been raised in his own dark trench, had lived
in his own atmosphere of high pressure. His father had been an
executive in the Bank of America, away from home for long
stretches of time, a caricature type-A overachiever. He drove his
only child as furiously and as unforgivingly as he drove himself.
The bedtime stories he told Craig in Craig's early years terrified
the boy. Nor was this surprising, because terror was exactly the
emotion Roger Toomy meant to awaken in the boy's breast. These
tales concerned themselves, for the most part, with a race of monstrous beings called the langoliers.

Their job, their mission in life (in the world of Roger Toomy,
everything had a job, *everything* had serious work to do), was to prey
on lazy, time-wasting children. By the time he was seven, Craig was
a dedicated type-A overachiever, just like Daddy. He had made up
his mind: the langoliers were never going to get *him*.

A report card which did not contain all A's was an unacceptable report card. An A— was the subject of a lecture fraught with dire warnings of what life would be like digging ditches or emptying garbage cans, and a B resulted in punishment—most commonly confinement to his room for a week. During that week, Craig was allowed out only for school and for meals. There was no time off for good behavior. On the other hand, extraordinary achievement— the time Craig won the tri-school decathlon, for instance— warranted no corresponding praise. When Craig showed his father the medal which had been awarded him on that occasion—in an assembly before the entire student body—his father glanced at it, grunted once, and went back to his newspaper. Craig was nine years old when his father died of a heart attack. He was actually sort of relieved that the Bank of America's answer to General Patton was gone.

His mother was an alcoholic whose drinking had been controlled only by her fear of the man she had married. Once Roger Toomy was safely in the ground, where he could no longer search out her bottles and break them, or slap her and tell her to get hold of herself, for God's sake, Catherine Toomy began her life's work in earnest. She alternately smothered her son with affection and froze him with rejection, depending on how much gin was currently perking through her bloodstream. Her behavior was often odd and sometimes bizarre. On the day Craig turned ten, she placed a wooden kitchen match between two of his toes, lit it, and sang "Happy Birthday to You" while it burned slowly down toward his flesh. She told him that if he tried to shake it out or kick it loose, she would take him to THE ORPHAN'S HOME at once. The threat of THE ORPHAN'S HOME was a frequent one when Catherine Toomy was loaded. "I ought to, anyway," she told him as she lit the match which stuck up between her weeping son's toes like a skinny birth-day candle. "You're just like your father. He didn't know how to have fun, and neither do you. You're a *bore*, Craiggy-weggy." She finished the song and blew out the match before the skin of Craig's second and third right toes was more than singed, but Craig never forgot the yellow flame, the curling, blackening stick of wood, and the growing heat as his mother warbled "Happy birthday, dear Craiggy-weggy, happy birthday to *yoooou*" in her droning, off-key drunk's voice.

Pressure.

Pressure in the trenches.

Craig Toomy continued to get all A's, and he continued to spend a lot of time in his room. The place which had been his Coventry had become his refuge. Mostly he studied there, but sometimes—when things were going badly, when he felt pressed to the wall—he would take one piece of notepaper after another and tear them into narrow strips. He would let them flutter around his feet in a growing drift while his eyes stared out blankly into space. But these blank periods were not frequent. Not then.

He graduated valedictorian from high school. His mother didn't come. She was drunk. He graduated ninth in his class from the UCLA Graduate School of Management. His mother didn't come. She was dead. In the dark trench which existed in the center of his own heart, Craig was quite sure that the langoliers had finally come for her.

Craig went to work for the Desert Sun Banking Corporation of California as part of the executive training program. He did very well, which was not surprising; Craig Toomy had been built, after all, to get all A's, built to thrive under the pressures which exist in the deep fathoms. And sometimes, following some small reverse at work (and in those days, only five short years ago, all the reverses had been small ones), he would go back to his apartment in West-wood, less than half a mile from the condo Brian Engle would occupy following his divorce, and tear small strips of paper for hours at a time. The paper-tearing episodes were gradually becoming more frequent.

During those five years, Craig ran the corporate fast track like a greyhound chasing a mechanical rabbit. Water-cooler gossips speculated that he might well become the youngest vice-president in Desert Sun's glorious forty-year history. But some fish are built to rise just so far and no farther; they explode if they transgress their built-in limits.

Eight months ago, Craig Toomy had been put in sole charge of his first big project—the corporate equivalent of a master's thesis. This project was created by the bonds department. Bonds—foreign bonds and junk bonds (they were frequently the same)—were Craig's specialty. This project proposed buying a limited number of questionable South American bonds—sometimes called Bad Debt Bonds—on a carefully set schedule. The theory behind these buys was sound enough, given the limited insurance on them that was available, and the much larger tax-breaks available on turn-overs resulting in a profit (Uncle Sam was practically falling all over himself to keep the complex structure of South American indebt-edness from collapsing like a house of cards). It just had to be done carefully.

Craig Toomy had presented a daring plan which raised a good many eyebrows. It centered upon a large buy of various Argentinian bonds, generally considered to be the worst of a bad lot. Craig had argued forcefully and persuasively for his plan, producing facts, figures, and projections to prove his contention that Argentinian bonds were a good deal more solid than they looked. In one bold stroke, he argued, Desert Sun could become the most important— and *richest*—buyer of foreign bonds in the American West. The money they made, he said, would be a lot less important than the long-run credibility they would establish.

After a good deal of discussion—some of it hot—Craig's take on the project got a green light. Tom Holby, a senior vice-president, had drawn Craig aside after the meeting to offer congratula-tions . . . and a word of warning. "If this comes off the way you expect at the end of the fiscal year, you're going to be everyone's fair-haired boy. If it doesn't, you are going to find yourself in a very windy place, Craig. I'd suggest that the next few months might be a good time to build a storm-shelter."

"I won't need a storm-shelter, Mr. Holby," Craig said confidently. "After this, what I'll need is a hang-glider. This is going to be the bond-buy of the century—like finding diamonds at a barn-sale. Just wait and see."

He had gone home early that night, and as soon as his apartment door was closed and triple-locked behind him, the confident smile had slipped from his face. What replaced it was that unsettling look of blankness. He had bought the news magazines on the way home. He took them into the kitchen, squared them up neatly in front of him on the table, and began to rip them into long, narrow strips. He went on doing this for over six hours. He ripped until *Newsweek, Time,* and *U.S. News & World Report* lay in shreds on the floor all around him. His Gucci loafers were buried. He looked like the lone survivor of an explosion in a tickertape factory.

The bonds he had proposed buying—the Argentinian bonds in particular—were a much higher risk than he had let on. He had pushed his proposal through by exaggerating some facts, suppressing others . . . and even making some up out of whole cloth. Quite a few of these latter, actually. Then he had gone home, ripped strips of paper for hours, and wondered why he had done it. He did not know about the fish that exist in trenches, living their lives and dying their deaths without ever seeing the sun. He did not know that there are both fish and men whose *bête noire* is not pressure but the lack of it. He only knew that he had been under an unbreakable compulsion to buy those bonds, to paste a target on his own forehead.

Now he was due to meet with bond representatives of five large banking corporations at the Prudential Center in Boston. There would be much comparing of notes, much speculation about the future of the world bond market, much discussion about the buys of the last sixteen months and the result of those buys. And before the first day of the three-day conference was over, they would all know what Craig Toomy had known for the last ninety days: the bonds he had purchased were now worth less than six cents on the dollar. And not long after that, the top brass at Desert Sun would discover the rest of the truth: that he had bought more than three times as much as he had been empowered to buy. He had also invested every penny of his personal savings . . . not that they would care about *that*.

Who knows how the fish captured in one of those deep trenches and brought swiftly toward the surface—toward the light of a sun it has never suspected—may feel? Is it not at least possible that its final moments are filled with ecstasy rather than horror? That it senses the crushing reality of all that pressure only as it finally falls away? That it thinks—as far as fish may be supposed to think, that is—in a kind of joyous frenzy, *I am free of that weight at last!* in the seconds before it explodes? Probably not. Fish from those dark depths may not feel at all, at least not in any way we could recognize, and they certainly do not think . . . but people do.

Instead of feeling shame, Craig Toomy had been dominated by vast relief and a kind of hectic, horrified happiness as he boarded American Pride's Flight 29 to Boston. He was going to explode, and he found he didn't give a damn. In fact, he found himself looking forward to it. He could feel the pressure peeling away from all the surfaces of his skin as he rose toward the surface. For the first time in weeks, there had been no paper-ripping. He had fallen asleep before Flight 29 even left the gate, and he had slept like a baby until that blind little brat had begun to caterwaul.

And now they told him everything had changed, and that simply could not be allowed. It must not be allowed. He had been firmly caught in the net, had felt the dizzying rise and the stretch of his skin as it tried to compensate. They could not now change their minds and drop him back into the deeps.

Bangor?

Bangor, *Maine?*

Oh no. No indeed.

Craig Toomy was vaguely aware that most of the people on Flight 29 had disappeared, but he didn't care. They weren't the important thing. They weren't part of what his father had always liked to call THE BIG PICTURE. The meeting at the Pru *was* part of THE BIG PICTURE.

This crazy idea of diverting to Bangor, Maine . . . whose scheme, exactly, had *that* been?

It had been the pilot's idea, of course. Engle's idea. The so-called captain.

Engle, now . . . Engle might very well be part of THE BIG PIC-TURE. He might, in fact, be an AGENT OF THE ENEMY. Craig had suspected this in his heart from the moment when Engle had begun to speak over the intercom, but in this case he hadn't needed to depend on his heart, had he? No indeed. He had been listening to the conversation between the skinny kid and the man in the fire-sale sport-coat. The man's taste in clothes was terrible, but what he had to say made perfect sense to Craig Toomy . . . at least, up to a point.

In that case, the pilot would be one of us, the kid had said.

Yes and no, the guy in the fire-sale sport-coat had said. *In my scenario, the pilot is the pilot. The pilot who just happened to be on board, supposedly deadheading to Boston, the pilot who just happened to be sitting less than thirty feet from the cockpit door.*

Engle, in other words.

And the other fellow, the one who had twisted Craig's nose, was clearly in on it with him, serving as a kind of sky-marshal to protect Engle from anyone who happened to catch on.

He hadn't eavesdropped on the conversation between the kid and the man in the fire-sale sport-coat much longer, because around that time the man in the fire-sale sport-coat stopped making sense and began babbling a lot of crazy shit about Denver and Des Moines and Omaha being gone. The idea that three large American cities could simply disappear was absolutely out to lunch . . . but that didn't mean *everything* the old guy had to say was out to lunch.

It *was* an experiment, of course. *That* idea wasn't silly, not a bit. But the old guy's idea that all of them were test subjects was just more crackpot stuff.

Me, Craig thought. *It's me. I'm the test subject.*

All his life Craig had felt himself a test subject in an experiment just like this one. *This is a question, gentlemen, of ratio: pressure to success. The right ratio produces some x-factor. What x-factor? That is what our test subject, Mr. Craig Toomy, will show us.*

But then Craig Toomy had done something they hadn't expected, something none of their cats and rats and guinea pigs had ever dared to do: he had told them he was pulling out.

But you can't do that! You'll explode!

Will I? Fine.

And now it had all become clear to him, so clear. These other people were either innocent bystanders or extras who had been hired to give this stupid little drama some badly needed verisimilitude. The whole thing had been rigged with one object in mind: to keep Craig Toomy away from Boston, to keep Craig Toomy from opting out of the experiment.

But I'll show them, Craig thought. He pulled another sheet from the in-flight magazine and looked at it. It showed a happy man, a man who had obviously never heard of the langoliers, who obviously did not know they were lurking everywhere, behind every bush and tree, in every shadow, just over the horizon. The happy man was driving down a country road behind the wheel of his Avis rental car. The ad said that when you showed your American Pride Frequent Flier Card at the Avis desk, they'd just about *give* you that rental car, and maybe a game-show hostess to drive it, as well. He began to tear a strip of paper from the side of the glossy ad. The long, slow ripping sound was at the same time excruciating and exquisitely calming.

I'll show them that when I say I'm getting out, I mean what I say.

He dropped the strip onto the floor and began on the next one. It was important to rip slowly. It was important that each strip should be as narrow as possible, but you couldn't make them *too* narrow or they got away from you and petered out before you got to the bottom of the page. Getting each one just right demanded sharp eyes and fearless hands. *And I've got them. You better believe it. You just better believe it.*

Rii-ip.

I might have to kill the pilot.

His hands stopped halfway down the page. He looked out the window and saw his own long, pallid face superimposed over the darkness.

I might have to kill the Englishman, too.

Craig Toomy had never killed anyone in his life. Could he do it? With growing relief, he decided that he could. Not while they were still in the air, of course; the Englishman was very fast, very strong, and up here there were no weapons that were sure enough. But once they landed?

Yes. If I have to, yes.

After all, the conference at the Pru was scheduled to last for three days. It seemed now that his late arrival was unavoidable, but at least he would be able to explain: he had been drugged and taken hostage by a government agency. It would stun them. He could see their startled faces as he stood before them, the three hundred bankers from all over the country assembled to discuss bonds and indebtedness, bankers who would instead hear the dirty truth about what the government was up to. *My friends, I was abducted by—*

Rii-ip.

—and was able to escape only when I—

Rii-ip.

If I have to, I can kill them both. In fact, I can kill them all.

Craig Toomy's hands began to move again. He tore off the rest of the strip, dropped it on the floor, and began on the next one. There were a lot of pages in the magazine, there were a lot of strips to each page, and that meant a lot of work lay ahead before the plane landed. But he wasn't worried.

Craig Toomy was a can-do type of guy.

5

Laurel Stevenson didn't go back to sleep but she did slide into a light doze. Her thoughts—which became something close to dreams in this mentally untethered state—turned to why she had really been going to Boston.

I'm supposed to be starting my first real vacation in ten years, she had said, but that was a lie. It contained a small grain of truth, but she doubted if she had been very believable when she told it; she had not been raised to tell lies, and her technique was not very good. Not that any of the people left on Flight 29 would have cared much either way, she supposed. Not in this situation. The fact that you were going to Boston to meet—and almost certainly sleep with—a man you had never met paled next to the fact that you were heading east in an airplane from which most of the passengers and all of the crew had disappeared.

Dear Laurel,
   I am so much looking forward to meeting you. You won't even have to double-check my photo when you step out of the jetway. I'll have so many butterflies in my stomach that all you need to do is look for the guy who's floating somewhere near the ceiling . . .

His name was Darren Crosby.

She wouldn't need to look at his photograph; that much was true. She had memorized his face, just as she had memorized most of his letters. The question was *why.* And to that question she had no answer. Not even a clue. It was just another proof of J. R. R. Tolkien's observation: you must be careful each time you step out of your door, because your front walk is really a road, and the road leads ever onward. If you aren't careful, you're apt to find yourself . . . well . . . simply swept away, a stranger in a strange land with no clue as to how you got there.

Laurel had told everyone where she was going, but she had told no one *why* she was going or what she was doing. She was a graduate of the University of California with a master's degree in library science. Although she was no model, she was cleanly built and pleasant enough to look at. She had a small circle of good friends, and they would have been flabbergasted by what she was up to: heading off to Boston, planning to stay with a man she knew only through correspondence, a man she had met through the extensive personals column of a magazine called *Friends and Lovers.*

She was, in fact, flabbergasted herself.

Darren Crosby was six-feet-one, weighed one hundred and eighty pounds, and had dark-blue eyes. He preferred Scotch (although not to excess), he had a cat named Stanley, he was a dedicated heterosexual, he was a perfect gentleman (or so he claimed), and he thought Laurel was the most beautiful name he had ever heard. The pictures he had sent showed a man with a pleasant, open, intelligent face. She guessed he was the sort of man who would look sinister if he didn't shave twice a day. And that was really all she knew.

Laurel had corresponded with half a dozen men over half a dozen years—it was a hobby, she supposed—but she had never expected to take the next step . . . this step. She supposed that Darren's wry and self-deprecating sense of humor was part of the attraction, but she was dismally aware that her real reasons were not in him at all, but in herself. And wasn't the real attraction her own inability to understand this strong desire to step out of character? To just fly off into the unknown, hoping for the right kind of lightning to strike?

What are you doing? she asked herself again.

The plane ran through some light turbulence and back into smooth air again. Laurel stirred out of her doze and looked around. She saw the young teenaged girl had taken the seat across from her. She was looking out the window.

"What do you see?" Laurel asked. "Anything?"

"Well, the sun's up," the girl said, "but that's all."

"What about the ground?" Laurel didn't want to get up and look for herself. Dinah's head was still resting on her, and Laurel didn't want to wake her.

"Can't see it. It's all clouds down there." She looked around. Her eyes had cleared and a little color—not much, but a little—had come back into her face. "My name's Bethany Simms. What's yours?"

"Laurel Stevenson."

"Do you think we'll be all right?"

"I think so," Laurel said, and then added reluctantly: "I hope so."

"I'm scared about what might be under those clouds," Bethany said, "but I was scared anyway. About Boston. My mother all at once decided how it would be a great idea if I spent a couple of weeks with my Aunt Shawna, even though school starts again in ten days. I think the idea was for me to get off the plane, just like

Mary's little lamb, and then Aunt Shawna pulls the string on me."

"What string?"

"Do not pass Go, do not collect two hundred dollars, go directly to the nearest rehab, and start drying out," Bethany said. She raked her hands through her short dark hair. "Things were already so weird that this seems like just more of the same." She looked Laurel over carefully and then added with perfect seriousness: "This *is* really happening, isn't it? I mean, I've already pinched myself. *Several* times. Nothing changed."

"It's real."

"It doesn't *seem* real," Bethany said. "It seems like one of those stupid disaster movies. *Airport 1990,* something like that. I keep looking around for a couple of old actors like Wilford Brimley and Olivia de Havilland. They're supposed to meet during the shitstorm and fall in love, you know?"

"I don't think they're on the plane," Laurel said gravely. They glanced into each other's eyes and for a moment they almost laughed together. It could have made them friends if it had happened . . . but it didn't. Not quite.

"What about you, Laurel? Do you have a disaster-movie problem?"

"I'm afraid not," Laurel replied . . . and then she *did* begin to laugh. Because the thought which shot across her mind in red neon was *Oh you liar!*

Bethany put a hand over her mouth and giggled.

"Jesus," she said after a minute. "I mean, this is the ultimate hairball, you know?"

Laurel nodded. "I know." She paused and then asked, "Do you need a rehab, Bethany?"

"I don't know." She turned to look out the window again. Her smile was gone and her voice was morose. "I guess I might. I used to think it was just party-time, but now I don't know. I guess it's out of control. But getting shipped off this way . . . I feel like a pig in a slaughterhouse chute."

"I'm sorry," Laurel said, but she was also sorry for herself. The blind girl had already adopted her; she did not need a second adoptee. Now that she was fully awake again she found herself scared— badly scared. She did not want to be behind this kid's dumpster if she was going to offload a big pile of disaster-movie angst. The thought made her grin again; she simply couldn't help it. It *was* the ultimate hairball. It really was.

"I'm sorry, too," Bethany said, "but I guess this is the wrong time to worry about it, huh?"

"I guess maybe it is," Laurel said.

"The pilot never disappeared in any of those *Airport* movies, did he?"

"Not that I remember."

"It's almost six o'clock. Two and a half hours to go."

"Yes."

"If only the world's still there," Bethany said, "that'll be enough for a start." She looked closely at Laurel again. "I don't suppose you've got any grass, do you?"

"I'm afraid not."

Bethany shrugged and offered Laurel a tired smile which was oddly winning. "Well," she said, "you're one ahead of me—I'm just afraid."

6

Some time later, Brian Engle rechecked his heading, his airspeed, his navigational figures, and his charts. Last of all he checked his wristwatch. It was two minutes past eight.

"Well," he said to Nick without looking around, "I think it's about that time. Shit or git."

He reached forward and flicked on the FASTEN SEATBELTS sign. The bell made its low, pleasant chime. Then he flicked the intercom toggle and picked up the mike.

"Hello, ladies and gentlemen. This is Captain Engle again. We're currently over the Atlantic Ocean, roughly thirty miles east of the Maine coast, and I'll be commencing our initial descent into the Bangor area very soon. Under ordinary circumstances I wouldn't turn on the seatbelt sign so early, but these circumstances aren't ordinary, and my mother always said prudence is the better part of valor. In that spirit, I want you to make sure your lap-belts are snug and secure. Conditions below us don't look especially threatening, but since I have no radio communication, the weather is going to be something of a surprise package for all of us. I kept hoping the clouds would break, and I did see a few small holes over Vermont, but I'm afraid they've closed up again. I can tell you from my experience as a pilot that the clouds you see below us don't suggest very bad weather to me. I think the weather in Bangor may be overcast, with some light rain. I'm beginning our descent now. Please be calm; my board is green across and all procedures here on the flight deck remain routine."

Brian had not bothered programming the autopilot for descent; he now began the process himself. He brought the plane around in a long, slow turn, and the seat beneath him canted slightly forward as the 767 began its slow slide down toward the clouds at 4,000 feet.

"Very comforting, that," Nick said. "You should have been a politician, matey."

"I doubt if they're feeling very comfortable right now," Brian said. "I know I'm not."

He was, in fact, more frightened than he had ever been while at the controls of an airplane. The pressure-leak on Flight 7 from Tokyo seemed like a minor glitch in comparison to this situation. His heart was beating slowly and heavily in his chest, like a funeral drum. He swallowed and heard a click in his throat. Flight 29 passed through 30,000 feet, still descending. The white, featureless clouds were closer now. They stretched from horizon to horizon like some strange ballroom floor.

"I'm scared shitless, mate," Nick Hopewell said in a strange, hoarse voice. "I saw men die in the Falklands, took a bullet in the leg there myself, got the Teflon knee to prove it, and I came within an ace of getting blown up by a truck bomb in Beirut—in '82, that was—but I've never been as scared as I am right now. Part of me would like to grab you and make you take us right back up. Just as far up as this bird will go."

"It wouldn't do any good," Brian replied. His own voice was no longer steady; he could hear his heartbeat in it, making it jig-jag up and down in minute variations. "Remember what I said before— we can't stay up here forever."

"I know it. But I'm afraid of what's under those clouds. Or *not* under them."

"Well, we'll all find out together."

"No help for it, is there, mate?"

"Not a bit."

The 767 passed through 25,000 feet, still descending.

7

All the passengers were in the main cabin; even the bald man, who had stuck stubbornly to his seat in business class for most of the flight, had joined them. And they were all awake, except for the bearded man at the very back of the plane. They could hear him snoring blithely away, and Albert Kaussner felt one moment of bitter jealousy, a wish that *he* could wake up after they were safely on the ground as the bearded man would most likely do, and say what the bearded man was most likely going to say: *Where the hell are we?*

The only other sound was the soft *rii-ip . . . rii-ip . . . rii-ip* of Craig Toomy dismembering the in-flight magazine. He sat with his shoes in a deep pile of paper strips.

"Would you mind stopping that?" Don Gaffney asked. His voice was tight and strained. "It's driving me up the wall, buddy."

Craig turned his head. Regarded Don Gaffney with a pair of wide, smooth, empty eyes. Turned his head back. Held up the page he was currently working on, which happened to be the eastern half of the American Pride route map.

Rii-ip.

Gaffney opened his mouth to say something, then closed it tight.

Laurel had her arm around Dinah's shoulders. Dinah was holding Laurel's free hand in both of hers.

Albert sat with Robert Jenkins, just ahead of Gaffney. Ahead of him was the girl with the short dark hair. She was looking out the window, her body held so stiffly upright it might have been wired together. And ahead of her sat Baldy from business class.

"Well, at least we'll be able to get some chow!" he said loudly.

No one answered. The main cabin seemed encased in a stiff shell of tension. Albert Kaussner felt each individual hair on his body standing at attention. He searched for the comforting cloak of Ace Kaussner, that duke of the desert, that baron of the Buntline, and could not find him. Ace had gone on vacation.

The clouds were much closer. They had lost their flat look; Laurel could now see fluffy curves and mild crenellations filled with early-morning shadows. She wondered if Darren Crosby was still down there, patiently waiting for her at a Logan Airport arrivals gate somewhere along the American Pride concourse. She was not terribly surprised to find she didn't care much, one way or another. Her gaze was drawn back to the clouds, and she forgot all about Darren Crosby, who liked Scotch (although not to excess) and claimed to be a perfect gentleman.

She imagined a hand, a huge green hand, suddenly slamming its way up through those clouds and seizing the 767 the way an angry child might seize a toy. She imagined the hand *squeezing*, saw the jet-fuel exploding in orange licks of flame between the huge knuckles, and closed her eyes for a moment.

Don't go down there! she wanted to scream. *Oh please, don't go down there!*

But what choice had they? What choice?

"I'm very scared," Bethany Simms said in a blurred, watery voice. She moved to one of the seats in the center section, fastened her lap-belt, and pressed her hands tightly against her middle. "I think I'm going to pass out."

Craig Toomy glanced at her, and then began ripping a fresh strip from the route map. After a moment, Albert unbuckled his seatbelt, got up, sat down beside Bethany, and buckled up again. As soon as he had, she grasped his hands. Her skin was as cold as marble.

"It's going to be all right," he said, striving to sound tough and unafraid, striving to sound like the fastest Hebrew west of the Mississippi. Instead he only sounded like Albert Kaussner, a seventeen-year-old violin student who felt on the verge of pissing his pants.

"I hope——" she began, and then Flight 29 began to bounce. Bethany screamed.

"What's wrong?" Dinah asked Laurel in a thin, anxious voice. "Is something wrong with the plane? Are we going to crash?"

"I don't——"

Brian's voice came over the speakers. "This is ordinary light turbulence, folks," he said. "Please be calm. We're apt to hit some heavier bumps when we go into the clouds. Most of you have been through this before, so just settle down."

Rii-ip.

Don Gaffney looked toward the man in the crew-neck jersey

again and felt a sudden, almost overmastering urge to rip the flight magazine out of the weird son of a bitch's hands and begin whacking him with it.

The clouds were very close now. Robert Jenkins could see the 767's black shape rushing across their white surfaces just below the plane. Shortly the plane would kiss its own shadow and disappear. He had never had a premonition in his life, but one came to him now, one which was sure and complete. *When we break through those clouds, we are going to see something no human being has ever seen before. It will be something which is utterly beyond belief . . . yet we will be forced to believe it. We will have no choice.*

His hands curled into tight knobs on the arms of his seat. A drop of sweat ran into one eye. Instead of raising a hand to wipe the eye clear, Jenkins tried to blink the sting away. His hands felt nailed to the arms of the seat.

"Is it going to be all right?" Dinah asked frantically. Her hands were locked over Laurel's. They were small, but they squeezed with almost painful force. "Is it really going to be all right?"

Laurel looked out the window. Now the 767 was skimming the tops of the clouds, and the first cotton-candy wisps drifted past her window. The plane ran through another series of jolts and she had to close her throat against a moan. For the first time in her life she felt physically ill with terror.

"I hope so, honey," she said. "I hope so, but I really don't know."

8

"What's on your radar, Brian?" Nick asked. "Anything unusual? Anything at all?"

"No," Brian said. "It says the world is down there, and that's all it says. We're—"

"Wait," Nick said. His voice had a tight, strangled sound, as if his throat had closed down to a bare pinhole. "Climb back up. Let's think this over. Wait for the clouds to break—"

"Not enough time and not enough fuel." Brian's eyes were locked on his instruments. The plane began to bounce again. He made the corrections automatically. "Hang on. We're going in."

He pushed the wheel forward. The altimeter needle began to move more swiftly beneath its glass circle. And Flight 29 slid into the clouds. For a moment its tail protruded, cutting through the fluffy surface like the fin of a shark. A moment later that was also gone and the sky was empty . . . as if no plane had ever been there at all.

CHAPTER FOUR

IN THE CLOUDS.
WELCOME TO BANGOR.
A ROUND OF APPLAUSE.
THE SLIDE AND THE
CONVEYOR BELT. THE
SOUND OF NO PHONES
RINGING. CRAIG TOOMY
MAKES A SIDE-TRIP. THE
LITTLE BLIND GIRL'S
WARNING.

1

The main cabin went from bright sunlight to the gloom of late twilight and the plane began to buck harder. After one particularly hard washboard bump, Albert felt a pressure against his right shoulder. He looked around and saw Bethany's head lying there, as heavy as a ripe October pumpkin. The girl had fainted.

The plane leaped again and there was a heavy thud in first class. This time it was Dinah who shrieked, and Gaffney let out a yell: "What was that? *For God's sake what was that?*"

"The drinks trolley," Bob Jenkins said in a low, dry voice. He tried to speak louder so they would all hear him and found himself unable. "The drinks trolley was left out, remember? I think it must have rolled across—"

The plane took a dizzying rollercoaster leap, came down with a jarring smack, and the drinks trolley fell over with a bang. Glass shattered. Dinah screamed again.

"It's all right," Laurel said frantically. "Don't hold me so tight, Dinah, honey, it's okay—"

"Please, I don't want to die! I just don't want to *die!*"

"Normal turbulence, folks." Brian's voice, coming through the speakers, sounded calm . . . but Bob Jenkins thought he heard barely controlled terror in that voice. "Just be—"

Another rocketing, twisting bump. Another crash as more glasses and mini-bottles fell out of the overturned drinks trolley.

"—calm," Brian finished.

From across the aisle on Don Gaffney's left: *rii-ip.*

Gaffney turned in that direction. "Quit it right now, mother-fucker, or I'll stuff what's left of that magazine right down your throat."

Craig looked at him blandly. "Try it, you old jackass."

The plane bumped up and down again. Albert leaned over Bethany toward the window. Her breasts pressed softly against his arm as he did, and for the first time in the last five years that sensation did not immediately drive everything else out of his mind. He stared out the window, desperately looking for a break in the clouds, trying to *will* a break in the clouds.

There was nothing but shades of dark gray.

2

"How low is the ceiling, mate?" Nick asked. Now that they were actually in the clouds, he seemed calmer.

"I don't know," Brian said. "Lower than I'd hoped, I can tell you that."

"What happens if you run out of room?"

"If my instruments are off even a little, we'll go into the drink," he said flatly. "I doubt if they are, though. If I get down to five hundred feet and there's still no joy, I'll take us up again and fly down to Portland."

"Maybe you ought to just head that way now."

Brian shook his head. "The weather there is almost always worse than the weather here."

"What about Presque Isle? Isn't there a long-range SAC base there?"

Brian had just a moment to think that this guy really did know much more than he should. "It's out of our reach. We'd crash in the woods."

"Then Boston is out of reach, too."

"You bet."

"This is starting to look like being a bad decision, matey."

The plane struck another invisible current of turbulence, and the 767 shivered like a dog with a bad chill. Brian heard faint screams from the main cabin even as he made the necessary corrections and wished he could tell them all that this was nothing, that the 767 could ride out turbulence twenty times this bad. The real problem was the ceiling.

"We're not struck out yet," he said. The altimeter stood at 2,200 feet.

"But we *are* running out of room."

"We—" Brian broke off. A wave of relief rushed over him like a cooling hand. "Here we are," he said. "Coming through."

Ahead of the 767's black nose, the clouds were rapidly thinning. For the first time since they had overflown Vermont, Brian saw a gauzy rip in the whitish-gray blanket. Through it he saw the leaden color of the Atlantic Ocean.

Into the cabin microphone, Brian said: "We've reached the ceiling, ladies and gentlemen. I expect this minor turbulence to ease off once we pass through. In a few minutes, you're going to hear a thump from below. That will be the landing gear descending and locking into place. I am continuing our descent into the Bangor area."

He clicked off and turned briefly to the man in the navigator's seat.

"Wish me luck, Nick."

"Oh, I do, matey—I do."

3

Laurel looked out the window with her breath caught in her throat. The clouds were unravelling fast now. She saw the ocean in a series of brief winks: waves, whitecaps, then a large chunk of rock poking out of the water like the fang of a dead monster. She caught a glimpse of bright orange that might have been a buoy.

They passed over a small, tree-shrouded island, and by leaning and craning her neck, she could see the coast dead ahead. Thin wisps of smoky cloud obscured the view for an endless forty-five seconds. When they cleared, the 767 was over land again. They passed above a field; a patch of forest; what looked like a pond.

But where are the houses? Where are the roads and the cars and the buildings and the high-tension wires?

Then a cry burst from her throat.

"What is it?" Dinah nearly screamed. "What is it, Laurel? What's wrong?"

"Nothing!" she shouted triumphantly. Down below she could see a narrow road leading into a small seaside village. From up here, it looked like a toy town with tiny toy cars parked along the main street. She saw a church steeple, a town gravel pit, a Little League baseball field. "Nothing's wrong! *It's all there! It's all still there!*"

From behind her, Robert Jenkins spoke. His voice was calm, level, and deeply dismayed. "Madam," he said, "I'm afraid you are quite wrong."

4

A long white passenger jet cruised slowly above the ground thirty-five miles east of Bangor International Airport. 767 was printed on its tail in large, proud numerals. Along the fuselage, the words AMERICAN PRIDE were written in letters which had been raked backward to indicate speed. On both sides of the nose was the airline's trademark: a large red eagle. Its spread wings were spangled with blue stars; its talons were flexed and its head was slightly bent. Like the airliner it decorated, the eagle appeared to be coming in for a landing.

The plane printed no shadow on the ground below it as it flew toward the cluster of city ahead; there was no rain, but the morning was gray and sunless. Its belly slid open. The undercarriage dropped down and spread out. The wheels locked into place below the body of the plane and the cockpit area.

American Pride Flight 29 slipped down the chute toward Bangor. It banked slightly left as it went; Captain Engle was now able to correct his course visually, and he did so.

"I see it!" Nick cried. "I see the airport! My God, what a beautiful sight!"

"If you see it, you're out of your seat," Brian said. He spoke without turning around. There was no time to turn around now. "Buckle up and shut up."

But that single long runway *was* a beautiful sight.

Brian centered the plane's nose on it and continued down the slide, passing through 1,000 to 800. Below him, a seemingly endless pine forest passed beneath Flight 29's wings. This finally gave way to a sprawl of buildings—Brian's restless eyes automatically recorded the usual litter of motels, gas stations, and fast-food restaurants—and then they were passing over the Penobscot River and into Bangor airspace. Brian checked the board again, noted he had green lights on his flaps, and then tried the airport again . . . although he knew it was hopeless.

"Bangor tower, this is Flight 29," he said. "I am declaring an emergency. Repeat, *I am declaring an emergency.* If you have runway traffic, get it out of my way. I'm coming in."

He glanced at the airspeed indicator just in time to see it drop below 140, the speed which theoretically committed him to landing. Below him, thinning trees gave way to a golf-course. He caught a quick glimpse of a green Holiday Inn sign and then the lights which marked the end of the runway—33 painted on it in big white numerals—were rushing toward him.

The lights were not red, not green.

They were simply dead.

No time to think about it. No time to think about what would happen to them if a Learjet or a fat little Doyka puddle-jumper suddenly trundled onto the runway ahead of them. No time to do anything now but land the bird.

They passed over a short strip of weeds and gravel and then concrete runway was unrolling thirty feet below the plane. They passed over the first set of white stripes and then the skidmarks—probably made by Air National Guard jets this far out—began just below them.

Brian babied the 767 down toward the runway. The second set of stripes flashed just below them . . . and a moment later there was a light bump as the main landing gear touched down. Now Flight 29 streaked along Runway 33 at a hundred and twenty miles an hour with its nose slightly up and its wings tilted at a mild angle. Brian applied full flaps and reversed the thrusters. There was another bump, even lighter than the first, as the nose came down.

Then the plane was slowing, from a hundred and twenty to a hundred, from a hundred to eighty, from eighty to forty, from forty to the speed at which a man might run.

It was done. They were down.

"Routine landing," Brian said. "Nothing to it." Then he let out a long, shuddery breath and brought the plane to a full stop still four hundred yards from the nearest taxiway. His slim body was suddenly twisted by a flock of shivers. When he raised his hand to his face, it wiped away a great warm handful of sweat. He looked at it and uttered a weak laugh.

A hand fell on his shoulder. "You all right, Brian?"

"Yes," he said, and picked up the intercom mike again. "Ladies and gentlemen," he said, "welcome to Bangor."

From behind him Brian heard a chorus of cheers and he laughed.

Nick Hopewell was not laughing. He was leaning over Brian's seat and peering out through the cockpit window. Nothing moved on the gridwork of runways; nothing moved on the taxiways. No trucks or security vehicles buzzed back and forth on the tarmac. He could see a few vehicles, he could see an Army transport plane— a C-12—parked on an outer taxiway and a Delta 727 parked at one of the jetways, but they were as still as statues.

"Thank you for the welcome, my friend," Nick said softly. "My deep appreciation stems from the fact that it appears you are the only one who is going to extend one. This place is utterly deserted."

6

In spite of the continued radio silence, Brian was reluctant to accept Nick's judgment . . . but by the time he had taxied to a point between two of the passenger terminal's jetways, he found it impossible to believe anything else. It was not just the absence of people; not just the lack of a single security car rushing out to see what was up with this unexpected 767; it was an air of utter lifelessness, as if Bangor International Airport had been deserted for a thousand years, or a hundred thousand. A Jeep-driven baggage train with a few scattered pieces of luggage on its flatties was parked beneath one wing of the Delta jet. It was to this that Brian's eyes kept returning as he brought Flight 29 as close to the terminal as he dared and parked it. The dozen or so bags looked as ancient as artifacts exhumed from the site of some fabulous ancient city. *I wonder if the guy who discovered King Tut's tomb felt the way I do now,* he thought.

He let the engines die and just sat there for a moment. Now there was no sound but the faint whisper of an auxiliary power unit—one of four—at the rear of the plane. Brian's hand moved toward a switch marked INTERNAL POWER and actually touched it before drawing his hand back. Suddenly he didn't want to shut down completely. There was no reason not to, but the voice of instinct was very strong.

Besides, he thought, *I don't think there's anyone around to bitch about wasting fuel . . . what little there is left to waste.*

Then he unbuckled his safety harness and got up.

"Now what, Brian?" Nick asked. He had also risen, and Brian noticed for the first time that Nick was a good four inches taller than he was. He thought: *I have been in charge. Ever since this weird thing happened—ever since we* discovered *it had happened, to be more accurate—I have been in charge. But I think that's going to change very shortly.*

He discovered he didn't care. Flying the 767 into the clouds had taken every ounce of courage he possessed, but he didn't expect any thanks for keeping his head and doing his job; courage was one of the things he got paid for. He remembered a pilot telling him once, "They pay us a hundred thousand dollars or more a year, Brian, and they really do it for just one reason. They know that in almost every pilot's career, there are thirty or forty seconds when he might actually make a difference. They pay us not to freeze when those seconds finally come."

It was all very well for your brain to tell you that you had to go down, clouds or no clouds, that there was simply no choice; your nerve-endings just went on screaming their old warning, telegraphing the old high-voltage terror of the unknown. Even Nick, whatever he was and whatever he did on the ground, had wanted to back away from the clouds when it came to the sticking point. He had needed Brian to do what needed to be done. He and all the others had needed Brian to be their guts. Now they were down and there were no monsters beneath the clouds; only this weird silence and one deserted luggage train sitting beneath the wing of a Delta 727.

So if you want to take over and be the captain, my nose-twisting friend, you have my blessing. I'll even let you wear my cap if you want to. But not until we're off the plane. Until you and the rest of the geese actually stand on the ground, you're my responsibility.

But Nick had asked him a question, and Brian supposed he deserved an answer.

"Now we get off the airplane and see what's what," he said, brushing past the Englishman.

Nick put a restraining hand on his shoulder. "Do you think—"

Brian felt a flash of uncharacteristic anger. He shook loose from Nick's hand. "I think we get off the plane," he said. "There's no one to extend a jetway or run us out a set of stairs, so I think we use the emergency slide. After that, *you* think. *Matey.*"

He pushed through into first class . . . and almost fell over the drinks trolley, which lay on its side. There was a lot of broken glass and an eye-watering stink of alcohol. He stepped over it. Nick caught up with him at the rear of the first-class compartment.

"Brian, if I said something to offend you, I'm sorry. You did a hell of a fine job."

"You didn't offend me," Brian said. "It's just that in the last ten hours or so I've had to cope with a pressure leak over the Pacific Ocean, finding out that my ex-wife died in a stupid apartment fire in Boston, and that the United States has been cancelled. I'm feeling a little zonked."

He walked through business class into the main cabin. For a moment there was utter silence; they only sat there, looking at him from their white faces with dumb incomprehension.

Then Albert Kaussner began to applaud.

After a moment, Bob Jenkins joined him . . . and Don Gaffney . . . and Laurel Stevenson. The bald man looked around and also began to applaud.

"What is it?" Dinah asked Laurel. "What's happening?"

"It's the captain," Laurel said. She began to cry. "It's the captain who brought us down safe."

Then Dinah began to applaud, too.

Brian stared at them, dumbfounded. Standing behind him, Nick joined in. They unbuckled their belts and stood in front of their seats, applauding him. The only three who did not join in were Bethany, who had fainted, the bearded man, who was still snoring in the back row, and Craig Toomy, who panned them all with his strange lunar gaze and then began to rip a fresh strip from the airline magazine.

6

Brian felt his face flush—this was just too goony. He raised his hands but for a moment they went on, regardless.

"Ladies and gentlemen, please . . . please . . . I assure you, it was a very routine landing—"

"Shucks, ma'am—t'warn't nothin," Bob Jenkins said, doing a very passable Gary Cooper imitation, and Albert burst out laughing. Beside him, Bethany's eyes fluttered open and she looked around, dazed.

"We got down alive, didn't we?" she said. "My God! That's great! I thought we were all dead meat!"

"Please," Brian said. He raised his arms higher and now he felt weirdly like Richard Nixon, accepting his party's nomination for four more years. He had to struggle against sudden shrieks of laughter. He couldn't do that; the passengers wouldn't understand. They wanted a hero, and he was elected. He might as well accept the position . . . and use it. He still had to get them off the plane, after all. "If I could have your attention, please!"

They stopped applauding one by one and looked at him expectantly—all except Craig, who threw his magazine aside in a sudden resolute gesture. He unbuckled his seatbelt, rose, and stepped out into the aisle, kicking a drift of paper strips aside. He began to rummage around in the compartment above his seat, frowning with concentration as he did so.

"You've looked out the windows, so you know as much as I do," Brian said. "Most of the passengers and all of the crew on this flight disappeared while we were asleep. That's crazy enough, but now we appear to be faced with an even crazier proposition. It looks like a lot of other people have disappeared as well . . . but logic suggests that other people must be around *somewhere*. We survived whatever-it-was, so others must have survived it as well."

Bob Jenkins, the mystery writer, whispered something under his breath. Albert heard him but could not make out the words. He half-turned in Jenkins's direction just as the writer muttered the two words again. This time Albert caught them. They were *false logic*.

"The best way to deal with this, I think, is to take things one step at a time. Step one is exiting the plane."

"I bought a ticket to Boston," Craig Toomy said in a calm, rational voice. "Boston is where I want to go."

Nick stepped out from behind Brian's shoulder. Craig glanced at him and his eyes narrowed. For a moment he looked like a bad-tempered housecat again. Nick raised one hand with the fingers curled in against his palm and scissored two of his knuckles together in a nose-pinching gesture. Craig Toomy, who had once been forced to stand with a lit match between his toes while his mother sang "Happy Birthday," got the message at once. He had always been a quick study. And he could wait.

"We'll have to use the emergency slide," Brian said, "so I want to review the procedures with you. Listen carefully, then form a single-file line and follow me to the front of the aircraft."

7

Four minutes later, the forward entrance of American Pride's Flight 29 swung inward. Some murmured conversation drifted out of the opening and seemed to fall immediately dead on the cool, still air. There was a hissing sound and a large clump of orange fabric suddenly bloomed in the doorway. For a moment it looked like a strange hybrid sunflower. It grew and took shape as it fell, its surface inflating into a plump ribbed slide. As the foot of the slide struck the tarmac there was a low *pop!* and then it just leaned there, looking like a giant orange air mattress.

Brian and Nick stood at the head of the short line in the portside row of first class.

"There's something wrong with the air out there," Nick said in a low voice.

"What do you mean?" Brian asked. He pitched his voice even lower. "Poisoned?"

"No . . . at least I don't think so. But it has no smell, no taste."

"You're nuts," Brian said uneasily.

"No I'm not," Nick said. "This is an *airport,* mate, not a bloody hayfield, but can you smell oil or gas? I can't."

Brian sniffed. And there was nothing. If the air was poisoned—he didn't believe it was, but *if*—it was a slow-acting toxin. His lungs seemed to be processing it just fine. But Nick was right. There was no smell. And that other, more elusive, quality that the Brit had called taste . . . that wasn't there, either. The air outside the open door tasted utterly neutral. It tasted canned.

"Is something wrong?" Bethany Simms asked anxiously. "I mean, I'm not sure if I really want to know if there is, but—"

"There's nothing wrong," Brian said. He counted heads, came up with ten, and turned to Nick again. "That guy in the back is still asleep. Do you think we should wake him up?"

Nick thought for a moment, then shook his head. "Let's not. Haven't we got enough problems for now without having to play nursemaid to a bloke with a hangover?"

Brian grinned. They were his thoughts exactly. "Yes, I think we do. All right—you go down first, Nick. Hold the bottom of the slide. I'll help the rest off."

"Maybe *you'd* better go first. In case my loudmouthed friend decides to cut up rough about the unscheduled stop again." He pronounced *unscheduled* as *un-shed-youled*.

Brian glanced at the man in the crew-necked jersey. He was standing at the rear of the line, a slim monogrammed briefcase in one hand, staring blankly at the ceiling. His face had all the expression of a department-store dummy. "I'm not going to have any trouble with him," he said, "because I don't give a crap what he does. He can go or stay, it's all the same to me."

Nick grinned. "Good enough for me, too. Let the grand exodus begin."

"Shoes off?"

Nick held up a pair of black kidskin loafers.

"Okay—away you go." Brian turned to Bethany. "Watch closely, miss—you're next."

"Oh god—I *hate* shit like this."

Bethany nevertheless crowded up beside Brian and watched apprehensively as Nick Hopewell addressed the slide. He jumped, raising both legs at the same time so he looked like a man doing a seat-drop on a trampoline. He landed on his butt and slid to the bottom. It was neatly done; the foot of the slide barely moved. He hit the tarmac with his stocking feet, stood up, twirled around, and made a mock bow with his arms held out behind him.

"Easy as pie!" he called up. "Next customer!"

"That's you, miss," Brian said. "Is it Bethany?"

"Yes," she said nervously. "I don't think I can do this. I flunked gym all three semesters and they finally let me take home ec again instead."

"You'll do fine," Brian told her. He reflected that people used the slide with much less coaxing and a lot more enthusiasm when there was a threat they could see—a hole in the fuselage or a fire in one of the portside engines. "Shoes off?"

Bethany's shoes—actually a pair of old pink sneakers—were off, but she tried to withdraw from the doorway and the bright-orange slide just the same. "Maybe if I could just have a drink before—"

"Mr. Hopewell's holding the slide and you'll be fine," Brian coaxed, but he was beginning to be afraid he might have to push her. He didn't want to, but if she didn't jump soon, he would. You couldn't let them go to the end of the line until their courage returned; that was the big no-no when it came to the escape slide. If you did that, they *all* wanted to go to the end of the line.

"Go on, Bethany," Albert said suddenly. He had taken his violin case from the overhead compartment and held it tucked under one arm. "I'm scared to death of that thing, and if you go, I'll have to."

She looked at him, surprised. "Why?"

Albert's face was very red. "Because you're a girl," he said simply. "I know I'm a sexist rat, but that's it."

Bethany looked at him a moment longer, then laughed and turned to the slide. Brian had made up his mind to push her if she looked around or drew back again, but she didn't. "Boy, I wish I had some grass," she said, and jumped.

She had seen Nick's seat-drop maneuver and knew what to do, but at the last moment she lost her courage and tried to get her feet under her again. As a result, she skidded to one side when she came down on the slide's bouncy surface. Brian was sure she was going to tumble off, but Bethany herself saw the danger and managed to roll back. She shot down the slope on her right side, one hand over her head, her blouse rucking up almost to the nape of her neck. Then Nick caught her and she stepped off.

"Oh boy," she said breathlessly. "Just like being a kid again."

"Are you all right?" Nick asked.

"Yeah. I think I might have wet my pants a little, but I'm okay."

Nick smiled at her and turned back to the slide.

Albert looked apologetically at Brian and extended the violin case. "Would you mind holding this for me? I'm afraid if I fall off the slide, it might get broken. My folks'd kill me. It's a Gretch."

Brian took it. His face was calm and serious, but he was smiling inside. "Could I look? I used to play one of these about a thousand years ago."

"Sure," Albert said.

Brian's interest had a calming effect on the boy . . . which was exactly what he had hoped for. He unsnapped the three catches and opened the case. The violin inside was indeed a Gretch, and not from the bottom of that prestigious line, either. Brian guessed you could buy a compact car for the amount of money this had cost.

"Beautiful," he said, and plucked out four quick notes along the neck: *My dog has fleas.* They rang sweetly and beautifully. Brian closed and latched the case again. "I'll keep it safe. Promise."

"Thanks." Albert stood in the doorway, took a deep breath, then let it out again. "Geronimo," he said in a weak little voice and jumped. He tucked his hands into his armpits as he did so—protecting his hands in any situation where physical damage was possible was so ingrained in him that it had become a reflex. He seat-dropped onto the slide and shot neatly to the bottom.

"Well done!" Nick said.

"Nothing to it," Ace Kaussner drawled, stepped off, and then nearly tripped over his own feet.

"Albert!" Brian called down. "Catch!" He leaned out, placed the violin case on the center of the slide, and let it go. Albert caught it easily five feet from the bottom, tucked it under his arm, and stood back.

Jenkins shut his eyes as he leaped and came down aslant on one scrawny buttock. Nick stepped nimbly to the left side of the slide and caught the writer just as he fell off, saving him a nasty tumble to the concrete.

"Thank you, young man."

"Don't mention it, matey."

Gaffney followed; so did the bald man. Then Laurel and Dinah Bellman stood in the hatchway.

"I'm scared," Dinah said in a thin, wavery voice.

"You'll be fine, honey," Brian said. "You don't even have to jump." He put his hands on Dinah's shoulders and turned her so she was facing him with her back to the slide. "Give me your hands and I'll lower you onto the slide."

But Dinah put them behind her back. "Not you. I want Laurel to do it."

Brian looked at the youngish woman with the dark hair. "Would you?"

"Yes," she said. "If you tell me what to do."

"Dinah already knows. Lower her onto the slide by her hands. When she's lying on her tummy with her feet pointed straight, she can shoot right down."

Dinah's hands were cold in Laurel's. "I'm scared," she repeated.

"Honey, it'll be just like going down a playground slide," Brian said. "The man with the English accent is waiting at the bottom to catch you. He's got his hands up just like a catcher in a baseball game." Not, he reflected, that Dinah would know what *that* looked like.

Dinah looked at him as if he were being quite foolish. "Not of *that*. I'm scared of this *place*. It smells funny."

Laurel, who detected no smell but her own nervous sweat, looked helplessly at Brian.

"Honey," Brian said, dropping to one knee in front of the little blind girl, "we have to get off the plane. You know that, don't you?"

The lenses of the dark glasses turned toward him. "*Why? Why* do we have to get off the plane? There's no one here."

Brian and Laurel exchanged a glance.

"Well," Brian said, "we won't really know that until we check, will we?"

"I know already," Dinah said. "There's nothing to smell and nothing to hear. But . . . but . . ."

"But what, Dinah?" Laurel asked.

Dinah hesitated. She wanted to make them understand that the way she had to leave the plane was really not what was bothering her. She had gone down slides before, and she trusted Laurel. Laurel would not let go of her hands if it was dangerous. Something was *wrong* here, *wrong,* and that was what she was afraid of—the wrong thing. It wasn't the quiet and it wasn't the emptiness. It might have to do with those things, but it was more than those things.

Something *wrong.*

But grownups did not believe children, especially not blind children, even more especially not blind *girl* children. She wanted to tell them they couldn't stay here, that it wasn't *safe* to stay here, that they had to start the plane up and get going again. But what would they say? Okay, sure, Dinah's right, everybody back on the plane? No *way.*

They'll see. They'll see that it's empty and then we'll get back on the airplane and go someplace else. Someplace where it doesn't feel wrong. There's still time.

I think.

"Never mind," she told Laurel. Her voice was low and resigned. "Lower me down."

Laurel lowered her carefully onto the slide. A moment later Dinah was looking up at her—*except she's not* really *looking,* Laurel thought, *she can't* really *look at all*—with her bare feet splayed out behind her on the orange slide.

"Okay, Dinah?" Laurel asked.

"No," Dinah said. "*Nothing's* okay here." And before Laurel could release her, Dinah unlocked her hands from Laurel's and released herself. She slid to the bottom, and Nick caught her.

Laurel went next, dropping neatly onto the slide and holding her skirt primly as she slid to the bottom. That left Brian, the snoozing drunk at the back of the plane, and that fun-loving paper-ripping party animal, Mr. Crew-Neck Jersey.

I'm not going to have any trouble with him, Brian had said, *because I don't give a crap what he does.* Now he discovered that was not really true. The man was not playing with a full deck. Brian suspected even the little girl knew that, and the little girl was blind. What if they left him behind and the guy decided to go on a rampage? What if, in the course of that rampage, he decided to trash the cockpit?

So what? You're not going anyplace. The tanks are almost dry.

Still, he didn't like the idea, and not just because the 767 was a multi-million-dollar piece of equipment, either. Perhaps what he felt was a vague echo of what he had seen in Dinah's face as she looked up from the slide. Things here seemed wrong, even wronger than they looked . . . and that was scary, because he didn't know how things could be wronger than that. The plane, however, was right. Even with its fuel tanks all but empty, it was a world he knew and understood.

"Your turn, friend," he said as civilly as he could.

"You know I'm going to report you for this, don't you?" Craig

Toomy asked in a queerly gentle voice. "You know I plan to sue this entire airline for thirty million dollars, and that I plan to name you a primary respondent?"

"That's your privilege, Mr.—"

"Toomy. Craig Toomy."

"Mr. Toomy," Brian agreed. He hesitated. "Mr. Toomy, are you aware of what has happened to us?"

Craig looked out the open doorway for a moment—looked at the deserted tarmac and the wide, slightly polarized terminal windows on the second level, where no happy friends and relatives stood waiting to embrace arriving passengers, where no impatient travellers waited for their flights to be called.

Of course he knew. It was the langoliers. The langoliers had come for all the foolish, lazy people, just as his father had always said they would.

In that same gentle voice, Craig said: "In the Bond Department of the Desert Sun Banking Corporation, I am known as The Wheelhorse. Did you know that?" He paused for a moment, apparently waiting for Brian to make some response. When Brian didn't, Craig continued. "Of course you didn't. No more than you know how important this meeting at the Prudential Center in Boston is. No more than you care. But let me tell you something, Captain: the economic fate of nations may hinge upon the results of that meeting—that meeting from which I will be absent when the roll is taken."

"Mr. Toomy, all that's very interesting, but I really don't have time—"

"*Time!*" Craig screamed at him suddenly. "What in the hell do *you* know about time? Ask me! Ask me! I know about time! I know *all about* time! Time is short, sir! Time is *very fucking short!*"

Hell with it, I'm going to push the crazy son of a bitch, Brian thought, but before he could, Craig Toomy turned and leaped. He did a perfect seat-drop, holding his briefcase to his chest as he did so, and Brian was crazily reminded of that old Hertz ad on TV, the one where O. J. Simpson went flying through airports in a suit and a tie.

"*Time is short as hell!*" Craig shouted as he slid down, briefcase over his chest like a shield, pantslegs pulling up to reveal his knee-high dress-for-success black nylon socks.

Brian muttered: "Jesus, what a fucking weirdo." He paused at the head of the slide, looked around once more at the comforting, known world of his aircraft . . . and jumped.

8

Ten people stood in two small groups beneath the giant wing of the 767 with the red-and-blue eagle on the nose. In one group were Brian, Nick, the bald man, Bethany Simms, Albert Kaussner, Robert Jenkins, Dinah, Laurel, and Don Gaffney. Standing slightly apart from them and constituting his own group was Craig Toomy, a.k.a. The Wheelhorse. Craig bent and shook out the creases of his pants with fussy concentration, using his left hand to do it. The right was tightly locked around the handle of his briefcase. Then he simply stood and looked around with wide, disinterested eyes.

"What now, Captain?" Nick asked briskly.

"You tell me. Us."

Nick looked at him for a moment, one eyebrow slightly raised, as if to ask Brian if he really meant it. Brian inclined his head half an inch. It was enough.

"Well, inside the terminal will do for a start, I reckon," Nick said. "What would be the quickest way to get there? Any idea?"

Brian nodded toward a line of baggage trains parked beneath the overhang of the main terminal. "I'd guess the quickest way in without a jetway would be the luggage conveyor."

"All right; let's hike on over, ladies and gentlemen, shall we?"

It was a short walk, but Laurel, who walked hand-in-hand with Dinah, thought it was the strangest one she had ever taken in her life. She could see them as if from above, less than a dozen dots trundling slowly across a wide concrete plain. There was no breeze. No birds sang. No motors revved in the distance, and no human voice broke the unnatural quiet. Even their footfalls seemed wrong to her. She was wearing a pair of high heels, but instead of the brisk click she was used to, she seemed to hear only small, dull thuds.

Seemed, she thought. *That's the key word. Because the situation is so strange,* everything *begins to seem strange. It's the concrete, that's all. High heels sound different on concrete.*

But she had walked on concrete in high heels before. She didn't remember ever hearing a sound precisely like this. It was . . . pallid, somehow. Strengthless.

They reached the parked luggage trains. Nick wove between them, leading the line, and stopped at a dead conveyor belt which emerged from a hole lined with hanging strips of rubber. The conveyor made a wide circle on the apron where the handlers normally stood to unload the flatties, then re-entered the terminal through another hole hung with rubber strips.

"What are those pieces of rubber for?" Bethany asked nervously.

"To keep out the draft in cold weather, I imagine," Nick said. "Just let me poke my head through and have a look. No fear; won't be a moment." And before anyone could reply, he had boosted himself onto the conveyor belt and was walking bent-over down to one of the holes cut into the building. When he got there, he dropped to his knees and poked his head through the rubber strips.

We're going to hear a whistle and then a thud, Albert thought wildly, *and when we pull him back, his head will be gone.*

There was no whistle, no thud. When Nick withdrew, his head was still firmly attached to his neck, and his face wore a thoughtful expression. "Coast's clear," he said, and to Albert his cheery tone now sounded manufactured. "Come on through, friends. When a body meet a body, and all that."

Bethany held back. "*Are* there bodies? Mister, are there dead people in there?"

"Not that I saw, miss," Nick said, and now he had dropped any attempt at lightness. "I was misquoting old Bobby Burns in an attempt to be funny. I'm afraid I achieved tastelessness instead of humor. The fact is, I didn't see anyone at all. But that's pretty much what we expected, isn't it?"

It was . . . but it struck heavily at their hearts just the same. Nick's as well, from his tone.

One after the other they climbed onto the conveyor belt and crawled after him through the hanging rubber strips.

Dinah paused just outside the entrance hole and turned her head back toward Laurel. Hazy light flashed across her dark glasses, turning them to momentary mirrors.

"It's really wrong here," she repeated, and pushed through to the other side.

9

One by one they emerged into the main terminal of Bangor International Airport, exotic baggage crawling along a stalled conveyor belt. Albert helped Dinah off and then they all stood there, looking around in silent wonder.

The shocked amazement at waking to a plane which had been magically emptied of people had worn off; now dislocation had taken the place of wonder. None of them had ever been in an airport terminal which was utterly empty. The rental-car stalls were deserted. The ARRIVALS/DEPARTURES monitors were dark and dead. No one stood at the bank of counters serving Delta, United, Northwest Air-Link, or Mid-Coast Airways. The huge tank in the middle of the floor with the BUY MAINE LOBSTERS banner stretched over it was full of water, but there were no lobsters in it. The overhead fluorescents were off, and the small amount of light entering through the doors on the far side of the large room petered out halfway across the floor, leaving the little group from Flight 29 huddled together in an unpleasant nest of shadows.

"Right, then," Nick said, trying for briskness and managing only unease. "Let's try the telephones, shall we?"

While he went to the bank of telephones, Albert wandered over to the Budget Rent A Car desk. In the slots on the rear wall he saw folders for BRIGGS, HANDLEFORD, MARCHANT, FENWICK and PESTLEMAN. There was, no doubt, a rental agreement inside each one, along with a map of the central Maine area, and on each map there would be an arrow with the legend YOU ARE HERE on it, pointing at the city of Bangor.

But where are we really? Albert wondered. *And where are Briggs, Handleford, Marchant, Fenwick, and Pestleman? Have they been transported to another dimension? Maybe it's the Grateful Dead. Maybe the Dead's playing somewhere downstate and everybody left for the show.*

There was a dry scratching noise just behind him. Albert nearly jumped out of his skin and whirled around fast, holding his violin case up like a cudgel. Bethany was standing there, just touching a match to the tip of her cigarette.

She raised her eyebrows. "Scare you?"

"A little," Albert said, lowering the case and offering her a small, embarrassed smile.

"Sorry." She shook out the match, dropped it on the floor, and drew deeply on her cigarette. "There. At least *that's* better. I didn't dare to on the plane. I was afraid something might blow up."

Bob Jenkins strolled over. "You know, I quit those about ten years ago."

"No lectures, please," Bethany said. "I've got a feeling that if we get out of this alive and sane, I'm in for about a month of lectures. Solid. Wall-to-wall."

Jenkins raised his eyebrows but didn't ask for an explanation. "Actually," he said, "I was going to ask you if I could have one. This seems like an excellent time to renew acquaintance with old habits."

Bethany smiled and offered him a Marlboro. Jenkins took it and she lit it for him. He inhaled, then coughed out a series of smoke-signal puffs.

"You *have* been away," she observed matter-of-factly.

Jenkins agreed. "But I'll get used to it again in a hurry. That's the real horror of the habit, I'm afraid. Did you two notice the clock?"

"No," Albert said.

Jenkins pointed to the wall above the doors of the men's and women's bathrooms. The clock mounted there had stopped at 4:07.

"It fits," he said. "We knew we had been in the air for awhile when—let's call it The Event, for want of a better term—when The Event took place. 4:07A.M. Eastern Daylight Time is 1:07A.M. PDT. So now we know the when."

"Gee, that's great," Bethany said.

"Yes," Jenkins said, either not noticing or preferring to ignore the light overlay of sarcasm in her voice. "But there's something wrong with it. I only wish the sun was out. Then I could be sure."

"What do you mean?" Albert asked.

"The clocks—the electric ones, anyway—are no good. There's no juice. But if the sun was out, we could get at least a rough idea of what time it is by the length and direction of our shadows. My watch says it's going on quarter of nine, but I don't trust it. It feels later to me that that. I have no proof for it, and I can't explain it, but it does."

Albert thought about it. Looked around. Looked back at Jenkins. "You know," he said, "it *does*. It feels like it's almost lunchtime. Isn't that nuts?"

"It's not nuts," Bethany said, "it's just jetlag."

"I disagree," Jenkins said. "We travelled west to east, young lady. Any temporal dislocation west–east travellers feel goes the other way. They feel it's *earlier* than it should be."

"I want to ask you about something you said on the plane," Albert said. "When the captain told us that there must be *some* other people here, you said 'false logic.' In fact, you said it twice. But it seems straight enough to me. We were all asleep, and *we're* here. And if this thing happened at"—Albert glanced toward the clock—"at 4:07, Bangor time, almost everyone in *town* must have been asleep."

"Yes," Jenkins said blandly. "So where are they?"

Albert was nonplussed. "Well . . ."

There was a bang as Nick forcibly hung up one of the pay telephones. It was the last in a long line of them; he had tried every one. "It's a washout," he said. "They're all dead. The coin-fed ones as well as the direct-dials. You can add the sound of no phones ringing to that of no dogs barking, Brian."

"So what do we do now?" Laurel asked. She heard the forlorn sound of her own voice and it made her feel very small, very lost. Beside her, Dinah was turning in slow circles. She looked like a human radar dish.

"Let's go upstairs," Baldy proposed. "That's where the restaurant must be."

They all looked at him. Gaffney snorted. "You got a one-track mind, mister."

The bald man looked at him from beneath one raised eyebrow. "First, the name is Rudy Warwick, not mister," he replied. "Second, people think better when their stomachs are full." He shrugged. "It's just a law of nature."

"I think Mr. Warwick is quite right," Jenkins said. "We all *could* use something to eat . . . and if we go upstairs, we may find some other clues pointing toward what has happened. In fact, I rather think we will."

Nick shrugged. He looked suddenly tired and confused. "Why not?" he said. "I'm starting to feel like Mr. Robinson Bloody Crusoe."

They started toward the escalator, which was also dead, in a straggling little group. Albert, Bethany, and Bob Jenkins walked together, toward the rear.

"You know something, don't you?" Albert asked abruptly. "What is it?"

"I *might* know something," Jenkins corrected. "I might not. For the time being I'm going to hold my peace . . . except for one suggestion."

"What?"

"It's not for you; it's for the young lady." He turned to Bethany. "Save your matches. That's my suggestion."

"What?" Bethany frowned at him.

"You heard me."

"Yeah, I guess I did, but I don't get what you mean. There's probably a newsstand upstairs, Mr. Jenkins. They'll have lots of matches. Cigarettes and disposable lighters, too."

"I agree," Jenkins said. "I still advise you to save your matches."

He's playing Philo Christie or whoever it was again, Albert thought.

He was about to point this out and ask Jenkins to please remember that this wasn't one of his novels when Brian Engle stopped at the foot of the escalator, so suddenly that Laurel had to jerk sharply on Dinah's hand to keep the blind girl from running into him.

"Watch where you're going, okay?" Laurel asked. "In case you didn't notice, the kid here can't see."

Brian ignored her. He was looking around at the little group of refugees. "Where's Mr. Toomy?"

"Who?" the bald man—Warwick—asked.

"The guy with the pressing appointment in Boston."

"Who cares?" Gaffney asked. "Good riddance to bad rubbish."

But Brian was uneasy. He didn't like the idea that Toomy had slipped away and gone off on his own. He didn't know why, but he didn't like that idea at all. He glanced at Nick. Nick shrugged, then shook his head. "Didn't see him go, mate. I was fooling with the phones. Sorry."

"*Toomy!*" Brian shouted. "*Craig Toomy! Where are you?*"

There was no response. Only that queer, oppressive silence. And Laurel noticed something then, something that made her skin cold. Brian had cupped his hands and shouted up the escalator. In a high-ceilinged place like this one, there should have been at least some echo.

But there had been none.

No echo at all.

10

While the others were occupied downstairs—the two teenagers and the old geezer standing by one of the car-rental desks, the others watching the British thug as he tried the phones—Craig Toomy had crept up the stalled escalator as quietly as a mouse. He knew exactly where he wanted to go; he knew exactly what to look for when he got there.

He strode briskly across the large waiting room with his briefcase swinging beside his right knee, ignoring both the empty chairs and an empty bar called The Red Baron. At the far end of the room was a sign hanging over the mouth of a wide, dark corridor. It read

GATE 5 INTERNATIONAL ARRIVALS
DUTY FREE SHOPS
U.S. CUSTOMS
AIRPORT SECURITY

He had almost reached the head of this corridor when he glanced out one of the wide windows at the tarmac again . . . and his pace faltered. He approached the glass slowly and looked out.

There was nothing to see but the empty concrete and the moveless white sky, but his eyes began to widen nonetheless and he felt fear begin to steal into his heart.

They're coming, a dead voice suddenly told him. It was the voice of his father, and it spoke from a small, haunted mausoleum tucked away in a gloomy corner of Craig Toomy's heart.

"No," he whispered, and the word spun a little blossom of fog on the window in front of his lips. "No one is coming."

You've been bad. Worse, you've been lazy.

"No!"

Yes. You had an appointment and you skipped it. You ran away. You ran away to Bangor, Maine, of all the silly places.

"It wasn't my fault," he muttered. He was gripping the handle of the briefcase with almost painful tightness now. "I was taken against my will. I . . . I was shanghaied!"

No reply from that interior voice. Only waves of disapproval. And once again Craig intuited the pressure he was under, the terrible never-ending pressure, the weight of the fathoms. The interior voice did not have to tell him there were no excuses; Craig knew that. He knew it of old.

THEY *were here . . . and they will be back. You know that, don't you?*

He knew. The langoliers would be back. They would be back for *him*. He could sense them. He had never seen them, but he knew how horrible they would be. And was he alone in his knowledge? He thought not.

He thought perhaps the little blind girl knew something about the langoliers as well.

But that didn't matter. The only thing which did was getting to Boston—getting to Boston before the langoliers could arrive in Bangor from their terrible, doomish lair to eat him alive and screaming. He had to get to that meeting at the Pru, had to let them know what he had done, and then he would be . . .

Free.

He would be free.

Craig pulled himself away from the window, away from the emptiness and the stillness, and plunged into the corridor beneath the sign. He passed the empty shops without a glance. Beyond them he came to the door he was looking for. There was a small rectangular plaque mounted on it, just above a bullseye peephole. AIRPORT SECURITY, it said.

He had to get in there. One way or another, he *had* to get in there.

All of this . . . this craziness . . . it doesn't have to belong to me. I don't have to own it. Not anymore.

Craig reached out and touched the doorknob of the Airport Security office. The blank look in his eyes had been replaced by an expression of clear determination.

I have been under stress for a long, a very long, time. Since I was seven? No—I think it started even before that. The fact is, I've been under stress for as long as I can remember. This latest piece of craziness is just a new variation. It's probably just what the man in the ratty sport-coat said it was: a test. Agents of some secret government agency or sinister foreign power running a test. But I choose not to participate in any more tests. I don't care if it's my father in charge, or my mother, or the dean of the Graduate School of Management, or the Desert Sun Banking Corporation's Board of Directors. I choose not to participate. I choose to escape. I choose to get to Boston and finish what I set out to do

*when I presented the Argentinian bond-buy in the first place. If I
don't . . .*

But he knew what would happen if he didn't.

He would go mad.

Craig tried the doorknob. It did not move beneath his hand, but
when he gave it a small, frustrated push, the door swung open.
Either it had been left slightly unlatched, or it had unlocked when
the power went off and the security systems went dead. Craig didn't
care which. The important thing was that he wouldn't need to muss
his clothes trying to crawl through an air-conditioning duct or something. He still had every intention of showing up at his meeting
before the end of the day, and he didn't want his clothes smeared
with dirt and grease when he got there. One of the simple, unex-
ceptioned truths of life was this: guys with dirt on their suits have
no credibility.

He pushed the door open and went inside.

11

Brian and Nick reached the top of the escalator first, and the others
gathered around them. This was BIA's central waiting room, a large
square box filled with contour plastic seats (some with coin-op TVs
bolted to the arms) and dominated by a wall of polarized floor-to-
ceiling windows. To their immediate left was the airport newsstand
and the security checkpoint which served Gate 1; to their right and
all the way across the room were The Red Baron Bar and The
Cloud Nine Restaurant. Beyond the restaurant was the corridor
leading to the Airport Security office and the International Arrivals
Annex.

"Come on—" Nick began, and Dinah said, "Wait."

She spoke in a strong, urgent voice and they all turned toward
her curiously.

Dinah dropped Laurel's hand and raised both of her own. She
cupped the thumbs behind her ears and splayed her fingers out like
fans. Then she simply stood there, still as a post, in this odd and
rather weird listening posture.

"What—" Brian began, and Dinah said *"Shhh!"* in an abrupt,
inarguable sibilant.

She turned slightly to the left, paused, then turned in the other direction until the white light coming through the windows fell directly on her, turning her already pale face into something which was ghostlike and eerie. She took off her dark glasses. The eyes beneath were wide, brown, and not quite blank.

"There," she said in a low, dreaming voice, and Laurel felt terror begin to stroke at her heart with chilly fingers. Nor was she alone. Bethany was crowding close to her on one side, and Don Gaffney moved in against her other side. "There—I can feel the light. They said that's how they know I can see again. I can always feel the light. It's like heat inside my head."

"Dinah, what—" Brian began.

Nick elbowed him. The Englishman's face was long and drawn, his forehead ribbed with lines. "Be quiet, mate."

"The light is . . . here."

She walked slowly away from them, her hands still fanned out by her ears, her elbows held out before her to encounter any object which might stand in her way. She advanced until she was less than two feet from the window. Then she slowly reached out until her fingers touched the glass. They looked like black starfish outlined against the white sky. She let out a small, unhappy murmur.

"The glass is wrong, too," she said in that dreaming voice.

"Dinah—" Laurel began.

"Shhh . . ." she whispered without turning around. She stood at the window like a little girl waiting for her father to come home from work. "*I hear something.*"

These whispered words sent a wordless, thoughtless horror through Albert Kaussner's mind. He felt pressure on his shoulders and looked down to see he had crossed his arms across his chest and was clutching himself hard.

Brian listened with all his concentration. He heard his own breathing, and the breathing of the others . . . but he heard nothing else. *It's her imagination,* he thought. *That's all it is.*

But he wondered.

"What?" Laurel asked urgently. "What do you hear, Dinah?"

"I don't know," she said without turning from the window. "It's very faint. I thought I heard it when we got off the airplane, and then I decided it was just my imagination. Now I can hear it better. I can hear it even through the glass. It sounds . . . a little like Rice Krispies after you pour in the milk."

Brian turned to Nick and spoke in a low voice. "Do you hear anything?"

"Not a bloody thing," Nick said, matching Brian's tone. "But she's blind. She's used to making her ears do double duty."

"I think it's hysteria," Brian said. He was whispering now, his lips almost touching Nick's ear.

Dinah turned from the window.

" 'Do you hear anything?' " she mimicked. " 'Not a bloody thing. But she's blind. She's used to making her ears do double duty.' " She paused, then added: " 'I think it's hysteria.' "

"Dinah, what are you talking about?" Laurel asked, perplexed and frightened. She had not heard Brian and Nick's muttered conversation, although she had been standing much closer to them than Dinah was.

"Ask *them,*" Dinah said. Her voice was trembling. "I'm not crazy! I'm blind, but I'm *not* crazy!"

"All right," Brian said, shaken. "All right, Dinah." And to Laurel he said: "I was talking to Nick. She heard us. From over there by the windows, she heard us."

"You've got great ears, hon," Bethany said.

"I hear what I hear," Dinah said. "And I hear something out there. In that direction." She pointed due east through the glass. Her unseeing eyes swept them. "And it's *bad.* It's an awful sound, a scary sound."

Don Gaffney said hesitantly: "If you knew what it was, little miss, that would help, maybe."

"I don't," Dinah said. "But I know that it's closer than it was." She put her dark glasses back on with a hand that was trembling. "We have to get out of here. And we have to get out soon. Because something is coming. The bad something making the cereal noise."

"Dinah," Brian said, "the plane we came in is almost out of fuel."

"Then you have to put some more in it!" Dinah screamed shrilly at him. *"It's coming,* don't you understand? It's *coming,* and if we haven't gone when it gets here, we're going to die! *We're all going to die!"*

Her voice cracked and she began to sob. She was not a sibyl or a medium but only a little girl forced to live her terror in a darkness which was almost complete. She staggered toward them, her self-possession utterly gone. Laurel grabbed her before she could stumble over one of the guide-ropes which marked the way to the security checkpoint and hugged her tight. She tried to soothe the girl, but those last words echoed and rang in Laurel's confused, shocked mind: *If we haven't gone when it gets here, we're going to die. We're all going to die.*

12

Craig Toomy heard the brat begin to caterwaul back there some-place and ignored it. He had found what he was looking for in the third locker he opened, the one with the name MARKEY Dymotaped to the front. Mr. Markey's lunch—a sub sandwich poking out of a brown paper bag—was on the top shelf. Mr. Markey's street shoes were placed neatly side by side on the bottom shelf. Hanging in between, from the same hook, were a plain white shirt and a gunbelt. Protruding from the holster was the butt of Mr. Markey's service revolver.

Craig unsnapped the safety strap and took the gun out. He didn't know much about guns—this could have been a .32, a .38, or even a .45, for all of him—but he was not stupid, and after a few moments of fumbling he was able to roll the cylinder. All six chambers were loaded. He pushed the cylinder back in, nodding slightly when he heard it click home, and then inspected the hammer area and both sides of the grip. He was looking for a safety catch, but there didn't appear to be one. He put his finger on the trigger and tightened until he saw both the hammer and the cylinder move slightly. Craig nodded, satisfied.

He turned around and without warning the most intense lone-liness of his adult life struck him. The gun seemed to take on weight and the hand holding it sagged. Now he stood with his shoulders slumped, the briefcase dangling from his right hand, the security guard's pistol dangling from his left. On his face was an expression of utter, abject misery. And suddenly a memory recurred to him, something he hadn't thought of in years: Craig Toomy, twelve years old, lying in bed and shivering as hot tears ran down his face. In the other room the stereo was turned up loud and his mother was singing along with Merrilee Rush in her droning off-key drunk's voice: "Just call me *angel* . . . of the *morn*-ing, *bay*-bee . . . just touch my cheek . . . before you leave me, *bay*-bee . . ."

Lying there in bed. Shaking. Crying. Not making a sound. And thinking: *Why can't you love me and leave me alone, Momma? Why can't you just love me and leave me alone?*

"I don't want to hurt anyone," Craig Toomy muttered through his tears. "I don't want to, but this . . . this is intolerable."

Across the room was a bank of TV monitors, all blank. For a moment, as he looked at them, the truth of what had happened, what was *still* happening, tried to crowd in on him. For a moment it almost broke through his complex system of neurotic shields and into the air-raid shelter where he lived his life.

Everyone is gone, Craiggy-weggy. The whole world is gone except for you and the people who were on that plane.

"No," he moaned, and collapsed into one of the chairs standing around the Formica-topped kitchen table in the center of the room. "No, that's not so. That's just not so. I refute that idea. I refute it *utterly.*"

The langoliers were here, and they will be back, his father said. It overrode the voice of his mother, as it always had. *You better be gone when they get here . . . or you know what will happen.*

He knew, all right. They would eat him. The langoliers would eat him up.

"But I don't want to hurt anyone," he repeated in a dreary, distraught voice. There was a mimeographed duty roster lying on the table. Craig let go of his briefcase and laid the gun on the table beside him. Then he picked up the duty roster, looked at it for a moment with unseeing eyes, and began to tear a long strip from the lefthand side.

Rii-ip.

Soon he was hypnotized as a pile of thin strips—maybe the thinnest ever!—began to flutter down onto the table. But even then the cold voice of his father would not entirely leave him:

Or you know what will happen.

CHAPTER FIVE

A BOOK OF MATCHES.
THE ADVENTURE OF THE
SALAMI SANDWICH.
ANOTHER EXAMPLE OF THE
DEDUCTIVE METHOD. THE
ARIZONA JEW PLAYS THE
VIOLIN. THE ONLY SOUND
IN TOWN.

1

The frozen silence following Dinah's warning was finally broken by Robert Jenkins. "We have some problems," he said in a dry lecture-hall voice. "If Dinah hears something—and following the remarkable demonstration she's just given us, I'm inclined to think she does—it would be helpful if we knew what it is. We don't. That's one problem. The plane's lack of fuel is another problem."

"There's a 727 out there," Nick said, "all cozied up to a jetway. Can you fly one of those, Brian?"

"Yes," Brian said.

Nick spread his hands in Bob's direction and shrugged, as if to say *There you are; one knot untied already.*

"Assuming we *do* take off again, where should we go?" Bob Jenkins went on. "A third problem."

"Away," Dinah said immediately. "Away from that sound. We *have* to get away from that sound, and what's making it."

"How long do you think we have?" Bob asked her gently. "How long before it gets here, Dinah? Do you have any idea at all?"

"No," she said from the safe circle of Laurel's arms. "I think it's still far. I think there's still time. But . . ."

"Then I suggest we do exactly as Mr. Warwick has suggested," Bob said. "Let's step over to the restaurant, have a bite to eat, and discuss what happens next. Food *does* have a beneficial effect on what Monsieur Poirot liked to call the little gray cells."

"We shouldn't *wait*," Dinah said fretfully.

"Fifteen minutes," Bob said. "No more than that. And even at your age, Dinah, you should know that useful thinking must always precede useful action."

Albert suddenly realized that the mystery writer had his own reasons for wanting to go to the restaurant. Mr. Jenkins's little gray cells were all in apple-pie working order—or at least he *believed* they were—and following his eerily sharp assessment of their situation on board the plane, Albert was willing at least to give him the benefit of the doubt. *He wants to show us something, or prove something to us,* he thought.

"Surely we have fifteen minutes?" he coaxed.

"Well . . ." Dinah said unwillingly. "I guess so . . ."

"Fine," Bob said briskly. "It's decided." And he struck off across the room toward the restaurant, as if taking it for granted that the others would follow him.

Brian and Nick looked at each other.

"We better go along," Albert said quietly. "I think he knows stuff."

"What kind of stuff?" Brian asked.

"I don't know, exactly, but I think it might be stuff worth finding out."

Albert followed Bob; Bethany followed Albert; the others fell in behind them, Laurel leading Dinah by the hand. The little girl was very pale.

2

The Cloud Nine Restaurant was really a cafeteria with a cold-case full of drinks and sandwiches at the rear and a stainless-steel counter running beside a long, compartmentalized steam-table. All the compartments were empty, all sparkling clean. There wasn't a speck of grease on the grill. Glasses—those tough cafeteria glasses with the ripply sides—were stacked in neat pyramids on rear shelves, along with a wide selection of even tougher cafeteria crockery.

Robert Jenkins was standing by the cash register. As Albert and Bethany came in, he said: "May I have another cigarette, Bethany?"

"Gee, you're a real mooch," she said, but her tone was good-natured. She produced her box of Marlboros and shook one out. He took it, then touched her hand as she also produced her book of matches.

"I'll just use one of these, shall I?" There was a bowl filled with paper matches advertising LaSalle Business School by the cash register. FOR OUR MATCHLESS FRIENDS, a little sign beside the bowl read. Bob took a book of these matches, opened it, and pulled one of the matches free.

"Sure," Bethany said, "but why?"

"That's what we're going to find out," he said. He glanced at the others. They were standing around in a semicircle, watching—all except Rudy Warwick, who had drifted to the rear of the serving area and was closely inspecting the contents of the cold-case.

Bob struck the match. It left a little smear of white stuff on the striker, but didn't light. He struck it again with the same result. On the third try, the paper match bent. Most of the flammable head was gone, anyway.

"My, my," he said in an utterly unsurprised tone. "I suppose they must be wet. Let's try a book from the bottom, shall we? *They* should be dry."

He dug to the bottom of the bowl, spilling a number of matchbooks off the top and onto the counter as he did so. They all looked perfectly dry to Albert. Behind him, Nick and Brian exchanged another glance.

Bob fished out another book of matches, pulled one, and tried to strike it. It didn't light.

"Son of a bee," he said. "We seem to have discovered yet another problem. May I borrow your book of matches, Bethany?"

She handed it over without a word.

"Wait a minute," Nick said slowly. "What do you know, matey?"

"Only that this situation has even wider implications than we at first thought," Bob said. His eyes were calm enough, but the face from which they looked was haggard. "And I have an idea that we all may have made one *big* mistake. Understandable enough under the circumstances . . . but until we've rectified our thinking on this subject, I don't believe we can make any progress. An error of perspective, I'd call it."

Warwick was wandering back toward them. He had selected a wrapped sandwich and a bottle of beer. His acquisitions seemed to have cheered him considerably. "What's happening, folks?"

"I'll be damned if I know," Brian said, "but I don't like it much."

Bob Jenkins pulled one of the matches from Bethany's book and struck it. It lit on the first strike. "Ah," he said, and applied the flame to the tip of his cigarette. The smoke smelled incredibly pungent, incredibly sweet to Brian, and a moment's reflection suggested a reason why: it was the only thing, save for the faint tang of Nick Hopewell's shaving lotion and Laurel's perfume, that he *could* smell. Now that he thought about it, Brian realized that he could hardly even smell his travelling companions' sweat.

Bob still held the lit match in his hand. Now he bent back the top of the book he'd taken from the bowl, exposing all the matches, and touched the lit match to the heads of the others. For a long moment nothing happened. The writer slipped the flame back and forth along the heads of the matches, but they didn't light. The others watched, fascinated.

At last there was a sickly *phsssss* sound, and a few of the matches erupted into dull, momentary life. They did not really burn at all; there was a weak glow and they went out. A few tendrils of smoke drifted up . . . smoke which seemed to have no odor at all.

Bob looked around at them and smiled grimly. "Even that," he said, "is more than I expected."

"All right," Brian said. "Tell us about it. I know—"

At that moment, Rudy Warwick uttered a cry of disgust. Dinah gave a little shriek and pressed closer to Laurel. Albert felt his heart take a high skip in his chest.

Rudy had unwrapped his sandwich—it looked to Brian like salami and cheese—and had taken a large bite. Now he spat it out onto the floor with a grimace of disgust.

"It's spoiled!" Rudy cried. "Oh, goddam! I *hate* that!"

"Spoiled?" Bob Jenkins said swiftly. His eyes gleamed like blue electrical sparks. "Oh, I doubt that. Processed meats are so loaded with preservatives these days that it takes eight hours or more in the hot sun to send them over. And we know by the clocks that the power in that cold-case went out less than five hours ago."

"Maybe not," Albert spoke up. "You were the one who said it felt later than our wristwatches say."

"Yes, but I don't think . . . Was the case still cold, Mr. Warwick? When you opened it, was the case still cold?"

"Not *cold,* exactly, but cool," Rudy said. "That sandwich is all fucked up, though. Pardon me, ladies. Here." He held it out. "If you don't think it's spoiled, *you* try it."

Bob stared at the sandwich, appeared to screw up his courage, and then did just that, taking a small bite from the untouched half. Albert saw an expression of disgust pass over his face, but he did not get rid of the food immediately. He chewed once . . . twice . . .

then turned and spat into his hand. He stuffed the half-chewed bite of sandwich into the trash-bin below the condiments shelf, and dropped the rest of the sandwich in after it.

"Not spoiled," he said. "Tasteless. And not just that, either. It seemed to have no texture." His mouth drew down in an involuntary expression of disgust. "We talk about things being bland—unseasoned white rice, boiled potatoes—but even the blandest food has *some* taste, I think. That had none. It was like chewing paper. No wonder you thought it was spoiled."

"It *was* spoiled," the bald man reiterated stubbornly.

"Try your beer," Bob invited. "*That* shouldn't be spoiled. The cap is still on, and a capped bottle of beer shouldn't spoil even if it isn't refrigerated."

Rudy looked thoughtfully at the bottle of Budweiser in his hand, then shook his head and held it out to Bob. "I don't want it anymore," he said. He glanced at the cold-case. His gaze was baleful, as if he suspected Jenkins of having played an unfunny practical joke on him.

"I will if I have to," Bob said, "but I've already offered my body up to science once. Will somebody else try this beer? I think it's very important."

"Give it to me," Nick said.

"No." It was Don Gaffney. "Give it to me. I could use a beer, by God. I've drunk em warm before and they don't cross my eyes none."

He took the beer, twisted off the cap, and upended it. A moment later he whirled and sprayed the mouthful he had taken onto the floor.

"*Jesus!*" he cried. "Flat! Flat as a pancake!"

"Is it?" Bob asked brightly. "Good! Great! Something we can all see!" He was around the counter in a flash, and taking one of the glasses down from the shelf. Gaffney had set the bottle down beside the cash register, and Brian looked at it closely as Bob Jenkins picked it up. He could see no foam clinging to the inside of the bottleneck. *It might as well be water in there,* he thought.

What Bob poured out didn't look like water, however; it looked like beer. Flat beer. There was no head. A few small bubbles clung to the inside of the glass, but none of them came pinging up through the liquid to the surface.

"All right," Nick said slowly, "it's flat. Sometimes that happens.

The cap doesn't get screwed on all the way at the factory and the gas escapes. Everyone's gotten a flat lager from time to time."

"But when you add in the tasteless salami sandwich, it's suggestive, isn't it?"

"Suggestive of *what?*" Brian exploded.

"In a moment," Bob said. "Let's take care of Mr. Hopewell's *caveat* first, shall we?" He turned, grabbed glasses with both hands (a couple of others fell off the shelf and shattered on the floor), then began to set them out along the counter with the agile speed of a bartender. "Bring me some more beer. And a couple of soft drinks, while you're at it."

Albert and Bethany went down to the cold-case and each took four or five bottles, picking at random.

"Is he nuts?" Bethany asked in a low voice.

"I don't think so," Albert said. He had a vague idea of what the writer was trying to show them . . . and he didn't like the shape it made in his mind. "Remember when he told you to save your matches? He knew something like this was going to happen. That's why he was so hot to get us to the restaurant. He wanted to show us."

3

The duty roster was ripped into three dozen narrow strips and the langoliers were closer now.

Craig could feel their approach at the back of his mind—more weight.

More insupportable weight.

It was time to go.

He picked up the gun and his briefcase, then stood up and left the security room. He walked slowly, rehearsing as he went: *I don't want to shoot you, but I will if I have to. Take me to Boston. I don't want to shoot you, but I will if I have to. Take me to Boston.*

"I will if I have to," Craig muttered as he walked back into the waiting room. "I will if I have to." His finger found the hammer of the gun and cocked it back.

Halfway across the room, his attention was once more snared by the pallid light which fell through the windows, and he turned in that direction. He could feel them out there. The langoliers. They had eaten all the useless, lazy people, and now they were returning for him. He *had* to get to Boston. It was the only way he knew to save the rest of himself . . . because *their* death would be horrible. Their death would be horrible indeed.

He walked slowly to the windows and looked out, ignoring—at least for the time being—the murmur of the other passengers behind him.

4

Bob Jenkins poured a little from each bottle into its own glass. The contents of each was as flat as the first beer had been. "Are you convinced?" he asked Nick.

"Yes," Nick said. "If you know what's going on here, mate, spill it. Please spill it."

"I have an idea," Bob said. "It's not . . . I'm afraid it's not very comforting, but I'm one of those people who believe that knowledge is always better—safer—in the long run than ignorance, no matter how dismayed one may feel when one first understands certain facts. Does that make any sense?"

"No," Gaffney said at once.

Bob shrugged and offered a small, wry smile. "Be that as it may, I stand by my statement. And before I say anything else, I want to ask you all to look around this place and tell me what you see."

They looked around, concentrating so fiercely on the little clusters of tables and chairs that no one noticed Craig Toomy standing on the far side of the waiting room, his back to them, gazing out at the tarmac.

"Nothing," Laurel said at last. "I'm sorry, but I don't see anything. Your eyes must be sharper than mine, Mr. Jenkins."

"Not a bit. I see what you see: nothing. But airports are open twenty-four hours a day. When this thing—this Event—happened, it was probably at the dead low tide of its twenty-four-hour cycle, but I find it difficult to believe there weren't at least a few people in here, drinking coffee and perhaps eating early breakfasts. Aircraft maintenance men. Airport personnel. Perhaps a handful of connecting passengers who elected to save money by spending the hours between midnight and six or seven o'clock in the terminal instead of in a nearby motel. When I first got off that baggage conveyor and looked around, I felt utterly dislocated. Why? Because airports are *never* completely deserted, just as police and fire stations are never completely deserted. Now look around again, and ask yourself this: where are the half-eaten meals, the half-empty glasses? Remember the drinks trolley on the airplane with the dirty glasses on the lower shelf? Remember the half-eaten pastry and the half-drunk cup of coffee beside the pilot's seat in the cockpit? There's nothing like that here. *Where is the least sign that there were people here at all when this Event occurred?"*

Albert looked around again and then said slowly, "There's no pipe on the foredeck, is there?"

Bob looked at him closely. "What? What do you say, Albert?"

"When we were on the plane," Albert said slowly, "I was thinking of this sailing ship I read about once. It was called the *Mary Celeste,* and someone spotted it, just floating aimlessly along. Well . . . not really *floating,* I guess, because the book said the sails were set, but when the people who found it boarded her, everyone on the *Mary Celeste* was gone. Their stuff was still there, though, and there was food cooking on the stove. Someone even found a pipe on the foredeck. It was still lit."

"Bravo!" Bob cried, almost feverishly. There were all looking at him now, and no one saw Craig Toomy walking slowly toward them. The gun he had found was no longer pointed at the floor.

"Bravo, Albert! You've put your finger on it! And there was another famous disappearance—an entire colony of settlers at a place called Roanoke Island . . . off the coast of North Carolina, I believe. All gone, but they had left remains of campfires, cluttered houses, and trash middens behind. Now, Albert, take this a step further. How else does this terminal differ from our airplane?"

For a moment Albert looked entirely blank, and then understanding dawned in his eyes. "The rings!" he shouted. "The purses! The wallets! The money! The surgical pins! None of that stuff is here!"

"Correct," Bob said softly. "One hundred per cent correct. As you say, none of that stuff is here. But it was on the airplane when we survivors woke up, wasn't it? There were even a cup of coffee and a half-eaten Danish in the cockpit. The equivalent of a smoking pipe on the foredeck."

"You think we've flown into another dimension, don't you?" Albert said. His voice was awed. "Just like in a science-fiction story."

Dinah's head cocked to one side, and for a moment she looked strikingly like Nipper, the dog on the old RCA Victor labels.

"No," Bob said. "I think—"

"Watch out!" Dinah cried sharply. "I hear some—"

She was too late. Once Craig Toomy broke the paralysis which had held him and he started to move, he moved fast. Before Nick or Brian could do more than begin to turn around, he had locked one forearm around Bethany's throat and was dragging her backward. He pointed the gun at her temple. The girl uttered a desperate, terrorized squawk.

"I don't want to shoot her, but I will if I have to," Craig panted. "Take me to Boston." His eyes were no longer blank; they shot glances full of terrified, paranoid intelligence in every direction. "Do you hear me? Take me to Boston!"

Brian started toward him, and Nick placed a hand against his chest without shifting his eyes away from Craig. "Steady down, mate," he said in a low voice. "It wouldn't be safe. Our friend here is quite bonkers."

Bethany was squirming under Craig's restraining forearm. "You're choking me! Please stop *choking* me!"

"What's happening?" Dinah cried. "What *is* it?"

"Stop that!" Craig shouted at Bethany. "Stop moving around! You're going to force me to do something I don't want to do!" He pressed the muzzle of the gun against the side of her head. She continued to struggle, and Albert suddenly realized she didn't know he had a gun—even with it pressed against her skull she didn't know.

"Quit it, girl!" Nick said sharply. "Quit fighting!"

For the first time in his waking life, Albert found himself not just thinking like The Arizona Jew but possibly called upon to *act* like that fabled character. Without taking his eyes off the lunatic in the crew-neck jersey, he slowly began to raise his violin case. He switched his grip from the handle and settled both hands around the neck of the case. Toomy was not looking at him; his eyes were shuttling rapidly back and forth between Brian and Nick, and he had his hands full—quite literally—holding onto Bethany.

"I don't want to shoot her—" Craig was beginning again, and then his arm slipped upward as the girl bucked against him, socking her behind into his crotch. Bethany immediately sank her teeth into his wrist. *"Ow!"* Craig screamed. *"OWWW!"*

His grip loosened. Bethany ducked under it. Albert leaped forward, raising the violin case, as Toomy pointed the gun at Bethany. Toomy's face was screwed into a grimace of pain and anger.

"No, Albert!" Nick bawled.

Craig Toomy saw Albert coming and shifted the muzzle toward him. For one moment Albert looked straight into it, and it was like none of his dreams or fantasies. Looking into the muzzle was like looking into an open grave.

I might have made a mistake here, he thought, and then Craig pulled the trigger.

5

Instead of an explosion there was a small pop—the sound of an old Daisy air rifle, no more. Albert felt something thump against the chest of his Hard Rock Cafe tee-shirt, had time to realize he had been shot, and then he brought the violin case down on Craig's head. There was a solid thud which ran all the way up his arms, and the indignant voice of his father suddenly spoke up in his mind: *What's the matter with you, Albert? That's no way to treat an expensive musical instrument!*

There was a startled *broink!* from inside the case as the violin jumped. One of the brass latches dug into Toomy's forehead and blood splashed outward in an amazing spray. Then the man's knees came unhinged and he went down in front of Albert like an express elevator. Albert saw his eyes roll up to whites, and then Craig Toomy was lying at his feet, unconscious.

A crazy but somehow wonderful thought filled Albert's mind for a moment: *By God, I never played better in my life!* And then he realized that he was no longer able to get his breath. He turned to the others, the corners of his mouth turning up in a thin-lipped, slightly confused smile. "I think I have been plugged," Ace Kaussner said, and then the world bleached out to shades of gray and his own knees came unhinged. He crumpled to the floor on top of his violin case.

6

He was out for less than thirty seconds. When he came around, Brian was slapping his cheeks lightly and looking anxious. Bethany was on her knees beside him, looking at Albert with shining my-hero eyes. Behind her, Dinah Bellman was still crying within the circle of Laurel's arms. Albert looked back at Bethany and felt his heart—apparently still whole—expand in his chest. "The Arizona Jew rides again," he muttered.

"What, Albert?" she asked, and stroked his cheek. Her hand was wonderfully soft, wonderfully cool. Albert decided he was in love.

"Nothing," he said, and then the pilot whacked him across the face again.

"Are you all right, kid?" Brian was asking. "Are you all right?"

"I think so," Albert said. "Stop doing that, okay? And the name is Albert. Ace, to my friends. How bad am I hit? I can't feel anything yet. Were you able to stop the bleeding?"

Nick Hopewell squatted beside Bethany. His face wore a be-mused, unbelieving smile. "I think you'll live, matey. I never saw anything like that in my life . . . and I've seen a lot. You Americans are too foolish not to love. Hold out your hand and I'll give you a souvenir."

Albert held out a hand which shook uncontrollably with reaction, and Nick dropped something into it. Albert held it up to his eyes and saw it was a bullet.

"I picked it up off the floor," Nick said. "Not even misshapen. It must have hit you square in the chest—there's a little powder mark on your shirt—and then bounced off. It was a misfire. God must like you, mate."

"I was thinking of the matches," Albert said weakly. "I sort of thought it wouldn't fire at all."

"That was very brave and very foolish, my boy," Bob Jenkins said. His face was dead white and he looked as if he might pass out himself in another few moments. "Never believe a writer. Listen to them, by all means, but never *believe* them. My God, what if I'd been wrong?"

"You almost were," Brian said. He helped Albert to his feet. "It was like when you lit the other matches—the ones from the bowl. There was just enough pop to drive the bullet out of the muzzle. A little more pop and Albert would have had a bullet in his lung."

Another wave of dizziness washed over Albert. He swayed on his feet, and Bethany immediately slipped an arm around his waist. "I thought it was really brave," she said, looking up at him with eyes which suggested she believed Albert Kaussner must shit diamonds from a platinum asshole. "I mean *incredible.*"

"Thanks," Ace said, smiling coolly (if a trifle woozily). "It wasn't much." The fastest Hebrew west of the Mississippi was aware that there was a great deal of girl pressed tightly against him, and that the girl smelled almost unbearably good. Suddenly *he* felt good. In fact, he believed he had never felt better in his life. Then he remembered his violin, bent down, and picked up the case. There was a deep dent in one side, and one of the catches had been sprung. There was blood and hair on it, and Albert felt his stomach turn over lazily. He opened the case and looked in. The instrument looked all right, and he let out a little sigh.

Then he thought of Craig Toomy, and alarm replaced relief.

"Say, I didn't kill that guy, did I? I hit him pretty hard." He looked toward Craig, who was lying near the restaurant door with Don Gaffney kneeling beside him. Albert suddenly felt like passing out again. There was a great deal of blood on Craig's face and forehead.

"He's alive," Don said, "but he's out like a light."

Albert, who had blown away more hardcases than The Man with No Name in his dreams, felt his gorge rise. "Jesus, there's so much *blood!*"

"Doesn't mean a thing," Nick said. "Scalp wounds tend to bleed a lot." He joined Don, picked up Craig's wrist, and felt for a pulse. "You want to remember he had a gun to that girl's head, matey. If he'd pulled the trigger at point-blank range, he might well have done for her. Remember the actor who killed himself with a blank round a few years ago? Mr. Toomy brought this on himself; he owns it completely. Don't take on."

Nick dropped Craig's wrist and stood up.

"Besides," he said, pulling a large swatch of paper napkins from the dispenser on one of the tables, "his pulse is strong and regular. I think he'll wake up in a few minutes with nothing but a bad headache. I also think it might be prudent to take a few precautions against that happy event. Mr. Gaffney, the tables in yonder watering hole actually appear to be equipped with tablecloths—strange but true. I wonder if you'd get a couple? We might be wise to bind old Mr. I've-Got-to-Get-to-Boston's hands behind him."

"Do you really have to do that?" Laurel asked quietly. "The man is unconscious, after all, and bleeding."

Nick pressed his makeshift napkin compress against Craig Toomy's head-wound and looked up at her. "You're Laurel, right?"

"Right."

"Well, Laurel, let's not paint it fine. This man is a lunatic. I don't know if our current adventure did that to him or if he just growed that way, like Topsy, but I *do* know he's dangerous. He would have grabbed Dinah instead of Bethany if she had been closer. If we leave him untied, he might do just that next time."

Craig groaned and waved his hands feebly. Bob Jenkins stepped away from him the moment he began to move, even though the revolver was now safely tucked into the waistband of Brian Engle's pants, and Laurel did the same, pulling Dinah with her.

"Is anybody dead?" Dinah asked nervously. "No one is, are they?"

"No, honey."

"I should have heard him sooner, but I was listening to the man who sounds like a teacher."

"It's okay," Laurel said. "It turned out all right, Dinah." Then she looked out at the empty terminal and her own words mocked her. *Nothing* was all right here. Nothing at all.

Don returned with a red-and-white-checked tablecloth in each fist.

"Marvellous," Nick said. He took one of them and spun it quickly and expertly into a rope. He put the center of it in his mouth, clamping his teeth on it to keep it from unwinding, and used his hands to flip Craig over like a human omelette.

Craig cried out and his eyelids fluttered.

"Do you have to be so *rough*?" Laurel asked sharply.

Nick gazed at her for a moment, and she dropped her eyes at once. She could not help comparing Nick Hopewell's eyes with the eyes in the pictures which Darren Crosby had sent her. Widely spaced, clear eyes in a good-looking—if unremarkable—face. But the eyes had also been rather unremarkable, hadn't they? And didn't Darren's eyes have something, perhaps even a great deal, to do with why she had made this trip in the first place? Hadn't she decided, after a great deal of close study, that they were the eyes of a man who would behave himself? A man who would back off it you told him to back off?

She had boarded Flight 29 telling herself that this was her great adventure, her one extravagant tango with romance—an impulsive transcontinental dash into the arms of the tall, dark stranger. But sometimes you found yourself in one of those tiresome situations where the truth could no longer be avoided, and Laurel reckoned the truth to be this: she had chosen Darren Crosby because his pictures and letters had told her he wasn't much different from the placid boys and men she had been dating ever since she was fifteen or so, boys and men who would learn quickly to wipe their feet on the mat before they came in on rainy nights, boys and men who would grab a towel and help with the dishes without being asked, boys and men who would let you go if you told them to do it in a sharp enough tone of voice.

Would she have been on Flight 29 tonight if the photos had shown Nick Hopewell's dark-blue eyes instead of Darren's mild brown ones? She didn't think so. She thought she would have written him a kind but rather impersonal note—*Thank you for your reply and your picture, Mr. Hopewell, but I somehow don't think we would be right for each other*—and gone on looking for a man like Darren. And, of course, she doubted very much if men like Mr. Hopewell even read the lonely-hearts magazines, let alone placed ads in their personals columns. All the same, she was here with him now, in this weird situation.

Well . . . she had wanted to have an adventure, just one adventure, before middle-age settled in for keeps. Wasn't that true? Yes. And here she was, proving Tolkien right—she had stepped out of her own door last evening, just the same as always, and look where she had ended up: a strange and dreary version of Fantasyland. But it was an adventure, all right. Emergency landings . . . deserted airports . . . a lunatic with a gun. Of course it was an adventure. Something she had read years ago suddenly popped into Laurel's mind. *Be careful what you pray for, because you just might get it.*

How true.

And how confusing.

There was no confusion in Nick Hopewell's eyes . . . but there was no mercy in them, either. They made Laurel feel shivery, and there was nothing romantic in the feeling.

Are you sure? a voice whispered, and Laurel shut it up at once.

Nick pulled Craig's hands out from under him, then brought his wrists together at the small of his back. Craig groaned again, louder this time, and began to struggle weakly.

"Easy now, my good old mate," Nick said soothingly. He wrapped the tablecloth rope twice around Craig's lower forearms and knotted it tightly. Craig's elbows flapped and he uttered a strange weak scream. "There!" Nick said, standing up. "Trussed as neatly as Father John's Christmas turkey. We've even got a spare if that one looks like not holding." He sat on the edge of one of the tables and looked at Bob Jenkins. "Now, what were you saying when we were so rudely interrupted?"

Bob looked at him, dazed and unbelieving. "What?"

"Go on," Nick said. He might have been an interested lecture-goer instead of a man sitting on a table in a deserted airport restaurant with his feet planted beside a bound man lying in a pool of his own blood. "You had just got to the part about Flight 29 being like the *Mary Celeste*. Interesting concept, that."

"And you want me to . . . to just go on?" Bob asked incredulously. "As if nothing had happened?"

"Let me *up*!" Craig shouted. His words were slightly muffled by the tough industrial carpet on the restaurant floor, but he still sounded remarkably lively for a man who had been coldcocked with a violin case not five minutes previous. "Let me up right *now*! I demand that you—"

Then Nick did something that shocked all of them, even those who had seen the Englishman twist Craig's nose like the handle of a bathtub faucet. He drove a short, hard kick into Craig's ribs. He pulled it at the last instant . . . but not much. Craig uttered a pained grunt and shut up.

"Start again, mate, and I'll stave them in," Nick said grimly. "My patience with you has run out."

"Hey!" Gaffney cried, bewildered. "What did you do that f—"

"Listen to me!" Nick said, and looked around. His urbane surface was entirely gone for the first time; his voice vibrated with anger and urgency. "You need waking up, fellows and girls, and I haven't the time to do it gently. That little girl—Dinah—says we are in bad trouble here, and I believe her. She says she hears something, something which may be coming our way, and I rather believe that, too. I don't hear a bloody thing, but my nerves are jumping like grease on a hot griddle, and I'm used to paying attention when they do that. I think something *is* coming, and I don't believe it's going to try and sell us vacuum-cleaner attachments or the latest insurance scheme when it gets here. Now we can make all the correct civilized noises over this bloody madman or we can try to understand what has happened to us. Understanding may not save our lives, but I'm rapidly becoming convinced that the lack of it may end them, and soon." His eyes shifted to Dinah. "Tell me I'm wrong if you believe I am, Dinah. I'll listen to *you,* and gladly."

"I don't want you to hurt Mr. Toomy, but I don't think you're wrong, either," Dinah said in a small, wavery voice.

"All right," Nick said. "Fair enough. I'll try my very best not to hurt him again . . . but I make no promises. Let's begin with a very simple concept. This fellow I've trussed up—"

"Toomy," Brian said. "His name is Craig Toomy."

"All right. Mr. Toomy is mad. Perhaps if we find our way back to our proper place, or if we find the place where all the people have gone, we can get some help for him. But for now, we can only help him by putting him out of commission—which I have done, with the generous if foolhardy assistance of Albert there—and getting back to our current business. Does anyone hold a view which runs counter to this?"

There was no reply. The other passengers who had been aboard Flight 29 looked at Nick uneasily.

"All right," Nick said. "Please go on, Mr. Jenkins."

"I . . . I'm not used to . . ." Bob made a visible effort to collect himself. "In books, I suppose I've killed enough people to fill every seat in the plane that brought us here, but what just happened is the first act of violence I've ever personally witnessed. I'm sorry if I've . . . er . . . behaved badly."

"I think you're doing great, Mr. Jenkins," Dinah said. "And I like listening to you, too. It makes me feel better."

Bob looked at her gratefully and smiled. "Thank you, Dinah." He stuffed his hands in his pockets, cast a troubled glance at Craig Toomy, then looked beyond them, across the empty waiting room.

"I think I mentioned a central fallacy in our thinking," he said at last. "It is this: we all assumed, when we began to grasp the dimensions of this Event, that something had happened to *the rest of the world.* That assumption is easy enough to understand, since we are all fine and everyone else—including those other passengers with whom we boarded at Los Angeles International—seems to have disappeared. But the evidence before us doesn't bear the assumption out. What has happened has happened to us and us alone. I am convinced that the world as we have always known it is ticking along just as it always has.

"It's us—the missing passengers and the eleven survivors of Flight 29—who are lost."

7

"Maybe I'm dumb, but I don't understand what you're getting at," Rudy Warwick said after a moment.

"Neither do I," Laurel added.

"We've mentioned two famous disappearances," Bob said quietly. Now even Craig Toomy seemed to be listening . . . he had stopped struggling, at any rate. "One, the case of the *Mary Celeste,* took place at sea. The second, the case of Roanoke Island, took place *near* the sea. They are not the only ones, either. I can think of at least two others which involved aircraft: the disappearance of the aviatrix Amelia Earhart over the Pacific Ocean, and the disappearance of several Navy planes over that part of the Atlantic known as the Bermuda Triangle. That happened in 1945 or 1946, I believe. There was some sort of garbled transmission from the lead aircraft's pilot, and rescue planes were sent out at once from an airbase in Florida, but no trace of the planes or their crews was ever found."

"I've heard of the case," Nick said. "It's the basis for the Triangle's infamous reputation, I think."

"No, there have been *lots* of ships and planes lost there," Albert put in. "I read the book about it by Charles Berlitz. Really interesting." He glanced around. "I just never thought I'd be *in* it, if you know what I mean."

Jenkins said, "I don't know if an aircraft has ever disappeared over the continental United States before, but—"

"It's happened lots of times with small planes," Brian said, "and once, about thirty-five years ago, it happened with a commercial passenger plane. There were over a hundred people aboard. 1955 or '56, this was. The carrier was either TWA or Monarch, I can't remember which. The plane was bound for Denver out of San

Francisco. The pilot made radio contact with the Reno tower—absolutely routine—and the plane was never heard from again. There was a search, of course, but . . . nothing."

Brian saw they were all looking at him with a species of dreadful fascination, and he laughed uncomfortably.

"Pilot ghost stories," he said with a note of apology in his voice. "It sounds like a caption for a Gary Larson cartoon."

"I'll bet they all went through," the writer muttered. He had begun to scrub the side of his face with his hand again. He looked distressed—almost horrified. "Unless they found bodies . . . ?"

"Please tell us what you know, or what you think you know," Laurel said. "The effect of this . . . this thing . . . seems to pile up on a person. If I don't get some answers soon, I think you can tie me up and put me down next to Mr. Toomy."

"Don't flatter yourself," Craig said, speaking clearly if rather obscurely.

Bob favored him with another uncomfortable glance and then appeared to muster his thoughts. "There's no mess here, but there's a mess on the plane. There's no electricity here, but there's electricity on the plane. That isn't conclusive, of course—the plane has its own self-contained power supply, while the electricity here comes from a power plant somewhere. But then consider the matches. Bethany was on the plane, and her matches work fine. The matches I took from the bowl in here wouldn't strike. The gun which Mr. Toomy took—from the Security office, I imagine—barely fired. I think that, if you tried a battery-powered flashlight, you'd find *that* wouldn't work, either. Or, if it did work, it wouldn't work for long."

"You're right," Nick said. "And we don't need to find a flashlight in order to test your theory." He pointed upward. There was an emergency light mounted on the wall behind the kitchen grill. It was as dead as the overhead lights. "That's battery-powered," Nick went on. "A light-sensitive solenoid turns it on when the power fails. It's dim enough in here for that thing to have gone into operation, but it didn't do so. Which means that either the solenoid's circuit failed or the battery is dead."

"I suspect it's both," Bob Jenkins said. He walked slowly toward the restaurant door and looked out. "We find ourselves in a world which appears to be whole, but it is also a world which seems almost exhausted. The carbonated drinks are flat. The food is tasteless.

The air is odorless. *We* still give off scents—I can smell Laurel's perfume and the captain's aftershave lotion, for instance—but everything else seems to have lost its smell."

Albert picked up one of the glasses with beer in it and sniffed deeply. There *was* a smell, he decided, but it was very, very faint. A flower-petal pressed for many years between the pages of a book might give off the same distant memory of scent.

"The same is true for sounds," Bob went on. "They are flat, one-dimensional, utterly without resonance."

Laurel thought of the listless *clup-clup* sound of her high heels on the cement, and the lack of echo when Captain Engle cupped his hands around his mouth and called up the escalator for Mr. Toomy.

"Albert, could I ask you to play something on your violin?" Bob asked.

Albert glanced at Bethany. She smiled and nodded.

"All right. Sure. In fact, I'm sort of curious about how it sounds after . . ." He glanced at Craig Toomy. "You know."

He opened the case, grimacing as his fingers touched the latch which had opened the wound in Craig Toomy's forehead, and drew out his violin. He caressed it briefly, then took the bow in his right hand and tucked the violin under his chin. He stood like that for a moment, thinking. What was the proper sort of music for this strange new world where no phones rang and no dogs barked? Ralph Vaughan Williams? Stravinsky? Mozart? Dvořák, perhaps? No. None of them were right. Then inspiration struck, and he began to play "Someone's in the Kitchen with Dinah."

Halfway through the tune the bow faltered to a stop.

"I guess you must have hurt your fiddle after all when you bopped that guy with it," Don Gaffney said. "It sounds like it's stuffed full of cotton batting."

"No," Albert said slowly. "My violin is perfectly okay. I can tell just by the way it feels, and the action of the strings under my fingers . . . but there's something else as well. Come on over here, Mr. Gaffney." Gaffney came over and stood beside Albert. "Now get as close to my violin as you can. No . . . not that close; I'd put out your eye with the bow. There. Just right. Listen again."

Albert began to play, singing along in his mind, as he almost always did when he played this corny but endlessly cheerful shit-kicking music:

Singing fee-fi-fiddly-I-oh,
Fee-fi-fiddly-I-oh-oh-oh-oh,
Fee-fi-fiddly-I-oh,
Strummin' on the old banjo.

"Did you hear the difference?" he asked when he had finished.

"It sounds a lot better close up, if that's what you mean," Gaffney said. He was looking at Albert with real respect. "You play good, kid."

Albert smiled at Gaffney, but it was really Bethany Simms he was talking to. "Sometimes, when I'm sure my music teacher isn't around, I play old Led Zeppelin songs," he said. "That stuff *really* cooks on the violin. You'd be surprised." He looked at Bob. "Anyway, it fits right in with what you were saying. The closer you get, the better the violin sounds. It's the *air* that's wrong, not the instrument. It's not conducting the sounds the way it should, and so what comes out sounds the way the beer tasted."

"Flat," Brian said.

Albert nodded.

"Thank you, Albert," Bob said.

"Sure. Can I put it away now?"

"Of course." Bob continued as Albert replaced his violin in its case, and then used a napkin to clean off the fouled latch and his own fingers. "Taste and sound are not the only off-key elements of the situation in which we find ourselves. Take the clouds, for instance."

"What about them?" Rudy Warwick asked.

"They haven't moved since we arrived, and I don't think they're *going* to move. I think the weather patterns we're all used to living with have either stopped or are running down like an old pocket-watch."

Bob paused for a moment. He suddenly looked old and helpless and frightened.

"As Mr. Hopewell would say, let's not draw it fine. *Everything* here feels wrong. Dinah, whose senses—including that odd, vague one we call the sixth sense—are more developed than ours, has perhaps felt it the most strongly, but I think we've all felt it to some degree. Things here are just *wrong*.

"And now we come to the very hub of the matter."

He turned to face them.

"I said not fifteen minutes ago that it felt like lunchtime. It now feels much later than that to me. Three in the afternoon, perhaps four. It isn't breakfast my stomach is grumbling for right now; it wants high tea. I have a terrible feeling that it may start to get dark outside before our watches tell us it's quarter to ten in the morning."

"Get to it, mate," Nick said.

"I think it's about time," Bob said quietly. "Not about dimension, as Albert suggested, but *time*. Suppose that, every now and then, a hole appears in the time stream? Not a time-*warp*, but a time-*rip*. A rip in the temporal fabric."

"That's the craziest shit I ever heard!" Don Gaffney exclaimed.

"Amen!" Craig Toomy seconded from the floor.

"No," Bob replied sharply. "If you want crazy shit, think about how Albert's violin sounded when you were standing six feet away from it. Or look around you, Mr. Gaffney. Just look around you. What's happening to us . . . what we're *in* . . . *that's* crazy shit."

Don frowned and stuffed his hands deep in his pockets.

"Go on," Brian said.

"All right. I'm not saying that I've got this right; I'm just offering a hypothesis that fits the situation in which we have found ourselves. Let us say that such rips in the fabric of time appear every now and then, but mostly over unpopulated areas . . . by which I mean the ocean, of course. I can't say why that would be, but it's still a logical assumption to make, since that's where most of these disappearances seem to occur."

"Weather patterns over water are almost always different from weather patterns over large land-masses," Brian said. "That could be it."

Bob nodded. "Right or wrong, it's a good way to think of it, because it puts it in a context we're all familiar with. This could be similar to rare weather phenomena which are sometimes reported: upside-down tornadoes, circular rainbows, daytime starlight. These time-rips may appear and disappear at random, or they may move, the way fronts and pressure systems move, but they very rarely appear over land.

"But a statistician will tell you that sooner or later whatever can happen will happen, so let us say that last night one *did* appear over land . . . and we had the bad luck to fly into it. And we know something else. Some unknown rule or property of this fabulous meteorological freak makes it impossible for any living being to travel through unless he or she is fast asleep."

"Aw, this is a fairy tale," Gaffney said.

"I agree completely," Craig said from the floor.

"Shut your cake-hole," Gaffney growled at him. Craig blinked, then lifted his upper lip in a feeble sneer.

"It feels right," Bethany said in a low voice. "It feels as if we're out of step with . . . with everything."

"What happened to the crew and the passengers?" Albert asked. He sounded sick. "If the plane came through, and *we* came through, what happened to the rest of them?"

His imagination provided him with an answer in the form of a sudden indelible image: hundreds of people falling out of the sky, ties and trousers rippling, dresses skating up to reveal garter-belts and underwear, shoes falling off, pens (the ones which weren't back on the plane, that was) shooting out of pockets; people waving their arms and legs and trying to scream in the thin air; people who had left wallets, purses, pocket-change, and, in at least one case, a pace-maker implant, behind. He saw them hitting the ground like dud bombs, squashing bushes flat, kicking up small clouds of stony dust, imprinting the desert floor with the shapes of their bodies.

"My guess is that they were vaporized," Bob said. "Utterly dis-corporated."

Dinah didn't understand at first; then she thought of Aunt Vicky's purse with the travellers' checks still inside and began to cry softly. Laurel crossed her arms over the little blind girl's shoulders and hugged her. Albert, meanwhile, was fervently thanking God that his mother had changed her mind at the last moment, deciding not to accompany him east after all.

"In many cases their things went with them," the writer went on. "Those who left wallets and purses may have had them out at the time of The . . . The Event. It's hard to say, though. What was taken and what was left behind—I suppose I'm thinking of the wig more than anything else—doesn't seem to have a lot of rhyme or reason to it."

"You got that right," Albert said. "The surgical pins, for instance. I doubt if the guy they belonged to took them out of his shoulder or knee to play with because he got bored."

"I agree," Rudy Warwick said. "It was too early in the flight to get *that* bored."

Bethany looked at him, startled, then burst out laughing.

"I'm originally from Kansas," Bob said, "and the element of ca-price makes me think of the twisters we used to sometimes get in the summer. They'd totally obliterate a farmhouse and leave the privy standing, or they'd rip away a barn without pulling so much as a shingle from the silo standing right next to it."

"Get to the bottom line, mate," Nick said. "Whatever time it is we're in, I can't help feeling that it's very late in the day."

Brian thought of Craig Toomy, Old Mr. I've-Got-to-Get-to-Boston, standing at the head of the emergency slide and screaming: *Time is short! Time is very fucking short!*

"All right," Bob said. "The bottom line. Let's suppose there *are* such things as time-rips, and we've gone through one. I think we've gone into the past and discovered the unlovely truth of time-travel: you can't appear in the Texas State School Book Depository on November 22, 1963, and put a stop to the Kennedy assassination; you can't watch the building of the pyramids or the sack of Rome; you can't investigate the Age of the Dinosaurs at first hand."

He raised his arms, hands outstretched, as if to encompass the whole silent world in which they found themselves.

"Take a good look around you, fellow time-travellers. This is the past. It is empty; it is silent. It is a world—perhaps a *universe*—with all the sense and meaning of a discarded paint-can. I believe we may have hopped an absurdly short distance in time, perhaps as little as fifteen minutes—at least initially. But the world is clearly unwinding around us. Sensory input is disappearing. Electricity has already disappeared. The weather is what the weather was when we made the jump into the past. But it seems to me that as the world winds down, time itself is winding up in a kind of spiral . . . crowding in on itself."

"Couldn't this be the future?" Albert asked cautiously.

Bob Jenkins shrugged. He suddenly looked very tired. "I don't know for sure, of course—how could I?—but I don't think so. This place we're in feels old and stupid and feeble and meaningless. It feels . . . I don't know . . ."

Dinah spoke then. They all looked toward her.

"It feels *over*," she said softly.

"Yes," Bob said. "Thank you, dear. That's the word I was looking for."

"Mr. Jenkins?"

"Yes?"

"The sound I told you about before? I can hear it again." She paused. "It's getting closer."

8

They all fell silent, their faces long and listening. Brian thought he heard something, then decided it was the sound of his own heart. Or simply imagination.

"I want to go out by the windows again," Nick said abruptly. He stepped over Craig's prone body without so much as a glance down and strode from the restaurant without another word.

"Hey!" Bethany cried. "Hey, I want to come, too!"

Albert followed her; most of the others trailed after. "What about you two?" Brian asked Laurel and Dinah.

"I don't want to go," Dinah said. "I can hear it as well as I want to from here." She paused and added: "But I'm going to hear it better, I think, if we don't get out of here soon."

Brian glanced at Laurel Stevenson.

"I'll stay here with Dinah," she said quietly.

"All right," Brian said. "Keep away from Mr. Toomy."

" 'Keep away from Mr. Toomy,' " Craig mimicked savagely from his place on the floor. He turned his head with an effort and rolled his eyes in their sockets to look at Brian. "You really can't get away with this, Captain Engle. I don't know what game you and your Limey friend think you're playing, but you can't get away with it. Your next piloting job will probably be running cocaine in from Colombia after dark. At least you won't be lying when you tell your friends all about what a crack pilot you are."

Brian started to reply, then thought better of it. Nick said this man was at least temporarily insane, and Brian thought Nick was right. Trying to reason with a madman was both useless and time-consuming.

"We'll keep our distance, don't worry," Laurel said. She drew Dinah over to one of the small tables and sat down with her. "And we'll be fine."

"All right," Brian said. "Yell if he starts trying to get loose."

Laurel smiled wanly. "You can count on it."

Brian bent, checked the tablecloth with which Nick had bound Craig's hands, then walked across the waiting room to join the others, who were standing in a line at the floor-to-ceiling windows.

9

He began to hear it before he was halfway across the waiting room and by the time he had joined the others, it was impossible to believe it was an auditory hallucination.

That girl's hearing is really remarkable, Brian thought.

The sound was very faint—to him, at least—but it was there, and it *did* seem to be coming from the east. Dinah had said it sounded like Rice Krispies after you poured milk over them. To Brian it sounded more like radio static—the exceptionally rough static you got sometimes during periods of high sunspot activity. He agreed with Dinah about one thing, though; it sounded *bad.*

He could feel the hairs on the nape of his neck stiffening in response to that sound. He looked at the others and saw identical expressions of frightened dismay on every face. Nick was controlling himself the best, and the young girl who had almost balked at using the slide—Bethany—looked the most deeply scared, but they all heard the same thing in the sound.

Bad.

Something bad on the way. *Hurrying.*

Nick turned toward him. "What do you make of it, Brian? Any ideas?"

"No," Brian said. "Not even a little one. All I know is that it's the only sound in town."

"It's not in town yet," Don said, "but it's going to be, I think. I only wish I knew how long it was going to take."

They were quiet again, listening to the steady hissing crackle from the east. And Brian thought: *I almost know that sound, I think. Not cereal in milk, not radio static, but . . . what? If only it wasn't so faint . . .*

But he didn't want to know. He suddenly realized that, and very strongly. He didn't want to know at all. The sound filled him with a bone-deep loathing.

"We *do* have to get out of here!" Bethany said. Her voice was loud and wavery. Albert put an arm around her waist and she gripped his hand in both of hers. Gripped it with panicky tightness. "We have to get out of here *right now!*"

"Yes," Bob Jenkins said. "She's right. That sound—I don't know what it is, but it's *awful*. We have to get out of here."

They were all looking at Brian and he thought, *It looks like I'm the captain again. But not for long.* Because they didn't understand. Not even Jenkins understood, sharp as some of his other deductions might have been, that they weren't going anywhere.

Whatever was making that sound was on its way, and it didn't matter, because they would still be here when it arrived. There was no way out of that. He understood the reason why it was so, even if none of the others did . . . and Brian Engle suddenly understood how an animal caught in a trap must feel as it hears the steady thud of the hunter's approaching boots.

CHAPTER SIX

STRANDED. BETHANY'S
MATCHES. TWO-WAY
TRAFFIC AHEAD. ALBERT'S
EXPERIMENT. NIGHTFALL.
THE DARK AND THE
BLADE.

1

Brian turned to look at the writer. "You say we have to get out of here, right?"

"Yes. I think we must do that just as soon as we possibly—"

"And where do you suggest we go? Atlantic City? Miami Beach? Club Med?"

"You are suggesting, Captain Engle, that there's no place we *can* go. I think—I *hope*—that you're wrong about that. I have an idea."

"Which is?"

"In a moment. First, answer one question for me. Can you refuel the airplane? Can you do that even if there's no power?"

"I think so, yes. Let's say that, with the help of a few able-bodied men, I could. Then what?"

"Then we take off again," Bob said. Little beads of sweat stood out on his deeply lined face. They looked like droplets of clear oil. "That sound—that crunchy sound—is coming from the east. The time-rip was several thousand miles west of here. If we retraced our original course . . . could you do that?"

"Yes," Brian said. He had left the auxiliary power units running, and that meant the INS computer's program was still intact. That program was an exact log of the trip they had just made, from the moment Flight 29 had left the ground in southern California until the moment it had set down in central Maine. One touch of a button would instruct the computer to simply reverse that course; the touch of another button, once in the air, would put the autopilot to work flying it. The Teledyne inertial navigation system would re-create the trip down to the smallest degree deviations. "I could do that, but why?"

"Because the rip may still be there. Don't you see? *We might be able to fly back through it.*"

Nick looked at Bob in sudden startled concentration, then turned to Brian. "He might have something there, mate. He just might."

Albert Kaussner's mind was diverted onto an irrelevant but fascinating side-track: if the rip were still there, and if Flight 29 had been on a frequently used altitude and heading—a kind of east-west avenue in the sky—then perhaps other planes had gone through it between 1:07 this morning and now (whenever *now* was). Perhaps there were other planes landing or landed at other deserted American airports, other crews and passengers wandering around, stunned . . .

No, he thought. *We happened to have a pilot on board. What are the chances of that happening twice?*

He thought of what Mr. Jenkins had said about Ted Williams's sixteen consecutive on-bases and shivered.

"He might or he might not," Brian said. "It doesn't really matter, because we're not going anyplace in that plane."

"Why not?" Rudy asked. "If you could refuel it, I don't see . . ."

"Remember the matches? The ones from the bowl in the restaurant? The ones that wouldn't light?"

Rudy looked blank, but an expression of huge dismay dawned on Bob Jenkins's face. He put his hand to his forehead and took a step backward. He actually seemed to shrink before them.

"What?" Don asked. He was looking at Brian from beneath drawn-together brows. It was a look which conveyed both confusion and suspicion. "What does that have to—"

But Nick knew.

"Don't you see?" he asked quietly. "Don't you see, mate? If batteries don't work, if matches don't light—"

"—then jet-fuel won't burn," Brian finished. "It will be as used up and worn out as everything else in this world." He looked at each one of them in turn. "I might as well fill up the fuel tanks with molasses."

2

"Have either of you fine young ladies ever heard of the langoliers?" Craig asked suddenly. His tone was light, almost vivacious.

Laurel jumped and looked nervously toward the others, who were still standing by the windows and talking. Dinah only turned toward Craig's voice, apparently not surprised at all.

"No," she said calmly. "What are those?"

"Don't talk to him, Dinah," Laurel whispered.

"I heard that," Craig said in the same pleasant tone of voice. "Dinah's not the only one with sharp ears, you know."

Laurel felt her face grow warm.

"I wouldn't hurt the child, anyway," Craig went on. "No more than I would have hurt that girl. I'm just frightened. Aren't you?"

"Yes," Laurel snapped, "but I don't take hostages and then try to shoot teenage boys when I'm frightened."

"*You* didn't have what looked like the whole front line of the Los Angeles Rams caving in on you at once," Craig said. "And that English fellow . . ." He laughed. The sound of his laughter in this quiet place was disturbingly merry, disturbingly *normal*. "Well, all I can say is that if you think *I'm* crazy, you haven't been watching *him* at all. That man's got a chainsaw for a mind."

Laurel didn't know what to say. She knew it hadn't been the way Craig Toomy was presenting it, but when he spoke it seemed as though it *should* have been that way . . . and what he said about the Englishman was too close to the truth. The man's eyes . . . and the kick he had chopped into Mr. Toomy's ribs after he had been tied up . . . Laurel shivered.

"What are the langoliers, Mr. Toomy?" Dinah asked.

"Well, I always used to think they were just make-believe," Craig said in that same good-humored voice. "Now I'm beginning to wonder . . . because I hear it, too, young lady. Yes I do."

"The sound?" Dinah asked softly. "That sound is the langoliers?"

Laurel put one hand on Dinah's shoulder. "I really wish you wouldn't talk to him anymore, honey. He makes me nervous."

"Why? He's tied up, isn't he?"

"Yes, but—"

"And you could always call for the others, couldn't you?"

"Well, I think—"

"I want to know about the langoliers."

With some effort, Craig turned his head to look at them . . . and now Laurel felt some of the charm and force of personality which had kept Craig firmly on the fast track as he worked out the high-pressure script his parents had written for him. She felt this even though he was lying on the floor with his hands tied behind him and his own blood drying on his forehead and left cheek.

"My father said the langoliers were little creatures that lived in closets and sewers and other dark places."

"Like elves?" Dinah wanted to know.

Craig laughed and shook his head. "Nothing so pleasant, I'm afraid. He said that all they really were was hair and teeth and fast little legs—their little legs were fast, he said, so they could catch up with bad boys and girls no matter how quickly they scampered."

"Stop it," Laurel said coldly. "You're scaring the child."

"No, he's not," Dinah said. "I know make-believe when I hear it. It's interesting, that's all." Her face said it was something more than interesting, however. She was intent, fascinated.

"It *is,* isn't it?" Craig said, apparently pleased by her interest. "I think what Laurel means is that I'm scaring *her.* Do I win the cigar, Laurel? If so, I'd like an El Producto, please. None of those cheap White Owls for me." He laughed again.

Laurel didn't reply, and after a moment Craig resumed.

"My dad said there were thousands of langoliers. He said there had to be, because there were *millions* of bad boys and girls scampering about the world. That's how he always put it. My father never saw a child run in his entire life. They always scampered. I think he liked that word because it implies senseless, directionless, nonproductive motion. But the langoliers . . . *they* run. *They* have purpose. In fact, you could say that the langoliers are purpose personified."

"What did the kids do that was so bad?" Dinah asked. "What did they do that was so bad the langoliers had to run after them?"

"You know, I'm glad you asked that question," Craig said. "Because when my father said someone was bad, Dinah, what he meant was lazy. A lazy person couldn't be part of THE BIG PICTURE. No way. In my house, you were either part of THE BIG PICTURE or you were LYING DOWN ON THE JOB, and that was the worst kind of bad you could be. Throat-cutting was a venial sin compared to LYING DOWN ON THE JOB. He said that if you weren't part of THE BIG PICTURE, the langoliers would come and take you out of the picture completely. He said you'd be in your bed one night and then you'd hear them coming . . . crunching and smacking their way toward you . . . and even if you tried to scamper off, they'd get you. Because of their fast little—"

"That's enough," Laurel said. Her voice was flat and dry.

"The sound *is* out there, though," Craig said. His eyes regarded her brightly, almost roguishly. "You can't deny that. The sound really is out th—"

"Stop it or I'll hit you with something myself."

"Okay," Craig said. He rolled over on his back, grimaced, and then rolled further, onto his other side and away from them. "A man gets tired of being hit when he's down and hog-tied."

Laurel's face grew not just warm but hot this time. She bit her lip and said nothing. She felt like crying. How was she supposed to handle someone like this? *How?* First the man seemed as crazy as a bedbug, and then he seemed as sane as could be. And meanwhile, the whole world—Mr. Toomy's BIG PICTURE—had gone to hell.

"I bet you were scared of your dad, weren't you, Mr. Toomy?"

Craig looked back over his shoulder at Dinah, startled. He smiled again, but this smile was different. It was a rueful, hurt smile with no public relations in it. "This time *you* win the cigar, miss," he said. "I was terrified of him."

"Is he dead?"

"Yes."

"Was he LYING DOWN ON THE JOB? Did the langoliers get him?"

Craig thought for a long time. He remembered being told that his father had had his heart attack while in his office. When his

secretary buzzed him for his ten o'clock staff meeting and there
was no answer, she had come in to find him dead on the carpet,
eyes bulging, foam drying on his mouth.

Did someone tell you that? he wondered suddenly. *That his eyes
were bugging out, that there was foam on his mouth? Did someone
actually tell you that—Mother, perhaps, when she was drunk—or was
it just wishful thinking?*

"Mr. Toomy? Did they?"

"Yes," Craig said thoughtfully. "I guess he was, and I guess they
did."

"Mr. Toomy?"

"What?"

"I'm not the way you see me. I'm not ugly. None of us are."

He looked at her, startled. "How would you know how you look
to me, little blind miss?"

"You might be surprised," Dinah said.

Laurel turned toward her, suddenly more uneasy than ever . . .
but of course there was nothing to see. Dinah's dark glasses defeated
curiosity.

3

The other passengers stood on the far side of the waiting room,
listening to that low rattling sound and saying nothing. It seemed
there was nothing left to say.

"What do we do now?" Don asked. He seemed to have wilted
inside his red lumberjack's shirt. Albert thought the shirt itself had
lost some of its cheerfully macho vibrancy.

"I don't know," Brian said. He felt a horrible impotence toiling
away in his belly. He looked out at the plane, which had been *his*
plane for a little while, and was struck by its clean lines and smooth
beauty. The Delta 727 sitting to its left at the jetway looked like
a dowdy matron by comparison. *It looks good to you because it's never
going to fly again, that's all. It's like glimpsing a beautiful woman for
just a moment in the back seat of a limousine—she looks even more
beautiful than she really is because you know she's not yours, can never
be yours.*

"How much fuel is left, Brian?" Nick asked suddenly. "Maybe

the burn-rate isn't the same over here. Maybe there's more than you realize."

"All the gauges are in apple-pie working order," Brian said. "When we landed, I had less than 600 pounds. To get back to where this happened, we'd need at least 50,000."

Bethany took out her cigarettes and offered the pack to Bob. He shook his head. She stuck one in her mouth, took out her matches, and struck one.

It didn't light.

"Oh-oh," she said.

Albert glanced over. She struck the match again . . . and again . . . and again. There was nothing. She looked at him, frightened.

"Here," Albert said. Let me."

He took the matches from her hand and tore another one loose. He struck it across the strip on the back. There was nothing.

"Whatever it is, it seems to be catching," Rudy Warwick observed.

Bethany burst into tears, and Bob offered her his handkerchief.

"Wait a minute," Albert said, and struck the match again. This time it lit . . . but the flame was low, guttering, unenthusiastic. He applied it to the quivering tip of Bethany's cigarette and a clear image suddenly filled his mind: a sign he had passed as he rode his ten-speed to Pasadena High School every day for the last three years. CAUTION, this sign said. TWO-WAY TRAFFIC AHEAD.

What in the hell does that mean?

He didn't know . . . at least not yet. All he knew for sure was that some idea wanted out but was, at least for the time being, stuck in the gears.

Albert shook the match out. It didn't take much shaking.

Bethany drew on her cigarette, then grimaced. "Blick! It tastes like a Carlton, or something."

"Blow smoke in my face," Albert said.

"What?"

"You heard me. Blow some in my face."

She did as he asked, and Albert sniffed at the smoke. Its former sweet fragrance was now muted.

Whatever it is, it seems to be catching.

CAUTION: TWO-WAY TRAFFIC AHEAD.

"I'm going back to the restaurant," Nick said. He looked depressed. "Yon Cassius has a lean and slippery feel. I don't like leaving him with the ladies for too long."

Brian started after him and the others followed. Albert thought there was something a little amusing about these tidal flows—they were behaving like cows which sense thunder in the air.

"Come on," Bethany said. "Let's go." She dropped her half-smoked cigarette into an ashtray and used Bob's handkerchief to wipe her eyes. Then she took Albert's hand.

They were halfway across the waiting room and Albert was looking at the back of Mr. Gaffney's red shirt when it struck him again, more forcibly this time: *TWO-WAY TRAFFIC AHEAD.*

"Wait a minute!" he yelled. He suddenly slipped an arm around Bethany's waist, pulled her to him, put his face into the hollow of her throat, and breathed in deeply.

"Oh my! We hardly know each other!" Bethany cried. Then she began to giggle helplessly and put her arms around Albert's neck. Albert, a boy whose natural shyness usually disappeared only in his daydreams, paid no notice. He took another deep breath through his nose. The smells of her hair, sweat, and perfume were still there, but they were faint; very faint.

They all looked around, but Albert had already let Bethany go and was hurrying back to the windows.

"Wow!" Bethany said. She was still giggling a little, and blushing brightly. "Strange dude!"

Albert looked at Flight 29 and saw what Brian had noticed a few minutes earlier: it was clean and smooth and almost impossibly white. It seemed to vibrate in the dull stillness outside.

Suddenly the idea came up for him. It seemed to burst behind his eyes like a firework. The central concept was a bright, burning ball; implications radiated out from it like fiery spangles and for a moment he quite literally forgot to breathe.

"Albert?" Bob asked. "Albert, what's wro—"

"*Captain Engle!*" Albert screamed. In the restaurant, Laurel sat bolt upright and Dinah clasped her arm with hands like talons. Craig Toomy craned his neck to look. "*Captain Engle, come here!*"

4

Outside, the sound was louder.

To Brian it was the sound of radio static. Nick Hopewell thought it sounded like a strong wind rattling dry tropical grasses. Albert, who had worked at McDonald's the summer before, was reminded of the sound of french fries in a deep-fat fryer, and to Bob Jenkins it was the sound of paper being crumpled in a distant room.

The four of them crawled through the hanging rubber strips and then stepped down into the luggage-unloading area, listening to the sound of what Craig Toomy called the langoliers.

"How much closer is it?" Brian asked Nick.

"Can't tell. It *sounds* closer, but of course we were inside before."

"Come on," Albert said impatiently. "How do we get back aboard? Climb the slide?"

"Won't be necessary," Brian said, and pointed. A rolling stairway stood on the far side of Gate 2. They walked toward it, their shoes clopping listlessly on the concrete.

"You know what a long shot this is, don't you, Albert?" Brian asked as they walked.

"Yes, but—"

"Long shots are better than no shots at all," Nick finished for him.

"I just don't want him to be too disappointed if it doesn't pan out."

"Don't worry," Bob said softly. "I will be disappointed enough for all of us. The lad's idea makes good logical sense. It *should* prove out . . . although, Albert, you do realize there may be factors here which we haven't discovered, don't you?"

"Yes."

They reached the rolling ladder, and Brian kicked up the footbrakes on the wheels. Nick took a position on the grip which jutted from the left railing, and Brian laid hold of the one on the right.

"I hope it still rolls," Brian said.

"It should," Bob Jenkins answered. "Some—perhaps even most—of the ordinary physical and chemical components of life seem to remain in operation; our bodies are able to process the air, doors open and close—"

"Don't forget gravity," Albert put in. "The earth still sucks."

"Let's quit talking about it and just try it," Nick said.

The stairway rolled easily. The two men trundled it across the tarmac toward the 767 with Albert and Bob walking behind them. One of the wheels squeaked rhythmically. The only other sound was that low, constant crunch-rattle-crunch from somewhere over the eastern horizon.

"Look at it," Albert said as they neared the 767. "Just *look* at it. Can't you see? Can't you see how much more *there* it is than anything else?"

There was no need to answer, and no one did. They could all see it. And reluctantly, almost against his will, Brian began to think the kid might have something.

They set the stairway at an angle between the escape slide and the fuselage of the plane, with the top step only a long stride away from the open door. "I'll go first," Brian said. "After I pull the slide in, Nick, you and Albert roll the stairs into better position."

"Aye, aye, Captain," Nick said, and clipped off a smart little salute, the knuckles of his first and second fingers touching his forehead.

Brian snorted. "Junior attaché," he said, and then ran fleetly up the stairs. A few moments later he had used the escape slide's lanyard to pull it back inside. Then he leaned out to watch as Nick and Albert carefully maneuvered the rolling staircase into position with its top step just below the 767's forward entrance.

5

Rudy Warwick and Don Gaffney were now babysitting Craig. Bethany, Dinah, and Laurel were lined up at the waiting-room windows, looking out. "What are they doing?" Dinah asked.

"They've taken away the slide and put a stairway by the door," Laurel said. "Now they're going up." She looked at Bethany. "You're sure you don't know what they're up to?"

Bethany shook her head. "All I know is that Ace—Albert, I mean—almost went nuts. I'd like to think it was this mad sexual attraction, but I don't think it was." She paused, smiled, and added: "At least, not yet. He said something about the plane being more *there.* And my perfume being *less* there, which probably wouldn't please Coco Chanel or whatever her name is. And two-way traffic. I didn't get it. He was really jabbering."

"I bet I know," Dinah said.

"What's your guess, hon?"

Dinah only shook her head. "I just hope they hurry up. Because poor Mr. Toomy is right. The langoliers are coming."

"Dinah, that's just something his father made up."

"Maybe once it was make-believe," Dinah said, turning her sightless eyes back to the windows, "but not anymore."

6

"All right, Ace," Nick said. "On with the show."

Albert's heart was thudding and his hands shook as he set the four elements of his experiment out on the shelf in first class, where, a thousand years ago and on the other side of the continent, a woman named Melanie Trevor had supervised a carton of orange juice and two bottles of champagne.

Brian watched closely as Albert put down a book of matches, a bottle of Budweiser, a can of Pepsi, and a peanut-butter-and-jelly sandwich from the restaurant cold-case. The sandwich had been sealed in plastic wrap.

"Okay," Albert said, and took a deep breath. "Let's see what we got here."

7

Don left the restaurant and walked over to the windows. "What's happening?"

"We don't know," Bethany said. She had managed to coax a flame from another of her matches and was smoking again. When she removed the cigarette from her mouth, Laurel saw she had torn off the filter. "They went inside the plane; they're still inside the plane; end of story."

Don gazed out for several seconds. "It looks different outside. I can't say just why, but it does."

"The light's going," Dinah said. "That's what's different." Her voice was calm enough, but her small face was an imprint of loneliness and fear. "I can feel it going."

"She's right," Laurel agreed. "It's only been daylight for two or three hours, but it's already getting dark again."

"I keep thinking this is a dream, you know," Don said. "I keep thinking it's the worst nightmare I ever had but I'll wake up soon."

Laurel nodded. "How is Mr. Toomy?"

Don laughed without much humor. "You won't believe it."

"Won't believe what?" Bethany asked.

"He's gone to sleep."

8

Craig Toomy, of course, was not sleeping. People who fell asleep at critical moments, like that fellow who was supposed to have been keeping an eye out while Jesus prayed in the Garden of Gethsemane, were most definitely not part of THE BIG PICTURE.

He had watched the two men carefully through eyes which were not quite shut and willed one or both of them to go away. Eventually the one in the red shirt *did* go away. Warwick, the bald man with the big false teeth, walked over to Craig and bent down. Craig let his eyes close all the way.

"Hey," Warwick said. "Hey, you 'wake?"

Craig lay still, eyes closed, breathing regularly. He considered manufacturing a small snore and thought better of it.

Warwick poked him in the side.

Craig kept his eyes shut and went on breathing regularly.

Baldy straightened up, stepped over him, and went to the restaurant door to watch the others. Craig cracked his eyelids and made sure Warwick's back was turned. Then, very quietly and very carefully, he began to work his wrists up and down inside the tight figure-eight of cloth which bound them. The tablecloth rope felt looser already.

He moved his wrists in short strokes, watching Warwick's back, ready to cease movement and close his eyes again the instant Warwick showed signs of turning around. He willed Warwick *not* to turn around. He wanted to be free before the assholes came back from the plane. Especially the English asshole, the one who had hurt his nose and then kicked him while he was down. The English asshole had tied him up pretty well; thank God it was only a tablecloth instead of a length of nylon line. Then he would have been out of luck, but as it was—

One of the knots loosened, and now Craig began to rotate his wrists from side to side. He could hear the langoliers approaching. He intended to be out of here and on his way to Boston before they arrived. In Boston he would be safe. When you were in a boardroom filled with bankers, no scampering was allowed.

And God help anyone—man, woman, or child—who tried to get in his way.

9

Albert picked up the book of matches he had taken from the bowl in the restaurant. "Exhibit A," he said. "Here goes."

He tore a match from the book and struck it. His unsteady hands betrayed him and he struck the match a full two inches above the rough strip which ran along the bottom of the paper folder. The match bent.

"Shit!" Albert cried.

"Would you like me to—" Bob began.

"Let him alone," Brian said. "It's Albert's show."

"Steady on, Albert," Nick said.

Albert tore another match from the book, offered them a sickly smile, and struck it.

The match didn't light.

He struck it again.

The match didn't light.

"I guess that does it," Brian said. "There's nothing—"

"I *smelled* it," Nick said. "I smelled the sulphur! Try another one, Ace!"

Instead, Albert snapped the same match across the rough strip a third time . . . and this time it flared alight. It did not just burn the flammable head and then gutter out; it stood up in the familiar little teardrop shape, blue at its base, yellow at its tip, and began to burn the paper stick.

Albert looked up, a wild grin on his face. "You see?" he said. *"You see?"*

He shook the match out, dropped it, and pulled another. This one lit on the first strike. He bent back the cover of the matchbook and touched the lit flame to the other matches, just as Bob Jenkins had done in the restaurant. This time they all flared alight with a dry *fsss!* sound. Albert blew them out like a birthday candle. It took two puffs of air to do the job.

"You see?" he asked. "You see what it means? Two-way traffic! *We brought our own time with us!* There's the past out there . . . and everywhere, I guess, east of the hole we came through . . . but the present is still in here! *Still caught inside this airplane!*"

"I don't know," Brian said, but suddenly everything seemed possible again. He felt a wild, almost unrestrainable urge to pull Albert into his arms and pound him on the back.

"Bravo, Albert!" Bob said. "The beer! Try the beer!"

Albert spun the cap off the beer while Nick fished an unbroken glass from the wreckage around the drinks trolley.

"Where's the smoke?" Brian asked.

"Smoke?" Bob asked, puzzled.

"Well, I guess it's not smoke, exactly, but when you open a beer there's usually something that looks like smoke around the mouth of the bottle."

Albert sniffed, then tipped the beer toward Brian. "Smell."

Brian did, and began to grin. He couldn't help it. "By God, it sure *smells* like beer, smoke or no smoke."

Nick held out the glass, and Albert was pleased to see that the Englishman's hand was not quite steady, either. "Pour it," he said. "Hurry up, mate—my sawbones says suspense is bad for the old ticker."

Albert poured the beer and their smiles faded.

The beer was flat. Utterly flat. It simply sat in the whiskey glass Nick had found, looking like a urine sample.

10

"Christ almighty, it's getting dark!"

The people standing at the windows looked around as Rudy Warwick joined them.

"You're supposed to be watching the nut," Don said.

Rudy gestured impatiently. "He's out like a light. I think that whack on the head rattled his furniture a little more than we thought at first. What's going on out there? And why is it getting dark so fast?"

"We don't know," Bethany said. "It just *is*. Do you think that weird dude is going into a coma, or something like that?"

"I don't know," Rudy said. "But if he is, we won't have to worry about him anymore, will we? Christ, is that sound *creepy*! It sounds like a bunch of coked-up termites in a balsa-wood glider." For the first time, Rudy seemed to have forgotten his stomach.

Dinah looked up at Laurel. "I think we better check on Mr. Toomy," she said. "I'm worried about him. I bet he's scared."

"If he's unconscious, Dinah, there isn't anything we can—"

"I don't think he's unconscious," Dinah said quietly. "I don't think he's even asleep."

Laurel looked down at the child thoughtfully for a moment and then took her hand. "All right," she said. "Let's have a look."

11

The knot Nick Hopewell had tied against Craig's right wrist finally loosened enough for him to pull his hand free. He used it to push down the loop holding his left hand. He got quickly to his feet. A bolt of pain shot through his head, and for a moment he swayed. Flocks of black dots chased across his field of vision and then slowly cleared away. He became aware that the terminal was being swallowed in gloom. Premature night was falling. He could hear the chew-crunch-chew sound of the langoliers much more clearly now, perhaps because his ears had become attuned to them, perhaps because they were closer.

On the far side of the terminal he saw two silhouettes, one tall and one short, break away from the others and start back toward the restaurant. The woman with the bitchy voice and the little blind girl with the ugly, pouty face. He couldn't let them raise the alarm. That would be very bad.

Craig backed away from the bloody patch of carpet where he had been lying, never taking his eyes from the approaching figures. He could not get over how rapidly the light was failing.

There were pots of eating utensils set into a counter to the left of the cash register, but it was all plastic crap, no good to him. Craig ducked around the cash register and saw something better: a butcher knife lying on the counter next to the grill. He took it and crouched behind the cash register to watch them approach. He watched the little girl with a particular anxious interest. The little girl knew a lot . . . too much, maybe. The question was, where had she come by her knowledge?

That was a very interesting question indeed.

Wasn't it?

12

Nick looked from Albert to Bob. "So," he said. "The matches work but the lager doesn't." He turned to set the glass of beer on the counter. "What does that mea—"

All at once a small mushroom cloud of bubbles burst from nowhere in the bottom of the glass. They rose rapidly, spread, and burst into a thin head at the top. Nick's eyes widened.

"Apparently," Bob said dryly, "it takes a moment or two for things to catch up." He took the glass, drank it off and smacked his lips. "Excellent," he said. They all looked at the complicated lace of white foam on the inside of the glass. "I can say without doubt that it's the best glass of beer I ever drank in my life."

Albert poured more beer into the glass. This time it came out foaming; the head overspilled the rim and ran down the outside. Brian picked it up.

"Are you sure you want to do that, matey?" Nick asked, grinning. "Don't you fellows like to say 'twenty-four hours from bottle to throttle'?"

"In cases of time-travel, the rule is suspended," Brian said. "You could look it up." He tilted the glass, drank, then laughed out loud. "You're right," he said to Bob. "It's the best goddam beer there ever was. Try the Pepsi, Albert."

Albert opened the can and they all heard the familiar *pop-hisss* of carbonation, mainstay of a hundred soft-drink commercials. He took a deep drink. When he lowered the can he was grinning . . . but there were tears in his eyes.

"Gentlemen, the Pepsi-Cola is also very good today," he said in plummy headwaiter's tones, and they all began to laugh.

13

Don Gaffney caught up with Laurel and Dinah just as they entered the restaurant. "I thought I'd better—" he began, and then stopped. He looked around, "Oh, shit. Where is he?"

"I don't—" Laurel began, and then, from beside her, Dinah Bellman said, *"Be quiet."*

Her head turned slowly, like the lamp of a dead searchlight. For a moment there was no sound at all in the restaurant . . . at least no sound Laurel could hear.

"There," Dinah said at last, and pointed toward the cash register. "He's hiding over there. Behind something."

"How do you know that?" Don asked in a dry, nervous voice. "I don't hear—"

"*I* do," Dinah said calmly. "I hear his fingernails on metal. And I hear his heart. It's beating very fast and very hard. He's scared to death. I feel so sorry for him." She suddenly disengaged her hand from Laurel's and stepped forward.

"Dinah, no!" Laurel screamed.

Dinah took no notice. She walked toward the cash register, arms out, fingers seeking possible obstacles. The shadows seemed to reach for her and enfold her.

"Mr. Toomy? Please come out. We don't want to hurt you. Please don't be afraid—"

A sound began to arise from behind the cash register. It was a high, keening scream. It was a word, or something which was trying to *be* a word, but there was no sanity in it.

"Youuuuuuuuuuu—"

Craig arose from his hiding place, eyes blazing, butcher knife upraised, suddenly understanding that it was *her,* she was one of *them,* behind those dark glasses she was one of *them,* she was not only a langolier but the *head* langolier, the one who was calling the others, calling them with her dead blind eyes.

"Youuuuuuuuuuu—"

He rushed at her, shrieking. Don Gaffney shoved Laurel out of his way, almost knocking her to the floor, and leaped forward. He was fast, but not fast enough. Craig Toomy was crazy, and he moved with the speed of a langolier himself. He approached Dinah at a dead-out run. No scampering for him.

Dinah made no effort to draw away. She looked up from her

darkness and into his, and now she held her arms out, as if to enfold him and comfort him.

"—*oooouuuuuuuu*—"

"It's all right, Mr. Toomy," she said. "Don't be afr—" And then Craig buried the butcher knife in her chest and ran past Laurel into the terminal, still shrieking.

Dinah stood where she was for a moment. Her hands found the wooden handle jutting out of the front of her dress and her fingers fluttered over it, exploring it. Then she sank slowly, gracefully, to the floor, becoming just another shadow in the growing darkness.

CHAPTER SEVEN

DINAH IN THE VALLEY OF THE SHADOW. THE FASTEST TOASTER EAST OF THE MISSISSIPPI. RACING AGAINST TIME. NICK MAKES A DECISION.

1

Albert, Brian, Bob, and Nick passed the peanut-butter-and-jelly sandwich around. They each got two bites and then it was gone . . . but while it lasted, Albert thought he had never sunk his teeth into such wonderful chow in his life. His belly awakened and immediately began clamoring for more.

"I think our bald friend Mr. Warwick is going to like this part best," Nick said, swallowing. He looked at Albert. "You're a genius, Ace. You know that, don't you? Nothing but a pure genius."

Albert flushed happily. "It wasn't much," he said. "Just a little of what Mr. Jenkins calls the deductive method. If two streams flowing in different directions come together, they mix and make a whirlpool. I saw what was happening with Bethany's matches and thought something like that might be happening here. And there was Mr. Gaffney's bright-red shirt. It started to lose its color. So I thought, well, if stuff starts to fade when it's not on the plane anymore, maybe if you brought faded stuff *onto* the plane, it would—"

"I hate to interrupt," Bob said softly, "but I think that if we intend to try and get back, we should start the process as soon as possible. The sounds we are hearing worry me, but there's something else that worries me more. This airplane is not a closed system. I think there's a good chance that before long it will begin to lose its . . . its . . ."

"Its temporal integrity?" Albert suggested.

"Yes. Well put. Any fuel we load into its tanks now may burn . . . but a few hours from now, it may not."

An unpleasant idea occurred to Brian: that the fuel might stop burning halfway across the country, with the 767 at 36,000 feet. He opened his mouth to tell them this . . . and then closed it again. What good would it do to put the idea in their minds, when they could do nothing about it?

"How do we start, Brian?" Nick asked in clipped, businesslike tones.

Brian ran the process over in his mind. It would be a little awkward, especially working with men whose only experience with aircraft probably began and ended with model planes, but he thought it could be done.

"We start by turning on the engines and taxiing as close to that Delta 727 as we can get," he said. "When we get there, I'll kill the starboard engine and leave the portside engine turning over. We're lucky. This 767 is equipped with wet-wing fuel tanks and an APU system that—"

A shrill, panicked scream drifted up to them, cutting across the low rattling background noise like a fork drawn across a slate blackboard. It was followed by running footfalls on the ladder. Nick turned in that direction and his hands came up in a gesture Albert recognized at once; he had seen some of the martial-arts freaks at school back home practicing the move. It was the classic Tae Kwan Do defensive position. A moment later Bethany's pallid, terrified face appeared in the doorway and Nick let his hands relax.

"*Come!*" Bethany screamed. "You've got to *come!*" She was panting, out of breath, and she reeled backward on the platform of the ladder. For a moment Albert and Brian were sure she was going to tumble back down the steep steps, breaking her neck on the way. Then Nick leaped forward, cupped a hand on the nape of her neck, and pulled her into the plane. Bethany did not even seem to realize she had had a close call. Her dark eyes blazed at them from the white circle of her face. "Please come! He's stabbed her! I think she's dying!"

Nick put his hands on her shoulders and lowered his face toward hers as if he intended to kiss her. "Who has stabbed whom?" he asked very quietly. "Who is dying?"

"I . . . she . . . Mr. T-T-Toomy—"

"Bethany, say teacup."

She looked at him, eyes shocked and uncomprehending. Brian was looking at Nick as though he had gone insane.

Nick gave the girl's shoulders a little shake.

"Say teacup. Right now."

"T-T-Teacup."

"Teacup and saucer. Say it, Bethany."

"Teacup and saucer."

"All right. Better?"

She nodded. "Yes."

"Good. If you feel yourself losing control again, say teacup at once and you'll come back. Now—who's been stabbed?"

"The blind girl. Dinah."

"Bloody *shit*. All right, Bethany. Just—" Nick raised his voice sharply as he saw Brian move behind Bethany, headed for the ladder, with Albert right behind him. "*No!*" he shouted in a bright, hard tone that stopped both of them. "Stay fucking *put!*"

Brian, who had served two tours in Vietnam and knew the sound of unquestionable command when he heard it, stopped so suddenly that Albert ran face-first into the middle of his back. *I knew it,* he thought. *I knew he'd take over. It was just a matter of time and circumstance.*

"Do you know how this happened or where our wretched travelling companion is now?" Nick asked Bethany.

"The guy . . . the guy in the red shirt said—"

"All right. Never mind." He glanced briefly up at Brian. His eyes were red with anger. "The bloody fools left him alone. I'd wager my pension on it. Well, it won't happen again. Our Mr. Toomy has cut his last caper."

He looked back at the girl. Her head drooped; her hair hung dejectedly in her face; she was breathing in great, watery swoops of breath.

"Is she alive, Bethany?" he asked gently.

"I . . . I . . . I . . ."

"Teacup, Bethany."

"Teacup!" Bethany shouted, and looked up at him from teary, red-rimmed eyes. "I don't know. She was alive when I . . . you know, came for you. She might be dead now. He really got her. Jesus, why did we have to get stuck with a fucking psycho? Weren't things bad enough without that?"

"And none of you who were supposed to be minding this fellow have the slightest idea where he went following the attack, is that right?"

Bethany put her hands over her face and began to sob. It was all the answer any of them needed.

"Don't be so hard on her," Albert said quietly, and slipped an arm around Bethany's waist. She put her head on his shoulder and began to sob more strenuously.

Nick moved the two of them gently aside. "If I was inclined to be hard on someone, it would be myself, Ace. I should have stayed behind."

He turned to Brian.

"I'm going back into the terminal. You're not. Mr. Jenkins here is almost certainly right; our time here is short. I don't like to think just *how* short. Start the engines but don't move the aircraft yet. If the girl is alive, we'll need the stairs to bring her up. Bob, bottom of the stairs. Keep an eye out for that bugger Toomy. Albert, you come with me."

Then he said something which chilled them all.

"I almost hope she's dead, God help me. It will save time if she is."

2

Dinah was not dead, not even unconscious. Laurel had taken off her sunglasses to wipe away the sweat which had sprung up on the girl's face, and Dinah's eyes, deep brown and very wide, looked up unseeingly into Laurel's blue-green ones. Behind her, Don and Rudy stood shoulder to shoulder, looking down anxiously.

"I'm sorry," Rudy said for the fifth time. "I really thought he was out. Out *cold.*"

Laurel ignored him. "How are you, Dinah?" she asked softly. She didn't want to look at the wooden handle growing out of the girl's dress, but couldn't take her eyes from it. There was very little blood, at least so far; a circle the size of a demitasse cup around the place where the blade had gone in, and that was all.

So far.

"It hurts," Dinah said in a faint voice. "It's hard to breathe. And it's *hot*."

"You're going to be all right," Laurel said, but her eyes were drawn relentlessly back to the handle of the knife. The girl was very small, and she couldn't understand why the blade hadn't gone all the way through her. Couldn't understand why she wasn't dead already.

". . . out of here," Dinah said. She grimaced, and a thick, slow curdle of blood escaped from the corner of her mouth and ran down her cheek.

"Don't try to talk, honey," Laurel said, and brushed damp curls back from Dinah's forehead.

"You have to get *out* of here," Dinah insisted. Her voice was little more than a whisper. "And you shouldn't blame Mr. Toomy. He's . . . he's scared, that's all. Of *them*."

Don looked around balefully. "If I find that bastard, *I'll* scare him," he said, and curled both hands into fists. A lodge ring gleamed above one knuckle in the growing gloom. "I'll make him wish he was born dead."

Nick came into the restaurant then, followed by Albert. He pushed past Rudy Warwick without a word of apology and knelt next to Dinah. His bright gaze fixed upon the handle of the knife for a moment, then moved to the child's face.

"Hello, love." He spoke cheerily, but his eyes had darkened. "I see you've been air-conditioned. Not to worry; you'll be right as a trivet in no time flat."

Dinah smiled a little. "What's a trivet?" she whispered. More blood ran out of her mouth as she spoke, and Laurel could see it on her teeth. Laurel's stomach did a slow, lazy roll.

"I don't know, but I'm sure it's something nice," Nick replied. "I'm going to turn your head to one side. Be as still as you can."

"Okay."

Nick moved her head, very gently, until her cheek was almost resting on the carpet. "Hurt?"

"Yes," Dinah whispered. "Hot. Hurts to . . . breathe." Her whispery voice had taken on a hoarse, cracked quality. A thin stream of blood ran from her mouth and pooled on the carpet less than ten feet from the place where Craig Toomy's blood was drying.

From outside came the sudden high-pressure whine of aircraft engines starting. Don, Rudy, and Albert looked in that direction. Nick never looked away from the girl. He spoke gently. "Do you feel like coughing, Dinah?"

"Yes . . . no . . . don't know."

"It's better if you don't," he said. "If you get that tickly feeling, try to ignore it. And don't talk anymore, right?"

"Don't . . . hurt . . . Mr. Toomy." Her words, whispered though they were, conveyed great emphasis, great urgency.

"No, love, wouldn't think of it. Take it from me."

". . . don't . . . trust . . . you . . ."

He bent, kissed her cheek, and whispered in her ear: "But you *can,* you know—trust me, I mean. For now, all you've got to do is lie still and let us take care of things."

He looked at Laurel.

"You didn't try to remove the knife?"

"I . . . no." Laurel swallowed. There was a hot, harsh lump in her throat. The swallow didn't move it. "Should I have?"

"If you had, there wouldn't be much chance. Do you have any nursing experience?"

"No."

"All right, I'm going to tell you what to do . . . but first I need to know if the sight of blood—quite a bit of it—is going to make you pass out. And I need the truth."

Laurel said, "I haven't really *seen* a lot of blood since my sister ran into a door and knocked out two of her teeth while we were playing hide-and-seek. But I didn't faint then."

"Good. And you're not going to faint now. Mr. Warwick, bring me half a dozen tablecloths from that grotty little pub around the corner." He smiled down at the girl. "Give me a minute or two, Dinah, and I think you'll feel much better. Young Dr. Hopewell is ever so gentle with the ladies—especially the ones who are young and pretty."

Laurel felt a sudden and absolutely absurd desire to reach out and touch Nick's hair.

What's the matter with you? This little girl is probably dying, and you're wondering what his hair feels like! Quit it! How stupid can you be?

Well, let's see . . . Stupid enough to have been flying across the country to meet a man I first contacted through the personals column of a so-called friendship magazine. Stupid enough to have been planning to sleep with him if he turned out to be reasonably presentable . . . and if he didn't have bad breath, of course.

Oh, quit it! Quit it, Laurel!

Yes, the other voice in her mind agreed. *You're absolutely right, it's crazy to be thinking things like that at a time like this, and I will quit it . . . but I wonder what Young Dr. Hopewell would be like in bed? I wonder if he would be gentle, or—*

Laurel shivered and wondered if this was the way your average nervous breakdown started.

"They're closer," Dinah said. "You really . . ." She coughed, and a large bubble of blood appeared between her lips. It popped, splattering her cheeks. Don Gaffney muttered and turned away. ". . . really have to hurry," she finished.

Nick's cheery smile didn't change a bit. "I know," he said.

3

Craig dashed across the terminal, nimbly vaulted the escalator's handrail, and ran down the frozen metal steps with panic roaring and beating in his head like the sound of the ocean in a storm; it even drowned out that other sound, the relentless chewing, crunching sound of the langoliers. No one saw him go. He sprinted across the lower lobby toward the exit doors . . . and crashed into them. He had forgotten everything, including the fact that the electric-eye door-openers wouldn't work with the power out.

He rebounded, the breath knocked out of him, and fell to the floor, gasping like a netted fish. He lay there for a moment, groping for whatever remained of his mind, and found himself gazing at his right hand. It was only a white blob in the growing darkness, but he could see the black splatters on it, and he knew what they were: the little girl's blood.

Except she wasn't a little girl, not really. She just looked *like a little girl. She was the head langolier, and with her gone the others won't be able to . . . won't be able to . . . to . . .*

To what?

To find him?

But he could still hear the hungry sound of their approach: that maddening chewing sound, as if somewhere to the east a tribe of huge, hungry insects was on the march.

His mind whirled. Oh, he was so confused.

Craig saw a smaller door leading outside, got up, and started in that direction. Then he stopped. There was a road out there, and the road undoubtedly led to the town of Bangor, but so what? He didn't care about *Bangor;* Bangor was most definitely not part of that fabled BIG PICTURE. It was *Boston* that he had to get to. If he could get there, everything would be all right. And what did that mean? His father would have known. It meant he had to STOP SCAMPERING AROUND and GET WITH THE PROGRAM.

His mind seized on this idea the way a shipwreck victim seizes upon a piece of wreckage—anything that still floats, even if it's only the shithouse door, is a prize to be cherished. If he could get to Boston, this whole experience would be . . . would be . . .

"Set aside," he muttered.

At the words, a bright beam of rational light seemed to shaft through the darkness inside his head, and a voice (it might have been his father's) cried out *YES!!* in affirmation.

But how was he to do that? Boston was too far to walk and the others wouldn't let him back on board the only plane that still worked. Not after what he had done to their little blind mascot.

"But they don't know," Craig whispered. "They don't know I did them a favor, because they don't know what she is." He nodded his head sagely. His eyes, huge and wet in the dark, gleamed.

Stow away, his father's voice whispered to him. *Stow away on the plane.*

Yes! his mother's voice added. *Stow away! That's the ticket, Craiggy-weggy! Only if you do that, you won't need a ticket, will you?*

Craig looked doubtfully toward the luggage conveyor belt. He could use it to get to the tarmac, but suppose they had posted a guard by the plane? The pilot wouldn't think of it—once out of his cockpit, the man was obviously an imbecile—but the Englishman almost surely would.

So what was he supposed to do?

If the Bangor side of the terminal was no good, and the runway side of the terminal was *also* no good, what was he supposed to do and where was he supposed to go?

Craig looked nervously at the dead escalator. They would be hunting him soon—the Englishman undoubtedly leading the pack— and here he stood in the middle of the floor, as exposed as a stripper who has just tossed her pasties and g-string into the audience.

I have to hide, at least for awhile.

He had heard the jet engines start up outside, but this did not worry him; he knew a little about planes and understood that Engle couldn't go anywhere until he had refuelled. And refuelling would take time. He didn't have to worry about them leaving without him.

Not yet, anyway.

Hide, Craiggy-weggy. That's what you have to do right now. You have to hide before they come for you.

He turned slowly, looking for the best place, squinting into the growing dark. And this time he saw a sign on a door tucked between the Avis desk and the Bangor Travel Agency.

AIRPORT SERVICES,

it read. A sign which could mean almost anything.

Craig hurried across to the door, casting nervous looks back over his shoulder as he went, and tried it. As with the door to Airport Security, the knob would not turn but the door opened when he pushed on it. Craig took one final look over his shoulder, saw no one, and closed the door behind him.

Utter, total dark swallowed him; in here, he was as blind as the little girl he had stabbed. Craig didn't mind. He was not afraid of the dark; in fact, he rather liked it. Unless you were with a woman, no one expected you to do anything significant in the dark. In the dark, performance ceased to be a factor.

Even better, the chewing sound of the langoliers was muffled.

Craig felt his way slowly forward, hands outstretched, feet shuffling. After three of these shuffling steps, his thigh came in contact with a hard object that felt like the edge of a desk. He reached forward and down. Yes. A desk. He let his hands flutter over it for a moment, taking comfort in the familiar accoutrements of white-collar America: a stack of paper, an IN/OUT basket, the edge of a blotter, a caddy filled with paper-clips, a pencil-and-pen set. He worked his way around the desk to the far side, where his hip bumped the arm of a chair. Craig maneuvered himself between the chair and the desk and then sat down. Being behind a desk made him feel better still. It made him feel like himself—calm, in control. He fumbled for the top drawer and pulled it open. Felt inside for a weapon—something sharp. His hand happened almost immediately upon a letter-opener.

He took it out, shut the drawer, and put it on the desk by his right hand.

He just sat there for a moment, listening to the muffled *whisk-thud* of his heartbeat and the dim sound of the jet engines, then sent his hands fluttering delicately over the surface of the desk again until they re-encountered the stack of papers. He took the top sheet and brought it toward him, but there wasn't a glimmer of white . . . not even when he held it right in front of his eyes.

That's all right, Craiggy-weggy. You just sit here in the dark. Sit here and wait until it's time to move. When the time comes—

I'll tell you, his father finished grimly.

"That's right," Craig said. His fingers spidered up the unseen sheet of paper to the righthand corner. He tore smoothly downward.

Riii-ip.

Calm filled his mind like cool blue water. He dropped the unseen strip on the unseen desk and returned his fingers to the top of the sheet. Everything was going to be fine. Just fine. He began to sing under his breath in a tuneless little whisper.

"Just call me angel . . . of the *morn*-ing, *ba*-by . . ."

Riii-ip.

"Just touch my cheek before you leave me . . . *ba*-by . . ."

Calm now, at peace, Craig sat and waited for his father to tell him what he should do next, just as he had done so many times as a child.

4

"Listen carefully, Albert," Nick said. "We have to take her on board the plane, but we'll need a litter to do it. There won't be one on board, but there must be one in here. Where?"

"Gee, Mr. Hopewell, Captain Engle would know better than—"

"But Captain Engle isn't here," Nick said patiently. "We shall have to manage on our own."

Albert frowned . . . then thought of a sign he had seen on the lower level. "Airport Services?" he asked. "Does that sound right?"

"It bloody well does," Nick said. "Where did you see that?"

"On the lower level. Next to the rent-a-car counters."

"All right," Nick said. "Here's how we're going to handle this. You and Mr. Gaffney are designated litter-finders and litter-bearers. Mr. Gaffney, I suggest you check by the grill behind the counter. I expect you'll find some sharp knives. I'm sure that's where our unpleasant friend found his. Get one for you and one for Albert."

Don went behind the counter without a word. Rudy Warwick returned from The Red Baron Bar with an armload of red-and-white-checked tablecloths.

"I'm really sorry—" he began again, but Nick cut him off. He was still looking at Albert, his face now only a circle of white above the deeper shadow of Dinah's small body. The dark had almost arrived.

"You probably won't see Mr. Toomy; my guess is that he left here unarmed, in a panic. I imagine he's either found a bolthole by now or has left the terminal. If you *do* see him, I advise you very strongly not to engage him unless he makes it necessary." He swung his head to look at Don as Don returned with a pair of butcher knives. "Keep your priorities straight, you two. Your mission isn't to recapture Mr. Toomy and bring him to justice. Your job is to get a stretcher and bring it here as quick as you can. We have to get out of here."

Don offered Albert one of the knives, but Albert shook his head and looked at Rudy Warwick. "Could I have one of those tablecloths instead?"

Don looked at him as if Albert had gone crazy. "A tablecloth? What in God's name for?"

"I'll show you."

Albert had been kneeling by Dinah. Now he got up and went behind the counter. He peered around, not sure exactly what he was looking for, but positive he would know it when he saw it. And so he did. There was an old-fashioned two-slice toaster sitting well back on the counter. He picked it up, jerking the plug out of the wall, and wrapped the cord tightly around it as he came back to where the others were. He took one of the tablecloths, spread it, and placed the toaster in one corner. Then he turned it over twice, wrapping the toaster in the end of the tablecloth like a Christmas present. He fashioned tight rabbit's-ear knots in the corners to make a pocket. When he gripped the loose end of the tablecloth and stood up, the wrapped toaster had become a rock in a makeshift sling.

"When I was a kid, we used to play Indiana Jones," Albert said apologetically. "I made something like this and pretended it was my whip. I almost broke my brother David's arm once. I loaded an old blanket with a sashweight I found in the garage. Pretty stupid, I guess. I didn't know hard it would hit. I got a hell of a spanking for it. It looks stupid, I guess, but it actually works pretty well. It always did, at least."

Nick looked at Albert's makeshift weapon dubiously but said nothing. If a toaster wrapped in a tablecloth made Albert feel more comfortable about going downstairs in the dark, so be it.

"Good enough, then. Now go find a stretcher and bring it back. If there isn't one in the Airport Services office, try someplace else. If you don't find anything in fifteen minutes—no, make that ten— just come back and we'll carry her."

"You can't do that!" Laurel cried softly. "If there's internal bleeding—"

Nick looked up at her. "There's internal bleeding already. And ten minutes is all the time I think we can spare."

Laurel opened her mouth to answer, to *argue,* but Dinah's husky whisper stopped her. "He's right."

Don slipped the blade of his knife into his belt. "Come on, son," he said. They crossed the terminal together and started down the escalator to the first floor. Albert wrapped the end of his loaded tablecloth around his hand as they went.

5

Nick turned his attention back to the girl on the floor. "How are you feeling, Dinah?"

"Hurts bad," Dinah said faintly.

"Yes, of course it does," Nick said. "And I'm afraid that what

I'm about to do is going to make it hurt a good deal more, for a few seconds, at least. But the knife is in your lung, and it's got to come out. You know that, don't you?"

"Yes." Her dark, unseeing eyes looked up at him. "Scared."

"So am I, Dinah. So am I. But it has to be done. Are you game?"

"Yes."

"Good girl." Nick bent and planted a soft kiss on her cheek. "That's a good, brave girl. It won't take long, and that's a promise. I want you to lie just as still as you can, Dinah, and try not to cough. Do you understand me? It's very important. *Try not to cough.*"

"I'll try."

"There may be a moment or two when you feel that you can't breathe. You may even feel that you're leaking, like a tire with a puncture. That's a scary feeling, love, and it may make you want to move around, or cry out. You mustn't do it. *And you mustn't cough.*"

Dinah made a reply none of them could hear.

Nick swallowed, armed sweat off his forehead in a quick gesture, and turned to Laurel. "Fold two of those tablecloths into square pads. Thick as you can. Kneel beside me. Close as you can get. Warwick, take off your belt."

Rudy began to comply at once.

Nick looked back at Laurel. She was again struck, and not unpleasantly this time, by the power of his gaze. "I'm going to grasp the handle of the knife and draw it out. If it's not caught on one of her ribs—and judging from its position, I don't think it is—the blade should come out in one slow, smooth pull. The moment it's out, I will draw back, giving you clear access to the girl's chest area. You will place one of your pads over the wound and press. Press *hard.* You're not to worry about hurting her, or compressing her chest so much she can't breathe. She's got at least one perforation in her lung, and I'm betting there's a pair of them. Those are what we've got to worry about. Do you understand?"

"Yes."

"When you've placed the pad, I'm going to lift her against the pressure you're putting on. Mr. Warwick here will then slip the other pad beneath her if we see blood on the back of her dress. Then we're going to tie the compresses in place with Mr. Warwick's belt." He glanced up at Rudy. "When I call for it, my friend, give it to me. Don't make me ask you twice."

"I won't."

"Can you see well enough to do this, Nick?" Laurel asked.

"I think so," Nick replied. "I hope so." He looked at Dinah again. "Ready?"

Dinah muttered something.

"All right," Nick said. He drew in a long breath and then let it out. "Jesus help me."

He wrapped his slim, long-fingered hands around the handle of the knife like a man gripping a baseball bat. He pulled. Dinah shrieked. A great gout of blood spewed from her mouth. Laurel had been leaning tensely forward, and her face was suddenly bathed in Dinah's blood. She recoiled.

"No!" Nick spat at her without looking around. "Don't you *dare* go weak-sister on me! Don't you *dare*!"

Laurel leaned forward again, gagging and shuddering. The blade, a dully gleaming triangle of silver in the deep gloom, emerged from Dinah's chest and glimmered in the air. The little blind girl's chest heaved and there was a high, unearthly whistling sound as the wound sucked inward.

"*Now!*" Nick grunted. "Press down! Hard as you can!"

Laurel leaned forward. For just a moment she saw blood pouring out of the hole in Dinah's chest, and then the wound was covered. The tablecloth pad grew warm and wet under her hands almost immediately.

"Harder!" Nick snarled at her. "Press harder! Seal it! Seal the wound!"

Laurel now understood what people meant when they talked about coming completely unstrung, because she felt on the verge of it herself. "I can't! I'll break her ribs if—"

"*Fuck her ribs!* You *have* to make a seal!"

Laurel rocked forward on her knees and brought her entire weight down on her hands. Now she could feel liquid seeping slowly between her fingers, although she had folded the tablecloth thick.

The Englishman tossed the knife aside and leaned forward until his face was almost touching Dinah's. Her eyes were closed. He rolled one of the lids. "I think she's finally out," he said. "Can't tell for sure because her eyes are so odd, but I hope to heaven she is." Hair had fallen over his brow. He tossed it back impatiently with a jerk of his head and looked at Laurel. "You're doing well.

Stay with it, all right? I'm rolling her now. Keep the pressure on as I do."

"There's so much blood," Laurel groaned. "Will she drown?"

"I don't know. Keep the pressure on. Ready, Mr. Warwick?"

"Oh Christ I guess so," Rudy Warwick croaked.

"Right. Here we go." Nick slipped his hands beneath Dinah's right shoulderblade and grimaced. "It's worse than I thought," he muttered. "Far worse. She's *soaked.*" He began to pull Dinah slowly upward against the pressure Laurel was putting on. Dinah uttered a thick, croaking moan. A gout of half-congealed blood flew from her mouth and spattered across the floor. And now Laurel could hear a rain of blood pattering down on the carpet from beneath the girl.

Suddenly the world began to swim away from her.

"Keep that pressure *on!*" Nick cried. "Don't let up!"

But she was fainting.

It was her understanding of what Nick Hopewell would think of her if she *did* faint which caused her to do what she did next. Laurel stuck her tongue out between her teeth like a child making a face and bit down on it as hard as she could. The pain was bright and exquisite, the salty taste of her own blood immediately filled her mouth . . . but that sensation that the world was swimming away from her like a big lazy fish in an aquarium passed. She was *here* again.

Downstairs, there was a sudden shriek of pain and surprise. It was followed by a hoarse shout. On the heels of the shout came a loud, drilling scream.

Rudy and Laurel both turned in that direction. "The boy!" Rudy said. "Him and Gaffney! They—"

"They've found Mr. Toomy after all," Nick said. His face was a complicated mask of effort. The tendons on his neck stood out like steel pulleys. "We'll just have to hope—"

There was a thud from downstairs, followed by a terrible howl of agony. Then a whole series of muffled thumps.

"—that they're on top of the situation. We can't do anything about it now. If we stop in the middle of what we're doing, this little girl is going to die for sure."

"But that sounded like the *kid!*"

"Can't be helped, can it? Slide the pad under her, Warwick. Do it right now, or I'll kick your bloody arse square."

6

Don led the way down the escalator, then stopped briefly at the bottom to fumble in his pocket. He brought out a square object that gleamed faintly in the dark. "It's my Zippo," he said. "Do you think it'll still work?"

"I don't know," Albert said. "It might . . . for awhile. You better not try it until you have to. I sure hope it does. We won't be able to see a thing without it."

"Where's this Airport Services place?"

Albert pointed to the door Craig Toomy had gone through less than five minutes before. "Right over there."

"Do you think it's unlocked?"

"Well," Albert said, "there's only one way to find out."

They crossed the terminal, Don still leading the way with his lighter in his right hand.

7

Craig heard them coming—more servants of the langoliers, no doubt. But he wasn't worried. He had taken care of the thing which had been masquerading as a little girl, and he would take care of these other things, as well. He curled his hand around the letter-opener, got up, and sidled back around the desk.

"Do you think it's unlocked?"

"Well, there's only one way to find out."

You're going to find out something, *anyway,* Craig thought. He reached the wall beside the door. It was lined with paper-stacked shelves. He reached out and felt doorhinges. Good. The opening door would block him off from them . . . not that they were likely to see him, anyway. It was as black as an elephant's asshole in here. He raised the letter-opener to shoulder height.

"The knob doesn't move." Craig relaxed . . . but only for a moment.

"Try pushing it." That was the smart-ass kid.

The door began to open.

8

Don stepped in, blinking at the gloom. He thumbed the cover of his lighter back, held it up, and flicked the wheel. There was a spark and the wick caught at once, producing a low flame. They saw what was apparently a combined office and storeroom. There was an untidy stack of luggage in one corner and a Xerox machine in another. The back wall was lined with shelves and the shelves were stacked with what looked like forms of various kinds.

Don stepped further into the office, lifting his lighter like a spelunker holding up a guttering candle in a dark cave. He pointed to the right wall. "Hey, kid! Ace! Look!"

A poster mounted there showed a tipsy guy in a business suit staggering out of a bar and looking at his watch. WORK IS THE CURSE OF THE DRINKING CLASS, the poster advised. Mounted on the wall beside it was a white plastic box with a large red cross on it. And leaning below it was a folded stretcher . . . the kind with wheels.

Albert wasn't looking at the poster or the first-aid kit or the stretcher, however. His eyes were fixed on the desk in the center of the room.

On it he saw a heaped tangle of paper strips.

"*Look out!*" he shouted. "*Look out, he's in h—*"

Craig Toomy stepped out from behind the door and struck.

9

"Belt," Nick said.

Rudy didn't move or reply. His head was turned toward the door of the restaurant. The sounds from downstairs had ceased. There was only the rattling noise and the steady, throbbing rumble of the jet engine in the dark outside.

Nick kicked backward like a mule, connecting with Rudy's shin. "*Ow!*"

"Belt! *Now!*"

Rudy dropped clumsily to his knees and moved next to Nick, who was holding Dinah up with one hand and pressing a second tablecloth pad against her back with the other.

"Slip it under the pad," Nick said. He was panting, and sweat was running down his face in wide streams. "Quick! I can't hold her up forever!"

Rudy slid the belt under the pad. Nick lowered Dinah, reached across the girl's small body, and lifted her left shoulder long enough to pull the belt out the other side. Then he looped it over her chest and cinched it tight. He put the belt's free end in Laurel's hand. "Keep the pressure on," he said, standing up. "You can't use the buckle—she's much too small."

"Are you going downstairs?" Laurel asked.

"Yes. That seems indicated."

"Be careful. Please be careful."

He grinned at her, and all those white teeth suddenly shining out in the gloom were startling . . . but not frightening, she discovered. Quite the opposite.

"Of course. It's how I get along." He reached down and squeezed her shoulder. His hand was warm, and at his touch a little shiver chased through her. "You did very well, Laurel. Thank you."

He began to turn away, and then a small hand groped out and caught the cuff of his blue-jeans. He looked down and saw that Dinah's blind eyes were open again.

"Don't . . ." she began, and then a choked sneezing fit shook her. Blood flew from her nose in a spray of fine droplets.

"Dinah, you mustn't—"

"Don't . . . you . . . kill him!" she said, and even in the dark Laurel could sense the fantastic effort she was making to speak at all.

Nick looked down at her thoughtfully. "The bugger stabbed you, you know. Why are you so insistent on keeping him whole?"

Her narrow chest strained against the belt. The bloodstained tablecloth pad heaved. She struggled and managed to say one thing more. They all heard it; Dinah was at great pains to speak clearly. "All . . . I know . . . is that we need him," she whispered, and then her eyes closed again.

10

Craig buried the letter-opener fist-deep in the nape of Don Gaffney's neck. Don screamed and dropped the lighter. It struck the floor and lay there, guttering sickishly. Albert shouted in surprise as he saw Craig step toward Don, who was now staggering in the direction of the desk and clawing weakly behind him for the protruding object.

Craig grabbed the opener with one hand and planted his other against Don's back. As he simultaneously pushed and pulled, Albert heard the sound of a hungry man pulling a drumstick off a well-done turkey. Don screamed again, louder this time, and went sprawling over the desk. His arms flew out ahead of him, knocking to the floor an IN/OUT box and the stack of lost-luggage forms Craig had been ripping.

Craig turned toward Albert, flicking a spray of blood-droplets from the blade of the letter-opener as he did so. "You're one of them, too," he breathed. "Well, fuck you. I'm going to Boston and you can't stop me. *None* of you can stop me." Then the lighter on the floor went out and they were in darkness.

Albert took a step backward and felt a warm swoop of air in his face as Craig swung the blade through the spot where he had been only a second before. He flailed behind him with his free hand, terrified of backing into a corner where Craig could use the knife (in the Zippo's pallid, fading light, that was what he had thought it was) on him at will and his own weapon would be useless as well as stupid. His fingers found only empty space, and he backed through the door into the lobby. He did not feel cool; he did not feel like the fastest Hebrew on *any* side of the Mississippi; he did not feel faster than blue blazes. He felt like a scared kid who had foolishly chosen a childhood playtoy instead of a real weapon because he had been unable to believe—really, really believe—that it could come to this in spite of what the lunatic asshole had done to the little girl upstairs. He could smell himself. Even in the dead air he could smell himself. It was the rancid monkeypiss aroma of fear.

Craig came gliding out through the door with the letter-opener raised. He moved like a dancing shadow in the dark. "I see you, sonny," he breathed. "I see you just like a cat."

He began to slide forward. Albert backed away from him. At the same time he began to pendulum the toaster back and forth, reminding himself that he would have only one good shot before Toomy moved in and planted the blade in his throat or chest.

And if the toaster goes flying out of the goddam pocket before it hits him, I'm a goner.

11

Craig closed in, weaving the top half of his body from side to side like a snake coming out of a basket. An absent little smile touched the corners of his lips and made small dimples there. *That's right,* Craig's father said grimly from his undying stronghold inside Craig's head. *If you have to pick them off one by one, you can do that. EPO, Craig, remember? EPO. Effort Pays Off.*

That's right, Craiggy-weggy, his mother chimed in. *You can do it, and you* have *to do it.*

"I'm sorry," Craig murmured to the white-faced boy through his smile. "I'm really, really sorry, but I have to do it. If you could see things from my perspective, you'd understand."

12

Albert shot a quick glance behind him and saw he was backing toward the United Airlines ticket desk. If he retreated much further, the backward arc of his swing would be restricted. It had to be soon. He began to pendulum the toaster more rapidly, his sweaty hand clutching the twist of tablecloth.

Craig caught the movement in the dark, but couldn't tell what it was the kid was swinging. It didn't matter. He couldn't *let* it matter. He gathered himself, then sprang forward.

"*I'M GOING TO BOSTON!*" he shrieked. "*I'M GOING TO—*"

Albert's eyes were adjusting to the dark, and he saw Craig make his move. The toaster was on the rearward half of its arc. Instead of snapping his wrist forward to reverse its direction, Albert let his arm go with the weight of the toaster, swinging it up and over his head in an exaggerated pitching gesture. At the same time he stepped to the left. The lump at the end of the tablecloth made a short, hard circlet in the air, held firmly in its pocket by centripetal force. Craig cooperated by stepping forward into the toaster's descending arc. It met his forehead and the bridge of his nose with a hard, toneless crunch.

Craig wailed with agony and dropped the letter-opener. His hands went to his face and he staggered backward. Blood from his broken nose poured between his fingers like water from a busted hydrant. Albert was terrified of what he had done but even more terrified of letting up now that Toomy was hurt. Albert took another step to the left and swung the tablecloth sidearm. It whipped through the air and smashed into the center of Craig's chest with a hard thump. Craig fell over backward, still howling.

For Albert "Ace" Kaussner, only one thought remained; all else was a tumbling, fragmented swirl of color, image, and emotion.

I have to make him stop moving or he'll get up and kill me. I have to make him stop moving or he'll get up and kill me.

At least Toomy had dropped his weapon; it lay glinting on the lobby carpet. Albert planted one of his loafers on it and unloaded with the toaster again. As it came down, Albert bowed from the waist like an old-fashioned butler greeting a member of the royal family. The lump at the end of the tablecloth smashed into Craig Toomy's gasping mouth. There was a sound like glass being crushed inside of a handkerchief.

Oh God, Albert thought. *That was his teeth.*

Craig flopped and squirmed on the floor. It was terrible to watch him, perhaps more terrible because of the poor light. There was something monstrous and unkillable and insectile about his horrible vitality.

His hand closed upon Albert's loafer. Albert stepped away from the letter-opener with a little cry of revulsion, and Craig tried to grasp it when he did. Between his eyes, his nose was a burst bulb of flesh. He could hardly see Albert at all; his vision was eaten up by a vast white corona of light. A steady high keening note rang in his head, the sound of a TV test-pattern turned up to full volume.

He was beyond doing any damage, but Albert didn't know it. In a panic, he brought the toaster down on Craig's head again. There was a metallic crunch-rattle as the heating elements inside it broke free.

Craig stopped moving.

Albert stood over him, sobbing for breath, the weighted tablecloth dangling from one hand. Then he took two long, shambling steps toward the escalator, bowed deeply again, and vomited on the floor.

13

Brian crossed himself as he thumbed back the black plastic shield which covered the screen of the 767's INS video-display terminal, half-expecting it to be smooth and blank. He looked at it closely . . . and let out a deep sigh of relief.

LAST PROGRAM COMPLETE

it informed him in cool blue-green letters, and below that:

NEW PROGRAM? Y   N

Brian typed Y, then:

REVERSE AP 29: LAX/LOGAN

The screen went dark for a moment. Then:

INCLUDE DIVERSION IN REVERSE PROGRAM AP 29?
Y   N

Brian typed Y.

COMPUTING REVERSE

the screen informed him, and less than five seconds later:

PROGRAM COMPLETE

"Captain Engle?"

He turned around. Bethany was standing in the cockpit doorway. She looked pale and haggard in the cabin lights.

"I'm a little busy right now, Bethany."

"Why aren't they back?"

"I can't say."

"I asked Bob—Mr. Jenkins—if he could see anyone moving inside the terminal, and he said he couldn't. What if they're all dead?"

"I'm sure they're not. If it will make you feel better, why don't you join him at the bottom of the ladder? I've got some more work to do here." *At least I hope I do.*

"Are you scared?" she asked.

"Yes. I sure am."

She smiled a little. "I'm sort of glad. It's bad to be scared all by yourself—totally bogus. I'll leave you alone now."

"Thanks. I'm sure they'll be out soon."

She left. Brian turned back to the INS monitor and typed:

ARE THERE PROBLEMS WITH THIS PROGRAM?

He hit EXECUTE.

NO PROBLEMS. THANK YOU FOR FLYING AMERICAN
PRIDE.

"You're welcome, I'm sure," Brian murmured, and wiped his forehead with his sleeve.

Now, he thought, *if only the fuel will burn.*

14

Bob heard footsteps on the ladder and turned quickly. It was only Bethany, descending slowly and carefully, but he still felt jumpy. The sound coming out of the east was gradually growing louder.

Closer.

"Hi, Bethany. May I borrow another of your cigarettes?"

She offered the depleted pack to him, then took one herself. She had tucked Albert's book of experimental matches into the cellophane covering the pack, and when she tried one it lit easily.

"Any sign of them?"

"Well, it all depends on what you mean by 'any sign,' I guess," Bob said cautiously. "I think I heard some shouting just before you came down." What he had heard actually sounded like screaming—*shrieking,* not to put too fine a point on it—but he saw no reason to tell the girl that. She looked as frightened as Bob felt, and he had an idea she'd taken a liking to Albert.

"I hope Dinah's going to be all right," she said, "but I don't know. He cut her really bad."

"Did you see the captain?"

Bethany nodded. "He sort of kicked me out. I guess he's programming his instruments, or something."

Bob Jenkins nodded soberly. "I hope so."

Conversation lapsed. They both looked east. A new and even more ominous sound now underlay the crunching, chewing noise: a high, inanimate screaming. It was a strangely mechanical sound, one that made Bob think of an automatic transmission low on fluid.

"It's a lot closer now, isn't it?"

Bob nodded reluctantly. He drew on his cigarette and the glowing ember momentarily illuminated a pair of tired, terrified eyes.

"What do you suppose it is, Mr. Jenkins?"

He shook his head slowly. "Dear girl, I hope we never have to find out."

15

Halfway down the escalator, Nick saw a bent-over figure standing in front of the useless bank of pay telephones. It was impossible to tell if it was Albert or Craig Toomy. The Englishman reached into his right front pocket, holding his left hand against it to prevent any jingling, and by touch selected a pair of quarters from his change. He closed his right hand into a fist and slipped the quarters between his fingers, creating a makeshift set of brass knuckles. Then he continued down to the lobby.

The figure by the telephones looked up as Nick approached. It was Albert. "Don't step in the puke," he said dully.

Nick dropped the quarters back into his pocket and hurried to where the boy was standing with his hands propped above his knees like an old man who has badly overestimated his capacity for exercise. He could smell the high, sour stench of vomit. That and the sweaty stink of fear coming off the boy were smells with which he was all too familiar. He knew them from the Falklands, and even more intimately from Northern Ireland. He put his left arm around the boy's shoulders and Albert straightened very slowly.

"Where are they, Ace?" Nick asked quietly. "Gaffney and Toomy—where are they?"

"Mr. Toomy's there." He pointed toward a crumpled shape on the floor. "Mr. Gaffney's in the Airport Services office. I think they're both dead. Mr. Toomy was in the Airport Services office. Behind the door, I guess. He killed Mr. Gaffney because Mr. Gaffney walked in first. If I'd walked in first, he would have killed me instead."

Albert swallowed hard.

"Then I killed Mr. Toomy. I had to. He came after me, see? He found another knife someplace and he came after me." He spoke in a tone which could have been mistaken for indifference, but Nick knew better. And it was not indifference he saw on the white blur of Albert's face.

"Can you get hold of yourself, Ace?" Nick asked.

"I don't know. I never k-k-killed anyone before, and—" Albert uttered a strangled, miserable sob.

"I know," Nick said. "It's a horrible thing, but it can be gotten over. I know. And you must get over it, Ace. We have miles to go before we sleep, and there's no time for therapy. The sound is louder."

He left Albert and went over to the crumpled form on the floor. Craig Toomy was lying on his side with one upraised arm partially obscuring his face. Nick rolled him onto his back, looked, whistled softly. Toomy was still alive—he could hear the harsh rasp of his breath—but Nick would have bet his bank account that the man was not shamming this time. His nose hadn't just been broken; it looked vaporized. His mouth was a bloody socket ringed with the shattered remains of his teeth. And the deep, troubled dent in the center of Toomy's forehead suggested that Albert had done some creative retooling of the man's skull-plate.

"He did all this with a *toaster?*" Nick muttered. "Jesus and Mary, Tom, Dick, and Harry." He got up and raised his voice. "He's not dead, Ace."

Albert had bent over again when Nick left him. Now he straightened slowly and took a step toward him. "He's not?"

"Listen for yourself. Out for the count, but still in the game." *Not for long, though; not by the sound of him.* "Let's check on Mr. Gaffney—maybe he got off lucky, too. And what about the stretcher?"

"Huh?" Albert looked at Nick as though he had spoken in a foreign language.

"The stretcher," Nick repeated patiently as they walked toward the open Airport Services door.

"We found it," Albert said.

"Did you? Super!"

Albert stopped just inside the door. "Wait a minute," he muttered, then squatted and felt around for Don's lighter. He found it after a moment or two. It was still warm. He stood up again. "Mr. Gaffney's on the other side of the desk, I think."

They walked around, stepping over the tumbled stacks of paper and the IN/OUT basket. Albert held out the lighter and flicked the wheel. On the fifth try the wick caught and burned feebly for three or four seconds. It was enough. Nick had actually seen enough in the spark-flashes the lighter's wheel had struck, but he hadn't liked to say so to Albert. Don Gaffney lay sprawled on his back, eyes open, a look of terrible surprise still fixed on his face. He hadn't gotten off lucky after all.

"How was it that Toomy didn't get you as well?" Nick asked after a moment.

"I knew he was in here," Albert said. "Even before he stuck Mr. Gaffney, I knew." His voice was still dry and shaky, but he felt a little better. Now that he had actually faced poor Mr. Gaffney—looked him in the eye, so to speak—he felt a little better.

"Did you hear him?"

"No—I saw those. On the desk." Albert pointed to the little heap of torn strips.

"Lucky you did." Nick put his hand on Albert's shoulder in the dark. "You deserve to be alive, mate. You earned the privilege. All right?"

"I'll try," Albert said.

"You do that, old son. It saves a lot of nightmares. You're looking at a man who knows."

Albert nodded.

"Keep it together, Ace. That's all there is to it—just keep things together and you'll be fine."

"Mr. Hopewell?"

"Yes?"

"Would you mind not calling me that? I—" His voice clogged, and Albert cleared his throat violently. "I don't think I like it anymore."

16

They emerged from the dark cave which was Airport Services thirty
seconds later, Nick carrying the folded stretcher by the handle.
When they reached the bank of phones, Nick handed the stretcher
to Albert, who accepted it wordlessly. The tablecloth lay on the
floor about five feet away from Toomy, who was snoring now in
great rhythmless snatches of air.

Time was short, time was very fucking short, but Nick had to
see this. He *had* to.

He picked up the tablecloth and pulled the toaster out. One of
the heating elements caught in a bread slot; the other tumbled out
onto the floor. The timer-dial and the handle you used to push the
bread down fell off. One corner of the toaster was crumpled inward.
The left side was bashed into a deep circular dent.

That's the part that collided with Friend Toomy's sniffer, Nick
thought. *Amazing.* He shook the toaster and listened to the loose
rattle of broken parts inside.

"A toaster," he marvelled. "I have friends, Albert—*professional*
friends—who wouldn't believe it. I hardly believe it myself. I
mean . . . a *toaster.*"

Albert had turned his head. "Throw it away," he said hoarsely.
"I don't want to look at it."

Nick did as the boy asked, then clapped him on the shoulder.
"Take the stretcher upstairs. I'll join you directly."

"What are you going to do?"

"I want to see if there's anything else we can use in that office."

Albert looked at him for a moment, but he couldn't make out
Nick's features in the dark. At last he said, "I don't believe you."

"Nor do you have to," Nick said in an oddly gentle voice. "Go
on, Ace . . . Albert, I mean. I'll join you soon. And don't look back."

Albert stared at him a moment longer, then began to trudge up
the frozen escalator, his head down, the stretcher dangling like a
suitcase from his right hand. He didn't look back.

17

Nick waited until the boy had disappeared into the gloom. Then
he walked back over to where Craig Toomy lay and squatted beside

him. Toomy was still out, but his breathing seemed a little more regular. Nick supposed it was not impossible, given a week or two of constant-care treatment in hospital, that Toomy might recover. He had proved at least one thing: he had an awesomely hard head.

Shame the brains underneath are so soft, mate, Nick thought. He reached out, meaning to put one hand over Toomy's mouth and the other over his nose—or what remained of it. It would take less than a minute, and they would not have to worry about Mr. Craig Toomy anymore. The others would have recoiled in horror at the act—would have called it cold-blooded murder—but Nick saw it as an insurance policy, no more and no less. Toomy had arisen once from what appeared to be total unconsciousness and now one of their number was dead and another was badly, perhaps mortally, wounded. There was no sense taking the same chance again.

And there was something else. If he left Toomy alive, what, exactly, would he be leaving him alive *for?* A short, haunted existence in a dead world? A chance to breathe dying air under a moveless sky in which all weather patterns appeared to have ceased? An opportunity to meet whatever was approaching from the east . . . approaching with a sound like that of a colony of giant, marauding ants?

No. Best to see him out of it. It would be painless, and that would have to be good enough.

"Better than the bastard deserves," Nick said, but still he hesitated.

He remembered the little girl looking up at him with her dark, unseeing eyes.

Don't you kill him! Not a plea; that had been a command. She had summoned up a little strength from some hidden last reserve in order to give him that command. *All I know is that we need him.*

Why is she so bloody protective of him?

He squatted a moment longer, looking into Craig Toomy's ruined face. And when Rudy Warwick spoke from the head of the escalator, he jumped as if it had been the devil himself.

"Mr. Hopewell? Nick? Are you coming?"

"In a jiffy!" he called back over his shoulder. He reached toward Toomy's face again and stopped again, remembering her dark eyes.

We need him.

Abruptly he stood up, leaving Craig Toomy to his tortured struggle for breath. "Coming now," he called, and ran lightly up the escalator.

CHAPTER EIGHT

*REFUELLING. DAWN'S
EARLY LIGHT.
THE APPROACH OF THE
LANGOLIERS. ANGEL OF
THE MORNING. THE TIME-
KEEPERS OF ETERNITY.
TAKE-OFF.*

1

Bethany had cast away her almost tasteless cigarette and was halfway up the ladder again when Bob Jenkins shouted: "I think they're coming out!"

She turned and ran back down the stairs. A series of dark blobs was emerging from the luggage bay and crawling along the conveyor belt. Bob and Bethany ran to meet them.

Dinah was strapped to the stretcher. Rudy had one end, Nick the other. They were walking on their knees, and Bethany could hear the bald man breathing in harsh, out-of-breath gasps.

"Let me help," she told him, and Rudy gave up his end of the stretcher willingly.

"Try not to jiggle her," Nick said, swinging his legs off the conveyor belt. "Albert, get on Bethany's end and help us take her up the stairs. We want this thing to stay as level as possible."

"How bad is she?" Bethany asked Albert.

"Not good," he said grimly. "Unconscious but still alive. That's all I know."

"Where are Gaffney and Toomy?" Bob asked as they crossed to the plane. He had to raise his voice slightly to be heard; the crunching sound was louder now, and that shrieking wounded-transmission undertone was becoming a dominant, maddening note.

"Gaffney's dead and Toomy might as well be," Nick said. "We'll discuss it later, if you like. Right now there's no time." He halted at the foot of the stairs. "Mind you keep your end up, you two."

They moved the stretcher slowly and carefully up the stairs, Nick walking backward and bent over the forward end, Albert and Bethany holding the stretcher up at forehead level and jostling hips on the narrow stairway at the rear. Bob, Rudy, and Laurel followed behind. Laurel had spoken only once since Albert and Nick had returned, to ask if Toomy was dead. When Nick told her he wasn't, she had looked at him closely and then nodded her head with relief.

Brian was standing at the cockpit door when Nick reached the top of the ladder and eased his end of the stretcher inside.

"I want to put her in first class," Nick said, "with this end of the stretcher raised so her head is up. Can I do that?"

"No problem. Secure the stretcher by looping a couple of seatbelts through the head-frame. Do you see where?"

"Yes." And to Albert and Bethany: "Come on up. You're doing fine."

In the cabin lights, the blood smeared on Dinah's cheeks and chin stood out starkly against her yellow-white skin. Her eyes were closed; her lids were a delicate shade of lavender. Under the belt (in which Nick had punched a new hole, high above the others), the makeshift compress was dark red. Brian could hear her breathing. It sounded like a straw dragging wind at the bottom of an almost empty glass.

"It's bad, isn't it?" Brian asked in a low voice.

"Well, it's her lung and not her heart, and she's not filling up anywhere near as fast as I was afraid she might . . . but it's bad, yes."

"Will she live until we get back?"

"How in hell should *I* know?" Nick shouted at him suddenly. "I'm a soldier, not a bloody sawbones!"

The other froze, looking at him with cautious eyes. Laurel felt her skin prickle again.

"I'm sorry," Nick muttered. "Time travel plays the very devil with one's nerves, doesn't it? I'm very sorry."

"No need to apologize," Laurel said, and touched his arm. "We're all under strain."

He gave her a tired smile and touched her hair. "You're a sweetheart, Laurel, and no mistake. Come on—let's strap her in and see what we can do about getting the hell out of here."

2

Five minutes later Dinah's stretcher had been secured in an inclined position to a pair of first-class seats, her head up, her feet down. The rest of the passengers were gathered in a tight little knot around Brian in the first-class serving area.

"We need to refuel the plane," Brian said. "I'm going to start the other engine now and pull over as close as I can to that 727-400 at the jetway." He pointed to the Delta plane, which was just a gray lump in the dark. "Because our aircraft sits higher, I'll be able to lay our right wing right over the Delta's left wing. While I do that, four of you are going to bring over a hose cart—there's one sitting by the other jetway. I saw it before it got dark."

"Maybe we better wake Sleeping Beauty at the back of the plane and get him to lend a hand," Bob said.

Brian thought it over briefly and then shook his head. "The last thing we need right now is another scared, disoriented passenger on our hands . . . and one with a killer hangover to boot. And we won't need him—two strong men can push a hose cart in a pinch. I've seen it done. Just check the transmission lever to make sure it's in neutral. It wants to end up directly beneath the overlapping wings. Got it?"

They all nodded. Brian looked them over and decided that Rudy and Bethany were still too blown from wrestling the stretcher to be of much help. "Nick, Bob, and Albert. You push. Laurel, you steer. Okay?"

They nodded.

"Go on and do it, then. Bethany? Mr. Warwick? Go down with them. Pull the ladder away from the plane, and when I've got the plane repositioned, place it next to the overlapping wings. The wings, not the door. Got it?"

They nodded. Looking around at them, Brian saw that their eyes looked clear and bright for the first time since they had landed. *Of course,* he thought. *They have something to do now. And so do I, thank God.*

3

As they approached the hose cart sitting off to the left of the unoccupied jetway, Laurel realized she could actually *see* it. "My

God," she said. "It's coming daylight again already. How long has it been since it got dark?"

"Less than forty minutes, by my watch," Bob said, "but I have a feeling that my watch doesn't keep very accurate time when we're outside the plane. I've also got a feeling time doesn't matter much here, anyway."

"What's going to happen to Mr. Toomey?" Laurel asked.

They had reached the cart. It was a small vehicle with a tank on the back, an open-air cab, and thick black hoses coiled on either side. Nick put an arm around her waist and turned her toward him. For a moment she had the crazy idea that he meant to kiss her, and she felt her heart speed up.

"I don't know what's going to happen to him," he said. "All I know is that when the chips were down, I chose to do what Dinah wanted. I left him lying unconscious on the floor. All right?"

"No," she said in a slightly unsteady voice, "but I guess it will have to do."

He smiled a little, nodded, and gave her waist a brief squeeze. "Would you like to go to dinner with me when and if we make it back to L.A.?"

"Yes," she said at once. "That would be something to look forward to."

He nodded again. "For me, too. But unless we can get this airplane refuelled, we're not going anywhere." He looked at the open cab of the hose cart. "Can you find neutral, do you think?"

Laurel eyed the stick-shift jutting up from the floor of the cab. "I'm afraid I only drive an automatic."

"I'll do it." Albert jumped into the cab, depressed the clutch, then peered at the diagram on the knob of the shift lever. Behind him, the 767's second engine whined into life and both engines began to throb harder as Brian powered up. The noise was very loud, but Laurel found she didn't mind it at all. It blotted out that other sound, at least temporarily. And she kept wanting to look at Nick. Had he actually invited her out to dinner? Already it seemed hard to believe.

Albert changed gears, then waggled the shift lever. "Got it," he said, and jumped down. "Up you go, Laurel. Once we get it rolling, you'll have to hang a hard right and bring it around in a circle."

"All right."

She looked back nervously as the three men lined themselves up along the rear of the hose cart with Nick in the middle.

"Ready, you lot?" he asked.

Albert and Bob nodded.

"Right, then—all together."

Bob had been braced to push as hard as he could, and damn the low back pain which had plagued him for the last ten years, but the hose cart rolled with absurd ease. Laurel hauled the stiff, balky steering wheel around with all her might. The yellow cart described a small circle on the gray tarmac and began to roll back toward the 767, which was trundling slowly into position on the righthand side of the parked Delta jet.

"The difference between the two aircraft is incredible," Bob said.

"Yes," Nick agreed. "You were right, Albert. We may have wandered away from the present, but in some strange way, that airplane is still a part of it."

"So are *we*," Albert said. "At least, so far."

The 767's turbines died, leaving only the steady low rumble of the APUs—Brian was now running all four of them. They were not loud enough to cover the sound in the east. Before, that sound had had a kind of massive uniformity, but as it neared it was fragmenting; there seemed to be sounds within sounds, and the sum total began to seem horribly familiar.

Animals at feeding time, Laurel thought, and shivered. *That's what it sounds like—the sound of feeding animals, sent through an amplifier and blown up to grotesque proportions.*

She shivered violently and felt panic begin to nibble at her thoughts, an elemental force she could control no more than she could control whatever was making that sound.

"Maybe if we could see it, we could deal with it," Bob said as they began to push the fuel cart again.

Albert glanced at him briefly and said, "I don't think so."

4

Brian appeared in the forward door of the 767 and motioned Bethany and Rudy to roll the ladder over to him. When they did, he stepped onto the platform at the top and pointed to the overlapping wings. As they rolled him in that direction, he listened to the approaching noise and found himself remembering a movie he had seen on the late show a long time ago. In it, Charlton Heston had owned a big plantation in South America. The plantation had been attacked by a vast moving carpet of soldier ants, ants which ate everything in their path—trees, grass, buildings, cows, men. What had that movie been called? Brian couldn't remember. He only remembered that Charlton had kept trying increasingly desperate tricks to stop the ants, or at least delay them. Had he beaten them in the end? Brian couldn't remember, but a fragment of his dream suddenly recurred, disturbing in its lack of association to anything: an ominous red sign which read SHOOTING STARS ONLY.

"Hold it!" he shouted down to Rudy and Bethany.

They ceased pushing, and Brian carefully climbed down the ladder until his head was on a level with the underside of the Delta jet's wing. Both the 767 and 727 were equipped with single-point fuelling ports in the left wing. He was now looking at a small square hatch with the words FUEL TANK ACCESS and CHECK SHUT-OFF VALVE BEFORE REFUELLING stencilled across it. And some wit had pasted a round yellow happy-face sticker to the fuel hatch. It was the final surreal touch.

Albert, Bob, and Nick had pushed the hose cart into position below him and were now looking up, their faces dirty gray circles in the brightening gloom. Brian leaned over and shouted down to Nick.

"There are two hoses, one on each side of the cart! I want the short one!"

Nick pulled it free and handed it up. Holding both the ladder and the nozzle of the hose with one hand, Brian leaned under the wing and opened the refuelling hatch. Inside was a male connector with a steel prong poking out like a finger. Brian leaned further out . . . and slipped. He grabbed the railing of the ladder.

"Hold on, mate," Nick said, mounting the ladder. "Help is on the way." He stopped three rungs below Brian and seized his belt. "Do me a favor, all right?"

"What's that?"

"Don't fart."

"I'll try, but no promises."

He leaned out again and looked down at the others. Rudy and Bethany had joined Bob and Albert below the wing. "Move away, unless you want a jet-fuel shower!" he called. "I can't control the Delta's shut-off valve, and it may leak!" As he waited for them to back away he thought, *Of course, it may not. For all I know, the tanks on this thing are as dry as a goddam bone.*

He leaned out again, using both hands now that Nick had him firmly anchored, and slammed the nozzle into the fuel port. There was a brief, spattering shower of jet-fuel—a very welcome shower, under the circumstances—and then a hard metallic click. Brian twisted the nozzle a quarter-turn to the right, locking it in place, and listened with satisfaction as jet-fuel ran down the hose to the cart, where a closed valve would dam its flow.

"Okay," he sighed, pulling himself back to the ladder. "So far, so good."

"What now, mate? How do we make that cart run? Do we jump-start it from the plane, or what?"

"I doubt if we could do that even if someone had remembered to bring the jumper cables," Brian said. "Luckily, it doesn't *have* to run. Essentially, the cart is just a gadget to filter and transfer fuel. I'm going to use the auxiliary power units on our plane to suck the fuel out of the 727 the way you'd use a straw to suck lemonade out of a glass."

"How long is it going to take?"

"Under optimum conditions—which would mean pumping with ground power—we could load 2,000 pounds of fuel a minute. Doing it like this makes it harder to figure. I've never had to use the APUs to pump fuel before. At least an hour. Maybe two."

Nick gazed anxiously eastward for a moment, and when he spoke again his voice was low. "Do me a favor, mate—don't tell the others that."

"Why not?"

"Because I don't think we *have* two hours. We may not even have one."

5

Alone in first class, Dinah Catherine Bellman opened her eyes.

And *saw.*

"Craig," she whispered.

6

Craig.

But he didn't want to hear his name again. When people called his name, something bad always happened. *Always.*

Craig! Get up, Craig!

No. He *wouldn't* get up. His head had become a vast chambered hive; pain roared and raved in each irregular room and crooked corridor. Bees had come. The bees had thought he was dead. They had invaded his head and turned his skull into a honeycomb. And now . . . now . . .

They sense my thoughts and are trying to sting them to death, he thought, and uttered a thick, agonized groan. His blood-streaked hands opened and closed slowly on the industrial carpet which covered the lower-lobby floor. *Let me die, oh please just let me die.*

Craig, you have to get up! Now!

It was his father's voice, the one voice he had never been able to refuse or shut out. But he would refuse it now. He would shut it out now.

"Go away," he croaked. "I hate you. Go away."

Pain blared through his head in a golden shriek of trumpets. Clouds of bees, furious and stinging, flew from the bells as they blew.

Oh let me die, he thought. *Oh let me die. This is hell. I am in a hell of bees and big-band horns.*

Get up, Craiggy-weggy. It's your birthday, and guess what? As soon as you get up, someone's going to hand you a beer and hit you over the head . . . because THIS thud's for you!

"No," he said. "No more hitting." His hands shuffled on the carpet. He made an effort to open his eyes, but a glue of drying blood had stuck them shut. "You're dead. Both of you are dead. You can't hit me, and you can't make me do things. Both of you are dead, and I want to be dead, too."

But he wasn't dead. Somewhere beyond these phantom voices he could hear the whine of jet engines . . . and that other sound. The sound of the langoliers on the march. On the *run.*

Craig, get up. You have to get up.

He realized that it wasn't the voice of his father, or of his mother, either. That had only been his poor, wounded mind trying to fool itself. This was a voice from . . . from

(above?)

some other place, some high bright place where pain was a myth and pressure was a dream.

Craig, they've come to you—all the people you wanted to see. They left Boston and came here. That's how important you are to them. You can still do it, Craig. You can still pull the pin. There's still time to hand in your papers and fall out of your father's army . . . if you're man enough to do it, that is.

If you're man enough to do it.

"Man enough?" he croaked. "*Man* enough? Whoever you are, you've *got* to be shitting me."

He tried again to open his eyes. The tacky blood holding them shut gave a little but would not let go. He managed to work one hand up to his face. It brushed the remains of his nose and he gave voice to a low, tired scream of pain. Inside his head the trumpets blared and the bees swarmed. He waited until the worst of the pain had subsided, then poked out two fingers and used them to pull his own eyelids up.

That corona of light was still there. It made a vaguely evocative shape in the gloom.

Slowly, a little at a time, Craig raised his head.

And saw *her.*

She stood within the corona of light.

It was the little girl, but her dark glasses were gone and she was looking at him, and her eyes were kind.

Come on, Craig. Get up. I know it's hard, but you have to get up— you have to. Because they are all here, they are all waiting . . . but they won't wait forever. The langoliers will see to that.

She was not standing on the floor, he saw. Her shoes appeared to float an inch or two above it, and the bright light was all around her. She was outlined in spectral radiance.

Come, Craig. Get up.

He started struggling to his feet. It was very hard. His sense of balance was almost gone, and it was hard to hold his head up— because, of course, it was full of angry honeybees. Twice he fell back, but each time he began again, mesmerized and entranced by the glowing girl with her kind eyes and her promise of ultimate release.

They are all waiting, Craig. For you.

They are waiting for you.

7

Dinah lay on the stretcher, watching with her blind eyes as Craig Toomy got to one knee, fell over on his side, then began trying to rise once more. Her heart was suffused with a terrible stern pity for this hurt and broken man, this murdering fish that only wanted to explode. On his ruined, bloody face she saw a terrible mixture of emotions: fear, hope, and a kind of merciless determination.

I'm sorry, Mr. Toomy, she thought. *In spite of what you did, I'm sorry. But we need you.*

Then called to him again, called with her own dying consciousness:

Get up, Craig! Hurry! It's almost too late!

And she sensed that it was.

8

Once the longer of the two hoses was looped under the belly of the 767 and attached to its fuel port, Brian returned to the cockpit, cycled up the APUs, and went to work sucking the 727-400's fuel tanks dry. As he watched the LED readout on his right tank slowly climb toward 24,000 pounds, he waited tensely for the APUs to start chugging and lugging, trying to eat fuel which would not burn.

The right tank had reached the 8,000-pound mark when he heard the note of the small jet engines at the rear of the plane change—they grew rough and labored.

"What's happening, mate?" Nick asked. He was sitting in the co-pilot's chair again. His hair was disarrayed, and there were wide streaks of grease and blood across his formerly natty button-down shirt.

"The APU engines are getting a taste of the 727's fuel and they don't like it," Brian said. "I hope Albert's magic works, Nick, but I don't know."

Just before the LED reached 9,000 pounds in the right tank, the first APU cut out. A red ENGINE SHUTDOWN light appeared on Brian's board. He flicked the APU off.

"What can you do about it?" Nick asked, getting up and coming to look over Brian's shoulder.

"Use the other three APUs to keep the pumps running and hope," Brian said.

The second APU cut out thirty seconds later, and while Brian was moving his hand to shut it down, the third went. The cockpit lights went with it; now there was only the irregular chug of the hydraulic pumps and the lights on Brian's board, which were flickering. The last APU was roaring choppily, cycling up and down, shaking the plane.

"I'm shutting down completely," Brian said. He sounded harsh and strained to himself, a man who was way out of his depth and tiring fast in the undertow. "We'll have to wait for the Delta's fuel to join our plane's time-stream, or time-frame, or whatever the fuck it is. We can't go on like this. A strong power-surge before the last APU cuts out could wipe the INS clean. Maybe even fry it."

But as Brian reached for the switch, the engine's choppy note suddenly began to smooth out. He turned and stared at Nick unbelievingly. Nick looked back, and a big, slow grin lit his face.

"We might have lucked out, mate."

Brian raised his hands, crossed both sets of fingers, and shook them in the air. "I hope so," he said, and swung back to the boards. He flicked the switches marked APU 1, 3, and 4. They kicked in smoothly. The cockpit lights flashed back on. The cabin bells binged. Nick whooped and clapped Brian on the back.

Bethany appeared in the doorway behind them. "What's happening? Is everything all right?"

"I think," Brian said without turning, "that we might just have a shot at this thing."

9

Craig finally managed to stand upright. The glowing girl now stood with her feet just above the luggage conveyor belt. She looked at him with a supernatural sweetness and something else . . . something he had longed for his whole life. What was it?

He groped for it, and at last it came to him.

It was compassion.

Compassion and understanding.

He looked around and saw that the darkness was draining away. That meant he had been out all night, didn't it? He didn't know.

And it didn't matter. All that mattered was that the glowing girl had brought *them* to *him*—the investment bankers, the bond specialists, the commission-brokers, and the stock-rollers. They were here, they would want an explanation of just what young Mr. Craiggy-Weggy Toomy-Woomy had been up to, and here was the ecstatic truth: *monkey-business!* That was what he had been up to— yards and yards of monkey-business—*miles* of monkey-business. And when he told them that . . .

"They'll have to let me go . . . won't they?"

Yes, she said. *But you have to hurry, Craig. You have to hurry before they decide you're not coming and leave.*

Craig began to make his slow way forward. The girl's feet did not move, but as he approached her she floated backward like a mirage, toward the rubber strips which hung between the luggage-retrieval area and the loading dock outside.

And . . . oh, glorious: she was *smiling.*

10

They were all back on the plane now, all except Bob and Albert, who were sitting on the stairs and listening to the sound roll toward them in a slow, broken wave.

Laurel Stevenson was standing at the open forward door and looking at the terminal, still wondering what they were going to do about Mr. Toomy, when Bethany tugged the back of her blouse.

"Dinah is talking in her sleep, or something. I think she might be delirious. Can you come?"

Laurel came. Rudy Warwick was sitting across from Dinah, holding one of her hands and looking at her anxiously.

"I dunno," he said worriedly. "I dunno, but I think she might be going."

Laurel felt the girl's forehead. It was dry and very hot. The bleeding had either slowed down or stopped entirely, but the girl's respiration came in a series of pitiful whistling sounds. Blood was crusted around her mouth like strawberry sauce.

Laurel began, "I think—" and then Dinah said, quite clearly, "You have to hurry before they decide you're not coming and leave."

Laurel and Bethany exchanged puzzled, frightened glances.

"I think she's dreaming about that guy Toomy," Rudy told Laurel. "She said his name once."

"Yes," Dinah said. Her eyes were closed, but her head moved slightly and she appeared to listen. "Yes I will be," she said. "If you want me to, I will. But hurry. I know it hurts, but you have to hurry."

"She *is* delirious, isn't she?" Bethany whispered.

"No," Laurel said. "I don't think so. I think she might be . . . dreaming."

But that was not what she thought at all. What she really thought was that Dinah might be

(seeing)

doing something else. She didn't think she wanted to know what that something might be, although an idea whirled and danced far back in her mind. Laurel knew she could summon that idea if she wanted to, but she didn't. Because something creepy was going on here, *extremely* creepy, and she could not escape the idea that it *did* have something to do with

(don't kill him . . . we need him)

Mr. Toomy.

"Leave her alone," she said in a dry, abrupt tone of voice. "Leave her alone and let her

(do what she has to do to him)

sleep."

"God, I hope we take off soon," Bethany said miserably, and Rudy put a comforting arm around her shoulders.

11

Craig reached the conveyor belt and fell onto it. A white sheet of agony ripped through his head, his neck, his chest. He tried to remember what had happened to him and couldn't. He had run down the stalled escalator, he had hidden in a little room, he had sat tearing strips of paper in the dark . . . and that was where memory stopped.

He raised his head, hair hanging in his eyes, and looked at the glowing girl, who now sat cross-legged in front of the rubber strips, an inch off the conveyor belt. She was the most beautiful thing he had ever seen in his life; how could he ever have thought she was one of *them?*

"Are you an angel?" he croaked.

Yes, the glowing girl replied, and Craig felt his pain overwhelmed with joy. His vision blurred and then tears—the first ones he had ever cried as an adult—began to run slowly down his cheeks. Suddenly he found himself remembering his mother's sweet, droning, drunken voice as she sang that old song.

"Are you an angel of the morning? Will you be *my* angel of the morning?"

Yes—I will be. If you want me to, I will. But hurry. I know it hurts, Mr. Toomy, but you have to hurry.

"Yes," Craig sobbed, and began to crawl eagerly along the luggage conveyor belt toward her. Every movement sent fresh pain jig-jagging through him on irregular courses; blood dripped from his smashed nose and shattered mouth. Yet he still hurried as much as he could. Ahead of him, the little girl faded back through the hanging rubber strips, somehow not disturbing them at all as she went.

"Just touch my cheek before you leave me, baby," Craig said. He hawked up a spongy mat of blood, spat it on the wall where it clung like a dead spider, and tried to crawl faster.

12

To the east of the airport, a large cracking, rending sound filled the freakish morning. Bob and Albert got to their feet, faces pallid and filled with dreadful questions.

"What was that?" Albert asked.

"I think it was a tree," Bob replied, and licked his lips.

"But there's no wind!"

"No," Bob agreed. "There's no wind."

The noise had now become a moving barricade of splintered sound. Parts of it would seem to come into focus . . . and then drop back again just before identification was possible. At one moment Albert could swear he heard something barking, and then the barks . . . or yaps . . . or whatever they were . . . would be swallowed up by a brief sour humming sound like evil electricity. The only constants were the crunching and the steady drilling whine.

"What's happening?" Bethany called shrilly from behind them.

"Noth—" Albert began, and then Bob seized his shoulder and pointed.

"*Look!*" he shouted. "*Look over there!*"

Far to the east of them, on the horizon, a series of power pylons marched north and south across a high wooded ridge. As Albert looked, one of the pylons tottered like a toy and then fell over, pulling a snarl of power cables after it. A moment later another pylon went, and another, and another.

"That's not all, either," Albert said numbly. "Look at the trees. The trees over there are shaking like shrubs."

But they were not just shaking. As Albert and the others looked, the trees began to fall over, to disappear.

Crunch, smack, crunch, thud, BARK!

Crunch, smack, BARK!, thump, crunch.

"We have to get out of here," Bob said. He gripped Albert with both hands. His eyes were huge, avid with a kind of idiotic terror. The expression stood in sick, jagged contrast to his narrow, intelligent face. "I believe we have to get out of here *right now.*"

On the horizon, perhaps ten miles distant, the tall gantry of a radio tower trembled, rolled outward, and crashed down to disappear into the quaking trees. Now they could feel the very earth beginning to vibrate; it ran up the ladder and shook their feet in their shoes.

"Make it stop!" Bethany suddenly screamed from the doorway above them. She clapped her hands to her ears. "*Oh please make it STOP!*"

But the sound-wave rolled on toward them—the crunching, smacking, eating sound of the langoliers.

13

"I don't like to tease, Brian, but how much longer?" Nick's voice was taut. "There's a river about four miles east of here—I saw it when we were coming down—and I reckon whatever's coming is just now on the other side of it."

Brian glanced at his fuel readouts. 24,000 pounds in the right wing; 16,000 pounds in the left. It was going faster now that he didn't have to pump the Delta's fuel overwing to the other side.

"Fifteen minutes," he said. He could feel sweat standing out on his brow in big drops. "We've got to have more fuel, Nick, or we'll come down dead in the Mojave Desert. Another ten minutes to unhook, button up, and taxi out."

"You can't cut that? You're sure you can't cut that?"

Brian shook his head and turned back to his gauges.

14

Craig crawled slowly through the rubber strips, feeling them slide down his back like limp fingers. He emerged in the white, dead light of a new—and vastly shortened—day. The sound was terrible, overwhelming, the sound of an invading cannibal army. Even the sky seemed to shake with it, and for a moment fear froze him in place.

Look, his angel of the morning said, and pointed.

Craig looked . . . and forgot his fear. Beyond the American Pride 767, in a triangle of dead grass bounded by two taxiways and a runway, there was a long mahogany boardroom table. It gleamed brightly in the listless light. At each place were a yellow legal pad, a pitcher of ice water, and a Waterford glass. Sitting around the table were two dozen men in sober bankers' suits, and now they were all turning to look at him.

Suddenly they began to clap their hands. They stood and faced him, applauding his arrival. Craig felt a huge, grateful grin begin to stretch his face.

15

Dinah had been left alone in first class. Her breathing had become very labored now, and her voice was a strangled choke.

"Run to them, Craig! Quick! Quick!"

16

Craig tumbled off the conveyor, struck the concrete with a bone-rattling thump, and flailed to his feet. The pain no longer mattered.

The angel had brought them! Of *course* she had brought them! Angels were like the ghosts in that story about Mr. Scrooge—they could do anything they wanted! The corona around her had begun to dim and she was fading out, but it didn't matter. She had brought his salvation: a net in which he was finally, blessedly caught.

Run to them, Craig! Run around the plane! Run away from the plane! Run to them now!

Craig began to run—a shambling stride that quickly became a crippled sprint. As he ran his head nodded up and down like a sunflower on a broken stalk. He ran toward humorless, unforgiving men who were his salvation, men who might have been fisher-folk standing in a boat beyond an unsuspected silver sky, retrieving their net to see what fabulous thing they had caught.

17

The LED readout for the left tank began to slow down when it reached 21,000 pounds, and by the time it topped 22,000 it had almost stopped. Brian understood what was happening and quickly flicked two switches, shutting down the hydraulic pumps. The 727-400 had given them what she had to give: a little over 46,000 pounds of jet-fuel. It would have to be enough.

"All right," he said, standing up.

"All right what?" Nick asked, also standing.

"We're uncoupling and getting the fuck out of here."

The approaching noise had reached deafening levels. Mixed into the crunching smacking sound and the transmission squeal were falling trees and the dull crump of collapsing buildings. Just before shutting the pumps down he had heard a number of crackling thuds followed by a series of deep splashes. A bridge falling into the river Nick had seen, he imagined.

"Mr. Toomy!" Bethany screamed suddenly. *"It's Mr. Toomy!"*

Nick beat Brian out the door and into first class, but they were both in time to see Craig go shambling and lurching across the taxiway. He ignored the plane completely. His destination appeared to be an empty triangle of grass bounded by a pair of crisscrossing taxiways.

"What's he doing?" Rudy breathed.

"Never mind him," Brian said. "We're all out of time. Nick? Go

down the ladder ahead of me. Hold me while I uncouple the hose."
Brian felt like a man standing naked on a beach as a tidal wave
humps up on the horizon and rushes toward the shore.

Nick followed him down and laid hold of Brian's belt again as
Brian leaned out and twisted the nozzle of the hose, unlocking it.
A moment later he yanked the hose free and dropped it to the
cement, where the nozzle-ring clanged dully. Brian slammed the
fuel-port door shut.

"Come on," he said after Nick had pulled him back. His face was
dirty gray. "Let's get out of here."

But Nick did not move. He was frozen in place, staring to the
east. His skin had gone the color of paper. On his face was an
expression of dreamlike horror. His upper lip trembled, and in that
moment he looked like a dog that is too frightened to snarl.

Brian turned his head slowly in that direction, hearing the tendons
in his neck creak like a rusty spring on an old screen door as he
did so. He turned his head and watched as the langoliers finally
entered stage left.

18

"So you see," Craig said, approaching the empty chair at the head
of the table and standing before the men seated around it, "the
brokers with whom I did business were not only unscrupulous;
many of them were actually CIA plants whose job it was to contact
and fake out just such bankers as myself—men looking to fill up
skinny portfolios in a hurry. As far as they are concerned, the end—
keeping communism out of South America—justifies any available
means."

"What procedures did you follow to check these fellows out?" a
fat man in an expensive blue suit asked. "Did you use a bond-
insurance company, or does your bank retain a specific investigation
firm in such cases?" Blue Suit's round, jowly face was perfectly
shaved; his cheeks glowed with either good health or forty years
of Scotch and sodas; his eyes were merciless chips of blue ice. They
were wonderful eyes; they were father-eyes.

Somewhere, far away from this boardroom two floors below the
top of the Prudential Center, Craig could hear a hell of a racket
going on. Road construction, he supposed. There was always road

construction going on in Boston, and he suspected that most of it was unnecessary, that in most cases it was just the old, old story— the unscrupulous taking cheerful advantage of the unwary. It had nothing to do with him. Nothing whatever. His job was to deal with the man in the blue suit, and he couldn't wait to get started.

"We're waiting, Craig," the president of his own banking insti- tution said. Craig felt momentary surprise—Mr. Parker hadn't been scheduled to attend this meeting—and then the feeling was over- whelmed by happiness.

"*No procedures at all!*" he screamed joyfully into their shocked faces. "*I just bought and bought and bought! I followed NO . . . PRO- CEDURES . . . AT ALL!*"

He was about to go on, to elaborate on this theme, to really *expound* on it, when a sound stopped him. *This* sound was not miles away; this sound was close, very close, perhaps in the boardroom itself.

A whickering chopping sound, like dry hungry teeth.

Suddenly Craig felt a deep need to tear some paper—any paper would do. He reached for the legal pad in front of his place at the table, but the pad was gone. So was the table. So were the bankers. So was *Boston.*

"Where *am* I?" he asked in a small, perplexed voice, and looked around. Suddenly he realized . . . and suddenly he saw *them.*

The langoliers had come.

They had come for *him.*

Craig Toomy began to scream.

19

Brian could see them, but could not understand what it was he was seeing. In some strange way they seemed to *defy* seeing, and he sensed his frantic, overstressed mind trying to change the incoming information, to make the shapes which had begun to appear at the east end of Runway 21 into something it could understand.

At first there were only two shapes, one black, one a dark to- mato red.

Are they balls? his mind asked doubtfully. *Could they be balls?*

Something actually seemed to *click* in the center of his head and they *were* balls, sort of like beachballs, but balls which rippled and contracted and then expanded again, as if he was seeing them through a heat-haze. They came bowling out of the high dead grass at the end of Runway 21, leaving cut swaths of blackness behind them. They were somehow cutting the grass—

No, his mind reluctantly denied. *They are not just cutting the grass, and you know it. They are cutting a lot more than the grass.*

What they left behind were narrow lines of perfect blackness. And now, as they raced playfully down the white concrete at the end of the runway, they were *still* leaving narrow dark tracks behind. They glistened like tar.

No, his mind reluctantly denied. *Not tar. You know what that blackness is. It's nothing. Nothing at all. They are eating a lot more than the surface of the runway.*

There was something malignantly joyful about their behavior. They crisscrossed each other's paths, leaving a wavery black X on the outer taxiway. They bounced high in the air, did an exuberant, crisscrossing maneuver, and then raced straight for the plane.

As they did, Brian screamed and Nick screamed beside him. *Faces* lurked below the surfaces of the racing balls—monstrous, alien faces. They shimmered and twitched and wavered like faces made of glowing swamp-gas. The eyes were only rudimentary indentations, but the mouths were huge: semicircular caves lined with gnashing, blurring teeth.

They ate as they came, rolling up narrow strips of the world.

A Texaco fuel truck was parked on the outer taxiway. The langoliers pounced upon it, high-speed teeth whirring and crunching and bulging out of their blurred bodies. They went through it without pause. One of them burrowed a path directly through the rear tires, and for a moment, before the tires collapsed, Brian could see the shape it had cut—a shape like a cartoon mouse-hole in a cartoon baseboard.

The other leaped high, disappeared for a moment behind the Texaco truck's boxy tank, and then blasted straight through, leaving a metal-ringed hole from which av-gas sprayed in a dull amber flood. They struck the ground, bounced as if on springs, crisscrossed again, and raced on toward the airplane. Reality peeled away in narrow strips beneath them, peeled away wherever and whatever they touched, and as they neared, Brian realized that they were unzipping more than the world—they were opening all the depths of forever.

They reached the edge of the tarmac and paused. They jittered uncertainly in place for a moment, looking like the bouncing balls that hopped over the words in old movie-house sing-alongs.

Then they turned and zipped off in a new direction.

Zipped off in the direction of Craig Toomy, who stood watching them and screaming into the white day.

With a huge effort, Brian snapped the paralysis which held him. He elbowed Nick, who was still frozen below him. "Come on!" Nick didn't move and Brian drove his elbow back harder this time, connecting solidly with Nick's forehead. "Come on, I said! Move your ass! *We're getting out of here!*"

Now more black and red balls were appearing at the edge of the airport. They bounced, danced, circled . . . and then raced toward them.

20

You can't get away from them, his father had said, *because of their legs. Their fast little legs.*

Craig tried, nevertheless.

He turned and ran for the terminal, casting horrified, grimacing looks behind him as he did. His shoes rattled on the pavement. He ignored the American Pride 767, which was now cycling up again, and ran for the luggage area instead.

No, Craig, his father said. *You may* THINK *you're running, but you're not. You know what you're really doing—you're* SCAMPERING!

Behind him the two ball-shapes sped up, closing the gap with effortless, happy speed. They crisscrossed twice, just a pair of daffy showoffs in a dead world, leaving spiky lines of blackness behind them. They rolled after Craig about seven inches apart, creating what looked like negative ski-tracks behind their weird, shimmering bodies. They caught him twenty feet from the luggage conveyor belt and chewed off his feet in a millisecond. At one moment his briskly scampering feet were there. At the next, Craig was three inches shorter; his feet, along with his expensive Bally loafers, had simply ceased to exist. There was no blood; the wounds were cauterized instantly in the langoliers' scorching passage.

Craig didn't know his feet had ceased to exist. He scampered on the stumps of his ankles, and as the first pain began to sizzle up his legs, the langoliers banked in a tight turn and came back, rolling up the pavement side by side. Their trails crossed twice this time, creating a crescent of cement bordered in black, like a depiction of the moon in a child's coloring book. Only this crescent began to *sink,* not into the earth—for there appeared to be no earth beneath the surface—but into nowhere at all.

This time the langoliers bounced upward in perfect tandem and clipped Craig off at the knees. He came down, still trying to run, and then fell sprawling, waving his stumps. His scampering days were over.

"*No!*" he screamed. "*No, Daddy! No! I'll be good! Please make them go away! I'll be good, I SWEAR I'LL BE GOOD FROM NOW ON IF YOU JUST MAKE THEM GO AW—*"

Then they rushed at him again, gibbering yammering buzzing whining, and he saw the frozen machine blur of their gnashing teeth and felt the hot bellows of their frantic, blind vitality in the half-instant before they began to cut him apart in random chunks.

His last thought was: *How can their little legs be fast? They* have *no le*

21

Scores of the black things had now appeared, and Laurel understood that soon there would be hundreds, thousands, millions, billions. Even with the jet engines screaming through the open forward door as Brian pulled the 767 away from the ladder and the wing of the Delta jet, she could hear their yammering, inhuman cry.

Great looping coils of blackness crisscrossed the end of Runway 21—and then the tracks narrowed toward the terminal, converging as the balls making them rushed toward Craig Toomy.

I guess they don't get live meat very often, she thought, and suddenly felt like vomiting.

Nick Hopewell slammed the forward door after one final, un-believing glance and dogged it shut. He began to stagger back down the aisle, swaying from side to side like a drunk as he came. His eyes seemed to fill his whole face. Blood streamed down his chin; he had bitten his lower lip deeply. He put his arms around Laurel and buried his burning face in the hollow where her neck met her shoulder. She put her arms around him and held him tight.

22

In the cockpit, Brian powered up as fast as he dared, and sent the 767 charging along the taxiway at a suicidal rate of speed. The eastern edge of the airport was now black with the invading balls; the end of Runway 21 had completely disappeared and the world beyond it was going. In that direction the white, unmoving sky now arched down over a world of scrawled black lines and fallen trees.

As the plane neared the end of the taxiway, Brain grabbed the microphone and shouted: "Belt in! Belt in! If you're not belted in, hold on!"

He slowed marginally, then slewed the 767 onto Runway 33. As he did so he saw something which made his mind cringe and wail: huge sections of the world which lay to the east of the runway, huge irregular pieces of *reality itself*, were falling into the ground like freight elevators, leaving big senseless chunks of emptiness behind.

They are eating the world, he thought. *My God, my dear God, they are eating the world.*

Then the entire airfield was turning in front of him and Flight 29 was pointed west again, with Runway 33 lying open and long and deserted before it.

23

Overhead compartments burst open when the 767 swerved onto the runway, spraying carry-on luggage across the main cabin in a deadly hail. Bethany, who hadn't had time to fasten her seatbelt, was hurled into Albert Kaussner's lap. Albert noticed neither his lapful of warm girl nor the attaché case that caromed off the curved wall three feet in front of his nose. He saw only the dark, speeding shapes rushing across Runway 21 to the left of them, and the glistening dark tracks they left behind. These tracks converged in a giant well of blackness where the luggage-unloading area had been.

They are being drawn to Mr. Toomy, he thought, *or to where Mr. Toomy was. If he hadn't come out of the terminal, they would have chosen the airplane instead. They would have eaten it—and us inside it—from the wheels up.*

Behind him, Bob Jenkins spoke in a trembling, awed voice. "Now we know, don't we?"

"*What?*" Laurel screamed in an odd, breathless voice she did not recognize as her own. A duffel-bag landed in her lap; Nick raised his head, let go of her, and batted it absently into the aisle. "*What do we know?*"

"Why, what happens to today when it becomes yesterday, what happens to the present when it becomes the past. It waits—dead and empty and deserted. It waits for *them*. It waits for the time-keepers of eternity, always running along behind, cleaning up the mess in the most efficient way possible . . . by eating it."

"Mr. Toomy knew about them," Dinah said in a clear, dreaming voice. "Mr. Toomy says they are the langoliers." Then the jet engines cycled up to full power and the plane charged down Runway 33.

24

Brian saw two of the balls zip across the runway ahead of him, peeling back the surface of reality in a pair of parallel tracks which gleamed like polished ebony. It was too late to stop. The 767 shuddered like a dog with a chill as it raced over the empty places, but he was able to hold it on the runway. He shoved his throttles forward, burying them, and watched his ground-speed indicator rise toward the commit point.

Even now he could hear those manic chewing, gobbling sounds . . . although he did not know if they were in his ears or only his reeling mind. And did not care.

25

Leaning over Laurel to look out the window, Nick saw the Bangor International terminal sliced, diced, chopped, and channelled. It tottered in its various jigsaw pieces and then began to tumble into loony chasms of darkness.

Bethany Simms screamed. A black track was speeding along next to the 767, chewing up the edge of the runway. Suddenly it jagged to the right and disappeared underneath the plane.

There was another terrific bump.

"Did it get us?" Nick shouted. *"Did it get us?"*

No one answered him. Their pale, terrified faces stared out the windows and no one answered him. Trees rushed by in a gray-green blur. In the cockpit, Brian sat tensely forward in his seat, waiting for one of those balls to bounce up in front of the cockpit window and bullet through. None did.

On his board, the last red lights turned green. Brian hauled back on the yoke and the 767 was airborne again.

26

In the main cabin, a black-bearded man with bloodshot eyes staggered forward, blinking owlishly at his fellow travellers. "Are we almost in Boston yet?" he inquired at large. "I hope so, because I want to go back to bed. I've got one *bastard* of a headache."

CHAPTER NINE

GOODBYE TO BANGOR.
HEADING WEST THROUGH
DAYS AND NIGHTS.
SEEING THROUGH THE
EYES OF OTHERS. THE
ENDLESS GULF. THE RIP.
THE WARNING. BRIAN'S
DECISION. THE LANDING.
SHOOTING STARS ONLY.

1

The plane banked heavily east, throwing the man with the black beard into a row of empty seats three-quarters of the way up the main cabin. He looked around at all the other empty seats with a wide, frightened gaze, and squeezed his eyes shut. "Jesus," he muttered. "DTs. Fucking DTs. This is the worst they've ever been." He looked around fearfully. "The bugs come next . . . where's the motherfuckin bugs?"

No bugs, Albert thought, *but wait till you see the balls. You're going to love those.*

"Buckle yourself in, mate," Nick said, "and shut u—"

He broke off, staring down incredulously at the airport . . . or where the airport had been. The main buildings were gone, and the National Guard base at the west end was going. Flight 29 overflew a growing abyss of darkness, an eternal cistern that seemed to have no end.

"Oh dear Jesus, Nick," Laurel said unsteadily, and suddenly put her hands over her eyes.

As they overflew Runway 33 at 1,500 feet, Nick saw sixty or a hundred parallel lines racing up the concrete, cutting the runway into long strips that sank into emptiness. The strips reminded him of Craig Toomy:

Rii-ip.

On the other side of the aisle, Bethany pulled down the window-shade beside Albert's seat with a bang.

"Don't you dare open that!" she told him in a scolding, hysterical voice.

"Don't worry," Albert said, and suddenly remembered that he had left his violin down there. Well . . . it was undoubtedly gone now. He abruptly put his hands over his own face.

2

Before Brian began to turn west again, he saw what lay east of Bangor. It was nothing. Nothing at all. A titanic river of blackness lay in a still sweep from horizon to horizon under the white dome of the sky. The trees were gone, the city was gone, the earth itself was gone.

This is what it must be like to fly in outer space, he thought, and he felt his rationality slip a cog, as it had on the trip east. He held onto himself desperately and made himself concentrate on flying the plane.

He brought them up quickly, wanting to be in the clouds, wanting that hellish vision to be blotted out. Then Flight 29 was pointed west again. In the moments before they entered the clouds, he saw the hills and woods and lakes which stretched to the west of the city, saw them being cut ruthlessly apart by thousands of black spiderweb lines. He saw huge swatches of reality go sliding soundlessly into the growing mouth of the abyss, and Brian did something he had never done before while in the cockpit of an airplane.

He closed his eyes. When he opened them again they were in the clouds.

3

There was almost no turbulence this time; as Bob Jenkins had suggested, the weather patterns appeared to be running down like an old clock. Ten minutes after entering the clouds, Flight 29 emerged into the bright-blue world which began at 18,000 feet. The remaining passengers looked around at each other nervously, then at the speakers as Brian came on the intercom.

"We're up," he said simply. "You all know what happens now: we go back exactly the way we came, and hope that whatever doorway we came through is still there. If it is, we'll try going through."

He paused for a moment, then resumed.

"Our return flight is going to take somewhere between four and a half and six hours. I'd like to be more exact, but I can't. Under ordinary circumstances, the flight west usually takes longer than the flight east, because of prevailing wind conditions, but so far as I can tell from my cockpit instruments, there *is* no wind." Brian paused for a moment and then added, "There's nothing moving up here but us." For a moment the intercom stayed on, as if Brian meant to add something else, and then it clicked off.

4

"What in God's name is going on here?" the man with the black beard asked shakily.

Albert looked at him for a moment and then said, "I don't think you want to know."

"Am I in the hospital again?" The man with the black beard blinked at Albert fearfully, and Albert felt sudden sympathy for him.

"Well, why don't you believe you are, if it will help?"

The man with the black beard continued to stare at him for a moment in dreadful fascination and then announced, "I'm going back to sleep. Right now." He reclined his seat and closed his eyes. In less than a minute his chest was moving up and down with deep regularity and he was snoring under his breath.

Albert envied him.

5

Nick gave Laurel a brief hug, then unbuckled his seatbelt and stood up. "I'm going forward," he said. "Want to come?"

Laurel shook her head and pointed across the aisle at Dinah. "I'll stay with her."

"There's nothing you can do, you know," Nick said. "It's in God's hands now, I'm afraid."

"I do know that," she said, "but I want to stay."

"All right, Laurel." He brushed at her hair gently with the palm of his hand. "It's such a pretty name. You deserve it."

She glanced up at him and smiled. "Thank you."

"We have a dinner date—you haven't forgotten, have you?"

"No," she said, still smiling. "I haven't and I won't."

He bent down and brushed a kiss lightly across her mouth. "Good, he said. "Neither will I."

He went forward and she pressed her fingers lightly against her mouth, as if to hold his kiss there, where it belonged. Dinner with Nick Hopewell—a dark, mysterious stranger. Maybe with candles and a good bottle of wine. More kisses afterward—real kisses. It all seemed like something which might happen in one of the Harlequin romances she sometimes read. So what? They were pleasant stories, full of sweet and harmless dreams. It didn't hurt to dream a little, did it?

Of course not. But why did she feel the dream was so unlikely to come true?

She unbuckled her own seatbelt, crossed the aisle, and put her hand on the girl's forehead. The hectic heat she had felt before was gone; Dinah's skin was now waxy-cool.

I think she's going, Rudy had said shortly before they started their headlong take-off charge. Now the words recurred to Laurel and rang in her head with sickening validity. Dinah was taking air in shallow sips, her chest barely rising and falling beneath the strap which cinched the tablecloth pad tight over her wound.

Laurel brushed the girl's hair off her forehead with infinite tenderness and thought of that strange moment in the restaurant, when Dinah had reached out and grasped the cuff of Nick's jeans. *Don't you kill him . . . we need him.*

Did you save us, Dinah? Did you do something to Mr. Toomy that saved us? Did you make him somehow trade his life for ours?

She thought that perhaps something like that had happened . . . and reflected that, if it was true, this little girl, blind and badly wounded, had made a dreadful decision inside her darkness.

She leaned forward and kissed each of Dinah's cool, closed lids. "Hold on," she whispered. "Please hold on, Dinah."

6

Bethany turned to Albert, grasped both of his hands in hers, and asked: "What happens if the fuel goes bad?"

Albert looked at her seriously and kindly. "You know the answer to that, Bethany."

"You can call me Beth, if you want."

"Okay."

She fumbled out her cigarettes, looked up at the NO SMOKING light, and put them away again. "Yeah," she said. "I know. We crash. End of story. And do you know what?"

He shook his head, smiling a little.

"If we can't find that hole again, I hope Captain Engle won't even try to land the plane. I hope he just picks out a nice high mountain and crashes us into the top of it. Did you see what happened to that crazy guy? I don't want that to happen to me."

She shuddered, and Albert put an arm around her. She looked up at him frankly. "Would you like to kiss me?"

"Yes," Albert said.

"Well, you better go ahead, then. The later it gets, the later it gets."

Albert went ahead. It was only the third time in his life that the fastest Hebrew west of the Mississippi had kissed a girl, and it was great. He could spend the whole trip back in a lip-lock with this girl and never worry about a thing.

"Thank you," she said, and put her head on his shoulder. "I needed that."

"Well, if you need it again, just ask," Albert said.

She looked up at him, amused. "Do you *need* me to ask, Albert?"

"I reckon not," drawled The Arizona Jew, and went back to work.

7

Nick had stopped on his way to the cockpit to speak to Bob Jenkins—an extremely nasty idea had occurred to him, and he wanted to ask the writer about it.

"Do you think there could be any of those things up here?"

Bob thought it over for a moment. "Judging from what we saw back at Bangor, I would think not. But it's hard to tell, isn't it? In a thing like this, all bets are off."

"Yes. I suppose so. All bets are off." Nick thought this over for a moment. "What about this time-rip of yours? Would you like to give odds on us finding it again?"

Bob Jenkins slowly shook his head.

Rudy Warwick spoke up from behind them, startling them both. "You didn't ask me, but I'll give you my opinion just the same. I put them at one in a thousand."

Nick thought this over. After a moment a rare, radiant smile burst across his face. "Not bad odds at all," he said. "Not when you consider the alternative."

8

Less than forty minutes later, the blue sky through which Flight 29 moved began to deepen in color. It cycled slowly to indigo, and then to deep purple. Sitting in the cockpit, monitoring his instruments and wishing for a cup of coffee, Brian thought of an old song: *When the deep purple falls . . . over sleepy garden walls . . .*

No garden walls up here, but he could see the first ice-chip stars gleaming in the firmament. There was something reassuring and calming about the old constellations appearing, one by one, in their old places. He did not know how they could be the same when so many other things were so badly out of joint, but he was very glad they were.

"It's going faster, isn't it?" Nick said from behind him.

Brian turned in his seat to face him. "Yes. It is. After awhile the 'days' and 'nights' will be passing as fast as a camera shutter can click, I think."

Nick sighed. "And now we do the hardest thing of all, don't we? We wait to see what happens. And pray a little bit, I suppose."

"It couldn't hurt." Brian took a long, measuring look at Nick Hopewell. "I was on my way to Boston because my ex-wife died in a stupid fire. Dinah was going because a bunch of doctors promised her a new pair of eyes. Bob was going to a convention, Albert to music school, Laurel on vacation. Why were you going to Boston, Nick? 'Fess up. The hour groweth late."

Nick looked at him thoughtfully for a long time and then laughed. "Well, why not?" he asked, but Brian was not so foolish as to believe this question was directed at him. "What does a Most Secret classification mean when you've just seen a bunch of killer fuzzballs rolling up the world like an old rug?"

He laughed again.

"The United States hasn't exactly cornered the market on dirty tricks and covert operations," he told Brian. "We Limeys have forgotten more nasty mischief than you johnnies ever knew. We've cut capers in India, South Africa, China, and the part of Palestine which became Israel. We certainly got into a pissing contest with the wrong fellows that time, didn't we? Nevertheless, we British are great believers in cloak and dagger, and the fabled MI5 isn't where it ends but only where it begins. I spent eighteen years in the armed services, Brian—the last five of them in Special Operations. Since then I've done various odd jobs, some innocuous, some fabulously nasty."

It was full dark outside now, the stars gleaming like spangles on a woman's formal evening gown.

"I was in Los Angeles—on vacation, actually—when I was contacted and told to fly to Boston. Extremely short notice, this was, and after four days spent backpacking in the San Gabriels, I was falling-down tired. That's why I happened to be sound asleep when Mr. Jenkins's Event happened.

"There's a man in Boston, you see . . . or was . . . or will be (time-travel plays hell on the old verb tenses, doesn't it?) . . . who is a politician of some note. The sort of fellow who moves and shakes with great vigor behind the scenes. This man—I'll call him Mr. O'Banion, for the sake of conversation—is very rich, Brian, and he is an enthusiastic supporter of the Irish Republican Army. He has channelled millions of dollars into what some like to call Boston's favorite charity, and there is a good deal of blood on his hands. Not just British soldiers but children in schoolyards, women in laundrettes, and babies blown out of their prams in pieces. He is an idealist of the most dangerous sort: one who never has to view the carnage at first hand, one who has never had to look at a severed leg lying in the gutter and been forced to reconsider his actions in light of that experience."

"You were supposed to kill this man O'Banion?"

"Not unless I had to," Nick said calmly. "He's very wealthy, but that's not the only problem. He's the total politician, you see, and he's got more fingers than the one he uses to stir the pot in Ireland. He has a great many powerful American friends, and some of his friends are our friends . . . that's the nature of politics; a cat's cradle woven by men who for the most part belong in rooms with rubber walls. Killing Mr. O'Banion would be a great political risk. But he keeps a little bit of fluff on the side. *She* was the one I was supposed to kill."

"As a warning," Brian said in a low, fascinated voice.

"Yes. As a warning."

Almost a full minute passed as the two men sat in the cockpit, looking at each other. The only sound was the sleepy drone of the jet engines. Brian's eyes were shocked and somehow very young. Nick only looked weary.

"If we get out of this," Brian said at last, "if we get back, will you carry through with it?"

Nick shook his head. He did this slowly, but with great finality. "I believe I've had what the Adventist blokes like to call a soul conversion, old mate of mine. No more midnight creeps or extreme-prejudice jobs for Mrs. Hopewell's boy Nicholas. If we get out of this—a proposition I find rather shaky just now—I believe I'll retire."

"And do what?"

Nick looked at him thoughtfully for a moment or two and then said, "Well . . . I suppose I could take flying lessons."

Brian burst out laughing. After a moment, Mrs. Hopewell's boy Nicholas joined him.

9

Thirty-five minutes later, daylight began to seep back into the main cabin of Flight 29. Three minutes later it might have been mid-morning; fifteen minutes after that it might have been noon.

Laurel looked around and saw that Dinah's sightless eyes were open.

Yet were they *entirely* sightless? There was something in them, something just beyond definition, which made Laurel wonder. She felt a sense of unknown awe creep into her, a feeling which almost touched upon fear.

She reached out and gently grasped one of Dinah's hands. "Don't try to talk," she said quietly. "If you're awake, Dinah, don't try to talk—just listen. We're in the air. We're going back, and you're going to be all right—I promise you that."

Dinah's hand tightened on hers, and after a moment Laurel realized the little girl was tugging her forward. She leaned over the secured stretcher. Dinah spoke in a tiny voice that seemed to Laurel a perfect scale model of her former voice.

"Don't worry about me, Laurel. I got . . . what I wanted."

"Dinah, you shouldn't—"

The unseeing brown eyes moved toward the sound of Laurel's voice. A little smile touched Dinah's bloody mouth. "I *saw*," that tiny voice, frail as a glass reed, told her. "I saw through Mr. Toomy's eyes. At the beginning, and then again at the end. It was better at the end. At the start, everything looked mean and nasty to him. It was better at the end."

Laurel looked at her with helpless wonder.

The girl's hand let go of Laurel's and rose waveringly to touch her cheek. "He wasn't such a bad guy, you know." She coughed. Small flecks of blood flew from her mouth.

"Please, Dinah," Laurel said. She had a sudden sensation that she could almost see through the little blind girl, and this brought a feeling of stifling, directionless panic. "Please don't try to talk any-more."

Dinah smiled. "I saw *you*," she said. "You are beautiful, Laurel.

Everything was beautiful . . . even the things that were dead. It was so wonderful to . . . you know . . . just to *see*."

She drew in one of her tiny sips of air, let it out, and simply didn't take the next one. Her sightless eyes now seemed to be looking far beyond Laurel Stevenson.

"Please breathe, Dinah," Laurel said. She took the girl's hands in hers and began to kiss them repeatedly, as if she could kiss life back into that which was now beyond it. It was not fair for Dinah to die after she had saved them all; no God could demand such a sacrifice, not even for people who had somehow stepped outside of time itself. "Please breathe, please, please, please breathe."

But Dinah did not breathe. After a long time, Laurel returned the girl's hands to her lap and looked fixedly into her pale, still face. Laurel waited for her own eyes to fill up with tears, but no tears came. Yet her heart ached with fierce sorrow and her mind beat with its own deep and outraged protest: *Oh, no! Oh, not fair! This is not fair! Take it back, God! Take it back, damn you, take it back, you just take it BACK!*

But God did not take it back. The jet engines throbbed steadily, the sun shone on the bloody sleeve of Dinah's good travelling dress in a bright oblong, and God did not take it back. Laurel looked across the aisle and saw Albert and Bethany kissing. Albert was touching one of the girl's breasts through her tee-shirt, lightly, delicately, almost religiously. They seemed to make a ritual shape, a symbolic representation of life and that stubborn, intangible spark which carries life on in the face of the most dreadful reversals and ludicrous turns of fate. Laurel looked hopefully from them to Dinah . . . and God had not taken it back.

God had not taken it back.

Laurel kissed the still slope of Dinah's cheek and then raised her hand to the little girl's face. Her fingers stopped only an inch from her eyelids.

I saw through Mr. Toomy's eyes. Everything was beautiful . . . even the things that were dead. It was so wonderful to see.

"Yes," Laurel said. "I can live with that."

She left Dinah's eyes open.

10

American Pride 29 flew west through the days and nights, going from light to darkness and light to darkness as if flying through a great, lazily shifting parade of fat clouds. Each cycle came slightly faster than the one before.

A little over three hours into the flight, the clouds below them ceased, and over exactly the same spot where they had begun on the flight east. Brian was willing to bet the front had not moved so much as a single foot. The Great Plains lay below them in a silent roan-colored expanse of land.

"No sign of them over here," Rudy Warwick said. He did not have to specify what he was talking about.

"No," Bob Jenkins agreed. "We seem to have outrun them, either in space or in time."

"Or in both," Albert put in.

"Yes—or both."

But they had not. As Flight 29 crossed the Rockies, they began to see the black lines below them again, thin as threads from this height. They shot up and down the rough, slabbed slopes and drew not-quite-meaningless patterns in the blue-gray carpet of trees. Nick stood at the forward door, looking out of the bullet porthole set into it. This porthole had a queer magnifying effect, and he soon discovered he could see better than he really wanted to. As he watched, two of the black lines split, raced around a jagged, snow-tipped peak, met on the far side, crossed, and raced down the other slope in diverging directions. Behind them the entire top of the mountain fell into itself, leaving something which looked like a volcano with a vast dead caldera at its truncated top.

"Jumping Jiminy Jesus," Nick muttered, and passed a quivering hand over his brow.

As they crossed the Western Slope toward Utah, the dark began to come down again. The setting sun threw an orange-red glare over a fragmented hellscape that none of them could look at for long; one by one, they followed Bethany's example and pulled their windowshades. Nick went back to his seat on unsteady legs and dropped his forehead into one cold, clutching hand. After a moment or two he turned toward Laurel and she took him wordlessly in her arms.

Brian was forced to look at it. There were no shades in the cockpit.

Western Colorado and eastern Utah fell into the pit of eternity piece by jagged piece below him and ahead of him. Mountains, buttes, mesas, and cols one by one ceased to exist as the crisscrossing langoliers cut them adrift from the rotting fabric of this dead past, cut them loose and sent them tumbling into sunless endless gulfs of forever. There was no sound up here, and somehow that was the most horrible thing of all. The land below them disappeared as silently as dust-motes.

Then darkness came like an act of mercy and for a little while he could concentrate on the stars. He clung to them with the fierceness of panic, the only real things left in this horrible world: Orion the hunter; Pegasus, the great shimmering horse of midnight; Cassiopeia in her starry chair.

11

Half an hour later the sun rose again, and Brian felt his sanity give a deep shudder and slide closer to the edge of its own abyss. The world below was gone; utterly and finally gone. The deepening blue sky was a dome over a cyclopean ocean of deepest, purest ebony.

The world had been torn from beneath Flight 29.

Bethany's thought had also crossed Brian's mind; if push came to shove, if worse came to worst, he had thought, he could put the 767 into a dive and crash them into a mountain, ending it for good and all. But now there were no mountains to crash into.

Now there was no *earth* to crash into.

What will happen to us if we can't find the rip again? he wondered. *What will happen if we run out of fuel? Don't try to tell me we'll crash, because I simply don't believe it—you can't crash into nothing. I think we'll simply fall . . . and fall . . . and fall. For how long? And how far? How far can you fall into nothing?*

Don't think about it.

But how, exactly, did one do that? How did one refuse to think about nothing?

He turned deliberately back to his sheet of calculations. He worked on them, referring frequently to the INS readout, until the light had begun to fade out of the sky again. He now put the elapsed time between sunrise and sunset at about twenty-eight minutes.

He reached for the switch that controlled the cabin intercom and opened the circuit.

"Nick? Can you come up front?"

Nick appeared in the cockpit doorway less than thirty seconds later.

"Have they got their shades pulled back there?" Brian asked him before he could come all the way in.

"You better believe it," Nick said.

"Very wise of them. I'm going to ask you not to look down yet, if you can help it. I'll *want* you to look out in a few minutes, and once you look out I don't suppose you'll be able to help looking down, but I advise you to put it off as long as possible. It's not . . . very nice."

"Gone, is it?"

"Yes. Everything."

"The little girl is gone, too. Dinah. Laurel was with her at the end. She's taking it very well. She liked that girl. So did I."

Brian nodded. He was not surprised—the girl's wound was the sort that demanded immediate treatment in an emergency room, and even then the prognosis would undoubtedly be cloudy—but it still rolled a stone against his heart. He had also liked Dinah, and he believed what Laurel believed—that the girl was somehow more responsible for their continued survival than anyone else. She had done something to Mr. Toomy, had used him in some strange way . . . and Brian had an idea that, somewhere inside, Toomy would not have minded being used in such a fashion. So, if her death was an omen, it was one of the worst sort.

"She never got her operation," he said.

"No."

"But Laurel is okay?"

"More or less."

"You like her, don't you?"

"Yes," Nick said. "I have mates who would laugh at that, but I do like her. She's a bit dewy-eyed, but she's got grit."

Brian nodded. "Well, if we get back, I wish you the best of luck."

"Thanks." Nick sat down in the co-pilot's seat again. "I've been thinking about the question you asked me before. About what I'll do when and if we get out of this mess . . . besides taking the lovely Laurel to dinner, that is. I suppose I might end up going after Mr.

O'Banion after all. As I see it, he's not all that much different from our friend Toomy."

"Dinah asked you to spare Mr. Toomy," Brian pointed out. "Maybe that's something you should add into the equation."

Nick nodded. He did this as if his head had grown too heavy for his neck. "Maybe it is."

"Listen, Nick. I called you up front because if Bob's time-rip actually exists, we've got to be getting close to the place where we went through it. We're going to man the crow's nest together, you and I. You take the starboard side and right center; I'll take port and left center. If you see anything that looks like a time-rip, sing out."

Nick gazed at Brian with wide, innocent eyes. "Are we looking for a thingumabob-type time-rip, or do you think it'll be one of the more or less fuckadelic variety, mate?"

"Very funny." Brian felt a grin touch his lips in spite of himself. "I don't have the slightest idea what it's going to look like or even if we'll be able to see it at all. If we can't, we're going to be in a hell of a jam if it's drifted to one side, or if its altitude has changed. Finding a needle in a haystack would be child's play in comparison."

"What about radar?"

Brian pointed to the RCA/TL color radar monitor. "Nothing, as you can see. But that's not surprising. If the original crew had acquired the damned thing on radar, they never would have gone through it in the first place."

"They wouldn't have gone through it if they'd seen it, either," Nick pointed out gloomily.

"That's not necessarily true. They might have seen it too late to avoid it. Jetliners move fast, and airplane crews don't spend the entire flight searching the sky for bogies. They don't have to; that's what ground control is for. Thirty or thirty-five minutes into the flight, the crew's major outbound tasks are completed. The bird is up, it's out of L.A. airspace, the anti-collision honker is on and beeping every ninety seconds to show it's working. The INS is all programmed—that happens before the bird ever leaves the ground—and it is telling the autopilot just what to do. From the look of the cockpit, the pilot and co-pilot were on their coffee break. They could have been sitting here, facing each other, talking about the last movie they saw or how much they dropped at Hollywood Park. If there had been a flight attendant up front just before

The Event took place, there would at least have been one more set of eyes, but we know there wasn't. The male crew had their coffee and Danish; the flight attendants were getting ready to serve drinks to the passengers when it happened."

"That's an extremely detailed scenario," Nick said. "Are you trying to convince me or yourself?"

"At this point, I'll settle for convincing anyone at all."

Nick smiled and stepped to the starboard cockpit window. His eyes dropped involuntarily downward, toward the place where the ground belonged, and his smile first froze, then dropped off his face. His knees buckled, and he gripped the bulkhead with one hand to steady himself.

"Shit on toast," he said in a tiny dismayed voice.

"Not very nice, is it?"

Nick looked around at Brian. His eyes seemed to float in his pallid face. "All my life," he said, "I've thought of Australia when I heard people talk about the great bugger-all, but it's not. *That's* the great bugger-all, right down there."

Brian checked the INS and the charts again, quickly. He had made a small red circle on one of the charts; they were now on the verge of entering the airspace that circle represented. "Can you do what I asked? If you can't, say so. Pride is a luxury we can't—"

"Of course I can," Nick murmured. He had torn his eyes away from the huge black socket below the plane and was scanning the sky. "I only wish I knew what I was looking *for*."

"I think you'll know it when you see it," Brian said. He paused and then added, "*If* you see it."

12

Bob Jenkins sat with his arms folded tightly across his chest, as if he were cold. Part of him *was* cold, but this was not a physical coldness. The chill was coming out of his head.

Something was wrong.

He did not know what it was, but something was wrong. Something was out of place . . . or lost . . . or forgotten. Either a mistake had been made or was going to be made. The feeling nagged at him like some pain not quite localized enough to be identified. That sense of wrongness would almost crystallize into a thought . . . and then it would skitter away again like some small, not-quite-tame animal.

Something wrong.

Or out of place. Or lost.

Or forgotten.

Ahead of him, Albert and Bethany were spooning contentedly. Behind him, Rudy Warwick was sitting with his eyes closed and his lips moving. The beads of a rosary were clamped in one fist. Across the aisle, Laurel Stevenson sat beside Dinah, holding one of her hands and stroking it gently.

Wrong.

Bob eased up the shade beside his seat, peeked out, and slammed it down again. Looking at *that* would not aid rational thought but erase it. What lay below the plane was utter madness.

I must warn them. I have to. They are going forward on my hypothesis, but if my hypothesis is somehow mistaken—and dangerous—then I must warn them.

Warn them of what?

Again it almost came into the light of his focussed thoughts, then slipped away, becoming just a shadow among shadows . . . but one with shiny feral eyes.

He abruptly unbuckled his seatbelt and stood up.

Albert looked around. "Where are you going?"

"Cleveland," Bob said grumpily, and began to walk down the aisle toward the tail of the aircraft, still trying to track the source of that interior alarm bell.

13

Brian tore his eyes away from the sky—which was already showing signs of light again—long enough to take a quick glance first at the INS readout and then at the circle on his chart. They were approaching the far side of the circle now. If the time-rip was still here, they should see it soon. If they didn't, he supposed he would have to take over the controls and send them circling back for another pass at a slightly different altitude and on a slightly different heading. It would play hell on their fuel situation, which was already tight, but since the whole thing was probably hopeless anyway, it didn't matter very—

"Brian?" Nick's voice was unsteady. "Brian? I think I see something."

14

Bob Jenkins reached the rear of the plane, made an about-face, and started slowly back up the aisle again, passing row after row of empty seats. He looked at the objects that lay in them and on the floor in front of them as he passed: purses . . . pairs of eyeglasses . . . wristwatches . . . a pocket-watch . . . two worn, crescent-shaped pieces of metal that were probably heel-taps . . . dental fillings . . . wedding rings . . .

Something is wrong.

Yes? Was that really so, or was it only his overworked mind nagging fiercely over nothing? The mental equivalent of a tired muscle which will not stop twitching?

Leave it, he advised himself, but he couldn't.

If something really is amiss, why can't you see it? Didn't you tell the boy that deduction is your meat and drink? Haven't you written forty mystery novels, and weren't a dozen of those actually quite good? Didn't Newgate Callendar call The Sleeping Madonna *"a masterpiece of logic" when he—*

Bob Jenkins came to a dead stop, his eyes widening. They fixed on a portside seat near the front of the cabin. In it, the man with the black beard was out cold again, snoring lustily. Inside Bob's head, the shy animal at last began to creep fearfully into the light. Only it wasn't small, as he had thought. That had been his mistake. Sometimes you couldn't see things because they were too small, but sometimes you ignored things because they were too big, too obvious.

The Sleeping Madonna.

The sleeping man.

He opened his mouth and tried to scream, but no sound came out. His throat was locked. Terror sat on his chest like an ape. He tried again to scream and managed no more than a breathless squeak.

Sleeping madonna, sleeping man.

They, the survivors, had all been asleep.

Now, with the exception of the bearded man, none of them were asleep.

Bob opened his mouth once more, tried once more to scream, and once more nothing came out.

15

"Holy Christ in the morning," Brian whispered.

The time-rip lay about ninety miles ahead, off to the starboard side of the 767's nose by no more than seven or eight degrees. If it had drifted, it had not drifted much; Brian's guess was that the slight differential was the result of a minor navigational error.

It was a lozenge-shaped hole in reality, but not a black void. It cycled with a dim pink-purple light, like the aurora borealis. Brian could see the stars beyond it, but they were also rippling. A wide white ribbon of vapor was slowly streaming either into or out of the shape which hung in the sky. It looked like some strange, ethereal highway.

We can follow it right in, Brian thought excitedly. *It's better than an ILS beacon!*

"We're in business!" he said, laughed idiotically, and shook his clenched fists in the air.

"It must be two miles across," Nick whispered. "My God, Brian, how many other planes do you suppose went through?"

"I don't know," Brian said, "but I'll bet you my gun and dog that we're the only one with a shot at getting back."

He opened the intercom.

"Ladies and gentlemen, we've found what we were looking for." His voice crackled with triumph and relief. "I don't know exactly what happens next, or how, or why, but we have sighted what appears to be an extremely large trapdoor in the sky. I'm going to take us straight through the middle of it. We'll find out what's on the other side together. Right now I'd like you all to fasten your seatbelts and—"

That was when Bob Jenkins came pelting madly up the aisle, screaming at the top of his lungs. "*No! No! We'll all die if you go into it! Turn back! You've got to turn back!*"

Brian swung around in his seat and exchanged a puzzled look with Nick.

Nick unbuckled his belt and stood up. "That's Bob Jenkins," he said. "Sounds like he's worked himself up to a good set of nerves. Carry on, Brian. I'll handle him."

"Okay," Brian said. "Just keep him away from me. I'd hate to have him grab me at the wrong second and send us into the edge of that thing."

He turned off the autopilot and took control of the 767 himself. The floor tilted gently to the right as he banked toward the long, glowing slot ahead of them. It seemed to slide across the sky until it was centered in front of the 767's nose. Now he could hear a sound mixing with the drone of the jet engines—a deep throbbing noise, like a huge diesel idling. As they approached the river of vapor—it was flowing into the hole, he now saw, not out of it—he began to pick up flashes of color travelling within it: green, blue, violet, red, candy pink. *It's the first real color I've seen in this world,* he thought.

Behind him, Bob Jenkins sprinted through the first-class section, up the narrow aisle which led to the service area . . . and right into Nick's waiting arms.

"Easy, mate," Nick soothed. "Everything's going to be all right now."

"No!" Bob struggled wildly, but Nick held him as easily as a man might hold a struggling kitten. "No, you don't understand! He's got to turn back! He's got to turn back before it's too late!"

Nick pulled the writer away from the cockpit door and back into first class. "We'll just sit down here and belt up tight, shall we?" he said in that same soothing, chummy voice. "It may be a trifle bumpy."

To Brian, Nick's voice was only a faint blur of sound. As he entered the wide flow of vapor streaming into the time-rip, he felt a large and immensely powerful hand seize the plane, dragging it eagerly forward. He found himself thinking of the leak on the flight from Tokyo to L.A., and of how fast air rushed out of a hole in a pressurized environment.

It's as if this whole world—or what is left of it—is leaking through that hole, he thought, and then that queer and ominous phrase from his dream recurred again: SHOOTING STARS ONLY.

The rip lay dead ahead of the 767's nose now, growing rapidly. *We're going in,* he thought. *God help us, we're really going in.*

16

Bob continued to struggle as Nick pinned him in one of the first-class seats with one hand and worked to fasten his seatbelt with the other. Bob was a small, skinny man, surely no more than a hundred and forty pounds soaking wet, but panic had animated him and he was making it extremely hard for Nick.

"We're really going to be all right, matey," Nick said. He finally managed to click Bob's seatbelt shut. "We were when we came through, weren't we?"

"*We were all asleep when we came through, you damned fool!*" Bob shrieked into his face. "*Don't you understand?* WE WERE ASLEEP! *You've got to stop him!*"

Nick froze in the act of reaching for his own belt. What Bob was saying—what he had been trying to say all along—suddenly struck him like a dropped load of bricks.

"Oh dear God," he whispered. "Dear God, what were we thinking of?"

He leaped out of his seat and dashed for the cockpit.

"Brian, stop! Turn back! *Turn back!*"

17

Brian had been staring into the rip, nearly hypnotized, as they approached. There was no turbulence, but that sense of tremendous power, of air rushing into the hole like a mighty river, had increased. He looked down at his instruments and saw the 767's airspeed was increasing rapidly. Then Nick began to shout, and a moment later the Englishman was behind him, gripping his shoulders, staring at the rip as it swelled in front of the jet's nose, its play of deepening colors racing across his cheeks and brow, making him look like a man staring at a stained-glass window on a sunny day. The steady thrumming sound had become dark thunder.

"*Turn back, Brian, you have to turn back!*"

Did Nick have a reason for what he was saying, or had Bob's panic been infectious? There was no time to make a decision on any rational basis; only a split-second to consult the silent tickings of instinct.

Brain Engle grabbed the steering yoke and hauled it hard over to port.

18

Nick was thrown across the cockpit and into a bulkhead; there was a sickening crack as his arm broke. In the main cabin, the luggage which had fallen from the overhead compartments when Brian swerved onto the runway at BIA now flew once more, striking the curved walls and thudding off the windows in a vicious hail. The man with the black beard was thrown out of his seat like a Cabbage Patch Kid and had time to utter one bleary squawk before his head collided with the arm of a seat and he fell into the aisle in an untidy tangle of limbs. Bethany screamed and Albert hugged her tight against him. Two rows behind, Rudy Warwick closed his eyes tighter, clutched his rosary harder, and prayed faster as his seat tilted away beneath him.

Now there was turbulence; Flight 29 became a surfboard with wings, rocking and twisting and thumping through the unsteady air. Brian's hands were momentarily thrown off the yoke and then he grabbed it again. At the same time he opened the throttle all the way to the stop and the plane's turbos responded with a deep snarl of power rarely heard outside of the airline's diagnostic hangars. The turbulence increased; the plane slammed viciously up and down, and from somewhere came the deadly shriek of overstressed metal.

In first class, Bob Jenkins clutched at the arms of his seat, numbly grateful that the Englishman had managed to belt him in. He felt as if he had been strapped to some madman's jet-powered pogo stick. The plane took another great leap, rocked up almost to the vertical on its portside wing, and his false teeth shot from his mouth.

Are we going in? Dear Jesus, are we?

He didn't know. He only knew that the world was a thumping, bucking nightmare . . . but he was still in it.

For the time being, at least, he was still in it.

19

The turbulence continued to increase as Brian drove the 767 across the wide stream of vapor feeding into the rip. Ahead of him, the hole continued to swell in front of the plane's nose even as it continued sliding off to starboard. Then, after one particularly vicious jolt, they came out of the rapids and into smoother air. The time-rip disappeared to starboard. They had missed it . . . by how little Brian did not like to think.

He continued to bank the plane, but at a less drastic angle. "Nick!" he shouted without turning around. "Nick, are you all right?"

Nick got slowly to his feet, holding his right arm against his belly with his left hand. His face was very white and his teeth were set in a grimace of pain. Small trickles of blood ran from his nostrils. "I've been better, mate. Broke my arm, I think. Not the first time for this poor old fellow, either. We missed it, didn't we?"

"We missed it," Brian agreed. He continued to bring the plane back in a big, slow circle. "And in just a minute you're going to tell me *why* we missed it, when we came all this way to find it. And it better be good, broken arm or no broken arm."

He reached for the intercom toggle.

20

Laurel opened her eyes as Brian began to speak and discovered that Dinah's head was in her lap. She stroked her hair gently and then readjusted her position on the stretcher.

"This is Captain Engle, folks. I'm sorry about that. It was pretty damned hairy, but we're okay; I've got a green board. Let me repeat that we've found what we were looking for, but—"

He clicked off suddenly.

The others waited. Bethany Simms was sobbing against Albert's chest. Behind them, Rudy was still saying his rosary.

21

Brian had broken his transmission when he realized that Bob Jenkins was standing beside him. The writer was shaking, there was a wet patch on his slacks, his mouth had an odd, sunken look Brian hadn't noticed before . . . but he seemed in charge of himself. Behind him, Nick sat heavily in the co-pilot's chair, wincing as he did so and still cradling his arm. It had begun to swell.

"What the hell is this all about?" Brian asked Bob sternly. "A little more turbulence and this bitch would have broken into about ten thousand pieces."

"Can I talk through that thing?" Bob asked, pointing to the switch marked INTERCOM.

"Yes, but—"

"Then let me do it."

Brian started to protest, then thought better of it. He flicked the switch. "Go ahead; you're on." Then he repeated: "And it better be good."

"Listen to me, all of you!" Bob shouted.

From behind them came a protesting whine of feedback. "We—"

"Just talk in your normal tone of voice," Brian said. "You'll blow their goddam eardrums out."

Bob made a visible effort to compose himself, then went on in a lower tone of voice. "We had to turn back, and we did. The captain has made it clear to me that we only just managed to do it. We have been extremely lucky . . . and extremely stupid, as well. We forgot the most elementary thing, you see, although it was right in front of us all the time. When we went through the time-rip in the first place, *everyone on the plane who was awake disappeared.*"

Brian jerked in his seat. He felt as if someone had slugged him. Ahead of the 767's nose, about thirty miles distant, the faintly glowing lozenge shape had appeared again in the sky, looking like some gigantic semi-precious stone. It seemed to mock him.

"*We* are all awake," Bob said. (In the main cabin, Albert looked at the man with the black beard lying out cold in the aisle and thought, *With one exception.*) "Logic suggests that if we try to go through that way, *we* will disappear." He thought about this and then said, "That is all."

Brian flicked the intercom link closed without thinking about it. Behind him, Nick voiced a painful, incredulous laugh.

"That is all? That is bloody *all*? What do we *do* about it?"

Brian looked at him and didn't answer. Neither did Bob Jenkins.

22

Bethany raised her head and looked into Albert's strained, bewildered face. "We have to go to sleep? How do we do *that*? I never felt less like sleeping in my whole *life*!"

"I don't know." He looked hopefully across the aisle at Laurel. She was already shaking her head. She wished she *could* go to sleep, just go to sleep and make this whole crazy nightmare *gone*—but, like Bethany, she had never felt less like it in her entire life.

23

Bob took a step forward and gazed out through the cockpit window in silent fascination. After a long moment he said in a soft, awed voice: "So that's what it looks like."

A line from some rock-and-roll song popped into Brian's head: *You can look but you better not touch.* He glanced down at the LED fuel indicators. What he saw there didn't ease his mind any, and he raised his eyes helplessly to Nick's. Like the others, he had never felt so wide awake in his life.

"I don't know what we do now," he said, "but if we're going to try that hole, it has to be soon. The fuel we've got will carry us for an hour, maybe a little more. After that, forget it. Got any ideas?"

Nick lowered his head, still cradling his swelling arm. After a moment or two he looked up again. "Yes," he said. "As a matter of fact, I do. People who fly rarely stick their prescription medicine in their checked baggage—they like to have it with them in case their luggage ends up on the other side of the world and takes a few days to get back to them. If we go through the hand-carry bags, we're sure to find scads of sedatives. We won't even have to take the bags out of the bins. Judging from the sounds, most of them are already lying on the floor . . . what? What's the matter with it?"

This last was directed at Bob Jenkins, who had begun shaking his head as soon as the phrase "prescription medicines" popped out of Nick's mouth.

"Do you know anything about prescription sedatives?" he asked Nick.

"A little," Nick said, but he sounded defensive. "A little, yeah."

"Well, I know a lot," Bob said dryly. "I've researched them exhaustively—from All-Nite to Xanax. Murder by sleeping potion has always been a great favorite in my field, you understand. Even if you happened to find one of the more potent medications in the very first bag you checked—unlikely in itself—you couldn't administer a safe dose which would act quickly enough."

"Why bloody *not?*"

"Because it would take at least forty minutes for the stuff to work . . . and I strongly doubt it *would* work on everyone. The natural reaction of minds under stress to such medication is to fight—to try to refuse it. There is absolutely no way to combat such a reaction, Nick . . . you might as well try to legislate your own heartbeat. What you'd do, always supposing you found a supply of medication large enough to allow it, would be to administer a series of lethal overdoses and turn the plane into Jonestown. We might all come through, but we'd be dead."

"Forty minutes," Nick said. "Christ. Are you sure? Are you absolutely *sure?*"

"Yes," Bob said unflinchingly.

Brian looked out at the glowing lozenge shape in the sky. He had put Flight 29 into a circling pattern and the rip was on the verge of disappearing again. It would be back shortly . . . but they would be no closer to it.

"I can't believe it," Nick said heavily. "To go through the things we've gone through . . . to have taken off successfully and come all this way . . . to have actually *found* the bloody thing . . . and then we find out we can't go through it and back to our own time just because we can't go to *sleep?*"

"We don't have forty minutes, anyway," Brian said quietly. "If we waited that long, this plane would crash sixty miles east of the airport."

"Surely there are other fields—"

"There are, but none big enough to handle an airplane of this size."

"If we went through and then turned back east again?"

"Vegas. But Vegas is going to be out of reach in . . ." Brian glanced at his instruments. ". . . less than eight minutes. I think it has to be LAX. I'll need at least thirty-five minutes to get there. That's cutting it extremely fine even if they clear everything out of our way and vector us straight in. That gives us . . ." He looked at the chronometer again. ". . . twenty minutes at most to figure this thing out and get through the hole."

Bob was looking thoughtfully at Nick. "What about you?" he asked.

"What do you mean, what about me?"

"I think you're a soldier . . . but I don't think you're an ordinary one. Might you be SAS, perhaps?"

Nick's face tightened. "And if I was that or something like it, mate?"

"Maybe *you* could put us to sleep," Bob said. "Don't they teach you Special Forces men tricks like that?"

Brian's mind flashed back to Nick's first confrontation with Craig Toomy. *Have you ever watched* Star Trek? he had asked Craig. *Marvellous American program . . . And if you don't shut your gob at once, you bloody idiot, I'll be happy to demonstrate Mr. Spock's famous Vulcan sleeper-hold for you.*

"What about it, Nick?" he said softly. "If we ever needed the famous Vulcan sleeper-hold, it's now."

Nick looked unbelievingly from Bob to Brian and then back to Bob again. "Please don't make me laugh, gents—it makes my arm hurt worse."

"What does that mean?" Bob asked.

"I've got my sedatives all wrong, have I? Well, let me tell you both that you've got it all wrong about me. I am *not* James Bond. There never *was* a James Bond in the real world. I suppose I might be able to kill you with a neck-chop, Bob, but I'd more likely just leave you paralyzed for life. Might not even knock you out. And then there's this." Nick held up his rapidly swelling right arm with a little wince. "My smart hand happens to be attached to my recently re-broken arm. I could perhaps defend myself with my left hand— against an unschooled opponent—but the kind of thing you're talking about? No. No way."

"You're all forgetting the most important thing of all," a new voice said.

They turned. Laurel Stevenson, white and haggard, was standing in the cockpit door. She had folded her arms across her breasts as if she was cold and was cupping her elbows in her hands.

"If we're all knocked out, who is going to fly the plane?" she asked. "Who is going to fly the plane into L.A.?"

The three men gaped at her wordlessly. Behind them, unnoticed, the large semi-precious stone that was the time-rip glided into view again.

"We're fucked," Nick said quietly. "Do you know that? We are absolutely dead-out fucked." He laughed a little, then winced as his stomach jogged his broken arm.

"Maybe not," Albert said. He and Bethany had appeared behind Laurel; Albert had his arm around the girl's waist. His hair was plastered against his forehead in sweaty ringlets, but his dark eyes were clear and intent. They were focussed on Brian. "I think *you* can put us to sleep," he said, "and I think *you* can land us."

"What are you talking about?" Brian asked roughly.

Albert replied: "Pressure. I'm talking about pressure."

24

Brian's dream recurred to him then, recurred with such terrible force that he might have been reliving it: Anne with her hand plastered over the crack in the body of the plane, the crack with the words SHOOTING STARS ONLY printed over it in red.

Pressure.

See, darling? It's all taken care of.

"What does he mean, Brian?" Nick asked. "I can see he's got *something*—your face says so. What is it?"

Brian ignored him. He looked steadily at the seventeen-year-old music student who might just have thought of a way out of the box they were in.

"What about after?" he asked. "What about after we come through? How do I wake up again so I can land the plane?"

"Will somebody please explain this?" Laurel pleaded. She had gone to Nick, who put his good arm around her waist.

"Albert is suggesting that I use this"—Brian tapped a rheostat on the control board, a rheostat marked CABIN PRESSURE—"to knock us all out cold."

"Can you do that, mate? Can you really do that?"

"Yes," Brian said. "I've known pilots—charter pilots . . . who *have* done it, when passengers who've had too much to drink started cutting up and endangering either themselves or the crew. Knocking out a drunk by lowering the air pressure isn't that difficult. To knock out everyone, all I have to do is lower it some more . . . to half sea-level pressure, say. It's like ascending to a height of two miles without an oxygen mask. Boom! You're out cold."

"If you can really do that, why hasn't it been used on terrorists?" Bob asked.

"Because there *are* oxygen masks, right?" Albert asked.

"Yes," Brian said. "The cabin crew demonstrates them at the start of every commercial jet-flight—put the gold cup over your mouth and nose and breathe normally, right? They drop automatically when cabin pressure falls below twelve psi. If a hostage pilot tried to knock out a terrorist by lowering the air pressure, all the terrorist would have to do is grab a mask, put it on, and start shooting. On smaller jets, like the Lear, that isn't the case. If the cabin loses pressure, the passenger has to open the overhead compartment himself."

Nick looked at the chronometer. Their window was now only fourteen minutes wide.

"I think we better stop talking about it and just do it," he said. "Time is getting very short."

"Not yet," Brian said, and looked at Albert again. "I can bring us back in line with the rip, Albert, and start decreasing pressure as we head toward it. I can control the cabin pressure pretty accurately, and I'm pretty sure I can put us all out before we go through. But that leaves Laurel's question: who flies the airplane if we're all knocked out?"

Albert opened his mouth; closed it again and shook his head.

Bob Jenkins spoke up then. His voice was dry and toneless, the voice of a judge pronouncing doom. "I think *you* can fly us home, Brian. But someone else will have to die in order for you to do it."

"Explain," Nick said crisply.

Bob did so. It didn't take long. By the time he finished, Rudy Warwick had joined the little group standing in the cockpit door.

"Would it work, Brian?" Nick asked.

"Yes," Brian said absently. "No reason why not." He looked at the chronometer again. Eleven minutes now. Eleven minutes to get across to the other side of the rip. It would take almost that long to line the plane up, program the autopilot, and move them along the forty-mile approach. "But who's going to do it? Do the rest of you draw straws, or what?"

"No need for that," Nick said. He spoke lightly, almost casually. "I'll do it."

"No!" Laurel said. Her eyes were very wide and very dark. "Why you? Why does it have to be you?"

"Shut up!" Bethany hissed at her. "If he wants to, let him!"

Albert glanced unhappily at Bethany, at Laurel, and then back at Nick. A voice—not a very strong one—was whispering that *he* should have volunteered, that this was a job for a tough Alamo survivor like The Arizona Jew. But most of him was only aware that he loved life very much . . . and did not want it to end just yet. So he opened his mouth and then closed it again without speaking.

"Why you?" Laurel asked again, urgently. "Why *shouldn't* we draw straws? Why not Bob? Or Rudy? Why not me?"

Nick took her arm. "Come with me a moment," he said.

"Nick, there's not much time," Brian said. He tried to keep his tone of voice even, but he could hear desperation—perhaps even panic—bleeding through.

"I know. Start doing the things you have to do."

Nick drew Laurel through the door.

25

She resisted for a moment, then came along. He stopped in the small galley alcove and faced her. In that moment, with his face less than four inches from hers, she realized a dismal truth—he was the man she had been hoping to find in Boston. He had been on the plane all the time. There was nothing at all romantic about this discovery; it was horrible.

"I think we might have had something, you and me," he said. "Do you think I could be right about that? If you do, say so— there's no time to dance. Absolutely none."

"Yes," she said. Her voice was dry, uneven. "I think that's right."

"But we don't know. We *can't* know. It all comes back to time, doesn't it? Time . . . and sleep . . . and not knowing. But I have to be the one, Laurel. I have tried to keep some reasonable account of myself, and all my books are deeply in the red. This is my chance to balance them, and I mean to take it."

"I don't understand what you mea—"

"No—but I do." He spoke fast, almost rapping his words. Now he reached out and took her forearm and drew her even closer to him. "You were on an adventure of some sort, weren't you, Laurel?"

"I don't know what you're—"

He gave her a brisk shake. "I told you—there's no time to dance! *Were* you on an adventure?"

"I . . . yes."

"Nick!" Brian called from the cockpit.

Nick looked rapidly in that direction. "Coming!" he shouted, and then looked back at Laurel. "I'm going to send you on another one. If you get out of this, that is, and if you agree to go."

She only looked at him, her lips trembling. She had no idea of what to say. Her mind was tumbling helplessly. His grip on her arm was very tight, but she would not be aware of that until later, when she saw the bruises left by his fingers; at that moment, the grip of his eyes was much stronger.

"Listen. Listen carefully." He paused and then spoke with peculiar, measured emphasis: "I was going to quit it. I'd made up my mind."

"Quit what?" she asked in a small, quivery voice.

Nick shook his head impatiently. "Doesn't matter. What matters is whether or not you believe me. Do you?"

"Yes," she said. "I don't know what you're talking about, but I believe you mean it."

"*Nick!*" Brian warned from the cockpit. "*We're heading toward it!*"

He shot a glance toward the cockpit again, his eyes narrow and gleaming. "Coming just now!" he called. When he looked at her again, Laurel thought she had never in her life been the focus of such ferocious, focussed intensity. "My father lives in the village of Fluting, south of London," he said. "Ask for him in any shop along the High Street. Mr. Hopewell. The older ones still call him the gaffer. Go to him and tell him I'd made up my mind to quit it. You'll need to be persistent; he tends to turn away and curse loudly when he hears my name. The old I-have-no-son bit. Can you be persistent?"

"Yes."

He nodded and smiled grimly. "Good! Repeat what I've told you, and tell him you believed me. Tell him I tried my best to atone for the day behind the church in Belfast."

"In Belfast."

"Right. And if you can't get him to listen any other way, tell him he *must* listen. Because of the daisies. The time I brought the daisies. Can you remember that, as well?"

"Because once you brought him daisies."

Nick seemed to almost laugh—but she had never seen a face filled with such sadness and bitterness. "No—not to him, but it'll do. That's your adventure. Will you do it?"

"Yes . . . but . . ."

"Good. Laurel, thank you." He put his left hand against the nape of her neck, pulled her face to his, and kissed her. His mouth was cold, and she tasted fear on his breath.

A moment later he was gone.

26

"Are we going to feel like we're—you know, choking?" Bethany asked. "Suffocating?"

"No," Brian said. He had gotten up to see if Nick was coming; now, as Nick reappeared with a very shaken Laurel Stevenson behind him, Brian dropped back into his seat. "You'll feel a little giddy . . . swimmy in the head . . . then, nothing." He glanced at Nick. "Until we all wake up."

"Right!" Nick said cheerily. "And who knows? I may still be right here. Bad pennies have a way of turning up, you know. Don't they, Brian?"

"Anything's possible, I guess," Brian said. He pushed the throttle forward slightly. The sky was growing bright again. The rip lay dead ahead. "Sit down, folks. Nick, right up here beside me. I'm going to show you what to do . . . and when to do it."

"One second, please," Laurel said. She had regained some of her color and self-possession. She stood on tiptoe and planted a kiss on Nick's mouth.

"Thank you," Nick said gravely.

"You were going to quit it. You'd made up your mind. And if

he won't listen, I'm to remind him of the day you brought the daisies. Have I got it right?"

He grinned. "Letter-perfect, my love. Letter-perfect." He encircled her with his left arm and kissed her again, long and hard. When he let her go, there was a gentle, thoughtful smile on his mouth. "That's the one to go on," he said. "Right enough."

27

Three minutes later, Brian opened the intercom. "I'm starting to decrease pressure now. Check your belts, everyone."

They did so. Albert waited tensely for some sound—the hiss of escaping air, perhaps—but there was only the steady, droning mumble of the jet engines. He felt more wide awake than ever.

"Albert?" Bethany said in a small, scared voice. "Would you hold me, please?"

"Yes," Albert said. "If you'll hold me."

Behind them, Rudy Warwick was telling his rosary again. Across the aisle, Laurel Stevenson gripped the arms of her seat. She could still feel the warm print of Nick Hopewell's lips on her mouth. She raised her head, looked at the overhead compartment, and began to take deep, slow breaths. She was waiting for the masks to fall . . . and ninety seconds or so later, they did.

Remember about the day in Belfast, too, she thought. *Behind the church. An act of atonement, he said. An act . . .*

In the middle of that thought, her mind drifted away.

28

"You know . . . what to do?" Brian asked again. He spoke in a dreamy, furry voice. Ahead of them, the time-rip was once more swelling in the cockpit windows, spreading across the sky. It was now lit with dawn, and a fantastic new array of colors coiled, swam, and then streamed away into its queer depths.

"I know," Nick said. He was standing beside Brian and his words were muffled by the oxygen mask he wore. Above the rubber seal, his eyes were calm and clear. "No fear, Brian. All's safe as houses. Off to sleep you go. Sweet dreams, and all that."

Brian was fading now. He could feel himself going . . . and yet he hung on, staring at the vast fault in the fabric of reality. It seemed to be swelling toward the cockpit windows, reaching for the plane. *It's so beautiful,* he thought. *God, it's so* beautiful*!*

He felt that invisible hand seize the plane and draw it forward again. No turning back this time.

"Nick," he said. It now took a tremendous effort to speak; he felt as if his mouth was a hundred miles away from his brain. He held his hand up. It seemed to stretch away from him at the end of a long taffy arm.

"Go to sleep," Nick said, taking his hand. "Don't fight it, unless you want to go with me. It won't be long now."

"I just wanted to say . . . thank you."

Nick smiled and gave Brian's hand a squeeze. "You're welcome, mate. It's been a flight to remember. Even without the movie and the free mimosas."

Brian looked back into the rip. A river of gorgeous colors flowed into it now. They spiralled . . . mixed . . . and seemed to form words before his dazed, wondering eyes:

SHOOTING STARS ONLY

"Is that . . . what we are?" he asked curiously, and now his voice came to him from some distant universe.

The darkness swallowed him.

29

Nick was alone now; the only person awake on Flight 29 was a man who had once gunned down three boys behind a church in Belfast, three boys who had been chucking potatoes painted dark gray to look like grenades. Why had they done such a thing? Had it been some mad sort of dare? He had never found out.

He was not afraid, but an intense loneliness filled him. The feeling wasn't a new one. This was not the first watch he had stood alone, with the lives of others in his hands.

Ahead of him, the rip neared. He dropped his hand to the rheostat which controlled the cabin pressure.

It's gorgeous, he thought. It seemed to him that the colors that now blazed out of the rip were the antithesis of everything which they had experienced in the last few hours; he was looking into a crucible of new life and new motion.

Why shouldn't it be beautiful? This is the place where life—all life, maybe—begins. The place where life is freshly minted every second of every day; the cradle of creation and the wellspring of time. No langoliers allowed beyond this point.

Colors ran across his cheeks and brows in a fountain-spray of hues: jungle green was overthrown by lava orange; lava orange was replaced by yellow-white tropical sunshine; sunshine was supplanted by the chilly blue of Northern oceans. The roar of the jet engines seemed muted and distant; he looked down and was not surprised to see that Brian Engle's slumped, sleeping form was being consumed by color, his form and features overthrown in an ever-changing kaleidoscope of brightness. He had become a fabulous ghost.

Nor was Nick surprised to see that his own hands and arms were as colorless as clay. *Brian's not the ghost; I am.*

The rip loomed.

Now the sound of the jets was lost entirely in a new sound; the 767 seemed to be rushing through a windtunnel filled with feathers. Suddenly, directly ahead of the airliner's nose, a vast nova of light exploded like a heavenly firework; in it, Nick Hopewell saw colors no man had ever imagined. It did not just fill the time-rip; it filled his mind, his nerves, his muscles, his very bones in a gigantic, coruscating fireflash.

"*Oh my God, SO BEAUTIFUL!*" he cried, and as Flight 29 plunged into the rip, he twisted the cabin-pressure rheostat back up to full.

A split-second later the fillings from Nick's teeth pattered onto the cockpit floor. There was a small thump as the Teflon disc which had been in his knee—souvenir of a conflict marginally more honorable than the one in Northern Ireland—joined them. That was all.

Nick Hopewell had ceased to exist.

30

The first things Brian was aware of were that his shirt was wet and his headache had returned.

He sat up slowly in his seat, wincing at the bolt of pain in his head, and tried to remember who he was, where he was, and why he felt such a vast and urgent need to wake up quickly. What had he been doing that was so important?

The leak, his mind whispered. *There's a leak in the main cabin, and if it isn't stabilized, there's going to be big tr—*

No, that wasn't right. The leak *had* been stabilized—or had in some mysterious way stabilized itself—and he had landed Flight 7 safely at LAX. Then the man in the green blazer had come, and—

It's Anne's funeral! My God, I've overslept!

His eyes flew open, but he was in neither a motel room nor the spare bedroom at Anne's brother's house in Revere. He was looking through a cockpit window at a sky filled with stars.

Suddenly it came back to him . . . everything.

He sat up all the way, too quickly. His head screamed a sickly hungover protest. Blood flew from his nose and splattered on the center control console. He looked down and saw the front of his shirt was soaked with it. There had been a leak, all right. In *him.*

Of course, he thought. *Depressurization often does that. I should have warned the passengers . . . How many passengers do I have left, by the way?*

He couldn't remember. His head was filled with fog.

He looked at his fuel indicators, saw that their situation was rapidly approaching the critical point, and then checked the INS. They were exactly where they should be, descending rapidly toward L.A., and at any moment they might wander into someone else's airspace while the someone else was still there.

Someone else had been sharing *his* airspace just before he passed out . . . who?

He fumbled, and it came. Nick, of course. Nick Hopewell. Nick was gone. He hadn't been such a bad penny after all, it seemed. But he must have done his job, or Brian wouldn't be awake now.

He got on the radio, fast.

"LAX ground control, this is American Pride Flight—" He stopped. What flight *were* they? He couldn't remember. The fog was in the way.

"Twenty-nine, aren't we?" a dazed, unsteady voice said from behind him.

"Thank you, Laurel." Brian didn't turn around. "Now go back and belt up. I may have to make this plane do some tricks."

He spoke into his mike again.

"American Pride Flight 29, repeat, two-niner. Mayday, ground control, I am declaring an emergency here. Please clear everything in front of me, I am coming in on heading 85 and I have no fuel. Get a foam truck out and—"

"Oh, quit it," Laurel said dully from behind him. "Just quit it."

Brian wheeled around then, ignoring the fresh bolt of pain through his head and the fresh spray of blood which flew from his nose. "Sit *down,* goddammit!" he snarled. "We're coming in un-announced into heavy traffic. If you don't want to break your neck—"

"There's no heavy traffic down there," Laurel said in the same dull voice. "No heavy traffic, no foam trucks. Nick died for nothing, and I'll never get a chance to deliver his message. Look for yourself."

Brian did. And, although they were now over the outlying sub-urbs of Los Angeles, he saw nothing but darkness.

There was no one down there, it seemed.

No one at all.

Behind him, Laurel Stevenson burst into harsh, raging sobs of terror and frustration.

31

A long white passenger jet cruised slowly above the ground sixteen miles east of Los Angeles International Airport. 767 was printed on its tail in large, proud numerals. Along the fuselage, the words AMERICAN PRIDE were written in letters which had been raked backward to indicate speed. On both sides of the nose was a large red eagle, its wings spangled with blue stars. Like the airliner it decorated, the eagle appeared to be coming in for a landing.

The plane printed no shadow on the deserted grid of streets as it passed above them; dawn was still an hour away. Below it, no car moved, no streetlight glowed. Below it, all was silent and move-less. Ahead of it, no runway lights gleamed.

The plane's belly slid open. The undercarriage dropped down and spread out. The landing gear locked in place.

American Pride Flight 29 slipped down the chute toward L.A. It banked slightly to the right as it came; Brian was now able to correct his course visually, and he did so. They passed over a cluster of airport motels, and for a moment Brian could see the monument that stood near the center of the terminal complex, a graceful tripod with curved legs and a restaurant in its center. They passed over a short strip of dead grass and then concrete runway was unrolling thirty feet below the plane.

There was no time to baby the 767 in this time; Brian's fuel indicators read zeros across and the bird was about to turn into a bitch. He brought it in hard, like a sled filled with bricks. There was a thud that rattled his teeth and started his nose bleeding again. His chest harness locked. Laurel, who was in the co-pilot's seat, cried out.

Then he had the flaps up and was applying reverse thrusters at full. The plane began to slow. They were doing a little over a hundred miles an hour when two of the thrusters cut out and the red ENGINE SHUTDOWN lights flashed on. He grabbed for the intercom switch.

"Hang on! We're going in hard! Hang on!"

Thrusters two and four kept running a few moments longer, and then they were gone, too. Flight 29 rushed down the runway in ghastly silence, with only the flaps to slow her now. Brian watched helplessly as the concrete ran away beneath the plane and the criss-cross tangle of taxiways loomed. And there, dead ahead, sat the carcass of a Pacific Airways commuter jet.

The 767 was still doing at least sixty-five. Brian horsed it to the right, leaning into the dead steering yoke with every ounce of his strength. The plane responded soupily, and he skated by the parked jet with only six feet to spare. Its windows flashed past like a row of blind eyes.

Then they were rolling toward the United terminal, where at least a dozen planes were parked at extended jetways like nursing infants. The 767's speed was down to just over thirty now.

"*Brace yourselves!*" Brian shouted into the intercom, momentarily forgetting that his own plane was now as dead as the rest of them and the intercom was useless. "*Brace yourselves for a collision! Bra—*"

American Pride 29 crashed into Gate 29 of the United Airlines terminal at roughly twenty-nine miles an hour. There was a loud, hollow bang followed by the sound of crumpling metal and breaking glass. Brian was thrown into his harness again, then snapped back into his seat. He sat there for a moment, stiff, waiting for the explosion . . . and then remembered there was nothing left in the tanks to explode.

He flicked all the switches on the control panel off—the panel was dead, but the habit ran deep—and then turned to check on Laurel. She looked at him with dull, apathetic eyes.

"That was about as close as I'd ever want to cut it," Brian said unsteadily.

"You should have let us crash. Everything we tried . . . Dinah . . . Nick . . . all for nothing. It's just the same here. Just the same."

Brian unbuckled his harness and got shakily to his feet. He took his handkerchief out of his back pocket and handed it to her. "Wipe your nose. It's bleeding."

She took the handkerchief and then only looked at it, as if she had never seen one before in her life.

Brian passed her and plodded slowly into the main cabin. He stood in the doorway, counting noses. His passengers—those few still remaining, that was—seemed all right. Bethany's head was pressed against Albert's chest and she was sobbing hard. Rudy Warwick unbuckled his seatbelt, got up, rapped his head on the overhead bin, and sat down again. He looked at Brian with dazed, uncomprehending eyes. Brian found himself wondering if Rudy was still hungry. He guessed not.

"Let's get off the plane," Brian said.

Bethany raised her head. "When do they come?" she asked him hysterically. "How long will it be before they come this time? Can anyone hear them yet?"

Fresh pain stroked Brian's head and he rocked on his feet, suddenly quite sure he was going to faint.

A steadying arm slipped around his waist and he looked around, surprised. It was Laurel.

"Captain Engle's right," she said quietly. "Let's get off the plane. Maybe it's not as bad as it looks."

Bethany uttered a hysterical bark of laughter. "How bad *can* it look?" she demanded. "Just how bad *can* it—"

"Something's different," Albert said suddenly. He was looking out the window. "Something's changed. I can't tell what it is . . . but it's not the same." He looked first at Bethany, then at Brian and Laurel. "It's just not the same."

Brian bent down next to Bob Jenkins and looked out the window.

He could see nothing very different from BIA—there were more planes, of course, but they were just as deserted, just as dead—yet he felt that Albert might be onto something, just the same. It was *feeling* more than seeing. Some essential difference which he could not quite grasp. It danced just beyond his reach, as the name of his ex-wife's perfume had done.

It's L'Envoi, darling. It's what I've always worn, don't you remember? Don't you remember?

"Come on," he said. "This time we use the cockpit exit."

32

Brian opened the trapdoor which lay below the jut of the instrument panel and tried to remember why he hadn't used it to offload his passengers at Bangor International; it was a hell of a lot easier to use than the slide. There didn't seem to *be* a why. He just hadn't thought of it, probably because he was trained to think of the escape slide before anything else in an emergency.

He dropped down into the forward-hold area, ducked below a cluster of electrical cables, and undogged the hatch in the floor of the 767's nose. Albert joined him and helped Bethany down. Brian helped Laurel, and then he and Albert helped Rudy, who moved as if his bones had turned to glass. Rudy was still clutching his rosary tight in one hand. The space below the cockpit was now very cramped, and Bob Jenkins waited for them above, propped on his hands and peering down at them through the trapdoor.

Brian pulled the ladder out of its storage clips, secured it in place, and then, one by one, they descended to the tarmac, Brian first, Bob last.

As Brian's feet touched down, he felt a mad urge to place his hand over his heart and cry out: *I claim this land of rancid milk and sour honey for the survivors of Flight 29 . . . at least until the langoliers arrive!*

He said nothing. He only stood there with the others below the loom of the jetliner's nose, feeling a light breeze against one cheek and looking around. In the distance he heard a sound. It was not the chewing, crunching sound of which they had gradually become aware in Bangor—nothing like it—but he couldn't decide exactly what it *did* sound like.

"What's that?" Bethany asked. "What's that humming? It sounds like electricity."

"No, it doesn't," Bob said thoughtfully. "It sounds like . . ." He shook his head.

"It doesn't sound like anything I've ever heard before," Brian said, but he wasn't sure if that was true. Again he was haunted by the sense that something he knew or should know was dancing just beyond his mental grasp.

"It's them, isn't it?" Bethany asked half-hysterically. "It's them, coming. It's the langoliers Dinah told us about."

"I don't think so. It doesn't sound the same at all." But he felt the fear begin in his belly just the same.

"Now what?" Rudy asked. His voice was as harsh as a crow's. "Do we start all over again?"

"Well, we won't need the conveyor belt, and that's a start," Brian said. "The jetway service door is open." He stepped out from beneath the 767's nose and pointed. The force of their arrival at Gate 29 had knocked the rolling ladder away from the door, but it would be easy enough to slip it back into position. "Come on."

They walked toward the ladder.

"Albert?" Brian said. "Help me with the lad—"

"Wait," Bob said.

Brian turned his head and saw Bob looking around with cautious wonder. And the expression in his previously dazed eyes . . . was that hope?

"What? What is it, Bob? What do you see?"

"Just another deserted airport. It's what I feel." He raised a hand to his cheek . . . then simply held it out in the air, like a man trying to flag a ride.

Brian started to ask him what he meant, and realized that he knew. Hadn't he noticed it himself while they had been standing under the liner's nose? Noticed it and then dismissed it?

There was a breeze blowing against his face. Not much of a breeze, hardly more than a puff, but it was a breeze. The air was in motion.

"Holy crow," Albert said. He popped a finger into his mouth, wetting it, and held it up. An unbelieving grin touched his face.

"That isn't all, either," Laurel said. "Listen!"

She dashed from where they were standing down toward the 767's wing. Then she ran back to them again, her hair streaming out behind her. The high heels she was wearing clicked crisply on the concrete.

"Did you hear it?" she asked them. "Did you *hear* it?"

They had heard. The flat, muffled quality was gone. Now, just listening to Laurel speak, Brian realized that in Bangor they had all sounded as if they had been talking with their heads poked inside bells which had been cast from some dulling metal—brass, or maybe lead.

Bethany raised her hands and rapidly clapped out the backbeat of the old Routers instrumental, "Let's Go." Each clap was as clean and clear as the pop of a track-starter's pistol. A delighted grin broke over her face.

"What does it m—" Rudy began.

"*The plane!*" Albert shouted in a high-pitched, gleeful voice, and for a moment Brian was absurdly reminded of the little guy on that old TV show, *Fantasy Island.* He almost laughed out loud. "I know what's different! Look at the plane! *Now it's the same as all the others!*"

They turned and looked. No one said anything for a long moment; perhaps no one was capable of speech. The Delta 727 standing next to the American Pride jetliner in Bangor had looked dull and dingy, somehow less real than the 767. Now all the aircraft—Flight 29 and the United planes lined up along the extended jetways behind it—looked equally bright, equally new. Even in the dark, their paintwork and trademark logos appeared to gleam.

"What does it mean?" Rudy asked, speaking to Bob. "What does it mean? If things have really gone back to normal, where's the electricity? Where are the *people?*"

"And what's that noise?" Albert put in.

The sound was already closer, already clearer. It was a humming sound, as Bethany had said, but there was nothing electrical about it. It sounded like wind blowing across an open pipe, or an inhuman choir which was uttering the same open-throated syllable in unison: *aaaaaaa . . .*

Bob shook his head. "I don't know," he said, turning away. "Let's push that ladder back into position and go in—"

Laurel grabbed his shoulder.

"You know something!" she said. Her voice was strained and tense. "I can see that you do. Let the rest of us in on it, why don't you?"

He hesitated for a moment before shaking his head. "I'm not

prepared to say right now, Laurel. I want to go inside and look around first."

With that they had to be content. Brian and Albert pushed the ladder back into position. One of the supporting struts had buckled slightly, and Brian held it as they ascended one by one. He himself came last, walking on the side of the ladder away from the buckled strut. The others had waited for him, and they walked up the jetway and into the terminal together.

They found themselves in a large, round room with boarding gates located at intervals along the single curving wall. The rows of seats stood ghostly and deserted, the overhead fluorescents were dark squares, but here Albert thought he could almost *smell* other people . . . as if they had all trooped out only seconds before the Flight 29 survivors emerged from the jetway.

From outside, that choral humming continued to swell, approaching like a slow invisible wave: —*aaaaaaaaaaaaaaa*—

"Come with me," Bob Jenkins said, taking effortless charge of the group. "Quickly, please."

He set off toward the concourse and the others fell into line behind him, Albert and Bethany walking together with arms linked about each other's waists. Once off the carpeted surface of the United boarding lounge and in the concourse itself, their heels clicked and echoed, as if there were two dozen of them instead of only six. They passed dim, dark advertising posters on the walls: Watch CNN, Smoke Marlboros, Drive Hertz, Read *Newsweek,* See Disneyland.

And that sound, that open-throated choral humming sound, continued to grow. Outside, Laurel had been convinced the sound had been approaching them from the west. Now it seemed to be right in here with them, as though the singers—if they *were* singers— had already arrived. The sound did not frighten her, exactly, but it made the flesh of her arms and back prickle with awe.

They reached a cafeteria-style restaurant, and Bob led them inside. Without pausing, he went around the counter and took a wrapped pastry from a pile of them on the counter. He tried to tear it open with his teeth . . . then realized his teeth were back on the plane. He made a small, disgusted sound and tossed it over the counter to Albert.

"You do it," he said. His eyes were glowing now. "Quickly, Albert! Quickly!"

"Quick, Watson, the game's afoot!" Albert said, and laughed
crazily. He tore open the cellophane and looked at Bob, who nodded. Albert took out the pastry and bit into it. Cream and raspberry
jam squirted out the sides. Albert grinned. "Ith delicious!" he said
in a muffled voice, spraying crumbs as he spoke. *"Delicious!"* He
offered it to Bethany, who took an even larger bite.

Laurel could smell the raspberry filling, and her stomach made a
goinging, boinging sound. She laughed. Suddenly she felt giddy,
joyful, almost stoned. The cobwebs from the depressurization experience were entirely gone; her head felt like an upstairs room
after a fresh sea breeze had blown in on a hot and horribly muggy
afternoon. She thought of Nick, who wasn't here, who had died so
the rest of them *could* be here, and thought that Nick would not
have minded her feeling this way.

The choral sound continued to swell, a sound with no direction
at all, a sourceless, singing sigh that existed all around them:

—AAAAAAAAAAAAAA—

Bob Jenkins raced back around the counter, cutting the corner
by the cash register so tightly that his feet almost flew out from
beneath him and he had to grab the condiments trolley to keep
from falling. He stayed up but the stainless-steel trolley fell over
with a gorgeous, resounding crash, spraying plastic cutlery and little
packets of mustard, ketchup, and relish everywhere.

"Quickly!" he cried. "We can't be here! It's going to happen
soon—at any moment, I believe—and we can't be here when it
does! I don't think it's safe!"

"*What* isn't sa—" Bethany began, but then Albert put his arm
around her shoulders and hustled her after Bob, a lunatic tour-
guide who had already bolted for the cafeteria door.

They ran out, following him as he dashed for the United boarding
lobby again. Now the echoing rattle of their footfalls was almost
lost in the powerful hum which filled the deserted terminal, echoing
and reechoing in the many throats of its spoked corridors.

Brian could hear that single vast note beginning to break up. It
was not shattering, not even really changing, he thought, but *focussing,* the way the sound of the langoliers had focussed as they
approached Bangor.

As they re-entered the boarding lounge, he saw an ethereal light
begin to skate over the empty chairs, the dark ARRIVALS and DE-
PARTURES TV monitors, and the boarding desks. Red followed blue;

yellow followed red; green followed yellow. Some rich and exotic expectation seemed to fill the air. A shiver chased through him; he felt all his body-hair stir and try to stand up. A clear assurance filled him like a morning sunray: *We are on the verge of something—some great and amazing thing.*

"Over here!" Bob shouted. He led them toward the wall beside the jetway through which they had entered. This was a passengers-only area, guarded by a red velvet rope. Bob jumped it as easily as the high-school hurdler he might once have been. "Against the wall!"

"Up against the wall, motherfuckers!" Albert cried through a spasm of sudden, uncontrollable laughter.

He and the rest joined Bob, pressing against the wall like suspects in a police line-up. In the deserted circular lounge which now lay before them, the colors flared for a moment . . . and then began to fade out. The sound, however, continued to deepen and become more real. Brian thought he could now hear voices in that sound, and footsteps, even a few fussing babies.

"I don't know what it is, but it's *wonderful!*" Laurel cried. She was half-laughing, half-weeping. "I *love* it!"

"I hope we're safe here," Bob said. He had to raise his voice to be heard. "I think we will be. We're out of the main traffic areas."

"What's going to happen?" Brian asked. "What do you know?"

"When we went through the time-rip headed east, we travelled back in time!" Bob shouted. "We went into the *past!* Perhaps as little as fifteen minutes . . . do you remember me telling you that?"

Brian nodded, and Albert's face suddenly lit up.

"This time it brought us into the future!" Albert cried. "That's it, isn't it? *This time the rip brought us into the future!"*

"I believe so, yes!" Bob yelled back. He was grinning helplessly. "And instead of arriving in a dead world—a world which had moved on without us—*we have arrived in a world waiting to be born!* A world as fresh and new as a rose on the verge of opening! *That* is what is happening now, I believe. *That* is what we hear, and what we sense . . . what has filled us with such marvellous, helpless joy. I believe we are about to see and experience something which no living man or woman has ever witnessed before. We have seen the death of the world; now I believe we are going to see it born. I believe that the present is on the verge of catching up to us."

As the colors had flared and faded, so now the deep, reverberating quality of the sound suddenly dropped. At the same time, the voices which had been within it grew louder, clearer. Laurel realized she could make out words, even whole phrases.

"—have to call her before she decides—"

"—I really don't think the option is a viable—"

"—home and dry if we can just turn this thing over to the parent company—"

That one passed directly before them through the emptiness on the other side of the velvet rope.

Brian Engle felt a kind of ecstasy rise within him, suffusing him in a glow of wonder and happiness. He took Laurel's hand and grinned at her as she clasped it and then squeezed it fiercely. Beside them, Albert suddenly hugged Bethany, and she began to shower kisses all over his face, laughing as she did it. Bob and Rudy grinned at each other delightedly, like long-lost friends who have met by chance in one of the world's more absurd backwaters.

Overhead, the fluorescent squares in the ceiling began to flash on. They went sequentially, racing out from the center of the room in an expanding circle of light that flowed down the concourse, chasing the night-shadows before it like a flock of black sheep.

Smells suddenly struck Brian with a bang: sweat, perfume, after-shave, cologne, cigarette smoke, leather, soap, industrial cleaner.

For a moment longer the wide circle of the boarding lounge remained deserted, a place haunted by the voices and footsteps of the not-quite-living. And Brian thought: *I am going to see it happen; I am going to see the moving present lock onto this stationary future and pull it along, the way hooks on moving express trains used to snatch bags of mail from the Postal Service poles standing by the tracks in sleepy little towns down south and out west. I am going to see time itself open like a rose on a summer morning.*

"Brace yourselves," Bob murmured. "There may be a jerk."

A bare second later Brian felt a thud—not just in his feet, but all through his body. At the same instant he felt as if an invisible hand had given him a strong push, directly in the center of his back. He rocked forward and felt Laurel rock forward with him. Albert had to grab Rudy to keep him from falling over. Rudy didn't seem to mind; a huge, goony smile split his face.

"Look!" Laurel gasped. "Oh, Brian—look!"

He looked . . . and felt his breath stop in his throat.

The boarding lounge was full of ghosts.

Ethereal, transparent figures crossed and crisscrossed the large central area: men in business suits toting briefcases, women in smart travelling dresses, teenagers in Levi's and tee-shirts with rock-group logos printed on them. He saw a ghost-father leading two small ghost-children, and through them he could see more ghosts sitting in the chairs, reading transparent copies of *Cosmopolitan* and *Esquire* and *U.S. News & World Report.* Then color dove into the shapes in a series of cometary flickers, solidifying them, and the echoing voices resolved themselves into the prosaic stereo swarm of real human voices.

Shooting stars, Brian thought wonderingly. *Shooting stars only.*

The two children were the only ones who happened to be looking directly at the survivors of Flight 29 when the change took place; the children were the only ones who saw four men and two women appear in a place where there had only been a wall the second before.

"Daddy!" the little boy exclaimed, tugging his father's right hand.

"Dad!" the little girl demanded, tugging his left.

"What?" he asked, tossing them an impatient glance. "I'm looking for your mother!"

"New people!" the little girl said, pointing at Brian and his be-draggled quintet of passengers. "Look at the new people!"

The man glanced at Brian and the others for a moment, and his mouth tightened nervously. It was the blood, Brian supposed. He, Laurel, and Bethany had all suffered nosebleeds. The man tightened his grip on their hands and began to pull them away fast. "Yes, great. Now help me look for your mother. What a mess *this* turned out to be."

"But they weren't there *before!*" the little boy protested. "They—"

Then they were gone into the hurrying crowds.

Brian glanced up at the monitors and noted the time as 4:17 A.M. *Too many people here,* he thought, *and I bet I know why.*

As if to confirm this, the overhead speaker blared: "*All eastbound flights out of Los Angeles International Airport continue to be delayed because of unusual weather patterns over the Mojave Desert. We are sorry for this inconvenience, but ask for your patience and understanding while this safety precaution is in force. Repeat: all eastbound flights . . .*"

Unusual weather patterns, Brian thought. *Oh yeah. Strangest goddam weather patterns ever.*

Laurel turned to Brian and looked up into his face. Tears streamed down her cheeks, and she made no effort to wipe them away. "Did you hear her? Did you hear what that little girl said?"

"Yes."

"Is that what we are, Brian? The new people? Do you think that's what we are?"

"I don't know," he said, "but that's what it feels like."

"That was wonderful," Albert said. "My God, that was the most wonderful thing."

"*Totally tubular!*" Bethany yelled happily, and then began to clap out "Let's Go" again.

"What do we do now, Brian?" Bob asked. "Any ideas?"

Brian glanced around at the choked boarding area and said, "I think I want to go outside. Breathe some fresh air. And look at the sky."

"Shouldn't we inform the authorities of what—"

"We will," Brian said. "But the sky first."

"And maybe something to eat on the way?" Rudy asked hopefully.

Brian laughed. "Why not?"

"My watch has stopped," Bethany said.

Brian looked down at his wrist and saw that his watch had also stopped. *All* their watches had stopped.

Brian took his off, dropped it indifferently to the floor, and put his arm around Laurel's waist. "Let's blow this joint," he said. "Unless any of you want to wait for the next flight east?"

"Not today," Laurel said, "but soon. All the way to England. There's a man I have to see in . . ." For one horrible moment the name wouldn't come to her . . . and then it did. "Fluting," she said. "Ask anyone along the High Street. The old folks still just call him the gaffer."

"What are you talking about?" Albert asked.

"Daisies," she said, and laughed. "I'm talking about daisies. Come on—let's go."

Bob grinned widely, exposing baby-pink gums. "As for me, I think that the next time I have to go to Boston, I'll take the train."

Laurel toed Brian's watch and asked, "Are you sure you don't want that? It looks expensive."

Brian grinned, shook his head, and kissed her forehead. The smell of her hair was amazingly sweet. He felt more than good; he felt reborn, every inch of him new and fresh and unmarked by the world. He felt, in fact, that if he spread his arms, he would be able to fly without the aid of engines. "Not at all," he said. "I know what time it is."

"Oh? And what time is that?"

"It's half past *now*."

Albert clapped him on the back.

They left the boarding lounge in a group, weaving their way through the disgruntled clots of delayed passengers. A good many of these looked curiously after them, and not just because some of them appeared to have recently suffered nosebleeds, or because they were laughing their way through so many angry, inconvenienced people.

They looked because the six people seemed somehow *brighter* then anyone else in the crowded lounge.

More actual.

More *there*.

Shooting stars only, Brian thought, and suddenly remembered that there was one passenger still back on the plane—the man with the black beard. *This is one hangover that guy will* never *forget,* Brian thought, grinning. He swept Laurel into a run. She laughed and hugged him.

The six of them ran down the concourse together toward the escalators and all the outside world beyond.

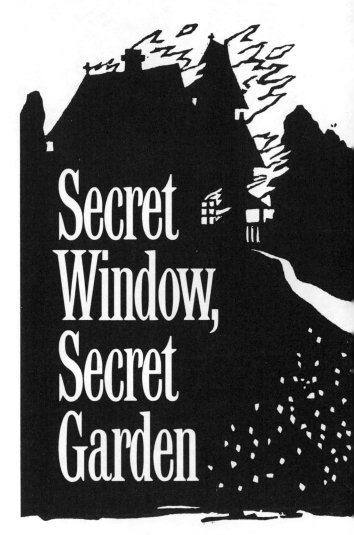

Secret Window, Secret Garden

THIS IS FOR
CHUCK VERRILL.

TWO PAST MIDNIGHT

*A NOTE ON
"SECRET WINDOW,
SECRET GARDEN"*

I'm one of those people who believe that life is a series of cycles—wheels within wheels, some meshing with others, some spinning alone, but all of them performing some finite, repeating function. I like that abstract image of life as something like an efficient factory machine, probably because actual life, up close and personal, seems so messy and strange. It's nice to be able to pull away every once in awhile and say, "There's a pattern there after all! I'm not sure what it means, but by God, I see it!"

All of these wheels seem to finish their cycles at roughly the same time, and when they do—about every twenty years would be my guess—we go through a time when we end things. Psychologists

have even lifted a parliamentary term to describe this phenomenon—they call it cloture.

I'm forty-two now, and as I look back over the last four years of
my life I can see all sorts of cloture. It's as apparent in my work as
anywhere else. In *It,* I took an outrageous amount of space to finish
talking about children and the wide perceptions which light their
interior lives. Next year I intend to publish the last Castle Rock
novel, *Needful Things* (the last story in this volume, "The Sun Dog,"
forms a prologue to that novel). And this story is, I think, the last
story about writers and writing and the strange no man's land which
exists between what's real and what's make-believe. I believe a good
many of my long-time readers, who have borne my fascination with
this subject patiently, will be glad to hear that.

A few years ago I published a novel called *Misery* which tried, at
least in part, to illustrate the powerful hold fiction can achieve over
the reader. Last year I published *The Dark Half,* where I tried to
explore the converse: the powerful hold fiction can achieve over
the writer. While that book was between drafts, I started to think
that there might be a way to tell both stories at the same time by
approaching some of the plot elements of *The Dark Half* from a
totally different angle. Writing, it seems to me, is a secret act—as
secret as dreaming—and that was one aspect of this strange and
dangerous craft I had never thought about much.

I knew that writers have from time to time revised old works—
John Fowles did it with *The Magus,* and I have done it myself with
The Stand—but revision was not what I had in mind. What I wanted
to do was to take familiar elements and put them together in an
entirely new way. This I had tried to do at least once before, re-
structuring and updating the basic elements of Bram Stoker's *Drac-
ula* to create *'Salem's Lot,* and I was fairly comfortable with the idea.

One day in the late fall of 1987, while these things were tumbling
around in my head, I stopped in the laundry room of our house to
drop a dirty shirt into the washing machine. Our laundry room is
a small, narrow alcove on the second floor. I disposed of the shirt
and then stepped over to one of the room's two windows. It was
casual curiosity, no more. We've been living in the same house for
eleven or twelve years now, but I had never taken a good hard look
out this particular window before. The reason is perfectly simple;
set at floor level, mostly hidden behind the drier, half blocked by
baskets of mending, it's a hard window to look out of.

I squeezed in, nevertheless, and looked out. That window looks down on a little brick-paved alcove between the house and the attached sunporch. It's an area I see just about every day . . . but the *angle* was new. My wife had set half a dozen pots out there, so the plants could take a little of the early-November sun, I suppose, and the result was a charming little garden which only I could see. The phrase which occurred to me was, of course, the title of this story. It seemed to me as good a metaphor as any for what writers— especially writers of fantasy—do with their days and nights. Sitting down at the typewriter or picking up a pencil is a physical act; the spiritual analogue is looking out of an almost forgotten window, a window which offers a common view from an entirely different angle . . . an angle which renders the common extraordinary. The writer's job is to gaze through that window and report on what he sees.

But sometimes windows break. I think that, more than anything else, is the concern of this story: what happens to the wide-eyed observer when the window between reality and unreality breaks and the glass begins to fly?

1

"You stole my story," the man on the doorstep said. "You stole my story and something's got to be done about it. Right is right and fair is fair and something has to be done."

Morton Rainey, who had just gotten up from a nap and who was still feeling only halfway into the real world, didn't have the slightest idea what to say. This was never the case when he was at work, sick or well, wide awake or half asleep; he was a writer, and hardly ever at a loss when it became necessary to fill a character's mouth with a snappy comeback. Rainey opened his mouth, found no snappy comeback there (not even a limp one, in fact), and so closed it again.

He thought: *This man doesn't look exactly real. He looks like a character out of a novel by William Faulkner.*

This was of no help in resolving the situation, but it was undeniably true. The man who had rung Rainey's doorbell out here in the western Maine version of nowhere looked about forty-five. He was very thin. His face was calm, almost serene, but carved with deep lines. They moved horizontally across his high brow in regular waves, cut vertically downward from the ends of his thin lips to his jawline, and radiated outward in tiny sprays from the corners of his eyes. The eyes were bright, unfaded blue. Rainey couldn't tell what color his hair was; he wore a large black hat with a round crown planted squarely on his head. The underside of the brim touched the tops of his ears. It looked like the sort of hat Quakers wore. He had no sideburns, either, and for all Morton Rainey knew, he might be as bald as Telly Savalas under that round-crowned felt hat.

He was wearing a blue work-shirt. It was buttoned neatly all the way to the loose, razor-reddened flesh of his neck, although he wore no tie. The bottom of the shirt disappeared into a pair of blue-jeans that looked a little too big for the man who was wearing them. They ended in cuffs which lay neatly on a pair of faded yellow work-shoes which looked made for walking in a furrow of played-out earth about three and a half feet behind a mule's ass.

"Well?" he asked when Rainey continued to say nothing.

"I don't know you," Rainey said finally. It was the first thing he'd said since he'd gotten up off the couch and come to answer the door, and it sounded sublimely stupid in his own ears.

"I know *that*," said the man. "*That* doesn't matter. I know *you,* Mr. Rainey. *That's* what matters." And then he reiterated: "You stole my story."

He held out his hand, and for the first time Rainey saw that he had something in it. It was a sheaf of paper. But not just any old sheaf of paper; it was a manuscript. After you've been in the business awhile, he thought, you always recognized the look of a manuscript. Especially an unsolicited one.

And, belatedly, he thought: *Good thing for you it wasn't a gun, Mort old kid. You would have been in hell before you knew you were dead.*

And, even more belatedly, he realized that he was probably dealing with one of the Crazy Folks. It was long overdue, of course;

although his last three books had been best-sellers, this was his first visit from one of that fabled tribe. He felt a mixture of fear and chagrin, and his thoughts narrowed to a single point: how to get rid of the guy as fast as possible, and with as little unpleasantness as possible.

"I don't read manuscripts—" he began.

"You read this one already," the man with the hard-working sharecropper's face said evenly. "You stole it." He spoke as if stating a simple fact, like a man noting that the sun was out and it was a pleasant fall day.

All of Mort's thoughts were belated this afternoon, it seemed; he now realized for the first time how alone he was out here. He had come to the house in Tashmore Glen in early October, after two miserable months in New York; his divorce had become final just last week.

It was a big house, but it was a summer place, and Tashmore Glen was a summer town. There were maybe twenty cottages on this particular road running along the north bay of Tashmore Lake, and in July or August there would be people staying in most or all of them . . . but this wasn't July or August. It was late October. The sound of a gunshot, he realized, would probably drift away unheard. If it *was* heard, the hearers would simply assume someone was shooting at quail or pheasant—it was the season.

"I can assure you—"

"I *know* you can," the man in the black hat said with that same unearthly patience. "I *know* that."

Behind him, Mort could see the car the man had come in. It was an old station wagon which looked as if it had seen a great many miles, very few of them on good roads. He could see that the plate on it wasn't from the State of Maine, but couldn't tell what state it *was* from; he'd known for some time now that he needed to go to the optometrist and have his glasses changed, had even planned early last summer to do that little chore, but then Henry Young had called him one day in April, asking who the fellow was he'd seen Amy with at the mall—some relative, maybe?—and the suspicions which had culminated in the eerily quick and quiet no-fault divorce had begun, the shitstorm which had taken up all his time and energy these last few months. During that time he had been doing well if he remembered to change his underwear, let alone handle more esoteric things like optometrist appointments.

"If you want to talk to someone about some grievance you feel you have," Mort began uncertainly, hating the pompous, talking-boilerplate sound of his own voice but not knowing how else to reply, "you could talk to my ag—"

"This is between you and me," the man on the doorstep said patiently. Bump, Mort's tomcat, had been curled up on the low cabinet built into the side of the house—you had to store your garbage in a closed compartment or the raccoons came in the night and pulled it all over hell—and now he jumped down and twined his way sinuously between the stranger's legs. The stranger's bright-blue eyes never left Rainey's face. "We don't need any outsiders, Mr. Rainey. It is strictly between you and me."

"I don't like being accused of plagiarism, if that's what you're doing," Mort said. At the same time, part of his mind was cautioning him that you had to be very careful when dealing with people of the Crazy Folks tribe. Humor them? Yes. But this man didn't seem to have a gun, and Mort outweighed him by at least fifty pounds. *I've also got five or ten years on him, by the look,* he thought. He had read that a bona-fide Crazy Guy could muster abnormal strength, but he was damned if he was simply going to stand here and let this man he had never seen before go on saying that he, Morton Rainey, had stolen his story. Not without some kind of rebuttal.

"I don't blame you for not liking it," the man in the black hat said. He spoke in the same patient and serene way. He spoke, Mort thought, like a therapist whose work is teaching small children who are retarded in some mild way. "But you did it. You stole my story."

"You'll have to leave," Mort said. He was fully awake now, and he no longer felt so bewildered, at such a disadvantage. "I have nothing to say to you."

"Yes, I'll go," the man said. "We'll talk more later." He held out the sheaf of manuscript, and Mort actually found himself reaching for it. He put his hand back down to his side just before his un-invited and unwanted guest could slip the manuscript into it, like a process server finally slipping a subpoena to a man who has been ducking it for months.

"I'm not taking that," Mort said, and part of him was marvelling at what a really accommodating beast a man was: when someone held something out to you, your first instinct was to take it. No matter if it was a check for a thousand dollars or a stick of dynamite with a lit and fizzing fuse, your first instinct was to take it.

"Won't do you any good to play games with me, Mr. Rainey," the man said mildly. "This has *got* to be settled."

"So far as I'm concerned, it is," Mort said, and closed the door on that lined, used, and somehow timeless face.

He had only felt a moment or two of fear, and those had come when he first realized, in a disoriented and sleep-befogged way, what this man was saying. Then it had been swallowed by anger—anger at being bothered during his nap, and more anger at the realization that he was being bothered by a representative of the Crazy Folks.

Once the door was closed, the fear returned. He pressed his lips together and waited for the man to start pounding on it. And when that didn't come, he became convinced that the man was just standing out there, still as a stone and as patient as same, waiting for him to reopen the door . . . as he would have to do, sooner or later.

Then he heard a low thump, followed by a series of light steps crossing the board porch. Mort walked into the master bedroom, which looked out on the driveway. There were two big windows in here, one giving on the driveway and the shoulder of hill behind it, the other providing a view of the slope which fell away to the blue and agreeable expanse of Tashmore Lake. Both windows were reflectorized, which meant he could look out but anyone trying to look in would see only his own distorted image, unless he put his nose to the glass and cupped his eyes against the glare.

He saw the man in the work-shirt and cuffed blue-jeans walking back to his old station wagon. From this angle, he could make out the license plate's state of issue—Mississippi. As the man opened the driver's-side door, Mort thought: *Oh shit. The gun's in the car. He didn't have it on him because he believed he could reason with me . . . whatever his idea of "reasoning" is. But now he's going to get it and come back. It's probably in the glove compartment or under the seat—*

But the man got in behind the wheel, pausing only long enough to take off his black hat and toss it down beside him. As he slammed the door and started the engine, Mort thought, *There's something different about him now.* But it wasn't until his unwanted afternoon visitor had backed up the driveway and out of sight behind the thick screen of bushes Mort kept forgetting to trim that he realized what it was.

When the man got into his car, he had no longer been holding the manuscript.

2

It was on the back porch. There was a rock on it to keep the individual pages from blowing all over the little dooryard in the light breeze. The small thump he'd heard had been the man putting the rock on the manuscript.

Mort stood in the doorway, hands in the pockets of his khaki pants, looking at it. He knew that craziness wasn't catching (except maybe in cases of prolonged exposure, he supposed), but he still didn't want to touch the goddam thing. He supposed he would have to, though. He didn't know just how long he would be here—a day, a week, a month, and a year all looked equally possible at this point—but he couldn't just let the fucking thing sit there. Greg Carstairs, his caretaker, would be down early this afternoon to give him an estimate on how much it would cost to reshingle the house, for one thing, and Greg would wonder what it was. Worse, he would probably assume it was Mort's, and that would entail more explanations than the damned thing was worth.

He stood there until the sound of his visitor's engine had merged into the low, slow hum of the afternoon, and then he went out on the porch, walking carefully in his bare feet (the porch had needed painting for at least a year now, and the dry wood was prickly with potential splinters), and tossed the rock into the juniper-choked gully to the left of the porch. He picked up the little sheaf of pages and looked down at it. The top one was a title page. It read:

SECRET WINDOW, SECRET GARDEN
By John Shooter

Mort felt a moment's relief in spite of himself. He had never heard of John Shooter, and he had never read *or* written a short story called "Secret Window, Secret Garden" in his life.

He tossed the manuscript in the kitchen wastebasket on his way by, went back to the couch in the living room, lay down again, and was asleep in five minutes.

He dreamed of Amy. He slept a great lot and he dreamed of Amy a great lot these days, and waking up to the sound of his own hoarse shouts no longer surprised him much. He supposed it would pass.

3

The next morning he was sitting in front of his word processor in the small nook off the living room which had always served as his study when they were down here. The word processor was on, but Mort was looking out the window at the lake. Two motor-boats were out there, cutting broad white wakes in the blue water. He had thought they were fishermen at first, but they never slowed down—just cut back and forth across each other's bows in big loops. Kids, he decided. Just kids playing games.

They weren't doing anything very interesting, but then, neither was he. He hadn't written anything worth a damn since he had left Amy. He sat in front of the word processor every day from nine to eleven, just as he had every day for the last three years (and for about a thousand years before that he had spent those two hours sitting in front of an old Royal office model), but for all the good he was doing with it, he might as well have traded it in on a motor-boat and gone out grab-assing with the kids on the lake.

Today, he had written the following lines of deathless prose during his two-hour stint:

```
    Four days after George had confirmed to his
own satisfaction that his wife was cheating on
him, he confronted her,
    "I have to talk to you, Abby," he said,
```

It was no good.

It was too close to real life to be good.

He had never been so hot when it came to real life. Maybe that was part of the problem.

He turned off the word processor, realizing just a second after he'd flicked the switch that he'd forgotten to save the document. Well, that was all right. Maybe it had even been the critic in his subconscious, telling him the document wasn't worth saving.

Mrs. Gavin had apparently finished upstairs; the drone of the Electrolux had finally ceased. She came in every Tuesday to clean, and she had been shocked into a silence very unlike her when Mort had told her two Tuesdays ago that he and Amy were quits. He suspected that she had liked Amy a good deal more than she had liked him. But she was still coming, and Mort supposed that was something.

He got up and went out into the living room just as Mrs. Gavin came down the main staircase. She was holding the vacuum-cleaner hose and dragging the small tubular machine after her. It came down in a series of thumps, looking like a small mechanical dog. *If I tried to pull the vacuum downstairs that way, it'd smack into one of my ankles and then roll all the way to the bottom,* Mort thought. *How does she get it to do that, I wonder?*

"Hi there, Mrs. G.," he said, and crossed the living room toward the kitchen door. He wanted a Coke. Writing shit always made him thirsty.

"Hello, Mr. Rainey." He had tried to get her to call him Mort, but she wouldn't. She wouldn't even call him Morton. Mrs. Gavin was a woman of her principles, but her principles had never kept her from calling his wife Amy.

Maybe I should tell her I caught Amy in bed with another man at one of Derry's finer motels, Mort thought as he pushed through the swing door. *She might go back to calling her Mrs. Rainey again, at the very least.*

This was an ugly and mean-spirited thought, the kind of thinking he suspected was at the root of his writing problems, but he didn't seem to be able to help it. Perhaps it would also pass . . . like the dreams. For some reason this idea made him think of a bumper sticker he'd seen once on the back of a very old VW beetle. CONSTIPATED—CANNOT PASS, the sticker had read.

As the kitchen door swung back, Mrs. Gavin called: "I found one of your stories in the trash, Mr. Rainey. I thought you might want it, so I put it on the counter."

"Okay," he said, having no idea what she might be talking about. He was not in the habit of tossing bad manuscripts or frags in the kitchen trash. When he produced a stinker—and lately he had produced more than his share—it went either directly to data heaven or into the circular file to the right of his word-processing station.

The man with the lined face and round black Quaker hat never even entered his mind.

He opened the refrigerator door, moved two small Tupperware dishes filled with nameless leftovers, discovered a bottle of Pepsi, and opened it as he nudged the fridge door closed with his hip. As he went to toss the cap in the trash, he saw the manuscript—its title page was spotted with something that looked like orange juice, but otherwise it was all right—sitting on the counter by the Silex. *Then* he remembered. John Shooter, right. Charter member of the Crazy Folks, Mississippi Branch.

He took a drink of Pepsi, then picked up the manuscript. He put the title page on the bottom and saw this at the head of the first page:

John Shooter
General Delivery
Dellacourt, Mississippi

30 pages
Approximately 7500 words
Selling 1st serial rights, North America

SECRET WINDOW, SECRET GARDEN
By John Shooter

The manuscript had been typed on a good grade of bond paper, but the machine must have been a sad case—an old office model, from the look, and not very well maintained. Most of the letters were as crooked as an old man's teeth.

He read the first sentence, then the second, then the third, and for a few moments clear thought ceased.

> Todd Downey thought that a woman who would steal
> your love when your love was really all you had was
> not much of a woman. He therefore decided to kill
> her. He would do it in the deep corner formed where
> the house and barn came together at an extreme
> angle—he would do it where his wife kept her
> garden.

"Oh shit," Mort said, and put the manuscript back down. His arm struck the Pepsi bottle. It overturned, foaming and fizzing across the counter and running down the cabinet facings. "Oh *SHIT*!" he yelled.

Mrs. Gavin came in a hurry, surveyed the situation, and said: "Oh, that's nothing. I thought from the sound that maybe you'd cut your own throat. Move a little, can't you, Mr. Rainey?"

He moved, and the first thing she did was to pick the sheaf of manuscript up off the counter and thrust it back into his hands. It was still okay; the soda had run the other way. He had once been a man with a fairly good sense of humor—*he* had always thought so, anyway—but as he looked down at the little pile of paper in his hands, the best he could manage was a sour sense of irony. *It's like the cat in the nursery rhyme,* he thought. *The one that kept coming back.*

"If you're trying to wreck that," Mrs. Gavin said, nodding at the manuscript as she got a dishrag from under the sink, "you're on the right track."

"It's not mine," he said, but it was funny, wasn't it? Yesterday, when he had almost reached out and taken the script from the man who had brought it to him, he'd thought about what an accommodating beast a man was. Apparently that urge to accommodate stretched in all directions, because the first thing he'd felt when he read those three sentences was guilt . . . and wasn't that just what Shooter (if that was really his name) had wanted him to feel? Of course it was. *You stole my story,* he'd said, and weren't thieves supposed to feel guilty?

"Pardon me, Mr. Rainey," Mrs. Gavin said, holding up the dishrag.

He stepped aside so she could get at the spill. "It's not mine," he repeated—insisted, really.

"Oh," she said, wiping up the spill on the counter and then stepping to the sink to wring out the cloth. "I thought it was."

"It says John Shooter," he said, putting the title page back on top and turning it toward her. "See?"

Mrs. Gavin favored the title page with the shortest glance politeness would allow and then began wiping the cabinet faces. "Thought it was one of those whatchacallums," she said. "Pseudonames. Or nyms. Whatever the word is for pen names."

"I don't use one," he said. "I never have."

This time she favored *him* with a brief glance—country shrewd and slightly amused—before getting down on her knees to wipe up the puddle of Pepsi on the floor. "Don't s'pose you'd tell me if you did," she said.

"I'm sorry about the spill," he said, edging toward the door.

"My job," she said shortly. She didn't look up again. Mort took the hint and left.

He stood in the living room for a moment, looking at the abandoned vacuum cleaner in the middle of the rug. In his head he heard the man with the lined face saying patiently, *This is between you and me. We don't need any outsiders, Mr. Rainey. It is strictly between you and me.*

Mort thought of that face, recalled it carefully to a mind which was trained to recall faces and actions, and thought: *It wasn't just a momentary aberration, or a bizarre way to meet an author he may or may not consider famous. He will be back.*

He suddenly headed back into his study, rolling the manuscript into a tube as he went.

4

Three of the four study walls were lined with bookshelves, and one of them had been set aside for the various editions, domestic and foreign, of his works. He had published six books in all: five novels and a collection of short stories. The book of short stories and his first two novels had been well received by his immediate family and a few friends. His third novel, *The Organ-Grinder's Boy,* had been an instant best-seller. The early works had been reissued after he became a success, and had done quite well, but they had never been as popular as his later books.

The short-story collection was called *Everybody Drops the Dime,* and most of the tales had originally been published in the men's magazines, sandwiched around pictures of women wearing lots of eye make-up and not much else. One of the stories, however, had been published in *Ellery Queen's Mystery Magazine.* It was called "Sowing Season," and it was to this story he now turned.

A woman who would steal your love when your love was all you had wasn't much of a woman—that, at least, was Tommy Havelock's opinion. He decided to kill her. He even knew the place he would do it, the exact place: the little patch of garden she kept in the extreme angle formed where the house and the barn came together.

Mort sat down and worked his way slowly through the two stories, reading back and forth. By the time he was halfway through, he understood he really didn't need to go any further. They varied in diction in some places; in many others even that was the same, word for word. Diction aside, they were *exactly* the same. In both of them, a man killed his wife. In both of them, the wife was a cold, loveless bitch who cared only for her garden and her canning. In both of them, the killer buried his spousal victim in her garden and then tended it, growing a really spectacular crop. In Morton Rainey's version, the crop was beans. In Shooter's, it was corn. In both versions, the killer eventually went crazy and was discovered by the police eating vast amounts of the vegetable in question and swearing he would be rid of her, that in the end he would finally be rid of her.

Mort had never considered himself much of a horror-story writer—and there was nothing supernatural about "Sowing Season"—but it had been a creepy little piece of work all the same. Amy had finished it with a little shiver and said, "I suppose it's good, but that man's mind . . . God, Mort, what a can of worms."

That had summed up his own feelings pretty well. The landscape of "Sowing Season" wasn't one he would care to travel through often, and it was no "Tell-Tale Heart," but he thought he had done a fair job of painting Tom Havelock's homicidal breakdown. The editor at *EQMM* had agreed, and so had the readers—the story had generated favorable mail. The editor had asked for more, but Mort had never come up with another story even remotely like "Sowing Season."

"I know I can do it," Todd Downey said, helping himself to another ear of corn from the steaming bowl. "I'm sure that in time all of her will be gone."

That was how Shooter's ended.

"I am confident I can take care of this business," Tom Havelock told them, and helped himself to another portion of beans from the brimming, steaming bowl. "I'm sure that, in time, her death will be a mystery even to me."

That was how Mort Rainey's ended.

Mort closed his copy of *Everybody Drops the Dime* and replaced it thoughtfully on his shelf of first editions.

He sat down and began to rummage slowly and thoroughly through the drawers of his desk. It was a big one, so big the furniture men had had to bring it into the room in sections, and it had a lot of drawers. The desk was solely his domain; neither Amy nor Mrs. G. had ever set a hand to it, and the drawers were full of ten years' worth of accumulated rick-rack. It had been four years since Mort had given up smoking, and if there were any cigarettes left in the house, this was where they would be. If he found some, he would smoke. Just about now, he was crazy for a smoke. If he didn't find any, that was all right, too; going through his junk was soothing. Old letters which he'd put aside to answer and never had, what had once seemed so important now looking antique, even arcane; postcards he'd bought but never mailed; chunks of manuscript in varying stages of completion; half a bag of very elderly Doritos; envelopes; paper-clips; cancelled checks. He could sense layers here which were almost geological—layers of summer life frozen in place. And it *was* soothing. He finished one drawer and went on to the next, thinking all the while about John Shooter and how John Shooter's story—*his* story, goddammit!—had made him feel.

The most obvious thing, of course, was that it had made him feel like he needed a cigarette. This wasn't the first time he'd felt that way in the last four years; there had been times when just seeing someone puffing away behind the wheel of a car next to his at a stoplight could set off a raging momentary lust for tobacco. But the key word there, of course, was "momentary." Those feelings passed in a hurry, like fierce rainsqualls—five minutes after a blinding silver curtain of rain has dropped out of the sky, the sun is shining again. He'd never felt the need to turn in to the next convenience store on his way for a deck of smokes . . . or go rummaging through his glove compartment for a stray or two as he was now rummaging through his desk.

He felt *guilty,* and that was absurd. Infuriating. He had not stolen John Shooter's story, and he knew he hadn't—if there had been stealing (and there must have been; for the two stories to be that close without prior knowledge on the part of one of the two players was impossible for Mort to believe), then it had been *Shooter* who had stolen from *him.*

Of course.

It was as plain as the nose on his face . . . or the round black hat on John Shooter's head.

Yet he still felt upset, unsettled, guilty . . . he felt *at a loss* in a way for which there was perhaps no word. And why? Well— because . . .

At that moment Mort lifted up a Xerox of *The Organ-Grinder's Boy* manuscript, and there, beneath it, was a package of L & M cigarettes. Did they even *make* L & M's anymore? He didn't know. The pack was old, crumpled, but definitely not flat. He took it out and looked at it. He reflected that he must have bought this particular pack in 1985, according to the informal science of stratification one might call—for want of a better word—Deskology.

He peered inside the pack. He saw three little coffin nails, all in a row.

Time-travellers from another age, Mort thought. He stuck one of the cigarettes in his mouth, then went out into the kitchen to get a match from the box by the stove. *Time-travellers from another age, riding up through the years, patient cylindrical voyagers, their mission to wait, to persevere, to bide until the proper moment to start me on the road to lung cancer again finally arrives. And it seems the time has finally come.*

"It'll probably taste like shit," he said aloud to the empty house (Mrs. Gavin had long since gone home), and set fire to the tip of the cigarette. It didn't taste like shit, though. It tasted pretty good. He wandered back toward his study, puffing away and feeling pleasantly lightheaded. *Ah, the dreadful patient persistence of addiction,* he thought. What had Hemingway said? Not this August, nor this September—this year you have to do what you like. But the time comes around again. It always does. Sooner or later you stick something back in your big dumb old mouth again. A drink, a smoke, maybe the barrel of a shotgun. Not this August, nor this September . . .

. . . unfortunately, this was October.

At an earlier point in his prospecting, he had found an old bottle half full of Planter's Peanuts. He doubted if the nuts would be fit to eat, but the lid of the bottle made a fine ashtray. He sat behind his desk, looked out at the lake (like Mrs. G., the boats which had been out there earlier were gone), relished his old, vile habit, and found he could think about John Shooter and John Shooter's story with a little more equanimity.

The man *was* one of the Crazy Folks, of course; that was now proven in brass if any further proof had been needed. As to how it had made him feel, finding that the similarity actually existed . . .

Well, a story was a thing, a *real* thing—you could think of it like that, anyway, especially if someone had paid you for it—but in another, more important, way, it wasn't a thing at all. It wasn't like a vase, or a chair, or an automobile. It was ink on paper, but it wasn't the ink and it wasn't the paper. People sometimes asked him where he got his ideas, and although he scoffed at the question, it always made him feel vaguely ashamed, vaguely spurious. They seemed to feel there was a Central Idea Dump somewhere (just as there was supposed to be an elephant graveyard somewhere, and a fabled lost city of gold somewhere else), and he must have a secret map which allowed him to get there and back, but Mort knew better. He could remember *where he had been* when certain ideas came to him, and he knew that the idea was often the result of seeing or sensing some odd connection between objects or events or people which had never seemed to have the slightest connection before, but that was the best he could do. As to why he should see these connections or want to make stories out of them after he had . . . to that he hadn't a clue.

If John Shooter had come to his door and said "You stole my car" instead of "You stole my story," Mort would have scotched the idea quickly and decisively. He could have done it even if the two cars in question had been the same year, make, model, and color. He would have shown the man in the round black hat his automobile registration, invited him to compare the number on the pink slip to the one on the doorpost, and sent him packing.

But when you got a story idea, no one gave you a bill of sale. There was no provenance to be traced. Why would there be? Nobody gave you a bill of sale when you got something for free. You charged whoever wanted to buy that thing from *you*—oh yes, all the traffic would bear, and a little more than that, if you could, to make up for all the times the bastards shorted you—magazines, newspapers, book publishers, movie companies. But the item came to you free, clear, and unencumbered. That was it, he decided. That was why he felt guilty even though he knew he hadn't plagiarized

Farmer John Shooter's story. He felt guilty because writing stories had *always* felt a little bit like stealing, and probably always would. John Shooter just happened to be the first person to show up on his doorstep and accuse him of it right out loud. He thought that, subconsciously, he had been expecting something like this for years.

Mort crushed out his cigarette and decided to take a nap. Then he decided that was a bad idea. It would be better, healthier both mentally and physically, to eat some lunch, read for half an hour or so, and then go for a nice long walk down by the lake. He was sleeping too much, and sleeping too much was a sign of depression. Halfway to the kitchen, he deviated to the long sectional couch by the window-wall in the living room. *The hell with it,* he thought, putting a pillow under his neck and another one behind his head. *I AM depressed.*

His last thought before drifting off was a repeat: *He's not done with me yet. Oh no, not this guy. He's a repeater.*

5

He dreamed he was lost in a vast cornfield. He blundered from one row to the next, and the sun glinted off the watches he was wearing—half a dozen on each forearm, and each watch set to a different time.

Please help me! he cried. *Someone please help me! I'm lost and afraid!*

Ahead of him, the corn on both sides of the row shook and rustled. Amy stepped out from one side. John Shooter stepped out from the other. Both of them held knives.

I am confident I can take care of this business, Shooter said as they advanced on him with their knives raised. *I'm sure that, in time, your death will be a mystery even to us.*

Mort turned to run, but a hand—Amy's, he was sure—seized him by the belt and pulled him back. And then the knives, glittering in the hot sun of this huge secret garden—

6

It was the telephone which woke him an hour and a quarter later. He struggled out of a terrible dream—someone had been chasing him, that was all he could clearly remember—to a sitting position on the couch. He was horribly hot; every inch of his skin seemed to be running with sweat. The sun had crept around to this side of the house while he was sleeping and had shone in on him through the window-wall for God knew how long.

Mort walked slowly toward the telephone table in the front hall, plodding like a man in a diver's suit walking in the bed of a river against the current, his head thumping slowly, his mouth tasting like old dead gopher-shit. For every step he took forward, the entrance to the hall seemed to retreat a step, and it occurred to Mort, not for the first time, that hell was probably like the way you felt after sleeping too long and too hard on a hot afternoon. The worst of it wasn't physical. The worst was that dismaying, disorienting sense of being outside yourself, somehow—just an observer looking through dual TV cameras with blurry lenses.

He picked up the phone thinking it would be Shooter.

Yeah, it'll be him, all right—the one person in the whole wide world I shouldn't be talking to with my guard down and one half of my mind feeling unbuttoned from the other half. Sure it'll be him—who else?

"Hello?"

It wasn't Shooter, but as he listened to the voice on the other end of the line reply to his greeting, he discovered there was at least one other person to whom he had no business talking while in a psychically vulnerable state.

"Hello, Mort," Amy said. "Are you all right?"

7

Some time later that afternoon, Mort donned the extra-large red flannel shirt he used as a jacket in the early fall and took the walk he should have taken earlier. Bump the cat followed him long enough to ascertain that Mort was serious, then returned to the house.

He walked slowly and deliberately through an exquisite afternoon which seemed to be all blue sky, red leaves, and golden air. He walked with his hands stuffed into his pockets, trying to let the lake's quiet work through his skin and calm him down, as it had always done before—he supposed that was the reason he had come here instead of staying in New York, as Amy had expected him to do, while they trundled steadily along toward divorce. He had come here because it was a magic place, especially in autumn, and he had felt, when he arrived, that if there was a sad sack anywhere on the planet who needed a little magic, he was that person. And if that old magic failed him now that the writing had turned so sour, he wasn't sure what he would do.

It turned out that he didn't need to worry about it. After awhile the silence and that queer atmosphere of suspension which always seemed to possess Tashmore Lake when fall had finally come and the summer people had finally gone began to work on him, loosening him up like gently kneading hands. But now he had something besides John Shooter to think about; he had Amy to think about as well.

"Of course I'm all right," he'd said, speaking as carefully as a drunk trying to convince people that he's sober. In truth, he was still so muzzy that he *felt* a little bit drunk. The shapes of words felt too big in his mouth, like chunks of soft, friable rock, and he had proceeded with great care, groping his way through the opening formalities and gambits of telephone conversation as if for the first time. "How are *you?*"

"Oh, fine, I'm fine," she said, and then trilled the quick little laugh which usually meant she was either flirting or nervous as hell, and Mort doubted that she was flirting with him—not at this point. The realization that she was nervous, too, set him a little more at ease. "It's just that you're alone down there, and almost anything could happen and nobody would know—" She broke off abruptly.

"I'm really not alone," he said mildly. "Mrs. Gavin was here today and Greg Carstairs is always around."

"Oh, I forgot about the roof repairs," Amy said, and for a moment he marvelled at how natural they sounded, how natural and undivorced. *Listening to us,* Mort thought, *you'd never guess there's a rogue real-estate agent in my bed . . . or what used to be my bed.* He waited for the anger to come back—the hurt, jealous, cheated anger—but only a ghost stirred where those lively if unpleasant feelings had been.

"Well, *Greg* didn't forget," he assured her. "He came down yesterday and crawled around on the roof for an hour and a half."

"How bad is it?"

He told her, and they talked about the roof for the next five minutes or so, while Mort slowly woke up; they talked about that old roof as if things were just the same as they always had been, talked about it as if they would be spending next summer under the new cedar shingles just as they had spent the last nine summers under the old cedar shingles. Mort thought: *Gimme a roof, gimme some shingles, and I'll talk to this bitch forever.*

As he listened to himself holding up his side of the conversation, he felt a deepening sense of unreality settling in. It felt as if he were returning to the half-waking, half-sleeping zombie state in which he had answered the phone, and at last he couldn't stand it anymore. If this was some sort of contest to see who could go the longest pretending that the last six months had never happened, then he was willing to concede. More than willing.

She was asking where Greg was going to get the cedar shakes and if he would be using a crew from town when Mort broke in. "Why *did* you call, Amy?"

There was a moment's silence in which he sensed her trying on responses and then rejecting them, like a woman trying on hats, and that *did* cause the anger to stir again. It was one of the things— one of the few things, actually—that he could honestly say he detested in her. That totally unconscious duplicity.

"I *told* you why," she said at last. "To see if you were all right." She sounded flustered and unsure of herself again, and that usually meant she was telling the truth. When Amy lied, she always sounded as if she was telling you the world was round. "I had one of my feelings—I know you don't believe in them, but I think you do know that I get them, and that *I* believe in them . . . don't you, Mort?" There was none of her usual posturing or defensive anger, that was the thing—she sounded almost as if she were pleading with him.

"Yeah, I know that."

"Well, I had one. I was making myself a sandwich for lunch, and I had a feeling that you . . . that you might not be all right. I held off for awhile—I thought it would go away, but it didn't. So I finally called. You *are* all right, aren't you?"

"Yes," he said.

"And nothing's happened?"

"Well, something *did* happen," he said, after only a moment of interior debate. He thought it was possible, maybe even likely, that John Shooter (*if that's really his name,* his mind insisted on adding) had tried to make contact with him in Derry before coming down here. Derry, after all, was where he usually was at this time of year. Amy might even have sent him down here.

"I *knew* it," she said. "Did you hurt yourself with that goddam chainsaw? Or—"

"Nothing requiring hospitalization," he said, smiling a little. "Just an annoyance. Does the name John Shooter ring a bell with you, Amy?"

"No, why?"

He let an irritated little sigh escape through his closed teeth like steam. Amy was a bright woman, but she had always had a bit of a dead-short between her brain and her mouth. He remembered once musing that she should have a tee-shirt reading SPEAK NOW, THINK LATER. "Don't say no right off the bat. Take a few seconds and really think about it. The guy is fairly tall, about six feet, and I'd guess he's in his mid-forties. His face looked older, but he *moved* like a man in his forties. He has a country kind of face. Lots of color, lots of sun-wrinkles. When I saw him, I thought he looked like a character out of Faulk—"

"What's this all about, Mort?"

Now he felt all the way back; now he could understand again why, as hurt and confused as he had been, he had rejected the urges he felt—mostly at night—to ask her if they couldn't at least *try* to reconcile their differences. He supposed he knew that, if he asked long enough and hard enough, she would agree. But facts were facts; there had been a lot more wrong with their marriage than Amy's real-estate salesman. The drilling quality her voice had taken on now—that was another symptom of what had killed them. *What have you done now?* the tone under the words asked . . . no, demanded. *What kind of a mess have you gotten yourself into now? Explain yourself.*

He closed his eyes and hissed breath through his clenched teeth again before answering. Then he told her about John Shooter, and Shooter's manuscript, and his own short story. Amy clearly remembered "Sowing Season," but said she had never heard of a man named John Shooter—it wasn't the kind of name you forget, she said, and Mort was inclined to agree—in her life. And she certainly hadn't seen him.

"You're sure? Mort pressed.

"Yes, I am," Amy said. She sounded faintly resentful of Mort's continued questioning. "I haven't seen anyone like that since you left. And before you tell me again not to say no right off the bat, let me assure you that I have a very clear memory of almost everything that's happened since then."

She paused, and he realized she was speaking with an effort now, quite possibly with real pain. That small, mean part of him rejoiced. Most of him did not; most of him was disgusted to find even a small part of him happy about any of this. That had no effect on the interior celebrant, however. That guy might be outvoted, but he also seemed impervious to Mort's—the larger Mort's—attempts to root him out.

"Maybe Ted saw him," he said. Ted Milner was the real-estate agent. He still found it hard to believe she had tossed him over for a real-estate agent, and he supposed that was part of the problem, part of the conceit which had allowed things to progress to this point in the first place. He certainly wasn't going to claim, especially to himself, that he had been as innocent as Mary's little lamb, was he?

"Is that supposed to be funny?" Amy sounded angry, ashamed, sorrowful, and defiant all at the same time.

"No," he said. He was beginning to feel tired again.

"Ted isn't here," she said. "Ted hardly ever comes here. I . . . I go to his place."

Thank you for sharing that with me, Amy, he almost said, and choked it off. It would be nice to get out of at least one conversation without a swap of accusations. So he didn't say thanks for sharing and he didn't say that'll change and most of all he didn't ask what in the hell's the matter with you, Amy?

Mostly because she might then have asked the same thing of him.

8

She had suggested he call Dave Newsome, the Tashmore constable—after all, the man might be dangerous. Mort told her he didn't think that would be necessary, at least not yet, but if "John Shooter" called by again, he would probably give Dave a jingle. After a few more stilted amenities, they hung up. He could tell she was still smarting over his oblique suggestion that Ted might currently be sitting in Mortybear's chair and sleeping in Mortybear's bed, but he honestly didn't know how he could have avoided mentioning Ted Milner sooner or later. The man had become a part of Amy's life, after all. And *she* had called *him,* that was the thing. She had gotten one of her funny feelings and called *him.*

Mort reached the place where the lakeside path forked, the right-hand branch climbing the steep bank back up to Lake Drive. He took that branch, walking slowly and savoring the fall color. As he came around the final curve in the path and into sight of the narrow ribbon of blacktop, he was somehow not surprised to see the dusty blue station wagon with the Mississippi plates parked there like an oft-whipped dog chained to a tree, nor the lean figure of John Shooter propped against the right front mudguard with his arms folded across his chest.

Mort waited for his heartbeat to speed up, for the surge of adrenaline into his body, but his heart went on maintaining its normal beat, and his glands kept their own counsel—which, for the time being, seemed to be to remain quiet.

The sun, which had gone behind a cloud, came out again, and fall colors which had already been bright now seemed to burst into flame. His own shadow reappeared, dark and long and clearcut. Shooter's round black hat looked blacker, his blue shirt bluer, and the air was so clear the man seemed scissored from a swatch of reality that was brighter and more vital than the one Mort knew as a rule. And he understood that he had been wrong about his reasons for not calling Dave Newsome—wrong, or practicing a little deception—on himself as well as on Amy. The truth was that he wanted to deal with this matter himself. *Maybe just to prove to myself that there are things I still* CAN *deal with,* he thought, and started up the hill again toward where John Shooter was leaning against his car and waiting for him.

9

His walk along the lake path had been both long and slow, and Amy's call hadn't been the only thing Mort had thought about as he picked his way over or around the occasional downed tree or paused to skip the occasional flat stone across the water (as a boy he had been able to get a really good one—what they called "a flattie"—to skip as many as nine times, but today four was the most he'd been able to manage). He had also thought about how to deal with Shooter, when and if Shooter turned up again.

It was true he had felt a transient—or maybe not-so-transient—guilt when he saw how close to identical the two stories were, but he had worked that one out; it was only the generalized guilt he guessed all writers of fiction felt from time to time. As for Shooter himself, the only feelings he had were annoyance, anger . . . and a kind of relief. He was full of an unfocussed rage; had been for months. It was good to finally have a donkey to pin this rotten, stinking tail on.

Mort had heard the old saw about how, if four hundred monkeys banged away on four hundred typewriters for four million years, one of them would produce the complete works of Shakespeare. He didn't believe it. Even if it were true, John Shooter was no monkey and he hadn't been alive anywhere near that long, no matter how lined his face was.

So Shooter had copied his story. Why he had picked "Sowing Season" was beyond Mort Rainey's powers of conjecture, but he knew that was what had happened because he had ruled out co-incidence, and he knew damned well that, while he might have stolen that story, like all his others, from The Great Idea Bank of the Universe, he most certainly had not stolen it from Mr. John Shooter of the Great State of Mississippi.

Where, then, had Shooter copied it *from*? Mort thought that was the most important question; his chance to expose Shooter as a fake and a cheat might lie buried within the answer to it.

There were only two possible answers, because "Sowing Season" had only been published twice—first in *Ellery Queen's Mystery Magazine,* and then in his collection, *Everybody Drops the Dime.* The dates of publication for the short stories in a collection are usually listed on the copyright page at the front of the book, and this format had been followed in *Everybody Drops the Dime.* He had looked up the acknowledgment for "Sowing Season" and found that it had been originally published in the June, 1980, issue of *EQMM.* The collection, *Everybody Drops the Dime,* had been issued by St. Martin's Press in 1983. There had been subsequent printings since then—all but one of them in paperback—but that didn't matter. All he really had to work with were those two dates, 1980 and 1983 . . . and his own hopeful belief that, aside from agents and publishing-company lawyers, no one paid much attention to those lines of fine print on the copyright page.

Hoping that this would prove true of John Shooter, hoping that Shooter would simply assume—as most general readers did—that a story he had read for the first time in a collection had no prior existence, Mort approached the man and finally stood before him on the edge of the road.

10

"I guess you must have had a chance to read my story by now," Shooter said. He spoke as casually as a man commenting on the weather.

"I did."

Shooter nodded gravely. "I imagine it rang a bell, didn't it?"

"It certainly did," Mort agreed, and then, with studied casualness: "When did you write it?"

"I thought you'd ask that," Shooter said. He smiled a secret little smile, but said no more. His arms remained crossed over his chest, his hands laid against his sides just below the armpits. He looked like a man who would be perfectly content to remain where he was forever, or at least until the sun sank below the horizon and ceased to warm his face.

"Well, sure," Mort said, still casually. "I have to, you know. When two fellows show up with the same story, that's serious."

"Serious," Shooter agreed in a deeply meditative tone of voice.

"And the only way to sort a thing like that out," Mort continued, "to decide who copied from whom, is to find out who wrote the words first." He fixed Shooter's faded blue eyes with his own dry and uncompromising gaze. Somewhere nearby a chickadee twittered self-importantly in a tangle of trees and was then quiet again. "Wouldn't you say that's true?"

"I suppose I would," Shooter agreed. "I suppose that's why I came all the way up here from Miss'ippi."

Mort heard the rumble of an approaching vehicle. They both turned in that direction, and Tom Greenleaf's Scout came over the nearest hill, pulling a little cyclone of fallen leaves behind it. Tom, a hale and healthy Tashmore native of seventy-something, was the caretaker for most of the places on this side of the lake that Greg Carstairs didn't handle. Tom raised one hand in salute as he passed. Mort waved back. Shooter removed one hand from its resting place and tipped a finger at Tom in a friendly gesture which spoke in some obscure way of a great many years spent in the country, of the uncountable and unrecollected number of times he had saluted the passing drivers of passing trucks and tractors and tedders and balers in that exact same casual way. Then, as Tom's Scout passed out of sight, he returned his hand to his ribcage so that his arms were crossed again. As the leaves rattled to rest on the road, his patient, unwavering, almost eternal gaze came back to Mort Rainey's face once more. "Now what were we saying?" he asked almost gently.

"We were trying to establish provenance," Mort said. "That means—"

"I know what it means," Shooter said, favoring Mort with a glance which was both calm and mildly contemptuous. "I know I am wearing shitkicker clothes and driving a shitkicker car, and I come from a long line of shitkickers, and maybe that makes me a shitkicker myself, but it doesn't necessarily make me a *stupid* shitkicker."

"No," Mort agreed. "I don't guess it does. But being smart doesn't necessarily make you honest, either. In fact, I think it's more often apt to go the other way."

"I could figure that much out from you, had I not known it," Shooter said dryly, and Mort felt himself flush. He didn't like to be zinged and rarely was, but Shooter had just done it with the effortless ease of an experienced shotgunner popping a clay pigeon.

His hopes of trapping Shooter dropped. Not all the way to zero, but quite a considerable way. Smart and sharp were not the same things, but he now suspected that Shooter might be both. Still, there was no sense drawing this out. He didn't want to be around the man any longer than he had to be. In some strange way he had looked forward to this confrontation, once he had become sure that another confrontation was inevitable—maybe only because it was a break in a routine which had already become dull and unpleasant. Now he wanted it over. He was no longer sure John Shooter was crazy—not completely, anyway—but he thought the man could be dangerous. He was so goddam implacable. He decided to take his best shot and get it over with—no more dancing around.

"When *did* you write your story, Mr. Shooter?"

"Maybe my name's not Shooter," the man said, looking faintly amused. "Maybe that's just a pen name."

"I see. What's your real one?"

"I didn't say it wasn't; I only said maybe. Either way, that's not part of our business." He spoke serenely, appearing to be more interested in a cloud which was making its way slowly across the high blue sky and toward the westering sun.

"Okay," Mort said, "but when you wrote that story *is*."

"I wrote it seven years ago," he said, still studying the cloud—it had touched the edge of the sun now and had acquired a gold fringe. "In 1982."

Bingo, Mort thought. *Wily old bastard or not, he stepped right into the trap after all. He got the story out of the collection, all right. And since* Everybody Drops the Dime *was published in 1983, he thought any date before then had to be safe. Should have read the copyright page, old son.*

He waited for a feeling of triumph, but there was none. Only a muted sense of relief that this nut could be sent on his merry way with no further fuss or muss. Still, he was curious; it was the curse of the writing class. For instance, why that particular story, a story which was so out of his usual run, so downright atypical? And if the guy was going to accuse him of plagiarism, why settle for an obscure short story when he could have cobbled up the same sort of almost identical manuscript of a best-seller like *The Organ-Grinder's Boy*? *That* would have been juicy; this was almost a joke.

I suppose knocking off one of the novels would have been too much like work, Mort thought.

"Why did you wait so long?" he asked. "I mean, my book of short stories was published in 1983, and that's six years ago. Going on seven now."

"Because I didn't know," Shooter said. He removed his gaze from the cloud and studied Mort with that discomfiting look of faint contempt again. "A man like you, I suppose that kind of man just assumes that everyone in America, if not everyone in every country where his books are published, reads what he has written."

"I know better than that, I think," Mort said, and it was his turn to be dry.

"But that's not true," Shooter went on, ignoring what Mort had said in his scarily serene and utterly fixated way. "That is not true at all. I never saw that story until the middle of June. *This* June."

Mort thought of saying: *Well, guess what, Johnny-me-boy? I never saw my wife in bed with another man until the middle of May!* Would it knock Shooter off his pace if he actually *did* say something like that out loud?

He looked into the man's face and decided not. The serenity had burned out of those faded eyes the way mist burns off the hills on a day which is going to be a real scorcher. Now Shooter looked like a fundamentalist preacher about to ladle a large helping of fire and brimstone upon the trembling, downcast heads of his flock, and for the first time Mort Rainey felt really and personally afraid of the man. Yet he was also still angry. The thought he'd had near the end of his first encounter with "John Shooter" now recurred: scared or not, he was damned if he was just going to stand here and take it while this man accused him of theft—especially now that the falsity had been revealed out of the man's own mouth.

"Let me guess," Mort said. "A guy like you is a little too picky about what he reads to bother with the sort of trash I write. You stick to guys like Marcel Proust and Thomas Hardy, right? At night, after the milking's done, you like to fire up one of those honest country kerosene lamps, plunk it down on the kitchen table—which is, of course, covered with a homey red-and-white-checked table-cloth—and unwind with a little *Tess* or *Remembrance of Things Past.* Maybe on the weekend you let your hair down a little, get a little funky, and drag out some Erskine Caldwell or Annie Dillard. It was one of your friends who told you about how I'd copied your honestly wrought tale. Isn't that how the story goes, Mr. Shooter . . . or whatever your name is?"

His voice had taken on a rough edge, and he was surprised to find himself on the edge of real fury. But, he discovered, not *totally* surprised.

"Nope. I don't *have* any friends." Shooter spoke in the dry tone of a man who is only stating a fact. "No friends, no family, no wife. I've got a little place about twenty miles south of Perkinsburg, and I do have a checked tablecloth on my kitchen table—now that you mention it—but we got electric lights in our town. I only bring out the kerosenes when there's a storm and the lines go down."

"Good for you," Mort said.

Shooter ignored the sarcasm. "I got the place from my father, and added to it with a little money that came to me from my gram.

I do have a dairy herd, about twenty milkers, you were right about that, too, and in the evenings I write stories. I suppose you've got one of those fancy computers with a screen, but I make do with an old typewriter."

He fell silent, and for a moment they could both hear the crisp rustle of the leaves in the light late-afternoon wind that had sprung up.

"As for your story being the same as mine, I found that out all on my own hook. You see, I'd been thinking about selling the farm. Thinking that with a little more money, I could write days, when my mind's fresh, instead of just after dark. The realtor in Perkinsburg wanted me to meet a fellow up in Jackson, who owns a lot of dairy farms in Miss'ippi. I don't like to drive more than ten or fifteen miles at a time—it gives me a headache, especially when some of it's city driving, because that's where they let all the fools loose—and so I took the bus. I got ready to get on, and then remembered I hadn't brought anything to read. I *hate* a long bus ride without something to read."

Mort found himself nodding involuntarily. He also hated a ride—bus, train, plane, or car—without something to read, something a little more substantial than the daily paper.

"There isn't any bus station in Perkinsburg—the Greyhound just stops at the Rexall for five minutes or so and then it's down the road. I was already inside the door of that 'hound and starting up the steps when I realized I was empty-handed. I asked the bus driver if he'd hold it for me and he said he was damned if he would, he was late already, and he was pulling out in another three minutes by his pocket-watch. If I was with him, that would be fine by him, and if I wasn't, then I could kiss his fanny when we met up again."

He TALKS *like a storyteller,* Mort thought. *Be damned if he doesn't.* He tried to cancel this thought—it didn't seem to be a good way to be thinking—and couldn't quite do it.

"Well, I ran inside that drugstore. They've got one of those old-fashioned wire paperback racks in the Perkinsburg Rexall, the ones that turn around and around, just like the one in the little general store up the road from you."

"Bowie's?"

Shooter nodded. "That's the place, all right. Anyway, I grabbed the first book my hand happened on. Could have been a paperback Bible, for all I saw of the cover. But it wasn't. It was your book of short stories. *Everybody Drops the Dime.* And for all I know, they *were* your short stories. All but that one."

Stop this now. He's working up a head of steam, so spike his boiler right now.

But he discovered he didn't want to. Maybe Shooter *was* a writer. He fulfilled both of the main requirements: he told a tale you wanted to hear to the end, even if you had a pretty good idea what the end was going to be, and he was so full of shit he squeaked.

Instead of saying what he should have said—that even if Shooter was by some wild stretch of the imagination telling the truth, he, Mort, had beaten him to that miserable story by two years—he said: "So you read 'Sowing Season' on a Greyhound bus while you were going to Jackson to sell your dairy farm last June."

"No. The way it happened, I read it on the way back. I sold the farm and went back on the Greyhound with a check for sixty thousand dollars in my pocket. I'd read the first half a dozen stories going down. I didn't think they were any great shakes, but they passed the time."

"Thank you."

Shooter studied him briefly. "Wasn't offering you any real compliment."

"Don't I know it."

Shooter thought about this for a moment, then shrugged. "Anyway, I read two more going back . . . and then that one. My story."

He looked at the cloud, which was now an airy mass of shimmering gold, and then back at Mort. His face was as dispassionate as ever, but Mort suddenly understood he had been badly mistaken in believing this man possessed even the slightest shred of peace or serenity. What he had mistaken for those things was the iron mantle of control Shooter had donned to keep himself from killing Morton Rainey with his bare hands. The face was dispassionate, but his eyes blazed with the deepest, wildest fury Mort had ever seen. He understood that he had stupidly walked up the path from the lake toward what might really be his own death at this fellow's hands. Here was a man mad enough—in both senses of that word— to do murder.

"I am surprised no one has taken that story up with you before— it's not like any of the others. Not a bit." Shooter's voice was still even, but Mort now recognized it as the voice of a man laboring mightily to keep from striking out, bludgeoning, perhaps throttling;

the voice of a man who knows that all the incentive he would ever need to cross the line between talking and killing would be to hear his own voice begin to spiral upward into the registers of cheated anger; the voice of a man who knows how fatally easy it would be to become his own lynch-mob.

Mort suddenly felt like a man in a dark room which is crisscrossed with hair-thin tripwires, all of them leading to packets of high explosive. It was hard to believe that only moments ago he had felt in charge of this situation. His problems—Amy, his inability to write—now seemed like unimportant figures in an unimportant landscape. In a sense, they had ceased to be problems at all. He only had one problem now, and that was staying alive long enough to get back to his house, let alone long enough to see the sun go down.

He opened his mouth, then closed it again. There was nothing he dared to say, not now. The room was full of tripwires.

"I am *very* surprised," Shooter repeated in that heavy even voice that now sounded like a hideous parody of calmness.

Mort heard himself say: "My wife. She didn't like it. *She* said that it wasn't like anything I'd ever written before."

"How did you get it?" Shooter asked slowly and fiercely. "That's what I really want to know. How in hell did a big-money scribbling asshole like you get down to a little shitsplat town in Mississippi and steal my goddam story? I'd like to know why, too, unless you stole all the other ones as well, but the how of it'll be enough to satisfy me right now."

The monstrous unfairness of this brought Mort's own anger back like an unslaked thirst. For a moment he forgot that he was out here on Lake Drive, alone except for this lunatic from Mississippi.

"Drop it," he said harshly.

"*Drop* it?" Shooter asked, looking at Mort with a kind of clumsy amazement. "*Drop* it? What in hell do you mean, *drop* it?"

"You said you wrote your story in 1982," Mort said. "I think I wrote mine in late 1979. I can't remember the exact date, but I do know that it was published for the first time in June of 1980. In a magazine. I beat you by two years, Mr. Shooter or whatever your name is. If anyone here has got a bitch about plagiarism, it's me."

Mort did not precisely see the man move. At one moment they were standing by Shooter's car, looking at each other; at the next he found himself pressed against the driver's door, with Shooter's hands wrapped around his upper arms and Shooter's face pressed against his own, forehead to forehead. In between his two positions, there was only a blurred sensation of being first grabbed and then whirled.

"You lie," Shooter said, and on his breath was a dry whiff of cinnamon.

"The fuck I *do*," Mort said, and lunged forward against the man's pressing weight.

Shooter was strong, almost certainly stronger than Mort Rainey, but Mort was younger, heavier, and he had the old blue station wagon to push against. He was able to break Shooter's hold and send him stumbling two or three steps backward.

Now he'll come for me, Mort thought. Although he hadn't had a fight since a schoolyard you-pull-me-and-I'll-push-you scuffle back in the fourth grade, he was astounded to find his mind was clear and cool. *We're going to duke it out over that dumb fucking story. Well, okay; I wasn't doing anything else today anyhow.*

But it didn't happen. Shooter raised his hands, looked at them, saw they were knotted into fists . . . and forced them to open. Mort saw the effort it took for the man to reimpose that mantle of control, and felt a kind of awe. Shooter put one of his open palms to his mouth and wiped his lips with it, very slowly and very deliberately.

"Prove it," he said.

"All right. Come back to the house with me. I'll show you the entry on the copyright page of the book."

"No," Shooter said. "I don't care about the *book*. I don't care a *pin* for the *book*. Show me the *story*. Show me the magazine with the story in it, so I can read it for myself."

"I don't have the magazine here."

He was about to say something else, but Shooter turned his face up toward the sky and uttered a single bark of laughter. The sound was as dry as an axe splitting kindling wood. "No," he said. The fury was still blazing and dancing in his eyes, but he seemed in charge of himself again. "No, I bet you *don't*."

"Listen to me," Mort said. "Ordinarily, this is just a place my wife and I come in the summer. I have copies of my books here, and some foreign editions, but I've published in a lot of magazines as well—articles and essays as well as stories. Those magazines are in our year-round house. The one in Derry."

"Then why aren't you there?" Shooter asked. In his eyes Mort read both disbelief and a galling satisfaction—it was clear that Shooter had expected him to try and squirm his way out of it, and in Shooter's mind, that was just what Mort was doing. Or trying to do.

"I'm here because—" He stopped. "How did *you* know I'd be here?"

"I just looked on the back of the book I bought," Shooter said, and Mort could have slapped his own forehead in frustration and sudden understanding. Of course—there had been a picture of him on the back of both the hardcover and paperback editions of *Everybody Drops the Dime.* Amy had taken it herself, and it had been an excellent shot. He was in the foreground; the house was in the middle distance; Tashmore Lake was in the background. The caption had read simply, *Morton Rainey at his home in western Maine.* So Shooter had come to western Maine, and he probably hadn't had to visit too many small-town bars and/or drugstores before he found someone who said, "Mort Rainey? Hell, yes! Got a place over in Tashmore. Personal friend of mine, in fact!"

Well, that answered one question, anyway.

"I'm here because my wife and I got a divorce," he said. "It just became final. She stayed in Derry. Any other year, the house down here would have been empty."

"Uh-huh," Shooter said. His tone of voice infuriated Mort all over again. *You're lying,* it said, *but in this case it doesn't much matter. Because I knew you'd lie. After all, lying is mostly what you're about, isn't it?* "Well, I would have found you, one place or the other."

He fixed Mort with a flinty stare.

"I would have found you if you'd moved to Brazil."

"I believe that," Mort said. "Nevertheless, you are mistaken. Or conning me. I'll do you the courtesy of believing it's only a mistake, because you *seem* sincere enough—"

Oh God, didn't he.

"—but I published that story two years before you say you wrote it."

He saw that mad flash in Shooter's eyes again, and then it was gone. Not extinguished but collared, the way a man might collar a dog with an evil nature.

"You say this magazine is at your other house?"

"Yes."

"And the magazine has your story in it."

"Yes."

"And the date of that magazine is June, 1980."

"Yes."

Mort had felt impatient with this laborious catechism (there was a long, thoughtful pause before each question) at first, but now he felt a little hope: it was as if the man was trying to teach himself the truth of what Mort had said . . . a truth, Mort thought, that part of "John Shooter" must have known all along, because the almost exact similarity between the two stories was *not* coincidence. He still believed that firmly, but he *had* come around to the idea that Shooter might have no conscious memory of committing the plagiarism. Because the man was clearly mad.

He wasn't quite as afraid as he had been when he first saw the hate and fury dancing in Shooter's eyes, like the reflection of a barn-fire blazing out of control. When he pushed the man, he had staggered backward, and Mort thought that if it came to a fight, he could probably hold his own . . . or actually put his man on the ground.

Still, it would be better if it didn't come to that. In an odd, backhand sort of way, he had begun to feel a bit sorry for Shooter.

That gentleman, meanwhile, was stolidly pursuing his course.

"This other house—the one your wife has now—it's here in Maine, too?"

"Yes."

"She's there?"

"Yes."

There was a much longer pause this time. In a weird way, Shooter reminded Mort of a computer processing a heavy load of information. At last he said: "I'll give you three days."

"That's very generous of you," Mort said.

Shooter's long upper lip drew back from teeth too even to be anything but mail-order dentures. "Don't you make light of me, son," he said. "I'm trying my best to hold my temper, and doing a pretty good job of it, but—"

"*You!*" Mort cried at him. "What about *me?* This is unbelievable! You come out of nowhere and make just about the most serious accusation a man can make against a writer, and when I tell you I've got proof you're either mistaken or lying through your damned teeth, you start patting yourself on the back for holding your temper! *Unbelievable!*"

Shooter's eyelids drooped, giving him a sly look. "Proof?" he said. "I don't see no proof. I hear you talking, but *talking* ain't *proof.*"

"I *told* you!" Mort shouted. He felt helpless, like a man trying to box cobwebs. "I *explained* all that!"

Shooter looked at Mort for a long moment, then turned and reached through the open window of his car.

"What are you doing?" Mort asked, his voice tight. *Now* he felt the adrenaline dump into his body, readying him for fight or flight . . . probably the latter, if Shooter was reaching for the big handgun Mort suddenly saw in the eye of his imagination.

"Just gettin m'smokes," Shooter said. "Hold your water."

When he pulled his arm out of the car, he had a red package of Pall Malls in his hand. He had taken them off the dashboard. "Want one?"

"I have my own," Mort said rather sulkily, and took the ancient pack of L & M's from the pocket beneath the red flannel overshirt.

They lit up, each from his own pack.

"If we keep on this way, we're going to have a fight," Shooter said finally. "I don't want that."

"Well, Jesus, neither do I!"

"Part of you does," Shooter contradicted. He continued to study Mort from beneath his dropped lids with that expression of country shrewdness. "Part of you wants *just* that. But I don't think it's just me or my story that's making you want to fight. You have got some other bee under your blanket that's got you all riled up, and *that* is making *this* harder. Part of you wants to fight, but what you don't understand is that, if we *do* start to fight, it's not going to end until one or the other of us is dead."

Mort looked for signs that Shooter was exaggerating for effect and saw none. He suddenly felt cold along the base of his spine.

"So I'm going to give you three days. You call your ex and get her to send down the magazine with your story in it, if there *is* such a magazine. And I'll be back. There *isn't* any magazine, of course; I think we both know that. But you strike me as a man who needs to do some long, hard thinking."

He looked at Mort with a disconcerting expression of stern pity.

"You didn't believe anybody would ever catch you out, did you?" he asked. "You really didn't."

"If I show you the magazine, will you go away?" Mort asked. He was speaking more to himself than to Shooter. "I guess what I really want to know is whether or not it's even worth it."

Shooter abruptly opened his car door and slid in behind the wheel. Mort found the speed with which the man could move a little creepy. "Three days. Use it the way you like, Mr. Rainey."

He started the engine. It ran with the low wheeze characteristic of valves which need to be reground, and the tang of oilsmoke from the old tailpipe polluted the air of the fading afternoon. "Right is right and fair is fair. The first thing is to get you to a place where you see I have really got you, and you can't wiggle out of this mess the way you've probably been wiggling out of the messes you have made all your life. That's the first thing."

He looked at Mort expressionlessly out of the driver's-side window.

"The second thing," he said, "is the real reason I come."

"What's that?" Mort heard himself say. It was strange and not a little infuriating, but he felt that sensation of guilt creeping relentlessly over him again, as if he really had done the thing of which this rustic lunatic was accusing him.

"We'll talk about it," Shooter said, and threw his elderly station wagon in gear. "Meantime, you think about what's right and what's fair."

"You're nuts!" Mort shouted, but Shooter was already rolling up Lake Drive toward where it spilled out onto Route 23.

He watched until the wagon was out of sight, then walked slowly back to the house. It felt emptier and emptier in his mind as he drew closer and closer to it. The rage and the fear were gone. He felt only cold, tired, and homesick for a marriage which no longer was, and which, it now began to seem to him, had never been at all.

11

The telephone started ringing when he was halfway along the driveway which ran down the steep hill from Lake Drive to the house. Mort broke into a run, knowing he wasn't going to make it but running anyway, cursing himself for his foolish reaction. Talk about Pavlov's dogs!

He had opened the screen door and was fumbling with the knob of the inside door when the phone silenced. He stepped in, closed the door behind him, and looked at the telephone, which stood on a little antique desk Amy had picked up at a flea market in Mechanic Falls. He could, in that moment, easily imagine that the phone was looking back at him with studied mechanical impatience: *Don't ask me, boss—I don't make the news, I only report it.* He thought that he ought to buy one of those machines that take messages . . . or maybe not. When he thought about it carefully, he realized that the telephone was hardly his favorite gadget. If people really wanted you, they eventually called back.

He made himself a sandwich and a bowl of soup and then discovered he didn't want them. He felt lonely, unhappy, and mildly infected by John Shooter's craziness. He was not much surprised to find that the sum of these feelings was sleepiness. He began to cast longing glances at the couch.

Okay, an interior voice whispered. *Remember, though—you can run but you can't hide. This shit is still gonna be here when you wake up.*

That was very true, he thought, but in the meantime, it would all be gone, gone, blessedly gone. The one thing you could definitely say for short-term solutions was that they were better than nothing. He decided he would call home (his mind persisted in thinking of the Derry house as home, and he suspected that was a circumstance which would not soon change), ask Amy to pull the copy of *EQMM* with "Sowing Season" in it and send it down by express mail. Then he would sack on the couch for a couple of hours. He would arise around seven or so, go into the study refreshed, and write a little more shit.

And shit is all you will write, with that attitude, the interior voice reproached him.

"Fuck you," Mort told it—one of the few advantages to living alone, so far as he could see, was that you could talk to yourself right out loud without having anyone wonder if you were crazy or what.

He picked up the phone and dialled the Derry number. He listened to the customary clicks of the long-distance connection being made, and then that most irritating of all telephone sounds: the dah-dah-dah of a busy signal. Amy was on the telephone with someone, and when Amy really got going, a conversation could go on for hours. Possibly days.

"Oh, fuck, great!" Mort cried, and jacked the handset back into the cradle hard enough to make the bell jingle faintly.

So—what now, little man?

He supposed he could call Isabelle Fortin, who lived across the street, but that suddenly seemed like too much work and a pain in the ass besides. Isabelle was already so deeply into his and Amy's breakup that she was doing everything but taking home movies. Also, it was already past five o'clock—the magazine couldn't actually start to move along the postal channel between Derry and Tashmore until tomorrow morning no matter what time it was mailed today. He would try Amy later on this evening, and if the line to the house was busy again (or if Amy was, perchance, still on the same call), he would call Isabelle with the message after all. For the moment, the siren-song of the couch in the living room was too strong to be denied.

Mort pulled the phone jack—whoever had tried to call him just as he was coming down the driveway would have to wait a little longer, please and thank you—and strolled into the living room.

He propped the pillows in their familiar positions, one behind his head and one behind his neck, and looked out at the lake, where the sun was setting at the end of a long and spectacular golden track. *I have never felt so lonely and so utterly horrible in my whole life,* he thought with some amazement. Then his lids closed slowly over his slightly bloodshot eyes, and Mort Rainey, who had yet to discover what true horror was all about, fell asleep.

12

He dreamed he was in a classroom.

It was a familiar classroom, although he couldn't have said just why. He was in the classroom with John Shooter. Shooter was holding a grocery bag in the curve of one arm. He took an orange out of the bag and bounced it reflectively up and down in his hand. He was looking in Mort's direction, but not *at* Mort; his gaze seemed fixed on something beyond Mort's shoulder. Mort turned and saw a cinderblock wall and a blackboard and a door with a frosted-glass upper panel. After a moment he could puzzle out the backward writing on the frosted glass.

WELCOME TO THE SCHOOL OF HARD KNOCKS,

it said. The writing on the blackboard was easier to read.

SOWING SEASON
A Short Story by Morton Rainey,

it said.

Suddenly something whizzed over Mort's shoulder, just missing his head. The orange. As Mort cringed back, the orange struck the blackboard, burst open with a rotten squashing sound, and splattered gore across what had been written there.

He turned back to Shooter. *Stop that!* he cried in a shaky scolding voice.

Shooter dipped into his bag again. *What's the matter?* Shooter asked in his calm, stern voice. *Don't you recognize blood oranges when you see them? What kind of writer are you?*

He threw another one. It splattered crimson across Mort's name and began to drip slowly down the wall.

No more! Mort screamed, but Shooter dipped slowly, implacably, into the bag again. His long, callused fingers sank into the skin of the orange he brought out; blood began to sweat its way onto the orange's skin in pinprick droplets.

No more! No more! Please! No more! I'll admit it, I'll admit anything, everything, if you just stop! Anything, if you'll just stop! If you'll—

13

"—stop, if you'll just stop—"

He was falling.

Mort grabbed at the edge of the couch just in time to save himself a short and probably painful trip to the living-room floor. He rolled toward the back of the couch and simply lay there for a moment, clutching the cushions, shivering, and trying to grasp at the ragged tails of the dream.

Something about a classroom, and blood oranges, and the school of hard knocks. Even this was going, and the rest was already gone. It had been real, whatever it was. Much too real.

At last he opened his eyes, but there was precious little to see;

he had slept until long past sundown. He was horribly stiff, especially at the base of his neck, and he suspected he had been asleep at least four hours, maybe five. He felt his way cautiously to the living-room light-switch, managing to avoid the octagonal glass-topped coffee table for a change (he had an idea the coffee table was semi-sentient, and given to shifting its position slightly after dark, the better to hack away at his shins), and then went into the front hall to try Amy again. On the way, he checked his watch. It was quarter past ten. He had slept over five hours . . . nor was this the first time. And he wouldn't even pay for it by tossing and turning all night. Judging by past experience, he would be asleep as soon as his head hit the pillow in the bedroom.

He picked up the phone, was momentarily puzzled by the dead silence in his ear, then remembered he had yanked the damn thing's fang. He pulled the wire through his fingers until he got to the jack, turned around to plug it in . . . and paused. From here he could look out the small window to the left of the door. This gave him an angle of vision on the back porch, where the mysterious and unpleasant Mr. Shooter had left his manuscript under a rock yesterday. He could also see the garbage cabinet, and there was something on it—two somethings, actually. A white something and a dark something. The dark something looked nasty; for one frightening second, Mort thought a giant spider was crouched there.

He dropped the phone cord and turned on the porch light in a hurry. Then there was a space of time—he didn't know just *how* long and didn't care to know—when he was incapable of further movement.

The white thing was a sheet of paper—a perfectly ordinary 8½" × 11" sheet of typing paper. Although the garbage cabinet was a good fifteen feet away from where Mort was standing, the few words on it were printed in large strokes and he could read them easily. He thought Shooter must have used either a pencil with an extremely soft lead or a piece of artist's charcoal. REMEMBER, YOU HAVE 3 DAYS, the message read. I AM NOT JOKING.

The black thing was Bump. Shooter had apparently broken the cat's neck before nailing him to the roof of the garbage cabinet with a screwdriver from Mort's own toolshed.

14

He wasn't aware of breaking the paralysis which held him. At one moment he was standing frozen in the hall by the telephone table, looking out at good old Bump, who seemed to have grown a screwdriver handle in the middle of his chest, where there was a ruff of white fur—what Amy had liked to call Bump's bib. At the next he was standing in the middle of the porch with the chilly night air biting through his thin shirt, trying to look six different ways at once.

He forced himself to stop. Shooter was gone, of course. That's why he had left the note. Nor did Shooter seem like the kind of nut who would enjoy watching Mort's obvious fear and horror. He was a nut, all right, but one which had fallen from a different tree. He had simply used Bump, used him on Mort the way a farmer might use a crowbar on a stubborn rock in his north forty. There was nothing personal in it; it was just a job that had to be done.

Then he thought of how Shooter's eyes had looked that afternoon and shivered violently. No, it was personal, all right. It was all kinds of personal.

"He believes I did it," Mort whispered to the cold western Maine night, and the words came out in ragged chunks, bitten off by his chattering teeth. "The crazy son of a bitch really believes I did it."

He approached the garbage cabinet and his stomach rolled over like a dog doing a trick. Cold sweat broke out on his forehead, and he wasn't sure he could take care of what needed taking care of. Bump's head was cocked far to the left, giving him a grotesque questioning look. His teeth, small, neat, and needle-sharp, were bared. There was a little blood around the blade of the screwdriver at the point where it was driven into his

(*bib*)

ruff, but not very much. Bump was a friendly cat; if Shooter had approached him, Bump would not have shied away. And that was what Shooter must have done, Mort thought, and wiped the sick sweat off his forehead. He had picked the cat up, snapped its neck between his fingers like a Popsicle stick, and then nailed it to the slanting roof of the garbage cabinet, all while Mort Rainey slept, if not the sleep of the just, that of the unheeding.

Mort crumpled up the sheet of paper, stuffed it in his back pocket, then put his hand on Bump's chest. The body, not stiff and not even entirely cold, shifted under his hand. His stomach rolled again, but he forced his other hand to close around the screwdriver's yellow plastic handle and pull it free.

He tossed the screwdriver onto the porch and held poor old Bump in his right hand like a bundle of rags. Now his stomach was in free fall, simply rolling and rolling and rolling. He lifted one of the two lids on top of the garbage cabinet, and secured it with the hook-and-eyelet that kept the heavy lid from crashing down on the arms or head of whoever was depositing trash inside. Three cans were lined up within. Mort lifted the lid from the center one and deposited Bump's body gently inside. It lay draped over the top of an olive-green Hefty bag like a fur stole.

He was suddenly furious with Shooter. If the man had appeared in the driveway at that second, Mort would have charged him without a second thought—driven him to the ground and choked him if he could.

Easy—it really IS catching.

Maybe it was. And maybe he didn't care. It wasn't just that Shooter had killed his only companion in this lonely October house by the lake; it was that he had done it while Mort was asleep, and in such a way that good old Bump had become an object of revulsion, something it was hard not to puke over.

Most of all it was the fact that he had been forced to put his good cat in a garbage can like a piece of worthless trash.

I'll bury him tomorrow. Right over in that soft patch to the left of the house. In sight of the lake.

Yes, but tonight Bump would lie in undignified state on top of a Hefty bag in the garbage cabinet because some man—some crazy son of a bitch—could be out there, and the man had a grudge over a story Mort Rainey hadn't even *thought* of for the last five years or so. The man was crazy, and consequently Mort was afraid to bury Bump tonight, because, note or no note, Shooter might be out there.

I want to kill him. And if the crazy bastard pushes me much more, I might just try to do it.

He went inside, slammed the door, and locked it. Then he walked deliberately through the house, locking all the doors and windows. When that was done, he went back to the window by the porch door and stared pensively out into the darkness. He could see the screwdriver lying on the boards, and the dark round hole the blade had made when Shooter plunged it into the right-hand lid of the garbage cabinet.

All at once he remembered he had been about to try Amy again.

He plugged the jack into the wall. He dialed rapidly, fingers tapping the old familiar keys which added up to home, and wondered if he would tell Amy about Bump.

There was an unnaturally long pause after the preliminary clicks. He was about to hang up when there was one final click—so loud it was almost a thud—followed by a robot voice telling him that the number he had dialled was out of service.

"Wonderful," he muttered. "What the hell did you do, Amy? Use it until it broke?"

He pushed the disconnect button down, thinking he would have to call Isabelle Fortin after all, and while he was conning his memory for her number, the telephone rang in his hand.

He hadn't realized how keyed up he was until that happened. He gave a screaky little cry and skipped backward, dropping the telephone handset on the floor and then almost tripping over the goddam bench Amy had bought and put by the telephone table, the bench absolutely no one, including Amy herself, ever used.

He pawed out with one hand, grabbed the bookcase, and kept himself from falling. Then he snatched up the phone and said, "Hello? Is that you, Shooter?" For in that moment, when it seemed that the whole world was slowly but surely turning topsy-turvy, he couldn't imagine who else it could be.

"Mort?" It was Amy, and she was nearly screaming. He knew the tone very well from the last two years of their marriage. It was either frustration or fury, more likely the latter. "Mort, is that you? Is it you, for God's sake? Mort? M—"

"Yes, it's me," he said. He suddenly felt weary.

"Where in the hell have you been? I've been trying to get you for the last *three hours!*"

"Asleep," he said.

"You pulled the jack." She spoke in the tired but accusatory tone of one who had been down this road before. "Well, you picked a great time to do it this time, champ."

"I tried to call around five—"

"I was at Ted's."

"Well, *somebody* was there," he said. "Maybe—"

"What do you mean, someone was there?" she asked, whiplash quick. "*Who* was there?"

"How the hell would I know, Amy? You're the one in Derry, remember? You Derry, me Tashmore. All I know is that the line was busy when I tried to call you. If you were over at Ted's, then I assume Isabelle—"

"I'm *still* at Ted's," she said, and now her voice was queerly flat. "I guess I'll be at Ted's for quite awhile to come, like it or not. Someone burned our house down, Mort. Someone burned it right to the ground." And suddenly Amy began to cry.

15

He had become so fixated on John Shooter that his immediate assumption, as he stood numbly in the hallway of the one remaining Rainey home with the telephone screwed against his ear, was that Shooter had burned the house down. Motive? Why, certainly, officer. He burned the house, a restored Victorian worth about $800,000, to get rid of a magazine. *Ellery Queen's Mystery Magazine,* to be precise; June of 1980 issue.

But *could* it have been Shooter? Surely not. The distance between Derry and Tashmore was over a hundred miles, and Bump's body had still been warm and flexible, the blood around the screwdriver blade tacky but not yet dry.

If he hurried—

Oh, quit it, why don't you? Pretty soon you'll be blaming Shooter for your divorce and thinking you've been sleeping sixteen hours out of every twenty-four because Shooter has been putting Phenobarb in your food. And after that? You can start writing letters to the paper saying that America's cocaine kingpin is a gentleman from Crow's Ass Mississippi named John Shooter. That he killed Jimmy Hoffa and also happened to be the famous second gun who fired at Kennedy from the grassy knoll in November of 1963. The man's crazy, okay . . . but do you really think he drove a hundred miles north and massacred your goddam house in order to kill a magazine? *Especially when there must be copies of that magazine still in existence all across America? Get serious.*

But still . . . if he hurried . . .

No. It was ridiculous. But, Mort suddenly realized, he wouldn't

be able to show the man his goddam proof, would he? Not unless . . .

The study was at the back of the house; they had converted what
had once been the loft of the carriage-barn.

"Amy," he said.

"It's so *horrible!*" she wept. "I was at Ted's and Isabelle called . . .
she said there were at least fifteen fire trucks there . . . hoses spraying . . . crowds . . . rubberneckers . . . *gawkers* . . . you know how I
hate it when people come and gawk at the house, even when it's
not burning down . . ."

He had to bite down hard on the insides of his cheeks to stifle
a wild bray of laughter. To laugh now would be the worst thing,
the cruellest thing he could possibly do, because he *did* know. His
success at his chosen trade after the years of struggle had been a
great and fulfilling thing for him; he sometimes felt like a man who
has won his way through a perilous jungle where most other ad-
venturers perish and has gained a fabulous prize by so doing. Amy
had been glad for him, at least initially, but for her there had been
a bitter downside: the loss of her identity not only as a private
person but as a *separate* person.

"Yes," he said as gently as he could, still biting at his cheeks to
protect against the laughter which threatened. If he laughed, it
would be at her unfortunate choice of phrasing, but she wouldn't
see it that way. So often during their years together she had mis-
interpreted his laughter. "Yes, I know, hon. Tell me what happened."

"Somebody burned down our *house!*" Amy cried tearily. "That's
what *happened!*"

"Is it a total loss?"

"Yes. That's what the fire chief said." He could hear her gulping,
trying to get herself under control, and then her tears stormed out
again. "It b-b-burned fuh-fuh-*flat!*"

"Even my study?"

"That's w-where it *st-started,*" she sniffled. "At least, that's what
the fire chief said they thought. And it fits with what Patty saw."

"Patty Champion?"

The Champions owned the house next to the Raineys' on the
right; the two lots were separated by a belt of yew trees that had
slowly run wild over the years.

"Yes. Just a second, Mort."

He heard a mighty honk as she blew her nose, and when she came back on the line, she seemed more composed. "Patty was walking her dog, she told the firemen. This was a little while after it got dark. She walked past our house and saw a car parked under the portico. Then she heard a crash from inside, and saw fire in your big study window."

"Did she see what kind of a car it was?" Mort asked. He felt sick in the pit of his stomach. As the news sank in, the John Shooter business began to dwindle in size and importance. It wasn't just the goddam June, 1980, issue of *EQMM;* it was almost *all* his manuscripts, both those which had been published and those which were incomplete, it was most of his first editions, his foreign editions, his contributors' copies.

Oh, but that was only the start. They had lost their books, as many as four thousand volumes. All of Amy's clothes would have burned, if the damage was as bad as she said it was, and the antique furniture she had collected—sometimes with his help, but mostly on her own—would all be cinders and clinkers now. Her jewelry and their personal papers—insurance policies and so on—would probably be okay (the safe hidden at the back of the upstairs closet was supposed to be fireproof), but the Turkish rugs would be ash, the thousand or so videotapes melted lumps of plastic, the audiovisual equipment . . . his clothes . . . their photographs, thousands of them. . . .

Good Christ, and the first thing he'd thought of was that goddam *magazine.*

"No," Amy was saying, answering the question he had almost forgotten asking in his realization of how enormous the personal loss must be, "she couldn't tell what kind of car it was. She said she thought somebody must have used a Molotov cocktail, or something like that. Because of the way the fire came up in the window right after the sound of breaking glass. She said she started up the driveway and then the kitchen door opened and a man ran out. Bruno started to bark at him, but Patty got scared and pulled him back, although she said he just about ripped the leash out of her hand.

"Then the man got into the car and started it up. He turned on the headlights, and Patty said they almost blinded her. She threw her arm up to shield her eyes and the car just roared out from under the portico . . . that's what she said . . . and she squeezed back against our front fence and pulled Bruno as hard as she could, or the man would have hit him. Then he turned out of the driveway and drove down the street, fast."

"And she never saw what kind of car it was?"

"No. First it was dark, and then, when the fire started to shine through your study window, the headlights dazzled her. She ran back to the house and called the fire department. Isabelle said they came fast, but you know how old our house is . . . was . . . and . . . and how fast dry wood burns . . . especially if you use gasoline . . ."

Yes, he knew. Old, dry, full of wood, the house had been an arsonist's wet dream. But who? If not Shooter, *who?* This terrible news, coming on top of the day's events like a hideous dessert at the end of a loathsome meal, had almost completely paralyzed his ability to think.

"He said it *was* probably gasoline . . . the fire chief, I mean . . . he was there first, but then the police came, and they kept asking questions, Mort, mostly about you . . . about any enemies you might have made . . . *enemies* . . . and I said I didn't think you h-had any enemies . . . I tried to answer all his questions . . ."

"I'm sure you did the best job you could," he said gently.

She went on as if she hadn't heard him, speaking in breathless ellipses, like a telegraph operator relating dire news aloud just as it spills off the wire. "I didn't even know how to tell them we were *divorced* . . . and of course they didn't know . . . it was Ted who had to tell them finally . . . Mort . . . my mother's Bible . . . it was on the nightstand in the bedroom . . . there were pictures in it of my family . . . and . . . and it was the only thing . . . only thing of hers I h-h-had . . ."

Her voice dissolved into miserable sobs.

"I'll be up in the morning," he said. "If I leave at seven, I can be there by nine-thirty. Maybe by nine, now that there's no summer traffic. Where will you stay tonight? At Ted's?"

"Yes," she said, sniffling. "I know you don't like him, Mort, but I don't know what I would have done without him tonight . . . how I could have handled it . . . you know . . . all their questions . . ."

"Then I'm glad you had him," he said firmly. He found the calmness, the *civilization,* in his voice really astounding. "Take care of yourself. Have you got your pills?" She'd had a tranquilizer prescription for the last six years of their marriage, but only took them when she had to fly . . . or, he remembered, when he had some public function to fulfill. One which required the presence of the Designated Spouse.

"They were in the medicine cabinet," she said dully. "It doesn't matter. I'm not stressed. Just heartsick."

Mort almost told her he believed they were the same thing, and decided not to.

"I'll be there as soon as I can," he said. "If you think I could do something by coming tonight—"

"No," she said. "Where should we meet? Ted's?"

Suddenly, unbidden, he saw his hand holding a chambermaid's passkey. Saw it turning in the lock of a motel-room door. Saw the door swinging open. Saw the surprised faces above the sheet, Amy's on the left, Ted Milner's on the right. His blow-dried look had been knocked all aslant and asprawl by sleep, and to Mort he had looked a little bit like Alfalfa in the old Little Rascals short subjects. Seeing Ted's hair in sleep corkscrews like that had also made the man look really real to Mort for the first time. He had seen their dismay and their bare shoulders. And suddenly, almost randomly, he thought: *A woman who would steal your love when your love was really all you had—*

"No," he said, "not Ted's. What about that little coffee shop on Witcham Street?"

"Would you prefer I came alone?" She didn't sound angry, but she sounded *ready* to be angry. How well I know her, he thought. Every move, every lift and drop of her voice, every turn of phrase. And how well she must know me.

"No," he said. "Bring Ted. That'd be fine." Not fine, but he could live with it. He thought.

"Nine-thirty, then," she said, and he could hear her standing down a little. "Marchman's."

"Is that the name of that place?"

"Yes—Marchman's Restaurant."

"Okay. Nine-thirty or a little earlier. If I get there first, I'll chalk a mark on the door—"

"—and if *I* get there first, I'll rub it out," she finished the old catechism, and they both laughed a little. Mort found that even the laugh hurt. They knew each other, all right. Wasn't that what the years together were supposed to be for? And wasn't that why it hurt so goddam bad when you discovered that, not only *could* the years end, they really had?

He suddenly thought of the note which had been stuck under one of the garbage cabinet's shake shingles—REMEMBER, YOU HAVE 3 DAYS. I AM NOT JOKING. He thought of saying, *I've had a little trouble of my own down here, Amy,* and then knew he couldn't add that to her current load of woe. It was his trouble.

"If it had happened later, at least you would have saved *your* stuff," she was saying. "I don't like to think about all the manuscripts you must have lost, Mort. If you'd gotten the fireproof drawers two years ago, when Herb suggested them, maybe—"

"I don't think it matters," Mort said. "I've got the manuscript of the new novel down here." He did, too. All fourteen shitty, wooden pages of it. "To hell with the rest. I'll see you tomorrow, Amy, I—"

(love you)

He closed his lips over it. They were divorced. *Could* he still love her? It seemed almost perverse. And even if he did, did he have any right to say so?

"I'm sorry as hell about this," he told her instead.

"So am I, Mort. So very sorry." She was starting to cry again. Now he could hear someone—a woman, probably Isabelle Fortin—comforting her.

"Get some sleep, Amy."

"You, too."

He hung up. All at once the house seemed much quieter than it had on any of the other nights he had been here alone; he could hear nothing but the night wind whispering around the eaves and, very far off, a loon calling on the lake. He took the note out of his pocket, smoothed it out, and read it again. It was the sort of thing you were supposed to put aside for the police. In fact, it was the sort of thing you weren't even supposed to touch until the police had had a chance to photograph it and work their juju on it. It was—ruffle of drums and blast of trumpets, please—EVIDENCE.

Well, fuck it, Mort thought, crumpling it up again. No police. Dave Newsome, the local constable, probably had trouble remembering what he'd eaten for breakfast by the time lunch rolled around, and he couldn't see taking the matter to either the county sheriff or the State Police. After all, it wasn't as though an attempt had been made on his life; his cat had been killed, but a cat wasn't a person. And in the wake of Amy's devastating news, John Shooter simply didn't seem as important anymore. He was one of the Crazy

Folks, he had a bee in his bonnet, and he might be dangerous . . . but Mort felt more and more inclined to try and handle the business himself, even if Shooter was dangerous. *Especially* if he was dangerous.

The house in Derry took precedence over John Shooter and John Shooter's crazy ideas. It even took precedence over who had done the deed—Shooter or some other fruitcake with a grudge, a mental problem, or both. The house, and, he supposed, Amy. She was clearly in bad shape, and it couldn't hurt either of them for him to offer her what comfort he could. Maybe she would even . . .

But he closed his mind to any speculation about what Amy might even do. He saw nothing but pain down that road. Better to believe that road was closed for good.

He went into the bedroom, undressed, and lay down with his hands behind his head. The loon called again, desperate and distant. It occurred to him again that Shooter could be out there, creeping around, his face a pale circle beneath his odd black hat. Shooter was nuts, and although he had used his hands and a screwdriver on Bump, that did not preclude the possibility that he still might have a gun.

But Mort didn't think Shooter was out there, armed or not.

Calls, he thought. *I'll have to make at least two on my way up to Derry. One to Greg Carstairs and one to Herb Creekmore. Too early to make them from here if I leave at seven, but I could use one of the pay phones at the Augusta tollbooths. . . .*

He turned over on his side, thinking it would be a long time before he fell asleep tonight after all . . . and then sleep rolled over him in a smooth dark wave, and if anyone came to peer in on him as he slept, he did not know it.

16

The alarm got him up at six-fifteen. He took half an hour to bury Bump in the sandy patch of ground between the house and the lake, and by seven he was rolling, just as planned. He was ten miles down the road and heading into Mechanic Falls, a bustling metropolis which consisted of a textile mill that had closed in 1970, five thousand souls, and a yellow blinker at the intersection of Routes 23 and 7, when he noticed that his old Buick was running on fumes. He pulled into Bill's Chevron, cursing himself for not having checked the gauge before setting out—if he had gotten through Mechanic Falls without noticing how low the gauge had fallen, he might have had a pretty good walk for himself and ended up very late for his appointment with Amy.

He went to the pay phone on the wall while the pump jockey tried to fill the Buick's bottomless pit. He dug his battered address book out of his left rear pocket and dialled Greg Carstairs's number. He thought he might actually catch Greg in this early, and he was right.

"Hello?"

"Hi, Greg—Mort Rainey."

"Hi, Mort. I guess you've got some trouble up in Derry, huh?"

"Yes," Mort said. "Was it on the news?"

"Channel 5."

"How did it look?"

"How did *what* look?" Greg replied. Mort winced . . . but if he had to hear that from anybody, he was glad it had been Greg Carstairs. He was an amiable, long-haired ex-hippie who had converted to some fairly obscure religious sect—the Swedenborgians, maybe—not long after Woodstock. He had a wife and two kids, one seven and one five, and so far as Mort could tell, the whole family was as laid back as Greg himself. You got so used to the man's small but constant smile that he looked undressed on the few occasions he was without it.

"That bad, huh?"

"Yes," Greg said simply. "It must have gone up like a rocket. I'm really sorry, man."

"Thank you. I'm on my way up there now, Greg. I'm calling from Mechanic Falls. Can you do me a favor while I'm gone?"

"If you mean the shingles, I think they'll be in by—"

"No, not the shingles. Something else. There's been a guy bothering me the last two or three days. A crackpot. He claims I stole a story he wrote six or seven years ago. When I told him I'd written my version of the same story before he claims to have written his, and told him I could prove it, he got wiggy. I was sort of hoping I'd seen the last of him, but no such luck. Last evening, while I was sleeping on the couch, he killed my cat."

"Bump?" Greg sounded faintly startled, a reaction that equalled roaring surprise in anyone else. "He killed *Bump*?"

"That's right."

"Did you talk to Dave Newsome about it?"

"No, and I don't want to, either. I want to handle him myself, if I can."

"The guy doesn't exactly sound like a pacifist, Mort."

"Killing a cat is a long way from killing a man," Mort said, "and I think maybe I could handle him better than Dave."

"Well, you could have something there," Greg agreed. "Dave's slowed down a little since he turned seventy. What can I do for you, Mort?"

"I'd like to know where the guy is staying, for one thing."

"What's his name?"

"I don't know. The name on the story he showed me was John Shooter, but he got cute about that later on, told me it might be a pseudonym. I think it is—it *sounds* like a pseudonym. Either way, I doubt if he's registered under that name if he's staying at an area motel."

"What does he look like?"

"He's about six feet tall and forty-something. He's got a kind of weatherbeaten face—sun-wrinkles around the eyes and lines going down from the corners of the mouth, kind of bracketing the chin."

As he spoke, the face of "John Shooter" floated into his consciousness with increasing clarity, like the face of a spirit swimming up to the curved side of a medium's crystal ball. Mort felt gooseflesh prick the backs of his hands and shivered a little. A voice in his midbrain kept muttering that he was either making a mistake or deliberately misleading Greg. Shooter was dangerous, all right. He hadn't needed to see what the man had done to Bump to know that. He had seen it in Shooter's eyes yesterday afternoon. Why was he playing vigilante, then?

Because, another, deeper, voice answered with a kind of dangerous firmness. *Just because, that's all.*

The midbrain voice spoke up again, worried: *Do you mean to hurt him? Is that what this is all about? Do you mean to hurt him?*

But the deep voice would not answer. It had fallen silent.

"Sounds like half the farmers around here," Greg was saying doubtfully.

"Well, there's a couple of other things that may help pick him out," Mort said. "He's Southern, for one thing—got an accent on him that sticks out a mile. He wears a big black hat—felt, I think—

with a round crown. It looks like the kind of hat Amish men wear. And he's driving a blue Ford station wagon, early or mid-sixties. Mississippi plates."

"Okay—better. I'll ask around. If he's in the area, somebody'll know where. Outta-state plates stand out this time of year."

"I know." Something else crossed his mind suddenly. "You might start by asking Tom Greenleaf. I was talking to this Shooter yesterday on Lake Drive, about half a mile north of my place. Tom came along in his Scout. He waved at us when he went by, and both of us waved back. Tom must have gotten a damned fine look at him."

"Okay. I'll probably see him up at Bowie's Store if I drop by for a coffee around ten."

"He's been there, too," Mort said. "I know, because he mentioned the paperback book-rack. It's one of the old-fashioned ones."

"And if I track him down, what?"

"Nothing," Mort said. "Don't do a thing. I'll call you tonight. Tomorrow night I should be back at the place on the lake. I don't know what the hell I can do up in Derry, except scuffle through the ashes."

"What about Amy?"

"She's got a guy," Mort said, trying not to sound stiff and probably sounding that way just the same. "I guess what Amy does next is something the two of them will have to work out."

"Oh. Sorry."

"No need to be," Mort said. He looked over toward the gas islands and saw that the jockey had finished filling his tank and was now washing the Buick's windshield, a sight he had never expected to witness again in his lifetime.

"Handling this guy yourself . . . are you really sure it's what you want to do?"

"Yes, I think so," Mort said.

He hesitated, suddenly understanding what was very likely going on in Greg's mind: he was thinking that if he found the man in the black hat and Mort got hurt as a result, he, Greg, would be responsible.

"Listen, Greg—you could go along while I talk to the guy, if you wanted to."

"I might just do that," Greg said, relieved.

"It's proof he wants," Mort said, "so I'll just have to get it for him."

"But you said you *had* proof."

"Yes, but he didn't exactly take my word for it. I guess I'm going to have to shove it in his face to get him to leave me alone."

"Oh." Greg thought it over. "The guy really is crazy, isn't he?"

"Yes indeed."

"Well, I'll see if I can find him. Give me a call tonight."

"I will. And thanks, Greg."

"Don't mention it. A change is as good as a rest."

"So they say."

He told Greg goodbye and checked his watch. It was almost seven-thirty, and that was much too early to call Herb Creekmore, unless he wanted to pry Herb out of bed, and this wasn't that urgent. A stop at the Augusta tollbooths would do fine. He walked back to the Buick, replacing his address book and digging out his wallet. He asked the pump jockey how much he owed him.

"That's twenty-two fifty, with the cash discount," the jockey said, and then looked at Mort shyly. "I wonder if I could have your autograph, Mr. Rainey? I've all your books."

That made him think of Amy again, and how Amy had hated the autograph seekers. Mort himself didn't understand them, but saw no harm in them. For her they had seemed to sum up an aspect of their lives which she found increasingly hateful. Toward the end, he had cringed inwardly every time someone asked *that* question in Amy's presence. Sometimes he could almost sense her thinking: *If you love me, why don't you STOP them?* As if he could, he thought. His job was to write books people like this guy would want to read . . . or so he saw it. When he succeeded at that, they asked for autographs.

He scribbled his name on the back of a credit slip for the pump jockey (who had, after all, actually washed his windshield) and reflected that if Amy had blamed him for doing something they liked—and he thought that, on some level she herself might not be aware of, she had—he supposed he was guilty. But it was only the way he had been built.

Right was right, after all, just as Shooter had said. And fair was fair.

He got back into his car and drove off toward Derry.

17

He paid his seventy-five cents at the Augusta toll plaza, then pulled into the parking area by the telephones on the far side. The day way sunny, chilly, and windy—coming out of the southwest from the direction of Litchfield and running straight and unbroken across the open plain where the turnpike plaza lay, that wind was strong enough to bring tears to Mort's eyes. He relished it, all the same. He could almost feel it blowing the dust out of rooms inside his head which had been closed and shuttered too long.

He used his credit card to call Herb Creekmore in New York— the apartment, not the office. Herb wouldn't actually make it to James and Creekmore, Mort Rainey's literary agency, for another hour or so, but Mort had known Herb long enough to guess that the man had probably been through the shower by now and was drinking a cup of coffee while he waited for the bathroom mirror to unsteam so he could shave.

He was lucky for the second time in a row. Herb answered in a voice from which most of the sleep-fuzz had departed. *Am I on a roll this morning, or what?* Mort thought, and grinned into the teeth of the cold October wind. Across the four lanes of highway, he could see men stringing snowfence in preparation for the winter which lay just over the calendar's horizon.

"Hi, Herb," he said. "I'm calling you from a pay telephone outside the Augusta toll plaza. My divorce is final, my house in Derry burned flat last night, some nut killed my cat, and it's colder than a well-digger's belt buckle—are we having fun yet?"

He hadn't realized how absurd his catalogue of woes sounded until he heard himself reciting them aloud, and he almost laughed. Jesus, it was cold out here, but didn't it feel good! Didn't it feel *clean*!

"Mort?" Herb said cautiously, like a man who suspects a practical joke.

"At your service," Mort said.

"What's this about your house?"

"I'll tell you, but only once. Take notes if you have to, because I plan to be back in my car before I freeze solid to this telephone." He began with John Shooter and John Shooter's accusation. He finished with the conversation he'd had with Amy last night.

Herb, who had spent a fair amount of time as Mort and Amy's

guest (and who had been entirely dismayed by their breakup, Mort guessed), expressed his surprise and sorrow at what had happened to the house in Derry. He asked if Mort had any idea who had done it. Mort said he didn't.

"Do you suspect this guy Shooter?" Herb asked. "I understand the significance of the cat being killed only a short time before you woke up, but—"

"I guess it's technically possible, and I'm not ruling it out completely," Mort said, "but I doubt it like hell. Maybe it's only because I can't get my mind around the idea of a man burning down a twenty-four-room house in order to get rid of a magazine. But I think it's mostly because I met him. He really believes I stole his story, Herb. I mean, he has no doubts at all. His attitude when I told him I could show him proof was 'Go ahead, motherfucker, make my day.' "

"Still . . . you called the police, didn't you?"

"Yeah, I made a call this morning," Mort said, and while this statement was a bit disingenuous, it was not an out-and-out lie. He *had* made a call this morning. To Greg Carstairs. But if he told Herb Creekmore, whom he could visualize sitting in the living room of his New York apartment in a pair of natty tweed pants and a strap-style tee shirt, that he intended to handle this himself, with only Greg to lend a hand, he doubted if Herb would understand. Herb was a good friend, but he was something of a stereotype: Civilized Man, late-twentieth-century model, urban and urbane. He was the sort of man who believed in counselling. The sort of man who believed in meditation and mediation. The sort of man who believed in discussion when reason was present, and the immediate delegation of the problem to Persons in Authority when it was absent. To Herb, the concept that sometimes a man has got to do what a man has got to do was one which had its place . . . but its place was in movies starring Sylvester Stallone.

"Well, that's good." Herb sounded relieved. "You've got enough on your plate without worrying about some psycho from Mississippi. If they find him, what will you do? Have him charged with harassment?"

"I'd rather convince him to take his persecution act and put it on the road," Mort said. His feeling of cheery optimism, so unwarranted but indubitably real, persisted. He supposed he would crash soon enough, but for the time being, he couldn't stop grinning.

So he wiped his leaking nose with the cuff of his coat and went right on doing it. He had forgotten how good it could feel to have a grin pasted onto your kisser.

"How will you do that?"

"With your help, I hope. You've got files of my stuff, right?"

"Right, but—"

"Well, I need you to pull the June, 1980, issue of *Ellery Queen's Mystery Magazine.* That's the one with 'Sowing Season' in it. I can't very well pull mine because of the fire, so—"

"I don't have it," Herb said mildly.

"You don't?" Mort blinked. This was one thing he hadn't expected. "Why not?"

"Because 1980 was two years before I came on board as your agent. I have at least one copy of everything *I* sold for you, but that's one of the stories you sold yourself."

"Oh, *shit!*" In his mind's eye, Mort could see the acknowledgment for "Sowing Season" in *Everybody Drops the Dime.* Most of the other acknowledgments contained the line, "Reprinted by permission of the author and the author's agents, James and Creekmore." The one for "Sowing Season" (and two or three other stories in the collection) read only, "Reprinted by permission of the author."

"Sorry," Herb said.

"Of *course* I sent it in myself—I remember writing the query letter before I submitted. It's just that it seems like you've been my agent forever." He laughed a little then and added, "No offense."

"None taken," Herb said. "Do you want me to make a call to *EQMM?* They must have back issues."

"Would you?" Mort asked gratefully. "That'd be great."

"I'll do it first thing. Only—" Herb paused.

"Only what?"

"Promise me you're not planning to confront this guy on your own once you have a copy of the printed story in hand."

"I promise," Mort agreed promptly. He was being disingenuous again, but what the hell—he *had* asked Greg to come along when he did it, and Greg had agreed, so he *wouldn't* be alone. And Herb Creekmore was his literary agent, after all, not his father. How he handled his personal problems wasn't really Herb's concern.

"Okay," Herb said. "I'll take care of it. Call me from Derry, Mort—maybe it isn't as bad as it seems."

"I'd like to believe that."

"But you don't?"

"Afraid not."

"Okay." Herb sighed. Then, diffidently, he added: "Is it okay to ask you to give Amy my best?"

"It is, and I will."

"Good. You go on and get out of the wind, Mort. I can hear it shrieking in the receiver. You must be freezing."

"Getting there. Thanks again, Herb."

He hung up and looked thoughtfully at the telephone for a moment. He'd forgotten that the Buick needed gas, which was minor, but he'd also forgotten that Herb Creekmore hadn't been his agent until 1982, and that wasn't so minor. Too much pressure, he supposed. It made a man wonder what else he might have forgotten.

The voice in his mind, not the midbrain voice but the one from the deep ranges, spoke up suddenly: *What about stealing the story in the first place? Maybe you forgot that.*

He snorted a laugh as he hurried back to his car. He had never been to Mississippi in his life, and even now, stuck in a writer's block as he was, he was a long way from stooping to plagiarism. He slid behind the wheel and started the engine, reflecting that a person's mind certainly got up to some weird shit every now and again.

18

Mort didn't believe that people—even those who tried to be fairly honest with themselves—knew when some things were over. He believed they often went on believing, or trying to believe, even when the handwriting was not only on the wall but writ in letters large enough to read a hundred yards away without a spyglass. If it was something you really cared about and felt that you needed, it was easy to cheat, easy to confuse your life with TV and convince yourself that what felt so wrong would eventually come right . . . probably after the next commercial break. He supposed that, without its great capacity for self-deception, the human race would be even crazier than it already was.

But sometimes the truth crashed through, and if you had consciously tried to think or dream your way around that truth, the results could be devastating: it was like being there when a tidal wave roared not over but straight through a dike which had been set in its way, smashing it and you flat.

Mort Rainey experienced one of these cataclysmic epiphanies after the representatives of the police and fire departments had gone and he and Amy and Ted Milner were left alone to walk slowly around the smoking ruin of the green Victorian house which had stood at 92 Kansas Street for one hundred and thirty-six years. It was while they were making that mournful inspection tour that he understood that his marriage to the former Amy Dowd of Portland, Maine, was over. It was no "period of marital stress." It was no "trial separation." It was not going to be one of those cases you heard of from time to time where both parties repented their decision and remarried. It was over. Their lives together were history. Even the house where they had shared so many good times was nothing but evilly smouldering beams tumbled into the cellar-hole like the teeth of a giant.

Their meeting at Marchman's, the little coffee shop on Witcham Street, had gone well enough. Amy had hugged him and he had hugged her back, but when he tried to kiss her mouth, she turned her head deftly aside so that his lips landed on her cheek instead. Kiss-kiss, as they said at the office parties. So good to see you, darling.

Ted Milner, blow-dried hair perfectly in place this morning and nary an Alfalfa corkscrew in sight, sat at the table in the corner, watching them. He was holding the pipe which Mort had seen clenched in his teeth at various parties over the last three years or so. Mort was convinced the pipe was an affectation, a little prop employed for the sole purpose of making its owner look older than he was. And how old was that? Mort wasn't sure, but Amy was thirty-six, and he thought Ted, in his impeccable stone-washed jeans and open-throated J. Press shirt, had to be at least four years younger than that, possibly more. He wondered if Amy knew she could be in for trouble ten years down the line—maybe even five— and then reflected it would take a better man than he was to suggest it to her.

He asked if there was anything new. Amy said there wasn't. Then Ted took over, speaking with a faintly Southern accent which was a good deal softer than John Shooter's nasal burr. He told Mort the fire chief and a lieutenant from the Derry Police Department would meet them at what Ted called "the site." They wanted to ask Mort a few questions. Mort said that was fine. Ted asked if he'd like a cup of coffee—they had time. Mort said that would also be fine. Ted asked how he had been. Mort used the word fine again. Each time it came out of his mouth it felt a little more threadbare. Amy watched the exchange between them with some apprehension, and Mort could understand that. On the day he had discovered the two of them in bed together, he had told Ted he would kill him. In fact, he might have said something about killing them both. His memory of the event was quite foggy. He suspected theirs might be rather foggy, too. He didn't know about the other two corners of the triangle, but he himself found that foggery not only understandable but merciful.

They had coffee. Amy asked him about "John Shooter." Mort said he thought that situation was pretty much under control. He did not mention cats or notes or magazines. And after awhile, they left Marchman's and went to 92 Kansas Street, which had once been a house instead of a site.

The fire chief and police detective were there as promised, and there were questions, also as promised. Most of the questions were about any people who might dislike him enough to have tossed a Texaco cocktail into his study. If Mort had been on his own, he would have left Shooter's name out of it entirely, but of course Amy would bring it up if he didn't, so he recounted the initial encounter just as it had happened.

The fire chief, Wickersham, said: "The guy was pretty angry?"

"Yes."

"Angry enough to have driven to Derry and torched your house?" the police detective, Bradley, asked.

He was almost positive Shooter hadn't done it, but he didn't want to delve into his brief dealings with Shooter any more deeply. It would mean telling them what Shooter had done to Bump, for one thing. That would upset Amy; it would upset her a great deal . . . and it would open up a can of worms he would prefer to leave closed. It was time, Mort reckoned, to be disingenuous again.

"He might have been at first. But after I discovered the two stories really *were* alike, I looked up the original date of publication on mine."

"His had never been published?" Bradley asked.

"No, I'm sure it hadn't been. Then, yesterday, he showed up

again. I asked him when he'd written his story, hoping he'd mention a date that was later than the one I had. Do you understand?"

Detective Bradley nodded. "You were hoping to prove you scooped him."

"Right. 'Sowing Season' was in a book of short stories I published in 1983, but it was *originally* published in 1980. I was hoping the guy would feel safe picking a date only a year or two before 1983. I got lucky. He said he'd written it in 1982. So you see, I had him."

He hoped it would end there, but Wickersham, the fire chief, pursued it. "You see and we see, Mr. Rainey, but did *he* see?"

Mort sighed inwardly. He supposed he had known that you could only be disingenuous for so long—if things went on long enough, they almost always progressed to a point where you had to either tell the truth or carve an outright lie. And here he was, at that point. But whose business was it? Theirs or his? His. Right. And he meant to see it stayed that way.

"Yes," he told them, "he saw."

"What did he do?" Ted asked. Mort looked at him with mild annoyance. Ted glanced away, looking as if he wished he had his pipe to play with. The pipe was in the car. The J. Press shirt had no pocket to carry it in.

"He went away," Mort said. His irritation with Ted, who had absolutely no business sticking *his* oar in, made it easier to lie. The fact that he was lying to Ted seemed to make it more all right, too. "He muttered some bullshit about what an incredible coincidence it all was, then jumped into his car like his hair was on fire and his ass was catching, and took off."

"Happen to notice the make of the car and the license plate, Mr. Rainey?" Bradley asked. He had taken out a pad and a ball-point pen.

"It was a Ford," Mort said. "I'm sorry, but I can't help you with the plate. It wasn't a Maine plate, but other than that . . ." He shrugged and tried to look apologetic. Inside, he felt increasingly uncomfortable with the way this was going. It had seemed okay when he was just being cute, skirting around any outright lies—it had seemed a way of sparing Amy the pain of knowing that the man had broken Bump's neck and then skewered him with a screwdriver. But now he had put himself in a position where he had told different stories to different people. If they got together and did a comparison, he wouldn't look so hot. Explaining his reasons for the lies might be sticky. He supposed that such comparisons were pretty unlikely, as long as Amy didn't talk to either Greg Carstairs or Herb Creekmore, but suppose there was a hassle with Shooter when he and Greg caught up to him and shoved the June, 1980, issue of *EQMM* in Shooter's face?

Never mind, he told himself, *we'll burn that bridge when we come to it, big guy.* At this thought, he experienced a brief return of the high spirits he'd felt while talking to Herb at the toll plaza, and almost cackled aloud. He held it in. They would wonder why he was laughing if he did something like that, and he supposed they would be right to wonder.

"I think Shooter must be bound for—"

(*Mississippi*)

"—for wherever he came from by now," he finished, with hardly a break.

"I imagine you're right," Lieutenant Bradley said, "but I'm inclined to pursue this, Mr. Rainey. You might have convinced the guy he was wrong, but that doesn't mean he left your place feeling mellow. It's possible that he drove up here in a rage and torched your house just because he was pissed off—pardon me, Mrs. Rainey."

Amy offered a crooked little smile and waved the apology away.

"Don't you think that's possible?"

No, Mort thought, *I don't. If he'd decided to torch the house, I think he would have killed Bump before he left for Derry, just in case I woke up before he got back. In that case, the blood would have been dry and Bump would have been stiff when I found him. That isn't the way it happened . . . but I can't say so. Not even if I wanted to. They'd wonder why I held back the stuff about Bump as long as I did, for one thing. They'd probably think I've got a few loose screws.*

"I guess so," he said, "but I met the guy. He didn't strike me as the house-burning type."

"You mean he wasn't a Snopes," Amy said suddenly.

Mort looked at her, startled—then smiled. "That's right," he said. "A Southerner, but not a Snopes."

"Meaning what?" Bradley asked, a little warily.

"An old joke, Lieutenant," Amy said. "The Snopeses were characters in some novels by William Faulkner. They got their start in business burning barns."

"Oh," Bradley said blankly.

Wickersham said: "There *is* no house-burning type, Mr. Rainey. They come in all shapes and sizes. Believe me."

"Well—"

"Give me a little more on the car, if you can," Bradley said. He poised a pencil over his notebook. "I want to make the State Police aware of this guy."

Mort suddenly decided he was going to lie some more. Quite a lot more, actually.

"Well, it was a sedan. I can tell you that much for sure."

"Uh-huh. Ford sedan. Year?"

"Somewhere in the seventies, I guess," Mort said. He was fairly sure Shooter's station wagon had actually been built around the time a fellow named Oswald had elected Lyndon Johnson President of the United States. He paused, then added: "The plate was a light color. It could have been Florida. I won't swear to it, but it could have been."

"Uh-huh. And the man himself?"

"Average height. Blonde hair. Eyeglasses. The round wire-framed ones John Lennon used to wear. That's really all I re—"

"Didn't you say he was wearing a hat?" Amy asked suddenly.

Mort felt his teeth come together with a click. "Yes," he said pleasantly. "That's right, I forgot. Dark gray or black. Except it was more of a cap. With a bill, you know."

"Okay." Bradley snapped his book closed. "It's a start."

"Couldn't this have been a simple case of vandalism, arson for kicks?" Mort asked. "In novels, everything has a connection, but my experience has been that in real life, things sometimes just happen."

"It could have been," Wickersham agreed, "but it doesn't hurt to check out the obvious connections." He dropped Mort a solemn little wink and said, "Sometimes life imitates art, you know."

"Do you need anything else?" Ted asked them, and put an arm around Amy's shoulders.

Wickersham and Bradley exchanged a glance and then Bradley shook his head. "I don't think so, at least not at the present."

"I only ask because Amy and Mort will have to put in some time with the insurance agent," Ted said. "Probably an investigator from the parent company, as well."

Mort found the man's Southern accent more and more irritating. He suspected that Ted came from a part of the South several states north of Faulkner country, but it was still a coincidence he could have done without.

The officials shook hands with Amy and Mort, expressed their sympathy, told them to get in touch if anything else occurred to either of them, and then took themselves off, leaving the three of them to take another turn around the house.

"I'm sorry about all of this, Amy," Mort said suddenly. She was walking between them, and looked over at him, apparently startled by something she had heard in his voice. Simple sincerity, maybe. "All of it. Really sorry."

"So am I," she said softly, and touched his hand.

"Well, Teddy makes three," Ted said with solemn heartiness. She turned back to him, and in that moment Mort could have cheerfully strangled the man until his eyes popped out jittering at the ends of their optic strings.

They were walking up the west side of the house toward the street now. Over here had been the deep corner where his study had met the house, and not far away was Amy's flower-garden. All the flowers were dead now, and Mort reflected that was probably just as well. The fire had been hot enough to crisp what grass had remained green in a twelve-foot border all around the ruin. If the flowers had been in bloom, it would have crisped them, as well, and that would have been just too sad. It would have been—

Mort stopped suddenly. He was remembering the stories. The *story.* You could call it "Sowing Season" or you could call it "Secret Window, Secret Garden," but they were the same thing once you took the geegaws off and looked underneath. He looked up. There was nothing to see but blue sky, at least now, but before last night's fire, there would have been a window right where he was looking. It was the window in the little room next to the laundry. The little room that was Amy's office. It was where she went to write checks, to write in her daily journal, to make the telephone calls that needed to be made . . . the room where, he suspected, Amy had several years ago started a novel. And, when it died, it was the room where she had buried it decently and quietly in a desk drawer. The desk had been by the window. Amy had liked to go there in the mornings. She could start the wash in the next room and then do paperwork while she waited for the buzzer which proclaimed it was time to strip the washer and feed the drier. The room was well away from the main house and she liked the quiet, she said. The quiet and the clear, sane morning light. She liked to look out the window every now and then, at her flowers growing in the deep corner formed by the house and the study ell. And he heard her saying, *It's the best room in the house, at least for me, because hardly anybody ever goes there but me. It's got a secret window, and it looks down on a secret garden.*

"Mort?" Amy was saying now, and for a moment Mort took no notice, confusing her real voice with her voice in his mind, which was the voice of memory. But was it a true memory or a false one? That was the real question, wasn't it? It *seemed* like a true memory, but he had been under a great deal of stress even before Shooter, and Bump, and the fire. Wasn't it at least possible that he was having a . . . well, a recollective hallucination? That he was trying to make his own past with Amy in some way conform to that goddam story where a man had gone crazy and killed his wife?

Jesus, I hope not. I hope not, because if I am, that's too close to nervous-breakdown territory for comfort.

"Mort, are you okay?" Amy asked. She plucked fretfully at his sleeve, at least temporarily breaking his trance.

"Yes," he said, and then, abruptly: "No. To tell you the truth, I'm feeling a little sick."

"Breakfast, maybe," Ted said.

Amy gave him a look that made Mort feel a bit better. It was not a very friendly look. "It *isn't* breakfast," she said a little indignantly. She swept her arm at the blackened ruins. "It's *this.* Let's get out of here."

"The insurance people are due at noon," Ted said.

"Well, that's more than an hour from now. Let's go to your place, Ted. I don't feel so hot myself. I'd like to sit down."

"All right." Ted spoke in a slightly nettled no-need-to-shout tone which also did Mort's heart good. And although he would have said at breakfast that morning that Ted Milner's place was the last one on earth he wanted to go, he accompanied them without protest.

19

They were all quiet on the ride across town to the split-level on the east side where Ted hung his hat. Mort didn't know what Amy and Ted were thinking about, although the house for Amy and whether or not they'd be on time to meet the wallahs from the insurance company for Ted would probably be a couple of good guesses, but he knew what *he* was thinking about. He was trying to decide if he was going crazy or not. Is it real, or is it Memorex?

He decided finally that Amy really *had* said that about her office next to the laundry room—it was not a false memory. Had she said it before 1982, when "John Shooter" claimed to have written a story called "Secret Window, Secret Garden"? He didn't know. No matter how earnestly he conned his confused and aching brain, what kept coming back was a single curt message: answer inconclusive. But if she *had* said it, no matter when, couldn't the title of Shooter's story still be simple coincidence? Maybe, but the coincidences were piling up, weren't they? He had decided the fire was, must be, a coincidence. But the memory which Amy's garden with its crop of dead flowers had prodded forth . . . well, it was getting harder and harder to believe all of this wasn't tied together in some strange, possibly even supernatural fashion.

And in his own way, hadn't "Shooter" himself been just as confused? *How did you get it?* he had asked; his voice had been fierce with rage and puzzlement. *That's what I really want to know. How in hell did a big-money scribbling asshole like you get down to a little shitsplat town in Mississippi and steal my goddam story?* At the time, Mort had thought either that it was another sign of the man's madness or that the guy was one hell of a good actor. Now, in Ted's car, it occurred to him for the first time that it was exactly the way he himself would have reacted, had the circumstances been reversed.

As, in a way, they had been. The one place where the two stories differed completely was in the matter of the title. They both fit, but now Mort found that he had a question to ask Shooter which was very similar to the one Shooter had already asked him: *How did you happen by that title, Mr. Shooter? That's what I really want to know. How did you happen to know that, twelve hundred miles away from your shitsplat town in Mississippi, the wife of a writer you claim you never heard of before this year had her own secret window, looking down on her own secret garden?*

Well, there was only one way to find out, of course. When Greg ran Shooter down, Mort would have to ask him.

20

Mort passed on the cup of coffee Ted offered and asked if he had a Coke or a Pepsi. Ted did, and after Mort had drunk it, his stomach settled. He had expected that just being here, here where Ted and Amy played house now that they no longer had to bother with the cheap little town-line motels, would make him angry and restless. It didn't. It was just a house, one where every room seemed to proclaim that the owner was a Swinging Young Bachelor Who Was Making It. Mort found that he could deal with that quite easily, although it made him feel a little nervous for Amy all over again. He thought of her little office with its clear, sane light and the soporific drone of the drier coming through the wall, her little office with its secret window, the only one in the whole place which looked down into the tight little angle of space formed by the house and the ell, and thought how much she had belonged there and how little she seemed to belong here. But that was something she would have to deal with herself, and he thought, after a few minutes in this other house which was not a dreaded den of iniquity at all but only a house, that he could live with that . . . that he could even be content with it.

She asked him if he would be staying in Derry overnight.

"Uh-uh. I'll be going back as soon as we finish with the insurance adjustors. If something else pops, they can get in touch with me . . . or you can."

He smiled at her. She smiled back and touched his hand briefly. Ted didn't like it. He frowned out the window and fingered his pipe.

21

They were on time for their meeting with the representatives of the insurance company, which undoubtedly relieved Ted Milner's mind. Mort was not particularly crazy about having Ted in attendance; it had never been Ted's house, after all, not even after the divorce. Still, it seemed to ease Amy's mind to have him there, and so Mort left it alone.

Don Strick, the Consolidated Assurance Company agent with whom they had done business, conducted the meeting at his office, where they went after another brief tour of "the site." At the office they met a man named Fred Evans, a Consolidated field investigator specializing in arson. The reason Evans hadn't been with Wickersham and Bradley that morning or at "the site" when Strick met them there at noon became obvious very quickly: he had spent most of the previous night poking through the ruins with a ten-cell flashlight and a Polaroid camera. He had gone back to his motel room, he said, to catch a few winks before meeting the Raineys.

Mort liked Evans very much. He seemed to really care about the loss he and Amy had suffered, while everyone else, including Mr. Teddy Makes Three, seemed to have only mouthed the traditional words of sympathy before going on to whatever they considered the business at hand (and in Ted Milner's case, Mort thought, the business at hand was getting him out of Derry and back to Tashmore Lake as soon as possible). Fred Evans did not refer to 92 Kansas Street as "the site." He referred to it as "the house."

His questions, while essentially the same as those asked by Wickersham and Bradley, were gentler, more detailed, and more probing. Although he'd had four hours' sleep at most, his eyes were bright, his speech quick and clear. After speaking with him for twenty minutes, Mort decided that he would deal with a company other than Consolidated Assurance if he ever decided to burn down a house for the insurance money. Or wait until this man retired.

When he had finished his questions, Evans smiled at them. "You've been very helpful, and I want to thank you again, both for your thoughtful answers and for your kind treatment of me. In a lot of cases, people's feathers get ruffled the second they hear the words 'insurance investigator.' They're already upset, understandably so, and quite often they take the presence of an investigator on the scene as an accusation that they torched their own property."

"Given the circumstances, I don't think we could have asked for better treatment," Amy said, and Ted Milner nodded so violently that his head might have been on a string—one controlled by a puppeteer with a bad case of nerves.

"This next part is hard," Evans said. He nodded to Strick, who opened a desk drawer and produced a clipboard with a computer printout on it. "When an investigator ascertains that a fire was as serious as this one clearly was, we have to show the clients a list of claimed insurable property. You look it over, then sign an affidavit swearing that the items listed still belong to you, and that they were still in the house when the fire occurred. You should put a check mark beside any item or items you've sold since your last insurance overhaul with Mr. Strick here, and any insured property which was not in the house at the time of the fire." Evans put a fist to his lips and cleared his throat before going on. "I'm told that there has been a separation of residence recently, so that last bit may be particularly important."

"We're divorced," Mort said bluntly. "I'm living in our place on Tashmore Lake. We only used it during the summers, but it's got a furnace and is livable during the cold months. Unfortunately, I hadn't got around to moving the bulk of my things out of the house up here. I'd been putting it off."

Don Strick nodded sympathetically. Ted crossed his legs, fiddled with his pipe, and generally gave the impression of a man who is trying not to look as deeply bored as he is.

"Do the best you can with the list," Evans said. He took the clipboard from Strick and handed it across the desk to Amy. "This can be a bit unpleasant—it's a little like a treasure hunt in reverse."

Ted had put his pipe down and was craning at the list, his boredom gone, at least for the time being; his eyes were as avid as those of any bystander gleeping the aftermath of a bad accident. Amy saw him looking and obligingly tipped the form his way. Mort, who was sitting on the other side of her, tipped it back the other way.

"Do you mind?" he asked Ted. He was angry, really angry, and they all heard it in his voice.

"Mort—" Amy said.

"I'm not going to make a big deal of this," Mort said to her, "but this was *our* stuff, Amy. *Ours.*"

"I hardly think—" Ted began indignantly.

"No, he's perfectly right, Mr. Milner," Fred Evans said with a mildness Mort felt might have been deceptive. "The law says you have no right to be looking at the listed items at all. We wink at something like that if nobody minds . . . but I think Mr. Rainey does."

"You're damned *tooting* Mr. Rainey does," Mort said. His hands were tightly clenched in his lap; he could feel his fingernails biting smile-shapes into the soft meat of his palms.

Amy switched her look of unhappy appeal from Mort to Ted. Mort expected Ted to huff and puff and try to blow somebody's house down, but Ted did not. Mort supposed it was a measure of his own hostile feeling toward the man that he'd made such an assumption; he didn't know Ted very well (although he *did* know he looked a bit like Alfalfa when you woke him up suddenly in a no-tell motel), but he knew Amy. If Ted had been a blowhard, she would have left him already.

Smiling a little, speaking to her and ignoring Mort and the others completely, Ted said: "Would it help matters if I took a walk around the block?"

Mort tried to restrain himself and couldn't quite do it. "Why not make it two?" he asked Ted with bogus amiability.

Amy shot him a narrow, dark stare, then looked back at Ted. "Would you? This might be a little easier . . ."

"Sure," he said. He kissed her high on her cheekbone, and Mort had another dolorous revelation: the man cared for her. He might not *always* care for her, but right now he did. Mort realized he had come halfway to thinking Amy was just a toy that had captivated Ted for a little while, a toy of which he would tire soon enough. But that didn't jibe with what he knew of Amy, either. She had better instincts about people than that . . . and more respect for herself.

Ted got up and left. Amy looked at Mort reproachfully. "Are you satisfied?"

"I suppose," he said. "Look, Amy—I probably didn't handle that as well as I could have, but my motives are honorable enough. We shared a lot over the years. I guess this is the last thing, and I think it belongs between the two of us. Okay?"

Strick looked uncomfortable. Fred Evans did not; he looked from Mort to Amy and then back to Mort again with the bright interest of a man watching a really good tennis match.

"Okay," Amy said in a low voice. He touched her hand lightly, and she gave him a smile. It was strained, but better than no smile at all, he reckoned.

He pulled his chair closer to hers and they bent over the list, heads close together, like kids studying for a test. It didn't take Mort long to understand why Evans had warned them. He thought he had grasped the size of the loss. He had been wrong.

Looking at the columns of cold computer type, Mort thought he could not have been more dismayed if someone had taken everything in the house at 92 Kansas Street and strewn it along the block for the whole world to stare at. He couldn't believe all the things he had forgotten, all the things that were gone.

Seven major appliances. Four TVs, one with a videotape editing hook-up. The Spode china, and the authentic Early American furniture which Amy had bought a piece at a time. The value of the antique armoire which had stood in their bedroom was listed at $14,000. They had not been serious art-collectors, but they had been appreciators, and they had lost twelve pieces of original art. Their value was listed at $22,000, but Mort didn't care about the dollar value; he was thinking about the N. C. Wyeth line-drawing of two boys putting to sea in a small boat. It was raining in the picture; the boys were wearing slickers and galoshes and big grins. Mort had loved that picture, and now it was gone. The Waterford glassware. The sports equipment stored in the garage—skis, ten-speed bikes, and the Old Town canoe. Amy's three furs were listed. He saw her make tiny check marks beside the beaver and the mink—still in storage, apparently—but she passed the short fox jacket without checking it off. It had been hanging in the closet, warm and stylish outerwear for fall, when the fire happened. He remembered giving her that coat for her birthday six or seven years ago. Gone now. His Celestron telescope. Gone. The big puzzle quilt Amy's mother had given them when they were married. Amy's mother was dead and the quilt was now so much ash in the wind.

The worst, at least for Mort, was halfway down the second column, and again it wasn't the dollar value that hurt. 124 BOTS. WINE, the item read. VALUE $4,900. Wine was something they had both liked. They weren't rabid about it, but they had built the little wine room in the cellar together, stocked it together, and had drunk the occasional bottle together.

"Even the wine," he said to Evans. "Even that."

Evans gave him an odd look that Mort couldn't interpret, then nodded. "The wine room itself didn't burn, because you had very little fuel oil in the cellar tank and there was no explosion. But it got very hot inside, and most of the bottles burst. The few that didn't . . . Well, I don't know much about wine, but I doubt if it would be good to drink. Perhaps I'm wrong."

"You're not," Amy said. A single tear rolled down her cheek and she wiped it absently away.

Evans offered her his handkerchief. She shook her head and bent over the list with Mort again.

Ten minutes later it was finished. They signed on the correct lines and Strick witnessed their signatures. Ted Milner showed up only instants later, as if he had been watching the whole thing on some private viewscreen.

"Is there anything else?" Mort asked Evans.

"Not now. There may be. Is your number down in Tashmore unlisted, Mr. Rainey?"

"Yes." He wrote it down for Evans. "Please get in touch if I can help."

"I will." He rose, hand outstretched. "This is always a nasty business. I'm sorry you two had to go through it."

They shook hands all around and left Strick and Evans to write reports. It was well past one, and Ted asked Mort if he'd like to have some lunch with him and Amy. Mort shook his head.

"I want to get back. Do some work and see if I can't forget all this for awhile." And he felt as if maybe he really could write. That was not surprising. In tough times—up until the divorce, anyway, which seemed to be an exception to the general rule—he had always found it easy to write. Necessary, even. It was good to have those make-believe worlds to fall back on when the real one had hurt you.

He half-expected Amy to ask him to change his mind, but she didn't. "Drive safe," she said, and planted a chaste kiss on the corner of his mouth. "Thanks for coming, and for being so . . . so reasonable about everything."

"Can I do anything for you, Amy?"

She shook her head, smiling a little, and took Ted's hand. If he had been looking for a message, this one was much too clear to miss.

They walked slowly toward Mort's Buick.

"You keepin well enough down there?" Ted asked. "Anything you need?"

For the third time he was struck by the man's Southern accent— just one more coincidence.

"Can't think of anything," he said, opening the Buick's door and fishing the car keys out of his pocket. "Where do you come from originally, Ted? You or Amy must have told me sometime, but I'll be damned if I can remember. Was it Mississippi?"

Ted laughed heartily. "A long way from there, Mort. I grew up in Tennessee. A little town called Shooter's Knob, Tennessee."

22

Mort drove back to Tashmore Lake with his hands clamped to the steering wheel, his spine as straight as a ruler, and his eyes fixed firmly on the road. He played the radio loud and concentrated ferociously on the music each time he sensed telltale signs of mental activity behind the center of his forehead. Before he had made forty miles, he felt a pressing sensation in his bladder. He welcomed this development and did not even consider stopping at a wayside comfort-station. The need to take a whizz was another excellent distraction.

He arrived at the house around four-thirty and parked the Buick in its accustomed place around the side of the house. Eric Clapton was throttled in the middle of a full-tilt-boogie guitar solo when Mort shut off the motor, and quiet crashed down like a load of stones encased in foam rubber. There wasn't a single boat on the lake, not a single bug in the grass.

Pissing and thinking have a lot in common, he thought, climbing out of the car and unzipping his fly. *You can put them both off . . . but not forever.*

Mort Rainey stood there urinating and thought about secret windows and secret gardens; he thought about those who might own the latter and those who might look through the former. He thought about the fact that the magazine he needed to prove a certain fellow was either a lunatic or a con man had just happened to burn up on the very evening he had tried to get his hands on it. He thought about the fact that his ex-wife's lover, a man he cordially detested, had come from a town called Shooter's Knob and that Shooter happened to be the pseudonym of the aforementioned loony-or-con-man who had come into Mort Rainey's life at the exact time when the aforementioned Mort Rainey was beginning to grasp his divorce not just as an academic concept but as a simple fact of his life forever after. He even thought about the fact that "John Shooter" claimed to have discovered Mort Rainey's act of plagiarism at about the same time Mort Rainey had separated from his wife.

Question: Were all of these things coincidences?
Answer: It was technically possible.
Question: Did he *believe* all these things were coincidences?
Answer: No.
Question: Did he believe he was going mad, then?
"The answer is no," Mort said. "He does not. At least not yet."
He zipped up his fly and went back around the corner to the door.

23

He found his housekey, started to put it in the lock, and then pulled
it out again. His hand went to the doorknob instead, and as his
fingers closed over it, he felt a clear certainty that it would rotate
easily. Shooter had been here . . . had been, or was still. And he
wouldn't have needed to force entry, either. Nope. Not *this* sucker.
Mort kept a spare key to the Tashmore Lake house in an old soap-
dish on a high shelf in the toolshed, which was where Shooter had
gone to get a screwdriver in a hurry when the time had come to
nail poor old Bump to the garbage cabinet. He was in the house
now, looking around . . . or maybe hiding. He was—
The knob refused to move; Mort's fingers simply slid around it.
The door was still locked.
"Okay," Mort said. "Okay, no big deal." He even laughed a little
as he socked the key home and turned it. Just because the door
was locked didn't mean Shooter wasn't in the house. In fact, it made
it more likely that he *was* in the house, when you really stopped
to think about it. He could have used the spare key, put it back,
then locked the door from the inside to lull his enemy's suspicions. All you had to do to lock it, after all, was to press the button
set into the knob. *He's trying to psych me out,* Mort thought as he
stepped in.
The house was full of dusty late-afternoon sunlight and silence.
But it did not feel like *unoccupied* silence.
"You're trying to psych me out, aren't you?" he called. He expected to sound crazy to himself: a lonely, paranoid man addressing
the intruder who only exists, after all, in his own imagination. But
he *didn't* sound crazy to himself. He sounded, instead, like a man
who has tumbled to at least *half* the trick. Only getting half a scam
wasn't so great, maybe, but half was better than nothing.

He walked into the living room with its cathedral ceiling, its window-wall facing the lake, and, of course, The World-Famous Mort Rainey Sofa, also known as The Couch of the Comatose Writer. An economical little smile tugged at his cheeks. His balls felt high and tight against the fork of his groin.

"Half a scam's better than none, right, Mr. Shooter?" he called.

The words died into dusty silence. He could smell old tobacco smoke in that dust. His eye happened on the battered package of cigarettes he had excavated from the drawer of his desk. It occurred to him that the house had a smell—almost a stink—that was horribly negative: it was an unwoman smell. Then he thought: *No. That's a mistake. That's not it. What you smell is Shooter. You smell the man, and you smell his cigarettes. Not yours,* his.

He turned slowly around, his head cocked back. A second-floor bedroom looked down on the living room halfway up the cream-colored wall; the opening was lined with dark-brown wooden slats. The slats were supposed to keep the unwary from falling out and splattering themselves all over the living-room floor, but they were also supposed to be decorative. Right then they didn't look partic-ularly decorative to Mort; they looked like the bars of a jail cell. All he could see of what he and Amy had called the guest bedroom was the ceiling and one of the bed's four posts.

"You up there, Mr. Shooter?" he yelled.

There was no answer.

"I *know* you're trying to psych me out!" *Now* he was beginning to feel just the tinest bit ridiculous. "It won't work, though!"

About six years before, they had plugged the big fieldstone fire-place in the living room with a Blackstone Jersey stove. A rack of fire-tools stood beside it. Mort grasped the handle of the ash-shovel, considered it for a moment, then let go of it and took the poker instead. He faced the barred guest-room overlook and held the poker up like a knight saluting his queen. Then he walked slowly to the stairs and began to climb them. He could feel tension worm-ing its way into his muscles now, but he understood it wasn't *Shooter* he was afraid of; what he was afraid of was finding nothing.

"I know you're here, and I know you're trying to psych me out! The only thing I don't know is what it's all about, Alfie, and when I find you, you better tell me!"

He paused on the second-floor landing, his heart pumping hard in his chest now. The guest-room door was to his left. The door to the guest bathroom was to the right. And he suddenly understood that Shooter was here, all right, but not in the bedroom. No; that was just a ploy. That was just what Shooter *wanted* him to believe.

Shooter was in the bathroom.

And, as he stood there on the landing with the poker clutched tightly in his right hand and sweat running out of his hair and down his cheeks, Mort *heard* him. A faint shuffle-shuffle. He was in there, all right. Standing in the tub, by the sound. He had moved the tiniest bit. Peekaboo, Johnny-boy, I hear you. Are you armed, fuckface?

Mort thought he probably was, but he didn't think it would turn out to be a gun. Mort had an idea that the man's pen-name was about as close to firearms as he had ever come. Shooter had looked like the sort of guy who would feel more at home with instruments of a blunter nature. What he had done to Bump seemed to bear this out.

I bet it's a hammer, Mort thought, and wiped sweat off the back of his neck with his free hand. He could feel his eyes pulsing in and out of their sockets in time with his heartbeat. *I'm betting it's a hammer from the toolshed.*

He had no more thought of this before he saw Shooter, saw him clearly, standing in the bathtub in his black round-crowned hat and his yellow shitkicker work-shoes, his lips split over his mail-order dentures in a grin which was really a grimace, sweat trickling down his own face, running down the deep lines grooved there like water running down a network of galvanized tin gutters, with the hammer from the toolshed raised to shoulder height like a judge's gavel. Just standing there in the tub, waiting to bring the hammer down. Next case, bailiff.

I know you, buddy. I got your number. I got it the first time I saw you. And guess what? You picked the wrong writer to fuck with. I think I've been wanting to kill somebody since the middle of May, and you'll do as well as anybody.

He turned his head toward the bedroom door. At the same time, he reached out with his left hand (after drying it on the front of his shirt so his grip wouldn't slip at the crucial moment) and curled it around the bathroom doorknob.

"*I know you're in there!*" he shouted at the closed bedroom door.

"If you're under the bed, you better get out! I'm counting to five! If you're not out by the time I get there, I'm coming in . . . and I'll come in swinging! You hear me?"

There was no answer . . . but then, he hadn't really expected one. Or *wanted* one. He tightened his grip on the bathroom doorknob, but would shout the numbers toward the guest-room door. He didn't know if Shooter would hear or sense the difference if he turned his head in the direction of the bathroom, but he thought Shooter might. The man was obviously clever. Hellishly clever.

In the instant before he started counting, he heard another faint movement in the bathroom. He would have missed it, even standing this close, if he hadn't been listening with every bit of concentration he could muster.

"One!"

Christ, he was sweating! Like a pig!

"Two!"

The knob of the bathroom door was like a cold rock in his clenched fist.

"Thr—"

He turned the knob of the bathroom door and slammed in, bouncing the door off the wall hard enough to chop through the wallpaper and pop the door's lower hinge, and there he was, *there he was,* coming at him with a raised weapon, his teeth bared in a killer's grin, and his eyes were insane, utterly insane, and Mort brought the poker down in a whistling overhand blow and he had just time enough to realize that Shooter was also swinging a poker, and to realize that Shooter was not wearing his round-crowned black hat, and to realize it wasn't Shooter at all, to realize it was *him,* the madman was *him,* and then the poker shattered the mirror over the washbasin and silver-backed glass sprayed every whichway, twinkling in the gloom, and the medicine cabinet fell into the sink. The bent door swung open like a gaping mouth, spilling bottles of cough syrup and iodine and Listerine.

"I killed a goddam fucking mirror!" he shrieked, and was about to sling the poker away when something *did* move in the tub, behind the corrugated shower door. There was a frightened little squeal. Grinning, Mort slashed sideways with the poker, tearing a jagged gash through the plastic door and knocking it off its tracks. He raised the poker over his shoulder, his eyes glassy and staring, his lips drawn into the grimace he had imagined on Shooter's face.

Then he lowered the poker slowly. He found he had to use the fingers of his left hand to pry open the fingers of his right so that the poker could fall to the floor.

"Wee sleekit cowerin' beastie," he said to the fieldmouse scurrying blindly about in the tub. "What a panic's in thy breastie." His voice sounded hoarse and flat and strange. It didn't sound like his own voice at all. It was like listening to himself on tape for the first time.

He turned and walked slowly out of the bathroom past the leaning door with its popped hinge, his shoes gritting on broken mirror glass.

All at once he wanted to go downstairs and lie on the couch and take a nap. All at once he wanted that more than anything else in the world.

24

It was the telephone that woke him up. Twilight had almost become night, and he made his way slowly past the glass-topped coffee table that liked to bite with a weird feeling that time had somehow doubled back on itself. His right arm ached like hell. His back wasn't in much better shape. Exactly how hard had he swung that poker, anyway? How much panic had been driving him? He didn't like to think.

He picked up the telephone, not bothering to guess who it might be. Life has been so dreadfully busy lately, darling, that it might even be the President. "Hello?"

"How you doin, Mr. Rainey?" the voice asked, and Mort recoiled, snatching the telephone away from his ear for a moment as if it were a snake which had tried to bite. He returned it slowly.

"I'm doing fine, Mr. Shooter," he said in a dry, spitless voice. "How are *you* doing?"

"I'm-a country fair," Shooter allowed, speaking in that thick crackerbarrel Southern accent that was somehow as bald and staring as an unpainted barn standing all by itself in the middle of a field. "But I don't think *you're* really all that well. Stealing from another man, that don't seem to have ever bothered you none. Being caught up on, though . . . that seems to have given you the pure miseries."

"What are you talking about?"

Shooter sounded faintly amused. "Well, I heard on the radio news that someone burned down your house. Your *other* house. And then, when you come back down here, it sounded like you pitched a fit or something once you got into the house. Shouting . . . whacking on things . . . or maybe it's just that successful writers like you throw tantrums when things don't go the way they expect. Is that it, maybe?"

My God, he was *here. He* was.

Mort found himself looking out the window as if Shooter *still* might be out there . . . hiding in the bushes, perhaps, while he spoke to Mort on some sort of cordless telephone. Ridiculous, of course.

"The magazine with my story in it is on the way," he said. "When it gets here, are you going to leave me alone?"

Shooter still sounded lazily amused. "There isn't any magazine with that story in it, Mr. Rainey. You and me, we *know* that. Not from 1980, there isn't. How could there be, when my story wasn't there for you to steal until 1982?"

"Goddammit, I did not steal your st—"

"When I heard about your house," Shooter said, "I went out and bought an *Evening Express*. They had a picture of what was left. Wasn't very much. Had a picture of your wife, too." There was a long, thoughtful pause. Then Shooter said, "She's purty." He used the country pronunciation purposely, sarcastically. "How'd an ugly son of a buck like you luck into such a purty wife, Mr. Rainey?"

"We're divorced," he said. "I told you that. Maybe she discovered how ugly I was. Why don't we leave Amy out of this? It's between you and me."

For the second time in two days, he realized he had answered the phone while he was only half awake and nearly defenseless. As a result, Shooter was in almost total control of the conversation. He was leading Mort by the nose, calling the shots.

Hang up, then.

But he couldn't. At least, not yet.

"Between you and me, is it?" Shooter asked. "Then I don't s'pose you even mentioned me to anyone else."

"What do you want? Tell me! What in the hell do you want?"

"You want the second reason I came, is that it?"

"*Yes!*"

"I want you to write me a story," Shooter said calmly. "I want

you to write a story and put my name on it and then give it to me.
You owe me that. Right is right and fair is fair."

Mort stood in the hallway with the telephone clutched in his
aching fist and a vein pulsing in the middle of his forehead. For a
few moments his rage was so total that he found himself buried
alive inside it and all he was capable of thinking was *So THAT'S it!
So THAT'S it! So THAT'S it!* over and over again.

"You there, Mr. Rainey?" Shooter asked in his calm, drawling
voice.

"The only thing I'll write for you," Mort said, his own voice slow
and syrupy-thick with rage, "is your death-warrant, if you don't
leave me alone."

"You talk big, pilgrim," Shooter said in the patient voice of a
man explaining a simple problem to a stupid child, "because you
know I can't put no hurtin on you. If you had stolen my dog or my
car, I could take *your* dog or car. I could do that just as easy as I
broke your cat's neck. If you tried to stop me, I could put a hurtin
on you and take it anyway. But this is different. The goods I want
are inside your head. You got the goods locked up like they were
inside a safe. Only I can't just blow off the door or torch open the
back. I have to find me the combination. Don't I?"

"I don't know what you're talking about," Mort said, "but the
day you get a story out of me will be the day the Statue of Liberty
wears a diaper. *Pilgrim.*"

Shooter said meditatively, "I'd leave her out of it if I could, but
I'm startin to think you ain't going to leave me that option."

All the spit in Mort's mouth was suddenly gone, leaving it dry
and glassy and hot. "What . . . what do you—"

"Do you want to wake up from one of your stupid naps and find
Amy nailed to your garbage bin?" Shooter asked. "Or turn on the
radio some morning and hear she came off second best in a match
with the chainsaw you keep in your garage up there? Or did the
garage burn, too?"

"Watch what you say," Mort whispered. His wide eyes began to
prickle with tears of rage and fear.

"You still have two days to think about it. I'd think about it real
close, Mr. Rainey. I mean I'd really hunker down over her, if I
were you. And I don't think I'd talk about this to anyone else.
That'd be like standing out in a thunderstorm and tempting the

lightning. Divorced or not, I have got an idea you still have some feeling for that lady. It's time for you to grow up a little. *You can't get away with it.* Don't you realize that yet? *I know what you did, and I ain't quitting until I get what's mine.*"

"*You're crazy!*" Mort screamed.

"Good night, Mr. Rainey," Shooter said, and hung up.

25

Mort stood there for a moment, the handset sinking away from his ear. Then he scooped up the bottom half of the Princess-style telephone. He was on the verge of throwing the whole combination against the wall before he was able to get hold of himself. He set it down again and took a dozen deep breaths—enough to make his head feel swimmy and light. Then he dialled Herb Creekmore's home telephone.

Herb's lady-friend, Delores, picked it up on the second ring and called Herb to the telephone.

"Hi, Mort," Herb said. "What's the story on the house?" His voice moved away from the telephone's mouthpiece a little. "Delores, will you move that skillet to the back burner?"

Suppertime in New York, Mort thought, *and he wants me to know it. Well, what the hell. A maniac has just threatened to turn my wife into veal cutlets, but life has to go on, right?*

"The house is gone," Mort said. "The insurance will cover the loss." He paused. "The *monetary* loss, anyway."

"I'm sorry," Herb said. "Can I do anything?"

"Well, not about the house," Mort said, "but thanks for offering. About the story, though—"

"What story is that, Mort?"

He felt his hand tightening down on the telephone's handset again and forced himself to loosen up. *He doesn't know what the situation up here is. You have to remember that.*

"The one my nutty friend is kicking sand about," he said, trying to maintain a tone which was light and mostly unconcerned. " 'Sowing Season.' *Ellery Queen's Mystery Magazine?*"

"Oh, *that!*" Herb said.

Mort felt a jolt of fear. "You didn't forget to call, did you?"

"No—I called," Herb reassured him. "I just forgot all about it for a minute. You losing your house and all . . ."

"Well? What did they say?"

"Don't worry about a thing. They're going to send a Xerox over to me by messenger tomorrow, and I'll send it right up to you by Federal Express. You'll have it by ten o'clock day after tomorrow."

For a moment it seemed that all of his problems were solved, and he started to relax. Then he thought of the way Shooter's eyes had blazed. The way he had brought his face down until his forehead and Mort's were almost touching. He thought of the dry smell of cinnamon on Shooter's breath as he said, "You lie."

A Xerox? He was by no means sure that Shooter would accept an *original* copy . . . but a *Xerox*?

"No," he said slowly. "That's no good, Herb. No Xerox, no phone-call from the editor. It has to be an original copy of the magazine."

"Well, that's a little tougher. They have their editorial offices in Manhattan, of course, but they store copies at their subscription offices in Pennsylvania. They only keep about five copies of each issue—it's really all they can *afford* to keep, when you consider that *EQMM* has been publishing since 1941. They really aren't crazy about lending them out."

"Come on, Herb! You can find those magazines at yard sales and in half the small-town libraries in America!"

"But never a complete run." Herb paused. "Not even a phone-call will do, huh? Are you telling me this guy is so paranoid he'd think he was talking to one of your thousands of stooges?"

From the background: "Do you want me to pour the wine, Herb?"

Herb spoke again with his mouth away from the phone. "Hold on a couple of minutes, Dee."

"I'm holding up your dinner," Mort said. "I'm sorry."

"It goes with the territory. Listen, Mort, be straight with me—is this guy as crazy as he sounds? Is he dangerous?"

I don't think I'd talk about this to anyone else. That'd be like standing out in a thunderstorm and tempting the lightning.

"I don't think so," he said, "but I want him off my back, Herb." He hesitated, searching for the right tone. "I've spent the last half-year or so walking through a shitstorm. This might be one thing I can do something about. I just want the doofus off my back."

"Okay," Herb said with sudden decision. "I'll call Marianne Jaf-

fery over at *EQMM*. I've known her for a long time. If I ask her
to ask the library curator—that's what they call the guy, honest,
the library curator—to send us a copy of the June, 1980, ish, she'll
do it. Is it okay if I say you might have a story for them at some
point in the future?"

"Sure," Mort said, and thought: *Tell her it'll be under the name
John Shooter,* and almost laughed aloud.

"Good. She'll have the curator send it on to you Federal Express,
direct from Pennsylvania. Just return it in good condition, or you'll
have to find a replacement copy at one of those yard sales you were
talking about."

"It there any chance all this could happen by the day after tomorrow?" Mort asked. He felt miserably sure that Herb would
think he was crazy for even asking . . . and he surely must feel that
Mort was making an awfully big mountain out of one small molehill.

"I think there's a very good chance," Herb said. "I won't guarantee it, but I'll *almost* guarantee it."

"Thanks, Herb," Mort said with honest gratitude. "You're swell."

"Aw, shucks, ma'am," Herb said, doing the bad John Wayne
imitation of which he was so absurdly proud.

"Now go get your dinner. And give Delores a kiss for me."

Herb was still in his John Wayne mode. "To heck with that. I'll
give 'er a kiss fer *me,* pilgrim."

You talk big, pilgrim.

Mort felt such a spurt of horror and fear that he almost cried out
aloud. Same word, same flat, staring drawl. Shooter had tapped his
telephone line, somehow, and no matter who Mort tried to call or
what number he dialled, it was John Shooter who answered. Herb
Creekmore had become just another one of his pen names, and—

"Mort? Are you still there?"

He closed his eyes. Now that Herb had dispensed with the bogus
John Wayne imitation, it was okay. It was just Herb again, and
always had been. Herb using that word, that had just been—

What?

*Just another float in the Parade of Coincidences? Okay. Sure. No
problem. I'll just stand on the curb and watch it slide past. Why not?
I've already watched half a dozen bigger ones go by.*

"Right here, Herb," he said, opening his eyes. "I was just trying
to figure out how do I love thee. You know, counting the ways?"

"You're thilly," Herb said, obviously pleased. "And you're going to handle this carefully and prudently, right?"

"Right."

"Then I think I'll go eat supper with the light of my life."

"That sounds like a good idea. Goodbye, Herb—and thanks."

"You're welcome. I'll try to make it the day after tomorrow. Dee says goodbye, too."

"If she wants to pour the wine, I *bet* she does," Mort said, and they both hung up laughing.

As soon as he put the telephone back on its table, the fantasy came back. Shooter. He do the police in different voices. Of course, he was alone and it was dark, a condition which bred fantasies. Nevertheless, he did not believe—at least in his head—that John Shooter was either a supernatural being or a supercriminal. If he had been the former, he would surely know that Morton Rainey had not committed plagiarism—at least not on that particular story—and if he had been the latter, he would have been off knocking over a bank or something, not farting around western Maine, trying to squeeze a short story out of a writer who made a lot more money from his novels.

He started slowly back toward the living room, intending to go through to the study and try the word processor, when a thought

(at least not that particular story)

struck him and stopped him.

What exactly did *that* mean, not that particular story? Had he *ever* stolen someone else's work?

For the first time since Shooter had turned up on his porch with his sheaf of pages, Mort considered this question seriously. A good many reviews of his books had suggested that he was not really an original writer; that most of his works consisted of twice-told tales. He remembered Amy reading a review of *The Organ-Grinder's Boy* which had first acknowledged the book's pace and readability, and then suggested a certain derivativeness in its plotting. She'd said, "So what? Don't these people know there are only about five really good stories, and writers just tell them over and over, with different characters?"

Mort himself believed there were at least six stories: success; failure; love and loss; revenge; mistaken identity; the search for a higher power, be it God or the devil. He had told the first four over and over, obsessively, and now that he thought of it, "Sowing Season" embodied at least three of those ideas. But was that plagiarism? If it was, every novelist at work in the world would be guilty of the crime.

Plagiarism, he decided, was outright theft. And he had never done it in his life. *Never.*

"Never," he said, and strode into his study with his head up and his eyes wide, like a warrior approaching the field of battle. And there he sat for the next one hour, and words he wrote none.

26

His dry stint on the word processor convinced him that it might be a good idea to drink dinner instead of eat it, and he was on his second bourbon and water when the telephone rang again. He approached it gingerly, suddenly wishing he had a phone answering machine after all. They did have at least one sterling quality: you could monitor incoming calls and separate friend from foe.

He stood over it irresolutely, thinking how much he disliked the sound modern telephones made. Once upon a time they had rung— jingled merrily, even. Now they made a shrill ululating noise that sounded like a migraine headache trying to happen.

Well, are you going to pick it up or just stand here listening to it do that?

I don't want to talk to him again. He scares me and he infuriates me, and I don't know which feeling I dislike more.

Maybe it's not him.

Maybe it is.

Listening to those two thoughts go around and around was even worse than listening to the warbling *beep-yawp* of the phone, so he picked it up and said hello gruffly and it was, after all, no one more dangerous than his caretaker, Greg Carstairs.

Greg asked the now-familiar questions about the house and Mort answered them all again, reflecting that explaining such an event was very similar to explaining a sudden death—if anything could get you over the shock, it was the constant repetition of the known facts.

"Listen, Mort, I finally caught up with Tom Greenleaf late this afternoon," Greg said, and Mort thought Greg sounded a little funny—a little cautious. "He and Sonny Trotts were painting the Methodist Parish Hall."

"Uh-huh? Did you speak to him about my buddy?"

"Yeah, I did," Greg said. He sounded more cautious than ever.

"Well?"

There was a short pause. Then Greg said, "Tom thought you must have been mixed up on your days."

"Mixed up on my . . . what do you mean?"

"Well," Greg said apologetically, "he says he *did* swing down Lake Drive yesterday afternoon, and he did see you; he said he waved to you and you waved back. But, Mort—"

"*What?*" But he was afraid he already knew what.

"Tom says you were alone," Greg finished.

27

For a long moment, Mort didn't say anything. He did not feel *capable* of saying anything. Greg didn't say anything, either, giving him time to think. Tom Greenleaf, of course, was no spring chicken; he was Dave Newsome's senior by at least three and perhaps as many as six years. But neither was he senile.

"Jesus," Mort said at last. He spoke very softly. The truth was, he felt a little winded.

"*My* idea," Greg said diffidently, "was maybe *Tom* was the one who got a little mixed up. You know he's not exactly—"

"A spring chicken," Mort finished. "I know it. But if there's anybody in Tashmore with a better eye for strangers than Tom, I don't know who it is. He's been remembering strangers all his *life,* Greg. That's one of the things caretakers *do,* right?" He hesitated, then burst out: "He looked at us! He looked right at *both* of us!"

Carefully, speaking as if he were only joshing, Greg said: "Are you sure you didn't just dream this fella, Mort?"

"I hadn't even considered it," Mort said slowly, "until now. If none of this happened, and I'm running around telling people it *did,* I guess that would make me crazy."

"Oh, I don't think *that* at all," Greg said hastily.

"*I* do," Mort replied. He thought: *But maybe that's what he really wants. To make people think you are crazy. And, maybe in the end, to make what people think the truth.*

Oh yes. Right. And he partnered up with old Tom Greenleaf to do the job. In fact, it was probably Tom who went up to Derry and burned the house, while Shooter stayed down here and wasted the cat—right?

Now, think about it. Really THINK. Was he there? Was he REALLY?

So Mort thought about it. He thought about it harder than he had ever thought about anything in his life; harder, even, than he had thought about Amy and Ted and what he should do about them after he had discovered them in bed together on that day in May. *Had* he hallucinated John Shooter?

He thought again of the speed with which Shooter had grabbed him and thrown him against the side of the car.

"Greg?"

"I'm here, Mort."

"Tom didn't see the car, either? Old station wagon, Mississippi plates?"

"He says he didn't see a car on Lake Drive at all yesterday. Just you, standing up by the end of the path that goes down to the lake. He thought you were admiring the view."

Is it live, or is it Memorex?

He kept coming back to the hard grip of Shooter's hands on his upper arms, the speed with which the man had thrown him against the car. "You lie," Shooter had said. Mort had seen the rage chained in his eyes, and had smelled dry cinnamon on his breath.

His hands.

The pressure of his hands.

"Greg, hold the phone a sec."

"Sure."

Mort put the receiver down and tried to roll up his shirtsleeves. He was not very successful, because his hands were shaking badly. He unbuttoned the shirt instead, pulled it off, then held out his arms. At first he saw nothing. Then he rotated them outward as far as they would go, and there they were, two yellowing bruises on the inside of each arm, just above the elbow.

The marks made by John Shooter's thumbs when he grabbed him and threw him against the car.

He suddenly thought he might understand, and was afraid. Not for himself, though.

For old Tom Greenleaf.

28

He picked up the telephone. "Greg?"

"I'm here."

"Did Tom seem all right when you talked to him?"

"He was exhausted," Greg said promptly. "Foolish old man has got no business crawling around on a scaffold and painting all day in a cold wind. Not at his age. He looked ready to fall into the nearest pile of leaves, if he couldn't get to a bed in a hurry. I see what you're getting at, Mort, and I suppose that if he was tired enough, it *could* have slipped his mind, but—"

"No, that's not what I'm thinking about. Are you sure exhaustion was all it was? Could he have been scared?"

Now there was a long, thinking silence at the other end of the line. Impatient though he was, Mort did not break it. He intended to allow Greg all the thinking time he needed.

"He didn't seem himself," Greg said at last. "He seemed distracted . . . *off,* somehow. I chalked it up to plain old tiredness, but maybe that wasn't it. Or not all of it."

"Could he have been hiding something from you?"

This time the pause was not so long. "I don't know. He might have been. That's all I can say for sure, Mort. You're making me wish I'd talked to him longer and pressed him a little harder."

"I think it might be a good idea if we went over to his place," Mort said. "Now. It happened the way I told you, Greg. If Tom said something different, it could be because my friend scared the bejesus out of him. I'll meet you there."

"Okay." Greg sounded worried all over again. "But, you know, Tom isn't the sort of man who'd scare easy."

"I'm sure that was true once, but Tom's seventy-five if he's a day. I think that the older you get, the easier to scare you get."

"Why don't I meet you there?"

"That sounds like a good idea." Mort hung up the telephone, poured the rest of his bourbon down the sink, and headed for Tom Greenleaf's house in the Buick.

29

Greg was parked in the driveway when Mort arrived. Tom's Scout was by the back door. Greg was wearing a flannel jacket with the collar turned up; the wind off the lake was keen enough to be uncomfortable.

"He's okay," he told Mort at once.

"How do you know?"

They both spoke in low tones.

"I saw his Scout, so I went to the back door. There's a note pinned there saying he had a hard day and went to bed early." Greg grinned and shoved his long hair out of his face. "It *also* says that if any of his regular people need him, they should call me."

"Is the note in his handwriting?"

"Yeah. Big old-man's scrawl. I'd know it anywhere. I went around and looked in his bedroom window. He's in there. The window's shut, but it's a wonder he doesn't break the damned glass, he's snoring so loud. Do you want to check for yourself?"

Mort sighed and shook his head. "But something's wrong, Greg. Tom saw us. *Both* of us. The man got hot under the collar a few minutes after Tom passed and grabbed me by the arms. I'm wearing his bruises. I'll show you, if you want to see."

Greg shook his head. "I believe you. The more I think about it, the less I like the way he sounded when he said you were all by yourself when he saw you. There was something . . . off about it. I'll talk to him again in the morning. Or we can talk to him together, if you want."

"That would be good. What time?"

"Why not come down to the Parish Hall around nine-thirty? He'll have had two-three cups of coffee—you can't say boo to him before he's had his coffee—and we can get him down off that damned scaffolding for awhile. Maybe save his life. Sound okay?"

"Yes." Mort held out his hand. "Sorry I got you out on a wild goosechase."

Greg shook his hand. "No need to be. Something's not right here. I'm good and curious to find out what it is."

Mort got back into his Buick, and Greg slipped behind the wheel of his truck. They drove off in opposite directions, leaving the old man to his exhausted sleep.

Mort himself did not sleep until almost three in the morning. He tossed and turned in the bedroom until the sheets were a battlefield and he could stand it no longer. Then he walked to the living-room couch in a kind of daze. He barked his shins on the rogue coffee table, cursed in a monotone, lay down, adjusted the cushions behind his head, and fell almost immediately down a black hole.

30

When he woke up at eight o'clock the next morning, he thought he felt fine. He went right on thinking so until he swung his legs off the couch and sat up. Then a groan so loud it was almost a muted scream escaped him and he could only sit for a moment, wishing he could hold his back, his knees, and his right arm all at the same time. The arm was the worst, so he settled for holding that. He had read someplace that people can accomplish almost supernatural acts of strength while in the grip of panic; that they feel nothing while lifting cars off trapped infants or strangling killer Dobermans with their bare hands, only realizing how badly they have strained their bodies after the tide of emotion has receded. Now he believed it. He had thrown open the door of the upstairs bathroom hard enough to pop one of the hinges. How hard had he swung the poker? Harder than he wanted to think about, according to the way his back and right arm felt this morning. Nor did he want to think what the damage up there might look like to a less inflamed eye. He *did* know that he was going to put the damage right himself—or as much of it as he could, anyway. Mort thought Greg Carstairs must have some serious doubts about his sanity already, his protestations to the contrary notwithstanding. A look at the broken bathroom door, smashed shower-stall door, and shattered medicine cabinet would do little to improve Greg's faith in his rationality. He remembered thinking that Shooter might be trying to make people believe he was crazy. The idea did not seem foolish at all now that he examined it in the light of day; it seemed, if anything, more logical and believable than ever.

But he had promised to meet Greg at the Parish Hall in ninety minutes—less than that, now—to talk to Tom Greenleaf. Sitting here and counting his aches wasn't going to get him there.

Mort forced himself to his feet and walked slowly through the house to the master bathroom. He turned the shower on hot enough to send up billows of steam, swallowed three aspirin, and climbed in.

By the time he emerged, the aspirin had started its work, and he thought he could get through the day after all. It wouldn't be fun, and he might feel as if it had lasted several years by the time it was over, but he thought he could get through it.

This is the second day, he thought as he dressed. A little cramp of apprehension went through him. *Tomorrow is his deadline.* That made him think first of Amy, and then of Shooter saying, *I'd leave her out of it if I could, but I'm startin to think you ain't going to leave me that option.*

The cramp returned. First the crazy son of a bitch had killed Bump, then he had threatened Tom Greenleaf (surely he *must* have threatened Tom Greenleaf), and, Mort had come to realize, it really *was* possible that Shooter could have torched the Derry house. He supposed he had known this all along, and had simply not wanted to admit it to himself. Torching the house and getting rid of the magazine had been his main mission—of course; a man as crazy as Shooter simply wouldn't think of all the other copies of that magazine that were lying around. Such things would not be a part of a lunatic's world view.

And Bump? The cat was probably just an afterthought. Shooter got back, saw the cat on the stoop waiting to be let back in, saw that Mort was still sleeping, and killed the cat on a whim. Making a round trip to Derry that fast would have been tight, but it could have been done. It all made sense.

And now he was threatening to involve Amy.

I'll have to warn her, he thought, stuffing his shirt into the back of his pants. *Call her up this morning and come totally clean. Handling the man myself is one thing; standing by while a madman involves the only woman I've ever really loved in something she doesn't know anything about . . . that's something else.*

Yes. But first he would talk with Tom Greenleaf and get the truth out of him. Without Tom's corroboration of the fact that Shooter was really around and really dangerous, Mort's own behavior was going to look suspicious or nutty, or both. Probably both. So, Tom first.

But before he met Greg at the Methodist Parish Hall, he intended to stop in at Bowie's and have one of Gerda's famous bacon-and-cheese omelettes. An army marches on its stomach, Private Rainey.

Right you are, sir. He went out to the front hallway, opened the little wooden box mounted on the wall over the telephone table, and felt for the Buick keys. The Buick keys weren't there.

Frowning, he walked out into the kitchen. There they were, on the counter by the sink. He picked them up and bounced them thoughtfully on the palm of his hand. Hadn't he put them back in the box when he returned from his run to Tom's house last night? He tried to remember, and couldn't—not for sure. Dropping the keys into the box after returning home was such a habit that one drop-off blended in with another. If you ask a man who likes fried eggs what he had for breakfast three days ago, he can't remember— he *assumes* he had fried eggs, because he has them so often, but he can't be sure. This was like that. He had come back tired, achy, and preoccupied. He just couldn't remember.

But he didn't like it.

He didn't like it at all.

He went to the back door and opened it. There, lying on the porch boards, was John Shooter's black hat with the round crown.

Mort stood in the doorway looking at it, his car keys clutched in one hand with the brass key-fob hanging down so it caught and reflected a shaft of morning sunlight. He could hear his heartbeat in his ears. It was beating slowly and deliberately. Some part of him had expected this.

The hat was lying exactly where Shooter had left his manuscript. And beyond it, in the driveway, was his Buick. He had parked it around the corner when he returned last night—that he *did* remember—but now it was here.

"*What did you do?*" Mort Rainey screamed suddenly into the morning sunshine, and the birds which had been twittering unconcernedly away in the trees fell suddenly silent. "*What in God's name did you do?*"

But if Shooter was there, watching him, he made no reply. Perhaps he felt that Mort would find out what he had done soon enough.

31

The Buick's ashtray was pulled open, and there were two cigarette butts in it. They were unfiltered. Mort picked one of them out with his fingernails, his face contorted into a grimace of distaste, sure it would be a Pall Mall, Shooter's brand. It was.

He turned the key and the engine started at once. Mort hadn't heard it ticking and popping when he came out, but it started as if it were warm, all the same. Shooter's hat was now in the trunk. Mort had picked it up with the same distaste he had shown for the cigarette butt, putting only enough of his fingers on the brim to get a grip on it. There had been nothing under it, and nothing inside it but a very old sweat-stained inner band. It had some other smell, however, one which was sharper and more acrid than sweat. It was a smell which Mort recognized in some vague way but could not place. Perhaps it would come to him. He put the hat in the back seat, then remembered he would be seeing Greg and Tom in a little less than an hour. He wasn't sure he wanted them to see the hat. He didn't know exactly why he felt that way, but this morning it seemed safer to follow his instincts than to question them, so he put the hat in the trunk and set off for town.

32

He passed Tom's house again on the way to Bowie's. The Scout was no longer in the driveway. For a moment this made Mort feel nervous, and then he decided it was a good sign, not a bad one— Tom must have already started his day's work. Or he might have gone to Bowie's himself—Tom was a widower, and he ate a lot of his meals at the lunch counter in the general store.

Most of the Tashmore Public Works Department was at the counter, drinking coffee and talking about the upcoming deer season, but Tom was

(*dead he's dead Shooter killed him and guess whose car he used*)

not among them.

"Mort Rainey!" Gerda Bowie greeted him in her usual hoarse, Bleacher Creature's shout. She was a tall woman with masses of frizzy chestnut hair and a great rounded bosom. "Ain't seen you in a coon's age! Writing any good books lately?"

"Trying," Mort said. "You wouldn't make me one of your special omelettes, would you?"

"Shit, no!" Gerda said, and laughed to show she was only joking. The PW guys in their olive-drab coveralls laughed right along with her. Mort wished briefly for a great big gun like the one Dirty Harry wore under his tweed sport-coats. Boom-bang-blam, and maybe they could have a little order around here. "Coming right up, Mort."

"Thanks."

When she delivered it, along with toast, coffee, and OJ, she said in a lower voice: "I heard about your divorce. I'm sorry."

He lifted the mug of coffee to his lips with a hand that was almost steady. "Thanks, Gerda."

"Are you taking care of yourself?"

"Well . . . trying."

"Because you look a little peaky."

"It's hard work getting to sleep some nights. I guess I'm not used to the quiet yet."

"Bullshit—it's sleeping alone you're not used to yet. But a man doesn't have to sleep alone forever, Mort, just because his woman don't know a good thing when she has it. I hope you don't mind me talking to you this way—"

"Not at all," Mort said. But he did. He thought Gerda Bowie made a shitty Ann Landers.

"—but you're the only famous writer this town has got."

"Probably just as well."

She laughed and tweaked his ear. Mort wondered briefly what she would say, what the big men in the olive-drab coveralls would say, if he were to bite the hand that tweaked him. He was a little shocked at how powerfully attractive the idea was. Were they all talking about him and Amy? Some saying she didn't know a good thing when she had it, others saying the poor woman finally got tired of living with a crazy man and decided to get out, none of them knowing what the fuck they were talking about, or what he and Amy had *been* about when they had been good? Of course they were, he thought tiredly. That's what people were best at. Big talk about people whose names they saw in the newspapers.

He looked down at his omelette and didn't want it.

He dug in just the same, however, and managed to shovel most of it down his throat. It was still going to be a long day. Gerda Bowie's opinions on his looks and his love-life wouldn't change that.

When he finished, paid for breakfast and a paper, and left the store (the Public Works crews had decamped *en masse* five minutes before him, one stopping just long enough to obtain an autograph for his niece, who was having a birthday), it was five past nine. He sat behind the steering wheel long enough to check the paper for a story about the Derry house, and found one on page three. DERRY FIRE INSPECTORS REPORT NO LEADS IN RAINEY ARSON, the headline read. The story itself was less than half a column long. The last sentence read, "Morton Rainey, known for such best-selling novels as *The Organ-Grinder's Boy* and *The Delacourt Family,* could not be reached for comment." Which meant that Amy hadn't given them the Tashmore number. Good deal. He'd thank her for that if he talked to her later on.

Tom Greenleaf came first. It would be almost twenty past the hour by the time he reached the Methodist Parish Hall. Close enough to nine-thirty. He put the Buick in gear and drove off.

33

When he arrived at the Parish Hall, there was a single vehicle parked in the drive—an ancient Ford Bronco with a camper on the back and a sign reading SONNY TROTTS PAINTING CARETAKING GENERAL CARPENTRY on each of the doors. Mort saw Sonny himself, a short man of about forty with no hair and merry eyes, on a scaffold. He was painting in great sweeps while the boom box beside him played something Las Vegasy by Ed Ames or Tom Jones—one of those fellows who sang with the top three buttons of their shirts undone, anyway.

"Hi, Sonny!" Mort called.

Sonny went on painting, sweeping back and forth in almost perfect rhythm as Ed Ames or whoever it was asked the musical questions what is a man, what has he got. They were questions Mort had asked himself a time or two, although without the horn section.

"*Sonny!*"

Sonny jerked. White paint flew from the end of his brush, and for an alarming moment Mort thought he might actually topple off the scaffold. Then he caught one of the ropes, turned, and looked down. "Why, Mr. Rainey!" he said. "You gave me a helluva turn!"

For some reason Mort thought of the doorknob in Disney's *Alice in Wonderland* and had to suppress a violent bray of laughter.

"Mr. Rainey? You okay?"

"Yes." Mort swallowed crooked. It was a trick he had learned in parochial school about a thousand years ago, and was the only foolproof way to keep from laughing he had ever found. Like most good tricks that worked, it hurt. "I thought you were going to fall off."

"Not me," Sonny said with a laugh of his own. He killed the voice coming from the boom box as it set off on a fresh voyage of emotion. "Tom might fall off, maybe, but not me."

"Where *is* Tom?" Mort asked. "I wanted to talk to him."

"He called early and said he couldn't make it today. I told him that was okay, there wasn't enough work for both of us anyways."

Sonny looked down upon Mort confidentially.

"There is, a' course, but Tom ladled too much onto his plate this time. This ain't no job for a older fella. He said he was all bound up in his back. Must be, too. Didn't sound like himself at all."

"What time was that?" Mort asked, trying hard to sound casual.

"Early," Sonny said. "Six or so. I was just about to step into the old shitatorium for my morning constitutional. Awful regular, I am." Sonny sounded extremely proud of this. "Course Tom, he knows what time I rise and commence my doins."

"But he didn't sound so good?"

"Nope. Not like himself at all." Sonny paused, frowning. He looked as if he was trying very hard to remember something. Then he gave a little shrug and went on. "Wind off the lake was fierce yesterday. Probably took a cold. But Tommy's iron. Give him a day or two and he'll be fine. I worry more about him gettin preoccupated and walkin the plank." Sonny indicated the floor of the scaffold with his brush, sending a riffle of white drops marching up the boards past his shoes. "Can I do anything for you, Mr. Rainey?"

"No," Mort said. There was a dull ball of dread, like a piece of crumpled canvas, under his heart. "Have you seen Greg, by the way?"

"Greg Carstairs?"

"Yes."

"Not this morning. Course, *he* deals with the carriage trade." Sonny laughed. "Rises later'n the rest of us, he does."

"Well, I thought he was going to come by and see Tom, too," Mort said. "Do you mind if I wait a little? He might show up."

"Be my guest," Sonny said. "You mind the music?"

"Not at all."

"You can get some wowser tapes off the TV these days. All you gotta do is give em your Mastercard number. Don't even have to pay for the call. It's a eight-hundred number." He bent toward the boom box, then looked earnestly down at Mort. "This is Roger Whittaker," he said in low and reverent tones.

"Oh."

Sonny pushed PLAY. Roger Whittaker told them there were times (he was sure they knew) when he bit off more than he could chew. That was also something Mort had done without the horn section. He strolled to the edge of the driveway and tapped absently at his shirt pocket. He was a little surprised to find that the old pack of L & M's, now reduced to a single hardy survivor, was in there. He lit the last cigarette, wincing in anticipation of the harsh taste. But it wasn't bad. It had, in fact, almost no taste at all . . . as if the years had stolen it away.

That's not the only thing the years have stolen.

How true. Irrelevant, but true. He smoked and looked at the road. Now Roger Whittaker was telling him and Sonny that a ship lay loaded in the harbor, and that soon for England they would sail. Sonny Trotts sang the last word of each line. No more; just the last word. Cars and trucks went back and forth on Route 23. Greg's Ford Ranger did not come. Mort pitched away his cigarette, looked at his watch, and saw it was quarter to ten. He understood that Greg, who was almost religiously punctual, was not coming, either.

Shooter got them both.

Oh, bullshit! You don't know that!

Yes I do. The hat. The car. The keys.

You're not just jumping to conclusions, you're leaping to them.

The hat. The car. The keys.

He turned and walked back toward the scaffold. "I guess he forgot," he said, but Sonny didn't hear him. He was swaying back and forth, lost in the art of painting and the soul of Roger Whittaker.

Mort got back into his car and drove away. Lost in his own thoughts, he never heard Sonny call after him.

The music probably would have covered it, anyway.

34

He arrived back at his house at quarter past ten, got out of the car, and started for the house. Halfway there, he turned back and opened the trunk. The hat sat inside, black and final, a real toad in an imaginary garden. He picked it up, not being so choosy of how he handled it this time, slammed the trunk shut, and went into the house.

He stood in the front hallway, not sure what he wanted to do next . . . and suddenly, for no reason at all, he put the hat on his head. He shuddered when he did it, the way a man will sometimes shudder after swallowing a mouthful of raw liquor. But the shudder passed.

And the hat felt like quite a good fit, actually.

He went slowly into the master bathroom, turned on the light, and positioned himself in front of the mirror. He almost burst out laughing—he looked like the man with the pitchfork in that Grant Wood painting, "American Gothic." He looked like that even though the guy in the picture was bareheaded. The hat covered Mort's hair completely, as it had covered Shooter's (if Shooter *had* hair—that was yet to be determined, although Mort supposed that he would know for sure the next time he saw him, since Mort now had his chapeau), and just touched the tops of his ears. It was pretty funny. A scream, in fact.

Then the restless voice in his mind asked, *Why'd you put it on? Who'd you think you'd look like? Him?* and the laughter died. Why *had* he put the hat on in the first place?

He wanted you to, the restless voice said quietly.

Yes? But why? Why would Shooter want Mort to put on his hat?

Maybe he wants you to . . .

Yes? he prompted the restless voice again. Wants me to what?

He thought the voice had gone away and was reaching for the light-switch when it spoke again.

. . . to get confused, it said.

The phone rang then, making him jump. He snatched the hat off guiltily (a little like a man who fears he may be caught trying on his wife's underwear) and went to answer it, thinking it would be Greg, and it would turn out Tom was at Greg's house. Yes, of course, that was what had happened; Tom had called Greg, had told him about Shooter and Shooter's threats, and Greg had taken the old man to *his* place. To protect him. It made such perfect sense that Mort couldn't believe he hadn't thought of it before.

Except it wasn't Greg. It was Herb Creekmore.

"Everything's arranged," Herb said cheerfully. "Marianne came through for me. She's a peach."

"Marianne?" Mort asked stupidly.

"Marianne Jaffery, at *EQMM*!" Herb said. "*EQMM*? 'Sowing Season'? June, 1980? You understand dese t'ings, bwana?"

"Oh," Mort said. "Oh, *good*! Thanks, Herb! Is it for sure?"

"Yep. You'll have it tomorrow—the actual magazine, not just a Xerox of the story. It's coming up from PA. Federal Express. Have you heard anything else from Mr. Shooter?"

"Not yet," Mort said, looking down at the black hat in his hand. He could still smell the odd, evocative aroma it held.

"Well, no news is good news, they say. Did you talk to the local law?"

Had he promised Herb he would do that? Mort couldn't remember for sure, but he might have. Best to play safe, anyway. "Yes. Old Dave Newsome didn't exactly burst a gasket. He thought the guy was probably just playing games." It was downright nasty to lie to Herb, especially after Herb had done him such a favor, but what sense would it make to tell him the truth? It was too crazy, too complicated.

"Well—you passed it along. I think that's important, Mort—I really do."

"Yes."

"Anything else?"

"No—but thanks a million for this. You saved my life." And maybe, he thought, that wasn't just a figure of speech.

"My pleasure. Remember that in small towns, FedEx usually delivers right to the local post office. Okay?"

"Yeah."

"How's the new book coming? I've really been wanting to ask."

"Great!" Mort cried heartily.

"Well, good. Get this guy off your back and turn to it. Work has saved many a better man than you or me, Mort."

"I know. Best to your lady."

"Thanks. Best to—" Herb stopped abruptly, and Mort could almost see him biting his lip. Separations were hard to get used to. Amputees kept feeling the foot which was no longer there, they said. "—to you," he finished.

"I got it," Mort said. "Take care, Herbert."

He walked slowly out to the deck and looked down at the lake.

There were no boats on it today. *I'm one step up, no matter what else happens. I can show the man the goddam magazine. It may not tame him . . . but then again, it may. He's crazy, after all, and you never know what people from the fabled tribe of the Crazy Folks will or won't do. That is their dubious charm. Anything is possible.*

It was even possible that Greg was at home after all, he thought—he might have forgotten their meeting at the Parish Hall, or something totally unrelated to this business might have come up. Feeling suddenly hopeful, Mort went to the telephone and dialled Greg's number. The phone was on the third ring when he remembered Greg saying the week before that his wife and kids were going to spend some time at his in-laws'. Megan starts school next year, and it'll be harder for them to get away, he'd said.

So Greg had been alone.

(*the hat*)

Like Tom Greenleaf.

(*the car*)

The young husband and the old widower.

(*the keys*)

And how does it work? Why, as simple as ordering a Roger Whittaker tape off the TV. Shooter goes to Tom Greenleaf's house, but not in his station wagon—oh no, that would be too much like advertising. He leaves his car parked in Mort Rainey's driveway, or maybe around the side of the house. He goes to Tom's in the Buick. Forces Tom to call Greg. Probably gets Greg out of bed, but Greg has got Tom on his mind and comes in a hurry. Then Shooter forces Tom to call Sonny Trotts and tell Sonny he doesn't feel well enough to come to work. Shooter puts a screwdriver against old Tom's jugular and suggests that if Tom doesn't make it good, he'll be one sorry old coot. Tom makes it good enough . . . although even Sonny, not too bright and just out of bed, realizes that Tom doesn't sound like himself at all. Shooter uses the screwdriver on Tom. And when Greg Carstairs arrives, he uses the screwdriver—or something like it—on *him.* And—

You've gone shit out of your mind. This is just a bad case of the screaming meemies and that's all. Repeat: that . . . is . . . ALL.

That was reasonable, but it didn't convince him. It wasn't a Chesterfield. It didn't satisfy.

Mort walked rapidly through the downstairs part of the house, tugging and twirling at his hair.

What about the trucks? Tom's Scout, Greg's Ranger? Add the Buick and you're thinking about three vehicles here—four if you count in Shooter's Ford wagon, and Shooter is just one man.

He didn't know . . . but he knew that enough was enough.

When he arrived at the telephone again, he pulled the phone book out of its drawer and started looking for the town constable's number. He stopped abruptly.

One of those vehicles was the Buick. MY *Buick.*

He put the telephone down slowly. He tried to think of a way Shooter could have handled all of the vehicles. Nothing came. It was like sitting in front of the word processor when you were tapped for ideas—you got nothing but a blank screen. But he *did* know he didn't want to call Dave Newsome. Not yet. He was walking away from the telephone, headed toward no place in particular, when it rang.

It was Shooter.

"Go to where we met the other day," Shooter said. "Walk down the path a little way. You impress me as a man who thinks the way old folks chew their food, Mr. Rainey, but I'm willing to give you all the time you need. I'll call back late this afternoon. Anybody you call between now and then is your responsibility."

"What did you do?" he asked again. This time his voice was robbed of all force, little more than a whisper. "What in the world did you *do?*"

But there was only a dead line.

35

He walked up to the place where the path and the road came together, the place where he had been talking to Shooter when Tom Greenleaf had had the misfortune to see them. For some reason he didn't like the idea of driving the Buick. The bushes on either side of the path were beaten down and skinned-looking, making a rough path. He walked jerkily down this path, knowing what he would find in the first good-sized copse of trees he came to . . . and he *did* find it. It was Tom Greenleaf's Scout. Both men were inside.

Greg Carstairs was sitting behind the wheel with his head thrown back and a screwdriver—a Phillips, this time—buried up to the hilt in his forehead, above his right eye. The screwdriver had come from a cupboard in the pantry of Mort's house. The red plastic handle was badly chipped and impossible not to recognize.

Tom Greenleaf was in the back seat with a hatchet planted in the top of his head. His eyes were open. Dried brains had trickled down around his ears. Written along the hatchet's ash handle in faded but still legible red letters was one word: RAINEY. It had come from the toolshed.

Mort stood silently. A chickadee called. A woodpecker used a hollow tree to send Morse code. A freshening breeze was producing whitecaps on the lake; the water was a dark cobalt today, and the whitecaps made a pretty contrast.

There was a rustling sound behind him. Mort wheeled around so fast he almost fell—would have fallen, if he'd not had the Scout to lean against. It wasn't Shooter. It was a squirrel. It looked down at him with bright hate from where it was frozen halfway up the trunk of a maple which blazed with red fall fire. Mort waited for his galloping heart to slow. He waited for the squirrel to dash up the tree. His heart did; the squirrel did not.

"He killed them both," he said at last, speaking to the squirrel. "He went to Tom's in my Buick. Then he went to Greg's in Tom's Scout, with Tom driving. He killed Greg. Then he had Tom drive down here, and killed *him.* He used my tools to do both of them. Then he walked back to Tom's house . . . or maybe he jogged. He looks rugged enough to have jogged. Sonny didn't think Tom sounded like himself, and I know why. By the time Sonny got that call, the sun was getting ready to come up and Tom was already dead. It was Shooter, *imitating* Tom. And it was probably easy. From the way Sonny had his music cranked this morning, he's a little deaf, anyway. Once he was done with Sonny Trotts, he got in my Buick again and drove it back to the house. Greg's Ranger is still parked in his own driveway, where it's been all along. And that's how—"

The squirrel scurried up the trunk and disappeared into the blazing red leaves.

"—that's how it worked," Mort finished dully.

Suddenly his legs felt watery. He took two steps back up the path, thought of Tom Greenleaf's brains drying on his cheeks, and his legs just gave up. He fell down and the world swam away for awhile.

36

When he came to, Mort rolled over, sat up groggily, and turned his wrist to look at his watch. It said quarter past two, but of course it must have stopped at that time last night; he had found Tom's Scout at mid-morning, and this *couldn't* be afternoon. He had fainted, and, considering the circumstances, that wasn't surprising. But no one faints for three and a half *hours*.

The watch's second hand was making its steady little circle, however.

Must have jogged it when I sat up, that's all.

But that *wasn't* all. The sun had changed position, and would soon be lost behind the clouds which were filling up the sky. The color of the lake had dulled to a listless chrome.

So he had started off fainting, or swooning, and then what? Well, it sounded incredible, but he supposed he must have fallen asleep. The last three days had been nerve-racking, and last night he had been sleepless until three. So call it a combination of mental and physical fatigue. His mind had just pulled the plug. And—

Shooter! Christ, Shooter said he'd call!

He tried to get to his feet, then fell back with a little *oof!* sound of mingled pain and surprise as his left leg buckled under him. It was full of pins and needles, all of them crazily dancing. He must have lain on the goddam thing. Why hadn't he brought the Buick, for Christ's sake? If Shooter called and Mort wasn't there to take the call, the man might do anything.

He lunged to his feet again, and this time made it all the way up. But when he tried to stride on the left leg, it refused his weight and spilled him forward again. He almost hit his head on the side of the truck going down and was suddenly looking at himself in one of the hubcaps of the Scout. The convex surface made his face look like a grotesque funhouse mask. At least he had left the god-damned hat back at the house; if he had seen *that* on his head, Mort thought he would have screamed. He wouldn't have been able to help himself.

All at once he remembered there were two dead men in the Scout. They were sitting above him, getting stiff, and there were tools sticking out of their heads.

He crawled out of the Scout's shadow, dragged his left leg across his right with his hands, and began to pound at it with his fists, like a man trying to tenderize a cheap cut of meat.

Stop it! a small voice cried—it was the last kernel of rationality at his command, a little sane light in what felt like a vast bank of black thunderheads between his ears. *Stop it! He said he'd call late in the afternoon, and it's only quarter past two! Plenty of time!*

But what if he called early? Or what if "late afternoon" started after two o'clock in the deep-dish, crackerbarrel South?

Keep beating on your leg like that and you'll wind up with a charley horse. Then you can see how you like trying to crawl *back in time to take his call.*

That did the trick. He was able to make himself stop. This time he got up more cautiously and just stood for a moment (he was careful to keep his back to Tom's Scout—he did not want to look inside again) before trying to walk. He found that the pins and needles were subsiding. He walked with a pronounced limp at first, but his gait began to smooth out after the first dozen strides.

He was almost clear of the bushes Shooter had stripped and beaten down with Tom's Scout when he heard a car approaching. Mort dropped to his knees without even thinking about it and watched as a rusty old Cadillac swept by. It belonged to Don Bassinger, who owned a place on the far side of the lake. Bassinger, a veteran alcoholic who spent most of his time drinking up what remained of his once-substantial inheritance, often used Lake Drive as a shortcut to what was known as Bassinger Road. Don was about the only year-round resident down here, Mort thought.

After the Caddy was out of sight, Mort got to his feet and hurried the rest of the way up to the road. Now he was glad he hadn't brought the Buick. He knew Don Bassinger's Cadillac, and Bassinger knew Mort's Buick. It was probably too early in the day for Don to be in a blackout, and he might well have remembered seeing Mort's car, if it had been there, parked not far from the place where, before too much longer, someone was going to make an *extremely* horrible discovery.

He's busy tying you to this business, Mort thought as he limped along Lake Drive toward his house. *He's been doing it all along. If anyone saw a car near Tom Greenleaf's last night, it will almost certainly turn out to be your Buick. He killed them with your tools—*

I could get rid of the tools, he thought suddenly. *I could throw them*

*in the lake. I might heave up a time or two getting them out, but I think
I could go through with it.*

*Could you? I wonder. And even if you did . . . well, Shooter almost
certainly will have thought of that possibility, too. He seems to have
thought of all the others. And he knows that if you tried to get rid of
the hatchet and the screwdriver and the police dragged the bottom for
them and they were found, things would look even worse for you. Do you
see what he's done? Do you?*

Yes. He saw. John Shooter had given him a present. It was a tar
baby. A large, glistening tar baby. Mort had smacked the tar baby
in the head with his left hand and it had stuck fast. So he had
whopped that old tar baby in the gut with his right hand to make
it let go, only his *right* hand had stuck, too. He had been—what
was the word he had kept using with such smug satisfaction? "Disingenuous," wasn't it? Yes, that was it. And all the time he had
been getting more entangled with John Shooter's tar baby. And
now? Well, he had told lies to all sorts of people, and that would
look bad if it came out, and a quarter of a mile behind him a man
was wearing a hatchet for a hat and Mort's name was written on
the handle, and that would look even worse.

Mort imagined the telephone ringing in the empty house and
forced himself into a trot.

37

Shooter didn't call.

The minutes stretched out like taffy, and Shooter didn't call. Mort
walked restlessly through the house, twirling and pulling at his hair.
He imagined this was what it felt like to be a junkie waiting for
the pusher-man.

Twice he had second thoughts about waiting, and went to the
phone to call the authorities—not old Dave Newsome, or even the
county sheriff, but the State Police. He would hew to the old
Vietnam axiom: Kill em all and let God sort em out. Why not? He
had a good reputation, after all; he was a respected member of two
Maine communities, and John Shooter was a—

Just what *was* Shooter?

The word "phantom" came to mind.

The word "will-o'-the-wisp" *also* came to mind.

But it was not this that stopped him. What stopped him was a horrible certainty that Shooter would be trying to call while Mort himself was using the line . . . that Shooter would hear the busy signal, hang up, and Mort would never hear from him again.

At quarter of four, it began to rain—a steady fall rain, cold and gentle, sighing down from a white sky, tapping on the roof and the stiff leaves around the house.

At ten of, the telephone rang. Mort leaped for it.

It was Amy.

Amy wanted to talk about the fire. Amy wanted to talk about how unhappy she was, not just for herself, but for both of them. Amy wanted to tell him that Fred Evans, the insurance investigator, was still in Derry, still picking over the site, still asking questions about everything from the most recent wiring inspection to who had keys to the wine cellar, and Ted was suspicious of his motives. Amy wanted Mort to wonder with her if things would have been different if they had had children.

Mort responded to all this as best he could, and all the time he was talking with her, he felt time—prime late-afternoon time—slipping away. He was half mad with worry that Shooter would call, find the line busy, and commit some fresh atrocity. Finally he said the only thing he could think of to get her off the line: that if he didn't get to the bathroom soon, he was going to have an accident.

"Is it booze?" she asked, concerned. "Have you been drinking?"

"Breakfast, I think," he said. "Listen, Amy, I—"

"At Bowie's?"

"Yes," he said, trying to sound strangled with pain and effort. The truth was, he *felt* strangled. It was all quite a comedy, when you really considered it. "Amy, really, I—"

"God, Mort, she keeps the dirtiest grill in town," Amy said. "Go. I'll call back later." The phone went dead in his ear. He put the receiver into its cradle, stood there a moment, and was amazed and dismayed to discover his fictional complaint was suddenly real: his bowels had drawn themselves into an aching, throbbing knot.

He ran for the bathroom, unclasping his belt as he went.

It was a near thing, but he made it. He sat on the ring in the rich odor of his own wastes, his pants around his ankles, catching his breath . . . and the phone began to ring again.

He sprang up like a jack released from its box, cracking one knee smartly on the side of the washstand, and ran for it, holding his pants up with one hand and mincing along like a girl in a tight skirt. He had that miserable, embarrassing I-didn't-have-time-to-wipe feeling, and he guessed it happened to everyone, but it suddenly occurred to him he had never read about it in a book—not one single book, ever.

Oh, life was such a comedy.

This time it *was* Shooter.

"I saw you down there," Shooter said. His voice was as calm and serene as ever. "Down where I left them, I mean. Looked like you had you a heat-stroke, only it isn't summer."

"What do you want?" Mort switched the telephone to his other ear. His pants slid down to his ankles again. He let them go and stood there with the waistband of his Jockey shorts suspended halfway between his knees and his hips. What an author photograph *this* would make, he thought.

"I almost pinned a note on you," Shooter said. "I decided not to." He paused, then added with a kind of absent contempt: "You scare too easy."

"What do you want?"

"Why, I told you that already, Mr. Rainey. I want a story to make up for the one you stole. Ain't you ready to admit it yet?"

Yes—tell him yes! Tell him anything, the earth is flat, John Kennedy and Elvis Presley are alive and well and playing banjo duets in Cuba, Meryl Streep's a transvestite, tell him ANYTHING—

But he wouldn't.

All the fury and frustration and horror and confusion suddenly burst out of his mouth in a howl.

"*I DIDN'T! I DIDN'T! YOU'RE CRAZY, AND I CAN PROVE IT! I HAVE THE MAGAZINE, YOU LOONY! DO YOU HEAR ME? I HAVE THE GODDAM MAGAZINE!*"

The response to this was no response. The line was silent and dead, without even the faraway gabble of a phantom voice to break that smooth darkness, like that which crept up to the window-wall each night he had spent here alone.

"Shooter?"

Silence.

"Shooter, are you still there?"

More silence. He was gone.

Mort let the telephone sag away from his ear. He was returning it to the cradle when Shooter's voice, tinny and distant and almost lost, said: ". . . now?"

Mort put the phone back to his ear. It seemed to weigh eight hundred pounds. "What?" he asked. "I thought you were gone."

"You have it? You *have* this so-called magazine? *Now?*" He thought Shooter sounded upset for the first time. Upset and unsure.

"No," Mort said.

"Well, *there!*" Shooter said, sounding relieved. "I think you might finally be ready to talk turk—"

"It's coming Federal Express," Mort interrupted. "It will be at the post office by ten tomorrow."

"*What* will be?" Shooter asked. "Some fuzzy old thing that's supposed to be a *copy?*"

"No," Mort said. The feeling that he had rocked the man, that he had actually gotten past his defenses and hit him hard enough to make it hurt, was strong and undeniable. For a moment or two Shooter had sounded almost afraid, and Mort was angrily glad. "The magazine. The actual *magazine.*"

There was another long pause, but this time Mort kept the telephone screwed tightly against his ear. Shooter was there. And suddenly the *story* was the central issue again, the story and the accusation of plagiarism; Shooter treating him like he was a goddam college kid was the issue, and maybe the man was on the run at last.

Once, in the same parochial school where Mort had learned the trick of swallowing crooked, he had seen a boy stick a pin in a beetle which had been trundling across his desk. The beetle had been caught—pinned, wriggling, and dying. At the time, Mort had been sad and horrified. Now he understood. Now he only wanted to do the same thing to this man. This crazy man.

"There can't be any magazine," Shooter said finally. "Not with that story in it. That story is *mine!*"

Mort could hear anguish in the man's voice. Real anguish. It made him glad. The pin was in Shooter. He was wriggling around on it.

"It'll be here at ten tomorrow," Mort said, "or as soon after as FedEx drops the Tashmore stuff. I'll be happy to meet you there. You can take a look. As long a look as you want, you goddamned maniac."

"Not there," Shooter said after another pause. "At your house."

"Forget it. When I show you that issue of *Ellery Queen*, I want to be someplace where I can yell for help if you go apeshit."

"You'll do it my way," Shooter said. He sounded a little more in control . . . but Mort did not believe Shooter had even half the control he'd had previously. "If you don't, I'll see you in the Maine State Prison for murder."

"Don't make me laugh." But Mort felt his bowels begin to knot up again.

"I hooked you to those two men in more ways than you know," Shooter said, "and you have told a right smart of lies. If I just disappear, Mr. Rainey, you are going to find yourself standing with your head in a noose and your feet in Crisco."

"You don't scare me."

"Yeah, I do," Shooter said. He spoke almost gently. "The only thing is, you're startin to scare me a little, too. I can't quite figure you out."

Mort was silent.

"It'd be funny," Shooter said in a strange, ruminating tone, "if we had come by the same story in two different places, at two different times."

"The thought had occurred to me."

"Did it?"

"I dismissed it," Mort said. "Too much of a coincidence. If it was just the same plot, that would be one thing. But the same language? The same goddam *diction?*"

"Uh-huh," Shooter said. "I thought the same thing, pilgrim. It's just too much. Coincidence is out. You stole it from me, all right, but I'm goddamned if I can figure out how or when."

"Oh, quit it!" Mort burst out. "I have the magazine! I have *proof*! Don't you understand that? It's over! Whether it was some nutty game on your part or just a delusion, it is over! *I have the magazine!*"

After a long silence, Shooter said: "Not yet, you don't."

"How true," Mort said. He felt a sudden and totally unwanted sense of kinship with the man. "So what do we do tonight?"

"Why, nothing," Shooter said. "Those men will keep. One has a wife and kids visiting family. The other lives alone. You go and get your magazine tomorrow morning. I will come to your place around noon."

"You'll kill me," Mort said. He found that the idea didn't carry much terror with it—not tonight, anyway. "If I show you the magazine, your delusion will break down and you'll kill me."

"No!" Shooter replied, and this time he seemed clearly surprised. "You? No, *sir*! But those others were going to get in the way of our business. I couldn't have that . . . and I saw that I could use them to make you deal with me. To face up to your responsibility."

"You're crafty," Mort said. "I'll give you that. I believe you're nuts, but I also believe you're just about the craftiest son of a bitch I ever ran across in my life."

"Well, you can believe this," Shooter said. "If I come tomorrow and find you gone, Mr. Rainey, I will make it my business to destroy every person in the world that you love and care for. I will burn your life like a canefield in a high wind. You will go to jail for killing those two men, but going to jail will be the least of your sorrows. Do you understand?"

"Yes," Mort said. "I understand. Pilgrim."

"Then you be there."

"And suppose—just suppose—I show you the magazine, and it has my name on the contents page and my story inside. What then?"

There was a short pause. Then Shooter said, "I go to the authorities and confess to the whole shooting match. But I'd take care of myself long before the trial, Mr. Rainey. Because if things turn out that way, then I suppose I am crazy. And that kind of a crazy man . . ." There was a sigh. "That kind of crazy man has no excuse or reason to live."

The words struck Mort with queer force. *He's unsure,* he thought. *For the first time, he's really unsure . . . which is more than I've ever been.*

But he cut that off, and hard. He had never had a *reason* to be unsure. This was Shooter's fault. Every bit of it was Shooter's fault.

He said: "How do I know you won't claim the magazine is a fake?"

He expected no response to this, except maybe something about how Mort would have to take his word, but Shooter surprised him.

"If it's real, I'll know," he said, "and if it's fake, we'll both know. I don't reckon you could have rigged a whole fake magazine in three days, no matter how many people you have got working for you in New York."

It was Mort's turn to think, and he thought for a long, long time. Shooter waited for him.

"I'm going to trust you," Mort said at last. "I don't know why, for sure. Maybe because I don't have a lot to live for myself these days. But I'm not going to trust you whole hog. You come down here. Stand in the driveway where I can see you, and see that you're unarmed. I'll come out. Is that satisfactory?"

"That'll do her."

"God help us both."

"Yessir. I'll be damned if I'm sure what I'm into anymore . . . and that is not a comfortable feeling."

"Shooter?"

"Right here."

"I want you to answer one question."

Silence . . . but an inviting silence, Mort thought.

"Did you burn down my house in Derry?"

"No," Shooter said at once. "I was keeping an eye on you."

"And Bump," Mort said bitterly.

"Listen," Shooter said. "You got my hat?"

"Yes."

"I'll want it," Shooter said, "one way or the other."

And the line went dead.

Just like that.

Mort put the phone down slowly and carefully and walked back to the bathroom—once again holding his pants up as he went—to finish his business.

38

Amy *did* call back, around seven, and this time Mort was able to talk to her quite normally—just as if the bathroom upstairs wasn't trashed and there weren't two dead men sitting behind a screen of bushes on the path down to the lake, stiffening as the twilight turned to dark around them.

She had spoken with Fred Evans herself since her last call, she said, and she was convinced he either knew something or suspected something about the fire he didn't want to tell them. Mort tried to soothe her, and thought he succeeded to some degree, but he was worried himself. If Shooter hadn't started the fire—and Mort felt

inclined to believe the man had been telling the truth about that—
then it must have been raw coincidence . . . right?

He didn't know if it was right or not.

"Mort, I've been so worried about you," she said suddenly.

That snapped him back from his thoughts. "Me? I'm okay."

"Are you sure? When I saw you yesterday, I thought you
looked . . . strained." She paused. "In fact, I thought you looked
like you did before you had the . . . you know."

"Amy, I did *not* have a nervous breakdown."

"Well, no," she said quickly. "But you know what I mean. When
the movie people were being so awful about *The Delacourt Family*."

That had been one of the bitterest experiences of Mort's life.
Paramount had optioned the book for $75,000 on a pick-up price
of $750,000—damned big money. And they had been on the verge
of exercising their option when someone had turned up an old
script in the files, something called *The Home Team,* which was
enough like *The Delacourt Family* to open up potential legal problems. It was the only time in his career—before *this* nightmare,
anyway—when he had been exposed to the possibility of a plagiarism charge. The execs had ended up letting the option lapse at the
eleventh hour. Mort still did not know if they had been really
worried about plagiarism or had simply had second thoughts about
his novel's film potential. If they really *had* been worried, he didn't
know how such a bunch of pansies could make *any* movies. Herb
Creekmore had obtained a copy of the *Home Team* screenplay, and
Mort had seen only the most casual similarity. Amy agreed.

The fuss happened just as he was reaching a dead end on a novel
he had wanted desperately to write. There had been a short PR
tour for the paperback version of *The Delacourt Family* at the same
time. All of that at once had put him under a great deal of strain.

But he had *not* had a nervous breakdown.

"I'm okay," he insisted again, speaking gently. He had discovered
an amazing and rather touching thing about Amy some years before:
if you spoke to her gently enough, she was apt to believe you about
almost anything. He had often thought that, if it had been a species-
wide trait, like showing your teeth to indicate rage or amusement,
wars would have ceased millennia ago.

"Are you *sure,* Mort?"

"Yes. Call me if you hear any more from our insurance friend."

"I will."

He paused. "Are you at Ted's?"

"Yes."

"How do you feel about him, these days?"

She hesitated, then said simply: "I love him."

"Oh."

"I didn't go with other men," she said suddenly. "I've always wanted to tell you that. I didn't go with other men. But Ted . . . he looked past your name and saw me, Mort. He saw *me*."

"You mean I didn't."

"You did when you were here," she said. Her voice sounded small and forlorn. "But you were gone so much."

His eyes widened and he was instantly ready to do battle. *Righteous* battle. "*What?* I haven't been on tour since *The Delacourt Family*! And that was a *short* one!"

"I don't want to argue with you, Mort," she said softly. "That part should be over. All I'm trying to say is that, even when you were here, you were gone a lot. You had your own lover, you know. Your work was your lover." Her voice was steady, but he sensed tears buried deep inside it. "How I hated that bitch, Mort. She was prettier than me, smarter than me, more fun than me. How could I compete?"

"Blame it all on me, why not?" he asked her, dismayed to find himself on the edge of tears. "What did you want me to do? Become a goddam plumber? We would have been poor and I would have been unemployed. There was nothing else I could fucking *do*, don't you understand that? There was nothing else I could *do*!" He had hoped the tears were over, at least for awhile, but here they were. Who had rubbed this horrible magic lamp again? Had it been him or her this time?

"I'm not blaming you. There's blame for me, too. You never would have found us . . . the way you did . . . if I hadn't been weak and cowardly. It wasn't Ted; Ted wanted us to go to you and tell you together. He kept asking. And I kept putting him off. I told him I wasn't sure. I told myself I still loved you, that things could go back to the way they were . . . but things never do, I guess. I'll—"

She caught her breath, and Mort realized she was crying, too. "I'll never forget the look on your face when you opened the door of that motel room. I'll carry that to my grave."

Good! he wanted to cry out at her. *Good! Because you only had to see it! I had to wear it!*

"You knew my love," he said unsteadily. "I never hid her from you. You knew from the start."

"But I never knew," she said, "how deep her embrace could be."

"Well, cheer up," Mort said. "She seems to have left me now."

Amy was weeping. "Mort, Mort—I only want you to live and be happy. Can't you see that? Can't you *do* that?"

What he had seen was one of her bare shoulders touching one of Ted Milner's bare shoulders. He had seen their eyes, wide and frightened, and Ted's hair stuck up in an Alfalfa corkscrew. He thought of telling her this—of trying, anyway—and let it go. It was enough. They had hurt each other enough. Another time, perhaps, they could go at it again. He wished she hadn't said that thing about the nervous breakdown, though. He had *not* had a nervous breakdown.

"Amy, I think I ought to go."

"Yes—both of us. Ted's out showing a house, but he'll be back soon. I have to put some dinner together."

"I'm sorry about the argument."

"Will you call if you need me? I'm still worried."

"Yes," he said, and said goodbye, and hung up. He stood there by the telephone for a moment, thinking he would surely burst into tears. But it passed. That was perhaps the real horror.

It passed.

39

The steadily falling rain made him feel listless and stupid. He made a little fire in the woodstove, drew a chair over, and tried to read the current issue of *Harper's,* but he kept nodding off and then jerking awake again as his chin dropped, squeezing his windpipe and producing a snore. *I should have bought some cigarettes today,* he thought. *A few smokes would have kept me awake.* But he hadn't bought any smokes, and he wasn't really sure they would have kept him awake, anyway. He wasn't just tired; he was suffering from shock.

At last he walked over to the couch, adjusted the pillows, and lay back. Next to his cheek, cold rain spickle-spackled against the dark glass.

Only once, he thought. *I only did it once.* And then he fell deeply asleep.

40

In his dream, he was in the world's biggest classroom.

The walls stretched up for miles. Each desk was a mesa, the gray tiles the endless plain which swept among them. The clock on the wall was a huge cold sun. The door to the hallway was shut, but Morton Rainey could read the words on the pebbled glass:

HOME TEAM WRITING ROOM
PROF. DELLACOURT

They spelled it wrong, Mort thought, *too many L's.*

But another voice told him this was not so.

Mort was standing on the giant blackboard's wide chalk gutter, stretching up. He had a piece of chalk the size of a baseball bat in his hand. He wanted to drop his arm, which ached ferociously, but he could not. Not until he had written the same sentence on the blackboard five hundred times: *I will not copy from John Kintner.* He must have written it four hundred times already, he thought, but four hundred wasn't enough. Stealing a man's work when a man's work was really all he had was unforgivable. So he would have to write and write and write, and never mind the voice in his mind trying to tell him that this was a dream, that his right arm ached for other reasons.

The chalk squeaked monstrously. The dust, acrid and some-how familiar—so familiar—sifted down into his face. At last he could go on no longer. His arm dropped to his side like a bag filled with lead shot. He turned on the chalk gutter, and saw that only one of the desks in the huge classroom was occupied. The occupant was a young man with a country kind of face; a face you expected to see in the north forty behind the ass end of a mule. His pale-brown hair stuck up in spikes from his head. His country-cousin hands, seemingly all knuckles, were folded on the desk before him. He was looking at Mort with pale, ab-sorbed eyes.

I know you, Mort said in the dream.

That's right, pilgrim, John Kintner said in his bald, drawling Southern accent. *You just put me together wrong. Now keep on writing. It's not five hundred. It's five thousand.*

Mort started to turn, but his foot slipped on the edge of the gutter, and suddenly he was spilling outward, screaming into the dry, chalky air, and John Kintner was laughing, and he—

41

—woke up on the floor with his head almost underneath the rogue coffee table, clutching at the carpet and crying out in high-pitched, whinnying shrieks.

He was at Tashmore Lake. Not in some weird, cyclopean classroom but at the lake . . . and dawn was coming up misty in the east.

I'm all right. It was just a dream and I'm all right.

But he wasn't. Because it *hadn't* just been a dream. John Kintner had been real. How in God's name could he have forgotten John Kintner?

Mort had gone to college at Bates, and had majored in creative writing. Later, when he spoke to classes of aspiring writers (a chore he ducked whenever possible), he told them that such a major was probably the worst mistake a man or woman could make, if he or she wanted to write fiction for a living.

"Get a job with the post office," he'd say. "It worked for Faulkner." And they would laugh. They liked to listen to him, and he supposed he was fairly good at keeping them entertained. That seemed very important, since he doubted that he or anyone else could teach them how to write creatively. Still, he was always glad to get out at the end of the class or seminar or workshop. The kids made him nervous. He supposed John Kintner was the reason why.

Had Kintner been from Mississippi? Mort couldn't remember, but he didn't think so. But he had been from some enclave of the Deep South all the same—Alabama, Louisiana, maybe the toolies of north Florida. He didn't know for sure. Bates College had been a long time ago, and he hadn't thought of John Kintner, who had suddenly dropped out one day for reasons known only to himself, in years.

That's not true. You thought about him last night.

Dreamed about him, you mean, Mort corrected himself quickly, but that hellish little voice inside would not let it go.

No, earlier than that. You thought about him while you were talking to Shooter on the telephone.

He didn't want to think about this. He *wouldn't* think about this.

John Kintner was in the past; John Kintner had nothing to do with what was happening now. He got up and walked unsteadily toward the kitchen in the milky, early light to make strong coffee. Lots and lots of strong coffee. Except the hellish little voice wouldn't let him be. Mort looked at Amy's set of kitchen knives hanging from their magnetized steel runners and thought that if he could cut that little voice out, he would try the operation immediately.

You were thinking that you rocked the man—that you finally rocked him. You were thinking that the story had become the central issue again, the story and the accusation of plagiarism. Shooter treating you like a goddam college kid was the issue. Like a goddam college kid. Like a—

"Shut up," Mort said hoarsely. "Just shut the fuck up."

The voice did, but he found himself unable to stop thinking about John Kintner anyway.

As he measured coffee with a shaking hand, he thought of his constant, strident protestations that he hadn't plagiarized Shooter's story, that he had never plagiarized *anything*.

But he had, of course.

Once.

Just once.

"But that was so long ago," he whispered. "And it doesn't have anything to do with this."

It might be true, but that did not stop his thoughts.

42

He had been a junior, and it was spring semester. The creative-writing class of which he was a part was focussing on the short story that semester. The teacher was a fellow named Richard Perkins, Jr., who had written two novels which had gotten very good reviews and sold very few copies. Mort had tried one, and thought the good reviews and bad sales had the same root cause: the books were incomprehensible. But the man hadn't been a bad teacher— he had kept them entertained, at least.

There had been about a dozen students in the class. One of them was John Kintner. Kintner was only a freshman, but he had gotten special permission to take the class. And had deserved it, Mort supposed. Southern-fried cracker or not, that sucker had been *good*.

The course required each of them to write either six short stories or three longer ones. Each week, Perkins dittoed off the ones he thought would make for the liveliest discussion and handed them out at the end of the class. The students were supposed to come the following week prepared to discuss and criticize. It was the usual way to run such a class. And one week Perkins had given them a story by John Kintner. It had been called . . . What *had* it been called?

Mort had turned on the water to fill the coffeemaker, but now he only stood, looking absently out at the fog beyond the window-wall and listening to the running water.

You know damned well what it was called. "Secret Window, Secret Garden."

"But it *wasn't!*" he yelled petulantly to the empty house. He thought furiously, determined to shut the hellish little voice up once and for all . . . and suddenly it came to him.

" 'Crowfoot Mile'!" he shrieked. "The name of the story was 'Crowfoot Mile,' and it doesn't have *anything* to do with *anything!*"

Except that was not quite true, either, and he didn't really need the little voice hunkered down someplace in the middle of his aching head to point out the fact.

Kintner had turned in three or maybe four stories before dis-appearing to wherever he had disappeared to (if asked to guess, Mort would have guessed Vietnam—it was where most of them had disappeared to at the end of the sixties—the young men, any-how). "Crowfoot Mile" hadn't been the best of Kintner's sto-ries . . . but it had been good. Kintner was clearly the best writer in Richard Perkins, Jr.'s class. Perkins treated the boy almost as an equal, and in Mort Rainey's not-so-humble estimation, Perkins had been right to do so, because he thought Kintner had been quite a bit *better* than Richard Perkins, Jr. As far as that went, Mort believed *he* had been better.

But had he been better than *Kintner?*

"Huh-uh," he said under his breath as he turned on the coffee-maker. "I was second."

Yes. He had been second, and he had hated that. He knew that most students taking writing courses were just marking time, pur-suing a whim before giving up childish things and settling into a study of whatever it was that would be their real life's work. The creative writing most of them would do in later life would consist of contributing items to the Community Calendar pages of their local newspapers or writing advertising copy for Bright Blue Breeze dish detergent. Mort had come into Perkins's class confidently expecting to be the best, because it had never been any other way with him. For that reason, John Kintner had come as an unpleasant shock.

He remembered trying to talk to the boy once . . . but Kintner, who contributed in class only when asked, had proved to be almost inarticulate. When he spoke out loud, he mumbled and stumbled like a poor-white sharecropper's boy whose education had stopped at the fourth-grade level. His writing was the only voice he had, apparently.

And you stole it.

"Shut up," he muttered. "Just shut up."

You were second best and you hated it. You were glad when he was gone, because then you could be first again. Just like you always had been.

Yes. True. And a year later, when he was preparing to graduate, he had been cleaning out the back closet of the sleazy Lewiston apartment he had shared with two other students, and had come upon a pile of offprints from Perkins's writing course. Only one of Kintner's stories had been in the stack. It happened to be "Crowfoot Mile."

He remembered sitting on the seedy, beer-smelling rug of his bedroom, reading the story, and the old jealousy had come over him again.

He threw the other offprints away, but he had taken that one with him . . . for reasons he wasn't sure he wanted to examine closely.

As a sophomore, Mort had submitted a story to a literary magazine called *Aspen Quarterly*. It came back with a note which said the readers had found it quite good "although the ending seemed rather jejune." The note, which Mort found both patronizing and tremendously exciting, invited him to submit other material.

Over the next two years, he had submitted four more stories. None were accepted, but a personal note accompanied each of the rejection slips. Mort went through an unpublished writer's agony of optimism alternating with deep pessimism. He had days when he was sure it was only a matter of time before he cracked *Aspen Quarterly*. And he had days when he was positive that the entire editorial staff—pencil-necked geeks to a man—was only playing with him, teasing him the way a man might tease a hungry dog by holding a piece of meat up over its head and then jerking the scrap out of reach when it leaps. He sometimes imagined one of them holding up one of his manuscripts, fresh out of its manila envelope, and shouting: "Here's another one from that putz in Maine! Who wants to write the letter this time?" And all of them cracking up, perhaps even rolling around on the floor under their posters of Joan Baez and Moby Grape at the Fillmore.

Most days, Mort had not indulged in this sort of sad paranoia. He understood that he was good, and that it was only a matter of time. And that summer, working as a waiter in a Rockland restaurant, he thought of the story by John Kintner. He thought it was probably still in his trunk, kicking around at the bottom. He had a sudden idea. He would change the title and submit "Crowfoot Mile" to *Aspen Quarterly* under his own name! He remembered thinking it would be a fine joke on them, although, looking back now, he could not imagine what the joke would have been.

He *did* remember that he'd had no intention of *publishing* the story under his own name . . . or, if he had had such an intention on some deeper level, he hadn't been aware of it. In the unlikely event of an acceptance, he would withdraw the story, saying he wanted to work on it some more. And if they rejected it, he could at least take some cheer in the thought that John Kintner wasn't good enough for *Aspen Quarterly,* either.

So he had sent the story.

And they had accepted it.

And he had *let* them accept it.

And they sent him a check for twenty-five dollars. "An honorarium," the accompanying letter had called it.

And then they had published it.

And Morton Rainey, overcome by belated guilt at what he had done, had cashed the check and had stuffed the bills into the poor box of St. Catherine's in Augusta one day.

But guilt hadn't been *all* he'd felt. Oh no.

Mort sat at the kitchen table with his head propped in one hand, waiting for the coffee to perk. His head ached. He didn't want to be thinking about John Kintner and John Kintner's story. What he had done with "Crowfoot Mile" had been one of the most shameful events of his life; was it really surprising that he had buried it for so many years? He wished he could bury it again now. This, after all, was going to be a big day—maybe the biggest of his life. Maybe even the *last* of his life. He should be thinking about going to the post office. He should be thinking about his confrontation with Shooter, but his mind would not let that sad old time alone.

When he'd seen the magazine, the actual *magazine* with his name in it above John Kintner's story, he felt like a man waking from a horrible episode of sleepwalking, an unconscious outing in which he has done some irrevocable thing. How had he let it go so *far*? It was supposed to have been a *joke*, for Christ's sake, just a little *giggle*—

But he *had* let it go so far. The story had been published, and there were at least a dozen other people in the world who knew it wasn't his—including Kintner himself. And if one of them happened to pick up *Aspen Quarterly*—

He himself told no one—of course. He simply waited, sick with terror. He slept and ate very little that late summer and early fall; he lost weight and dark shadows brushed themselves under his eyes. His heart began to triphammer every time the telephone rang. If the call was for him, he would approach the instrument with dragging feet and cold sweat on his brow, sure it would be Kintner, and the first words out of Kintner's mouth would be, *You stole my story, and something has got to be done about it. I think I'll start by telling everybody what kind of thief you are.*

The most incredible thing was this: he had *known* better. He had *known* the possible consequences of such an act for a young man who hoped to make a career of writing. It was like playing Russian roulette with a bazooka. Yet still . . . still . . .

But as that fall slipped uneventfully past, he began to relax a little. *The* issue of *Aspen Quarterly* had been replaced by a new issue. *The* issue was no longer lying out on tables in library periodical rooms all across the country; it had been tucked away into the stacks or transferred to microfiche. It might still cause trouble— he bleakly supposed he would have to live with that possibility for the rest of his life—but in most cases, out of sight meant out of mind.

Then, in November of that year, a letter from *Aspen Quarterly* came.

Mort held it in his hands, looking at his name on the envelope, and began to shake all over. His eyes filled with some liquid that felt too hot and corrosive to be tears, and the envelope first doubled and then trebled.

Caught. They caught me. They'll want me to respond to a letter they have from Kintner . . . or Perkins . . . or one of the others in the class . . . I'm caught.

He had thought of suicide then—quite calmly and quite rationally. His mother had sleeping pills. He would use those. Somewhat eased by this prospect, he tore the envelope open and pulled out a single sheet of stationery. He held it folded in one hand for a long moment and considered burning it without even looking at it. He wasn't sure he could stand to see the accusation held baldly up in front of him. He thought it might drive him mad.

Go ahead, dammit—look. The least you can do is look at the consequences. You may not be able to stand up to them, but you can by-God look at them.

He unfolded the letter.

Dear Mort Rainey,

Your short story, "Eye of the Crow," was extremely well received here. I'm sorry this follow-up letter has been so slow in coming, but, frankly, *we* expected to hear from *you*. You have been so faithful in your submissions over the years that your silence now that you have finally succeeded in "making it" is a little perplexing. If there was anything about the way your story was handled—typesetting, design, placement, etc.— that you didn't like, we hope you'll bring it up. Meantime, how about another tale?

Respectfully yours,

Charlie

Charles Palmer
Assistant Editor

Mort had read this letter twice, and then began to peal hoarse bursts of laughter at the house, which was luckily empty. He had heard of side-splitting laughter, and this was surely it—he felt that if he didn't stop soon, his sides really *would* split, and send his guts spewing out all over the floor. He had been ready to kill himself with his mother's sleeping pills, and they wanted to know if he was upset with the way the story had been typeset! He had expected to find that his career was ruined even before it was fairly begun, and they wanted more! *More!*

He laughed—howled, actually—until his side-splitting laughter turned to hysterical tears. Then he sat on the sofa, reread Charles Palmer's letter, and cried until he laughed again. At last he had gone into his room and lain down with the pillows arranged behind him just the way he liked, and then he had fallen asleep.

He had gotten away with it. That was the upshot. He had gotten away with it, and he had never done anything even remotely like it again, and it had all happened about a thousand years ago, and so why had it come back to haunt him now?

He didn't know, but he intended to stop thinking about it.

"And right now, too," he told the empty room, and walked briskly over to the coffeemaker, trying to ignore his aching head.

You know why you're thinking about it now.

"Shut up." He spoke in a conversational tone which was rather cheery . . . but his hands were shaking as he picked up the Silex.

Some things you can't hide forever. You might be ill, Mort.

"Shut up, I'm warning you," he said in his cheery conversational voice.

You might be very ill. In fact, you might be having a nervous br—

"*Shut up!*" he cried, and threw the Silex as hard as he could. It sailed over the counter, flew across the room, turning over and over as it went, crunched into the window-wall, shattered, and fell dead on the floor. He looked at the window-wall and saw a long, silvery crack zig-zagging up to the top. It started at the place where the Silex had impacted. He felt very much like a man who might have a similar crack running right through the middle of his brain.

But the voice had shut up.

He walked stolidly into the bedroom, got the alarm clock, and walked back into the living room. He set the alarm for ten-thirty as he walked. At ten-thirty he was going to go to the post office, pick up his Federal Express package, and go stolidly about the task of putting this nightmare behind him.

In the meantime, though, he would sleep.

He would sleep on the couch, where he had always slept best.

"I am *not* having a nervous breakdown," he whispered to the little voice, but the little voice was having none of the argument. Mort thought that he might have frightened the little voice. He hoped so, because the little voice had certainly frightened *him.*

His eyes found the silvery crack in the window-wall and traced it dully. He thought of using the chambermaid's key. How the room had been dim, and it had taken his eyes a moment to adjust. Their naked shoulders. Their frightened eyes. He had been shouting, he couldn't remember what—and had never dared to ask Amy—but it must have been some scary shit, judging from the look in their eyes.

If I was ever going to have a nervous breakdown, he thought, looking at the lightning-bolt senselessness of the crack, *it would have been then. Hell, that letter from* Aspen Quarterly *was nothing compared to opening a motel-room door and seeing your wife with another man, a slick real-estate agent from some shitsplat little town in Tennessee—*

Mort closed his eyes, and when he opened them again it was because another voice was clamoring. This one belonged to the alarm clock. The fog had cleared, the sun had come out, and it was time to go to the post office.

43

On the way, he became suddenly sure that Federal Express would have come and gone . . . and Juliet would stand there at the window with her bare face hanging out and shake her head and tell him there was nothing for him, sorry. And his proof? It would be gone like smoke. This feeling was irrational—Herb was a cautious man, one who did not make promises that couldn't be kept—but it was almost too strong to deny.

He had to force himself out of the car, and the walk from the door of the post office to the window where Juliet Stoker stood sorting mail seemed at least a thousand miles long.

When he got there, he tried to speak and no words came out. His lips moved, but his throat was too dry to make the sounds. Juliet looked up at him, then took a step back. She looked alarmed. Not, however, as alarmed as Amy and Ted had looked when he opened the motel-room door and pointed the gun at them.

"Mr. Rainey? Are you all right?"

He cleared his throat. "Sorry, Juliet. My throat kind of double-clutched on me for a second."

"You're very pale," she said, and he could hear in her voice that tone so many of the Tashmore residents used when they spoke to him—it was a sort of pride, but it held an undertaste of irritation and condescension, as though he was a child prodigy who needed special care and feeding.

"Something I ate last night, I guess," he said. "Did Federal Express leave anything for me?"

"No, not a thing."

He gripped the underside of the counter desperately, and for a moment thought he would faint, although he had understood almost immediately that that was not what she had said.

"Pardon me?"

She had already turned away; her sturdy country bum was presented to him as she shuffled through some packages on the floor.

"Just the one thing, I said," she replied, and then turned around and slid the package across the counter to him. He saw the return address was *EQMM* in Pennsylvania, and felt relief course through him. It felt like cool water pouring down a dry throat.

"Thank you."

"Welcome. You know, the post office would have a *cow* if they knew we handle that Federal Express man's mail."

"Well, I certainly appreciate it," Mort said. Now that he had the magazine, he felt a need to get away, to get back to the house. This need was so strong it was almost elemental. He didn't know why— it was an hour and a quarter until noon—but it was there. In his distress and confusion, he actually thought of giving Juliet a tip to shut her up . . . and *that* would have caused her soul, Yankee to its roots, to rise up in a clamor.

"*You* won't tell them, will you?" she asked archly.

"No way," he said, managing a grin.

"Good," Juliet Stoker said, and smiled. "Because I saw what you did."

He stopped by the door. "Pardon me?"

"I said they'd shoot me if you did," she said, and looked closely at his face. "You ought to go home and lie down, Mr. Rainey. You really don't look well at all."

I feel like I spent the last three days lying down, Juliet—the time I didn't spend hitting things, that is.

"Well," he said, "maybe that's not such a bad idea. I still feel weak."

"There's a virus going around. You probably caught it."

Then the two women from Camp Wigmore—the ones everybody in town suspected of being lesbians, albeit discreet ones—came in, and Mort made good his escape. He sat in the Buick with the blue package on his lap, not liking the way everybody kept saying he looked sick, liking the way his mind had been working even less.

It doesn't matter. It's almost over.

He started to pull the envelope open, and then the ladies from Camp Wigmore came back out and looked at him. They put their heads together. One of them smiled. The other laughed out loud. And Mort suddenly decided he would wait until he got back home.

44

He parked the Buick around the side of the house, in its customary place, turned off the ignition . . . and then a soft grayness came over his vision. When it drew back, he felt strange and frightened. Was something wrong with him, then? Something physical?

No—he was just under strain, he decided.

He heard something—or thought he did—and looked around quickly. Nothing there. *Get hold of your nerves,* he told himself shakily. *That's really all you have to do—just get hold of your mother-fucking nerves.*

And then he thought: *I did have a gun. That day. But it was unloaded. I told them that, later. Amy believed me. I don't know about Milner, but Amy did, and—*

Was it, Mort? Was it really unloaded?

He thought of the crack in the window-wall again, senseless silver lightning-bolt zig-zagging right up through the middle of things. *That's how it happens,* he thought. *That's how it happens in a person's life.*

Then he looked down at the Federal Express package again. *This* was what he should be thinking about, not Amy and Mr. Ted Kiss-My-Ass from Shooter's Knob, Tennessee, but *this.*

The flap was already half open—everyone was careless these days. He pulled it up and shook the magazine out into his lap. *Ellery Queen's Mystery Magazine,* the logo said in bright red letters. Beneath that, in much smaller type, *June, 1980.* And below that, the names of some of the writers featured in the issue. Edward D. Hoch. Ruth Rendell. Ed McBain. Patricia Highsmith. Lawrence Block.

His name wasn't on the cover.

Well, of course not. He was scarcely known as a writer at all then, and certainly not as a writer of mystery stories; "Sowing Season" had been a oner. His name would have meant nothing to regular readers of the magazine, so the editors would not have put it on. He turned the cover back.

There was no contents page beneath.

The contents page had been cut out.

He thumbed frantically through the magazine, dropping it once and then picking it up with a little cry. He didn't find the excision the first time, but on the second pass, he realized that pages 83 to 97 were gone.

"*You cut it out!*" he screamed. He screamed so loudly that his eyeballs bulged from their sockets. He began to bring his fists down on the steering wheel of the Buick, again and again and again. The horn burped and blared. "*You cut it out, you son of a bitch! How did you do that? You cut it out! You cut it out! You cut it out!*"

45

He was halfway to the house before the deadly little voice again wondered how Shooter could have done that. The envelope had come Federal Express from Pennsylvania, and Juliet had taken possession of it, so how, how in God's name—

He stopped.

Good, Juliet had said. *Good, because I saw what you did.*

That was it; that explained it. Juliet was in on it. Except—

Except Juliet had been in Tashmore since forever.

Except that hadn't been what she said. That had only been his mind. A little paranoid flatulence.

"He's doing it, though," Mort said. He went into the house and once he was inside the door, he threw the magazine as hard as he could. It flew like a startled bird, pages riffling, and landed on the floor with a slap. "Oh yeah, you bet, you bet your fucking *ass,* he's doing it. But I don't have to wait around for him. I—"

He saw Shooter's hat. Shooter's hat was lying on the floor in front of the door to his study.

Mort stood where he was for a moment, heart thundering in his ears, and then walked over to the stove in great cartoon tippy-toe steps. He pulled the poker from the little clutch of tools, wincing when the poker's tip clanged softly against the ash-shovel. He took the poker and walked carefully back to the closed door again, holding the poker as he had held it before crashing into the bathroom. He had to skirt the magazine he'd thrown on the way.

He reached the door and stood in front of it.

"Shooter?"

There was no answer.

"Shooter, you better come out under your own power! If I have to come in and get you, you'll never walk out of anyplace under your own power again!"

There was still no answer.

He stood a moment longer, nerving himself (but not really sure he had the nerve), and then twisted the knob. He hit the door with his shoulder and barrelled in, screaming, waving the poker—

And the room was empty.

But Shooter had been here, all right. Yes. The VDT unit of Mort's word cruncher lay on the floor, its screen a shattered staring eye. Shooter had killed it. On the desk where the VDT had stood was an old Royal typewriter. The steel surfaces of this dinosaur were dull and dusty. Propped on the keyboard was a manuscript. Shooter's manuscript, the one he had left under a rock on the porch a million years ago.

It was "Secret Window, Secret Garden."

Mort dropped the poker on the floor. He walked toward the typewriter as if mesmerized and picked up the manuscript. He shuffled slowly through its pages, and came to understand why Mrs. Gavin had been so sure it was his . . . sure enough to rescue it from the trash. Maybe she hadn't known *consciously,* but her eye had recognized the irregular typeface. And why not? She had seen manuscripts which looked like "Secret Window, Secret Garden" for years. The Wang word processor and the System Five laser printer were relative newcomers. For most of his writing career he had used this old Royal. The years had almost worn it out, and it was a sad case now—when you typed on it, it produced letters as crooked as an old man's teeth.

But it had been here all the time, of course—tucked away at the back of the study closet behind piles of old galleys and manuscripts . . . what editors called "foul matter." Shooter must have stolen it, typed his manuscript on it, and then sneaked it back when

Mort was out at the post office. Sure. That made sense, didn't it?

No, Mort. That doesn't make sense. Would you like to do something that does make sense? Call the police, then. That makes sense. Call the police and tell them to come down here and lock you up. Tell them to do it fast, before you can do any more damage. Tell them to do it before you kill anyone else.

Mort dropped the pages with a great wild cry and they seesawed lazily down around him as all of the truth rushed in on him at once like a jagged bolt of silver lightning.

46

There *was* no John Shooter.

There never had been.

"No," Mort said. He was striding back and forth through the big living room again. His headache came and went in waves of pain. "No, I do not accept that. I do not accept that at *all*."

But his acceptance or rejection didn't make much difference. All the pieces of the puzzle were there, and when he saw the old Royal typewriter, they began to fly together. Now, fifteen minutes later, they were *still* flying together, and he seemed to have no power to will them apart.

The picture which kept coming back to him was of the gas jockey in Mechanic Falls, using a squeegee to wash his windshield. A sight he had never expected to witness again in his lifetime. Later, he had assumed that the kid had given him a little extra service because he had recognized Mort and liked Mort's books. Maybe that was so, but the windshield had *needed* washing. Summer was gone, but plenty of stuff still splatted on your windshield if you drove far enough and fast enough on the back roads. And he must have used the back roads. He must have sped up to Derry and back again in record time, only stopping long enough to burn down his house. He hadn't even stopped long enough to get gas on the way back. After all, he'd had places to go and cats to kill, hadn't he? Busy, busy, busy.

He stopped in the middle of the floor and whirled to stare at the window-wall. "If I did all that, why can't I remember?" he asked the silvery crack in the glass. "Why can't I remember even *now*?"

He didn't know . . . but he *did* know where the name had come from, didn't he? One half from the Southern man whose story he had stolen in college; one half from the man who had stolen his wife. It was like some bizarre literary in-joke.

She says she loves him, Mort. She says she loves him now.

"Fuck that. A man who sleeps with another man's wife is a thief. And the woman is his accomplice."

He looked defiantly at the crack.

The crack said nothing.

Three years ago, Mort had published a novel called *The Delacourt Family*. The return address on Shooter's story had been Dellacourt, Mississippi. It—

He suddenly ran for the encyclopedias in the study, slipping and almost falling in the mess of pages strewn on the floor in his hurry. He pulled out the M volume and at last found the entry for Mississippi. He ran a trembling finger down the list of towns—it took up one entire page—hoping against hope.

It was no good.

There was no Dellacourt or Delacourt, Mississippi.

He thought of looking for Perkinsburg, the town where Shooter had told him he'd picked up a paperback copy of *Everybody Drops the Dime* before getting on the Greyhound bus, and then simply closed the encyclopedia. Why bother? There might be a Perkinsburg in Mississippi, but it would mean nothing if there was.

The name of the novelist who'd taught the class in which Mort had met John Kintner had been Richard Perkins, Jr. *That* was where the name had come from.

Yes, but I don't remember any of this, so how—?

Oh, Mort, the small voice mourned. *You're very sick. You're a very sick man.*

"I don't accept that," he said again, horrified by the wavery weakness of his voice, but what other choice was there? Hadn't he even thought once that it was almost as if he were doing things, taking irrevocable steps, in his sleep?

You killed two men, the little voice whispered. *You killed Tom because he knew you were alone that day, and you killed Greg so he wouldn't find out for sure. If you had just killed Tom, Greg would have called the police. And you didn't want that, COULDN'T have that. Not until this horrible story you've been telling is all finished. You were so sore when you got up yesterday. So stiff and sore. But it wasn't just from breaking in the bathroom door and trashing the shower stall, was it?*

*You were a lot busier than that. You had Tom and Greg to take care
of. And you were right about how the vehicles got moved around . . . but
YOU were the one who called up Sonny Trotts and pretended to be Tom.
A man who just got into town from Mississippi wouldn't know Sonny
was a little deaf, but YOU would. You killed them, Mort, you KILLED
those men!*

"I do not accept that I did!" he shrieked. "This is all just part of
his plan! This is just part of his little game! His little mind-game!
And I do not . . . I do not accept . . ."

Stop, the little voice whispered inside his head, and Mort stopped.

For a moment there was utter silence in both worlds: the one
inside his head, and the one outside of it.

And, after an interval, the little voice asked quietly: *Why did you
do it, Mort? This whole elaborate and homicidal episode? Shooter kept
saying he wanted a story, but there IS no Shooter. What do YOU want,
Mort? What did you create John Shooter FOR?*

Then, from outside, came the sound of a car rolling down the
driveway. Mort looked at his watch and saw that the hands were
standing straight up at noon. A blaze of triumph and relief roared
through him like flames shooting up the neck of a chimney. That
he had the magazine but still no proof did not matter. That Shooter
might kill him did not matter. He could die happily, just knowing
that there *was* a John Shooter and that he himself was not responsible for the horrors he had been considering.

"He's here!" he screamed joyfully, and ran out of the study. He
waved his hands wildly above his head, and actually cut a little caper
as he rounded the corner and came into the hall.

He stopped, looking out at the driveway past the sloping roof of
the garbage cabinet where Bump's body had been nailed up. His
hands dropped slowly to his sides. Dark horror stole over his brain.
No, not *over* it; it came down, as if some merciless hand were pulling
a shade. The last piece fell into place. It had occurred to him moments before in the study that he might have created a fantasy
assassin because he lacked the courage to commit suicide. Now he
realized that Shooter had told the truth when he said he would
never kill Mort.

It wasn't John Shooter's imaginary station wagon but Amy's no-
nonsense little Subaru which was just now coming to a stop. Amy
was behind the wheel. She had stolen his love, and a woman who

would steal your love when your love was really all you had to give was not much of a woman.

He loved her, all the same.

It was *Shooter* who hated her. It was *Shooter* who meant to kill her and then bury her down by the lake near Bump, where she would before long be a mystery to both of them.

"Go away, Amy," he whispered in the palsied voice of a very old man. "Go away before it's too late."

But Amy was getting out of the car, and as she closed the door behind her, the hand pulled the shade in Mort's head all the way down and he was in darkness.

47

Amy tried the door and found it unlocked. She stepped in, started to call for Mort, and then didn't. She looked around, wide-eyed and startled.

The place was a mess. The trash can was full and had overflowed onto the floor. A few sluggish autumn flies were crawling in and out of an aluminum pot-pie dish that had been kicked into the corner. She could smell stale cooking and musty air. She thought she could even smell spoiled food.

"Mort?"

There was no answer. She walked further into the house, taking small steps, not entirely sure she wanted to look at the rest of the place. Mrs. Gavin had been in only three days ago—how had things gotten so out of hand since then? What had happened?

She had been worried about Mort during the entire last year of their marriage, but she had been even more worried since the divorce. Worried, and, of course, guilty. She held part of the blame for herself, and supposed she always would. But Mort had never been strong . . . and his greatest weakness was his stubborn (and sometimes almost hysterical) refusal to recognize the fact. This morning he had sounded like a man on the point of suicide. And the only reason she had heeded his admonition not to bring Ted was because she thought the sight of him might set Mort off if he really was poised on the edge of such an act.

The thought of murder had never crossed her mind, nor did it do so now. Even when he had brandished the gun at them that horrible afternoon at the motel, she had not been afraid. Not of *that*. Mort was no killer.

"Mort? M—"

She came around the kitchen counter and the word died. She stared at the big living room with wide, stunned eyes. Paper was littered everywhere. It looked as if Mort must at some point have exhumed every copy of every manuscript he had in his desk drawers and in his files and strewn the pages about in here like confetti at some black New Year's Eve celebration. The table was heaped with dirty dishes. The Silex was lying shattered on the floor by the window-wall, which was cracked.

And everywhere, everywhere, everywhere was one word. The word was SHOOTER.

SHOOTER had been written on the walls in colored chalks he must have taken from her drawer of art supplies. SHOOTER was sprayed on the window twice in what looked like dried whipped cream— and yes, there was the Redi-Whip pressure-can, lying discarded under the stove. SHOOTER was written over and over on the kitchen counters in ink, and on the wooden support posts of the deck on the far side of the house in pencil—a neat column like adding that went down in a straight line and said SHOOTER SHOOTER SHOOTER SHOOTER.

Worst of all, it had been carved into the polished cherrywood surface of the table in great jagged letters three feet high, like a grotesque declaration of love: SHOOTER.

The screwdriver he had used to do this last was lying on a chair nearby. There was red stuff on its steel shaft—stain from the cherry-wood, she assumed.

"Mort?" she whispered, looking around.

Now she was frightened that she would find him dead by his own hand. And where? Why, in the study, of course. Where else? He had lived all the most important parts of his life in there; surely he had chosen to die there.

Although she had no wish to go in, no wish to be the one to find him, her feet carried her in that direction all the same. As she went, she kicked the issue of *EQMM* Herb Creekmore had had sent out of her way. She did not look down. She reached the study door and pushed it slowly open.

48

Mort stood in front of his old Royal typewriter; the screen-and-keyboard unit of his word processor lay overturned in a bouquet of glass on the floor. He looked strangely like a country preacher. It was partly the posture he had adopted, she supposed; he was standing almost primly with his hands behind his back. But most of it was the hat. The black hat, pulled down so it almost touched the tops of his ears. She thought he looked a little bit like the old man in that picture, "American Gothic," even though the man in the picture wasn't wearing a hat.

"Mort?" she asked. Her voice was weak and uncertain.

He made no reply, only stared at her. His eyes were grim and glittering. She had never seen Mort's eyes look this way, not even on the horrible afternoon at the motel. It was almost as if this was not Mort at all, but some stranger who looked like Mort.

She recognized the hat, though.

"Where did you find that old thing? The attic?" Her heartbeat was in her voice, making it stagger.

He *must* have found it in the attic. The smell of mothballs on it was strong, even from where she was standing. Mort had gotten the hat years ago, at a gift shop in Pennsylvania. They had been travelling through Amish country. She had kept a little garden at the Derry house, in the angle where the house and the study addition met. It was her garden, but Mort often went out to weed it when he was stuck for an idea. He usually wore the hat when he did this. He called it his thinking cap. She remembered him looking at himself in a mirror once when he was wearing it and joking that he ought to have a bookjacket photo taken in it. "When I put this on," he'd said, "I look like a man who belongs out in the north forty, walking plow-furrows behind a mule's ass."

Then the hat had disappeared. It must have migrated down here and been stored. But—

"It's *my* hat," he said at last in a rusty, bemused voice. "Wasn't ever anybody else's."

"Mort? What's wrong? What's—"

"You got you a wrong number, woman. Ain't no Mort here. Mort's dead." The gimlet eyes never wavered. "He did a lot of squirmin around, but in the end he couldn't lie to himself anymore, let alone to me. I never put a hand on him, Mrs. Rainey. I swear. He took the coward's way out."

"Why are you talking that way?" Amy asked.

"This is just the way I talk," he said with mild surprise. "Everybody down in Miss'ippi talks this way."

"Mort, *stop!*"

"Don't you understand what I *said?*" he asked. "You ain't deaf, are you? He's *dead.* He killed himself."

"Stop it, Mort," she said, beginning to cry. "You're scaring me, and I don't like it."

"Don't matter," he said. He took his hands out from behind his back. In one of them he held the scissors from the top drawer of the desk. He raised them. The sun had come out, and it sent a starflash glitter along the blades as he snicked them open and then closed. "You won't be scared long." He began walking toward her.

49

For a moment she stood where she was. Mort would not kill her; if there had been killing in Mort, then surely he would have done some that day at the motel.

Then she saw the look in his eyes and understood that Mort knew that, too.

But this wasn't him.

She screamed and wheeled around and lunged for the door.

Shooter came after her, bringing the scissors down in a silver arc. He would have buried them up to the handles between her shoulderblades if his feet had not slid on the papers scattered about the hardwood floor. He fell full-length with a cry of mingled perplexity and anger. The blades stabbed down through page nine of "Secret Window, Secret Garden" and the tips broke off. His mouth struck the floor and sprayed blood. The package of Pall Malls—the brand John Kintner had silently smoked during the breaks halfway through the writing class he and Mort Rainey had shared—shot out of his pocket and slid along the slick wood like the weight in a barroom shuffleboard game. He got up on his knees, his mouth snarling and smiling through the blood which ran over his lips and teeth.

"Won't do you no help, Mrs. Rainey!" he cried, getting to his feet. He looked at the scissors, snicked them open to study the blunted tips a little better, and then tossed them impatiently aside. "I got a place in the garden for you! I got it all picked out. You mind me, now!"

He ran out the door after her.

50

Halfway across the living room, Amy took her own spill. One of her feet came down on the discarded issue of *EQMM* and she fell sprawling on her side, hurting her hip and right breast. She cried out.

Behind her, Shooter ran across to the table and snatched up the screwdriver he had used on the cat.

"Stay right there, and be still," he said as she turned over on her back and stared at him with wide eyes which looked almost drugged. "If you move around, I'm only goin to hurt you before it's over. I don't want to hurt you, missus, but I will if I have to. I've got to have something, you see. I have come all this way, and I've got to have something for my trouble."

As he approached, Amy propped herself up on her elbows and shoved herself backward with her feet. Her hair hung in her face. Her skin was coated with sweat; she could smell it pouring out of her, hot and stinking. The face above her was the solemn, judgmental face of insanity.

"No, Mort! Please! Please, Mort—"

He flung himself at her, raising the screwdriver over his head and then bringing it down. Amy shrieked and rolled to the left. Pain burned a line across her hip as the screwdriver blade tore her dress and grooved her flesh. Then she was scrambling to her knees, hearing and feeling the dress shred out a long unwinding strip as she did it.

"No, ma'am," Shooter panted. His hand closed upon her ankle. "No, ma'am." She looked over her shoulder and through the tangles of her hair and saw he was using his other hand to work the screwdriver out of the floor. The round-crowned black hat sat askew on his head.

He yanked the screwdriver free and drove it into her right calf. The pain was horrid. The pain was the whole world. She screamed and kicked backward, connecting with his nose, breaking it. Shooter grunted and fell on his side, clutching at his face, and Amy got to her feet. She could hear a woman howling. It sounded like a dog howling at the moon. She supposed it wasn't a dog. She supposed it was her.

Shooter was getting to his feet. His lower face was a mask of blood. The mask split open, showing Mort Rainey's crooked front teeth. She could remember licking across those teeth with her tongue.

"Feisty one, ain't you?" he said, grinning. "That's all right, ma'am. You go right on."

He lunged for her.

Amy staggered backward. The screwdriver fell out of her calf and rolled across the floor. Shooter glanced at it, then lunged at her again, almost playfully. Amy grabbed one of the living-room chairs and dumped it in front of him. For a moment they only stared at each other over it . . . and then he snatched for the front of her dress. Amy recoiled.

"I'm about done fussin with you," he panted.

Amy turned and bolted for the door.

He was after her at once, flailing at her back, his fingertips skating and skidding down the nape of her neck, trying to close on the top of the dress, catching it, then just missing the hold which would have coiled her back to him for good.

Amy bolted past the kitchen counter and toward the back door. Her right loafer squelched and smooched on her foot. It was full of blood. Shooter was after her, puffing and blowing bubbles of blood from his nostrils, clutching at her.

She struck the screen door with her hands, then tripped and fell full-length on the porch, the breath whooshing out of her. She fell exactly where Shooter had left his manuscript. She rolled over and saw him coming. He only had his bare hands now, but they looked like they would be more than enough. His eyes were stern and unflinching and horribly kind beneath the brim of the black hat.

"I am so sorry, missus," he said.

"*Rainey!*" a voice cried. "*Stop!*"

She tried to look around and could not. She had strained something in her neck. Shooter never even tried. He simply came on toward her.

"*Rainey! Stop!*"

"There is no Rainey h—" Shooter began, and then a gunshot rapped briskly across the fall air. Shooter stopped where he was, and looked curiously, almost casually, down at his chest. There was a small hole there. No blood issued from it—at least, not at first— but the hole was there. He put his hand to it, then brought it away. His index finger was marked by a small dot of blood. It looked like a bit of punctuation—the period which ends a sentence. He looked at this thoughtfully. Then he dropped his hands and looked at Amy.

"Babe?" he asked, and then fell full-length beside her on the porch boards.

She rolled over, managed to get up on her elbows, and crawled to where he lay, beginning to sob.

"Mort?" she cried. "Mort? Please, Mort, try to say something!"

But he was not going to say anything, and after a moment she let this realization fill her up. She would reject the simple fact of his death again and again over the next few weeks and months, and would then weaken, and the realization would fill her up again. He was dead. He was dead. He had gone crazy down here and he was dead.

He, and whoever had been inside him at the end.

She put her head down on his chest and wept, and when someone came up behind her and put a comforting hand on her shoulder, Amy did not look around.

EPILOGUE

Ted and Amy Milner came to see the man who had shot and killed Amy's first husband, the well-known writer Morton Rainey, about three months after the events at Tashmore Lake.

They had seen the man at one other time during the three-month period, at the inquest, but that had been a formal situation, and Amy had not wanted to speak to him personally. Not there. She was grateful that he had saved her life . . . but Mort had been her husband, and she had loved him for many years, and in her deepest heart she felt that Fred Evans's finger hadn't been the only one which pulled the trigger.

She would have come in time anyway, she suspected, in order

to clarify it as much as possible in her mind. Her time might have been a year, or two, possibly even three. But things had happened in the meanwhile which made her move more quickly. She had hoped Ted would let her come to New York alone, but he was emphatic. Not after the last time he had let her go someplace alone. *That* time she had almost gotten killed.

Amy pointed out with some asperity that it would have been hard for Ted to "let her go," since she had never told him she was going in the first place, but Ted only shrugged. So they went to New York together, rode up to the fifty-third floor of a large skyscraper together, and were together shown to the small cubicle in the offices of the Consolidated Assurance Company which Fred Evans called home during the working day . . . unless he was in the field, of course.

She sat as far into the corner as she could get, and although the offices were quite warm, she kept her shawl wrapped around her.

Evans's manner was slow and kind—he seemed to her almost like the country doctor who had nursed her through her childhood illnesses—and she liked him. *But that's something he'll never know,* she thought. *I might be able to summon up the strength to tell him, and he would nod, but his nod wouldn't indicate belief. He only knows that to me he will always be the man who shot Mort, and he had to watch me cry on Mort's chest until the ambulance came, and one of the paramedics had to give me a shot before I would let him go. And what he won't know is that I like him just the same.*

He buzzed a woman from one of the outer offices and had her bring in three big, steaming mugs of tea. It was January outside now, the wind high, the temperature low. She thought with some brief longing of how it would be in Tashmore, with the lake finally frozen and that killer wind blowing long, ghostly snakes of powdered snow across the ice. Then her mind made some obscure but nasty association, and she saw Mort hitting the floor, saw the package of Pall Malls skidding across the wood like a shuffleboard weight. She shivered, her brief sense of longing totally dispelled.

"Are you okay, Mrs. Milner?" Evans asked.

She nodded.

Frowning ponderously and playing with his pipe, Ted said, "My wife wants to hear everything you know about what happened, Mr. Evans. I tried to discourage her at first, but I've come to think that it might be a good thing. She's had bad dreams ever since—"

"Of course," Evans said, not exactly ignoring Ted, but speaking directly to Amy. "I suppose you will for a long time. I've had a few of my own, actually. I never shot a man before." He paused, then added, "I missed Vietnam by a year or so."

Amy offered him a smile. It was wan, but it was a smile.

"She heard it all at the inquest," Ted went on, "but she wanted to hear it again, from you, and with the legalese omitted."

"I understand," Evans said. He pointed at the pipe. "You can light that, if you want to."

Ted looked at it, then dropped it into the pocket of his coat quickly, as if he were slightly ashamed of it. "I'm trying to give it up, actually."

Evans looked at Amy. "What purpose do you think this will serve?" he asked her in the same kind, rather sweet voice. "Or maybe a better question would be what purpose do you *need* it to serve?"

"I don't know." Her voice was low and composed. "But we were in Tashmore three weeks ago, Ted and I, to clean the place out— we've put it up for sale—and something happened. Two things, actually." She looked at her husband and offered the wan smile again. "Ted knows *something* happened, because that's when I got in touch with you and made this appointment. But he doesn't know what, and I'm afraid he's put out with me. Perhaps he's right to be."

Ted Milner did not deny that he was put out with Amy. His hand stole into his coat pocket, started to remove the pipe, and then let it drop back again.

"But these two things—they bear on what happened at your lake home in October?"

"I don't know. Mr. Evans . . . what *did* happen? How much do *you* know?"

"Well," he said, leaning back in his chair and sipping from his mug, "if you came expecting all the answers, you're going to be sorely disappointed. I can tell you about the fire, but as for why your husband did what he did . . . you can probably fill in more of those blanks than I can. What puzzled us most about the fire was where it started—not in the main house but in Mr. Rainey's office, which is an addition. That made the act seem directed against him, but he wasn't even there.

"Then we found a large chunk of bottle in the wreckage of the office. It had contained wine—champagne, to be exact—but there wasn't any doubt that the last thing it had contained was gasoline. Part of the label was intact, and we sent a Fax copy to New York. It was identified as Moët et Chandon, nineteen-eighty-something. That wasn't proof indisputable that the bottle used for the Molotov cocktail came from your own wine room, Mrs. Milner, but it was very persuasive, since you listed better than a dozen bottles of Moët et Chandon, some from 1983 and some from 1984.

"This led us toward a supposition which seemed clear but not very sensible: that you or your ex-husband might have burned down your own house. Mrs. Milner here said she went off and left the house unlocked—"

"I lost a lot of sleep over that," Amy said. "I often forgot to lock up when I was only going out for a little while. I grew up in a little town north of Bangor and country habits die hard. Mort used to . . ." Her lips trembled and she stopped speaking for a moment, pressing them together so tightly they turned white. When she had herself under control again, she finished her thought in a low voice. "He used to scold me about it."

Ted took her hand.

"It didn't matter, of course," Evans said. "If you had locked the house, Mr. Rainey still could have gained access, because he still had his keys. Correct?"

"Yes," Ted said.

"It might have sped up the detection end a little if you'd locked the door, but it's impossible to say for sure. Monday-morning quarterbacking is a vice we try to steer clear of in my business, anyway. There's a theory that it causes ulcers, and that's one I subscribe to. The point is this: given Mrs. Rainey's—excuse me, Mrs. Milner's—testimony that the house was left unlocked, we at first believed the arsonist could have been literally anyone. But once we started playing around with the assumption that the bottle used had come from the cellar wine room, it narrowed things down."

"Because *that* room was locked," Ted said.

Evans nodded. "Do you remember me asking who held keys to that room, Mrs. Milner?"

"Call me Amy, won't you?"

He nodded. "Do you remember, Amy?"

"Yes. We started locking the little wine closet three or four years ago, after some bottles of red table wine disappeared. Mort thought it was the housekeeper. I didn't like to believe it, because I liked her, but I knew he could be right, and probably was. We started locking it then so nobody else would be tempted."

Evans looked at Ted Milner.

"Amy had a key to the wine room, and she believed Mr. Rainey still had his. So that limited the possibilities. Of course, if it had been Amy, you would have had to have been in collusion with her, Mr. Milner, since you were each other's alibis for that evening. Mr. Rainey didn't have an alibi, but he was at a considerable distance. And the main thing was this: we could see no motive for the crime. His work had left both Amy and himself financially comfortable. Nevertheless, we dusted for fingerprints and came up with two good ones. This was the day after we had our meeting in Derry. Both prints belonged to Mr. Rainey. It still wasn't proof—"

"It *wasn't?*" Ted asked, looking startled.

Evans shook his head. "Lab tests were able to confirm that the prints were made before what remained of the bottle was charred in the fire, but not how long before. The heat had cooked the oils in them, you see. And if our assumption that the bottle came from the wine room was correct, why, someone had to physically pick it up out of the bag or carton it came in and store it in its cradle. That someone would have been either Mr. or Mrs. Rainey, and he could have argued that that was where the prints came from."

"He was in no shape to argue anything," Amy said softly. "Not at the end."

"I guess that's true, but *we* didn't know that. All we knew is that when people carry bottles, they generally pick them up by the neck or the upper barrel. These two prints were near the bottom, and the angle was very odd."

"As if he had been carrying it sideways or even upside down," Ted broke in. "Isn't that what you said at the hearing?"

"Yes—and people who know anything about wine don't do it. With most wines, it disturbs the sediment. And with champagne—"

"It shakes it up," Ted said.

Evans nodded. "If you shake a bottle of champagne really hard, it will burst from the pressure."

"But there was no champagne in it, anyway," Amy said quietly.

"No. Still, it was not proof. I canvassed the area gas stations to see if anyone who looked like Mr. Rainey had bought a small amount of gas that night, but had no luck. I wasn't too surprised; he could have bought the gasoline in Tashmore or at half a hundred service stations between the two places.

"Then I went to see Patricia Champion, our one witness. I took a picture of a 1986 Buick—the make and model we assumed Mr. Rainey would have been driving. She said it *might* have been the car, but she still couldn't be sure. So I was up against it. I went back out to the house to look around, and *you* came, Amy. It was early morning. I wanted to ask you some questions, but you were clearly upset. I *did* ask you why you were there, and you said a peculiar thing. You said you were going down to Tashmore Lake to see your husband, but you came by first to look in the garden."

"On the phone he kept talking about what he called my secret window . . . the one that looked down on the garden. He said he'd left something there. But there wasn't anything. Not that I could see, anyway."

"I had a feeling about the man when we met," Evans said slowly. "A feeling that he wasn't . . . quite on track. It wasn't that he was lying about some things, although I was pretty sure he was. It was something else. A kind of distance."

"Yes—I felt it in him more and more. That distance."

"You looked almost sick with worry. I decided I could do worse than follow you down to the other house, Amy, especially when you told me not to tell Mr. Milner here where you'd gone if he came looking for you. I didn't believe that idea was original with you. I thought I might just find something out. And I also thought . . ." He trailed off, looking bemused.

"You thought something might happen to me," she said. "Thank you, Mr. Evans. He would have killed me, you know. If you hadn't followed me, he would have killed me."

"I parked at the head of the driveway and walked down. I heard a terrific rumpus from inside the house and I started to run. That was when you more or less fell out through the screen door, and he came out after you."

Evans looked at them both earnestly.

"I asked him to stop," he said. "I asked him twice."

Amy reached out, squeezed his hand gently for a moment, then let it go.

"And that's it," Evans said. "I know a little more, mostly from the newspapers and two chats I had with Mr. Milner—"

"Call me Ted."

"Ted, then." Evans did not seem to take to Ted's first name as easily as he had to Amy's. "I know that Mr. Rainey had what was probably a schizophrenic episode in which he was two people, and that neither one of them had any idea they were actually existing in the same body. I know that one of them was named John Shooter. I know from Herbert Creekmore's deposition that Mr. Rainey imagined this Shooter was hounding him over a story called 'Sowing Season,' and that Mr. Creekmore had a copy of the magazine in which that story appeared sent up so Mr. Rainey could prove that he had published first. The magazine arrived shortly before you did, Amy—it was found in the house. The Federal Express envelope it came in was on the seat of your ex-husband's Buick."

"But he cut the story out, didn't he?" Ted asked.

"Not just the story—the contents page as well. He was careful to remove every trace of himself. He carried a Swiss-army knife, and that was probably what he used. The missing pages were in the Buick's glove compartment."

"In the end, the existence of that story became a mystery even to him," Amy said softly.

Evans looked at her, eyebrows raised. "Beg pardon?"

She shook her head. "Nothing."

"I think I've told you everything I can," Evans said. "Anything else would be pure speculation. I'm an insurance investigator, after all, not a psychiatrist."

"He *was* two men," Amy said. "He was himself . . . and he became a character he created. Ted believes that the last name, Shooter, was something Mort picked up and stored in his head when he found out Ted came from a little town called Shooter's Knob, Tennessee. I'm sure he's right. Mort was always picking out character names just that way . . . like anagrams, almost.

"I don't know the rest of it—I can only guess. I *do* know that when a film studio dropped its option on his novel *The Delacourt Family,* Mort almost had a nervous breakdown. They made it clear— and so did Herb Creekmore—that they were concerned about an accidental similarity, and they understood he never could have seen the screenplay, which was called *The Home Team.* There was no question of plagiarism . . . except in Mort's head. His reaction was exaggerated, abnormal. It was like stirring a stick around in what looks like a dead campfire and uncovering a live coal."

"You don't think he created John Shooter just to punish you, do you?" Evans asked.

"No. Shooter was there to punish *Mort*. I think . . ." She paused and adjusted her shawl, pulling it a little more tightly about her shoulders. Then she picked up her teacup with a hand which wasn't quite steady. "I think that Mort stole somebody's work sometime in the past," she said. "Probably quite far in the past, because everything he wrote from *The Organ-Grinder's Boy* on was widely read. It would have come out, I think. I doubt that he even actually published what he stole. But I think that's what happened, and I think that's where John Shooter *really* came from. Not from the film company dropping his novel, or from my . . . my time with Ted, and not from the divorce. Maybe all those things contributed, but I think the root goes back to a time before I knew him. Then, when he was alone at the lake house . . ."

"Shooter came," Evans said quietly. "He came and accused him of plagiarism. Whoever Mr. Rainey stole from never did, so in the end he had to punish himself. But I doubt if that was all, Amy. He *did* try to kill you."

"No," she said. "That was Shooter."

He raised his eyebrows. Ted looked at her carefully, and then drew the pipe out of his pocket again.

"The *real* Shooter."

"I don't understand you."

She smiled her wan smile. "I don't understand myself. That's why I'm here. I don't think telling this serves any practical purpose— Mort's dead, and it's over—but it may help me. It may help me to sleep better."

"Then tell us, by all means," Evans said.

"You see, when we went down to clean out the house, we stopped at the little store in town—Bowie's. Ted filled the gas tank—it's always been self-service at Bowie's—and I went in to get some things. There was a man in there, Sonny Trotts, who used to work with Tom Greenleaf. Tom was the older of the two caretakers who were killed. Sonny wanted to tell me how sorry he was about Mort, and he wanted to tell me something else, too, because he saw Mort the day before Mort died, and meant to tell him. So he said. It was about Tom Greenleaf—something Tom told Sonny while they were painting the Methodist Parish Hall together. Sonny saw Mort after that, but didn't think to tell him right away, he said. Then he remembered that it had something to do with Greg Carstairs—"

"The other dead man?"

"Yes. So he turned around and called, but Mort didn't hear him. And the next day, Mort was dead."

"What did Mr. Greenleaf tell this guy?"

"That he thought he might have seen a ghost," Amy said calmly. They looked at her, not speaking.

"Sonny said Tom had been getting forgetful lately, and that Tom was worried about it. Sonny thought it was no more than the ordinary sort of forgetfulness that settles in when a person gets a little older, but Tom had nursed his wife through Alzheimer's disease five or six years before, and he was terrified of getting it himself and going the same way. According to Sonny, if Tom forgot a paintbrush, he spent half the day obsessing about it. Tom said that was why, when Greg Carstairs asked him if he recognized the man he'd seen Mort Rainey talking to the day before, or if he would recognize him if he saw him again, Tom said he hadn't seen *anyone* with Mort—that Mort had been alone."

There was the snap of a match. Ted Milner had decided to light his pipe after all. Evans ignored him. He was leaning forward in his chair, his gaze fixed intently on Amy Milner.

"Let's get this straight. According to this Sonny Troots—"

"Trotts."

"Okay, Trotts. According to him, Tom Greenleaf *did* see Mort with someone?"

"Not exactly," Amy said. "Sonny thought if Tom believed that, believed it for sure, he wouldn't have lied to Greg. What Tom said was that he didn't know *what* he'd seen. That he was confused. That it seemed safer to say nothing about it at all. He didn't want anybody—particularly Greg Carstairs, who was also in the caretaking business—to know how confused he was, and most of all he didn't want anybody to think that he might be getting sick the way his late wife had gotten sick."

"I'm not sure I understand this—I'm sorry."

"According to Sonny," she said, "Tom came down Lake Drive in his Scout and saw Mort, standing by himself where the lakeside path comes out."

"Near where the bodies were found?"

"Yes. Very near. Mort waved. Tom waved back. He drove by. Then, according to what Sonny says, Tom looked in his rear-view mirror and saw another man with Mort, and an old station wagon, although neither the man nor the car had been there ten seconds before. The man was wearing a black hat, he said . . . *but you could see right through him, and the car, too.*"

"Oh, Amy," Ted said softly. "The man was bullshitting you. Big time."

She shook her head. "I don't think Sonny is smart enough to make up such a story. He told me Tom thought he ought to get in touch with Greg and tell him he might have seen such a man after all; that it would be all right if he left out the see-through part. But Sonny said the old man was terrified. He was convinced that it was one of two things: either he was coming down with Alzheimer's disease, or he'd seen a ghost."

"Well, it's certainly creepy," Evans said, and it was—the skin on his arms and back had crinkled into gooseflesh for a moment or two. "But it's hearsay . . . hearsay from a dead man, in fact."

"Yes . . . but there's the other thing." She set her teacup on the desk, picked up her purse, and began to rummage in it. "When I was cleaning out Mort's office, I found that hat—that awful black hat—behind his desk. It gave me a shock, because I wasn't expecting it. I thought the police must have taken it away as evidence, or something. I hooked it out from behind there with a stick. It came out upside down, with the stick inside it. I used the stick to carry it outside and dump it in the trash cabinet. Do you understand?"

Ted clearly didn't; Evans clearly did. "You didn't want to touch it."

"That's right. I didn't want to touch it. It landed right side up on one of the green trash bags—I'd swear to that. Then, about an hour later, I went out with a bag of old medicines and shampoos and things from the bathroom. When I opened the lid of the garbage cabinet to put it in, the hat was turned over again. And this was tucked into the sweatband." She pulled a folded sheet of paper from her purse and offered it to Evans with a hand that still trembled minutely. "It wasn't there when the hat came out from behind the desk. I *know* that."

Evans took the folded sheet and just held it for a moment. He didn't like it. It felt too heavy, and the texture was somehow wrong.

"I think there *was* a John Shooter," she said. "I think he was

Mort's greatest creation—a character so vivid that he actually *did* become real.

"And I think that this is a message from a ghost."

He took the slip of paper and opened it. Written halfway down was this message:

Missus—I am sorry for all the trouble. Things got out of hand. I am going back to my home now. I got my story, which is all I came for in the first place. It is called "Crowfoot Mile," and it is a crackerjack.

Yours truly,

John Shooter

The signature was a bald scrawl below the neat lines of script.

"Is this your late husband's signature, Amy?" Evans asked.

"No," she said. "Nothing like it."

The three of them sat in the office, looking at one another. Fred Evans tried to think of something to say and could not. After awhile, the silence (and the smell of Ted Milner's pipe) became more than any of them could stand. So Mr. and Mrs. Milner offered their thanks, said their goodbyes, and left his office to get on with their lives as best they could, and Fred Evans got on with his own as best *he* could, and sometimes, late at night, both he and the woman who had been married to Morton Rainey woke from dreams in which a man in a round-crowned black hat looked at them from sun-faded eyes caught in nets of wrinkles. He looked at them with no love . . . but, they both felt, with an odd kind of stern pity.

It was not a kind expression, and it left no feeling of comfort, but they also both felt, in their different places, that they could find room to live with that look. And to tend their gardens.

The
Library
Policeman

THREE PAST MIDNIGHT

A NOTE ON
"THE LIBRARY
POLICEMAN"

On the morning when this story started to happen, I was sitting at the breakfast table with my son Owen. My wife had already gone upstairs to shower and dress. Those two vital seven o'clock divisions had been made: the scrambled eggs and the newspaper. Willard Scott, who visits our house five days out of every seven, was telling us about a lady in Nebraska who had just turned a hundred and four, and I think Owen and I had one whole pair of eyes open between us. A typical weekday morning *chez* King, in other words.

Owen tore himself away from the sports section just long enough to ask me if I'd be going by the mall that day—there was a book he wanted me to pick up for a school report. I can't remember what it was—it might have been *Johnny Tremain* or *April Morning,* Howard Fast's novel of the American Revolution—but it was one of those tomes you can never quite lay your hands on in a bookshop; it's always just out of print or just about to come back into print or some damned thing.

I suggested that Owen try the local library, which is a very good one. I was sure they'd have it. He muttered some reply. I only caught two words of it, but, given my interests, those two words were more than enough to pique my interest. They were "library police."

I put my half of the newspaper aside, used the MUTE button on the remote control to strangle Willard in the middle of his ecstatic report on the Georgia Peach Festival, and asked Owen to kindly repeat himself.

He was reluctant to do so, but I pressed him. Finally he told me that he didn't like to use the library because he worried about the Library Police. He knew there *were* no Library Police, he hastened to add, but it was one of those stories that burrowed down into your subconscious and just sort of lurked there. He had heard it from his Aunt Stephanie when he was seven or eight and much more gullible, and it had been lurking ever since.

I, of course, was delighted, because I had been afraid of the Library Police myself as a kid—the faceless enforcers who would *actually come to your house* if you didn't bring your overdue books back. That would be bad enough . . . but what if you couldn't find the books in question when those strange lawmen turned up? What then? What would they do to you? What might they take to make up for the missing volumes? It had been years since I'd thought of the Library Police (although not since childhood; I can clearly remember discussing them with Peter Straub and his son, Ben, six or eight years ago), but now all those old questions, both dreadful and somehow enticing, recurred.

I found myself musing on the Library Police over the next three or four days, and as I mused, I began to glimpse the outlines of the story which follows. This is the way stories usually happen for me, but the musing period usually lasts a lot longer than it did in this case. When I began, the story was titled "The Library Police," and I had no clear idea of where I was going with it. I thought it would probably be a funny story, sort of like the suburban nightmares the late Max Shulman used to bolt together. After all, the idea *was* funny, wasn't it? I mean, the Library Police! How absurd!

What I realized, however, was something I knew already: the fears of childhood have a hideous persistence. Writing is an act of self-hypnosis, and in that state a kind of total emotional recall often takes place and terrors which should have been long dead start to walk and talk again.

As I worked on this story, that began to happen to me. I knew, going in, that I had loved the library as a kid—why not? It was the only place a relatively poor kid like me could get all the books he wanted—but as I continued to write, I became reacquainted with a deeper truth: I had also feared it. I feared becoming lost in the dark stacks, I feared being forgotten in a dark corner of the reading room and ending up locked in for the night, I feared the old librarian with the blue hair and the cat's-eye glasses and the almost lipless mouth who would pinch the backs of your hands with her long, pale fingers and hiss *"Shhhh!"* if you forgot where you were and started to talk too loud. And yes, I feared the Library Police.

What happened with a much longer work, a novel called *Christine,* began to happen here. About thirty pages in, the humor began to go out of the situation. And about fifty pages in, the whole story took a screaming left turn into the dark places I have travelled so often and which I still know so little about. Eventually I found the guy I was looking for, and managed to raise my head enough to look into his merciless silver eyes. I have tried to bring back a sketch of him for you, Constant Reader, but it may not be very good.

My hands were trembling quite badly when I made it, you see.

CHAPTER ONE

THE STAND-IN

1

Everything, Sam Peebles decided later, was the fault of the god-damned acrobat. If the acrobat hadn't gotten drunk at exactly the wrong time, Sam never would have ended up in such trouble.

It is not bad enough, he thought with a perhaps justifiable bitter-ness, *that life is like a narrow beam over an endless chasm, a beam we have to walk blindfolded. It's bad, but not bad enough. Sometimes, we also get pushed.*

But that was later. First, even before the Library Policeman, was the drunken acrobat.

2

In Junction City, the last Friday of every month was Speaker's Night at the local Rotarians' Hall. On the last Friday in March of 1990, the Rotarians were scheduled to hear—and to be entertained by— The Amazing Joe, an acrobat with Curry & Trembo's All-Star Circus and Travelling Carnival.

The telephone on Sam Peebles's desk at Junction City Realty and Insurance rang at five past four on Thursday afternoon. Sam picked it up. It was always Sam who picked it up—either Sam in person or Sam on the answering machine, because he was Junction City Realty and Insurance's owner and sole employee. He was not a rich man, but he was a reasonably happy one. He liked to tell people that his first Mercedes was still quite a distance in the future, but he had a Ford which was almost new and owned his own home on Kelton Avenue. "Also, the business keeps me in beer and skittles," he liked to add . . . although in truth, he hadn't drunk much beer since college and wasn't exactly sure what skittles were. He thought they might be pretzels.

"Junction City Realty and In—"

"Sam, this is Craig. The acrobat broke his neck."

"*What?*"

"You heard me!" Craig Jones cried in deeply aggrieved tones. "The acrobat broke his fucking neck!"

"Oh," Sam said. "Gee." He thought about this for a moment and then asked cautiously, "Is he dead, Craig?"

"No, he's not dead, but he might as well be as far as we're concerned. He's in the hospital over in Cedar Rapids with his neck dipped in about twenty pounds of plaster. Billy Bright just called me. He said the guy came on drunk as a skunk at the matinee this afternoon, tried to do a back-over flip, and landed outside the center ring on the nape of his neck. Billy said he could hear it way up in the bleachers, where he was sitting. He said it sounded like when you step in a puddle that just iced over."

"Ouch!" Sam exclaimed, wincing.

"I'm not surprised. After all—The Amazing Joe. What kind of name is that for a circus performer? I mean, The Amazing Randix, okay. The Amazing Tortellini, still not bad. But The Amazing *Joe?* It sounds like a prime example of brain damage in action to me."

"Jesus, that's too bad."

"Fucking shit on toast is what it is. It leaves us without a speaker tomorrow night, good buddy."

Sam began to wish he had left the office promptly at four. Craig would have been stuck with Sam the answering machine, and that would have given Sam the living being a little more time to think. He felt he would soon *need* time to think. He also felt that Craig Jones was not going to give him any.

"Yes," he said, "I guess that's true enough." He hoped he sounded philosophical but helpless. "What a shame."

"It sure is," Craig said, and then dropped the dime. "But I know you'll be happy to step in and fill the slot."

"*Me?* Craig, you've got to be kidding! I can't even do a somersault, let alone a back-over fl—"

"I thought you could talk about the importance of the independently owned business in small-town life," Craig Jones pressed on relentlessly. "If that doesn't do it for you, there's baseball. Lacking *that,* you could always drop your pants and wag your wing-wang at the audience. Sam, I am not just the head of the Speakers Committee—that would be bad enough. But since Kenny moved away and Carl quit coming, I *am* the Speakers Committee. Now, you've got to help me. I *need* a speaker tomorrow night. There are about five guys in the whole damn club I feel I can trust in a pinch, and you're one of them."

"But—"

"You're also the only one who hasn't filled in already in a situation like this, so you're elected, buddy-boy."

"Frank Stephens—"

"—pinch-hit for the guy from the trucking union last year when the grand jury indicted him for fraud and he couldn't show up. Sam—it's your turn in the barrel. You can't let me down, man. You *owe* me."

"I run an *insurance* business!" Sam cried. "When I'm not writing insurance, I sell farms! Mostly to banks! Most people find it *boring*! The ones who don't find it boring find it *disgusting*!"

"None of that matters." Craig was now moving in for the kill, marching over Sam's puny objection in grim hobnailed boots. "They'll all be drunk by the end of dinner and you know it. They won't remember a goddam word you said come Saturday morning, but in the meantime, *I need someone to stand up and talk for half an hour and you're elected*!"

Sam continued to object a little longer, but Craig kept coming down on the imperatives, italicizing them mercilessly. *Need. Gotta. Owe.*

"All right!" he said at last. "All right, all right! Enough!"

"My man!" Craig exclaimed. His voice was suddenly full of sunshine and rainbows. "Remember, it doesn't have to be any longer than thirty minutes, plus maybe another ten for questions. If anybody *has* any questions. And you really *can* wag your wing-wang if you want to. I doubt that anybody could actually *see* it, but—"

"Craig," Sam said, "that's enough."

"Oh! *Sorry!* Shet mah mouf!" Craig, perhaps lightheaded with relief, cackled.

"Listen, why don't we terminate this discussion?" Sam reached for the roll of Tums he kept in his desk drawer. He suddenly felt he might need quite a few Tums during the next twenty-eight hours or so. "It looks as if I've got a speech to write."

"You got it," Craig said. "Just remember—dinner at six, speech at seven-thirty. As they used to say on *Hawaii Five-0,* be there! Aloha!"

"Aloha, Craig," Sam said, and hung up. He stared at the phone. He felt hot gas rising slowly up through his chest and into his throat. He opened his mouth and uttered a sour burp—the product of a stomach which had been reasonably serene until five minutes ago.

He ate the first of what would prove to be a great many Tums indeed.

3

Instead of going bowling that night as he had planned, Sam Peebles shut himself in his study at home with a yellow legal pad, three sharpened pencils, a package of Kent cigarettes, and a six-pack of Jolt. He unplugged the telephone from the wall, lit a cigarette, and stared at the yellow pad. After five minutes of staring, he wrote this on the top line of the top sheet:

SMALL-TOWN BUSINESSES: THE LIFEBLOOD OF AMERICA

He said it out loud and liked the sound of it. Well . . . maybe he didn't exactly *like* it, but he could *live* with it. He said it louder and liked it better. A *little* better. It actually wasn't *that* good; in fact, it probably sucked the big hairy one, but it beat the shit out of "Communism: Threat or Menace." And Craig was right—most of them would be too hung over on Saturday morning to remember what they'd heard on Friday night, anyway.

Marginally encouraged, Sam began to write.

"When I moved to Junction City from the more or less thriving metropolis of Ames in 1984 . . ."

4

". . . and that is why I feel now, as I did on that bright September morn in 1984, that small businesses are not just the lifeblood of America, but the bright and sparkly lifeblood of the entire Western world."

Sam stopped, crushed out a cigarette in the ashtray on his office desk, and looked hopefully at Naomi Higgins.

"Well? What do you think?"

Naomi was a pretty young woman from Proverbia, a town four miles west of Junction City. She lived in a ramshackle house by the Proverbia River with her ramshackle mother. Most of the Rotarians knew Naomi, and wagers had been offered from time to time on whether the house or the mother would fall apart first. Sam didn't know if any of these wagers had ever been taken, but if so, their resolution was still pending.

Naomi had graduated from Iowa City Business College, and could actually retrieve whole legible sentences from her shorthand. Since she was the only local woman who possessed such a skill, she was in great demand among Junction City's limited business population. She also had extremely good legs, and that didn't hurt. She worked mornings five days a week, for four men and one woman—two lawyers, one banker, and two realtors. In the afternoons she went back to the ramshackle house, and when she was not caring for her ramshackle mother, she typed up the dictation she had taken.

Sam Peebles engaged Naomi's services each Friday morning from ten until noon, but this morning he had put aside his correspondence—even though some of it badly needed to be answered—and asked Naomi if she would listen to something.

"Sure, I guess so," Naomi had replied. She looked a little worried, as if she thought Sam—whom she had briefly dated—might be planning to propose marriage. When he explained that Craig Jones had drafted him to stand in for the wounded acrobat, and that he wanted her to listen to his speech, she'd relaxed and listened to the whole thing—all twenty-six minutes of it—with flattering attention.

"Don't be afraid to be honest," he added before Naomi could do more than open her mouth.

"It's good," she said. "Pretty interesting."

"No, that's okay—you don't have to spare my feelings. Let it all hang out."

"I *am*. It's really okay. Besides, by the time you start talking, they'll all be—"

"Yes, they'll all be hammered, I know." This prospect had comforted Sam at first, but now it disappointed him a little. Listening to himself read, he'd actually thought the speech *was* pretty good.

"There *is* one thing," Naomi said thoughtfully.

"Oh?"

"It's kind of . . . you know . . . *dry*."

"Oh," Sam said. He sighed and rubbed his eyes. He had been up until nearly one o'clock this morning, first writing and then revising.

"But that's easy to fix," she assured him. "Just go to the library and get a couple of those books."

Sam felt a sudden sharp pain in his lower belly and grabbed his roll of Tums. Research for a stupid Rotary Club speech? *Library* research? That was going a little overboard, wasn't it? He had never been to the Junction City Library before, and he didn't see a reason to go there now. Still, Naomi had listened very closely, Naomi was trying to help, and it would be rude not to at least listen to what she had to say.

"What books?"

"*You* know—books with stuff in them to liven up speeches. They're like . . ." Naomi groped. "Well, you know the hot sauce they give you at China Light, if you want it?"

"Yes—"

"They're like that. They have jokes. Also, there's this one book, *Best Loved Poems of the American People*. You could probably find something in there for the end. Something sort of uplifting."

"There are poems in this book about the importance of small businesses in American life?" Sam asked doubtfully.

"When you quote poetry, people get *uplifted,*" Naomi said. "Nobody cares what it's *about,* Sam, let alone what it's *for.*"

"And they really have joke-books especially for speeches?" Sam found this almost impossible to believe, although hearing that the library carried books on such esoterica as small-engine repair and wig-styling wouldn't have surprised him in the least.

"Yes."

"How do you know?"

"When Phil Brakeman was running for the State House, I used to type up speeches for him all the time," Naomi said. "He had one of those books. I just can't remember what the name of it was. All I can think of is *Jokes for the John,* and of course *that's* not right."

"No," Sam agreed, thinking that a few choice tidbits from *Jokes for the John* would probably make him a howling success. But he began to see what Naomi was getting at, and the idea appealed to him despite his reluctance to visit the local library after all his years of cheerful neglect. A little spice for the old speech. Dress up your leftovers, turn your meatloaf into a masterpiece. And a library, after all, was just a library. If you didn't know how to find what you wanted, all you had to do was ask a librarian. Answering questions was one of their jobs, right?

"Anyway, you *could* leave it just the way it is," Naomi said. "I mean, they *will* be drunk." She looked at Sam kindly but severely and then checked her watch. "You have over an hour left—did you want to do some letters?"

"No, I guess not. Why don't you type up my speech instead?" He had already decided to spend his lunch hour at the library.

CHAPTER TWO

THE LIBRARY (I)

1

Sam had gone by the Library hundreds of times during his years in Junction City, but this was the first time he had really *looked* at it, and he discovered a rather amazing thing: he hated the place on sight.

The Junction City Public Library stood on the corner of State

Street and Miller Avenue, a square granite box of a building with
windows so narrow they looked like loopholes. A slate roof over-
hung all four sides of the building, and when one approached it
from the front, the combination of the narrow windows and the
line of shadow created by the roof made the building look like the
frowning face of a stone robot. It was a fairly common style of Iowa
architecture, common enough so Sam Peebles, who had been selling
real estate for nearly twenty years, had given it a name: Midwestern
Ugly. During spring, summer, and fall, the building's forbidding
aspect was softened by the maples which stood around it in a kind
of grove, but now, at the end of a hard Iowa winter, the maples
were still bare and the Library looked like an oversized crypt.

He didn't like it; it made him uneasy; he didn't know why. It
was, after all, just a library, not the dungeons of the Inquisition.
Just the same, another acidic burp rose up through his chest as he
made his way along the flagstone walk. There was a funny sweet
undertaste to the burp that reminded him of something . . .
something from a long time ago, perhaps. He put a Tum in his
mouth, began to crunch it up, and came to an abrupt decision. His
speech was good enough as it stood. Not great, but good enough.
After all, they were talking Rotary Club here, not the United Nations. It was time to stop playing with it. He was going to go back
to the office and do some of the correspondence he had neglected
that morning.

He started to turn, then thought: *That's dumb. Really dumb. You
want to be dumb? Okay. But you agreed to give the goddam speech; why
not give a good one?*

He stood on the Library walk, frowning and undecided. He liked
to make fun of Rotary. Craig did, too. And Frank Stephens. Most
of the young business types in Junction City laughed about the
meetings. But they rarely missed one, and Sam supposed he knew
why: it was a place where connections could be made. A place
where a fellow like him could meet some of the not-so-young business types in Junction City. Guys like Elmer Baskin, whose bank
had helped float a strip shopping center in Beaverton two years
ago. Guys like George Candy—who, it was said, could produce
three million dollars in development money with one phone
call . . . if he chose to make it.

These were small-town fellows, high-school basketball fans, guys who got their hair cut at Jimmy's, guys who wore boxer shorts and strappy tee-shirts to bed instead of pajamas, guys who still drank their beer from the bottle, guys who didn't feel comfortable about a night on the town in Cedar Rapids unless they were turned out in Full Cleveland. They were also Junction City's movers and shakers, and when you came right down to it, wasn't that why Sam kept going on Friday nights? When you came right down to it, wasn't that why Craig had called in such a sweat after the stupid acrobat broke his stupid neck? You wanted to get noticed by the movers and shakers . . . but not because you had fucked up. *They'll all be drunk,* Craig had said, and Naomi had seconded the motion, but it now occurred to Sam that he had never seen Elmer Baskin take anything stronger than coffee. Not once. And he probably wasn't the only one. Some of them might be drunk . . . but not all of them. And the ones who weren't might well be the ones who really mattered.

Handle this right, Sam, and you might do yourself some good. It's not impossible.

No. It wasn't. Unlikely, of course, but not impossible. And there was something else, quite aside from the shadow politics which might or might not attend a Friday-night Rotary Club speaker's meeting: he had always prided himself on doing the best job possible. So it was just a dumb little speech. So what?

Also, it's just a dumb little small-town library. What's the big deal? There aren't even any bushes growing along the sides.

Sam had started up the walk again, but now he stopped with a frown creasing his forehead. That was a strange thought to have; it seemed to have come right out of nowhere. So there were no bushes growing along the sides of the Library—what difference did *that* make? He didn't know . . . but he did know it had an almost magical effect on him. His uncharacteristic hesitation fell away and he began to move forward once more. He climbed the four stone steps and paused for a moment. The place felt deserted, somehow. He grasped the door-handle and thought, *I bet it's locked. I bet the place is closed Friday afternoons.* There was something strangely comforting in this thought.

But the old-fashioned latch-plate depressed under his thumb, and the heavy door swung noiselessly inward. Sam stepped into a small foyer with a marble floor in checkerboard black and white squares.

An easel stood in the center of this antechamber. There was a sign propped on the easel; the message consisted of one word in very large letters.

SILENCE!

it read. Not

SILENCE IS GOLDEN

or

QUIET, PLEASE

but just that one staring, glaring word:

SILENCE!

"You bet," Sam said. He only murmured the words, but the acoustics of the place were very good, and his low murmur was magnified into a grouchy grumble that made him cringe. It actually seemed to bounce back at him from the high ceiling. At that moment he felt as if he was in the fourth grade again, and about to be called to task by Mrs. Glasters for cutting up rough at exactly the wrong moment. He looked around uneasily, half-expecting an ill-natured librarian to come swooping out of the main room to see who had dared profane the silence.

Stop it, for Christ's sake. You're forty years old. Fourth grade was a long time ago, buddy.

Except it didn't seem like a long time ago. Not in here. In here, fourth grade seemed almost close enough to reach out and touch.

He crossed the marble floor to the left of the easel, unconsciously walking with his weight thrown forward so the heels of his loafers would not click, and entered the main lobby of the Junction City Library.

There were a number of glass globes hanging down from the ceiling (which was at least twenty feet higher than the ceiling of the foyer), but none of them were on. The light was provided by two large, angled skylights. On a sunny day these would have been quite enough to light the room; they might even have rendered it cheery and welcoming. But this Friday was overcast and dreary, and the light was dim. The corners of the lobby were filled with gloomy webs of shadow.

What Sam Peebles felt was a sense of *wrongness*. It was as if he had done more than step through a door and cross a foyer; he felt as if he had entered another world, one which bore absolutely no resemblance to the small Iowa town that he sometimes liked, sometimes hated, but mostly just took for granted. The air in here seemed heavier than normal air, and did not seem to conduct light as well as normal air did. The silence was thick as a blanket. As cold as snow.

The library was deserted.

Shelves of books stretched above him on every side. Looking up toward the skylights with their crisscrosses of reinforcing wire made Sam a little dizzy, and he had a momentary illusion: he felt that he was upside down, that he had been hung by his heels over a deep square pit lined with books.

Ladders leaned against the walls here and there, the kind that were mounted on tracks and rolled along the floor on rubber wheels. Two wooden islands broke the lake of space between the place where he stood and the checkout desk on the far side of the large, high room. One was a long oak magazine rack. Periodicals, each encased in a clear plastic cover, hung from this rack on wooden dowels. They looked like the hides of strange animals which had been left to cure in this silent room. A sign mounted on top of the rack commanded:

RETURN ALL MAGAZINES TO THEIR PROPER PLACES!

To the left of the magazine rack was a shelf of brand-new novels and nonfiction books. The sign mounted on top of the shelf proclaimed them to be seven-day rentals.

Sam passed down the wide aisle between the magazines and the seven-day bookshelf, his heels rapping and echoing in spite of his effort to move quietly. He found himself wishing he had heeded his original impulse to just turn around and go back to the office. This place was spooky. Although there was a small, hooded microfilm camera alight and humming on the desk, there was no one manning—or womaning—it. A small plaque reading

A. LORTZ

stood on the desk, but there was no sign of A. Lortz or anyone else.

Probably taking a dump and checking out the new issue of Library Journal.

Sam felt a crazy desire to open his mouth and yell, "Everything coming out all right, A. Lortz?" It passed quickly. The Junction City Public Library was not the sort of place that encouraged amusing sallies.

Sam's thoughts suddenly spun back to a little rhyme from his childhood. *No more laughing, no more fun; Quaker meeting has begun. If you show your teeth or tongue, you may pay a forfeit.*

If you show your teeth or tongue in here, does A. Lortz make you pay a forfeit? he wondered. He looked around again, let his nerve endings feel the frowning quality of the silence, and thought you could make book on it.

No longer interested in obtaining a joke-book or *Best Loved Poems of the American People,* but fascinated by the library's suspended, dreamy atmosphere in spite of himself, Sam walked toward a door to the right of the seven-day books. A sign over the door said this was the Children's Library. Had he used the Children's Library when he had been growing up in St. Louis? He thought so, but those memories were hazy, distant, and hard to hold. All the same, approaching the door of the Children's Library gave him an odd and haunting feeling. It was almost like coming home.

The door was closed. On it was a picture of Little Red Riding Hood, looking down at the wolf in Grandma's bed. The wolf was wearing Grandma's nightgown and Grandma's nightcap. It was snarling. Foam dripped from between its bared fangs. An expression of almost exquisite horror had transfixed Little Red Riding Hood's face, and the poster seemed not just to suggest but to actually proclaim that the happy ending of this story—of all fairy tales—was a convenient lie. Parents might believe such guff, Red Riding Hood's ghastly-sick face said, but the little ones knew better, didn't they?

Nice, Sam thought. *With a poster like that on the door, I bet lots of kids use the Children's Library. I bet the little ones are especially fond of it.*

He opened the door and poked his head in.

His sense of unease left him; he was charmed at once. The poster on the door was all wrong, of course, but what was behind it seemed perfectly right. Of *course* he had used the library as a child; it only took one look into this scale-model world to refresh those memories. His father had died young; Sam had been an only child raised by a working mother he rarely saw except on Sundays and holidays. When he could not promote money for a movie after school—and that was often—the library had to do, and the room he saw now brought those days back in a sudden wave of nostalgia that was sweet and painful and obscurely frightening.

It had been a *small* world, and this was a small world; it had been a well-lighted world, even on the grimmest, rainiest days, and so was this one. No hanging glass globes for this room; there were shadow-banishing fluorescent lights behind frosted panels in the suspended ceiling, and all of them were on. The tops of the tables were only two feet from the floor; the seats of the chairs were even closer. In this world the adults would be the interlopers, the uncomfortable aliens. They would balance the tables on their knees if they tried to sit at them, and they would be apt to crack their skulls bending to drink from the water fountain which was mounted on the far wall.

Here the shelves did not stretch up in an unkind trick of perspective which made one giddy if one looked up too long; the ceiling was low enough to be cozy, but not low enough to make a child feel cramped. Here were no rows of gloomy bindings but books which fairly shouted with raucous primary colors: bright blues, reds, yellows. In this world Dr. Seuss was king, Judy Blume was queen, and all the princes and princesses attended Sweet Valley High. Here Sam felt all that old sense of benevolent after-school welcome, a place where the books did all but beg to be touched, handled, looked at, explored. Yet these feelings had their own dark undertaste.

His clearest sense, however, was one of almost wistful pleasure. On one wall was a photograph of a puppy with large, thoughtful eyes. Written beneath the puppy's anxious-hopeful face was one of the world's great truths: IT IS HARD TO BE GOOD. On the other wall was a drawing of mallards making their way down a riverbank to the reedy verge of the water. MAKE WAY FOR DUCKLINGS! the poster trumpeted.

Sam looked to his left, and the faint smile on his lips first faltered and then died. Here was a poster which showed a large, dark car speeding away from what he supposed was a school building. A little boy was looking out of the passenger window. His hands were plastered against the glass and his mouth was open in a scream. In the background, a man—only a vague, ominous shape—was hunched over the wheel, driving hell for leather. The words beneath this picture read:

NEVER TAKE RIDES FROM STRANGERS!

Sam recognized that this poster and the Little Red Riding Hood picture on the door of the Children's Library both appealed to the same primitive emotions of dread, but he found this one much more disturbing. Of *course* children shouldn't accept rides from strangers, and of course they had to be taught not to do so, but was *this* the right way to make the point?

How many kids, he wondered, *have had a week's worth of nightmares thanks to that little public-service announcement?*

And there was another one, posted right on the front of the checkout desk, that struck a chill as deep as January down Sam's back. It showed a dismayed boy and girl, surely no older than eight, cringing back from a man in a trenchcoat and gray hat. The man looked at least eleven feet tall; his shadow fell on the upturned faces of the children. The brim of his 1940s-style fedora threw its own shadow, and the eyes of the man in the trenchcoat gleamed relentlessly from its black depths. They looked like chips of ice as they studied the children, marking them with the grim gaze of Authority. He was holding out an ID folder with a star pinned to it—an odd sort of star, with at least nine points on it. Maybe as many as a dozen. The message beneath read:

AVOID THE LIBRARY POLICE!
GOOD BOYS AND GIRLS RETURN THEIR BOOKS *ON TIME*!

That taste was in his mouth again. That sweet, unpleasant taste. And a queer, frightening thought occurred to him: *I have seen this man before.* But that was ridiculous, of course. Wasn't it?

Sam thought of how such a poster would have intimidated him as a child—of how much simple, unalloyed pleasure it would have stolen from the safe haven of the library—and felt indignation rise in his chest. He took a step toward the poster to examine the odd star more closely, taking his roll of Tums out of his pocket at the same time.

He was putting one of them into his mouth when a voice spoke up from behind him. "Well, hello there!"

He jumped and turned around, ready to do battle with the library dragon, now that it had finally disclosed itself.

2

No dragon presented itself. There was only a plump, white-haired woman of about fifty-five, pushing a trolley of books on silent rubber tires. Her white hair fell around her pleasant, unlined face in neat beauty-shop curls.

"I suppose you were looking for me," she said. "Did Mr. Peckham direct you in here?"

"I didn't see anybody at all."

"No? Then he's gone along home," she said. "I'm not really surprised, since it's Friday. Mr. Peckham comes in to dust and read the paper every morning around eleven. He's the janitor—only part-time, of course. Sometimes he stays until one—one-thirty on most Mondays, because that's the day when both the dust and the paper are thickest—but you know how thin Friday's paper is."

Sam smiled. "I take it you're the librarian?"

"I am she," Mrs. Lortz said, and smiled at him. But Sam didn't think her *eyes* were smiling; her eyes seemed to be watching him carefully, almost coldly. "And you are . . . ?"

"Sam Peebles."

"Oh yes! Real estate and insurance! That's *your* game!"

"Guilty as charged."

"I'm sorry you found the main section of the library deserted—you must have thought we were closed and someone left the door open by mistake."

"Actually," he said, "the idea did cross my mind."

"From two until seven there are three of us on duty," said Mrs. Lortz. "Two is when the schools begin to let out, you know—the grammar school at two, the middle school at two-thirty, the high school at two-forty-five. The children are our most faithful clients, and the most welcome, as far as I am concerned. I love the little

ones. I used to have an all-day assistant, but last year the Town
Council cut our budget by eight hundred dollars and . . ." Mrs. Lortz
put her hands together and mimed a bird flying away. It was an
amusing charming gesture.

So why, Sam wondered, *aren't I charmed or amused?*

The posters, he supposed. He was still trying to make Red Riding
Hood, the screaming child in the car, and the grim-eyed Library
Policeman jibe with this smiling small-town librarian.

She put her left hand out—a small hand, as plump and round as
the rest of her—with perfect unstudied confidence. He looked at
the third finger and saw it was ringless; she wasn't Mrs. Lortz after
all. The fact of her spinsterhood struck him as utterly typical, utterly
small-town. Almost a caricature, really. Sam shook it.

"You haven't been to our library before, have you, Mr. Peebles?"

"No, I'm afraid not. And please make it Sam." He did not know
if he really wanted to be Sam to this woman or not, but he was a
businessman in a small town—a salesman, when you got right down
to it—and the offer of his first name was automatic.

"Why, thank you, Sam."

He waited for her to respond by offering her own first name,
but she only looked at him expectantly.

"I've gotten myself into a bit of a bind," he said. "Our scheduled
speaker tonight at Rotary Club had an accident, and—"

"Oh, that's too bad!"

"For me as well as him. I got drafted to take his place."

"Oh-oh!" Ms. Lortz said. Her tone was alarmed, but her eyes
crinkled with amusement. And still Sam did not find himself warm-
ing to her, although he was a person who warmed up to other
people quickly (if superficially) as a rule; the kind of man who had
few close friends but felt compelled nonetheless to start conversations with strangers in elevators.

"I wrote a speech last night and this morning I read it to the
young woman who takes dictation and types up my correspondence—"

"Naomi Higgins, I'll bet."

"Yes—how did you know that?"

"Naomi is a regular. She borrows a great many romance novels—
Jennifer Blake, Rosemary Rogers, Paul Sheldon, people like that."
She lowered her voice and said, "She says they're for her mother,
but actually I think she reads them herself."

Sam laughed. Naomi *did* have the dreamy eyes of a closet romance reader.

"Anyway, I know she's what would be called an office temporary in a big city. I imagine that here in Junction City she's the whole secretarial pool. It seemed reasonable that she was the young woman of whom you spoke."

"Yes. She liked my speech—or so she said—but she thought it was a bit dry. She suggested—"

"*The Speaker's Companion,* I'll bet!"

"Well, she couldn't remember the exact title, but that sure *sounds* right." He paused, then asked a little anxiously: "Does it have jokes?"

"Only three hundred pages of them," she said. She reached out her right hand—it was as innocent of rings as her left—and tugged at his sleeve with it. "Right this way." She led him toward the door by the sleeve. "I am going to solve all your problems, Sam. I only hope it won't take a crisis to bring you back to our library. It's small, but it's very fine. I think so, anyway, although of course I'm prejudiced."

They passed through the door into the frowning shadows of the Library's main room. Ms. Lortz flicked three switches by the door, and the hanging globes lit up, casting a soft yellow glow that warmed and cheered the room considerably.

"It gets so *gloomy* in here when it's overcast," she said in a confidential we're-in-the-real-Library-now voice. She was still tugging firmly on Sam's sleeve. "But of course you know how the Town Council complains about the electricity bill in a place like this . . . or perhaps you don't, but I'll bet you can *guess.*"

"I can," Sam agreed, also dropping his voice to a near-whisper.

"But that's a holiday compared to what they have to say about the heating expenses in the winter." She rolled her eyes. "Oil is so *dear.* It's the fault of those Arabs . . . and *now* look what they are up to—hiring religious hit-men to try and kill *writers.*"

"It *does* seem a little harsh," Sam said, and for some reason he found himself thinking of the poster of the tall man again—the one with the odd star pinned to his ID case, the one whose shadow was falling so ominously over the upturned faces of the children. Falling over them like a stain.

"And of course, I've been fussing in the Children's Library. I lose all track of time when I'm in there."

"That's an interesting place," Sam said. He meant to go on, to ask her about the posters, but Ms. Lortz forestalled him. It was clear to Sam exactly who was in charge of this peculiar little side-trip in an otherwise ordinary day.

"You bet it is! Now, you just give me one minute." She reached up and put her hands on his shoulders—she had to stand on tiptoe to do it—and for one moment Sam had the absurd idea that she meant to kiss him. Instead she pressed him down onto a wooden bench which ran along the far side of the seven-day bookshelf. "I know right where to find the books you need, Sam. I don't even have to check the card catalogue."

"I could get them myself—"

"I'm *sure*," she said, "but they're in the Special Reference section, and I don't like to let people in there if I can help it. I'm very bossy about that, but I *always* know where to put my hand right on the things I need . . . back there, anyway. People are so *messy*, they have so little regard for *order*, you know. Children are the worst, but even adults get up to didos if you let them. Don't worry about a thing. I'll be back in two shakes."

Sam had no intention of protesting further, but he wouldn't have had time even if he had wanted to. She was gone. He sat on the bench, once more feeling like a fourth-grader . . . like a fourth-grader who had done something wrong this time, who had gotten up to didos and so couldn't go out and play with the other children at recess.

He could hear Ms. Lortz moving about in the room behind the checkout desk, and he looked around thoughtfully. There was nothing to see except books—there was not even one old pensioner reading the paper or leafing through a magazine. It seemed odd. He wouldn't have expected a small-town library like this to be doing a *booming* business on a weekday afternoon, but no one at all?

Well, there was Mr. Peckham, he thought, *but he finished the paper and went home. Dreadfully thin paper on Friday, you know. Thin dust, too.* And then he realized he only had the word of Ms. Lortz that a Mr. Peckham had ever been here at all.

True enough—but why would she lie?

He didn't know, and doubted very much that she had, but the fact that he was questioning the honesty of a sweet-faced woman he had just met highlighted the central puzzling fact of this meeting: he didn't like her. Sweet face or not, he didn't like her one bit.

It's the posters. You were prepared not to like ANYBODY *that would put up posters like that in a children's room. But it doesn't matter, because a side-trip is all it is. Get the books and get out.*

He shifted on the bench, looked up, and saw a motto on the wall:

> *If you would know how a man treats his*
> *wife and his children, see how he treats his*
> *books.*
> —Ralph Waldo Emerson

Sam didn't care much for *that* little homily, either. He didn't know exactly why . . . except that maybe he thought a man, even a bookworm, might be expected to treat his family a little better than his reading matter. The motto, painted in gold leaf on a length of varnished oak, glared down at him nevertheless, seeming to suggest he better think again.

Before he could, Ms. Lortz returned, lifting a gate in the checkout desk, stepping through it, and lowering it neatly behind her again.

"I think I've got what you need," she said cheerfully. "I hope you'll agree."

She handed him two books. One was *The Speaker's Companion,* edited by Kent Adelmen, and the other was *Best Loved Poems of the American People.* The contents of this latter book, according to the jacket (which was, in its turn, protected by a tough plastic over-jacket), had not been edited, exactly, but *selected* by one Hazel Felleman. "Poems of life!" the jacket promised. "Poems of home and mother! Poems of laughter and whimsey! The poems most frequently asked for by the readers of the *New York Times Book Review!*" It further advised that Hazel Felleman "has been able to keep her finger on the poetry pulse of the American people."

Sam looked at her with some doubt, and she read his mind effortlessly.

"Yes, I know, they look old-fashioned," she said. "Especially nowadays, when self-help books are all the rage. I imagine if you went to one of the chain bookstores in the Cedar Rapids mall, you could find a dozen books designed to help the beginning public speaker. But none of them would be as good as these, Sam. I really believe these are the best helps there are for men and women who are new to the art of public speaking."

"Amateurs, in other words," Sam said, grinning.

"Well, yes. Take *Best Loved Poems,* for instance. The second section of the book—it begins on page sixty-five, if memory serves—is called 'Inspiration.' You can almost surely find something there which will make a suitable climax to your little talk, Sam. And you're apt to find that your listeners will remember a well-chosen verse even if they forget everything else. Especially if they're a little—"

"Drunk," he said.

"*Tight* was the word I would have used," she said with gentle reproof, "although I suppose you know them better than I do." But the gaze she shot at him suggested that she was only saying this because she was polite.

She held up *The Speaker's Companion.* The jacket was a cartoonist's drawing of a bunting-draped hall. Small groups of men in old-fashioned evening dress were seated at tables with drinks in front of them. They were all yucking it up. The man behind the podium— also in evening dress and clearly the after-dinner speaker—was grinning triumphantly down at them. It was clear he was a roaring success.

"There's a section at the beginning on the *theory* of after-dinner speeches," said Ms. Lortz, "but since you don't strike me as the sort of man who wants to make a *career* out of this—"

"You've got *that* right, " Sam agreed fervently.

"—I suggest you go directly to the middle section, which is called 'Lively Speaking.' There you will find jokes and stories divided into three categories: 'Easing Them In,' 'Softening Them Up,' and 'Finishing Them Off.' "

Sounds like a manual for gigolos, Sam thought but did not say.

She read his mind again. "A little suggestive, I suppose—but these books were published in a simpler, more innocent time. The late thirties, to be exact."

"Much more innocent, right," Sam said, thinking of deserted dust-bowl farms, little girls in flour-sack dresses, and rusty, thrown-together Hoovervilles surrounded by police wielding truncheons.

"But both books still *work,*" she said, tapping them for emphasis, "and that's the important thing in business, isn't it, Sam? Results!"

"Yes . . . I guess it is."

He looked at her thoughtfully, and Ms. Lortz raised her eyebrows—a trifle defensively, perhaps. "A penny for your thoughts," she said.

"I was thinking that this has been a fairly rare occurrence in my adult life," he said. "Not unheard-of, nothing like that, but *rare,* I came in here to get a couple of books to liven up my speech, and you seem to have given me exactly what I came for. How often does something like that happen in a world where you usually can't even get a couple of good lambchops at the grocery store when you've got your face fixed for them?"

She smiled. It appeared to be a smile of genuine pleasure . . . except Sam noticed once again that her *eyes* did not smile. He didn't think they had changed expression since he had first come upon her—or she upon him—in the Children's Library. They just went on watching. "I think I've just been paid a compliment!"

"Yes, ma'am. You have."

"I thank you, Sam. I thank you very kindly. They say flattery will get you everywhere, but I'm afraid I'm still going to have to ask you for two dollars."

"You are?"

"That's the charge for issuing an adult library card," she said, "but it's good for three years, and renewal is only fifty cents. Now, is that a deal, or what?"

"It sounds fine to me."

"Then step right this way," she said, and Sam followed her to the checkout desk.

3

She gave him a card to fill out—on it he wrote his name, address, telephone numbers, and place of business.

"I see you live on Kelton Avenue. Nice!"

"Well, *I* like it."

"The houses are lovely and big—you should be married."

He started a little. "How did you know I wasn't married?"

"The same way you knew *I* wasn't," she said. Her smile had become a trifle sly, a trifle catlike. "Nothing on the third left."

"Oh," he said lamely, and smiled. He didn't think it was his usual sparkly smile, and his cheeks felt warm.

"Two dollars, please."

He gave her two singles. She went over to a small desk where an aged, skeletal typewriter stood, and typed briefly on a bright-orange card. She brought it back to the checkout desk, signed her name at the bottom with a flourish, and then pushed it across to him.

"Check and make sure all the information's correct, please."

Sam did so. "It's all fine." Her first name, he noted, was Ardelia. A pretty name, and rather unusual.

She took his new library card back—the first one he'd owned since college, now that he thought about it, and he had used that one precious little—and placed it under the microfilm recorder beside a card she took from the pocket of each book. "You can only keep these out for a week, because they're from Special Reference. That's a category I invented myself for books which are in great demand."

"Helps for the beginning speaker are in great demand?"

"Those, and books on things like plumbing repair, simple magic tricks, social etiquette . . . You'd be surprised what books people call for in a pinch. But I know."

"I'll bet you do."

"I've been in the business a long, long time, Sam. And they're not renewable, so be sure to get them back by April sixth." She raised her head, and the light caught in her eyes. Sam almost dismissed what he saw there as a twinkle . . . but that wasn't what it was. It was a shine. A flat, hard shine. For just a moment Ardelia Lortz looked as if she had a nickel in each eye.

"Or?" he asked, and his smile suddenly didn't feel like a smile— it felt like a mask.

"Or else I'll have to send the Library Policeman after you," she said.

4

For a moment their gazes locked, and Sam thought he saw the *real* Ardelia Lortz, and there was nothing charming or soft or spinster-librarian about *that* woman at all.

This woman might actually be dangerous, he thought, and then dismissed it, a little embarrassed. The gloomy day—and perhaps the pressure of the impending speech—was getting to him. *She's about as dangerous as a canned peach . . . and it isn't the gloomy day or the Rotarians tonight, either. It's those goddam posters.*

He had *The Speaker's Companion* and *Best Loved Poems of the American People* under his arm and they were almost to the door before
he realized she was showing him out. He planted his feet firmly
and stopped. She looked at him, surprised.

"Can I ask you something, Ms. Lortz?"

"Of course, Sam. That's what I'm here for—to answer questions."

"It's about the Children's Library," he said, "and the posters.
Some of them surprised me. Shocked me, almost." He expected
that to come out sounding like something a Baptist preacher might
say about an issue of *Playboy* glimpsed beneath the other magazines
on a parishioner's coffee table, but it didn't come out that way at
all. *Because,* he thought, *it's not just a conventional sentiment. I really
was shocked. No almost about it.*

"Posters?" she asked, frowning, and then her brow cleared. She
laughed. "Oh! You must mean the Library Policeman . . . and Simple Simon, of course."

"Simple Simon?"

"You know the poster that says NEVER TAKE RIDES FROM
STRANGERS? That's what the kids call the little boy in the picture.
The one who is yelling. They call him Simple Simon—I suppose
they feel contempt for him because he did such a foolish thing. I
think that's very healthy, don't you?"

"He's not yelling," Sam said slowly. "He's *screaming.*"

She shrugged. "Yelling, screaming, what's the difference? We
don't hear much of either in here. The children are very good—
very respectful."

"I'll bet," Sam said. They were back in the foyer again now, and
he glanced at the sign on the easel, the sign which didn't say

SILENCE IS GOLDEN

or

PLEASE TRY TO BE QUIET

but just offered that one inarguable imperative:

SILENCE!

"Besides—it's all a matter of interpretation, isn't it?"

"I suppose," Sam said. He felt that he was being maneuvered—

and very efficiently—into a place where he would not have a moral leg to stand on, and the field of dialectic would belong to Ardelia Lortz. She gave him the impression that she was used to doing this, and that made him feel stubborn. "But they struck me as extreme, those posters."

"Did they?" she asked politely. They had halted by the outer door now.

"Yes. Scary." He gathered himself and said what he really believed. "Not appropriate to a place where small children gather."

He found he still did not sound prissy or self-righteous, at least to himself, and this was a relief.

She was smiling, and the smile irritated him. "You're not the first person who ever expressed that opinion, Sam. Childless adults aren't frequent visitors to the Children's Library, but they *do* come in from time to time—uncles, aunts, some single mother's boyfriend who got stuck with pick-up duty . . . or people like you, Sam, who are looking for me."

People in a pinch, her cool blue-gray eyes said. *People who come for help and then, once they HAVE been helped, stay to criticize the way we run things here at the Junction City Public Library. The way I run things at the Junction City Public Library.*

"I guess you think I was wrong to put my two cents in," Sam said good-naturedly. He didn't feel good-natured, all of a sudden he didn't feel good-natured at all, but it was another trick of the trade, one he now wrapped around himself like a protective cloak.

"Not at all. It's just that you don't understand. We had a poll last summer, Sam—it was part of the annual Summer Reading Program. We call our program Junction City's Summer Sizzlers, and each child gets one vote for every book he or she reads. It's one of the strategies we've developed over the years to encourage children to read. That is one of our most important responsibilities, you see."

We know what we're doing, her steady gaze told him. *And I'm being very polite, aren't I? Considering that you, who have never been here in your life before, have presumed to poke your head in once and start shotgunning criticisms.*

Sam began to feel very much in the wrong. That dialectical battlefield did not belong to the Lortz woman yet—at least not entirely—but he recognized the fact that he was in retreat.

"According to the poll, last summer's favorite movie among the children was *A Nightmare on Elm Street, Part 5.* Their favorite rock group is called Guns n' Roses—the runner-up was something named Ozzy Osbourne, who, I understand, has a reputation for biting the heads off live animals during his concerts. Their favorite novel was a paperback original called *Swan Song.* It's a horror novel by a man named Robert McCammon. We can't keep it in stock, Sam. They read each new copy to rags in weeks. I had a copy put in Vinabind, but of course it was stolen. By one of the bad children."

Her lips pursed in a thin line.

"Runner-up was a horror novel about incest and infanticide called *Flowers in the Attic.* That one was the champ for five years running. Several of them even mentioned *Peyton Place!*"

She looked at him sternly.

"I myself have never seen any of the *Nightmare on Elm Street* movies. I have never heard an Ozzy Osbourne record and have no desire to do so, nor to read a novel by Robert McCammon, Stephen King, or V. C. Andrews. Do you see what I'm getting at, Sam?"

"I suppose. You're saying it wouldn't be fair to . . ." He needed a word, groped for it, and found it. ". . . to usurp the children's tastes."

She smiled radiantly—everything but the eyes, which seemed to have nickels in them again.

"That's *part* of it, but that's not *all* of it. The posters in the Children's Library—both the nice, uncontroversial ones and the ones which put you off—came to us from the Iowa Library Association. The ILA is a member of the Midwest Library Association, and that is, in turn, a member of The National Library Association, which gets the majority of its funding from tax money. From John Q. Public—which is to say from me. And you."

Sam shifted from one foot to the other. He didn't want to spend the afternoon listening to a lecture on How Your Library Works for You, but hadn't he invited it? He supposed so. The only thing he was absolutely sure of was that he was liking Ardelia Lortz less and less all the time.

"The Iowa Library Association sends us a sheet every other month, with reproductions of about forty posters," Ms. Lortz continued relentlessly. "We can pick any five free; extras cost three dollars each. I see you're getting restless, Sam, but you *do* deserve an explanation, and we are finally reaching the nub of the matter."

"Me? I'm not restless," Sam said restlessly.

She smiled at him, revealing teeth too even to be anything but dentures. "We have a Children's Library Committee," she said. "Who is on it? Why, children, of course! Nine of them. Four high-school students, three middle-school students, and two grammar-school students. Each child has to have an overall B average in his schoolwork to qualify. They pick some of the new books we order, they picked the new drapes and tables when we redecorated last fall . . . and, of course, they pick the posters. That is, as one of our younger Committeemen once put it, 'the funnest part.' *Now* do you understand?"

"Yes," Sam said. "The kids picked out Little Red Riding Hood, and Simple Simon, and the Library Policeman. They like them because they're scary."

"Correct!" she beamed.

Suddenly he'd had enough. It was something about the Library. Not the posters, not the librarian, exactly, but the Library itself. Suddenly the Library was like an aggravating, infuriating splinter jammed deep in one buttock. Whatever it was, it was . . . *enough.*

"Ms. Lortz, do you keep a videotape of *A Nightmare on Elm Street, Part 5,* in the Children's Library? Or a selection of albums by Guns n' Roses and Ozzy Osbourne?"

"Sam, you miss the *point,*" she began patiently.

"What about *Peyton Place?* Do you keep a copy of that in the Children's Library just because some of the kids have read it?"

Even as he was speaking, he thought, *Does ANYBODY still read that old thing?*

"No," she said, and he saw that an ill-tempered flush was rising in her cheeks. This was not a woman who was used to having her judgments called into question. "But we *do* keep stories about housebreaking, parental abuse, and burglary. I am speaking, of course, of 'Goldilocks and the Three Bears,' 'Hansel and Gretel,' and 'Jack and the Beanstalk.' I expected a man such as yourself to be a little more understanding, Sam."

A man you helped out in a pinch is what you mean, Sam thought, *but what the hell, lady—isn't that what the town pays you to do?*

Then he got hold of himself. He didn't know exactly what she meant by "a man such as himself," wasn't sure he *wanted* to know, but he did understand that this discussion was on the edge of getting out of hand—of becoming an argument. He had come in here to find a little tenderizer to sprinkle over his speech, not to get in a hassle about the Children's Library with the head librarian.

"I apologize if I've said anything to offend you," he said, "and I really ought to be going."

"Yes," she said. "I think you ought." *Your apology is not accepted,* her eyes telegraphed. *It is not accepted at all.*

"I suppose," he said, "that I'm a little nervous about my speaking debut. And I was up late last night working on this." He smiled his old good-natured Sam Peebles smile and hoisted the briefcase.

She stood down—a little—but her eyes were still snapping. "That's understandable. We are here to serve, and, of course, we're always interested in constructive criticism from the taxpayers." She accented the word *constructive* ever so slightly, to let him know, he supposed, that *his* had been anything but.

Now that it was over, he had an urge—almost a need—to make it *all* over, to smooth it down like the coverlet on a well-made bed. And this was also part of the businessman's habit, he supposed . . . or the businessman's protective coloration. An odd thought occurred to him—that what he should really talk about tonight was his encounter with Ardelia Lortz. It said more about the small-town heart and spirit than his whole written speech. Not all of it was flattering, but it surely wasn't dry. And it would offer a sound rarely heard during Friday-night Rotary speeches: the unmistakable ring of truth.

"Well, we got a little feisty there for a second or two," he heard himself saying, and saw his hand go out. "I expect I overstepped my bounds. I hope there are no hard feelings."

She touched his hand. It was a brief, token touch. Cool, smooth flesh. Unpleasant, somehow. Like shaking hands with an umbrella stand. "None at all," she said, but her eyes continued to tell a different story.

"Well then . . . I'll be getting along."

"Yes. Remember—one week on those, Sam." She lifted a finger. Pointed a well-manicured nail at the books he was holding. And smiled. Sam found something extremely disturbing about that smile, but he could not for the life of him have said exactly what it was. "I wouldn't want to have to send the Library Cop after you."

"No," Sam agreed. "I wouldn't want that, either."

"That's right," said Ardelia Lortz, still smiling. "You wouldn't."

5

Halfway down the walk, the face of that screaming child

(*Simple Simon, the kids call him Simple Simon I think that's very healthy, don't you*)

recurred to him, and with it came a thought—one simple enough and practical enough to stop him in his tracks. It was this: given a chance to pick such a poster, a jury of kids might very well do so . . . but would *any* Library Association, whether from Iowa, the Midwest, or the country as a whole, actually send one out?

Sam Peebles thought of the pleading hands plastered against the obdurate, imprisoning glass, the screaming, agonized mouth, and suddenly found that more than difficult to believe. He found it *impossible* to believe.

And *Peyton Place.* What about that? He guessed that most of the *adults* who used the Library had forgotten about it. Did he really believe that some of their children—the ones young enough to use the Children's Library—had rediscovered that old relic?

I don't believe that one, either.

He had no wish to incur a second dose of Ardelia Lortz's anger—the first had been enough, and he'd had a feeling her dial hadn't been turned up to anything near full volume—but these thoughts were strong enough to cause him to turn around.

She was gone.

The library doors stood shut, a vertical slot of mouth in that brooding granite face.

Sam stood where he was a moment longer, then hurried down to where his car was parked at the curb.

CHAPTER THREE

SAM'S SPEECH

1

It was a rousing success.

He began with his own adaptations of two anecdotes from the "Easing Them In" section of *The Speaker's Companion*—one was about a farmer who tried to wholesale his own produce and the other was about selling frozen dinners to Eskimos—and used a third in the middle (which really *was* pretty arid). He found another good one in the subsection titled "Finishing Them Off," started to pencil it in, then remembered Ardelia Lortz and *Best Loved Poems of the American People. You're apt to find your listeners remember a well-chosen verse even if they forget everything else,* she had said, and Sam found a good short poem in the "Inspiration" section, just as she had told him he might.

He looked down on the upturned faces of his fellow Rotarians and said: "I've tried to give you some of the reasons why I live and work in a small town like Junction City, and I hope they make at least some sense. If they don't, I'm in a lot of trouble."

A rumble of good-natured laughter (and a whiff of mixed Scotch and bourbon) greeted this.

Sam was sweating freely, but he actually felt pretty good, and he had begun to believe he was going to get out of this unscathed. The microphone had produced feedback whine only once, no one had walked out, no one had thrown food, and there had only been a few catcalls—good-natured ones, at that.

"I think a poet named Spencer Michael Free summed up the things I've been trying to say better than I ever could. You see, almost everything we have to sell in our small-town businesses can be sold cheaper in big-city shopping centers and suburban malls. Those places like to boast that you can get just about all the goods and services you'd ever need right there, and park for free in the bargain. And I guess they're almost right. But there is still one thing the small-town business has to offer that the malls and shopping centers don't, and that's the thing Mr. Free talks about in his poem. It isn't a very long one, but it says a lot. It goes like this.

> " 'Tis the human touch in this world that counts,
>   The touch of your hand and mine,
> Which means far more to the fainting heart
>   Than shelter and bread and wine;
> For shelter is gone when the night is o'er,
>   And bread lasts only a day,
> But the touch of the hand and the sound of a voice
>   Sing on in the soul alway."

Sam looked up at them from his text, and for the second time that day was surprised to find that he meant every word he had just said. He found that his heart was suddenly full of happiness and simple gratitude. It was good just to find out you still *had* a heart, that the ordinary routine of ordinary days hadn't worn it away, but it was even better to find it could still speak through your mouth.

"We small-town businessmen and businesswomen offer that human touch. On the one hand, it isn't much . . . but on the other, it's just about everything. I know that it keeps me coming back for more. I want to wish our originally scheduled speaker, The Amazing Joe, a speedy recovery; I want to thank Craig Jones for asking me to sub for him; and I want to thank all of you for listening so patiently to my boring little talk. So . . . thanks very much."

The applause started even before he finished his last sentence; it swelled while he gathered up the few pages of text which Naomi had typed and which he had spent the afternoon amending; it rose to a crescendo as he sat down, bemused by the reaction.

Well, it's just the booze, he told himself. *They would have applauded you if you'd told them about how you managed to quit smoking after you found Jesus at a Tupperware party.*

Then they started to rise to their feet and he thought he must have spoken too long if they were *that* anxious to get out. But they went on applauding, and then he saw Craig Jones was flapping his hands at him. After a moment, Sam understood. Craig wanted him to stand up and take a bow.

He twirled a forefinger around his ear: *You're nuts!*

Craig shook his head emphatically and began elevating his hands so energetically that he looked like a revival preacher encouraging the faithful to sing louder.

So Sam stood up and was amazed when they actually *cheered* him.

After a few moments, Craig approached the lectern. The cheers at last died down when he tapped the microphone a few times, producing a sound like a giant fist wrapped in cotton knocking on a coffin.

"I think we'll all agree," he said, "that Sam's speech more than made up for the price of the rubber chicken."

This brought another hearty burst of applause.

Craig turned toward Sam and said, "If I'd known you had *that* in you, Sammy, I would have booked you in the first place!"

This produced more clapping and whistling. Before it died out,

Craig Jones had seized Sam's hand and began pumping it briskly up and down.

"That was great!" Craig said. "Where'd you copy it from, Sam?"

"I didn't," Sam said. His cheeks felt warm, and although he'd only had one gin and tonic—a weak one—before getting up to speak, he felt a little drunk. "It's mine. I got a couple of books from the Library, and they helped."

Other Rotarians were crowding around now; Sam's hand was shaken again and again. He started to feel like the town pump during a summer drought.

"Great!" someone shouted in his ear. Sam turned toward the voice and saw it belonged to Frank Stephens, who had filled in when the trucking-union official was indicted for malfeasance. "We shoulda had it on tape, we coulda sold it to the goddam JayCees! Damn, that was a good talk, Sam!"

"Oughtta take it on the road!" Rudy Pearlman said. His round face was red and sweating. "I darn near cried! Honest to God! Where'd you find that pome?"

"At the Library," Sam said. He still felt dazed . . . but his relief at having actually finished in one piece was being supplanted by a kind of cautious delight. He thought he would have to give Naomi a bonus. "It was in a book called—"

But before he could tell Rudy what the book had been called, Bruce Engalls had grasped him by the elbow and was guiding him toward the bar. "Best damned speech I've heard at this foolish club in two years!" Bruce was exclaiming. "Maybe five! Who needs a goddam acrobat, anyway? Let me buy you a drink, Sam. Hell, let me buy you two!"

2

Before he was able to get away, Sam consumed a total of six drinks, all of them free, and ended his triumphant evening by puking on his own WELCOME mat shortly after Craig Jones let him out in front of his house on Kelton Avenue. When his stomach vapor-locked, Sam had been trying to get his housekey in the lock of his front door—it was a job, because there appeared to be three locks and four keys—and there was just no time to get rid of it in the bushes at the side of the stoop. So when he finally succeeded in getting the door open, he simply picked the WELCOME mat up (carefully, holding it by the sides so the gunk would pool in the middle) and tossed *it* over the side.

He got a cup of coffee to stay down, but the phone rang twice while he was drinking it. More congratulations. The second call was from Elmer Baskin, who hadn't even *been* there. He felt a little like Judy Garland in *A Star Is Born,* but it was hard to enjoy the feeling while his stomach was still treading water and his head was beginning to punish him for his overindulgence.

Sam put on the answering machine in the living room to field any further calls, then went upstairs to his bedroom, unplugged the phone by the bed, took two aspirin, stripped, and lay down.

Consciousness began to fade fast—he was tired as well as bombed—but before sleep took him, he had time to think: *I owe most of it to Naomi . . . and to that unpleasant woman at the Library. Horst. Borscht. Whatever her name was. Maybe I ought to give her a bonus, too.*

He heard the telephone start to ring downstairs, and then the answering machine cut in.

Good boy, Sam thought sleepily. *Do your duty—I mean, after all, isn't that what I pay you to do?*

Then he was in blackness, and knew no more until ten o'clock Saturday morning.

3

He returned to the land of the living with a sour stomach and a slight headache, but it could have been a lot worse. He was sorry about the WELCOME mat, but glad he'd offloaded at least some of the booze before it could swell his head any worse than it already was. He stood in the shower for ten minutes, making only token washing motions, then dried off, dressed, and went downstairs with a towel draped over his head. The red message light on the telephone answering machine was blinking. The tape only rewound a short way when he pushed the PLAY MESSAGES button; apparently the call he'd heard just as he was drifting off had been the last.

Beep! "Hello, Sam." Sam paused in the act of removing the towel, frowning. It was a woman's voice, and he knew it. Whose? "I heard your speech was a great success. I'm so glad for you."

It was the Lortz woman, he realized.

Now how did she get my number? But that was what the telephone book was for, of course . . . and he had written it on his library-card application as well, hadn't he? Yes. For no reason he could rightly tell, a small shiver shook its way up his back.

"Be sure to get your borrowed books back by the sixth of April," she continued, and then, archly: "Remember the Library Policeman."

There was the click of the connection being broken. On Sam's answering machine, the ALL MESSAGES PLAYED lamp lit up.

"You're a bit of a bitch, aren't you, lady?" Sam said to the empty house, and then went into the kitchen to make himself some toast.

4

When Naomi came in at ten o'clock on the Friday morning a week after Sam's triumphant debut as an after-dinner speaker, Sam handed her a long white envelope with her name written on the front.

"What's this?" Naomi asked suspiciously, taking off her cloak. It was raining hard outside, a driving, dismal early-spring rain.

"Open it and see."

She did. It was a thank-you card. Taped inside was a portrait of Andrew Jackson.

"Twenty dollars!" She looked at him more suspiciously than ever. "Why?"

"Because you saved my bacon when you sent me to the Library," Sam said. "The speech went over very well, Naomi. I guess it wouldn't be wrong to say I was a big hit. I would have put in fifty, if I'd thought you would take it."

Now she understood, and was clearly pleased, but she tried to give the money back just the same. "I'm really glad it worked, Sam, but I can't take th—"

"Yes you can," he said, "and you will. You'd take a commission if you worked for me as a salesperson, wouldn't you?"

"I don't, though. I could never sell anything. When I was in the Girl Scouts, my mother was the only person who ever bought cookies from me."

"Naomi. My dear girl. No—don't start looking all nervous and cornered. I'm not going to make a pass at you. We went through all of that two years ago."

"We certainly *did*," Naomi agreed, but she still looked nervous and checked to make sure that she had a clear line of retreat to the door, should she need one.

"Do you realize I've sold two houses and written almost two hundred thousand dollars' worth of insurance since that damn speech? Most of it was common group coverage with a high top-off and a low commission rate, true, but it still adds up to the price of a new car. If you don't take that twenty, I'm going to feel like shit."

"Sam, *please!*" she said, looking shocked. Naomi was a dedicated Baptist. She and her mother went to a little church in Proverbia which was almost as ramshackle as the house they lived in. He knew; he had been there once. But he was happy to see that she also looked pleased . . . and a little more relaxed.

In the summer of 1988, Sam had dated Naomi twice. On the second date, he made a pass. It was as well behaved as a pass can be and still remain a pass, but a pass it was. Much good it had done him; Naomi, it turned out, was a good enough pass deflector to play in the Denver Broncos' defensive backfield. It wasn't that she didn't like him, she explained; it was just that she had decided the two of them could never get along "that way." Sam, bewildered, had asked her why not. Naomi only shook her head. *Some things are hard to explain, Sam, but that doesn't make them less true. It could never work. Believe me, it just couldn't.* And that had been all he could get out of her.

"I'm sorry I said the s-word, Naomi," he told her now. He spoke humbly, although he doubted somehow that Naomi was even half as priggish as she liked to sound. "What I mean to say is that if you don't take that twenty, I'll feel like caca-poopie."

She tucked the bill into her purse and then endeavored to look at him with an expression of dignified primness. She almost made it . . . but the corners of her lips quivered slightly.

"There. Satisfied?"

"Short of giving you fifty," he said. "Would you take fifty, Omes?"

"No," she said. "And please don't call me Omes. You know I don't like it."

"I'm sorry."

"Apology accepted. Now why don't we just drop the subject?"

"Okay," Sam said agreeably.

"I heard several people say your speech was good. Craig Jones just *raved* about it. Do you really think that's the reason you've done more business?"

"Does a bear—" Sam began, and then retraced his steps. "Yes. I do. Things work that way sometimes. It's funny, but it's true. The old sales graph has really spiked this week. It'll drop back, of course, but I don't think it'll drop back all the way. If the new folks like the way I do business—and I like to think they will—there'll be a carry-over."

Sam leaned back in his chair, laced his hands together behind his neck, and looked thoughtfully up at the ceiling.

"When Craig Jones called up and put me on the spot, I was ready to shoot him. No joke, Naomi."

"Yes," she said. "You looked like a man coming down with a bad case of poison ivy."

"Did I?" He laughed. "Yeah, I suppose so. It's funny how things work out sometimes—purest luck. If there *is* a God, it makes you wonder sometimes if He tightened all the screws in the big machine before He set it going."

He expected Naomi to scold him for his irreverence (it wouldn't be the first time), but she didn't take the gambit today. Instead she said, "You're luckier than you know, if the books you got at the Library really did help you out. It usually doesn't open until five o'clock on Fridays. I meant to tell you that, but then I forgot."

"Oh?"

"You must have found Mr. Price catching up on his paperwork or something."

"Price?" Sam asked. "Don't you mean Mr. Peckham? The newspaper-reading janitor?"

Naomi shook her head. "The only Peckham I ever heard of around here was old Eddie Peckham, and he died years ago. I'm talking about Mr. *Price*. The *librarian*." She was looking at Sam as though he were the thickest man on earth . . . or at least in Junction City, Iowa. "Tall man? Thin? About fifty?"

"Nope," Sam said. "I got a lady named Lortz. Short, plump, somewhere around the age when women form lasting attachments to bright-green polyester."

A rather strange mix of expressions crossed Naomi's face—

surprise was followed by suspicion; suspicion was followed by a species of faintly exasperated amusement. That particular sequence of expressions almost always indicates the same thing: someone is coming to realize that his or her leg is being shaken vigorously. Under more ordinary circumstances Sam might have wondered about that, but he had done a land-office business all week long, and as a result he had a great deal of his own paperwork to catch up on. Half of his mind had already wandered off to examine it.

"*Oh*," Naomi said and laughed. "Miss *Lortz,* was it? That must have been fun."

"She's peculiar, all right," Sam said.

"You bet," Naomi agreed. "In fact, she's absolutely—"

If she had finished what she had started to say she probably would have startled Sam Peebles a great deal, but luck—as he had just pointed out—plays an absurdly important part in human affairs, and luck now intervened.

The telephone rang.

It was Burt Iverson, the spiritual chief of Junction City's small legal tribe. He wanted to talk about a really *huge* insurance deal— the new medical center, comp-group coverage, still in the planning stages but you know how big this could be, Sam—and by the time Sam got back to Naomi, thoughts of Ms. Lortz had gone entirely out of his mind. He knew how big it could be, all right; it could land him behind the wheel of that Mercedes-Benz after all. And he really didn't like to think just how much of all this good fortune he might be able to trace back to that stupid little speech, if he really wanted to.

Naomi *did* think her leg was being pulled; she knew perfectly well who Ardelia Lortz was, and thought Sam must, too. After all, the woman had been at the center of the nastiest piece of business to occur in Junction City in the last twenty years . . . maybe since World War II, when the Moggins boy had come home from the Pacific all funny in the head and had killed his whole family before sticking the barrel of his service pistol in his right ear and taking care of himself as well. Ira Moggins had done that before Naomi's time; it did not occur to her that *l'affaire Ardelia* had occurred long before Sam had come to Junction City.

At any rate, she had dismissed the whole thing from her mind and was trying to decide between Stouffer's lasagna and something from Lean Cuisine for supper by the time Sam put the telephone down. He dictated letters steadily until twelve o'clock, then asked Naomi if she would like to step down to McKenna's with him for a spot of lunch. Naomi declined, saying she had to get back to her mother, who had Failed Greatly over the course of the winter. No more was said about Ardelia Lortz.

That day.

CHAPTER FOUR

THE MISSING BOOKS

1

Sam wasn't much of a breakfast-eater through the week—a glass of orange juice and an oat-bran muffin did him just fine—but on Saturday mornings (at least on Saturday mornings when he wasn't dealing with a Rotary-inspired hangover) he liked to rise a little late, stroll down to McKenna's on the square, and work his way slowly through an order of steak and eggs while he really *read* the paper instead of just scanning it between appointments.

He followed this routine the next morning, the seventh of April. The previous day's rain was gone, and the sky was a pale, perfect blue—the very image of early spring. Sam took the long way home following his breakfast, pausing to check out whose tulips and crocuses were in good order and whose were a little late. He arrived back at his own house at ten minutes past ten.

The PLAY MESSAGES lamp on his answering machine was lit. He pushed the button, got out a cigarette, and struck a match.

"Hello, Sam," Ardelia Lortz's soft and utterly unmistakable voice said, and the match paused six inches shy of Sam's cigarette. "I'm very disappointed in you. Your books are overdue."

"Ah, *shit!*" Sam exclaimed.

Something had been nagging at him all week long, the way a word you want will use the tip of your tongue for a trampoline, bouncing just out of reach. The books. The goddam *books*. The woman would undoubtedly regard him as exactly the sort of Philistine she wanted him to be—him with his gratuitous judgments of which posters belonged in the Children's Library and which ones didn't. The only real question was whether she had put her tongue-lashing on the answering machine or was saving it until she saw him in person.

He shook out the match and dropped it in the ashtray beside the telephone.

"I explained to you, I believe," she was going on in her soft and just a little too reasonable voice, "that *The Speaker's Companion* and *Best Loved Poems of the American People* are from the Library's Special Reference section, and cannot be kept out for longer than one week. I expected better things of you, Sam. I really did."

Sam, to his great exasperation, found he was standing here in his own house with an unlit cigarette between his lips and a guilty flush climbing up his neck and beginning to overrun his cheeks. Once more he had been deposited firmly back in the fourth grade—this time sitting on a stool facing into the corner with a pointed dunce-cap perched firmly on his head.

Speaking as one who is conferring a great favor, Ardelia Lortz went on: "I have decided to give you an extension, however; you have until Monday afternoon to return your borrowed books. Please help me avoid any unpleasantness." There was a pause. "Remember the Library Policeman, Sam."

"That one's getting old, Ardelia-baby," Sam muttered, but he wasn't even speaking to the recording. She had hung up after mentioning the Library Policeman, and the machine switched itself quietly off.

2

Sam used a fresh match to light his smoke. He was still exhaling the first drag when a course of action popped into his mind. It might be a trifle cowardly, but it would close his accounts with Ms. Lortz for good. And it also had a certain rough justice to it.

He had given Naomi *her* just reward, and he would do the same for Ardelia. He sat down at the desk in his study, where he had composed the famous speech, and drew his note-pad to him. Below the heading (*From the Desk of SAMUEL PEEBLES*), he scrawled the following note:

Dear Ms. Lortz,

I apologize for being late returning your books. This is a sincere apology, because the books were extremely helpful in preparing my speech. Please accept this money in payment of the fine on tardy books. I want you to keep the rest as a token of my thanks.

Sincerely yours

Sam Peebles

Sam Peebles

Sam read the note over while he fished a paper clip out of his desk drawer. He considered changing ". . . returning your books" to ". . . returning the library's books" and decided to leave it as it was. Ardelia Lortz had impressed him very much as the sort of woman who subscribed to the philosophy of *l'état c'est moi,* even if *l'état* in this case was just the local library.

He removed a twenty-dollar bill from his wallet and used the clip to attach it to the note. He hesitated a moment longer, drumming his fingers restlessly on the edge of the desk.

She's going to look at this as a bribe. She'll probably be offended and mad as hell.

That might be true, but Sam didn't care. He knew what was behind the Lortz woman's arch little call this morning—behind *both* arch little calls, probably. He had pulled her chain a little too hard about the posters in the Children's Library, and she was getting back at him—or trying to. But this wasn't the fourth grade, he wasn't a scurrying, terrified little kid (not anymore, at least), and he wasn't going to be intimidated. Not by the ill-tempered sign in the library foyer, nor by the librarian's you're-one-whole-day-late-you-bad-boy-you nagging.

"Fuck it!" he said out loud. "If you don't want the goddam money, stick it in the Library Defense Fund, or something."

He laid the note with the twenty paper-clipped to it on the desk. He had no intention of presenting it in person so she could get shirty on him. He would bind the two volumes together with a couple of rubber bands after laying the note and the money into one of them so it stuck out. Then he would simply dump the whole shebang into the book-drop. He had spent six years in Junction

City without making Ardelia Lortz's acquaintance; with any luck, it would be six years before he saw her again.

Now all he had to do was find the books.

They were not on his study desk, that was for sure. Sam went out into the dining room and looked on the table. It was where he usually stacked things which needed to be returned. There were two VHS tapes ready to go back to Bruce's Video Stop, an envelope with *Paperboy* written across the front, two folders with insurance policies in them . . . but no *Speaker's Companion.* No *Best Loved Poems of the American People,* either.

"Crap," Sam said, and scratched his head. "Where the hell—?"

He went out into the kitchen. Nothing on the kitchen table but the morning paper; he'd put it down there when he came in. He tossed it absently in the cardboard carton by the woodstove as he checked the counter. Nothing on the counter but the box from which he had taken last night's frozen dinner.

He went slowly upstairs to check the rooms on the second story, but he was already starting to get a very bad feeling.

3

By three o'clock that afternoon, the bad feeling was a lot worse. Sam Peebles was, in fact, fuming. After going through the house twice from top to bottom (on the second pass he even checked the cellar), he had gone down to the office, even though he was pretty sure he had brought the two books home with him when he left work late last Monday afternoon. Sure enough, he had found nothing there. And here he was, most of a beautiful spring Saturday shot in a fruitless search for two library books, no further ahead.

He kept thinking of her arch tone—*remember the Library Police-man, Sam*—and how happy she would feel if she knew just how far under his skin she had gotten. If there really *were* Library Police, Sam had no doubt at all that the woman would be happy to sic one on him. The more he thought about it, the madder he got.

He went back into his study. His note to Ardelia Lortz, with the twenty attached, stared at him blandly from the desk.

"Balls!" he cried, and was almost off on another whirlwind search of the house before he caught himself and stopped. That would accomplish nothing.

Suddenly he heard the voice of his long-dead mother. It was soft and sweetly reasonable. *When you can't find a thing, Samuel, tearing around and looking for it usually does no good. Sit down and think things over instead. Use your head and save your feet.*

It had been good advice when he was ten; he guessed it was just as good now that he was forty. Sam sat down behind his desk, closed his eyes, and set out to trace the progress of those goddamned library books from the moment Ms. Lortz had handed them to him until . . . whenever.

From the Library he had taken them back to the office, stopping at Sam's House of Pizza on the way for a pepperoni-and-double-mushroom pie, which he had eaten at his desk while he looked through *The Speaker's Companion* for two things: good jokes and how to use them. He remembered how careful he'd been not to get even the smallest dollop of pizza sauce on the book—which was sort of ironic, considering the fact that he couldn't find either of them now.

He had spent most of the afternoon on the speech, working in the jokes, then rewriting the whole last part so the poem would fit better. When he went home late Friday afternoon, he'd taken the finished speech but not the books. He was sure of that. Craig Jones had picked him up when it was time for the Rotary Club dinner, and Craig had dropped him off later on—just in time for Sam to baptize the WELCOME mat.

Saturday morning had been spent nursing his minor but annoying hangover; for the rest of the weekend he had just stayed around the house, reading, watching TV, and—let's face it, gang—basking in his triumph. He hadn't gone near the office all weekend. He was sure of it.

Okay, he thought. *Here comes the hard part. Now concentrate.* But he didn't need to concentrate all that hard after all, he discovered.

He had started out of the office around quarter to five on Monday afternoon, and then the phone had rung, calling him back. It had been Stu Youngman, wanting him to write a large homeowner's policy. That had been the start of this week's shower of bucks. While he was talking with Stu, his eye had happened on the two library books, still sitting on the corner of his desk. When he left the second time, he'd had his briefcase in one hand and the books in the other. He was positive of that much.

He had intended to return them to the Library that evening, but then Frank Stephens had called, wanting him to come out to dinner with him and his wife and their niece, who was visiting from Omaha (when you were a bachelor in a small town, Sam had discovered, even your casual acquaintances became relentless matchmakers). They had gone to Brady's Ribs, had returned late—around eleven, late for a weeknight—and by the time he got home again, he had forgotten all about the library books.

After that, he lost sight of them completely. He hadn't thought of returning them—his unexpectedly brisk business had taken up most of his thinking time—until the Lortz woman's call.

Okay—I probably haven't moved them since then. They must be right where I left them when I got home late Monday afternoon.

For a moment he felt a burst of hope—maybe they were still in the car! Then, just as he was getting up to check, he remembered how he'd shifted his briefcase to the hand holding the books when he'd arrived home on Monday. He'd done that so he could get his housekey out of his right front pocket. He hadn't left them in the car at all.

So what did you do when you got in?

He saw himself unlocking the kitchen door, stepping in, putting his briefcase on a kitchen chair, turning with the books in his hand—

"Oh *no*," Sam muttered. The bad feeling returned in a rush.

There was a fair-sized cardboard carton sitting on the shelf by his little kitchen woodstove, the kind of carton you could pick up at the liquor store. It had been there for a couple of years now. People sometimes packed their smaller belongings into such cartons when they were moving house, but the cartons also made great hold-alls. Sam used the one by the stove for newspaper storage. He put each day's paper into the box after he had finished reading it; he had tossed today's paper in only a short time before. And, once every month or so—

"Dirty Dave!" Sam muttered.

He got up from behind his desk and hurried into the kitchen.

4

The box, with Johnnie Walker's monocled ain't-I-hip image on the side, was almost empty. Sam thumbed through the thin sheaf of newspapers, knowing he would find nothing but looking anyway, the way people do when they are so exasperated they half-believe that just *wanting* a thing badly enough will make it *be* there. He found the Saturday *Gazette*—the one he had so recently disposed of—and the Friday paper. No books between or beneath them, of course. Sam stood there for a moment, thinking black thoughts, then went to the telephone to call Mary Vasser, who cleaned house for him every Thursday morning.

"Hello?" a faintly worried voice answered.

"Hi, Mary. This is Sam Peebles."

"Sam?" The worry deepened. "Is something wrong?"

Yes! By Monday afternoon the bitch who runs the local Library is going to be after me! Probably with a cross and a number of very long nails!

But of course he couldn't say anything like that, not to Mary; she was one of those unfortunate human beings who have been born under a bad sign and live in their own dark cloud of doomish premonition. The Mary Vassers of the world believe that there are a great many large black safes dangling three stories above a great many sidewalks, held by fraying cables, waiting for a destiny to carry the doom-fated into the drop zone. If not a safe, then a drunk driver; if not a drunk driver, a tidal wave (in Iowa? yes, in Iowa); if not a tidal wave, a meteorite. Mary Vasser was one of those afflicted folks who *always* want to know if something is wrong when you call them on the phone.

"Nothing," Sam said. "Nothing wrong at all. I just wondered if you saw Dave on Thursday." The question wasn't much more than a formality; the papers, after all, were gone, and Dirty Dave was the only Newspaper Fairy in Junction City.

"Yes," Mary agreed. Sam's hearty assurance that nothing was wrong seemed to have put her wind up even higher. Now barely concealed terror positively vibrated in her voice. "He came to get the papers. Was I wrong to let him? He's been coming for *years,* and I thought—"

"Not at all," Sam said with insane cheerfulness. "I just saw they were gone and thought I'd check that—"

"You never checked *before.*" Her voice caught. "Is he all right? Has something happened to Dave?"

"No," Sam said. "I mean, I don't know. I just—" An idea flashed into his mind. "The coupons!" he cried wildly. "I forgot to clip the coupons on Thursday, so—"

"*Oh!*" she said. "You can have mine, if you want."

"No, I couldn't do th—"

"I'll bring them next Thursday," she overrode him. "I have thousands." *So many I'll never get a chance to use them all,* her voice implied. *After all, somewhere out there a safe is waiting for me to walk under it, or a tree is waiting to fall over in a windstorm and squash me, or in some North Dakota motel a hair-dryer is waiting to fall off the shelf and into the bathtub. I'm living on borrowed time, so what do I need a bunch of fucking Folger's Crystals coupons for?*

"All right," Sam said. "That would be great. Thanks, Mary, you're a peach."

"And you're sure nothing else is wrong?"

"Not a thing," Sam replied, speaking more heartily than ever. To himself he sounded like a lunatic top-sergeant urging his few remaining men to mount a final fruitless frontal assault on a fortified machine-gun nest. *Come on, men, I think they might be asleep!*

"All right," Mary said doubtfully, and Sam was finally permitted to escape.

He sat down heavily in one of the kitchen chairs and regarded the almost empty Johnnie Walker box with a bitter eye. Dirty Dave had come to collect the newspapers, as he did during the first week of every month, but this time he had unknowingly taken along a little bonus: *The Speaker's Companion* and *Best Loved Poems of the American People.* And Sam had a very good idea of what they were now.

Pulp. Recycled pulp.

Dirty Dave was one of Junction City's functioning alcoholics. Unable to hold down a steady job, he eked out a living on the discards of others, and in that way he was a fairly useful citizen. He collected returnable bottles, and, like twelve-year-old Keith Jordan, he had a paper route. The only difference was that Keith delivered the Junction City *Gazette* every day, and Dirty Dave Duncan collected it—from Sam and God knew how many other homeowners in the Kelton Avenue section of town—once a month. Sam had seen him many times, trundling his shopping cart full of green plastic garbage bags across town toward the Recycling Center which stood between the old train depot and the small homeless shelter where Dirty Dave and a dozen or so of his *compadres* spent most of their nights.

He sat where he was for a moment longer, drumming his fingers on the kitchen table, then got up, pulled on a jacket, and went out to the car.

CHAPTER FIVE

ANGLE STREET (I)

1

The intentions of the sign-maker had undoubtedly been the best, but his spelling had been poor. The sign was nailed to one of the porch uprights of the old house by the railroad tracks, and it read:

ANGLE STREET

Since there were no angles on Railroad Avenue that Sam could see—like most Iowa streets and roads, it was as straight as a string—he reckoned the sign-maker had meant *Angel* Street. Well, so what? Sam thought that, while the road of good intentions might end in hell, the people who tried to fill the potholes along the way deserved at least some credit.

Angle Street was a big building which, Sam guessed, had housed railroad-company offices back in the days when Junction City really *had* been a railway junction point. Now there were just two sets of working tracks, both going east-west. All the others were rusty and overgrown with weeds. Most of the cross-ties were gone, appropriated for fires by the same homeless people Angle Street was here to serve.

Sam arrived at quarter to five. The sun cast a mournful, failing light over the empty fields which took over here at the edge of town. A seemingly endless freight was rumbling by behind the few buildings which stood out here. A breeze had sprung up, and as he stopped his car and got out, he could hear the rusty squeak of the old JUNCTION CITY sign swinging back and forth above the deserted platform where people had once boarded passenger trains for St. Louis and Chicago—even the old Sunnyland Express, which

had made its only Iowa stop in Junction City on its way west to the
fabulous kingdoms of Las Vegas and Los Angeles.

The homeless shelter had once been white; now it was a paintless
gray. The curtains in the windows were clean but tired and limp.
Weeds were trying to grow in the cindery yard. Sam thought they
might gain a foothold by June, but right now they were making a
bad job of it. A rusty barrel had been placed by the splintery steps
leading up to the porch. Opposite the Angle Street sign, nailed to
another porch support, was this message:

NO DRINKING ALOWED AT THIS SHELTER!
IF YOU HAVE A BOTTLE,
IT MUST GO HERE BEFORE YOU ENTER!

His luck was in. Although Saturday night had almost arrived and
the ginmills and beerjoints of Junction City awaited, Dirty Dave
was here, and he was sober. He was, in fact, sitting on the porch
with two other winos. They were engaged in making posters on
large rectangles of white cardboard, and enjoying varying degrees
of success. The fellow sitting on the floor at the far end of the porch
was holding his right wrist with his left hand in an effort to offset
a bad case of the shakes. The one in the middle worked with his
tongue peeking from the corner of his mouth, and looked like a
very old nursery child trying his level best to draw a tree which
would earn him a gold star to show Mommy. Dirty Dave, sitting
in a splintered rocking chair near the porch steps, was easily in the
best shape, but all three of them looked folded, stapled, and mu-
tilated.

"Hello, Dave," Sam said, mounting the steps.

Dave looked up, squinted, and then offered a tentative smile.
All of his remaining teeth were in front. The smile revealed all five
of them.

"Mr. Peebles?"

"Yes," he said. "How you doing, Dave?"

"Oh, purty fair, I guess. Purty fair." He looked around. "Say,
you guys! Say hello to Mr. Peebles! He's a lawyer!"

The fellow with the tip of his tongue sticking out looked up,
nodded briefly, and went back to his poster. A long runner of snot
depended from his left nostril.

"Actually," Sam said, "real estate's my game, Dave. Real estate and insur—"

"You got me my Slim Jim?" the man with the shakes asked abruptly. He did not look up at all, but his frown of concentration deepened. Sam could see his poster from where he stood; it was covered with long orange squiggles which vaguely resembled words.

"Pardon?" Sam asked.

"That's Lukey," Dave said in a low voice. "He ain't havin one of his better days, Mr. Peebles."

"Got me my Slim Jim, got me my Slim Jim, got me my Slim Fuckin Slim Jim?" Lukey chanted without looking up.

"Uh, I'm sorry—" Sam began.

"He ain't got no Slim Jims!" Dirty Dave yelled. "Shut up and do your poster, Lukey! Sarah wants em by six! She's comin out special!"

"I'll *get* me a fuckin Slim Jim," Lukey said in a low intense voice. "If I don't, I guess I'll eat rat-turds."

"Don't mind him, Mr. Peebles," Dave said. "What's up?"

"Well, I was just wondering if you might have found a couple of books when you picked up the newspapers last Thursday. I've misplaced them, and I thought I'd check. They're overdue at the Library."

"You got a quarter?" the man with the tip of his tongue sticking out asked abruptly. "What's the word? Thunderbird!"

Sam reached automatically into his pocket. Dave reached out and touched his wrist, almost apologetically.

"Don't give him any money, Mr. Peebles," he said. "That's Rudolph. He don't need no Thunderbird. Him and the Bird don't agree no more. He just needs a night's sleep."

"I'm sorry," Sam said. "I'm tapped, Rudolph."

"Yeah, you and everybody else," Rudolph said. As he went back to his poster he muttered: "What's the price? Fifty twice."

"I didn't see any books," Dirty Dave said. "I'm sorry. I just got the papers, like usual. Missus V. was there, and she can tell you. I didn't do nothing wrong." But his rheumy, unhappy eyes said he did not expect Sam to believe this. Unlike Mary, Dirty Dave Duncan did not live in a world where doom lay just up the road or around the corner; his surrounded him. He lived in it with what little dignity he could muster.

"I believe you." Sam laid a hand on Dave's shoulder.

"I just dumped your box of papers into one of my bags, like always," Dave said.

"If I had a thousand Slim Jims, I'd eat them all," Lukey said abruptly. "I would snark those suckers right *down*! That's *chow*! That's *chow*! That's *chow*-de-*dow*!"

"I believe you," Sam repeated, and patted Dave's horribly bony shoulder. He found himself wondering, God help him, if Dave had fleas. On the heels of this uncharitable thought came another: he wondered if any of the other Rotarians, those hale and hearty fellows with whom he had made such a hit a week ago, had been down to this end of town lately. He wondered if they even knew about Angle Street. And he wondered if Spencer Michael Free had been thinking about such men as Lukey and Rudolph and Dirty Dave when he wrote that it was the human touch in this world that counted—the touch of your hand and mine. Sam felt a sudden burst of shame at the recollection of his speech, so full of innocent boosterism and approval for the simple pleasures of small-town life.

"That's good," Dave said. "Then I can come back next month?"

"Sure. You took the papers to the Recycling Center, right?"

"Uh-huh." Dirty Dave pointed with a finger which ended in a yellow, ragged nail. "Right over there. But they're closed."

Sam nodded. "What are you doing?" he asked.

"Aw, just passin the time," Dave said, and turned the poster around so Sam could see it.

It showed a picture of a smiling woman holding a platter of fried chicken, and the first thing that struck Sam was that it was good—really good. Wino or not, Dirty Dave had a natural touch. Above the picture, the following was neatly printed:

CHICKEN DINNER AT THE 1ST METHODIST CHURCH
TO BENEFIT "ANGEL STREET" HOMELESS SHELTER
SUNDAY APRIL 15TH
6:00 TO 8:00 P.M.
COME ONE COME ALL

"It's before the AA meeting," Dave said, "but you can't put nothing on the poster about AA. That's because it's sort of secret."

"I know," Sam said. He paused, then asked: "Do you go to AA? You don't have to answer if you don't want to. I know it's really none of my business."

"I go," Dave said, "but it's hard, Mr. Peebles. I got more white chips than Carter has got liver pills. I'm good for a month, sometimes two, and once I went sober almost a whole year. But it's hard." He shook his head. "Some people can't never get with the program, they say. I must be one of those. But I keep tryin.'"

Sam's eyes were drawn back to the woman with her platter of chicken. The picture was too detailed to be a cartoon or a sketch, but it wasn't a painting, either. It was clear that Dirty Dave had done it in a hurry, but he had caught a kindness about the eyes and a faint slant of humor, like one last sunbeam at the close of the day, in the mouth. And the oddest thing was that the woman looked familiar to Sam.

"Is that a real person?" he asked Dave.

Dave's smile widened. He nodded. "That's Sarah. She's a great gal, Mr. Peebles. This place would have closed down five years ago except for her. She finds people to give money just when it seems the taxes will be too much or we won't be able to fix the place up enough to satisfy the building inspectors when they come. She calls the people who give the money angels, but *she's* the angel. We named the place for Sarah. Of course, Tommy St. John spelled part of it wrong when he made the sign, but he meant well." Dirty Dave fell silent for a moment, looking at his poster. Without looking up, he added: "Tommy's dead now, a course. Died this last winter. His liver busted."

"Oh," Sam said, and then he added lamely, "I'm sorry."

"Don't be. He's well out of it."

"Chow-de-dow!" Lukey exclaimed, getting up. "Chow-de-dow! Ain't that some fuckin chow-de-dow!" He brought his poster over to Dave. Below the orange squiggles he had drawn a monster woman whose legs ended in sharkfins Sam thought were meant to be shoes. Balanced on one hand was a misshapen plate which appeared to be loaded with blue snakes. Clutched in the other was a cylindrical brown object.

Dave took the poster from Lukey and examined it. "This is *good*, Lukey."

Lukey's lips peeled back in a gleeful smile. He pointed at the brown thing. "Look, Dave! She got her a Slim Fuckin Slim Jim!"

"She sure does. Purty good. Go on inside and turn on the TV, if you want. *Star Trek's* on right away. How you doin, Dolph?"

"I draw better when I'm stewed," Rudolph said, and gave his

poster to Dave. On it was a gigantic chicken leg with stick men and women standing around and looking up at it. "It's the fantasy approach," Rudolph said to Sam. He spoke with some truculence.

"I like it," Sam said. He did, actually. Rudolph's poster reminded him of a *New Yorker* cartoon, one of the ones he sometimes couldn't understand because they were so surreal.

"Good." Rudolph studied him closely. "You sure you ain't got a quarter?"

"No," Sam said.

Rudolph nodded. "In a way, that's good," he said. "But in another way, it really shits the bed." He followed Lukey inside, and soon the *Star Trek* theme drifted out through the open door. William Shatner told the winos and burnouts of Angle Street that their mission was to boldly go where no man had gone before. Sam guessed that several members of this audience were already there.

"Nobody much comes to the dinners but us guys and some of the AA's from town," Dave said, "but it gives us something to do. Lukey hardly talks at all anymore, 'less he's drawing."

"You're awfully good," Sam told him. "You really are, Dave. Why don't you—" He stopped.

"Why don't I what, Mr. Peebles?" Dave asked gently. "Why don't I use my right hand to turn a buck? The same reason I don't get myself a regular job. The day got late while I was doin other things."

Sam couldn't think of a thing to say.

"I had a shot at it, though. Do you know I went to the Lorillard School in Des Moines on full scholarship? The best art school in the Midwest. I flunked out my first semester. Booze. It don't matter. Do you want to come in and have a cup of coffee, Mr. Peebles? Wait around? You could meet Sarah."

"No, I better get back. I've got an errand to run."

He did, too.

"All right. Are you sure you're not mad at me?"

"Not a bit."

Dave stood up. "I guess I'll go in awhile, then," he said. "It was a beautiful day, but it's gettin nippy now. You have a nice night, Mr. Peebles."

"Okay," Sam said, although he doubted that he was going to enjoy himself very much *this* Saturday evening. But his mother had had another saying: the way to make the best of bad medicine is to swallow it just as fast as you can. And that was what he intended to do.

He walked back down the steps of Angle Street, and Dirty Dave Duncan went on inside.

2

Sam got almost all the way back to his car, then detoured in the direction of the Recycling Center. He walked across the weedy, cindery ground slowly, watching the long freight disappear in the direction of Camden and Omaha. The red lamps on the caboose twinkled like dying stars. Freight trains always made him feel lonely for some reason, and now, following his conversation with Dirty Dave, he felt lonelier than ever. On the few occasions when he had met Dave while Dave was collecting his papers, he had seemed a jolly, almost clownish man. Tonight Sam thought he had seen behind the make-up, and what he had seen made him feel unhappy and helpless. Dave was a lost man, calm but totally lost, using what was clearly a talent of some size to make posters for a church supper.

One approached the Recycling Center through zones of litter— first the yellowing ad supplements which had escaped old copies of the *Gazette*, then the torn plastic garbage bags, finally an asteroid belt of busted bottles and squashed cans. The shades of the small clapboard building were drawn. The sign hanging in the door simply read CLOSED.

Sam lit a cigarette and started back to his car. He had gone only half a dozen steps when he saw something familiar lying on the ground. He picked it up. It was the bookjacket of *Best Loved Poems of the American People*. The words PROPERTY OF THE JUNCTION CITY PUBLIC LIBRARY were stamped across it.

So now he knew for sure. He had set the books on top of the papers in the Johnnie Walker box and then forgotten them. He had put other papers—Tuesday's, Wednesday's, and Thursday's— on top of the books. Then Dirty Dave had come along late Thursday morning and had dumped the whole shebang into his plastic collection bag. The bag had gone into his shopping-cart, the shopping-cart had come here, and this was all that was left—a bookjacket with a muddy sneaker-print tattooed on it.

Sam let the bookjacket flutter out of his fingers and walked slowly back to his car. He had an errand to run, and it was fitting that he should run it at the dinner hour.

It seemed he had some crow to eat.

CHAPTER SIX

THE LIBRARY (II)

1

Halfway to the library, an idea suddenly struck him—it was so obvious he could hardly believe it hadn't occurred to him already. He had lost a couple of library books; he had since discovered they had been destroyed; he would have to pay for them.

And that was all.

It occurred to him that Ardelia Lortz had been more successful in getting him to think like a fourth-grader than he had realized. When a kid lost a book, it was the end of the world; powerless, he cringed beneath the shadow of bureaucracy and waited for the Library Policeman to show up. But there *were* no Library Police, and Sam, as an adult, knew that perfectly well. There were only town employees like Ms. Lortz, who sometimes got overinflated ideas of their place in the scheme of things, and taxpayers like him, who sometimes forgot they were the dog which wagged the tail, and not the other way around.

I'm going to go in, I'm going to apologize, and then I'm going to ask her to send me a bill for the replacement copies, Sam thought. *And that's all. That's the end.*

It was so simple it was amazing.

Still feeling a little nervous and a little embarrassed (but much more in control of this teapot tempest), Sam parked across the street from the Library. The carriage lamps which flanked the main entrance were on, casting soft white radiance down the steps and across the building's granite façade. Evening lent the building a kindness and a welcoming air it had definitely been lacking on his first visit—or maybe it was just that spring was clearly on the rise now, something which had not been the case on the overcast March day when he had first met the resident dragon. The forbidding face of the stone robot was gone. It was just the public library again.

Sam started to get out of the car and then stopped. He had been granted one revelation; now he was suddenly afforded another.

The face of the woman in Dirty Dave's poster came back to him, the woman with the platter of fried chicken. The one Dave had called Sarah. That woman had looked familiar to Sam, and all at once some obscure circuit fired off in his brain and he knew why.

It had been Naomi Higgins.

2

He passed two kids in JCHS jackets on the steps and caught the door before it could swing all the way closed. He stepped into the foyer. The first thing that struck him was the sound. The reading room beyond the marble steps was by no means rowdy, but neither was it the smooth pit of silence which had greeted Sam on Friday noon just over a week ago.

Well, but it's Saturday evening now, he thought. *There are kids here, maybe studying for their midterm exams.*

But would Ardelia Lortz condone such chatter, muted as it was? The answer seemed to be yes, judging from the sound, but it surely didn't seem in character.

The second thing had to do with that single mute adjuration which had been mounted on the easel.

SILENCE!

was gone. In its place was a picture of Thomas Jefferson. Below it was this quotation:

"I cannot live without books."
—Thomas Jefferson (in a letter to John Adams)
June 10th, 1815

Sam studied this for a moment, thinking that it changed the whole flavor in one's mouth as one prepared to enter the library.

SILENCE!

induced feelings of trepidation and disquiet (what if one's belly was rumbling, for instance, or if one felt an attack of not necessarily silent flatulence might be imminent?).

"I cannot live without books,"

on the other hand, induced feelings of pleasure and anticipation— it made one feel as hungry men and women feel when the food is finally arriving.

Puzzling over how such a small thing could make such an essential difference, Sam entered the Library . . . and stopped dead.

3

It was much brighter in the main room than it had been on his first visit, but that was only one of the changes. The ladders which had stretched up to the dim reaches of the upper shelves were gone. There was no need of them, because the ceiling was now only eight or nine feet above the floor instead of thirty or forty. If you wanted to take a book from one of the higher shelves, all you needed was one of the stools which were scattered about. The magazines were placed in an inviting fan on a wide table by the circulation desk. The oak rack from which they had hung like the skins of dead animals was gone. So was the sign reading

RETURN ALL MAGAZINES TO THEIR PROPER PLACES!

The shelf of new novels was still there, but the 7-DAY RENTALS sign had been replaced with one which said READ A BEST SELLER— JUST FOR THE FUN OF IT!

People—mostly young people—came and went, talking in low tones. Someone chuckled. It was an easy, unselfconscious sound.

Sam looked up at the ceiling, trying desperately to understand what in hell had happened here. The slanted skylights were gone. The upper reaches of the room had been hidden by a modern suspended ceiling. The old-fashioned hanging globes had been re- placed by panelled fluorescent lighting set into the new ceiling.

A woman on her way up to the main desk with a handful of mystery novels followed Sam's gaze up to the ceiling, saw nothing unusual there, and looked curiously at Sam instead. One of the boys sitting at a long desk to the right of the magazine table nudged his fellows and pointed Sam out. Another tapped his temple and they all snickered.

Sam noticed neither the stares nor the snickers. He was unaware that he was simply standing in the entrance to the main reading room, gawking up at the ceiling with his mouth open. He was trying to get this major change straight in his mind.

Well, they've put in a suspended ceiling since you were here last. So what? It's probably more heat-efficient.

Yes, but the Lortz woman never said anything about changes.

No, but why would she say anything to him? Sam was hardly a library regular, was he?

She should have been upset, though. She struck me as a rock-ribbed traditionalist. She wouldn't like this. Not at all.

That was true, but there was something else, something even more troubling. Putting in a suspended ceiling was a major renovation. Sam didn't see how it could have been accomplished in just a week. And what about the high shelves, and all the books which had been on them? Where had the shelves gone? Where had the *books* gone?

Other people were looking at Sam now; even one of the library assistants was staring at him from the other side of the circulation desk. Most of the lively, hushed chatter in the big room had stilled.

Sam rubbed his eyes—actually rubbed his eyes—and looked up at the suspended ceiling with its inset fluorescent squares again. It was still there.

I'm in the wrong library! he thought wildly. *That's what it is!*

His confused mind first jumped at this idea and then backed away again, like a kitten that has been tricked into pouncing on a shadow. Junction City was fairly large by central Iowa standards, with a population of thirty-five thousand or so, but it was ridiculous to think it could support two libraries. Besides, the location of the building and the configuration of the room were right . . . it was just everything else that was wrong.

Sam wondered for just a moment if he might be going insane, and then dismissed the thought. He looked around and noticed for the first time that everyone had stopped what they were doing.

They were all looking at him. He felt a momentary, mad urge to say, "Go back to what you were doing—I was just noticing that the whole library is different this week." Instead, he sauntered over to the magazine table and picked up a copy of *U.S. News & World Report*. He began leafing through it with a show of great interest, and watched out of the corners of his eyes as the people in the room went back to what they had been doing.

When he felt that he could move without attracting undue attention, Sam replaced the magazine on the table and sauntered toward the Children's Library. He felt a little like a spy crossing enemy territory. The sign over the door was exactly the same, gold letters on warm dark oak, but the poster was different. Little Red Riding Hood at the moment of her terrible realization had been replaced by Donald Duck's nephews, Huey, Dewey, and Louie. They were wearing bathing trunks and diving into a swimming pool filled with books. The tag-line beneath read:

COME ON IN! THE READING'S FINE!

"What's going *on* here?" Sam muttered. His heart had begun to beat too fast; he could feel a fine sweat breaking out on his arms and back. If it had been just the poster, he could have assumed that La Lortz had been fired . . . but it *wasn't* just the poster. It was *everything*.

He opened the door of the Children's Library and peeked inside. He saw the same agreeable small world with its low tables and chairs, the same bright-blue curtains, the same water fountain mounted on the wall. Only now the suspended ceiling in here matched the suspended ceiling in the main reading room, and all the posters had been changed. The screaming child in the black sedan

(*Simple Simon they call him Simple Simon they feel contempt for him I think that's very healthy, don't you*)

was gone, and so was the Library Policeman with his trenchcoat and his strange star of many points. Sam drew back, turned around, and walked slowly to the main circulation desk. He felt as if his whole body had turned to glass.

Two library assistants—a college-age boy and girl—watched him approach. Sam was not too upset himself to see that they looked a trifle nervous.

Be careful. No . . . be NORMAL. *They already think you're halfway to being nuts.*

He suddenly thought of Lukey and a horrible, destructive impulse tried to seize him. He could see himself opening his mouth and yelling at these two nervous young people, demanding at the top of his voice that they give him a few Slim Fucking Slim Jims, because that was *chow*, that was *chow*, that was *chow*-de-*dow*.

He spoke in a calm, low voice instead.

"Perhaps you could help me. I need to speak to the librarian."

"Gee, I'm sorry," the girl said. "Mr. Price doesn't come in on Saturday nights."

Sam glanced down at the desk. As on his previous trip to the library, there was a small name-plaque standing next to the micro-film recorder, but it no longer said

A. LORTZ.

Now it said

MR. PRICE.

In his mind he heard Naomi say, *Tall man? About fifty?*

"No," he said. "Not Mr. Price. Not Mr. Peckham, either. The other one. Ardelia Lortz."

The boy and girl exchanged a puzzled glance. "No one named Ardelia Lord works here," the boy said. "You must be thinking of some other library."

"Not Lord," Sam told them. His voice seemed to be coming from a great distance. "*Lortz.*"

"No," the girl said. "You really must be mistaken, sir."

They were starting to look cautious again, and although Sam felt like insisting, telling them of *course* Ardelia Lortz worked here, he had met her only *eight days ago*, he made himself pull back. And in a way, it all made perfect sense, didn't it? It was perfect sense within a framework of utter lunacy, granted, but that didn't change the fact that the interior logic was intact. Like the posters, the skylights, and the magazine rack, Ardelia Lortz had simply ceased to exist.

Naomi spoke up again inside his head. *Oh? Miss Lortz, was it? That must have been fun.*

"*Naomi* recognized the name," he muttered.

Now the library assistants were looking at him with identical expressions of consternation.

"Pardon me," Sam said, and tried to smile. It felt crooked on his face. "I'm having one of those days."

"Yes," the boy said.

"You bet," the girl said.

They think I'm crazy, Sam thought, *and do you know what? I don't blame them a bit.*

"Was there anything else?" the boy asked.

Sam opened his mouth to say no—after which he would beat a hasty retreat—and then changed his mind. He was in for a penny; he might as well go in for a pound.

"How long has Mr. Price been the head librarian?"

The two assistants exchanged another glance. The girl shrugged. "Since we've been here," she said, "but that's not very long, Mr.—?"

"Peebles," Sam said, offering his hand. "Sam Peebles. I'm sorry. My manners seem to have flown away with the rest of my mind."

They both relaxed a little—it was an indefinable thing, but it was there, and it helped Sam do the same. Upset or not, he had managed to hold onto at least some of his not inconsiderable ability to put people at ease. A real-estate-and-insurance salesman who couldn't do that was a fellow who ought to be looking for a new line of work.

"I'm Cynthia Berrigan," she said, giving his hand a tentative shake. "This is Tom Stanford."

"Pleased to meet you," Tom Stanford said. He didn't look entirely sure of this, but he also gave Sam's hand a quick shake.

"Pardon me?" the woman with the mystery novels asked. "Could someone help me, please? I'll be late for my bridge game."

"I'll do it," Tom told Cynthia, and walked down the desk to check out the woman's books.

She said, "Tom and I go to Chapelton Junior College, Mr. Peebles. This is a work-study job. I've been here three semesters now—Mr. Price hired me last spring. Tom came during the summer."

"Mr. Price is the only full-time employee?"

"Uh-huh." She had lovely brown eyes and now he could see a touch of concern in them. "Is something wrong?"

"I don't know." Sam looked up again. He couldn't help it. "Has this suspended ceiling been here since you came to work?"

She followed his glance. "Well," she said, "I didn't know that was what it's called, but yes, it's been this way since I've been here."

"I had an idea there were skylights, you see."

Cynthia smiled. "Well, sure. I mean, you can see them from the outside, if you go around to the side of the building. And, of course, you can see them from the stacks, but they're boarded over. The skylights, I mean—not the stacks. I think they've been that way for years."

For years.

"And you've never heard of Ardelia Lortz."

She shook her head. "Uh-uh. Sorry."

"What about the Library Police?" Sam asked impulsively.

She laughed. "Only from my old aunt. She used to tell me the Library Police would get me if I didn't bring my books back on time. But that was back in Providence, Rhode Island, when I was a little girl. A long time ago."

Sure, Sam thought. *Maybe as long as ten, twelve years ago. Back when dinosaurs walked the earth.*

"Well," he said, "thanks for the information. I didn't mean to freak you out."

"You didn't."

"I think I did, a little. I was just confused for a second."

"Who is this Ardelia Lortz?" Tom Stanford asked, coming back. "That name rings a bell, but I'll be darned if I know why."

"That's just it. I don't really know," Sam said.

"Well, we're closed tomorrow, but Mr. Price will be in Monday afternoon and Monday evening," he said. "Maybe he can tell you what you want to know."

Sam nodded. "I think I'll come and see him. Meantime, thanks again."

"We're here to help if we can," Tom said. "I only wish we could have helped you more, Mr. Peebles."

"Me too," Sam said.

4

He was okay until he got to the car, and then, as he was unlocking the driver's-side door, all the muscles in his belly and legs seemed to drop dead. He had to support himself with a hand on the roof of his car to keep from falling down while he swung the door open. He did not really get in; he simply collapsed behind the wheel and then sat there, breathing hard and wondering with some alarm if he was going to faint.

What's going on here? I feel like a character in Rod Serling's old show. "*Submitted for your examination, one Samuel Peebles, ex-resident of Junction City, now selling real estate and whole life in . . . the Twilight Zone.*"

Yes, that was what it was like. Only watching people cope with inexplicable happenings on TV was sort of fun. Sam was discovering that the inexplicable lost a lot of its charm when *you* were the one who had to struggle with it.

He looked across the street at the Library, where people came and went beneath the soft glow of the carriage lamps. The old lady with the mystery novels was headed off down the street, presumably bound for her bridge game. A couple of girls were coming down the steps, talking and laughing together, books held to their blooming chests. Everything looked perfectly normal . . . and of course it was. The *abnormal* Library had been the one he had entered a week ago. The only reason the oddities hadn't struck him more forcibly, he supposed, was because his mind had been on that damned speech of his.

Don't think about it, he instructed himself, although he was afraid that this was going to be one of those times when his mind simply wouldn't take instruction. *Do a Scarlett O'Hara and think about it tomorrow. Once the sun is up, all this will make a lot more sense.*

He put the car in gear and thought about it all the way home.

CHAPTER SEVEN

NIGHT TERRORS

1

The first thing he did after letting himself in was to check the answering machine. His heartbeat cranked up a notch when he saw the MESSAGE WAITING lamp was lit.

It'll be her. I don't know who she really is, but I'm beginning to think she won't be happy until she's driven me completely crackers.

Don't listen to it, then, another part of his mind spoke up, and Sam was now so confused he couldn't tell if that was a reasonable idea or not. It *seemed* reasonable, but it also seemed a little cowardly. In fact—

He realized that he was standing here in a sweat, gnawing his fingernails, and suddenly grunted—a soft, exasperated noise.

From the fourth grade to the mental ward, he thought. *Well, I'll be damned if it's going to work that way, hon.*

He pushed the button.

"Hi!" a man's whiskey-roughened voice said. "This is Joseph Randowski, Mr. Peebles. My stage name is The Amazing Joe. I just called to thank you for filling in for me at that Kiwanis meeting or whatever it was. I wanted to tell you that I'm feeling a lot better— my neck was only sprained, not broke like they thought at first. I'm sending you a whole bunch of free tickets to the show. Pass em out to your friends. Take care of yourself. Thanks again. Bye."

The tape stopped. The ALL MESSAGES PLAYED lamp came on. Sam snorted at his case of nerves—if Ardelia Lortz wanted him jumping at shadows, she was getting exactly what she wanted. He pushed the REWIND button, and a new thought struck him. Rewinding the tape that took his messages was a habit with him, but it meant that the old messages disappeared under the new ones. The Amazing Joe's message would have erased Ardelia's earlier message. His only evidence that the woman actually existed was gone.

But that wasn't true, was it? There was his library card. He had stood in front of that goddamned circulation desk and watched her sign her name on it in large, flourishing letters.

Sam pulled out his wallet and went through it three times before admitting to himself that the library card was gone, too. And he thought he knew why. He vaguely remembered tucking it into the inside pocket of *Best Loved Poems of the American People.*

For safekeeping.

So he wouldn't lose it.

Great. Just great.

Sam sat down on the couch and put his forehead in his hand. His head was starting to ache.

2

He was heating a can of soup on the stove fifteen minutes later, hoping a little hot food would do something for his head, when he thought of Naomi again—Naomi, who looked so much like the woman in Dirty Dave's poster. The question of whether or not Naomi was leading a secret life of some sort under the name of Sarah had taken a back seat to something that seemed a lot more important, at least right now: Naomi had known who Ardelia Lortz was. But her reaction to the name . . . it had been a little odd, hadn't it? It had startled her for a moment or two, and she'd started to make a joke, and then the phone had rung and it had been Burt Iverson, and—

Sam tried to replay the conversation in his mind and was chagrined at how little he remembered. Naomi had said Ardelia was peculiar, all right; he was sure of that, but not much else. It hadn't seemed important then. The important thing then was that his career seemed to have taken a quantum leap forward. And that was still important, but this other thing seemed to dwarf it. In truth, it seemed to dwarf *everything*. His mind kept going back to that modern no-nonsense suspended ceiling and the short bookcases. He didn't believe he was crazy, not at all, but he was beginning to feel that if he didn't get this thing sorted out, he might *go* crazy. It was as if he had uncovered a hole in the middle of his head, one so deep you could throw things into it and not hear a splash no matter how big the things you threw were or how long you waited with your ear cocked for the sound. He supposed the feeling would pass—maybe—but in the meantime it was horrible.

He turned the burner under the soup to LO, went into the study, and found Naomi's telephone number. It rang three times and then a cracked, elderly voice said, "Who is it, please?" Sam recognized the voice at once, although he hadn't seen its owner in person for almost two years. It was Naomi's ramshackle mother.

"Hello, Mrs. Higgins," he said. "It's Sam Peebles."

He stopped, waited for her to say *Oh, hello, Sam* or maybe *How are you?* but there was only Mrs. Higgins's heavy, emphysemic breathing. Sam had never been one of her favorite people, and it seemed that absence had not made her heart grow fonder.

Since she wasn't going to ask it, Sam decided he might as well. "How are you, Mrs. Higgins?"

"I have my good days and my bad ones."

For a moment Sam was nonplussed. It seemed to be one of those remarks to which there was no adequate reply. *I'm sorry to hear that* didn't fit, but *That's great, Mrs. Higgins!* would sound even worse.

He settled for asking if he could speak to Naomi.

"She's out this evening. I don't know when she'll be back."

"Could you ask her to call me?"

"I'm going to bed. And don't ask me to leave her a note, either. My arthritis is very bad."

Sam sighed. "I'll call tomorrow."

"We'll be in church tomorrow morning," Mrs. Higgins stated in the same flat, unhelpful voice, "and the first Baptist Youth Picnic of the season is tomorrow afternoon. Naomi has promised to help."

Sam decided to call it off. It was clear that Mrs. Higgins was sticking as close to name, rank, and serial number as she possibly could. He started to say goodbye, then changed his mind. "Mrs. Higgins, does the name Lortz mean anything to you? Ardelia Lortz?"

The heavy wheeze of her respiration stopped in mid-snuffle. For a moment there was total silence on the line and then Mrs. Higgins spoke in a low, vicious voice. "How long are you Godless heathens going to go on throwing that woman in our faces? Do you think it's *funny*? Do you think it's *clever*?"

"Mrs. Higgins, you don't understand. I just want to know—"

There was a sharp little click in his ear. It sounded as if Mrs. Higgins had broken a small dry stick over her knee. And then the line went dead.

3

Sam ate his soup, then spent half an hour trying to watch TV. It was no good. His mind kept wandering away. It might start with the woman in Dirty Dave's poster, or with the muddy footprint on the cover of *Best Loved Poems of the American People*, or with the missing poster of Little Red Riding Hood. But no matter where it started, it always ended up in the same place: that completely different ceiling above the main reading room of the Junction City Public Library.

Finally he gave it up and crawled into bed. It had been one of the worst Saturdays he could remember, and might well have been the worst Saturday of his life. The only thing he wanted now was a quick trip into the land of dreamless unconsciousness.

But sleep didn't come.

The horrors came instead.

Chief among them was the idea that he was losing his mind. Sam had never realized just how terrible such an idea could be. He had seen movies where some fellow would go to see a psychiatrist and say "I feel like I'm losing my mind, doc," while dramatically clutching his head, and he supposed he had come to equate the onset of mental instability with an Excedrin headache. It wasn't like that, he discovered as the long hours passed and April 7 gradually became April 8. It was more like reaching down to scratch your balls and finding a large lump there, a lump that was probably a tumor of some kind.

The Library *couldn't* have changed so radically in just over a week. He *couldn't* have seen the skylights from the reading room. The girl, Cynthia Berrigan, had said they were boarded over, had been since she had arrived, at least a year ago. So this was some sort of a mental breakdown. Or a brain tumor. Or what about Alzheimer's disease? *There* was a pleasant thought. He had read someplace— *Newsweek*, perhaps—that Alzheimer's victims were getting younger and younger. Maybe the whole weird episode was a signal of creeping, premature senility.

An unpleasant billboard began to fill his thoughts, a billboard with three words written on it in greasy letters the color of red licorice. These words were

LOSING MY MIND.

He had lived an ordinary life, full of ordinary pleasures and ordinary regrets; a pretty-much-unexamined life. He had never seen his name in lights, true, but he had never had any reason to question his sanity, either. Now he found himself lying in his rumpled bed and wondering if this was how you came untethered from the real, rational world. If this was how it started when you

LOST YOUR MIND.

The idea that the angel of Junction City's homeless shelter was Naomi—Naomi going under an alias—was another nutso idea. It

just couldn't be . . . could it? He even began to question the strong
upsurge in his business. Maybe he had hallucinated the whole thing.

Toward midnight, his thoughts turned to Ardelia Lortz, and that
was when things really began to get bad. He began to think of how
awful it would be if Ardelia Lortz was in his closet, or even under
his bed. He saw her grinning happily, secretly, in the dark, wriggling
fingers tipped with long, sharp nails, her hair sprayed out all around
her face in a weird fright-wig. He imagined how his bones would
turn to jelly if she began to whisper to him.

*You lost the books, Sam, so it will have to be the Library Police-
man . . . you lost the books . . . you loooossst them . . .*

At last, around twelve-thirty, Sam couldn't stand it any longer.
He sat up and fumbled in the dark for the bedside lamp. And as
he did, he was gripped by a new fantasy, one so vivid it was almost
a certainty: he was not alone in his bedroom, but his visitor was
not Ardelia Lortz. Oh no. His visitor was the Library Policeman
from the poster that was no longer in the Children's Library. He
was standing here in the dark, a tall, pale man wrapped in a trenchcoat, a man with a bad complexion and a white, jagged scar lying
across his left cheek, below his left eye, and over the bridge of his
nose. Sam hadn't seen that scar on the face in the poster, but that
was only because the artist hadn't wanted to put it in. It was there.
Sam knew it was there.

You were wrong about the bushes, the Library Policeman would say
in his lightly lisping voice. *There* are *bushes growing along the sideth.
Loth of bushes. And we're going to ecthplore them. We're going to ecthplore
them together.*

No! Stop it! Just . . . STOP it!

As his trembling hand finally found the lamp, a board creaked in
the room and he uttered a breathless little scream. His hand
clenched, squeezing the switch. The light came on. For a moment
he actually thought he *saw* the tall man, and then he realized it was
only a shadow cast on the wall by the bureau.

Sam swung his feet out onto the floor and put his face in his
hands for a moment. Then he reached for the pack of Kents on
the nightstand.

"You've got to get hold of yourself," he muttered. "What the
fuck were you thinking about?"

I don't know, the voice inside responded promptly. *Furthermore,
I don't want to know. Ever. The bushes were a long time ago. I never*

have to remember the bushes again. Or the taste. That sweet sweet taste.

He lit a cigarette and inhaled deeply.

The worst thing was this: Next time he might really *see* the man in the trenchcoat. Or Ardelia. Or Gorgo, High Emperor of Pellucidar. Because if he'd been able to create a hallucination as complete as his visit to the Library and his meeting with Ardelia Lortz, he could hallucinate *anything*. Once you started thinking about skylights that weren't there, and people who weren't there, and even *bushes* that weren't there, everything seemed possible. How did you quell a rebellion in your own *mind?*

He went down to the kitchen, turning on lights as he went, resisting an urge to look over his shoulder and see if anyone was creeping after him. A man with a badge in his hand, for instance. He supposed that what he needed was a sleeping pill, but since he didn't have any—not even one of the over-the-counter preparations like Sominex—he would just have to improvise. He splashed milk into a saucepan, heated it, poured it into a coffee mug, and then added a healthy shot of brandy. This was something else he had seen in the movies. He took a taste, grimaced, almost poured the evil mixture down the sink, and then looked at the clock on the microwave. Quarter to one in the morning. It was a long time until dawn, a long time to spend imagining Ardelia Lortz and the Library Policeman creeping up the stairs with knives gripped between their teeth.

Or arrows, he thought. *Long black arrows. Ardelia and the Library Policeman creeping up the stairs with long black arrows clamped between their teeth. How about* that *image, friends and neighbors?*

Arrows?

Why arrows?

He didn't want to think about it. He was tired of thoughts which came whizzing out of the previously unsuspected darkness inside him like horrid, stinking Frisbees.

I don't want to think about it. I won't *think about it.*

He finished the brandy-laced milk and went back to bed.

4

He left the bedside lamp on, and that made him feel a little calmer. He actually began to think he might go to sleep at some point before the heat-death of the universe. He pulled the comforter up to his chin, laced his hands behind his head, and looked at the ceiling.

SOME of it must have really happened, he thought. *It can't ALL have been a hallucination . . . unless this is part of it, and I'm really in one of the rubber rooms up in Cedar Rapids, wrapped in a straitjacket and only imagining I'm lying here in my own bed.*

He *had* delivered the speech. He *had* used the jokes from *The Speaker's Companion,* and Spencer Michael Free's verse from *Best Loved Poems of the American People.* And since he had neither volume in his own small collection of books, he must have gotten them from the Library. Naomi had known Ardelia Lortz—had known her name, anyway—and so had Naomi's mother. Had she! It was as if he'd set a firecracker off under her easy chair.

I can check around, he thought. *If Mrs. Higgins knows the name, other people will, too. Not work-study kids from Chapelton, maybe, but people who've been in Junction City a long time. Frank Stephens, maybe. Or Dirty Dave . . .*

At this point, Sam finally drifted off. He crossed the almost seamless border between waking and sleeping without knowing it; his thoughts never ceased but began instead to twist themselves into ever more strange and fabulous shapes. The shapes became a dream. And the dream became a nightmare. He was at Angle Street again, and the three alkies were on the porch, laboring over their posters. He asked Dirty Dave what he was doing.

Aw, just passin the time, Dave said, and then, shyly, he turned the poster around so Sam could see it.

It was a picture of Simple Simon. He had been impaled on a spit over an open fire. He was clutching a great bundle of melting red licorice in one hand. His clothes were burning but he was still alive. He was screaming. The words written above this terrible image were:

CHILDREN DINNER IN THE PUBLIC LIBRARY BUSHES
TO BENEFIT THE LIBRARY POLICE FUND
MIDNITE TO 2 A.M.
COME ONE COME ALL
"THAT'S CHOW-DE-DOW!"

Dave, that's horrible, Sam said in the dream.

Not at all, Dirty Dave replied. *The children call him Simple Simon. They love to eat him. I think that's very healthy, don't you?*

Look! Rudolph cried. *Look, it's Sarah!*

Sam looked up and saw Naomi crossing the littered, weedy ground between Angle Street and the Recycling Center. She was moving very slowly, because she was pushing a shopping-cart filled with copies of *The Speaker's Companion* and *Best Loved Poems of the American People.* Behind her, the sun was going down in a sullen furnace glare of red light and a long passenger train was rumbling slowly along the track, headed out into the emptiness of western Iowa. It was at least thirty coaches long, and every car was black. Crepe hung and swung in the windows. It was a funeral train, Sam realized.

Sam turned back to Dirty Dave and said, *Her name isn't Sarah. That's Naomi. Naomi Higgins from Proverbia.*

Not at all, Dirty Dave said. *It's Death coming, Mr. Peebles. Death is a woman.*

Lukey began to squeal then. In the extremity of his terror he sounded like a human pig. *She got Slim Jims! She got Slim Jims! Oh my God, she got all Slim Fuckin Slim Jims!*

Sam turned back to see what Lukey was talking about. The woman was closer, but it was no longer Naomi. It was Ardelia. She was dressed in a trenchcoat the color of a winter stormcloud. The shopping cart was not full of Slim Jims, as Lukey had said, but thousands of intertwined red licorice whips. While Sam watched, Ardelia snatched up handfuls of them and began to cram them into her mouth. Her teeth were no longer dentures; they were long and discolored. They looked like vampire teeth to Sam, both sharp and horribly strong. Grimacing, she bit down on her mouthful of candy. Bright blood squirted out, spraying a pink cloud in the sunset air and dribbling down her chin. Severed chunks of licorice tumbled to the weedy earth, still jetting blood.

She raised hands which had become hooked talons.

"*Youuuu losst the BOOOOOKS!*" she screamed at Sam, and charged at him.

5

Sam came awake in a breathless jerk. He had pulled all the bed-clothes loose from their moorings, and was huddled beneath them near the foot of the bed in a sweaty ball. Outside, the first thin light of a new day was peeking under the drawn shade. The bedside clock said it was 5:53 A.M.

He got up, the bedroom air cool and refreshing on his sweaty skin, went into the bathroom, and urinated. His head ached vaguely, either as a result of the early-morning shot of brandy or stress from the dream. He opened the medicine cabinet, took two aspirin, and then shambled back to his bed. He pulled the covers up as best he could, feeling the residue of his nightmare in every damp fold of the sheet. He wouldn't go back to sleep again—he knew that—but he could at least lie here until the nightmare started to dissolve.

As his head touched the pillow, he suddenly realized he knew something else, something as surprising and unexpected as his sudden understanding that the woman in Dirty Dave's poster had been his part-time secretary. This new understanding also had to do with Dirty Dave . . . and with Ardelia Lortz.

It was the dream, he thought. *That's where I found out.*

Sam fell into a deep, natural sleep. There were no more dreams and when he woke up it was almost eleven o'clock. Churchbells were calling the faithful to worship, and outside it was a beautiful day. The sight of all that sunshine lying on all that bright new grass did more than make him feel good; it made him feel almost reborn.

CHAPTER EIGHT

ANGLE STREET (II)

1

He made himself brunch—orange juice, a three-egg omelette loaded with green onions, lots of strong coffee—and thought about going back to Angle Street. He could still remember the moment of illumination he had experienced during his brief period of waking and was perfectly sure that his insight was true, but he wondered if he really wanted to pursue this crazy business any further.

In the bright light of a spring morning, his fears of the previous night seemed both distant and absurd, and he felt a strong temptation—almost a need—to simply let the matter rest. Something had happened to him, he thought, something which had no reasonable, rational explanation. The question was, so what?

He had read about such things, about ghosts and premonitions and possessions, but they held only minimal interest for him. He liked a spooky movie once in awhile, but that was about as far as it went. He was a practical man, and he could see no practical use for paranormal episodes . . . if they did indeed occur. He had experienced . . . well, call it an *event,* for want of a better word. Now the event was over. Why not leave it at that?

Because she said she wanted the books back by tomorrow—what about that?

But this seemed to have no power over him now. In spite of the messages she had left on his answering machine, Sam no longer exactly believed in Ardelia Lortz.

What *did* interest him was his own reaction to what had happened. He found himself remembering a college biology lecture. The instructor had begun by saying that the human body had an extremely efficient way of dealing with the incursion of alien organisms. Sam remembered the teacher saying that because the bad news—cancer, influenza, sexually transmitted diseases such as syphilis—got all the headlines, people tended to believe they were a lot more vulnerable to disease than they really were. "The human body," the instructor had said, "has its own Green Beret force at its disposal. When the human body is attacked by an outsider, ladies and gentlemen, the response of this force is quick and without mercy. No quarter is given. Without this army of trained killers, each of you would have been dead twenty times over before the end of your first year."

The prime technique the body employed to rid itself of invaders was isolation. The invaders were first surrounded, cut off from the nutrients they needed to live, then either eaten, beaten, or starved. Now Sam was discovering—or thought he was—that the mind employed exactly the same technique when it was attacked. He could remember many occasions when he had felt he was coming down with a cold only to wake up the next morning feeling fine. The body had done its work. A vicious war had been going on even as he slept, and the invaders had been wiped out to the last man . . . or bug. They had been eaten, beaten, or starved.

Last night he had experienced the mental equivalent of an impending cold. This morning the invader, the threat to his clear, rational perceptions, had been surrounded. Cut off from its nutrients. Now it was only a matter of time. And part of him was warning the rest of him that, by investigating this business further, he might be feeding the enemy.

This is how it happens, he thought. *This is why the world isn't full of reports of strange happenings and inexplicable phenomena. The mind experiences them . . . reels around for awhile . . . then counterattacks.*

But he was curious. That was the thing. And didn't they say that, although curiosity killed the cat, satisfaction brought the beast back?

Who? Who says?

He didn't know . . . but he supposed he could find out. At his local library. Sam smiled a little as he took his dishes over to the sink. And discovered he had already made his decision: he *would* pursue this crazy business just a little further.

Just a little bit.

2

Sam arrived back at Angle Street around twelve-thirty. He was not terribly surprised to see Naomi's old blue Datsun parked in the driveway. Sam parked behind it, got out, and climbed the rickety steps past the sign telling him he'd have to drop any bottles he might have in the trash barrel. He knocked, but there was no answer. He pushed the door open, revealing a wide hall that was barren of furniture . . . unless the pay telephone halfway down counted. The wallpaper was clean but faded. Sam saw a place where it had been mended with Scotch tape.

"Hello?"

There was no answer. He went in, feeling like an intruder, and walked down the hall. The first door on the left opened into the common room. Two signs had been thumbtacked to this door.

FRIENDS OF BILL ENTER HERE!

read the top one. Below this was another, which seemed at once utterly sensible and exquisitely dumb to Sam. It read:

TIME TAKES TIME.

The common room was furnished with mismatched, cast-off chairs and a long sofa which had also been mended with tape— electrician's tape, this time. More slogans had been hung on the wall. There was a coffeemaker on a little table by the TV. Both the TV and the coffeemaker were off.

Sam walked on down the hall past the stairs, feeling more like an intruder than ever. He glanced into the three other rooms which opened off the corridor. Each was furnished with two plain cots, and all were empty. The rooms were scrupulously clean, but they told their tales just the same. One smelled of Musterole. Another smelled unpleasantly of some deep sickness. *Either someone has died recently in this room,* Sam thought, *or someone is going to.*

The kitchen, also empty, was at the far end of the hall. It was a big, sunny room with faded linoleum covering the floor in uneven dunes and valleys. A gigantic stove, combination wood and gas, filled an alcove. The sink was old and deep, its enamel discolored with rust stains. The faucets were equipped with old-fashioned pro-peller handles. An ancient Maytag washing machine and a gas-fired Kenmore drier stood next to the pantry. The air smelled faintly of last night's baked beans. Sam liked the room. It spoke to him of pennies which had been pinched until they screamed, but it also spoke of love and care and some hard-won happiness. It reminded him of his grandmother's kitchen, and that had been a good place. A safe place.

On the old restaurant-sized Amana refrigerator was a magnetized plaque which read:

GOD BLESS OUR BOOZELESS HOME.

Sam heard faint voices outside. He crossed the kitchen and looked through one of the windows, which had been raised to admit as much of the warm spring day as the mild breeze could coax in.

The back lawn of Angle Street was showing the first touches of green; at the rear of the property, by a thin belt of just-budding trees, an idle vegetable garden waited for warmer days. To the left, a volleyball net sagged in a gentle arc. To the right were two horse-shoe pits, just beginning to sprout a few weeds. It was not a pre-possessing back yard—at this time of year, few country yards were—but Sam saw it had been raked at least once since the snow had released its winter grip, and there were no cinders, although he could see the steely shine of the railroad tracks less than fifty feet from the garden. The residents of Angle Street might not have a lot to take care of, he thought, but they were taking care of what they did have.

About a dozen people were sitting on folding camp chairs in a rough circle between the volleyball net and the horseshoe pits. Sam recognized Naomi, Dave, Lukey, and Rudolph. A moment later he realized he also recognized Burt Iverson, Junction City's most prosperous lawyer, and Elmer Baskin, the banker who hadn't gotten to his Rotary speech but who had called later to congratulate him just the same. The breeze gusted, blowing back the homely checked curtains which hung at the sides of the window through which Sam was looking. It also ruffled Elmer's silver hair. Elmer turned his face up to the sun and smiled. Sam was struck by the simple pleasure he saw, not on Elmer's face but *in* it. At that moment he was both more and less than a small city's richest banker; he was every man who ever greeted spring after a long, cold winter, happy to still be alive, whole, and free of pain.

Sam felt struck with unreality. It was weird enough that Naomi Higgins should be out here consorting with the unhomed winos of Junction City—and under another name, at that. To find that the town's most respected banker and one of its sharpest legal eagles were also here was a bit of a mind-blower.

A man in ragged green pants and a Cincinnati Bengals sweatshirt raised his hand. Rudolph pointed at him. "My name's John, and I'm an alcoholic," the man in the Bengals sweatshirt said.

Sam backed away from the window quickly. His face felt hot. Now he felt not only like an intruder but a spy. He supposed they usually held their Sunday-noon AA meeting in the common room— the coffeepot suggested it, anyway—but today the weather had been so nice that they had taken their chairs outside. He bet it had been Naomi's idea.

We'll be in church tomorrow morning, Mrs. Higgins had said, *and the first Baptist Youth Picnic of the season is tomorrow afternoon. Naomi has promised to help.* He wondered if Mrs. Higgins knew her daughter was spending the afternoon with the alkies instead of the Baptists and supposed she did. He thought he also understood why Naomi had abruptly decided two dates with Sam Peebles was enough. He had thought it was the religion thing at the time, and Naomi hadn't ever tried to suggest it was anything else. But after the first date, which had been a movie, she had agreed to go out with him again. After the *second* date, any romantic interest she'd had in him ceased. Or seemed to. The second date had been dinner. And he had ordered wine.

Well for Christ's sake—how was I supposed to know she's an alcoholic? Am I a mind-reader?

The answer, of course, was he *couldn't* have known . . . but his face felt hotter, just the same.

Or maybe it's not booze . . . or not just *booze. Maybe she's got other problems, too.*

He also found himself wondering what would happen if Burt Iverson and Elmer Baskin, both powerful men, found out that he knew they belonged to the world's largest secret society. Maybe nothing; he didn't know enough about AA to be sure. He *did* know two things, however: that the second A stood for Anonymous, and that these were men who could squash his rising business aspirations flat if they chose to do so.

Sam decided to leave as quickly and quietly as he could. To his credit, this decision was not based on personal considerations. The people sitting out there on the back lawn of Angle Street shared a serious problem. He had discovered this by accident; he had no intention of staying—and eavesdropping—on purpose.

As he went back down the hallway again, he saw a pile of cut-up paper resting on top of the pay phone. A stub of pencil had been tacked to the wall on a short length of string beside the phone. On impulse he took a sheet of paper and printed a quick note on it.

Dave,

I stopped by this morning to see you, but nobody was around. I want to talk to you about a woman named Ardelia Lortz. I've got an idea you know who she is, and I'm anxious to find out about her. Will you give me a call this afternoon or this evening, if you get a chance? The number is 555-8699. Thanks very much.

He signed his name at the bottom, folded the sheet in half, and printed Dave's name on the fold. He thought briefly about taking it back down to the kitchen and putting it on the counter, but he didn't want any of them—Naomi most of all—worrying that he might have seen them at their odd but perhaps helpful devotions. He propped it on top of the TV in the common room instead, with Dave's name facing out. He thought about placing a quarter for the telephone beside the note and then didn't. Dave might take that wrong.

He left then, glad to be out in the sun again undiscovered. As he got back into his car, he saw the bumper sticker on Naomi's Datsun.

LET GO AND LET GOD,

it said.

"Better God than Ardelia," Sam muttered, and backed out the driveway to the road.

3

By late afternoon, Sam's broken rest of the night before had begun to tell, and a vast sleepiness stole over him. He turned on the TV, found a Cincinnati-Boston exhibition baseball game wending its slow way into the eighth inning, lay down on the sofa to watch it, and almost immediately dozed off. The telephone rang before the doze had a chance to spiral down into real sleep, and Sam got up to answer it, feeling woozy and disoriented.

"Hello?"

"You don't want to be talking about that woman," Dirty Dave said with no preamble whatsoever. His voice was trembling at the far edge of control. "You don't even want to be *thinking* about her."

How long are you Godless heathens going to go on throwing that woman in our faces? Do you think it's funny? Do you think it's clever?

All of Sam's drowsiness was gone in an instant. "Dave, what *is* it about that woman? Either people react as though she were the devil or they don't know anything about her. Who is she? What in the hell did she do to freak you out this way?"

There was a long period of silence. Sam waited through it, his heart beating heavily in his chest and throat. He would have thought the connection had been broken if not for the sound of Dave's broken breathing in his ear.

"Mr. Peebles," he said at last, "you've been a real good help to me over the years. You and some others helped me stay alive when I wasn't even sure I wanted to myself. But I can't talk about that bitch. I can't. And if you know what's good for you, you won't talk to anybody else about her, neither."

"That sounds like a threat."

"No!" Dave said. He sounded more than surprised; he sounded shocked. "No—I'm just warnin you, Mr. Peebles, same as I'd do if I saw you wanderin around an old well where the weeds were all grown up so you couldn't see the hole. Don't talk about her and don't think about her. Let the dead stay dead."

Let the dead stay dead.

In a way it didn't surprise him; everything that had happened (with, perhaps, the exception of the messages left on his answering machine) pointed to the same conclusion: that Ardelia Lortz was no longer among the living. He—Sam Peebles, small-town realtor and insurance agent—had been speaking to a ghost without even knowing it. Spoken to her? Hell! Had done *business* with her! He had given her two bucks and she had given him a library card.

So he was not exactly surprised . . . but a deep chill began to radiate out along the white highways of his skeleton just the same. He looked down and saw pale knobs of gooseflesh standing out on his arms.

You should have left it alone, part of his mind mourned. *Didn't I tell you so?*

"When did she die?" Sam asked. His voice sounded dull and listless to his own ears.

"I don't want to talk about it, Mr. Peebles!" Dave sounded nearly frantic now. His voice trembled, skipped into a higher register which was almost falsetto, and splintered there. *"Please!"*

Leave him alone, Sam cried angrily at himself. *Doesn't he have enough problems without this crap to worry about?*

Yes. And he *could* leave Dave alone—there must be other people in town who would talk to him about Ardelia Lortz . . . if he could find a way to approach them that wouldn't make them want to call for the men with the butterfly nets, that was. But there was one other thing, a thing perhaps only Dirty Dave Duncan could tell him for sure.

"You drew some posters for the Library once, didn't you? I think I recognized your style from the poster you were doing yesterday on the porch. In fact, I'm almost sure. There was one showing a little boy in a black car. And a man in a trenchcoat—the Library Policeman. Did you—"

Before he could finish, Dave burst out with such a shriek of shame and grief and fear that Sam was silenced.

"Dave? I—"

"*Leave it alone!*" Dave wept. "*I couldn't help myself, so can't you just please leave—*"

His cries abruptly diminished and there was a rattle as someone took the phone from him.

"Stop it," Naomi said. She sounded near tears herself, but she also sounded furious. "Can't you just stop it, you horrible man?"

"Naomi—"

"My name is Sarah when I'm here," she said slowly, "but I hate you equally under both names, Sam Peebles. I'm never going to set foot in your office again." Her voice began to rise. "Why couldn't you leave him alone? Why did you have to rake up all this old *shit*? *Why?*"

Unnerved, hardly in control of himself, Sam said: "Why did you send me to the Library? If you didn't want me to meet her, Naomi, why did you send me to the goddam Library in the first place?"

There was a gasp on the other end of the line.

"Naomi? Can we—"

There was a click as she hung up the telephone.

Connection broken.

4

Sam sat in his study until almost nine-thirty, eating Tums and writing one name after another on the same legal pad he had used when composing the first draft of his speech. He would look at each name for a little while, then cross it off. Six years had seemed like a long time to spend in one place . . . at least until tonight. Tonight it seemed like a much shorter period of time—a weekend, say.

Craig Jones, he wrote.

He stared at the name and thought, *Craig might know about Ardelia . . . but he'd want to know why I was interested.*

Did he know Craig well enough to answer that question truth-fully? The answer to that question was a firm no. Craig was one of Junction City's younger lawyers, a real wannabe. They'd had a few business lunches . . . and there was Rotary Club, of course—and Craig had invited him to his house for dinner once. When they happened to meet on the street they spoke cordially, sometimes about business, more often about the weather. None of that added up to friendship, though, and if Sam meant to spill this nutty busi-ness to someone, he wanted it to be a friend, not an associate that called him *ole buddy* after the second sloe-gin fizz.

He scratched Craig's name off the list.

He'd made two fairly close friends since coming to Junction City, one a physician's assistant with Dr. Melden's practice, the other a city cop. Russ Frame, his PA friend, had jumped to a better-paying family practice in Grand Rapids early in 1989. And since the first of January, Tom Wycliffe had been overseeing the Iowa State Pa-trol's new Traffic Control Board. He had fallen out of touch with both men since—he was slow making friends, and not good at keeping them, either.

Which left him just where?

Sam didn't know. He *did* know that Ardelia Lortz's name affected some people in Junction City like a satchel charge. He knew—or believed he knew—that he had met her even though she was dead. He couldn't even tell himself that he had met a relative, or some nutty woman *calling* herself Ardelia Lortz. Because—

I think I met a ghost. In fact, I think I met a ghost inside of a ghost. I think that the library I entered was the Junction City Library as it was when Ardelia Lortz was alive and in charge of the place. I think that's why it felt so weird and off-kilter. It wasn't like time-travel, or the way I imagine time-travel would be. It was more like stepping into limbo for a little while. And it was real. I'm sure it was real.

He paused, drumming his fingers on the desk.

Where did she call me from? Do they have telephones in limbo?

He stared at the list of crossed-off names for a long moment, then tore the yellow sheet slowly off the pad. He crumpled it up and tossed it in the wastebasket.

You should have left it alone, part of him continued to mourn.

But he hadn't. So now what?

Call one of the guys you trust. Call Russ Frame or Tom Wycliffe. Just pick up the phone and make a call.

But he didn't want to do that. Not tonight, at least. He recognized this as an irrational, half-superstitious feeling—he had given and gotten a lot of unpleasant information over the phone just lately, or so it seemed—but he was too tired to grapple with it tonight. If he could get a good night's sleep (and he thought he could, if he left the bedside lamp on again), maybe something better, something more concrete, would occur to him tomorrow morning, when he was fresh. Further along, he supposed he would have to try and mend his fences with Naomi Higgins and Dave Duncan—but first he wanted to find out just what kind of fences they were.

If he could.

CHAPTER NINE

THE LIBRARY POLICEMAN (I)

He *did* sleep well. There were no dreams, and an idea came to him naturally and easily in the shower the next morning, the way ideas sometimes did when your body was rested and your mind hadn't been awake long enough to get cluttered up with a load of shit. The Public Library was not the only place where information was available, and when it was local history—*recent* local history—you were interested in, it wasn't even the best place.

"The *Gazette*!" he cried, and stuck his head under the shower nozzle to rinse the soap out of it.

Twenty minutes later he was downstairs, dressed except for his coat and tie, and drinking coffee in his study. The legal pad was once more in front of him, and on it was the start of another list.

1. *Ardelia Lortz—who is she? Or who was she?*
2. *Ardelia Lortz—what did she do?*
3. *Junction City Public Library—renovated? When? Pictures?*

At this point the doorbell rang. Sam glanced at the clock as he got up to answer it. It was going on eight-thirty, time to get to work. He could shoot over to the *Gazette* office at ten, the time he usually took his coffee break, and check some back issues. Which ones? He was still mulling this over—some would undoubtedly bear fruit quicker than others—as he dug in his pocket for the paperboy's money. The doorbell rang again.

"I'm coming as fast as I can, Keith!" he called, stepping into the kitchen entryway and grabbing the doorknob. "Don't punch a hole in the damn d—"

At that moment he looked up and saw a shape much larger than Keith Jordan's bulking behind the sheer curtain hung across the window in the door. His mind had been preoccupied, more concerned with the day ahead than this Monday-morning ritual of paying the newsboy, but in that instant an icepick of pure terror stabbed its way through his scattered thoughts. He did not have to see the face; even through the sheer he recognized the shape, the set of the body . . . and the trenchcoat, of course.

The taste of red licorice, high, sweet, and sickening, flooded his mouth.

He let go of the doorknob, but an instant too late. The latch had clicked back, and the moment it did, the figure standing on the back porch rammed the door open. Sam was thrown backward into the kitchen. He flailed his arms to keep his balance and managed to knock all three coats hanging from the rod in the entryway to the floor.

The Library Policeman stepped in, wrapped in his own pocket of cold air. He stepped in slowly, as if he had all the time in the world, and closed the door behind him. In one hand he held Sam's copy of the *Gazette* neatly rolled and folded. He raised it like a baton.

"I brought you your paper," the Library Policeman said. His voice was strangely distant, as if it was coming to Sam through a heavy pane of glass. "I was going to pay the boy as well, but he theemed in a hurry to get away. I wonder why."

He advanced toward the kitchen—toward Sam, who was cowering against the counter and staring at the intruder with the huge, shocked eyes of a terrified child, of some poor fourth-grade Simple Simon.

I am imagining this, Sam thought, *or I'm having a nightmare—a nightmare so horrible it makes the one I had two nights ago look like a sweet dream.*

But it was no nightmare. It was terrifying, but it was no nightmare.

Sam had time to hope he had gone crazy after all. Insanity was no day at the beach, but nothing could be as awful as this man-shaped thing which had come into his house, this thing which walked in its own wedge of winter.

Sam's house was old and the ceilings were high, but the Library Policeman had to duck his head in the entry, and even in the kitchen the crown of his gray felt hat almost brushed the ceiling. That meant he was over seven feet tall.

His body was wrapped in a trenchcoat the leaden color of fog at twilight. His skin was paper white. His face was dead, as if he could understand neither kindness nor love nor mercy. His mouth was set in lines of ultimate, passionless authority and Sam thought for one confused moment of how the closed library door had looked, like the slotted mouth in the face of a granite robot. The Library Policeman's eyes appeared to be silver circles which had been punc- tured by tiny shotgun pellets. They were rimmed with pinkish-red flesh that looked ready to bleed. They were lashless. And the worst thing of all was this: it was a face Sam *knew*. He did not think this was the first time he had cringed in terror beneath that black gaze, and far back in his mind, Sam heard a voice with the slightest trace of a lisp say: *Come with me, son . . . I'm a poleethman.*

The scar overlaid the geography of that face exactly as it had in Sam's imagination—across the left cheek, below the left eye, across the bridge of the nose. Except for the scar, it was the man in the poster . . . or was it? He could no longer be sure.

Come with me, son . . . I'm a poleethman.

Sam Peebles, darling of the Junction City Rotary Club, wet his pants. He felt his bladder let go in a warm gush, but that seemed far away and unimportant. What was important was that there was a monster in his kitchen, and the most terrible thing about this monster was that Sam almost knew his face. Sam felt a triple-locked door far back in his mind straining to burst open. He never thought of running. The idea of flight was beyond his capacity to imagine. He was a child again, a child who has been caught red-handed

(*the book isn't* The Speaker's Companion)

doing some awful bad thing. Instead of running

(*the book isn't* Best Loved Poems of the American People)

he folded slowly over his own wet crotch and collapsed between the two stools which stood at the counter, holding his hands up blindly above his head.

(the book is)

"No," he said in a husky, strengthless voice. "No, please—no, please, please don't do it to me, please, I'll be good, please don't hurt me that way."

He was reduced to this. But it didn't matter; the giant in the fog-colored trenchcoat

(the book is The Black Arrow *by Robert Louis Stevenson)*

now stood directly over him.

Sam dropped his head. It seemed to weigh a thousand pounds. He looked at the floor and prayed incoherently that when he looked up—when he had the *strength* to look up—the figure would be gone.

"Look at me," the distant, thudding voice instructed. It was the voice of an evil god.

"No," Sam cried in a shrieky, breathless voice, and then burst into helpless tears. It was not just terror, although the terror was real enough, bad enough. Separate from it was a cold deep drift of childish fright and childish shame. Those feelings clung like poison syrup to whatever it was he dared not remember, the thing that had something to do with a book he had never read: *The Black Arrow,* by Robert Louis Stevenson.

Whack!

Something struck Sam's head and he screamed.

"Look at me!"

"No, please don't make me," Sam begged.

Whack!

He looked up, shielding his streaming eyes with one rubbery arm, just in time to see the Library Policeman's arm come down again.

Whack!

He was hitting Sam with Sam's own rolled-up copy of the *Gazette,* whacking him the way you might a heedless puppy that has piddled on the floor.

"That'th better," said the Library Policeman. He grinned, lips parting to reveal the points of sharp teeth, teeth which were almost fangs. He reached into the pocket of his trenchcoat and brought out a leather folder. He flipped it open and revealed the strange star of many points. It glinted in the clean morning light.

Sam was now helpless to look away from that merciless face, those silver eyes with their tiny birdshot pupils. He was slobbering and knew it but was helpless to stop that, either.

"You have two books which belong to uth," the Library Policeman said. His voice still seemed to be coming from a distance, or
from behind a thick pane of glass. "Mith Lorth is very upthet with
you, Mr. Peebles."

"I lost them," Sam said, beginning to cry harder. The thought of
lying to this man about

(*The Black Arrow*)

the books, about *anything,* was out of the question. He was all
authority, all power, all force. He was judge, jury, and executioner.

Where's the janitor? Sam wondered incoherently. *Where's the janitor who checks the dials and then goes back into the sane world? The
sane world where things like this don't have to happen?*

"I . . . I . . . I . . ."

"I don't want to hear your thick ecthcuses," the Library Policeman
said. He flipped his leather folder closed and stuffed it into his right
pocket. At the same time he reached into his left pocket and drew
out a knife with a long, sharp blade. Sam, who had spent three
summers earning money for college as a stockboy, recognized it.
It was a carton-slitter. There was undoubtedly a knife like that in
every library in America. "You have until midnight. Then . . ."

He leaned down, extending the knife in one white, corpselike
hand. That freezing envelope of air struck Sam's face, numbed it.
He tried to scream and could produce only a glassy whisper of silent air.

The tip of the blade pricked the flesh of his throat. It was like
being pricked with an icicle. A single bead of scarlet oozed out and
then froze solid, a tiny seed-pearl of blood.

" . . . then I come again," the Library Policeman said in his odd,
lisp-rounded voice. "You better find what you lotht, Mr. Peebles."

The knife disappeared back into the pocket. The Library Policeman drew back up to his full height.

"There is another thing," he said. "You have been athking questions, Mr. Peebles. Don't athk any more. Do you underthand me?"

Sam tried to answer and could only utter a deep groan.

The Library Policeman began to bend down, pushing chill air
ahead of him the way the flat prow of a barge might push a chunk
of river-ice. "Don't pry into things that don't conthern you. *Do you
underthand me?*"

"*Yes!*" Sam screamed. "*Yes! Yes! Yes!*"

"Good. Because I will be watching. And I am not alone."

He turned, his trenchcoat rustling, and recrossed the kitchen toward the entry. He spared not a single backward glance for Sam. He passed through a bright patch of morning sun as he went, and Sam saw a wonderful, terrible thing: the Library Policeman cast no shadow.

He reached the back door. He grasped the knob. Without turning around he said in a low, terrible voice: "If you don't want to thee me again, Mr. Peebles, *find those bookth.*"

He opened the door and went out.

A single frantic thought filled Sam's mind the minute the door closed again and he heard the Library Policeman's feet on the back porch: he had to lock the door.

He got halfway to his feet and then grayness swam over him and he fell forward, unconscious.

CHAPTER TEN

CHRON-O-LODGE-ICK-A-LEE SPEAKING

1

"May I . . . help you?" the receptionist asked. The slight pause came as she took a second look at the man who had just approached the desk.

"Yes," Sam said. "I want to look at some back issues of the *Gazette,* if that's possible."

"Of course it is," she said. "But—pardon me if I'm out of line—do you feel all right, sir? Your color is very bad."

"I think I may be coming down with something, at that," Sam said.

"Spring colds are the worst, aren't they?" she said, getting up. "Come right through the gate at the end of the counter, Mr.—?"

"Peebles. Sam Peebles."

She stopped, a chubby woman of perhaps sixty, and cocked her head. She put one red-tipped nail to the corner of her mouth. "You sell insurance, don't you?"

"Yes, ma'am," he said.

"I thought I recognized you. Your picture was in the paper last week. Was it some sort of award?"

"No, ma'am," Sam said, "I gave a speech. At the Rotary Club." *And would give anything to be able to turn back the clock,* he thought. *I'd tell Craig Jones to go fuck himself.*

"Well, that's wonderful," she said . . . but she spoke as if there might be some doubt about it. "You looked different in the picture."

Sam came in through the gate.

"I'm Doreen McGill," the woman said, and put out a plump hand.

Sam shook it and said he was pleased to meet her. It took an effort. He thought that speaking to people—and touching people, especially that—was going to be an effort for quite awhile to come. All of his old ease seemed to be gone.

She led him toward a carpeted flight of stairs and flicked a light-switch. The stairway was narrow, the overhead bulb dim, and Sam felt the horrors begin to crowd in on him at once. They came eagerly, as fans might congregate around a person offering free tickets to some fabulous sold-out show. The Library Policeman could be down there, waiting in the dark. The Library Police-man with his dead white skin and red-rimmed silver eyes and small but hauntingly familiar lisp.

Stop it, he told himself. *And if you can't stop it, then for God's sake control it. You have to. Because this is your only chance. What will you do if you can't go down a flight of stairs to a simple office basement? Just cower in your house and wait for midnight?*

"That's the morgue," Doreen McGill said, pointing. This was clearly a lady who pointed every chance she got. "You only have to—"

"Morgue?" Sam asked, turning toward her. His heart had begun to knock nastily against his ribs. *"Morgue?"*

Doreen McGill laughed. "Everyone says it just like that. It's awful, isn't it? But that's what they call it. Some silly newspaper tradition, I guess. Don't worry, Mr. Peebles—there are no bodies down there; just reels and reels of microfilm."

I wouldn't be so sure, Sam thought, following her down the carpeted stairs. He was very glad she was leading the way.

She flicked on a line of switches at the foot of the stairs. A number of fluorescent lights, embedded in what looked like oversized in-verted ice-cube trays, went on. They lit up a large low room carpeted in the same dark blue as the stairs. The room was lined with shelves of small boxes. Along the left wall were four microfilm readers that looked like futuristic hair-driers. They were the same blue as the carpet.

"What I started to say was that you have to sign the book," Doreen said. She pointed again, this time at a large book chained to a stand by the door. "You also have to write the date, the time you came in, which is"—she checked her wristwatch—"twenty past ten, and the time you leave."

Sam bent over and signed the book. The name above his was Arthur Meecham. Mr. Meecham had been down here on December 27th, 1989. Over three months ago. This was a well-lighted, well-stocked, efficient room that apparently did very little business.

"It's nice down here, isn't it?" Doreen asked complacently. "That's because the federal government helps subsidize newspaper morgues—or libraries, if you like that word better. I know *I* do."

A shadow danced in one of the aisles and Sam's heart began to knock again. But it was only Doreen McGill's shadow; she had bent over to make sure he had entered the correct time of day, and—

—and HE *didn't cast a shadow. The Library Policeman. Also ...*

He tried to duck the rest and couldn't.

Also, I can't live like this. I can't live with this kind of fear. I'd stick my head in a gas oven if it went on too long. And if it does, I will. It's not just fear of him—that man, or whatever he is. It's the way a person's mind feels, the way it screams when it feels everything it ever believed in slipping effortlessly away.

Doreen pointed to the right wall, where three large folio volumes stood on a single shelf. "That's January, February, and March of 1990," she said. "Every July the paper sends the first six months of the year to Grand Island, Nebraska, to be microfilmed. The same thing when December is over." She extended the plump hand and pointed a red-tipped nail at the shelves, counting over from the shelf at the right toward the microfilm readers at the left. She appeared to be admiring her fingernail as she did it. "The microfilms go that way, chronologically," she said. She pronounced the word carefully, producing something mildly exotic: *chron-o-lodge-ick-a-lee.* "Modern times on your right; ancient days on your left."

She smiled to show that this was a joke, and perhaps to convey a sense of how wonderful she thought all this was. Chron-o-lodge-ick-a-lee speaking, the smile said, it was all sort of a gas.

"Thank you," Sam said.

"Don't mention it. It's what we're here for. *One* of the things, anyway." She put her nail to the corner of her mouth and gave him her peek-a-boo smile again. "Do you know how to run a microfilm reader, Mr. Peebles?"

"Yes, thanks."

"All right. If I can help you further, I'll be right upstairs. Don't hesitate to ask."

"Are you—" he began, and then snapped his mouth shut on the rest: —*going to leave me here alone?*

She raised her eyebrows.

"Nothing," he said, and watched her go back upstairs. He had to resist a strong urge to pelt up the stairs behind her. Because, cushy blue carpet or not, this was another Junction City library.

And this one was called the morgue.

2

Sam walked slowly toward the shelves with their weight of square microfilm boxes, unsure of where to begin. He was very glad that the overhead fluorescents were bright enough to banish most of the troubling shadows in the corners.

He hadn't dared ask Doreen McGill if the name Ardelia Lortz rang a bell, or even if she knew roughly when the city Library had last undergone renovations. *You have been athking questions,* the Library Policeman had said. *Don't pry into things that don't concern you. Do you underthand?*

Yes, he understood. And he supposed he was risking the Library Policeman's wrath by prying anyway . . . but he wasn't asking questions, at least not exactly, and these *were* things that concerned him. They concerned him desperately.

I will be watching. And I am not alone.

Sam looked nervously over his shoulder. Saw nothing. And still found it impossible to move with any decision. He had gotten this far, but he didn't know if he could get any further. He felt more than intimidated, more than frightened. He felt shattered.

"You've got to," he muttered harshly, and wiped at his lips with a shaking hand. "You've just *got* to."

He made his left foot move forward. He stood that way a moment, legs apart, like a man caught in the act of fording a small stream. Then he made his right foot catch up with his left one. He made his way across to the shelf nearest the bound folios in this hesitant, reluctant fashion. A card on the end of the shelf read:

1987–1989.

That was almost certainly too recent—in fact, the Library renovations must have taken place before the spring of 1984, when he had moved to Junction City. If it had happened since, he would have noticed the workmen, heard people talking about it, and read about it in the *Gazette*. But, other than guessing that it must have happened in the last fifteen or twenty years (the suspended ceilings had not looked any older than that), he could narrow it down no further. If only he could *think* more clearly! But he couldn't. What had happened that morning screwed up any normal, rational effort to think the way heavy sunspot activity screwed up radio and TV transmissions. Reality and unreality had come together like vast stones, and Sam Peebles, one tiny, screaming, struggling speck of humanity, had had the bad luck to get caught between them.

He moved two aisles to the left, mostly because he was afraid that if he stopped moving for too long he might freeze up entirely, and walked down the aisle marked

1981–1983.

He picked a box almost at random and took it over to one of the microfilm readers. He snapped it on and tried to concentrate on the spool of microfilm (the spool was also blue, and Sam wondered if there was any reason why everything in this clean, well-lighted place was color coordinated) and nothing else. First you had to mount it on one of the spindles, right; then you had to thread it, check; then you had to secure the leader in the core of the take-up reel, okay. The machine was so simple an eight-year-old could have executed these little tasks, but it took Sam almost five minutes; he had his shaking hands and shocked, wandering mind to deal with. When he finally got the microfilm mounted and scrolled to the first frame, he discovered he had mounted the reel backward. The printed matter was upside down.

He patiently rewound the microfilm, turned it around, and re-threaded it. He discovered he didn't mind this little setback in the least; repeating the operation, one simple step at a time, seemed to calm him. This time the front page of the April 1, 1981, issue of the Junction city *Gazette* appeared before him, right side up. The headline bannered the surprise resignation of a town official Sam had never heard of, but his eyes were quickly drawn to a box at the bottom of the page. Inside the box was this message:

> RICHARD PRICE AND THE ENTIRE STAFF OF
> THE JUNCTION CITY PUBLIC LIBRARY
> REMIND YOU THAT
> APRIL 6TH–13TH IS
> NATIONAL LIBRARY WEEK
> COME AND SEE US!

Did I know that? Sam wondered. *Is that why I grabbed this particular box? Did I subconsciously remember that the second week of April is National Library Week?*

Come with me, a tenebrous, whispering voice answered. *Come with me, son . . . I'm a poleethman.*

Gooseflesh gripped him; a shudder shook him. Sam pushed both the question and that phantom voice away. After all, it didn't really matter why he had picked the April, 1981, issues of the *Gazette*; the important thing was that he had, and it was a lucky break.

Might be a lucky break.

He advanced the reel quickly to April 6th, and saw exactly what he had hoped for. Over the *Gazette* masthead, in red ink, it said:

> SPECIAL LIBRARY SUPPLEMENT ENCLOSED!

Sam advanced to the supplement. There were two photos on the first page of the supplement. One was of the Library's exterior. The other showed Richard Price, the head librarian, standing at the circulation desk and smiling nervously into the camera. He looked exactly as Naomi Higgins had described him—a tall, bespectacled man of about forty with a narrow little mustache. Sam was more interested in the background. He could see the suspended ceiling which had so shocked him on his second trip to the Library. So the renovations had been done prior to April of 1981.

The stories were exactly the sort of self-congratulatory puff-pieces he expected—he had been reading the *Gazette* for six years now and was very familiar with its ain't-we-a-jolly-bunch-of-JayCees editorial slant. There were informative (and rather breathless) items about National Library Week, the Summer Reading Program, the Junction County Bookmobile, and the new fund drive which had just commenced. Sam glanced over these quickly. On the last page of the supplement he found a much more interesting story, one written by Price himself. It was titled

THE JUNCTION CITY PUBLIC LIBRARY
One Hundred Years of History

Sam's eagerness did not last long. Ardelia's name wasn't there. He reached for the power switch to rewind the microfilm and then stopped. He saw a mention of the renovation project—it had happened in 1970—and there was something else. Something just a little off-key. Sam began to read the last part of Mr. Price's chatty historical note again, this time more carefully.

With the end of the Great Depression our Library turned the corner. In 1942, the Junction City Town Council voted $5,000 to repair the extensive water damage the Library sustained during the Flood of '32, and Mrs. Felicia Culpepper took on the job of Head Librarian, donating her time without recompense. She never lost sight of her goal: a completely renovated Library, serving a Town which was rapidly becoming a City.

Mrs. Culpepper stepped down in 1951, giving way to Christopher Lavin, the first Junction City Librarian with a degree in Library Science. Mr. Lavin inaugurated the Culpepper Memorial Fund, which raised over $15,000 for the acquisition of new books in its first year, and the Junction City Public Library was on its way into the modern age!

Shortly after I became Head Librarian in 1964, I made major renovations my number one goal. The funds needed to achieve this goal were finally raised by the end of 1969, and while both City and Federal money helped in the construction of the splen-

did building Junction City "bookworms" enjoy today, this
project could not have been completed without the help of all
those volunteers who later showed up to swing a hammer or
run a bench-saw during "Build Your Library Month" in August
of 1970!

Other notable projects during the 1970's and 1980's
included . . .

Sam looked up thoughtfully. He believed there was something
missing from Richard Price's careful, droning history of the town
Library. No; on second thought, missing was the wrong word. The
essay made Sam decide Price was a fussbudget of the first water—
probably a nice man, but a fussbudget just the same—and such
men did not miss things, especially when they were dealing with
subjects which were clearly close to their hearts.

So—not missing. Concealed.

It didn't quite add up, chron-o-lodge-ick-a-lee speaking. In 1951,
a man named Christopher Lavin had succeeded that saint Felicia
Culpepper as head librarian. In 1964, Richard Price had become
city librarian. Had Price succeeded Lavin? Sam didn't think so. He
thought that at some point during those thirteen blank years, a
woman named Ardelia Lortz had succeeded Lavin. Price, Sam
thought, had succeeded *her*. She wasn't in Mr. Price's fussbudgety
account of the Library because she had done . . . *something*. Sam was
no closer to knowing what that something might have been, but he
had a better idea of the magnitude. Whatever it was, it had been
bad enough for Price to make her an unperson in spite of his very
obvious love of detail and continuity.

Murder, Sam thought. *It must have been murder. It's really the only
thing bad enough to f—*

At that second a hand dropped on Sam's shoulder.

3

If he had screamed, he would undoubtedly have terrified the hand's
owner almost as much as she had already terrorized him, but Sam
was unable to scream. Instead, all the air whooshed out of him and
the world went gray again. His chest felt like an accordion being
slowly crushed under an elephant's foot. All of his muscles seemed

to have turned to macaroni. He did not wet his pants again. That was perhaps the only saving grace.

"Sam?" he heard a voice ask. It seemed to come from quite a distance—somewhere in Kansas, say. "Is that you?"

He swung around, almost falling out of his chair in front of the microfilm reader, and saw Naomi. He tried to get his breath back so he could say something. Nothing but a tired wheeze came out. The room seemed to waver in front of his eyes. The grayness came and went.

Then he saw Naomi take a stumble-step backward, her eyes widening in alarm, her hand going to her mouth. She struck one of the microfilm shelves almost hard enough to knock it over. It rocked, two or three of the boxes tumbled to the carpet with soft thumps, and then it settled back again.

"Omes," he managed at last. His voice came out in a whispery squeak. He remembered once, as a boy in St. Louis, trapping a mouse under his baseball cap. It had made a sound like that as it scurried about, looking for an escape hatch.

"Sam, what's *happened* to you?" She also sounded like someone who would have been screaming if shock hadn't whipped the breath out of her. We make quite a pair, Sam thought, Abbott and Costello Meet the Monsters.

"What are you doing here?" he said. "You scared the living shit out of me!"

There, he thought. *I went and used the s-word again. Called you Omes again, too. Sorry about that.* He felt a little better, and thought of getting up, but decided against it. No sense pressing his luck. He was still not entirely sure his heart wasn't going to vapor-lock.

"I went to the office to see you," she said. "Cammy Harrington said she thought she saw you come in here. I wanted to apologize. Maybe. I thought at first you must have played some cruel trick on Dave. He said you'd never do a thing like that, and I started to think that it *didn't* seem like you. You've always been so nice . . ."

"Thanks," Sam said. "I guess."

". . . and you seemed so . . . so bewildered on the telephone. I asked Dave what it was about, but he wouldn't tell me anything else. All I know is what I heard . . . and how he looked when he was talking to you. He looked like he'd seen a ghost."

No, Sam thought of telling her. *I was the one who saw the ghost. And this morning I saw something even worse.*

"Sam, you have to understand something about Dave . . . and about me. Well, I guess you already know about Dave, but I'm—"

"I guess I know," Sam told her. "I said in my note to Dave that I didn't see anyone at Angle Street, but that wasn't the truth. I didn't see anyone at first, but I walked through the downstairs, looking for Dave. I saw you guys out back. So . . . I know. But I don't know on purpose, if you see what I mean."

"Yes," she said. "It's all right. But . . . Sam . . . dear God, what's happened? Your hair . . ."

"What about my hair?" he asked her sharply.

She fumbled her purse open with hands that shook slightly and brought out a compact. "Look," she said.

He did, but he already knew what he was going to see.

Since eight-thirty this morning, his hair had gone almost completely white.

4

"I see you found your friend," Doreen McGill said to Naomi as they climbed back up the stairs. She put a nail to the corner of her mouth and smiled her cute-little-me smile.

"Yes."

"Did you remember to sign out?"

"Yes," Naomi said again. Sam hadn't, but she had done it for both of them.

"And did you return any microfilms you might have used?"

This time Sam said yes. He couldn't remember if either he or Naomi had returned the one spool of microfilm he had mounted, and he didn't care. All he wanted was to get out of here.

Doreen was still being coy. Finger tapping the edge of her lower lip, she cocked her head and said to Sam, "You *did* look different in the newspaper picture. I just can't put my finger on what it *is*."

As they went out the door, Naomi said: "He finally got smart and quit dyeing his hair."

On the steps outside, Sam exploded with laughter. The force of his bellows doubled him over. It was hysterical laughter, its sound only half a step removed from the sound of screams, but he didn't care. It felt good. It felt enormously cleansing.

Naomi stood beside him, seeming to be bothered neither by

Sam's laughing fit nor the curious glances they were drawing from passersby on the street. She even lifted one hand and waved to someone she knew. Sam propped his hands on his upper thighs, still caught in his helpless gale of laughter, and yet there was a part of him sober enough to think: *She has seen this sort of reaction before. I wonder where?* But he knew the answer even before his mind had finished articulating the question. Naomi was an alcoholic, and she had made working with other alcoholics, helping them, part of her own therapy. She had probably seen a good deal more than a hysterical laughing fit during her time at Angle Street.

She'll slap me, he thought, still howling helplessly at the image of himself at his bathroom mirror, patiently combing Grecian Formula into his locks. *She'll slap me, because that's what you do with hysterical people.*

Naomi apparently knew better. She only stood patiently beside him in the sunshine, waiting for him to regain control. At last his laughter began to taper off to wild snorts and runaway snickers. His stomach muscles ached and his vision was water-wavery and his cheeks were wet with tears.

"Feel better?" she asked.

"Oh, Naomi—" he began, and then another hee-haw bray of laughter escaped him and galloped off into the sunshiny morning. "You don't *know* how much better."

"Sure I do," she said. "Come on—we'll take my car."

"Where . . ." He hiccupped. "Where are we going?"

"Angel Street," she said, pronouncing it the way the sign-painter had intended it to be pronounced. "I'm very worried about Dave. I went there first this morning, but he wasn't there. I'm afraid he may be out drinking."

"That's nothing new, is it?" he asked, walking beside her down the steps. Her Datsun was parked at the curb, behind Sam's own car.

She glanced at him. It was a brief glance, but a complex one: irritation, resignation, compassion. Sam thought that if you boiled that glance down it would say *You don't know what you're talking about, but it's not your fault.*

"Dave's been sober almost a year this time, but his general health isn't good. As you say, falling off the wagon isn't anything new for him, but another fall may kill him."

"And that would be my fault." The last of his laughter dried up.

She looked at him, a little surprised. "No," she said. "That would be nobody's fault . . . but that doesn't mean I want it to happen. Or that it has to. Come on. We'll take my car. We can talk on the way."

6

"Tell me what happened to you," she said as they headed toward the edge of town. "Tell me everything. It isn't just your hair, Sam; you look ten years older."

"Bullshit," Sam said. He had seen more than his hair in Naomi's compact mirror; he had gotten a better look at himself than he wanted. "More like twenty. And it feels like a hundred."

"What happened? What was it?"

Sam opened his mouth to tell her, thought of how it would sound, then shook his head. "No," he said, "not yet. You're going to tell me something first. You're going to tell me about Ardelia Lortz. You thought I was joking the other day. I didn't realize that then, but I do now. So tell me all about her. Tell me who she was and what she did."

Naomi pulled over to the curb beyond Junction City's old granite firehouse and looked at Sam. Her skin was very pale beneath her light make-up, and her eyes were wide. "You *weren't*? Sam, are you trying to tell me you *weren't* joking?"

"That's right."

"But Sam . . ." She stopped, and for a moment she seemed not to know how she should go on. At last she spoke very softly, as though to a child who has done something he doesn't know is wrong. "But Sam, Ardelia Lortz is dead. She has been dead for thirty years."

"I know she's dead. I mean, I know it *now*. What I want to know is the rest."

"Sam, whoever you think you saw—"

"I *know* who I saw."

"Tell me what makes you think—"

"First, you tell me."

She put her car back in gear, checked her rear-view mirror, and began to drive toward Angle Street again. "I don't know very much," she said. "I was only five when she died, you see. Most of what I *do* know comes from overheard gossip. She belonged to The First Baptist Church of Proverbia—she went there, at least—but my mother doesn't talk about her. Neither do any of the older parishioners. To them it's like she never existed."

Sam nodded. "That's just how Mr. Price treated her in the article he wrote about the Library. The one I was reading when you put your hand on my shoulder and took about twelve more years off my life. It also explains why your mother was so mad at me when I mentioned her name Saturday night."

Naomi glanced at him, startled. "*That's* what you called about?" Sam nodded.

"Oh, Sam—if you weren't on Mom's s-list before, you are now."

"Oh, I was on before, but I've got an idea she's moved me up." Sam laughed, then winced. His stomach still hurt from his fit on the steps of the newspaper office, but he was very glad he had had that fit—an hour ago he never would have believed he could have gotten so much of his equilibrium back. In fact, an hour ago he had been quite sure that Sam Peebles and equilibrium were going to remain mutually exclusive concepts for the rest of his life. "Go ahead, Naomi."

"Most of what I've heard I picked up at what AA people call 'the real meeting,' " she said. "That's when people stand around drinking coffee before and then after, talking about everything under the sun."

He looked at her curiously. "How long have you been in AA, Naomi?"

"Nine years," Naomi said evenly. "And it's been six since I had to take a drink. But I've been an alcoholic forever. Drunks aren't made, Sam. They're born."

"Oh," he said lamely. And then: "Was *she* in the program? Ardelia Lortz?"

"God, no—but that doesn't mean there aren't people in AA who remember her. She showed up in Junction City in 1956 or '57, I think. She went to work for Mr. Lavin in the Public Library. A year or two later, he died very suddenly—it was a heart attack or a stroke, I think—and the town gave the job to the Lortz woman. I've heard she was very good at it, but judging by what happened, I'd say the thing she was best at was fooling people."

"What did she do, Naomi?"

"She killed two children and then herself," Naomi said simply. "In the summer of 1960. There was a search for the kids. No one thought of looking for them in the Library, because it was supposed to be closed that day. They were found the next day, when the Library was supposed to be open but wasn't. There are skylights in the Library roof—"

"I know."

"—but these days you can only see them from the outside, because they changed the Library inside. Lowered the ceiling to conserve heat, or something. Anyway, those skylights had big brass catches on them. You grabbed the catches with a long pole to open the skylights and let in fresh air, I guess. She tied a rope to one of the catches—she must have used one of the track-ladders that ran along the bookcases to do it—and hanged herself from it. She did that after she killed the children."

"I see." Sam's voice was calm, but his heart was beating slowly and very hard. "And how did she . . . how did she kill the children?"

"I don't know. No one's ever said, and I've never asked. I suppose it was horrible."

"Yes. I suppose it was."

"Now tell me what happened to you."

"First I want to see if Dave's at the shelter."

Naomi tightened up at once. "*I'll* see if Dave's at the shelter," she said. "You're going to sit tight in the car. I'm sorry for you, Sam, and I'm sorry I jumped to the wrong conclusion last night. But you won't upset Dave anymore. I'll see to that."

"Naomi, he's a *part* of this!"

"That's impossible," she said in a brisk this-closes-the-discussion tone of voice.

"Dammit, the whole *thing* is impossible!"

They were nearing Angle Street now. Ahead of them was a pickup truck rattling toward the Recycling Center, its bed full of cardboard cartons filled with bottles and cans.

"I don't think you understand what I told you," she said. "It doesn't surprise me; Earth People rarely do. So open your ears, Sam. I'm going to say it in words of one syllable. *If Dave drinks, Dave dies.* Do you follow that? Does it get through?"

She tossed another glance Sam's way. This one was so furious it was still smoking around the edges, and even in the depths of his own distress, Sam realized something. Before, even on the two occasions when he had taken Naomi out, he had thought she was pretty. Now he saw she was beautiful.

"What does that mean, Earth People?" he asked her.

"People who don't have a problem with booze or pills or pot or cough medicine or any of the other things that mess up the human head," she nearly spat. "People who can afford to moralize and make judgments."

Ahead of them, the pick-up truck turned off onto the long, rutted driveway leading to the redemption center. Angle Street lay ahead. Sam could see something parked in front of the porch, but it wasn't a car. It was Dirty Dave's shopping-cart.

"Stop a minute," he said.

Naomi did, but she wouldn't look at him. She stared straight ahead through the windshield. Her jaw was working. There was high color in her cheeks.

"You care about him," he said, "and I'm glad. Do you also care about me, Sarah? Even though I'm an Earth Person?"

"You have no right to call me Sarah. I can, because it's part of my name—I was christened Naomi Sarah Higgins. And *they* can, because they are, in a way, closer to me than blood relatives could ever be. We *are* blood relatives, in fact—because there's something in us that makes us the way we are. Something in our blood. *You,* Sam—you have no right."

"Maybe I do," Sam said. "Maybe I'm one of you now. You've got booze. This Earth Person has got the Library Police."

Now she looked at him, and her eyes were wide and wary. "Sam, I don't underst—"

"Neither do I. All I know is that I need help. I need it desperately. I borrowed two books from a library that doesn't exist anymore, and now the books don't exist, either. I lost them. Do you know where they ended up?"

She shook her head.

Sam pointed over to the left, where two men had gotten out of the pick-up's cab and were starting to unload the cartons of returnables. "There. That's where they ended up. They've been pulped. I've got until midnight, Sarah, and then the Library Police are going to pulp *me.* And I don't think they'll even leave my jacket behind."

6

Sam sat in the passenger seat of Naomi Sarah Higgins's Datsun for what seemed like a long, long time. Twice his hand went to the door-handle and then fell back. She had relented . . . a little. *If* Dave wanted to talk to him, and *if* Dave was still in any condition to talk, she would allow it. Otherwise, no soap.

At last the door of Angle Street opened. Naomi and Dave Duncan came out. She had an arm around his waist, his feet were shuffling, and Sam's heart sank. Then, as they stepped out into the sun, he saw that Dave wasn't drunk . . . or at least not necessarily. Looking at him was, in a weird way, like looking into Naomi's compact mirror all over again. Dave Duncan looked like a man trying to weather the worst shock of his life . . . and not doing a very good job of it.

Sam got out of the car and stood by the door, indecisive.

"Come up on the porch," Naomi said. Her voice was both resigned and fearful. "I don't trust him to make it down the steps."

Sam came up to where they stood. Dave Duncan was probably sixty years old. On Saturday he had looked seventy or seventy-five. That was the booze, Sam supposed. And now, as Iowa turned slowly on the axis of noon, he looked older than all the ages. And that, Sam knew, was his fault. It was the shock of things Dave had assumed were long buried.

I didn't know, Sam thought, but this, however true it might be, had lost its power to comfort. Except for the burst veins in his nose and cheeks, Dave's face was the color of very old paper. His eyes were watery and stunned. His lips had a bluish tinge, and little beads of spittle pulsed in the deep pockets at the corners of his mouth.

"I didn't want him to talk to you," Naomi said. "I wanted to take him to Dr. Melden, but he refuses to go until he talks to you."

"Mr. Peebles," Dave said feebly. "I'm sorry, Mr. Peebles, it's all my fault, isn't it? I—"

"You have nothing to apologize for," Sam said. "Come on over here and sit down."

He and Naomi led Dave to a rocking chair at the corner of the porch and Dave eased himself into it. Sam and Naomi drew up chairs with sagging wicker bottoms and sat on either side of him.

They sat without speaking for some little time, looking out across the railroad tracks and into the flat farm country beyond.

"She's after you, isn't she?" Dave asked. "That bitch from the far side of hell."

"She's sicced someone on me," Sam said. "Someone who was in one of those posters you drew. He's a . . . I know this sounds crazy, but he's a Library Policeman. He came to see me this morning. He did . . ." Sam touched his hair. "He did this. And this." He pointed to the small red dot in the center of his throat. "And he says he isn't alone."

Dave was silent for a long time, looking out into the emptiness, looking at the flat horizon which was broken only by tall silos and, to the north, the apocalyptic shape of the Proverbia Feed Company's grain elevator. "The man you saw isn't real," he said at last. "None of them are real. Only her. Only the devil-bitch."

"Can you tell us, Dave?" Naomi asked gently. "If you can't, say so. But if it will make it better for you . . . easier . . . tell us."

"Dear Sarah," Dave said. He took her hand and smiled. "I love you—have I ever told you so?"

She shook her head, smiling back. Tears glinted in her eyes like tiny specks of mica. "No. But I'm glad, Dave."

"I *have* to tell," he said. "It isn't a question of better or easier. It can't be allowed to go on. Do you know what I remember about my first AA meeting, Sarah?"

She shook her head.

"How they said it was a program of honesty. How they said you had to tell everything, not just to God, but to God and another person. I thought, 'If that's what it takes to live a sober life, I've had it. They'll throw me in a plot up on Wayvern Hill in that part of the boneyard they set aside for the drunks and all-time losers who never had a pot to piss in nor a window to throw it out of. Because I could never tell all the things I've seen, all the things I've done.' "

"We all think that at first," she said gently.

"I know. But there can't be many that've seen the things I have, or done what I have. I did the best I could, though. Little by little I did the best I could. I set my house in order. But those things I saw and did back then . . . those I never told. Not to any person, not to no man's God. I found a room in the basement of my heart, and I put those things in that room and then I locked the door."

He looked at Sam, and Sam saw tears rolling slowly and tiredly down the deep wrinkles in Dave's blasted cheeks.

"Yes. I did. And when the door was locked, I nailed boards across it. And when the boards was nailed, I put sheet steel across the boards and riveted it tight. And when the riveting was done, I drawed a bureau up against the whole works, and before I called it good and walked away, I piled bricks on top of the bureau. And all these years since, I've spent telling myself I forgot all about Ardelia and her strange ways, about the things she wanted me to do and the things she told me and the promises she made and what she really was. I took a lot of forgetting medicine, but it never did the job. And when I got into AA, that was the one thing that always drove me back. The thing in that room, you know. That thing has a name, Mr. Peebles—its name is Ardelia Lortz. After I was sobered up awhile, I would start having bad dreams. Mostly I dreamed of the posters I did for her—the ones that scared the children so bad—but they weren't the worst dreams."

His voice had fallen to a trembling whisper.

"They weren't the worst ones by a long chalk."

"Maybe you better rest a little," Sam said. He had discovered that no matter how much might depend on what Dave had to say, a part of him didn't want to hear it. A part of him was *afraid* to hear it.

"Never mind resting," he said. "Doctor says I'm diabetic, my pancreas is a mess, and my liver is falling apart. Pretty soon I'm going on a permanent vacation. I don't know if it'll be heaven or hell for me, but I'm pretty sure the bars and package stores are closed in both places, and thank God for that. But the time for restin isn't now. If I'm ever goin to talk, it has to be now." He looked carefully at Sam. "You know you're in trouble, don't you?"

Sam nodded.

"Yes. But you don't know just how bad your trouble is. That's why I have to talk. I think she has to . . . has to lie still sometimes. But her time of bein still is over, and she has picked you, Mr. Peebles. That's why I have to talk. Not that I want to. I went out last night after Sarah was gone and bought myself a jug. I took it down to the switchin yard and sat where I've sat many times before, in the weeds and cinders and busted glass. I spun the cap off and held that jug up to my nose and smelled it. You know how that jug wine smells? To me it always smells like the wallpaper in cheap hotel rooms, or like a stream that has flowed its way through a town dump somewhere. But I have always liked that smell just the same, because it smells like sleep, too.

"And all the time I was holdin that jug up, smellin it, I could hear the bitch queen talkin from inside the room where I locked her up. From behind the bricks, the bureau, the sheet steel, the boards and locks. Talkin like someone who's been buried alive. She was a little muffled, but I could still hear her just fine. I could hear her sayin, 'That's right, Dave, that's the answer, it's the only answer there is for folks like you, the only one that works, and it will be the only answer you need until answers don't matter anymore.'

"I tipped that jug up for a good long drink, and then at the last second it smelled like *her* . . . and I remembered her face at the end, all covered with little threads . . . and how her mouth changed . . . and I threw that jug away. Smashed it on a railroad tie. Because this shit has got to end. I won't let her take another nip out of this town!"

His voice rose to a trembling but powerful old man's shout. "*This shit has gone on long enough!*"

Naomi laid a hand on Dave's arm. Her face was frightened and full of trouble. "What, Dave? What is it?"

"I want to be sure," Dave said. "You tell me first, Mr. Peebles. Tell me everything that's been happening to you, and don't leave out nothing."

"I will," Sam said, "on one condition."

Dave smiled faintly. "What condition is that?"

"You have to promise to call me Sam . . . and in return, I'll never call you Dirty Dave again."

His smile broadened. "You got a deal there, Sam."

"Good." He took a deep breath. "Everything was the fault of the goddam acrobat," he began.

7

It took longer than he had thought it would, but there was an inexpressible relief—a joy, almost—in telling it all, holding nothing back. He told Dave about The Amazing Joe, Craig's call for help, and Naomi's suggestion about livening up his material. He told them about how the Library had looked, and about his meeting with Ardelia Lortz. Naomi's eyes grew wider and wider as he spoke. When he got to the part about the Red Riding Hood poster on the door to the Children's Library, Dave nodded.

"That's the only one I didn't draw," he said. "She had that one with her. I bet they never found it, either. I bet she *still* has that one with her. She liked mine, but that one was her favorite."

"What do you mean?" Sam asked.

Dave only shook his head and told Sam to go on.

He told them about the library card, the books he had borrowed, and the strange little argument they had had on Sam's way out.

"That's it," Dave said flatly. "That's all it took. You might not believe it, but I know her. You made her mad. Goddam if you didn't. You made her mad . . . and now she's set her cap for you."

Sam finished his story as quickly as he could, but his voice slowed and nearly halted when he came to the visit from the Library Policeman in his fog-gray trenchcoat. When Sam finished, he was nearly weeping and his hands had begun to shake again.

"Could I have a glass of water?" he asked Naomi thickly.

"Of course," she said, and got up to get it. She took two steps, then returned and kissed Sam on the cheek. Her lips were cool and soft. And before she left to get his water, she spoke three blessed words into his ear: "I believe you."

8

Sam raised the glass to his lips, using both hands to be sure he wouldn't spill it, and drank half of it at a draught. When he put it down he said, "What about you, Dave? Do you believe me?"

"Yeah," Dave said. He spoke almost absently, as if this were a foregone conclusion. Sam supposed that, to Dave, it was. After all, he had known the mysterious Ardelia Lortz firsthand, and his ravaged, too-old face suggested that theirs had not been a loving relationship.

Dave said nothing else for several moments, but a little of his color had come back. He looked out across the railroad tracks toward the fallow fields. They would be green with sprouting corn in another six or seven weeks, but now they looked barren. His eyes watched a cloud shadow flow across that Midwestern emptiness in the shape of a giant hawk.

At last he seemed to rouse himself and turned to Sam.

"My Library Policeman—the one I drew for her—didn't have no scar," he said at last.

Sam thought of the stranger's long, white face. The scar had been there, all right—across the cheek, under the eye, over the bridge of the nose in a thin flowing line.

"So?" he asked. "What does that mean?"

"It don't mean nothing to me, but I think it must mean somethin to you, Mr.—Sam. I know about the badge . . . what you called the star of many points. I found that in a book of heraldry right there in the Junction City Library. It's called a Maltese Cross. Christian knights wore them in the middle of their chests when they went into battle durin the Crusades. They were supposed to be magical. I was so taken with the shape that I put it into the picture. But . . . a scar? No. Not on *my* Library Policeman. Who was *your* Library Policeman, Sam?"

"I don't . . . I don't know what you're talking about," Sam said slowly, but that voice—faint, mocking, haunting—recurred: *Come with me, son . . . I'm a poleethman.* And his mouth was suddenly full of that taste again. The sugar-slimy taste of red licorice. His taste-buds cramped; his stomach rolled. But it was stupid. Really quite stupid. He had never eaten red licorice in his life. He hated it.

If you've never eaten it, how do you know you hate it?

"I really don't get you," he said, speaking more strongly.

"You're getting *something*," Naomi said. "You look like someone just kicked you in the stomach."

Sam glanced at her, annoyed. She looked back at him calmly, and Sam felt his heart rate speed up.

"Let it alone for now," Dave said, "although you can't let it alone for long, Sam—not if you want to hold onto any hope of getting out of this. Let me tell you my story. I've never told it before, and I'll never tell it again . . . but it's time."

CHAPTER ELEVEN

DAVE'S STORY

1

"I wasn't always Dirty Dave Duncan," he began. "In the early fifties I was just plain old Dave Duncan, and people liked me just fine. I was a member of that same Rotary Club you talked to the other night, Sam. Why not? I had my own business, and it made money. I was a sign-painter, and I was a damned good one. I had all the work I could handle in Junction City and Proverbia, but I sometimes did a little work up in Cedar Rapids, as well. Once I painted a Lucky Strike cigarette ad on the right-field wall of the minor-league ball-park all the way to hell and gone in Omaha. I was in great demand, and I deserved to be. I was good. I was just the best sign-painter around these parts.

"I stayed here because serious painting was what I was really interested in, and I thought you could do that anywhere. I didn't have no formal art education—I tried but I flunked out—and I knew that put me down on the count, so to speak, but I knew that there were artists who made it without all that speed-shit bushwah—Gramma Moses, for one. She didn't need no driver's license; she went right to town without one.

"I might even have made it. I sold some canvases, but not many—I didn't need to, because I wasn't married and I was doing well with my sign-painting business. Also, I kept most of my pitchers so I could put on shows, the way artists are supposed to. I had some, too. Right here in town at first, then in Cedar Rapids, and then in Des Moines. That one was written up in the *Democrat*, and they made me sound like the second coming of James Whistler."

Dave fell silent for a moment, thinking. Then he raised his head and looked out at the empty, fallow fields again.

"In AA, they talk about folks who have one foot in the future and the other in the past and spend their time pissin all over today because of it. But sometimes it's hard not to wonder what might have happened if you'd done things just a little different."

He looked almost guiltily at Naomi, who smiled and pressed his hand.

"Because I *was* good, and I *did* come close. But I was drinkin heavy, even back then. I didn't think much of it—hell, I was young, I was strong, and besides, don't all great artists drink? *I* thought they did. And I still might have made it—made something, anyway, for awhile—but then Ardelia Lortz came to Junction City.

"And when she came, I was lost."

He looked at Sam.

"I recognize her from your story, Sam, but that wasn't how she looked back then. You expected to see an old-lady librarian, and that suited her purpose, so that's just what you *did* see. But when she came to Junction City in the summer of '57, her hair was ash-blonde, and the only places she was plump was where a woman is supposed to be plump.

"I was living out in Proverbia then, and I used to go to the Baptist Church. I wasn't much on religion, but there were some fine-looking women there. Your mom was one of em, Sarah."

Naomi laughed in the way women do when they are told something they cannot quite believe.

"Ardelia caught on with the home folks right away. These days, when the folks from that church talk about her—if they ever do— I bet they say things like 'I knew from the very start there was *somethin* funny about that Lortz woman' or 'I never trusted the look in that woman's eye,' but let me tell you, that wasn't how it was. They buzzed around her—the women as well as the men—like bees around the first flower of spring. She got a job as Mr. Lavin's assistant before she was in town a month, but she was teachin the little ones at the Sunday School out there in Proverbia two weeks before that.

"Just *what* she was teachin em I don't like to think—you can bet your bottom dollar it wasn't the Gospel According to Matthew— but she was teachin em. And everyone swore on how much the little ones loved her. *They* swore on it, too, but there was a look in their eyes when they said so . . . a far-off look, like they wasn't really sure where they were, or even *who* they were.

"Well, she caught my eye . . . and I caught hers. You wouldn't know it from the way I am now, but I was a pretty good-lookin fella in those days. I always had a tan from workin outdoors, I had muscles, my hair was faded almost blonde from the sun, and my belly was as flat as your ironin board, Sarah.

"Ardelia had rented herself a farmhouse about a mile and a half from the church, a tight enough little place, but it needed a coat of paint as bad as a man in the desert needs a drink of water. So after church the second week I noticed her there—I didn't go often and by then it was half-past August—I offered to paint it for her.

"She had the biggest eyes you've ever seen. I guess most people would have called them gray, but when she looked right at you, hard, you would have sworn they were silver. And she looked at *me* hard that day after church. She was wearin some kind of perfume that I never smelled before and ain't never smelled since. Lavender, I think. I can't think how to describe it, but I know it always made me think of little white flowers that only bloom after the sun has gone down. And I was smitten. Right there and then.

"She was close to me—almost close enough for our bodies to touch. She was wearin this dowdy black dress, the kind of dress an old lady would wear, and a hat with a little net veil, and she was holdin her purse in front of her. All prim and proper. Her *eyes* weren't prim, though. Nossir. Nor proper. Not a bit.

" 'I hope you don't want to put advertisements for bleach and chewing tobacco all over my new house,' she says.

" 'No ma'am,' I says back. 'I thought just two coats of plain old white. Houses aren't what I do for a livin, anyway, but with you bein new in town and all, I thought it would be neighborly—'

" 'Yes indeed,' she says, and touches my shoulder."

Dave looked apologetically at Naomi.

"I think I ought to give you a chance to leave, if you want to. Pretty soon I'm gonna start tellin some dirty stuff, Sarah. I'm ashamed of it, but I want to clean the slate of my doins with her."

She patted his old, chapped hand. "Go ahead," she told him quietly. "Say it all."

He fetched in a deep breath and went on again.

"When she touched me, I knew I had to have her or die tryin. Just that one little touch made me feel better—and crazier—than any woman-touch ever made me feel in my whole life. She knew it, too. I could see it in her eyes. It was a sly look. It was a mean look, too, but somethin about that excited me more than anything else.

" 'It *would* be neighborly, Dave,' she says, 'and I want to be a *very* good neighbor.'

"So I walked her home. Left all the other young fellows standin at the church door, you might say, fumin and no doubt cursin my name. They didn't know how lucky they were. None of them.

"My Ford was in the shop and she didn't have no car, so we were stuck with shank's mare. I didn't mind a bit, and she didn't seem to, neither. We went out the Truman Road, which was still dirt in those days, although they sent a town truck along to oil it every two or three weeks and lay the dust.

"We got about halfway to her place, and she stopped. It was just the two of us, standin in the middle of Truman Road at high noon on a summer's day, with about a million acres of Sam Orday's corn on one side and about two million of Bill Humpe's corn on the other, all of it growin high over our heads and rustlin in that secret way corn has, even when there's no breeze. My granddad used to say it was the sound of the corn growin. I dunno if that's the truth or not, but it's a spooky sound. I can tell you that.

" 'Look!' she says, pointin to the right. 'Do you see it?'

"I looked, but I didn't see nothing—only corn. I told her so.

" 'I'll show you!' she says, and runs into the corn, Sunday dress and high heels and all. She didn't even take off that hat with the veil on it.

"I stood there for a few seconds, sorta stunned. Then I heard her laughin. I heard her laughin in the corn. So I ran in after her, partly to see whatever it was she'd seen, but mostly because of that laugh. I was *so* randy. I can't begin to tell you.

"I seen her standin way up the row I was in, and then she faded into the next one, still laughin. I started to laugh, too, and went on through myself, not carin that I was bustin down some of Sam Orday's plants. He'd never miss em, not in all those acres. But when I got through, trailin cornsilk off my shoulders and a green leaf stuck in my tie like some new kind of clip, I stopped laughin in a hurry, because she wasn't there. Then I heard her on the other side of me. I didn't have no idea how she could have got back there without me seein her, but she had. So I busted back through just in time to see her runnin into the next row.

"We played hide n seek for half an hour, I guess, and I couldn't catch her. All I did was get hotter and randier. I'd think she was a row over, in front of me, but I'd get there and hear her *two* rows over, *behind* me. Sometimes I'd see her foot, or her leg, and of course she left tracks in the soft dirt, but they weren't no good, because they seemed to go every which way at once.

"Then, just when I was startin to get mad—I'd sweat through my good shirt, my tie was undone, and my shoes was full of dirt—

I come through to a row and seen her hat hangin off a corn-plant with the veil flippin in the little breeze that got down there into the corn.

" 'Come and get me, Dave!' she calls. I grabbed her hat and busted through to the next row on a slant. She was gone—I could just see the corn waverin where she'd went through—but both her shoes were there. In the next row I found one of her silk stockins hung over an ear of corn. And still I could hear her laughin. Over on my blind side, she was, and how the bitch got there, God only knows. Not that it mattered to me by then.

"I ripped off my tie and tore after her, around and around and dosey-doe, pantin like a stupid dog that don't know enough to lie still on a hot day. And I'll tell you somethin—I broke the corn down everywhere I went. Left a trail of trampled stalks and leaners behind me. But *she* never busted a one. They'd just waver a bit when she passed, as if there was no more to her than there was to that little summer breeze.

"I found her dress, her slip, and her garter-belt. Then I found her bra and step-ins. I couldn't hear her laughin no more. There wasn't no sound but the corn. I stood there in one of the rows, puffin like a leaky boiler, with all her clothes bundled up against my chest. I could smell her perfume in em, and it was drivin me crazy.

" 'Where are you?' I yelled, but there wasn't no answer. Well, I finally lost what little sanity I had left . . . and of course, that was just what she wanted. '*Where the fuck are you?*' I screamed, and her long white arm reached through the corn-plants right beside me and she stroked my neck with one finger. It jumped the shit out of me.

" 'I've been waiting for you,' she said. 'What took you so long? Don't you want to see it?' She grabbed me and drawed me through the corn, and there she was with her feet planted in the dirt, not a stitch on her, and her eyes as silver as rain on a foggy day."

2

Dave took a long drink of water, closed his eyes, and went on.

"We didn't make love there in the corn—in all the time I knew her, we never made love. But we made *somethin*. I had Ardelia in just about every way a man can have a woman, and I think I had her in some ways you'd think would be impossible. I can't remember all the ways, but I can remember her body, how white it was; how her legs looked; how her toes curled and seemed to feel along the shoots of the plants comin out of the dirt; I can remember how she pulled her fingernails back and forth across the skin of my neck and my throat.

"We went on and on and on. I don't know how many times, but I know I didn't never get tired. When we started I felt horny enough to rape the Statue of Liberty, and when we finished I felt the same way. I couldn't get enough of her. It was like the booze, I guess. Wasn't any way I could *ever* get enough of her. And she knew it, too.

"But we finally *did* stop. She put her hands behind her head and wriggled her white shoulders in the black dirt we was layin in and looked up at me with those silvery eyes of hers and she says, 'Well, Dave? Are we neighbors yet?'

"I told her I wanted to go again and she told me not to push my luck. I tried to climb on just the same, and she pushed me off as easy as a mother pushes a baby off'n her tit when she don't want to feed it no more. I tried again and she swiped at my face with her nails and split the skin open in two places. That finally damped my boiler down. She was quick as a cat and twice as strong. When she saw I knew playtime was over, she got dressed and led me out of the corn. I went just as meek as Mary's little lamb.

"We walked the rest of the way to her house. Nobody passed us, and that was probably just as well. My clothes were all covered with dirt and cornsilk, my shirttail was out, my tie was stuffed into my back pocket and flappin along behind me like a tail, and every place that the cloth rubbed I felt raw. *Her*, though—she looked as smooth and cool as an ice-cream soda in a drugstore glass. Not a hair out of place, not a speck of dirt on her shoes, not a strand of cornsilk on her skirt.

"We got to the house and while I was lookin it over, tryin to decide how much paint it would take, she brought me a drink in a tall glass. There was a straw in it, and a sprig of mint. I thought it was iced tea until I took a sip. It was straight Scotch.

" 'Jesus!' I says, almost chokin.

" 'Don't you want it?' she asks me, smilin in that mockin way she had. 'Maybe you'd prefer some iced coffee.'

" 'Oh, I want it,' I says, but it was more than that. I *needed* it. I was tryin not to drink in the middle of the day back then, because that's what alcoholics do. But that was the end of that. For the rest of the time I knew her, I drank pretty near all day, every day. For me, the last two and a half years Ike was President was one long souse.

"While I was paintin her house—and doin everything she'd let me do to her whenever I could—she was settlin in at the Library. Mr. Lavin hired her first crack outta the box, and put her in charge of the Children's Library. I used to go there every chance I got, which was a lot, since I was self-employed. When Mr. Lavin spoke to me about how much time I was spendin there, I promised to paint the whole inside of the Library for free. Then he let me come and go as much as I wanted. Ardelia told me it would work out just that way, and she was right—as usual.

"I don't have any connected memories of the time I spent under her spell—and that's what I was, an enchanted man livin under the spell of a woman who wasn't really a woman at all. It wasn't the blackouts that drunks sometimes get; it was wantin to forget things after they were over. So what I have is memories that stand apart from each other but seem to lie in a chain, like those islands in the Pacific Ocean. Archie Pelligos, or whatever they call em.

"I remember she put the poster of Little Red Ridin Hood up on the door to the Children's Room about a month before Mr. Lavin died, and I remember her takin one little boy by the hand and leadin him over to it. 'Do you see that little girl?' Ardelia asked him. 'Yes,' he says. 'Do you know why that Bad Thing is getting ready to eat her?' Ardelia asks. 'No,' the kid says back, his eyes all big and solemn and full of tears. 'Because he forgot to bring back his library book on time,' she says. 'You won't ever do that, Willy, will you?' 'No, never,' the little boy says, and Ardelia says, 'You better not.' And then she led him into the Children's Room for Story Hour, still holdin him by the hand. That kid—it was Willy Klemmart, who got killed in Vietnam—looked back over his shoulder at where I was, standin on my scaffold with a paintbrush in my hand, and I could read his eyes like they were a newspaper headline. *Save me from her*, his eyes said. *Please, Mr. Duncan.* But how could I? I couldn't even save myself."

Dave produced a clean but badly wrinkled bandanna from the depths of one back pocket and blew a mighty honk into it.

"Mr. Lavin began by thinkin Ardelia just about walked on water, but he changed his mind after awhile. They got into a hell of a scrap over that Red Ridin Hood poster about a week before he died. He never liked it. Maybe he didn't have a very good idea of what went on durin Story Hour—I'll get to that pretty soon—but he wasn't *entirely* blind. He saw the way the kids looked at that poster. At last he told her to take it down. That was when the argument started. I didn't hear it all because I was on the scaffold, high above them, and the acoustics were bad, but I heard enough. He said somethin about scaring the children, or maybe it was *scarring* the children, and she said somethin back about how it helped her keep 'the rowdy element' under control. She called it a teachin tool, just like the hickory stick.

"But he stuck to his guns and she finally had to take it down. That night, at her house, she was like a tiger in the zoo after some kid has spent all day pokin it with a stick. She went back and forth in great big long strides, not a stitch on, her hair flyin out behind her. I was in bed, drunk as a lord. But I remember she turned around and her eyes had gone from silver to bright red, as if her brains had caught afire, and her mouth looked funny, like it was tryin to pull itself right out of her face, or somethin. It almost scared me sober. I hadn't ever seen nothin like that, and never wanted to see it again.

" 'I'm going to fix him,' she said. 'I'm going to fix that fat old whoremaster, Davey. You wait and see.'

"I told her not to do anything stupid, not to let her temper get the best of her, and a lot of other stuff that didn't stand knee-high to jack shit. She listened to me for awhile and then she ran across the room so fast that . . . well, I don't know how to say it. One second she was standin all the way across the room by the door, and the next second she was jumpin on top of me, her eyes red and glaring, her mouth all pooched out of her face like she wanted to kiss me so bad she was stretchin her skin somehow to do it, and I had an idea that instead of just scratchin me this time, she was gonna put her nails into my throat and peel me to the backbone.

"But she didn't. She put her face right down to mine and looked at me. I don't know what she saw—how scared I was, I guess—but it must have made her happy, because she tipped her head back so her hair fell all the way down to my thighs, and she laughed. 'Stop talking, you damned souse,' she said, 'and stick it in me. What else are you good for?'

"So I did. Because stickin it in her—and drinkin—*was* all I was good for by then. I surely wasn't paintin pitchers anymore, I lost my license after I got clipped for my third OUI—in '58 or early '59, that was—and I was gettin bad reports on some of my jobs. I didn't care much how I did them anymore, you see; all I wanted was her. Talk started to circulate about how Dave Duncan wasn't trustworthy no more . . . but the *reason* they said I wasn't was always the booze. The word of what we were to each other never got around much. She was careful as the devil about that. My reputation went to hell in a handbasket, but she never got so much as a splash of mud on the hem of her skirts.

"I think Mr. Lavin suspected. At first he thought I just had a crush on her and she never so much as knew I was makin calf's eyes at her from up on my scaffold, but I think that in the end he suspected. But then Mr. Lavin died. They said it was a heart attack, but I know better. We were in the hammock on her back porch that night after it happened, and that night it was *her* that couldn't get enough of it. She screwed me until I hollered uncle. Then she lay down next to me and looked at me as content as a cat that's had its fill of cream, and her eyes had that deep-red glow again. I am not talking about something in my imagination; I could see the reflection of that red glow on the skin of my bare arm. And I could *feel* it. It was like sittin next to a woodstove that's been stoked and then damped down. 'I told you I'd fix him, Davey,' she says all at once in this mean, teasin voice.

"Me, I was drunk and half killed with fuckin—what she said hardly registered on me. I felt like I was fallin asleep in a pit of quicksand. 'What'd you do to him?' I asked, half in a doze.

" 'I hugged him,' she said. 'I give special hugs, Davey—you don't know about my special hugs, and if you're lucky, you never will. I got him in the stacks and put my arms around him and showed him what I really looked like. Then he began to cry. That's how scared he was. He began to cry his special tears, and I kissed them away, and when I was done, he was dead in my arms.'

" 'His special tears.' That's what she called them. And then her face . . . it *changed*. It rippled, like it was underwater. And I seen something . . . "

Dave trailed off, looking out into the flatlands, looking at the grain elevator, looking at nothing. His hands had gripped the porch rail. They flexed, loosened, flexed again.

"I don't remember," he said at last. "Or maybe I don't *want* to remember. Except for two things: it had red eyes with no lids, and there was a lot of loose flesh around its mouth, lyin in folds and flaps, but it wasn't skin. It looked . . . dangerous. Then that flesh around its mouth started to move somehow and I think I started to scream. Then it was gone. All of it was gone. It was only Ardelia again, peepin up at me and smilin like a pretty, curious cat.

" 'Don't worry,' she says. 'You don't have to see, Davey. As long as you do what I tell you, that is. As long as you're one of the Good Babies. As long as you behave. Tonight I'm very happy, because that old fool is gone at last. The Town Council is going to appoint me in his place, and I'll run things the way I want.'

"God help us all, then, I thought, but I didn't say it. You wouldn't't've, either, if you'd looked down and seen that thing with those starin red eyeballs curled up next to you in a hammock way out in the country, so far out nobody would hear you screamin even if you did it at the top of your lungs.

"A little while later she went into the house and come back out with two of those tall glasses full of Scotch, and pretty soon I was twenty thousand leagues under the sea again, where nothing mattered.

"She kept the Library closed for a week . . . 'out of respect for Mr. Lavin' was how she put it, and when she opened up again, Little Red Ridin Hood was back on the door of the Children's Room. A week or two after that, she told me she wanted me to make some new posters for the Children's Room."

He paused, then went on in a lower, slower voice.

"There's a part of me, even now, that wants to sugarcoat it, make my part in it better than it was. I'd like to tell you that I fought with her, argued, told her I didn't want nothin to do with scarin a bunch of kids . . . but it wouldn't be true. I went right along with what she wanted me to do. God help me, I did. Partly it was because I was scared of her by then. But mostly it was because I was still besotted with her. And there was something else, too. There was a mean, nasty part of me—I don't think it's in everyone, but I think it's in a lot of us—that liked what she was up to. *Liked* it.

"Now, you're wonderin what I *did* do, and I can't really tell you all of it. I really don't remember. Those times is all jumbled up, like the broken toys you send to the Salvation Army just to get the damned things out of the attic.

"I didn't kill anyone. That's the only thing I'm sure of. She wanted me to . . . and I almost did . . . but in the end I drew back. That's the only reason I've been able to go on livin with myself, because in the end I was able to crawl away. She kept part of my soul with her—the best part, maybe—but she never kept all of it."

He looked at Naomi and Sam thoughtfully. He seemed calmer now, more in control; perhaps even at peace with himself, Sam thought.

"I remember going in one day in the fall of 1959—I *think* it was '59—and her telling me that she wanted me to make a poster for the Children's Room. She told me exactly what she wanted, and I agreed willingly enough. I didn't see nothing wrong with it. I thought it was kind of funny, in fact. What she wanted, you see, was a poster that showed a little kid flattened by a steamroller in the middle of the street. Underneath it was supposed to say HASTE MAKES WASTE! GET YOUR LIBRARY BOOKS BACK IN PLENTY OF TIME!

"I thought it was just a joke, like when the coyote is chasing the Road Runner and gets flattened by a freight train or something. So I said sure. She was pleased as Punch. I went into her office and drew the poster. It didn't take long, because it was just a cartoon.

"I thought she'd like it, but she didn't. Her brows drew down and her mouth almost disappeared. I'd made a cartoon boy with crosses for eyes, and as a joke I had a word-balloon comin out of the mouth of the guy drivin the steamroller. 'If you had a stamp, you could mail him like a postcard,' he was saying.

"She didn't even crack a smile. 'No, Davey,' she says, 'you don't understand. *This* won't make the children bring their books back on time. *This* will only make them laugh, and they spend too much time doing that as it is.'

" 'Well,' I says, 'I guess I didn't understand what you wanted.'

"We were standin behind the circulation desk, so nobody could see us except from the waist up. And she reached down and took my balls in her hand and looked at me with those big silver eyes of hers and said, 'I want you to make it *realistic*.'

"It took me a second or two to understand what she really meant. When I did, I couldn't believe it. 'Ardelia,' I says, 'you don't understand what you're sayin. If a kid really *did* get run over by a steamroller—'

"She gave my balls a squeeze, one that hurt—as if to remind me just how she had me—and said: 'I understand, all right. Now *you* understand *me*. I don't want them to *laugh,* Davey; I want them to *cry*. So why don't you go on back in there and do it right this time?'

"I went back into her office. I don't know what I meant to do, but my mind got made up in a hurry. There was a fresh piece of posterboard on the desk, and a tall glass of Scotch with a straw and a sprig of mint in it, and a note from Ardelia that said 'D.—Use a lot of *red* this time.' "

He looked soberly at Sam and Naomi.

"But she'd never been in there, you see. Never for a minute."

3

Naomi brought Dave a fresh glass of water, and when she came back, Sam noticed that her face was very pale and that the corners of her eyes looked red. But she sat down very quietly and motioned for Dave to go on.

"I did what alcoholics do best," he said. "I drank the drink and did what I was told. A kind of ... of frenzy, I suppose you'd say ... fell over me. I spent two hours at her desk, workin with a box of five-and-dime watercolors, sloppin water and paint all over her desk, not givin a shit what flew where. What I came out with was somethin I don't like to remember ... but I *do* remember. It was a little boy splattered all over Rampole Street with his shoes knocked off and his head all spread out like a pat of butter that's melted in the sun. The man drivin the steamroller was just a sil-houette, but he was lookin back, and you could see the grin on his face. That guy showed up again and again in the posters I did for her. He was drivin the car in the poster you mentioned, Sam, the one about never takin rides from strangers.

"My father left my mom about a year after I was born, just left her flat, and I got an idea now that was who I was tryin to draw in all those posters. I used to call him the dark man, and I think it was my dad. I think maybe Ardelia prodded him out of me some-how. And when I took the second one out, she liked it fine. She laughed over it. 'It's *perfect,* Davey!' she said. 'It'll scare a whole *mountain* of do-right into the little snotnoses! I'll put it up right away!' She did, too, on the front of the checkout desk in the Children's Room. And when she did, I saw somethin that really chilled my blood. I *knew* the little boy I'd drawn, you see. It was Willy Klemmart. I'd drawn him without even knowin it, and the expression on what was left of his face was the one I'd seen that day when she took his hand and led him into the Children's Room.

"I was there when the kids came in for Story Hour and saw that poster for the first time. They were scared. Their eyes got big, and one little girl started to cry. And I *liked* it that they were scared. I thought, 'That'll pound the do-right into em, all right. That'll teach em what'll happen if they cross her, if they don't do what she says.' And part of me thought, *You're gettin to think like her, Dave. Pretty soon you'll get to* be *like her, and then you'll be lost. You'll be lost forever.*

"But I went on, just the same. I felt like I had a one-way ticket and I wasn't goin to get off until I rode all the way to the end of the line. Ardelia hired some college kids, but she always put em in the circulation room and the reference room and on the main desk. *She* kept complete charge of the kids . . . they were the easiest to scare, you see. And I think they were the *best* scares, the ones that fed her the best. Because that's what she lived on, you know—she fed on their fright. And I made more posters. I can't remember them all, but I remember the Library Policeman. He was in a lot of them. In one—it was called LIBRARY POLICEMEN GO ON VACATION, TOO—he was standin on the edge of a stream and fishin. Only what he'd baited his hook with was that little boy the kids called Simple Simon. In another one, he had Simple Simon strapped to the nose of a rocket and was pullin the switch that would send him into outer space. That one said LEARN MORE ABOUT SCIENCE AND TECHNOLOGY AT THE LIBRARY—BUT BE SURE TO DO RIGHT AND GET YOUR BOOKS BACK ON TIME.

"We turned the Children's Room into a house of horrors for the kids who came there," Dave said. He spoke slowly, and his voice was full of tears. "She and I. We did that to the children. But do you know what? They always came back. They always came back for more. And they never, never told. *She* saw to that."

"But the parents!" Naomi exclaimed suddenly, and so sharply that Sam jumped. "Surely when the parents saw—"

"No!" Dave told her. "Their parents never saw *nothing*. The only scary poster they ever saw was the one of Little Red Ridin Hood and the wolf. Ardelia left that one up all the time, but the others only went up during Story Hour—after school, on Thursday nights, and Saturday mornings. She wasn't a human bein, Sarah. You've got to get that straight in your mind. *She was not human.* She *knew* when grownups was comin, and she always got the posters I'd drawn off the walls and other ones—regular posters that said things like READ BOOKS JUST FOR THE FUN OF IT—up before they came.

"I can remember times when I'd be there for Story Hour—in those days I never left her if I could stay close, and I had lots of time to stay close, because I'd quit paintin pictures, all my regular jobs had fell through, and I was livin on the little I'd managed to save up. Before long the money was gone, too, and I had to start sellin things—my TV, my guitar, my truck, finally my house. But that don't matter. What matters is that I was there a lot, and I saw what went on. The little ones would have their chairs drawn up in a circle with Ardelia sittin in the middle. I'd be in the back of the room, sittin in one of those kid-sized chairs myself, wearing my old paint-spotted duster more often than not, drunk as a skunk, needin a shave, reekin of Scotch. And she'd be readin—readin one of her special Ardelia-stories—and then she'd break off and cock her head to one side, like she was listenin. The kids would stir around and look uneasy. They looked another way, too—like they was wakin out of a deep sleep she'd put em into.

" 'We're going to have company,' she'd say, smiling. 'Isn't that special, children? Do I have some Good-Baby volunteers to help me get ready for our Big People company?' They'd *all* raise their hands when she said that, because they all wanted to be Good Babies. The posters I'd made showed em what happened to Bad Babies who didn't do right. Even I'd raise my hand, sittin drunk in the back of the room in my filthy old duster, lookin like the world's oldest, tiredest kid. And then they'd get up and some would take down my posters and others would take the regular posters out of the bottom drawer of her desk. They'd swap em. Then they'd sit down and she'd switch from whatever horrible thing she'd been tellin em to a story like 'The Princess and the Pea,' and sure enough, a few minutes later some mother'd poke her head in and see all the do-right Good Babies listenin to that nice Miss Lortz readin em a story, and they'd smile at whatever kid was theirs, and the kid would smile back, and things would go on."

"What do you mean, 'whatever horrible thing she'd been telling them'?" Sam asked. His voice was husky and his mouth felt dry. He had been listening to Dave with a mounting sense of horror and revulsion.

"Fairy tales," Dave said. "But she'd change em into horror stories. You'd be surprised how little work she had to do on most of em to make the change."

"*I* wouldn't," Naomi said grimly. "I remember those stories."

"I'll bet you do," he said, "but you never heard em like Ardelia told em. And the kids *liked* them—part of them liked the stories, and they liked her, because she drew on them and fascinated them the same way she drew on me. Well, not *exactly*, because there was never the sex thing—at least, I don't think so—but the darkness in her called to the darkness in them. Do you understand me?"

And Sam, who remembered his dreadful fascination with the story of Bluebeard and the dancing brooms in *Fantasia*, thought he *did* understand. Children hated and feared the darkness . . . but it drew them, didn't it? It beckoned to them,

(*come with me, son*)

didn't it? It sang to them,

(*I'm a poleethman*)

didn't it?

Didn't it?

"I know what you mean, Dave," he said.

He nodded. "Have you figured it out yet, Sam? Who *your* Library Policeman was?"

"I still don't understand that part," Sam said, but he thought part of him did. It was as if his mind was some deep, dark body of water and there was a boat sunk at the bottom of it—but not just any boat. No—this was a pirate schooner, full of loot and dead bodies, and now it had begun to shift in the muck which had held it so long. Soon, he feared, this ghostly, glaring wreck would surface again, its blasted masts draped with black seaweed and a skeleton with a million-dollar grin still lashed to the rotting remains of the wheel.

"I think maybe you do," Dave said, "or that you're beginning to. And it will have to come out, Sam. Believe me."

"I still don't really understand about the stories," Naomi said.

"One of her favorites, Sarah—and it was a favorite of the children, too; you have to understand that, and believe it—was 'Goldilocks and the Three Bears.' You know the story, but you don't know it the way some people in this town—people who are grown-ups now, bankers and lawyers and big-time farmers with whole fleets of John Deere tractors—know it. Deep in their hearts, it's the Ardelia Lortz version they keep, you see. It may be that some of them have told those same stories to their own children, never knowing there are other ways to tell them. I don't like to think that's so, but in my heart I know it is.

"In Ardelia's version, Goldilocks is a Bad Baby who won't do right. She comes into the house of the Three Bears and wrecks it on purpose—pulls down Mamma Bear's curtains and drags the washin through the mud and tears up all of Papa Bear's magazines and business papers and uses one of the steak-knives to cut holes in his favorite chair. Then she tears up all their books. That was Ardelia's favorite part, I think, when Goldilocks spoiled the books. And she don't eat the porridge, oh no! Not when Ardelia told the story! The way Ardelia told it, Goldilocks got some rat poison off a high shelf and shook it all over the porridge like powdered sugar. She didn't know anything about who lived in the house, but she wanted to kill them anyway, because that's the kind of Bad Baby she was."

"That's *horrible!*" Naomi exclaimed. She had lost her composure—really lost it—for the first time. Her hands were pressed over her mouth, and her wide eyes regarded Dave from above them.

"Yes. It was. But it wasn't the end. Goldilocks was so tired from wreckin the house, you see, that when she went upstairs to tear their bedrooms apart, she fell asleep in Baby Bear's bed. And when the Three Bears came home and saw her, they fell upon her—that was just how Ardelia used to say it—they fell upon her and ate that wicked Bad Baby alive. They ate her from the feet up, while she screamed and struggled. All except for her head. They saved that, because they knew what she had done to their porridge. They smelled the poison. 'They could do that, children, because they were *bears*,' Ardelia used to say, and all the children—Ardelia's Good Babies—would nod their heads, because they saw how that could be. 'They took Goldilocks' head down to the kitchen and boiled it and ate her brains for their breakfast. They all agreed it was very tasty . . . and they lived happily ever after.' "

4

There was a thick, almost deathly silence on the porch. Dave reached for his glass of water and almost knocked it off the railing with his trembling fingers. He rescued it at the last moment, held it in both hands, and drank deeply. Then he put it down and said to Sam, "Are you surprised that my boozing got a little bit out of control?"

Sam shook his head.

Dave looked at Naomi and said, "Do you understand now why I was never able to tell this story? Why I put it in that room?"

"Yes," she said in a trembling, sighing voice that was not much more than a whisper. "And I think I understand why the kids never told, either. Some things are just too . . . too monstrous."

"For us, maybe," Dave said. "For kids? I don't know, Sarah. I don't think kids know monsters so well at first glance. It's their folks that tell em how to recognize the monsters. And she had somethin else goin for her. You remember me tellin you about how, when she told the kids a parent was comin, they looked like they were wakin up from a deep sleep? They *were* sleepin, in some funny way. It wasn't hypnosis—at least, I don't think it was—but it was *like* hypnosis. And when they went home, they didn't re-member, in the top part of their minds, anyway, about the stories or the posters. Down underneath, I think they remembered plenty . . . just like down underneath Sam knows who his Library Policeman is. I think they still remember today—the bankers and lawyers and big-time farmers who were once Ardelia's Good Babies. I can still see em, wearin pinafores and short pants, sittin in those little chairs, lookin at Ardelia in the middle of the circle, their eyes so big and round they looked like pie-plates. And I think that when it gets dark and the storms come, or when they are sleepin and the nightmares come, they go *back* to bein kids. I think the doors open and they see the Three Bears—*Ardelia's* Three Bears—eatin the brains out of Goldilocks' head with their wooden porridge-spoons, and Baby Bear wearin Goldilocks' scalp on his head like a long golden wig. I think they wake up sweaty, feelin sick and afraid. I think that's what she left this town. I think she left a legacy of secret nightmares.

"But I still haven't got to the worst thing. Those stories, you see—well, sometimes it was the posters, but mostly it was the

stories—would scare one of them into a crying fit, or they'd start
to faint or pass out or whatever. And when that happened, she'd
tell the others, 'Put your heads down and rest while I take
Billy . . . or Sandra . . . or Tommy . . . to the bathroom and make
him feel better.'

"They'd all drop their heads at the same instant. It was like they
were dead. The first time I seen it happen, I waited about two
minutes after she took some little girl out of the room, and then I
got up and went over to the circle. I went to Willy Klemmart first.

" 'Willy!' I whispered, and poked him in the shoulder. 'You okay,
Will?'

"He never moved, so I poked him harder and said his name
again. He still didn't move. I could hear him breathin—kinda snotty
and snory, the way kids are so much of the time, always runnin
around with colds like they do—but it was still like he was dead.
His eyelids were partway open, but I could only see the whites,
and this long thread of spit was hangin off his lower lip. I got scared
and went to three or four of the others, but wouldn't none of them
look up at me or make a sound."

"You're saying she enchanted them, aren't you?" Sam asked.
"That they were like Snow White after she ate the poisoned apple."

"Yes," Dave agreed. "That's what they were like. In a different
kind of way, that's what I was like, too. Then, just as I was gettin
ready to take hold of Willy Klemmart and shake the shit out of
him, I heard her comin back from the bathroom. I ran to my seat
so she wouldn't catch me. Because I was more scared of what she
might do to me than anything she might have done to them.

"She came in, and that little girl, who'd been as gray as a dirty
sheet and half unconscious when Ardelia took her out, looked like
somebody had just filled her up with the finest nerve-tonic in the
world. She was wide awake, with roses in her cheeks and a sparkle
in her eye. Ardelia patted her on the bottom and she ran for her
seat. Then Ardelia clapped her hands together and said, 'All Good
Babies lift your heads up! Sonja feels much better, and she wants
us to finish the story, don't you, Sonja?'

" 'Yes, ma'am,' Sonja pipes up, just as pert as a robin in a birdbath.
And their heads all came up. You never would have known that
two seconds before that room looked like it was full of dead kids.

"The third or fourth time this happened, I let her get out of the
room and then I followed her. I knew she was scarin them on

purpose, you see, and I had an idea there was a *reason* for it. I was scared almost to death myself, but I wanted to see what it was.

"That time it was Willy Klemmart she'd taken down to the bathroom. He'd started havin hysterics during Ardelia's version of 'Hansel and Gretel.' I opened the door real easy and quiet, and I seen Ardelia kneelin in front of Willy down by where the washbasin was. He had stopped cryin, but beyond that I couldn't tell anything. Her back was to me, you see, and Willy was so short she blocked him right out of my view, even on her knees. I could see his hands were on the shoulders of the jumper she was wearin, and I could see one sleeve of his red sweater, but that was all. Then I heard somethin—a thick suckin sound, like a straw makes when you've gotten just about all of your milkshake out of the glass. I had an idea then she was . . . you know, molestin him, and she was, but not the way I thought.

"I walked in a little further, and slipped over to the right, walkin high up on the toes of my shoes so the heels wouldn't clack. I expected her to hear me just the same, though . . . she had ears like goddam radar dishes, and I kept waitin for her to turn around and pin me with those red eyes of hers. But I couldn't stop. I *had* to see. And little by little, as I angled over to the right, I began to.

"Willy's face came into my sight over her shoulder, a little piece at a time, like a moon coming out of a 'clipse. At first all I could see of her was her blonde hair—there was masses of it, all in curls and ringlets—but then I began to see *her* face, as well. And I seen what she was doin. All the strength ran out of my legs just like water down a pipe. There was no way they were goin to see me, not unless I reached up and started hammerin on one of the overhead pipes. Their eyes were closed, but that wasn't the reason. They were lost in what they were doin, you see, and they were both lost in the same place, because they were hooked together.

"Ardelia's face wasn't human anymore. It had run like warm taffy and made itself into this funnel shape that flattened her nose and pulled her eyesockets all long and Chinese to the sides and made her look like some kind of insect . . . a fly, maybe, or a bee. Her mouth was gone again. It had turned into that thing I started to see just after she killed Mr. Lavin, the night we were layin in the hammock. It had turned into the narrow part of the funnel. I could see these funny red streaks on it, and at first I thought it was blood, or maybe veins under her skin, and then I realized it was lipstick.

She didn't *have* lips anymore, but that red paint marked where her lips had been.

"She was usin that sucker thing to drink from Willy's eyes."

Sam looked at Dave, thunderstruck. He wondered for a moment if the man had lost his mind. Ghosts were one thing; this was something else. He didn't have the slightest idea what *this* was. And yet sincerity and honesty shone on Dave's face like a lamp, and Sam thought: *If he's lying, he doesn't know it.*

"Dave, are you saying Ardelia Lortz was drinking his tears?" Naomi asked hesitantly.

"Yes . . . and no. It was his *special* tears she was drinkin. Her face was all stretched out to him, it was beatin like a heart, and her features were drawn out flat. She looked like a face you might draw on a shoppin bag to make a Halloween mask.

"What was comin out of the corners of Willy's eyes was gummy and pink, like bloody snot, or chunks of flesh that have almost liquefied. She sucked it in with that slurpin sound. It was his *fear* she was drinkin. She had made it real, somehow, and made it so big that it had to come out in those awful tears or kill him."

"You're saying that Ardelia was some kind of vampire, aren't you?" Sam asked.

Dave looked relieved. "Yes. That's right. When I've thought of that day since—when I've *dared* to think of it—I believe that's *just* what she was. All those old stories about vampires sinking their teeth into people's throats and drinkin their blood are wrong. Not by much, but in this business, close is not good enough. They drink, but not from the neck; they grow fat and healthy on what they take from their victims, but what they take isn't blood. Maybe the stuff they take is redder, *bloodier*, when the victims are grownups. Maybe she took it from Mr. Lavin. I think she did. But it's not blood.

"It's fear."

5

"I dunno how long I stood there, watchin her, but it couldn't have been too long—she was never gone much more than five minutes. After awhile, the stuff comin from the corners of Willy's eyes started to get paler and paler, and there was less and less of it. I could see that . . . you know, that thing of hers . . ."

"Proboscis," Naomi said quietly. "I think it must have been a proboscis."

"Is it? All right. I could see that probos-thing stretchin further and further out, not wanting to miss any, wanting to get every last bit, and I knew she was almost done. And when she was, they'd wake up and she'd see me. And when she did, I thought she'd probably kill me.

"I started to back up, slow, one step at a time. I didn't think I was going to make it, but at last my butt bumped the bathroom door. I almost screamed when that happened, because I thought she'd got behind me somehow. I was sure of that even though I could see her kneelin there right in front of me.

"I clapped my hand over my mouth to keep the scream in and pushed out through the door. I stood there while it swung shut on the pneumatic hinge. It seemed to take forever. When it was closed, I started for the main door. I was half crazy; all I wanted to do was get out of there and never go back. I wanted to run forever.

"I got down into the foyer, where she'd put up that sign you saw, Sam—the one that just said SILENCE!—and then I caught hold of myself. If she led Willy back to the Children's Room and saw I was gone, she'd know I'd seen. She'd chase me, and she'd catch me, too. I didn't even think she'd have to try hard. I kept rememberin that day in the corn, and how she'd run rings all around me and never even worked up a sweat.

"So I turned around and walked back to my seat in the Children's Room instead. It was the hardest thing I've ever done in my life, but somehow I managed to do it. My ass wasn't on the chair two seconds before I heard them coming. And of course Willy was all happy and smilin and full of beans, and so was she. Ardelia looked ready to go three fast rounds with Carmen Basilio and whip him solid.

" 'All Good Babies lift your heads up!' she called, and clapped her hands. They all raised their heads and looked at her. 'Willy feels lots better, and he wants me to finish the story. Don't you, Willy?'

" 'Yes, ma'am,' Willy said. She kissed him and he ran back to his seat. She went on with the story. I sat there and listened. And when that Story Hour was done, I started drinkin. And from then until the end, I never really stopped."

6

"How *did* it end?" Sam asked. "What do you know about that?"

"Not as much as I would have known if I hadn't been so dog-drunk all the time, but more than I wish I knew. That last part of it, I'm not even sure how long it was. About four months, I think, but it might have been six, or even eight. By then I wasn't even noticin the seasons much. When a drunk like me really starts to slide, Sam, the only weather he notices is inside of a bottle. I know two things, though, and they are really the only two things that matter. Somebody *did* start to catch onto her, that was one thing. And it was time for her to go back to sleep. To change. That was the other.

"I remember one night at her house—she never came to mine, not once—she said to me, 'I'm getting sleepy, Dave. All the time now I'm sleepy. Soon it will be time for a long rest. When that time comes, I want you to sleep with me. I've grown fond of you, you see.'

"I was drunk, of course, but what she said still gave me a chill. I thought I knew what she was talkin about, but when I asked her, she only laughed.

" 'No, not *that*,' she said, and gave me a scornful, amused kind of look. 'I'm talking about *sleep*, not death. But you'll need to feed with me.'

"That sobered me up in a hurry. She didn't think I knew what she was talkin about, but I did. I'd seen.

"After that, she began to ask me questions about the kids. About which ones I didn't like, which ones I thought were sneaky, which ones were too loud, which ones were the brattiest. 'They're Bad Babies, and they don't deserve to live,' she'd say. 'They're rude, they're destructive, they bring their books back with pencil marks in them and ripped pages. Which ones do *you* think deserve to die, Davey?'

"That was when I knew I had to get away from her, and if killin myself was the only way, I'd have to take that way out. Something was happenin to her, you see. Her hair was gettin dull, and her skin, which had always been perfect, started to show up with blemishes. And there was something else—I could see that *thing,* that thing her mouth turned into—all the time, just under the surface of her skin. But it was starting to look all wrinkled and dewlapped, and there were strings like cobwebs on it.

"One night while we were in bed she saw me lookin at her hair and said, 'You see the change in me, don't you, Davey?' She patted my face. 'It's all right; it's perfectly natural. It's always this way when I'm getting ready to go to sleep again. I will have to do it soon, and if you mean to come with me, you will have to take one of the children soon. Or two. Or three. The more the merrier!' She laughed in the crazy way she had, and when she looked back at me, her eyes had gone red again. 'In any case, I don't mean to leave you behind. All else aside, it wouldn't be safe. You know that, don't you?'

"I said I did.

" 'So if you don't want to die, Davey, it has to be soon. Very soon. And if you've made up your mind not to, you should tell me now. We can end our time together pleasantly and painlessly, to-night.'

"She leaned over me and I could smell her breath. It was like spoiled dogfood, and I couldn't believe I'd ever kissed the mouth that smell was coming out of, sober *or* drunk. But there was some part of me—some little part—that must have still wanted to live, because I told her I *did* want to come with her, but I needed a little more time to get ready. To prepare my mind.

" 'To drink, you mean,' she said. 'You ought to get down on your knees and thank your miserable, unlucky stars for me, Dave Duncan. If not for me, you'd be dead in the gutter in a year, or even less. With me, you can live almost forever.'

"Her mouth stretched out for just a second, stretched out until it touched my cheek. And somehow I managed to keep from screaming."

Dave looked at them with his deep, haunted eyes. Then he smiled. Sam Peebles never forgot the eldritch quality of that smile; it haunted his dreams ever after.

"But that's all right," he said. "Somewhere, down deep inside of me, I have been screaming ever since."

7

"I'd like to say that in the end I broke her hold over me, but that'd be a lie. It was just happenstance—or what Program people call a higher power. You have to understand that by 1960, I was entirely cut off from the rest of the town. Remember me tellin you that once I was a member of the Rotary Club, Sam? Well, by February of '60, those boys wouldn't have hired me to clean the urinals in their john. As far as Junction City was concerned, I was just another Bad Baby livin the life of a bum. People I'd known all my life would cross the street to get out of my way when they saw me comin. I had the constitution of a brass eagle in those days, but the booze was rustin me out just the same, and what the booze wasn't takin, Ardelia Lortz was.

"I wondered more'n once if she wouldn't turn to me for what she needed, but she never did. Maybe I was no good to her that way . . . but I don't really think that was it. I don't think she loved me—I don't think Ardelia could love anybody—but I *do* think she was lonely. I think she's lived, if you can call what she does living, a very long time, and that she's had . . ."

Dave trailed off. His crooked fingers drummed restlessly on his knees and his eyes sought the grain elevator on the horizon again, as if for comfort.

"*Companions* seems like the word that comes closest to fittin. I think she's had companions for some of her long life, but I don't think she'd had one for a very long time when she came to Junction City. Don't ask what she said to make me feel that way, because I don't remember. It's lost, like so much of the rest. But I'm pretty sure it's true. And she had me tapped for the job. I'm pretty sure I would have gone with her, too, if she hadn't been found out."

"Who found her out, Dave?" Naomi asked, leaning forward. "Who?"

"Deputy Sheriff John Power. In those days, the Homestead County sheriff was Norman Beeman, and Norm's the best argument I know for why sheriffs should be appointed rather than elected. The voters gave him the job when he got back to Junction City in '45 with a suitcase full of medals he'd won when Patton's army was drivin into Germany. He was a hell of a scrapper, no one could take that away from him, but as county sheriff he wasn't worth a fart in a windstorm. What he had was the biggest, whitest smile you

ever saw, and a load of bullshit two mules wide. And he was a
Republican, of course. That's always been the most important thing
in Homestead County. I think Norm would be gettin elected still
if he hadn't dropped dead of a stroke in Hughie's Barber Shop in
the summer of 1963. I remember *that* real clear; by then Ardelia
had been gone awhile and I'd come around a little bit.

"There were two secrets to Norm's success—other than that big
grin and the line of bullshit, I mean. First, he was honest. So far as
I know, he never took a dime. Second, he always made sure he had
at least one deputy sheriff under him who could think fast and
didn't have no interest in runnin for the top job himself. He always
played square with those fellows; every one of them got a rock-
solid recommendation when he was ready to move on and move
up. Norm took care of his own. I think, if you looked, you'd find
there are six or eight town police chiefs and State Police colonels
scattered across the Midwest who spent two or three years here in
Junction City, shovelling shit for Norm Beeman.

"Not John Power, though. He's dead. If you looked up his obit-
uary, it'd say he died of a heart attack, although he wasn't yet thirty
years old and with none of the bad habits that cause people's tickers
to seize up early sometimes. I know the truth—it wasn't a heart
attack killed John any more than it was a heart attack that killed
Lavin. *She* killed him."

"How do you know that, Dave?" Sam asked.

"I know because there were supposed to be *three* children killed
in the Library on that last day."

Dave's voice was still calm, but Sam heard the terror this man
had lived with so long running just below the surface like a low-
voltage electrical charge. Supposing that even half of what Dave
had told them this afternoon was true, then he must have lived
these last thirty years with terrors beyond Sam's capacity to imagine.
No wonder he had used a bottle to keep the worst of them at bay.

"Two *did* die—Patsy Harrigan and Tom Gibson. The third was
to be my price of admission to whatever circus it is that Ardelia
Lortz is ringmaster of. That third was the one she really wanted,
because she was the one who turned the spotlight on Ardelia just
when Ardelia most needed to operate in the dark. That third had
to be mine, because that one wasn't allowed to come to the Library
anymore, and Ardelia couldn't be sure of gettin near her. That third
Bad Baby was Tansy Power, Deputy Power's daughter."

"You aren't talking about Tansy *Ryan*, are you?" Naomi asked, and her voice was almost pleading.

"Yeah, I am. Tansy Ryan from the post office, Tansy Ryan who goes to meetins with us, Tansy Ryan who used to be Tansy Power. A lot of the kids who used to come to Ardelia's Story Hours are in AA around these parts, Sarah—make of it what you will. In the summer of 1960, I came very close to killin Tansy Power . . . and that's not the worst of it. I only wish it were."

8

Naomi excused herself, and after several minutes had dragged by, Sam got up to go after her.

"Let her be," Dave said. "She's a wonderful woman, Sam, but she needs a little time to put herself back in order. You would, too, if you found out that one of the members of the most important group in your life once came close to murderin your closest friend. Let her abide. She'll be back—Sarah's strong."

A few minutes later, she did come back. She had washed her face—the hair at her temples was still wet and slick—and she was carrying a tray with three glasses of iced tea on it.

"Ah, we're getting down to the hard stuff at last, ain't we, dear?" Dave said.

Naomi did her best to return his smile. "You bet. I just couldn't hold out any longer."

Sam thought her effort was better than good; he thought it was noble. All the same, the ice was talking to the glasses in brittle, chattery phrases. Sam rose again and took the tray from her unsteady hands. She looked at him gratefully.

"Now," she said, sitting down. "Finish, Dave. Tell it to the end."

9

"A lot of what's left is stuff she told me," Dave resumed, "because by then I wasn't in a position to see anything that went on first hand. Ardelia told me sometime late in '59 that I wasn't to come around the Public Library anymore. If she saw me in there, she said she'd turn me out, and if I hung around outside, she'd sic the cops on me. She said I was gettin too seedy, and talk would start if I was seen goin in there anymore.

" 'Talk about you and me?' I asked. 'Ardelia, who'd believe it?'

" 'Nobody,' she said. 'It's not talk about you and me that concerns me, you idiot.'

" 'Well then, what does?'

" 'Talk about you and the children,' she said. I guess that was the first time I really understood how low I'd fallen. You've seen me low in the years since we started goin to the AA meetins together, Sarah, but you've never seen me that low. I'm glad, too.

"That left her house. It was the only place I was allowed to see her, and the only time I was allowed to come was long after dark. She told me not to come by the road any closer than the Orday farm. After that I was to cut through the fields. She told me she'd know if I tried to cheat on that, and I believed her—when those silver eyes of hers turned red, Ardelia saw *everything.* I'd usually show up sometime between eleven o'clock and one in the morning, dependin on how much I'd had to drink, and I was usually frozen almost to the bone. I can't tell you much about those months, but I can tell you that in 1959 and 1960 the state of Iowa had a damned cold winter. There were lots of nights when I believe a sober man would have frozen to death out there in those cornfields.

"There wasn't no problem on the night I want to tell you about next, though—it must have been July of 1960 by then, and it was hotter than the hinges of hell. I remember how the moon looked that night, bloated and red, hangin over the fields. It seemed like every dog in Homestead County was yarkin up at that moon.

"Walkin into Ardelia's house that night was like walkin under the skirt of a cyclone. That week—that whole month, I guess— she'd been slow and sleepy, but not that night. That night she was wide awake, and she was in a fury. I hadn't seen her that way since the night after Mr. Lavin told her to take the Little Red Ridin Hood poster down because it was scarin the children. At first she didn't even know I was there. She went back and forth through the down-stairs, naked as the day she was born—if she ever *was* born—with her head down and her hands rolled into fists. She was madder'n a bear with a sore ass. She usually wore her hair up in an old-maidy bun when she was at home, but it was down when I let myself in through the kitchen door and she was walkin so fast it went flyin out behind her. I could hear it makin little crackly sounds, like it was full of static electricity. Her eyes were red as blood and glowin like those railroad lamps they used to put out in the old days when the tracks were blocked someplace up the line, and they seemed to be poppin right out of her face. Her body was oiled with sweat, and bad as I was myself, I could smell her; she stank like a bobcat in heat. I remember I could see big oily drops rollin down her bosom and her belly. Her hips and thighs shone with it. It was one of those still, muggy nights we get out here in the summer sometimes, when the air smells green and sits on your chest like a pile of junk iron, and it seems like there's cornsilk in every breath you pull in. You wish it would thunder and lightnin and pour down a gusher on nights like that, but it never does. You wish the wind would blow, at least, and not just because it would cool you off if it did, but because it would make the sound of the corn a little easier to bear . . . the sound of it pushin itself up out of the ground all around you, soundin like an old man with arthritis tryin to get out of bed in the mornin without wakin his wife.

"Then I noticed she was scared as well as mad this time—someone had really looped the fear of God into her. And the change in her was speedin up. Whatever it was that happened to her, it had knocked her into a higher gear. She didn't look older, exactly; she looked less *there*. Her hair had started to look finer, like a baby's hair. You could see her scalp through it. And her skin looked like it was startin to grow its own skin—this fine, misty webbing over her cheeks, around her nostrils, at the corners of her eyes, between her fingers. Wherever there was a fold in the skin, that was where you could see it best. It fluttered a little as she walked. You want to hear something crazy? When the County Fair comes to town these days, I can't bear to go near the cotton-candy stands on the midway. You know the machine they make it with? Looks like a doughnut and goes round and round, and the man sticks in a paper cone and winds the pink sugar up on it? *That's* what Ardelia's skin was starting to look like—those fine strands of spun sugar. I think I know now what I was seein. She was doin what caterpillars do when they go to sleep. She was spinnin a cocoon around herself.

"I stood in the doorway for some time, watchin her go back and forth. She didn't notice me for a long while. She was too busy rollin around in whatever bed of nettles it was she'd stumbled into. Twice she hammered her fist against a wall and smashed all the way through it—paper, plaster, and lath. It sounded like breakin bones, but it didn't seem to do her no hurt at all, and there was no blood. She screamed each time, too, but not with pain. What I heard was the sound of a pissed-off she-cat . . . but, like I said, there was fear underneath her anger. And what she screamed was that deputy's name.

" *'John Power!'* she'd scream, and *whack!* Right through the wall her fist would go. 'God *damn* you, John Power! I'll teach you to stay out of my business! You want to look at me? Fine! But I'll teach you how to do it! I'll teach you, little baby of mine!' Then she'd walk on, so fast she was almost runnin, and her bare feet'd come down so hard they shook the whole damn house, it seemed like. She'd be mutterin to herself while she walked. Then her lip would curl, her eyes would glare redder'n ever, and *whack!* would go her fist, right through the wall and a little puff of plaster dust comin out through the hole. 'John Power, you don't *dare!*' she'd snarl. 'You don't *dare* cross me!'

"But you only had to look into her face to know she was afraid he *did* dare. And if you'd known Deputy Power, you'd have known she was right to be worried. He was smart, and he wasn't afraid of nothing. He was a good deputy and a bad man to cross.

"She got into the kitchen doorway on her fourth or fifth trip through the house, and all at once she saw me. Her eyes glared into mine, and her mouth began to stretch out into that horn shape—only now it was all coated with those spidery, smoky threads—and I thought I was dead. If she couldn't lay hands on John Power, she'd have me in his place.

"She started toward me and I slid down the kitchen door in a kind of puddle. She saw that and she stopped. The red light went out of her eyes. She changed in the wink of an eye. She looked and spoke as if I'd come into a fancy cocktail party she was throwin instead of walking into her house at midnight to find her rammin around naked and smashin holes in the walls.

" 'Davey!' she says. 'I'm so glad you're here! Have a drink. In fact, have two!'

"She wanted to kill me—I saw it in her eyes—but she needed me, and not just for a companion no more, neither. She needed me to kill Tansy Power. She knew she could take care of the cop, but she wanted him to know his daughter was dead before she did him. For that she needed me.

" 'There isn't much time,' she said. 'Do you know this Deputy Power?'

"I said I ought to. He'd arrested me for public drunkenness half a dozen times.

" 'What do you make of him?' she asked.

" 'He's got a lot of hard bark on him,' I says.

" 'Well, fuck him and fuck you, too!'

"I didn't say nothing to that. It seemed wiser not to.

" 'That goddam squarehead came into the Library this afternoon and asked to see my references. And he kept asking me questions. He wanted to know where I'd been before I came to Junction City, where I went to school, where I grew up. You should have seen the way he looked at me, Davey—but I'll teach him the right way to look at a lady like me. You see if I don't.'

" 'You don't want to make a mistake with Deputy Power,' I said. 'I don't think he's afraid of anything.'

" 'Yes, he is—he's afraid of me. He just doesn't know it yet,' she said, but I caught the gleam of fear in her eyes again. He had picked the worst possible time to start askin questions, you see—she was gettin ready for her time of sleeping and change, and it weakened her somehow."

"Did Ardelia tell you how he caught on?" Naomi asked.

"It's obvious," Sam said. "His daughter told him."

"No," Dave said. "I didn't ask—I didn't dare, not with her in the mood she was in—but I don't think Tansy told her dad. I don't think she could have—not in so many words, at least. When they left the Children's Room, you see, they'd forget all about what she'd told them . . . and done to them in there. And it wasn't *just* forgetting, either—she put other memories, false memories, into their heads, so they'd go home just as jolly as could be. Most of their parents thought Ardelia was just about the greatest thing that ever happened to the Junction City Library.

"I think it was what she took from Tansy that put her father's wind up, and I think Deputy Power must have done a good deal of investigating before he ever went to see Ardelia at the Library. I don't know what difference he noticed in Tansy, because the kids weren't all pale and listless, like the people who get their blood sucked in the vampire movies, and there weren't any marks on their necks. But she was takin *something* from them, just the same, and John Power saw it or sensed it."

"Even if he did see something, why did it make him suspicious of Ardelia?" Sam asked.

"I told you his nose was keen. I think he must have asked Tansy some questions—nothing direct, all on the slant, if you see what I mean—and the answers he got must have been just enough to point him in the right direction. When he came to the Library that day he didn't *know* anything . . . but he *suspected* something. Enough to put Ardelia on her mettle. I remember what made her the maddest—and scared her the most—was how he looked at her. 'I'll teach you how to look at me,' she said. Over and over again. I've wondered since how long it had been since anyone looked at her with real suspicion . . . how long since anyone got into sniffin distance of what she was. I bet it scared her in more ways than one. I bet it made her wonder if she wasn't finally losin her touch."

"He might have talked to some of the other children, too," Naomi said hesitantly. "Compared stories and got answers that didn't quite jibe. Maybe they even saw her in different ways. The way you and Sam saw her in different ways."

"It could be—any of those things could be. Whatever it was, he scared her into speedin up her plans.

" 'I'll be at the Library all day tomorrow,' she told me. 'I'll make sure plenty of people see me there, too. But *you*—you're going to pay a visit to Deputy Power's house, Davey. You're going to watch and wait until you see that child alone—I don't think you'll have to wait long—and then you're going to snatch her and take her into the woods. Do whatever you want to her, but you make sure that the *last* thing you do is cut her throat. Cut her throat and leave her where she'll be found. I want that bastard to know before I see him.'

"I couldn't say nothing. It was probably just as well for me that I was tongue-tied, because anything I said she would have taken wrong, and she probably would have ripped my head off. But I only sat at her kitchen table with my drink in my hand, starin at her, and she must have taken my silence for agreement.

"After that we went into the bedroom. It was the last time. I remember thinkin I wouldn't be able to have it off with her; that a scared man can't get it up. But it was fine, God help me. Ardelia had that kind of magic, too. We went and went and went, and at some point I either fell asleep or just went unconscious. The next thing I remember was her pushin me out of bed with her bare feet, dumpin me right into a patch of early-morning sun. It was quarter past six, my stomach felt like an acid bath, and my head was throbbin like a swollen gum with an abscess in it.

" 'It's time for you to be about your business,' she said. 'Don't let anybody see you on your way back to town, Davey, and remember what I told you. Get her this morning. Take her into the woods and do for her. Hide until dark. If you're caught before then, there's nothing I can do for you. But if you get here, you'll be safe. I'll make sure today that there'll be a couple of kids at the Library tomorrow, even though it's closed. I've got them picked out already, the two worst little brats in town. We'll go to the Library together . . . they'll come . . . and when the rest of the fools find us, they'll think we're all dead. But you and I won't be dead, Davey; we'll be free. The joke will be on them, won't it?'

"Then she started to laugh. She sat naked on her bed with me grovellin at her feet, sick as a rat full of poison bait, and she laughed and laughed and laughed. Pretty soon her face started to change into the insect face again, that probos-thing pushin out of her face, almost like one of those Viking horns, and her eyes drawin off to the side. I knew everything in my guts was going to come up in a rush so I beat it out of there and puked into her ivy. Behind me I could her laughin . . . laughin . . . and laughin.

"I was puttin on my clothes by the side of the house when she spoke to me out the window. I didn't see her, but I heard her just fine. 'Don't let me down, Davey,' she said. 'Don't let me down, or I'll kill you. And you won't die fast.'

" 'I won't let you down, Ardelia,' I said, but I didn't turn around to see her hangin out of her bedroom window. I knew I couldn't stand to see her even one more time. I'd come to the end of my string. And still . . . part of me wanted to go with her even if it meant goin mad first, and most of me thought I *would* go with her. Unless it was her plan to set me up somehow, to leave me holdin the bag for all of it. I wouldn't have put it past her. I wouldn't have put *nothin* past her.

"I set off through the corn back toward Junction City. Usually those walks would sober me up a little, and I'd sweat out the worst of the hangover. Not that day, though. Twice I had to stop to vomit, and the second time I didn't think I was goin to be able to quit. I finally did, but I could see blood all over the corn I'd stopped to kneel in, and by the time I got back to town, my head was achin worse than ever and my vision was doubled. I thought I was dyin, but I still couldn't stop thinkin about what she'd said: *Do whatever you want to her, but you make sure that the last thing you do is cut her throat.*

"I didn't want to hurt Tansy Power, but I thought I was goin to, just the same. I wouldn't be able to stand against what Ardelia wanted . . . and then I would be damned forever. And the worst thing, I thought, might be if Ardelia was tellin the truth, and I just went on livin . . . livin almost forever with that thing on my mind.

"In those days, there was two freight depots at the station, and a loading dock that wasn't much used on the north side of the second one. I crawled under there and fell asleep for a couple of hours. When I woke up, I felt a little better. I knew there wasn't any way I could stop her or myself, so I set out for John Power's house, to find that little girl and snatch her away. I walked right through downtown, not lookin at anyone, and all I kept thinkin over and over was, 'I can make it quick for her—I can do that, at least. I'll snap her neck in a wink and she'll never know a thing.' "

Dave produced his bandanna again and wiped his forehead with a hand which was shaking badly.

"I got as far as the five-and-dime. It's gone now, but in those days it was the last business on O'Kane Street before you got into the residential district again. I had less than four blocks to go, and I thought that when I got to the Power house, I'd see Tansy in the yard. She'd be alone . . . and the woods weren't far.

"Only I looked into the five-and-dime show window and what I saw stopped me cold. It was a pile of dead children, all staring eyes, tangled arms, and busted legs. I let out a little scream and clapped my hands against my mouth. I closed my eyes tight. When I looked again, I saw it was a bunch of dolls old Mrs. Seger was gettin ready to make into a display. She saw me and flapped one of em at me— get away, you old drunk. But I didn't. I kept lookin in at those dolls. I tried to tell myself dolls were all they were; *anyone* could see that. But when I closed my eyes tight and then opened em again, they were dead bodies again. Mrs. Seger was settin up a bunch of little corpses in the window of the five-and-dime and didn't even know it. It came to me that someone was tryin to send me a message, and that maybe the message was that it wasn't too late, even then. Maybe I couldn't stop Ardelia, but maybe I could. And even if I couldn't, maybe I could keep from bein dragged into the pit after her.

"That was the first time I really prayed, Sarah. I prayed for strength. I didn't want to kill Tansy Power, but it was more than that—I wanted to save them all if I could.

"I started back toward the Texaco station a block down—it was where the Piggly Wiggly is now. On the way I stopped and picked a few pebbles out of the gutter. There was a phone booth by the side of the station—and it's still there today, now that I think of it. I got there and then realized I didn't have a cent. As a last resort, I felt in the coin return. There was a dime in there. Ever since that morning, when somebody tells me they don't believe there's a God, I think of how I felt when I poked my fingers into that coin-return slot and found that ten-cent piece.

"I thought about calling Mrs. Power, then decided it'd be better to call the Sheriff's Office. Someone would pass the message on to John Power, and if he was as suspicious as Ardelia seemed to think, he might take the proper steps. I closed the door of the booth and looked up the number—this was back in the days when you could sometimes still find a telephone book in a telephone booth, if you were lucky—and then, before I dialled it, I stuck the pebbles I'd picked up in my mouth.

"John Power himself answered the phone, and I think now that's why Patsy Harrigan and Tom Gibson died . . . why John Power himself died . . . and why Ardelia wasn't stopped then and there. I expected the dispatcher, you see—it was Hannah Verrill in those days—and I'd tell her what I had to say, and she'd pass it on to the deputy.

"Instead, I heard this hard don't-fuck-with-me voice say, 'Sheriff's Office, Deputy Power speaking, how can I help you?' I almost swallowed the mouthful of pebbles I had, and for a minute I couldn't say anything.

"He goes 'Damn kids,' and I knew he was gettin ready to hang up.

" 'Wait!' I says. The pebbles made it sound like I was talkin through a mouthful of cotton. 'Don't hang up, Deputy!'

" 'Who is this?' he asked.

" 'Never mind,' I says back. 'Get your daughter out of town, if you value her, and *whatever* you do, don't let her near the Library. It's serious. She's in danger.'

"And then I hung up. Just like that. If Hannah had answered, I think I would have told more. I would have spoken names—Tansy's, Tom's, Patsy's . . . and Ardelia's, too. But he scared me—I felt like if I stayed on that line, he'd be able to look right through it and see me on the other end, standin in that booth and stinkin like a bag of used-up peaches.

"I spat the pebbles out into my palm and got out of the booth in a hurry. Her power over me was broken—makin the call had done that much, anyway—but I was in a panic. Did you ever see a bird that's flown into a garage and goes swoopin around, bashin itself against the walls, it's so crazy to get out? That's what I was like. All of a sudden I wasn't worryin about Patsy Harrigan, or Tom Gibson, or even Tansy Power. I felt like *Ardelia* was the one who was lookin at me, that Ardelia knew what I'd done, and she'd be after me.

"I wanted to hide—hell, I *needed* to hide. I started walkin down Main Street, and by the time I got to the end, I was almost runnin. By then Ardelia had gotten all mixed up in my mind with the Library Policeman and the dark man—the one who was drivin the steamroller, and the car with Simple Simon in it. I expected to see all three of them turn onto Main Street in the dark man's old Buick, lookin for me. I got out to the railway depot and crawled under the loadin platform again. I huddled up in there, shiverin and shakin, even cryin a little, waitin for her to show up and do for me. I kept thinkin I'd look up and I'd see her face pokin under the platform's concrete skirt, her eyes all red and glaring, her mouth turnin into that horn thing.

"I crawled all the way to the back, and I found half a jug of wine under a pile of dead leaves and old spiderwebs. I'd stashed it back there God knows when and forgot all about it. I drank the wine in about three long swallows. Then I started to crawl back to the front of that space under the platform, but halfway there I passed out. When I woke up again, I thought at first that no time at all had gone by, because the light and the shadows were just about the same. Only my headache was gone, and my belly was roarin for food."

"You'd slept the clock around, hadn't you?" Naomi guessed.

"No—almost *twice* around. I'd made my call to the Sheriff's Office around ten o'clock on Monday mornin. When I came to under the loadin platform with that empty jug of wine still in my hand, it was just past seven on Wednesday morning. Only it wasn't sleep, not really. You have to remember that I hadn't been on an all-day drunk or even a week-long toot. I'd been roaring drunk for the best part of *two years*, and that wasn't all—there was Ardelia, and the Library, and the kids, and Story Hour. It was two years on a merry-go-round in hell. I think the part of my mind that still wanted to live and be sane decided the only thing to do was to pull the plug for awhile and shut down. And when I woke up, it was all over. They hadn't found the bodies of Patsy Harrigan and Tom Gibson yet, but it was over, just the same. And I knew it even before I poked my head out from under the loadin platform. There was an empty place in me, like an empty socket in your gum after a tooth falls out. Only that empty place was in my *mind*. And I understood. She was gone. Ardelia was gone.

"I crawled out from under and almost fainted again from hunger. I saw Brian Kelly, who used to be freightmaster back in those days. He was countin sacks of somethin on the other loadin platform and makin marks on a clipboard. I managed to walk over to him. He saw me, and an expression of disgust came over his face. There had been a time when we'd bought each other drinks in The Domino— a roadhouse that burned down long before your time, Sam—but those days were long gone. All he saw was a dirty, filthy drunk with leaves and dirt in his hair, a drunk that stank of piss and Old Duke.

" 'Get outta here, daddy-O, or I'll call the cops,' he says.

"That day was another first for me. One thing about bein a drunk—you're always breakin new ground. That was the first time I ever begged for money. I asked him if he could spare a quarter so I could get a cuppa joe and some toast at the Route 32 Diner. He dug into his pocket and brought out some change. He didn't hand it to me; he just tossed it in my general direction. I had to get down in the cinders and grub for it. I don't think he threw the money to shame me. He just didn't want to touch me. I don't blame him, either.

"When he saw I had the money he said, 'Get in the wind, daddy-O. And if I see you down here again, I *will* call the cops.'

" 'You bet,' I said, and went on my way. He never even knew who I was, and I'm glad.

"About halfway to the diner, I passed one of those newspaper boxes, and I seen that day's *Gazette* inside. That was when I realized I'd been out of it two days instead of just one. The date didn't mean much to me—by then I wasn't much interested in calendars—but I knew it was Monday morning when Ardelia booted me out of her bed for the last time and I made that call. Then I saw the headlines. I'd slept through just about the biggest day for news in Junction City's history, it seemed like. SEARCH FOR MISSING CHILDREN CONTINUES, it said on one side. There was pictures of Tom Gibson and Patsy Harrigan. The headline on the other side read COUNTY CORONER SAYS DEPUTY DIED OF HEART ATTACK. Below that one there was a picture of John Power.

"I took one of the papers and left a nickel on top of the pile, which was how it was done back in the days when people still mostly trusted each other. Then I sat down, right there on the curb, and read both stories. The one about the kids was shorter. The thing was, nobody was very worried about em just yet—Sheriff Beeman was treatin it as a runaway case.

"She'd picked the right kids, all right; those two really *were* brats, and birds of a feather flock together. They was always chummin around. They lived on the same block, and the story said they'd gotten in trouble the week before when Patsy Harrigan's mother caught em smokin cigarettes in the back shed. The Gibson boy had a no-account uncle with a farm in Nebraska, and Norm Beeman was pretty sure that's where they were headed—I told you he wasn't much in the brains department. But how could he know? And he was right about one thing—they weren't the kind of kids who fall down wells or get drownded swimmin in the Proverbia River. But *I* knew where they were, and I knew Ardelia had beaten the clock again. I knew they'd find all three of them together, and later on that day, they did. I'd saved Tansy Power, and I'd saved myself, but I couldn't find much consolation in that.

"The story about Deputy Power was longer. It was the second one, because Power had been found late Monday afternoon. His death'd been reported in Tuesday's paper, but not the cause. He'd been found slumped behind the wheel of his cruiser about a mile west of the Orday farm. That was a place I knew pretty well, because it was where I usually left the road and went into the corn on my way to Ardelia's.

"I could fill in the blanks pretty well. John Power wasn't a man to let the grass grow under his feet, and he must have headed out to Ardelia's house almost as soon as I hung up that pay telephone beside the Texaco station. He might have called his wife first, and told her to keep Tansy in the house until she heard from him. That wasn't in the paper, of course, but I bet he did.

"When he got there, she must have known that I'd told on her and the game was up. So she killed him. She . . . she hugged him to death, the way she did Mr. Lavin. He had a lot of hard bark on him, just like I told her, but a maple tree has hard bark on it, too, and you can still get the sap to run out of it, if you drive your plug in deep enough. I imagine she drove hers plenty deep.

"When he was dead, she must have driven him in his own cruiser out to the place where he was found. Even though that road—Garson Road—wasn't much travelled back then, it still took a heap of guts to do that. But what else *could* she do? Call the Sheriff's Office and tell em John Power'd had a heart attack while he was talkin to her? That would have started up a lot more questions at the very time when she didn't want nobody thinkin of her at all. And, you know, even Norm Beeman would have been curious about why John Power had been in such a tearin hurry to talk to the city librarian.

"So she drove him out Garson Road almost to the Orday farm, parked his cruiser in the ditch, and then she went back to her own house the same way I always went—through the corn."

Dave looked from Sam to Naomi and then back to Sam again.

"I'll bet I know what she did next, too. I'll bet she started lookin for me.

"I don't mean she jumped in her car and started drivin around Junction City, pokin her head into all my usual holes; she didn't have to. Time and time again over those years she would show up where I was when she wanted me, or she would send one of the kids with a folded-over note. Didn't matter if I was sittin in a pile of boxes behind the barber shop or fishin out at Grayling's Stream or if I was just drunk behind the freight depot, she knew where I was to be found. That was one of her talents.

"Not that last time, though—the time she wanted to find me most of all—and I think I know why. I told you that I didn't fall asleep or even black out after makin that call; it was more like goin into a coma, or being dead. And when she turned whatever eye she had in her mind outward, lookin for me, it couldn't see me. I don't know how many times that day and that night her eye might have passed right over where I lay, and I don't want to know. I only know if she'd found me, it wouldn't have been any kid with a folded-over note that showed up. It would have been *her*, and I can't even imagine what she would have done to me for interfering with her plans the way I did.

"She probably would have found me anyway if she'd had more time, but she didn't. Her plans were laid, that was one thing. And then there was the way her change was speedin up. Her time of sleep was comin on, and she couldn't waste time lookin for me. Besides, she must have known she'd have another chance, further up the line. And now her chance has come."

"I don't understand what you mean," Sam said.

"Of course you do," Dave replied. "Who took the books that have put you in this jam? Who sent em to the pulper, along with your newspapers? *I* did. Don't you think she knows that?"

"Do you think that she still wants you?" Naomi asked.

"Yes, but not the way she did. Now she only wants to kill me." His head turned and his bright, sorrowful eyes gazed into Sam's. "*You're* the one she wants now."

Sam laughed uneasily. "I'm sure she was a firecracker thirty years ago," he said, "but the lady has aged. She's really not my type."

"I guess you don't understand after all," Dave said. "She doesn't want to *fuck* you, Sam; she wants to *be* you."

10

After a few moments Sam said, "Wait. Just hold on a second."

"You've heard me, but you haven't taken it to heart the way you need to," Dave told him. His voice was patient but weary; terribly weary. "So let me tell you a little more.

"After Ardelia killed John Power, she put him far enough away so she wouldn't be the first one to fall under suspicion. Then she went ahead and opened the Library that afternoon, just like always. Part of it was because a guilty person looks more suspicious if they swerve away from their usual routines, but that wasn't all of it. Her change was right upon her, *and she had to have those children's lives.* Don't even think about asking me why, because I don't know. Maybe she's like a bear that has to stuff itself before it goes into hibernation. All I can be sure of is that she had to make sure there was a Story Hour that Monday afternoon . . . and she did.

"Sometime during that Story Hour, when all the kids were sittin around her in the trance she could put em into, she told Tom and Patsy that she wanted em to come to the Library on Tuesday morning, even though the Library was closed Tuesdays and Thursdays in the summer. They did, and she did for em, and then she went to sleep . . . that sleep that looks so much like death. And now you come along, Sam, thirty years later. You know me, and Ardelia still owes me a settling up, so that is a start . . . but there's something a lot better than that. You also know about the Library Police."

"I don't know how—"

"No, you don't know *how* you know, and that makes you even better. Because secrets that are so bad that we even have to hide them from ourselves . . . for someone like Ardelia Lortz, those are the best secrets of all. Plus, look at the bonuses—you're young, you're single, and you have no close friends. That's true, isn't it?"

"I would have said so until today," Sam said after a moment's thought. "I would have said the only good friends I made since I came to Junction City have moved away. But I consider you and Naomi my friends, Dave. I consider you very good friends indeed. The best."

Naomi took Sam's hand and squeezed it briefly.

"I appreciate that," Dave said, "but it doesn't matter, because she intends to do for me and Sarah as well. The more the merrier, as she told me once. She has to take lives to get through her time of change . . . and waking up must be a time of change for her, too."

"You're saying that she means to possess Sam somehow, aren't you?" Naomi asked.

"I think I mean a little more than that, Sarah. I think she means to destroy whatever there is inside Sam that *makes* him Sam—I think she means to clean him out the way a kid cleans out a pumpkin to make a Halloween jack-o-lantern, and then she's going to put him on like you'd put on a suit of new clothes. And after that happens—if it does—he'll go on lookin like a man named Sam Peebles, but he won't *be* a man anymore, no more than Ardelia Lortz was ever a woman. There's somethin not human, some *it* hidin inside her skin, and I think I always knew that. It's inside . . . but it's forever an outsider. Where did Ardelia Lortz come from? Where did she live before she came to Junction City? I think, if you checked, you'd find that everything she put on the references she showed Mr. Lavin was a lie, and that nobody in town really knew. I think it was John Power's curiosity about that very thing that sealed his fate. But I think there was a *real* Ardelia Lortz at one time . . . in Pass Christian, Mississippi . . . or Harrisburg, Pennsylvania . . . or Portland, Maine . . . and the *it* took her over and put her on. Now she wants to do it again. If we let that happen, I think that later this year, in some other town, in San Francisco, California . . . or Butte, Montana . . . or Kingston, Rhode Island . . . a man named Sam Peebles will show up. Most people will like him. Children in particular will like him . . . although they may be afraid of him, too, in some way they don't understand and can't talk about.

"And, of course, he will be a librarian."

CHAPTER TWELVE

BY AIR TO DES MOINES

1

Sam looked at his wristwatch and was astounded to see it was almost 3:00 P.M. Midnight was only nine hours away, and then the tall man with the silver eyes would be back. Or Ardelia Lortz would be back. Or maybe both of them together.

"What do you think I should do, Dave? Go out to the local graveyard and find Ardelia's body and pound a stake through her heart?"

"A good trick if you could do it," he replied, "since the lady was cremated."

"Oh," Sam said. He settled back into his chair with a little helpless sigh.

Naomi took his hand again. "In any case, you won't be doing anything alone," she said firmly. "Dave says she means to do us as well as you, but that's almost beside the point. Friends stand by when there's trouble. *That's* the point. What else are they for?"

Sam lifted her hand to his lips and kissed it. "Thank you—but I don't know what you can do. Or me, either. There doesn't seem to be anything *to* do. Unless . . ." He looked at Dave hopefully. "Unless I ran?"

Dave shook his head. "She—or it—*sees.* I told you that. I guess you could drive most of the way to Denver before midnight if you really put your foot down and the cops didn't catch you, but Ardelia Lortz would be right there to greet you when you got out of your car. Or you'd look over in some dark mile and see the Library Policeman sittin next to you on the seat."

The thought of that—the white face and silver eyes, illuminated only by the green glow of the dashboard lights—made Sam shiver.

"What, then?"

"I think you both know what has to be done first," Dave said. He drank the last of his iced tea and then set the glass on the porch. "Just think a minute, and you'll see."

Then they all looked out toward the grain elevator for awhile. Sam's mind was a roaring confusion; all he could catch hold of were isolated snatches of Dave Duncan's story and the voice of the Library Policeman, with his strange little lisp, saying *I don't want to hear your sick ecthcuses . . . You have until midnight . . . then I come again.*

It was on Naomi's face that light suddenly dawned.

"Of course!" she said. "How stupid! But . . ."

She asked Dave a question, and Sam's own eyes widened in understanding.

"There's a place in Des Moines, as I recall," Dave said. "Pell's. If any place can help, it'll be them. Why don't you make a call, Sarah?"

2

When she was gone, Sam said: "Even if they *can* help, I don't think we could get there before the close of business hours. I can try, I suppose . . ."

"I never expected you'd drive," Dave said. "No—you and Sarah have to go out to the Proverbia Airport."

Sam blinked. "I didn't know there *was* an airport in Proverbia."

Dave smiled. "Well . . . I guess that *is* stretchin it a little. There's a half-mile of packed dirt Stan Soames calls a runway. Stan's front parlor is the office of Western Iowa Air Charter. You and Sarah talk to Stan. He's got a little Navajo. He'll take you to Des Moines and have you back by eight o'clock, nine at the latest."

"What if he's not there?"

"Then we'll try to figure out something else. I think he will be, though. The only thing Stan loves more than flyin is farmin, and come the spring of the year, farmers don't stray far. He'll probably tell you he can't take you because of his garden, come to that— he'll say you shoulda made an appointment a few days in advance so he could get the Carter boy to come over and babysit his back ninety. If he says that, you tell him Dave Duncan sent you, and Dave says it's time to pay for the baseballs. Can you remember that?"

"Yes, but what does it mean?"

"Nothing that concerns this business," Dave said. "He'll take you, that's the important thing. And when he lands you again, never mind comin here. You and Sarah drive straight into town."

Sam felt dread begin to seep into his body. "To the Library."

"That's right."

"Dave, what Naomi said about friends is all very sweet—and maybe even true—but I think I have to take it from here. Neither one of you has to be a part of this. I was the one responsible for stirring her up again—"

Dave reached out and seized Sam's wrist in a grip of surprising strength. "If you really think that, you haven't heard a word I've said. You're not responsible for *anything.* I carry the deaths of John Power and two little children on my conscience—not to mention the terrors I don't know how many other children may have suffered—but I'm not responsible, either. Not really. I didn't set out to be Ardelia Lortz's companion any more than I set out to be a thirty-year drunk. Both things just happened. But she bears me a grudge, and she will be back for me, Sam. If I'm not with you when she comes, she'll visit me first. And I won't be the only one she visits. Sarah was right, Sam. She and I don't have to stay close to protect you; the three of us have to stay close to protect each other. Sarah *knows* about Ardelia, don't you see? If Ardelia don't know that already, she will as soon as she shows up tonight. She plans to go on from Junction City as *you,* Sam. Do you think she'll leave anybody behind who knows her new identity?"

"But—"

"But nothin," Dave said. "In the end it comes down to a real simple choice, one even an old souse like me can understand: we share this together or we're gonna die at her hands."

He leaned forward.

"If you want to save Sarah from Ardelia, Sam, forget about bein a hero and start rememberin who *your* Library Policeman was. You *have* to. Because I don't believe Ardelia can take just anyone. There's only one coincidence in this business, but it's a killer: once *you* had a Library Policeman, too. And you have to get that memory back."

"I've tried," Sam said, and knew that was a lie. Because every time he turned his mind toward

(*come with me, son . . . I'm a poleethman*)

that voice, it shied away. He tasted red licorice, which he had never eaten and always hated—and that was all.

"You have to try harder," Dave said, "or there's no hope."

Sam drew in a deep breath and let it out. Dave's hand touched the back of his neck, then squeezed it gently.

"It's the key to this," Dave said. "You may even find it's the key to everything that has troubled you in your life. To your loneliness and your sadness."

Sam looked at him, startled. Dave smiled.

"Oh yes," he said. "You're lonely, you're sad, and you're closed off from other people. You talk a good game, but you don't walk what you talk. Up until today I wasn't nothing to you but Dirty Dave who comes to get your papers once a month, but a man like me sees a lot, Sam. And it takes one to know one."

"The key to everything," Sam mused. He wondered if there really were such conveniences, outside of popular novels and movies-of-the-week populated with Brave Psychiatrists and Troubled Patients.

"It's true," Dave persisted. "Such things are dreadful in their power, Sam. I don't blame you for not wantin to search for it. But you can, you know, if you want to. You have that choice."

"Is that something else you learn in AA, Dave?"

He smiled. "Well, they teach it there," he said, "but that's one I guess I always knew."

Naomi came out onto the porch again. She was smiling and her eyes were sparkling.

"Ain't she some gorgeous?" Dave asked quietly.

"Yes," Sam said. "She sure is." He was clearly aware of two things: that he was falling in love, and that Dave Duncan knew it.

3

"The man took so long checking that I got worried," she said, "but we're in luck."

"Good," Dave said. "You two are goin out to see Stan Soames, then. Does the Library still close at eight during the school year, Sarah?"

"Yes—I'm pretty sure it does."

"I'll be payin a visit there around five o'clock, then. I'll meet you in back, where the loadin platform is, between eight and nine. Nearer eight would be better—n safer. For Christ's sake, try not to be late."

"How will we get in?" Sam asked.

"I'll take care of that, don't worry. You just get goin."

"Maybe we ought to call this guy Soames from here," Sam said. "Make sure he's available."

Dave shook his head. "Won't do no good. Stan's wife left him for another man four years ago—claimed he was married to his work, which always makes a good excuse for a woman who's got a yen to make a change. There aren't any kids. He'll be out in his field. Go on, now. Daylight's wastin."

Naomi bent over and kissed Dave's cheek. "Thank you for telling us," she said.

"I'm glad I did it. It's made me feel ever so much better."

Sam started to offer Dave his hand, then thought better of it. He bent over the old man and hugged him.

4

Stan Soames was a tall, rawboned man with angry eyes burning out of a gentle face, a man who already had his summer sunburn although calendar spring had not yet run its first month. Sam and Naomi found him in the field behind his house, just as Dave had told them they would. Seventy yards north of Soames's idling, mud-

splashed Rototiller, Sam could see what looked like a dirt
road . . . but since there was a small airplane with a tarpaulin thrown
over it at one end and a windsock fluttering from a rusty pole at
the other, he assumed it was the Proverbia Airport's single runway.

"Can't do it," Soames said. "I got fifty acres to turn this week
and nobody but me to do it. You should have called a couple-three
days ahead."

"It's an emergency," Naomi said. "Really, Mr. Soames."

He sighed and spread his arms, as if to encompass his entire farm.
"You want to know what an emergency is?" he asked. "What the
government's doing to farms like this and people like me. *That's* a
dad-ratted emergency. Look, there's a fellow over in Cedar Rapids
who might—"

"We don't have time to go to Cedar Rapids," Sam said. "Dave
told us you'd probably say—"

"Dave?" Stan Soames turned to him with more interest than he
had heretofore shown. "Dave who?"

"Duncan. He told me to say it's time to pay for the baseballs."

Soames's brows drew down. His hands rolled themselves up into
fists, and for just a moment Sam thought the man was going to slug
him. Then, abruptly, he laughed and shook his head.

"After all these years, Dave Duncan pops outta the woodwork
with his IOU rolled up in his hand! Goddam!"

He began walking toward the Rototiller. He turned his head to
them as he did, yelling to make himself heard over the machine's
enthusiastic blatting. "*Walk on over to the airplane while I put this
goddam thing away! Mind the boggy patch just on the edge of the
runway, or it'll suck your damned shoes off!*"

Soames threw the Rototiller into gear. It was hard to tell with
all the noise, but Sam thought he was still laughing. "*I thought that
drunk old bastard was gonna die before I could quit evens with him!*"

He roared past them toward his barn, leaving Sam and Naomi
looking at each other.

"What was that all about?" Naomi asked.

"I don't know—Dave wouldn't tell me." He offered her his arm.
"Madam, will you walk with me?"

She took it. "Thank you, sir."

They did their best to skirt the mucky place Stan Soames had
told them about, but didn't entirely make it. Naomi's foot went in
to the ankle, and the mud pulled her loafer off when she jerked

her foot back. Sam bent down, got it, and then swept Naomi into his arms.

"Sam, no!" she cried, startled into laughter. "You'll break your *back!*"

"Nope," he said. "You're light."

She was . . . and his head suddenly felt light, too. He carried her up the graded slope of the runway to the airplane and set her on her feet. Naomi's eyes looked up into his with calmness and a sort of luminous clarity. Without thinking, he bent and kissed her. After a moment, she put her arms around his neck and kissed him back.

When he looked at her again, he was slightly out of breath. Naomi was smiling.

"You can call me Sarah anytime you want to," she said. Sam laughed and kissed her again.

5

Riding in the Navajo behind Stan Soames was like riding piggyback on a pogo stick. They bounced and jounced on uneasy tides of spring air, and Sam thought once or twice that they might cheat Ardelia in a way not even that strange creature could have foreseen: by spreading themselves all over an Iowa cornfield.

Stan Soames didn't seem to be worried, however; he bawled out such hoary old ballads as "Sweet Sue" and "The Sidewalks of New York" at the top of his voice as the Navajo lurched toward Des Moines. Naomi was transfixed, peering out of her window at the roads and fields and houses below with her hands cupped to the sides of her face to cut the glare.

At last Sam tapped her on the shoulder. "You act like you've never flown before!" he yelled over the mosquito-drone of the engine.

She turned briefly toward him and grinned like an enraptured schoolgirl. "I haven't!" she said, and returned at once to the view.

"I'll be damned," Sam said, and then tightened his seatbelt as the plane took another of its gigantic, bucking leaps.

6

It was twenty past four when the Navajo skittered down from the sky and landed at County Airport in Des Moines. Soames taxied to the Civil Air Terminal, killed the engine, then opened the door. Sam was a little amused at the twinge of jealousy he felt as Soames put his hands on Naomi's waist to help her down.

"Thank you!" she gasped. Her cheeks were now deeply flushed and her eyes were dancing. "That was *wonderful!*"

Soames smiled, and suddenly he looked forty instead of sixty. "I've always liked it myself," he said, "and it beats spendin an afternoon abusin my kidneys on that Rototiller . . . I have to admit that." He looked from Naomi to Sam. "Can you tell me what this big emergency is? I'll help if I can—I owe Dave a little more'n a puddle-jump from Proverbia to Des Moines and back again."

"We need to go into town," Sam said. "To a place called Pell's Book Shop. They're holding a couple of books for us."

Stan Soames looked at them, eyes wide. "Come again?"

"Pell's—"

"I know Pell's," he said. "New books out front, old books in the back. Biggest Selection in the Midwest, the ads say. What I'm tryin to get straight is this: you took me away from my garden and got me to fly you all the way across the state to get a couple of *books?*"

"They're very important books, Mr. Soames," Naomi said. She touched one of his rough farmer's hands. "Right now, they're just about the most important things in my life . . . or Sam's."

"Dave's, too," Sam said.

"If you told me what was going on," Soames asked, "would I be apt to understand it?"

"No," Sam said.

"No," Naomi agreed, and smiled a little.

Soames blew a deep sigh out of his wide nostrils and stuffed his hands into the pockets of his pants. "Well, I guess it don't matter that much, anyway. I've owed Dave this one for ten years, and there have been times when it's weighed on my mind pretty heavy." He brightened. "And I got to give a pretty young lady her first airplane ride. The only thing prettier than a girl after her first plane ride is a girl after her first—"

He stopped abruptly and scuffed at the tar with his shoes. Naomi looked discreetly off toward the horizon. Just then a fuel truck drove up. Soames walked over quickly and fell into deep conversation with the driver.

Sam said, "You had quite an effect on our fearless pilot."

"Maybe I did, at that," she said. "I feel wonderful, Sam. Isn't that crazy?"

He stroked an errant lock of her hair back into place behind her ear. "It's been a crazy day. The craziest day I can ever remember."

But the inside voice spoke then—it drifted up from that deep place where great objects were still in motion—and told him that wasn't quite true. There was one other that had been just as crazy. More crazy. The day of *The Black Arrow* and the red licorice.

That strange, stifled panic rose in him again, and he closed his ears to that voice.

If you want to save Sarah from Ardelia, Sam, forget about bein a hero and start rememberin who your Library Policeman was.

I don't! I can't! I . . . I mustn't!

You have to get that memory back.

I mustn't! It's not allowed!

You have to try harder or there's no hope.

"I really have to go home now," Sam Peebles muttered.

Naomi, who had strolled away to look at the Navajo's wing-flaps, heard him and came back.

"Did you say something?"

"Nothing. It doesn't matter."

"You look very pale."

"I'm very tense," he said edgily.

Stan Soames returned. He cocked a thumb at the driver of the fuel truck. "Dawson says I can borrow his car. I'll run you into town."

"We could call a cab—" Sam began.

Naomi was shaking her head. "Time's too short for that," she said. "Thank you very much, Mr. Soames."

"Aw, hell," Soames said, and then flashed her a little-boy grin. "You go on and call me Stan. Let's go. Dawson says there's low pressure movin in from Colorado. I want to get back to Junction City before the rain starts."

7

Pell's was a big barnlike structure on the edge of the Des Moines business district—the very antithesis of the mall-bred chain bookstore. Naomi asked for Mike. She was directed to the customer-service desk, a kiosk which stood like a customs booth between the section which sold new books and the larger one which sold old books.

"My name is Naomi Higgins. I talked to you on the telephone earlier?"

"Ah, yes," Mike said. He rummaged on one of his cluttered shelves and brought out two books. One was *Best Loved Poems of the American People;* the other was *The Speaker's Companion,* edited by Kent Adelmen. Sam Peebles had never been so glad to see two books in his life, and he found himself fighting an impulse to snatch them from the clerk's hands and hug them to his chest.

"*Best Loved Poems* is easy," Mike said, "but *The Speaker's Companion* is out of print. I'd guess Pell's is the only bookshop between here and Denver with a copy as nice as this one . . . except for library copies, of course."

"They both look great to me," Sam said with deep feeling.

"Is it a gift?"

"Sort of."

"I can have it gift-wrapped for you, if you like; it would only take a second."

"That won't be necessary," Naomi said.

The combined price of the books was twenty-two dollars and fifty-seven cents.

"I can't believe it," Sam said as they left the store and walked toward the place where Stan Soames had parked the borrowed car. He held the bag tightly in one hand. "I can't believe it's as simple as just . . . just returning the books."

"Don't worry," Naomi said. "It won't be."

8

As they drove back to the airport, Sam asked Stan Soames if he could tell them about Dave and the baseballs.

"If it's personal, that's okay. I'm just curious."

Soames glanced at the bag Sam held in his lap. "I'm sorta curious about those, too," he said. "I'll make you a deal. The thing with the baseballs happened ten years ago. I'll tell you about that if you'll tell me about the books ten years from now."

"Deal," Naomi said from the back seat, and then added what Sam himself had been thinking. "If we're all still around, of course."

Soames laughed. "Yeah . . . I suppose there's always *that* possibility, isn't there?"

Sam nodded. "Lousy things sometimes happen."

"They sure do. One of em happened to my only boy in 1980. The doctors called it leukemia, but it's really just what you said— one of those lousy things that sometimes happens."

"Oh, I'm so sorry," Naomi said.

"Thanks. Every now and then I start to think I'm over it, and then it gets on my blind side and hits me again. I guess some things take a long time to shake out, and some things don't ever shake out."

Some things don't ever shake out.

Come with me, son . . . I'm a poleethman.

I really have to go home now . . . is my fine paid?

Sam touched the corner of his mouth with a trembling hand.

"Well, hell, I'd known Dave a long time before it ever happened," Stan Soames said. They passed a sign which read AIRPORT 3 MI. "We grew up together, went to school together, sowed a mess of wild oats together. The only thing was, I reaped my crop and quit. Dave just went on sowin."

Soames shook his head.

"Drunk or sober, he was one of the sweetest fellows I ever met. But it got so he was drunk more'n he was sober, and we kinda fell out of touch. It seemed like the worst time for him was in the late fifties. During those years he was drunk *all* the time. After that he started goin to AA, and he seemed to get a little better . . . but he'd always fall off the wagon with a crash.

"I got married in '68, and I wanted to ask him to be my best man, but I didn't dare. As it happened, he turned up sober—that time—but you couldn't *trust* him to turn up sober."

"I know what you mean," Naomi said quietly.

Stan Soames laughed. "Well, I sort of doubt that—a little sweetie like you wouldn't know what miseries a dedicated boozehound can get himself into—but take it from me. If I'd asked Dave to stand up for me at the weddin, Laura—that's my ex—would have shit bricks. But Dave *did* come, and I saw him a little more frequently after our boy Joe was born in 1970. Dave seemed to have a special feeling for all kids during those years when he was tryin to pull himself out of the bottle.

"The thing Joey loved most was baseball. He was nuts for it— he collected sticker books, chewing-gum cards . . . he even pestered me to get a satellite dish so we could watch all the Royals games— the Royals were his favorites—and the Cubs, too, on WGN from Chicago. By the time he was eight, he knew the averages of all the Royals starting players, and the won-lost records of damn near every pitcher in the American League. Dave and I took him to games three or four times. It was a lot like takin a kid on a guided tour of heaven. Dave took him alone twice, when I had to work. Laura had a cow about that—said he'd show up drunk as a skunk, with the boy left behind, wandering the streets of K.C. or sittin in a police station somewhere, waitin for someone to come and get him. But nothing like that ever happened. So far as I know, Dave never took a drink when he was around Joey.

"When Joe got the leukemia, the worst part for him was the doctors tellin him he wouldn't be able to go to any games that year at least until June and maybe not at all. He was more depressed about that than he was about having cancer. When Dave came to see him, Joe cried about it. Dave hugged him and said, 'If you can't go to the games, Joey, that's okay; I'll bring the Royals to you.'

"Joe stared up at him and says, 'You mean in *person*, Uncle Dave?' That's what he called him—Uncle Dave.

" 'I can't do that,' Dave said, 'but I can do somethin almost as good.' "

Soames drove up to the Civil Air Terminal gate and blew the horn. The gate rumbled back on its track and he drove out to where the Navajo was parked. He turned off the engine and just sat behind the wheel for a moment, looking down at his hands.

"I always knew Dave was a talented bastard," he said finally. "What I don't know is how he did what he did so damned *fast*. All I can figure is that he must have worked days and nights both, because he was done in ten days—and those suckers were *good*.

"He knew he had to go fast, though. The doctors had told me and Laura the truth, you see, and I'd told Dave. Joe didn't have much chance of pulling through. They'd caught onto what was wrong with him too late. It was roaring in his blood like a grassfire.

"About ten days after Dave made that promise, he comes into my son's hospital room with a paper shopping-bag in each arm. 'What you got there, Uncle Dave?' Joe asks, sitting up in bed. He had been pretty low all that day—mostly because he was losin his hair, I think; in those days if a kid didn't have hair most of the way down his back, he was considered to be pretty low-class—but when Dave came in, he brightened right up.

" 'The Royals, a course,' Dave says back. 'Didn't I tell you?'

"Then he put those two shopping-bags down on the bed and spilled em out. And you never, ever, in your whole life, saw such an expression on a little boy's face. It lit up like a Christmas tree . . . and . . . and shit, I dunno . . ."

Stan Soames's voice had been growing steadily thicker. Now he leaned forward against the steering wheel of Dawson's Buick so hard that the horn honked. He pulled a large bandanna from his back pocket, wiped his eyes with it, then blew his nose.

Naomi had also leaned forward. She pressed one of her hands against Soames's cheek. "If this is too hard for you, Mr. Soames—"

"No," he said, and smiled a little. Sam watched as a tear Stan Soames had missed ran its sparkling, unnoticed course down his cheek in the late-afternoon sun. "It's just that it brings him back so. How he was. That hurts, miss, but it feels good, too. Those two feelings are all wrapped up together."

"I understand," she said.

"When Dave tipped over those bags, what spilled out was baseballs—over two dozen of them. But they weren't *just* baseballs, because there was a face painted on every one, and each one was the face of a player on the 1980 Kansas City Royals baseball team. They weren't those whatdoyoucallums, caricatures, either. They were as good as the faces Norman Rockwell used to paint for the covers of the *Saturday Evening Post.* I've seen Dave's work—the work he did before he got drinkin real heavy—and it was good, but none of it was as good as this. There was Willie Aikens and Frank White and U. L. Washington and George Brett . . . Willie Wilson and Amos Otis . . . Dan Quisenberry, lookin as fierce as a gunslinger in an old Western movie . . . Paul Splittorff and Ken Brett . . . I can't remember all the names, but it was the whole damned roster, including Jim Frey, the field manager.

"And sometime between when he finished em and when he gave em to my son, he took em to K.C. and got all the players but one to sign em. The one who didn't was Darrell Porter, the catcher. He was out with the flu, and he promised to sign the ball with *his* face on it as soon as he could. He did, too."

"Wow," Sam said softly.

"And it was all Dave's doing—the man I hear people in town laugh about and call Dirty Dave. I tell you, sometimes when I hear people say that and I remember what he did for Joe when Joey was dying of the leukemia, I could—"

Soames didn't finish, but his hands curled themselves into fists on his broad thighs. And Sam—who had used the name himself until today, and laughed with Craig Jones and Frank Stephens over the old drunk with his shopping-cart full of newspapers—felt a dull and shameful heat mount into his cheeks.

"That was a wonderful thing to do, wasn't it?" Naomi asked, and touched Stan Soames's cheek again. She was crying.

"You shoulda seen his face," Soames said dreamily. "You wouldn't have believed how he looked, sittin up in his bed and lookin down at all those faces with their K.C. baseball caps on their round heads. I can't describe it, but I'll never forget it.

"You shoulda seen his face.

"Joe got pretty sick before the end, but he didn't ever get too sick to watch the Royals on TV—or listen to em on the radio—and he kept those balls all over his room. The windowsill by his bed was the special place of honor, though. That's where he'd line up the nine men who were playin in the game he was watchin or listenin to on the radio. If Frey took out the pitcher, Joe would take that one down from the windowsill and put up the relief pitcher in his place. And when each man batted, Joe would hold that ball in his hands. So—"

Stan Soames broke off abruptly and hid his face in his bandanna. His chest hitched twice, and Sam could see his throat locked against a sob. Then he wiped his eyes again and stuffed the bandanna briskly into his back pocket.

"So now you know why I took you two to Des Moines today, and why I would have taken you to New York to pick up those two books if that's where you'd needed to go. It wasn't my treat; it was Dave's. He's a special sort of man."

"I think maybe you are, too," Sam said.

Soames gave him a smile—a strange, crooked smile—and opened the door of Dawson's Buick. "Well, thank you," he said. "Thank you kindly. And now I think we ought to be rolling along if we want to beat the rain. Don't forget your books, Miss Higgins."

"I won't," Naomi said as she got out with the top of the bag wrapped tightly in one hand. "Believe me, I won't."

CHAPTER THIRTEEN

THE LIBRARY POLICEMAN (II)

1

Twenty minutes after they took off from Des Moines, Naomi tore herself away from the view—she had been tracing Route 79 and marvelling at the toy cars bustling back and forth along it—and turned to Sam. What she saw frightened her. He had fallen asleep with his head resting against one of the windows, but there was no peace on his face; he looked like a man suffering some deep and private pain.

Tears trickled slowly from beneath his closed lids and ran down his face.

She leaned forward to shake him awake and heard him say in a trembling little-boy's voice: "Am I in trouble, sir?"

The Navajo arrowed its way into the clouds now massing over western Iowa and began to buck, but Naomi barely noticed. Her hand paused just above Sam's shoulder for a moment, then withdrew.

Who was YOUR Library Policeman, Sam?

Whoever it was, Naomi thought, *he's found him again, I think. I think he's with him now. I'm sorry, Sam . . . but I can't wake you. Not now. Right now I think you're where you're supposed to be . . . where you have to be. I'm sorry, but dream on. And remember what you dreamed when you wake up. Remember.*

Remember.

2

In his dream, Sam Peebles watched as Little Red Riding Hood set off from a gingerbread house with a covered basket over one arm; she was bound for Gramma's house, where the wolf was waiting to eat her from the feet up. It would finish by scalping her and then eating her brains out of her skull with a long wooden spoon.

Except none of that was right, because Little Red Riding Hood was a boy in this dream and the gingerbread house was the two-story duplex in St. Louis where he had lived with his mother after Dad died and there was no food in the covered basket. There was a book in the basket, *The Black Arrow* by Robert Louis Stevenson, and he *had* read it, every word, and he was not bound for Gramma's house but for the Briggs Avenue Branch of the St. Louis Public Library, and he had to hurry because his book was already four days overdue.

This was a watching dream.

He watched as Little White Walking Sam waited at the corner of Dunbar Street and Johnstown Avenue for the light to change. He watched as he scampered across the street with the book in his hand . . . the basket was gone now. He watched as Little White Walking Sam went into the Dunbar Street News and then he was inside, too, smelling the old mingled smells of camphor, candy, and pipe tobacco, watching as Little White Walking Sam approached the counter with a nickel package of Bull's Eye red licorice—his favorite. He watched as the little boy carefully removed the dollar bill his mother had tucked into the card-pocket in the back of *The Black Arrow*. He watched as the clerk took the dollar and returned ninety-five cents . . . more than enough to pay the fine. He watched as Little White Walking Sam left the store and paused on the street outside long enough to put the change in his pocket and tear open the package of licorice with his teeth. He watched as Little White Walking Sam went on his way—only three blocks to the Library now—munching the long red whips of candy as he went.

He tried to scream at the boy.

Beware! Beware! The wolf is waiting, little boy! Beware the wolf! Beware the wolf!

But the boy walked on, eating his red licorice; now he was on Briggs Avenue and the Library, a great pile of red brick, loomed ahead.

At this point Sam—Big White Plane-Riding Sam—tried to pull himself out of the dream. He sensed that Naomi and Stan Soames and *the world of real things* were just outside this hellish egg of nightmare in which he found himself. He could hear the drone of the Navajo's engine behind the sounds of the dream: the traffic on Briggs Avenue, the brisk *brrrinnng!-brrrinnng!* of some kid's bike-bell, the birds squabbling in the rich leaves of the midsummer elms. He closed his dreaming eyes and *yearned* toward that world outside the shell, the world of real things. And more: he sensed he could reach it, that he could hammer through the shell—

No, Dave said. *No, Sam, don't do that. You* mustn't *do that. If you want to save Sarah from Ardelia, forget about breaking out of this dream. There's only one coincidence in this business, but it's a killer: once* YOU *had a Library Policeman, too. And you have to get that memory back.*

I don't want to see. I don't want to know. Once was bad enough.

Nothing is as bad as what's waiting for you, Sam. Nothing.

He opened his eyes—not his outer eyes but the inside ones; the dreaming eyes.

Now Little White Walking Sam is on the concrete path which approaches the east side of the Public Library, the concrete path which leads to the Children's Wing. He moves in a kind of portentous slow motion, each step the soft swish of a pendulum in the glass throat of a grandfather clock, and everything is clear: the tiny sparks of mica and quartz gleaming in the concrete walk; the cheerful roses which border the concrete walk; the thick drift of green bushes along the side of the building; the climbing ivy on the red brick wall; the strange and somehow frightening Latin motto, *Fuimus, non sumus,* carved in a brief semicircle over the green doors with their thick panes of wire-reinforced glass.

And the Library Policeman standing by the steps is clear, too.

He is not pale. He is flushed. There are pimples on his forehead, red and flaring. He is not tall but of medium height with extremely broad shoulders. He is wearing not a trenchcoat but an overcoat, and that's very odd because this is a summer day, a hot St. Louis summer day. His eyes might be silver; Little White Walking Sam cannot see what color they are, because the Library Policeman is wearing little round black glasses—blind man's glasses.

He's not a Library Policeman! He's the wolf! Beware! He's the wolf! The Library WOLF!

But Little White Walking Sam doesn't hear. Little White Walking

Sam isn't afraid. It is, after all, bright daylight, and the city is full of strange—and sometimes amusing—people. He has lived all his life in St. Louis, and he's not afraid of it. That is about to change.

He approaches the man, and as he draws closer he notices the scar: a tiny white thread which starts high on the left cheek, dips beneath the left eye, and peters out on the bridge of the nose.

Hello there, son, the man in the round black glasses says.

Hello, says Little White Walking Sam.

Do you mind telling me thomething about the book you have before you go inthide? the man asks. His voice is soft and polite, not a bit threatening. A faint lisp clips lightly along the top of his speech, turning some of his s-sounds into diphthongs. *I work for the Library, you thee.*

It's called The Black Arrow, Little White Walking Sam says politely, *and it's by Mr. Robert Louis Stevenson. He's dead. He died of toober-clue-rosis. It was very good. There were some great battles.*

The boy waits for the man in the little round black glasses to step aside and let him go in, but the man in the little round black glasses does not stand aside. The man only bends down to look at him more closely. Grandpa, what little round black eyes you have.

One other quethion, the man says. *Is your book overdue?*

Now Little White Walking Sam is more afraid.

Yes . . . but only a little. Only four days. It was very long, you see, and I have Little League, and day camp, and—

Come with me, son . . . I'm a poleethman.

The man in the black glasses and the overcoat extends a hand. For a moment Sam almost runs. But he is a kid; this man is an adult. This man works for the Library. This man is a policeman. Suddenly this man—this scary man with his scar and his round black glasses—is all Authority. One cannot run from Authority; it is everywhere.

Sam timidly approaches the man. He begins to lift his hand—the one holding the package of red licorice, which is now almost empty—and then tries to pull it back at the last second. He is too late. The man seizes it. The package of Bull's Eye licorice falls to the walk. Little White Walking Sam will never eat red licorice again.

The man pulls Sam toward him, reels him in the way a fisherman would reel in a trout. The hand clamped over Sam's is very strong. It hurts. Sam begins to cry. The sun is still out, the grass is still green, but suddenly the whole world seems distant, no more than a cruel mirage in which he was for a little while allowed to believe.

He can smell Sen-Sen on the man's breath. *Am I in trouble, sir?* he asks, hoping with every fiber of his being that the man will say no.

Yes, the man says. *Yes, you are. In a LOT of trouble. And if you want to get out of trouble, son, you have to do ecthactly as I thay. Do you underthand?*

Sam cannot reply. He has never been so afraid. He can only look up at the man with wide, streaming eyes.

The man shakes him. *Do you underthand or not?*

Ye—yes! Sam gasps. He feels an almost irresistible heaviness in his bladder.

Let me tell you exthactly who I am, the man says, breathing little puffs of Sen-Sen into Sam's face. *I am the Briggth Avenue Library Cop, and I am in charge of punishing boyth and girlth who bring their books back late.*

Little White Walking Sam begins to cry harder. *I've got the money!* he manages through his sobs. *I've got ninety-five cents! You can have it! You can have it all!*

He tries to pull the change out of his pocket. At the same moment the Library Cop looks around and his broad face suddenly seems sharp, suddenly the face of a fox or wolf who has successfully broken into the chicken house but now smells danger.

Come on, he says, and jerks Little White Walking Sam off the path and into the thick bushes which grow along the side of the library. *When the poleethman tellth you to come, you COME!* It is dark in here; dark and mysterious. The air smells of pungent juniper berries. The ground is dark with mulch. Sam is crying very loudly now.

Thut up! the Library Policeman grunts, and gives Sam a hard shake. The bones in Sam's hand grind together painfully. His head wobbles on his neck. They have reached a little clearing in the jungle of bushes now, a cove where the junipers have been smashed flat and the ferns broken off, and Sam understands that this is more than a place the Library Cop knows; it is a place he has *made.*

Thut up, or the fine will only be the beginning! I'll have to call your mother and tell her what a bad boy you've been! Do you want that?

No! Sam weeps. *I'll pay the fine! I'll pay it, mister, but please don't hurt me!*

The Library Policeman spins Little White Walking Sam around. *Put your hands up on the wall! Thpread your feet! Now! Quick!*

Still sobbing, but terrified that his mother may find out he has done something bad enough to merit this sort of treatment, Little White Walking Sam does as the Library Cop tells him. The red bricks are cool, cool in the shade of the bushes which lie against this side of the building in a tangled, untidy heap. He sees a narrow window at ground level. It looks down into the Library's boiler room. Bare bulbs shaded with rounds of tin like Chinese coolie hats hang over the giant boiler; the duct-pipes throw weird octopus-tangles of shadow. He sees a janitor standing at the far wall, his back to the window, reading dials and making notes on a clipboard.

The Library Cop seizes Sam's pants and pulls them down. His underpants come with them. He jerks as the cool air strikes his bum.

Thdeady, the Library Policeman pants. *Don't move. Once you pay the fine, son, it's over . . . and no one needth to know.*

Something heavy and hot presses itself against his bottom. Little White Walking Sam jerks again.

Thdeady, the Library Policeman says. He is panting harder now; Sam feels hot blurts of breath on his left shoulder and smells Sen-Sen. He is lost in terror now, but terror isn't all that he feels: there is shame, as well. He has been dragged into the shadows, is being forced to submit to this grotesque, unknown punishment, because he has been late returning *The Black Arrow.* If he had only known that fines could run this high—!

The heavy thing jabs into his bottom, thrusting his buttocks apart. A horrible, tearing pain laces upward from Little White Walking Sam's vitals. There has never been pain like this, never in the world.

He drops *The Black Arrow* and shoves his wrist sideways into his mouth, gagging his own cries.

Thdeady, the Library Wolf pants, and now his hands descend on Sam's shoulders and he is rocking back and forth, in and out, back and forth, in and out. *Thdeady . . . thdeaady . . . oooh! Thdeeeaaaaaaddyyyyy—*

Gasping and rocking, the Library Cop pounds what feels like a huge hot bar of steel in and out of Sam's bum; Sam stares with wide eyes into the Library basement, which is in another universe, an *orderly* universe where gruesome things like this don't ever happen. He watches the janitor nod, tuck his clipboard under his arm, and walk toward the door at the far end of the room. If the janitor turned his head just a little and raised his eyes slightly, he would see a face peering in the window at him, the pallid, wide-eyed face of a little boy with red licorice on his lips. Part of Sam wants the janitor to do just that—to rescue him the way the woodcutter rescued Little Red Riding Hood—but most of him knows the janitor would only turn away, disgusted, at the sight of another bad little boy submitting to his just punishment at the hands of the Briggs Avenue Library Cop.

Thdeadeeeeeeeeeeee! the Library Wolf whisper-screams as the janitor goes out the door and into the rest of his orderly universe without looking around. The Wolf thrusts even further forward and for one agonized second the pain becomes so bad Little White Walking Sam is sure his belly will explode, that whatever it is the Library Cop has stuck up his bottom will simply come raving out the front of him, pushing his guts ahead of it.

The Library Cop collapses against him in a smear of rancid sweat, panting harshly, and Sam slips to his knees under his weight. As he does, the massive object—no longer quite so massive—pulls out of him, but Sam can feel wetness all over his bottom. He is afraid to put his hands back there. He is afraid that when they come back he will discover he has become Little Red Bleeding Sam.

The Library Cop suddenly grasps Sam's arm and pulls him around to face him. His face is redder than ever, flushed in puffy, hectic bands like warpaint across his cheeks and forehead.

Look at you! the Library Cop says. His face pulls together in a knot of contempt and disgust. *Look at you with your panth down and your little dingle out! You liked it, didn't you? You LIKED it!*

Sam cannot reply. He can only weep. He pulls his underwear and his pants up together, as they were pulled down. He can feel mulch inside them, prickling his violated bottom, but he doesn't care. He squirms backward from the Library Cop until his back is to the Library's red brick wall. He can feel tough branches of ivy, like the bones of a large, fleshless hand, poking into his back. He doesn't care about this, either. All he cares about is the shame and terror and the sense of worthlessness that now abide in him, and of these three the shame is the greatest. The shame is beyond comprehension.

Dirty boy! the Library Cop spits at him. *Dirty little boy!*

I really have to go home now, Little White Walking Sam says, and the words come out minced into segments by his hoarse sobs: *Is my fine paid?*

The Library Cop crawls toward Sam on his hands and knees, his little round black eyes peering into Sam's face like the blind eyes of a mole, and this is somehow the final grotesquerie. Sam thinks, *He is going to punish me again,* and at this idea something in his mind, some overstressed strut or armature, gives way with a soggy snap he can almost hear. He does not cry or protest; he is now past that. He only looks at the Library Cop with silent apathy.

No, the Library Cop says. *I'm letting you go, thatth all. I'm taking pity on you, but if you ever tell anyone . . . ever . . . I'll come back and do it again. I'll do it until the fine is paid. And don't you ever let me catch you around here again, son. Do you underthand?*

Yes, Sam says. Of course he will come back and do it again if Sam tells. He will be in the closet late at night; under the bed; perched in a tree like some gigantic, misshapen crow. When Sam looks up into a troubled sky, he will see the Library Policeman's twisted, contemptuous face in the clouds. He will be anywhere; he will be everywhere.

This thought makes Sam tired, and he closes his eyes against that lunatic mole-face, against everything.

The Library Cop grabs him, shakes him again. *Yeth, what?* he hisses. *Yeth what, son?*

Yes, I understand, Sam tells him without opening his eyes.

The Library Policeman withdraws his hand. *Good,* he says. *You better not forget. When bad boys and girls forget, I kill them.*

Little White Walking Sam sits against the wall with his eyes closed for a long time, waiting for the Library Cop to begin punishing him again, or to simply kill him. He wants to cry, but there are no tears. It will be years before he cries again, over anything. At last he opens his eyes and sees he is alone in the Library Cop's den in the bushes. The Library Cop is gone. There is only Sam, and his copy of *The Black Arrow,* lying open on its spine.

Sam begins to crawl toward daylight on his hands and knees. Leaves tickle his sweaty, tear-streaked face, branches scrape his back and spank against his hurt bottom. He takes *The Black Arrow* with him, but he will not bring it into the Library. He will never go into the Library, any library, ever again: this is the promise he makes to himself as he crawls away from the place of his punishment. He makes another promise, as well: nobody will ever find out about this terrible thing, because he intends to forget it ever happened. He senses he can do this. He can do it if he tries very, very hard, and he intends to start trying very, very hard right now.

When he reaches the edge of the bushes, he looks out like a small hunted animal. He sees kids crossing the lawn. He doesn't see the Library Cop, but of course this doesn't matter; the Library Cop sees *him*. From today on, the Library Cop will always be close.

At last the lawn is empty. A small, dishevelled boy, Little White Crawling Sam, wriggles out of the bushes with leaves in his hair and dirt on his face. His untucked shirt billows behind him. His eyes are wide and staring and no longer completely sane. He sidles over to the concrete steps, casts one cringing, terrified look up at the cryptic Latin motto inscribed over the door, and then lays his book down on one of the steps with all the care and terror of an orphan girl leaving her nameless child on some stranger's doorstep. Then Little White Walking Sam becomes Little White Running Sam: he runs across the lawn, he sets the Briggs Avenue Branch of the St. Louis Public Library to his back and runs, but it doesn't matter how fast he runs because he can't outrun the taste of red licorice on his tongue and down his throat, sweet and sugar-slimy, and no matter how fast he runs the Library Wolf of course runs with him, the Library Wolf is just behind his shoulder where he cannot see, and the Library Wolf is whispering *Come with me, son . . . I'm a poleethman,* and he will *always* whisper that, through all the years he will whisper that, in those dark dreams Sam dares not remember he will whisper that, Sam will always run from that voice screaming *Is it paid yet? Is the fine paid yet? Oh dear God please, IS MY FINE PAID YET?* And the answer which comes back is always the same: *It will never be paid, son; it will never be paid.*

Never.

Nev—

CHAPTER FOURTEEN

THE LIBRARY (III)

1

The final approach to the dirt runway which Stan called the Proverbia Airport was bumpy and scary. The Navajo came down, feeling its way through stacks of angry air, and landed with a final jarring thump. When it did, Sam uttered a pinched scream. His eyes flew open.

Naomi had been waiting patiently for something like this. She leaned forward at once, ignoring the seatbelt which cut into her middle, and put her arms around him. She ignored his raised arms and first instinctive drawing away, just as she ignored the first hot and unpleasant outrush of horrified breath. She had comforted a great many drunks in the grip of the d.t.'s; this wasn't much different. She could feel his heart as she pressed against him. It seemed to leap and skitter just below his shirt.

"It's okay. Sam, it's okay—it's just me, and you're back. It was a dream. You're back."

For a moment he continued trying to push himself into his seat. Then he collapsed, limp. His hands came up and hugged her with panicky tightness.

"Naomi," he said in a harsh, choked voice. "Naomi, oh Naomi, oh dear Jesus, what a nightmare I had, what a terrible dream."

Stan had radioed ahead, and someone had come out to turn on the runway landing lights. They were taxiing between them toward the end of the runway now. They had not beaten the rain after all; it drummed hollowly on the body of the plane. Up front, Stan Soames was bellowing out something which might have been "Camptown Races."

"*Was* it a nightmare?" Naomi asked, drawing back from Sam so she could look into his bloodshot eyes.

"Yes. But it was also true. All true."

"Was it the Library Policeman, Sam? *Your* Library Policeman?"

"Yes," he whispered, and pressed his face into her hair.

"Do you know who he is? Do you know who he is now, Sam?"

After a long, long moment, Sam whispered: "I know."

2

Stan Soames took a look at Sam's face as he and Naomi stepped from the plane and was instantly contrite. "Sorry it was so rough. I really thought we'd beat the rain. It's just that with a headwind—"

"I'll be okay," Sam said. He was, in fact, looking better already.

"Yes," Naomi said. "He'll be fine. Thank you, Stan. Thank you so much. And Dave thanks you, too."

"Well, as long as you got what you needed—"

"We did," Sam assured him. "We really did."

"Let's walk around the end of the runway," Stan told them. "That boggy place'd suck you right in to your waist if you tried the shortcut this evening. Come on into the house. We'll have coffee. There's some apple pie, too, I think."

Sam glanced at his watch. It was quarter past seven.

"We'll have to take a raincheck, Stan," he said. "Naomi and I have to get these books into town right away."

"You ought to at least come in and dry off. You're gonna be soaked by the time you get to your car."

Naomi shook her head. "It's very important."

"Yeah," Stan said. "From the look of you two, I'd say it is. Just remember that you promised to tell me the story."

"We will, too," Sam said. He glanced at Naomi and saw his own thought reflected in her eyes: *If we're still alive to tell it.*

3

Sam drove, resisting an urge to tromp the gas pedal all the way to the floor. He was worried about Dave. Driving off the road and turning Naomi's car over in the ditch wasn't a very effective way of showing concern, however, and the rain in which they had landed was now a downpour driven by a freshening wind. The wipers could not keep up with it, even on high, and the headlights petered out after twenty feet. Sam dared drive no more than twenty-five. He glanced at his watch, then looked over at where Naomi sat, with the bookshop bag in her lap.

"I hope we can make it by eight," he said, "but I don't know."

"Just do the best you can, Sam."

Headlights, wavery as the lights of an undersea diving bell, loomed ahead. Sam slowed to ten miles an hour and squeezed left as a ten-wheeler rumbled by—a half-glimpsed hulk in the rainy darkness.

"Can you talk about it? The dream you had?"

"I could, but I'm not going to," he said. "Not now. It's the wrong time."

Naomi considered this, then nodded her head. "All right."

"I can tell you this much—Dave was right when he said children made the best meal, and he was right when he said that what she really lives on is fear."

They had reached the outskirts of town. A block further on, they drove through their first light-controlled intersection. Through the Datsun's windshield, the signal was only a bright-green smear dancing in the air above them. A corresponding smear danced across the smooth wet hide of the pavement.

"I need to make one stop before we get to the Library," Sam said. "The Piggly Wiggly's on the way, isn't it?"

"Yes, but if we're going to meet Dave behind the Library at eight, we really don't have much time to spare. Like it or not, this is go-slow weather."

"I know—but this won't take long."

"What do you need?"

"I'm not sure," he said, "but I think I'll know it when I see it."

She glanced at him, and for the second time he found himself amazed by the foxlike, fragile quality of her beauty, and unable to understand why he had never seen it before today.

Well, you dated her, didn't you? You must have seen SOMETHING.

Except he hadn't. He had dated her because she was pretty, presentable, unattached, and approximately his own age. He had dated her because bachelors in cities which were really just over-grown small towns were *supposed* to date . . . if they were bachelors interested in making a place for themselves in the local business community, that was. If you didn't date, people . . . some people . . . might think you were

(*a poleethman*)

a little bit funny.

I WAS *a little funny,* he thought. *On second thought, I was a* LOT *funny. But whatever I was, I think I'm a little different now. And I am seeing her. There's that. I'm really* SEEING *her.*

For Naomi's part, she was struck by the strained whiteness of his face and the look of tension around his eyes and mouth. He looked strange . . . but he no longer looked terrified. Naomi thought: *He looks like a man who has been granted the opportunity to return to his worst nightmare . . . with some powerful weapon in his hands.*

She thought it was a face she might be falling in love with, and this made her deeply uneasy.

"This stop . . . it's important, isn't it?"

"I think so, yes."

Five minutes later he stopped in the parking lot of the Piggly Wiggly store. Sam was out at once and dashing for the door through the rain.

Halfway there, he stopped. A telephone booth stood at the side of the parking lot—the same booth, undoubtedly, where Dave had made his call to the Junction City Sheriff's Office all those years before. The call made from that booth had not killed Ardelia . . . but it *had* driven her off for a good long while.

Sam stepped into it. The light went on. There was nothing to see; it was just a phone booth with numbers and graffiti scribbled on the steel walls. The telephone book was gone, and Sam remembered Dave saying, *This was back in the days when you could sometimes still find a telephone book in a telephone booth, if you were lucky.*

Then he glanced at the floor, and saw what he had been looking for. It was a wrapper. He picked it up, smoothed it out, and read what was written there in the dingy overhead light: Bull's Eye Red Licorice.

From behind him, Naomi beat an impatient tattoo on the Datsun's horn. Sam left the booth with the wrapper in his hand, waved to her, and ran into the store through the pouring rain.

4

The Piggly Wiggly clerk looked like a young man who had been cryogenically frozen in 1969 and thawed out just that week. His eyes had the red and slightly glazed look of the veteran dope-smoker. His hair was long and held with a rawhide Jesus thong. On one pinky he wore a silver ring beaten into the shape of the peace sign. Beneath his Piggly Wiggly tunic was a billowy shirt in an extravagant flower-print. Pinned to the collar was a button which read

MY FACE IS LEAVING IN 5 MINUTES
BE ON IT!

Sam doubted if this was a sentiment of which the store manager would have approved . . . but it was a rainy night, and the store manager was nowhere in sight. Sam was the only customer in the place, and the clerk watched him with a bemused and uninvolved eye as he went to the candy rack and began to pick up packages of Bull's Eye Red Licorice. Sam took the entire stock—about twenty packages.

"You sure you got enough, dude?" the clerk asked him as Sam approached the counter and laid his trove upon it. "I think there might be another carton or two of the stuff out back in the storeroom. I know how it is when you get a serious case of the munchies."

"This should do. Ring it up, would you? I'm in a hurry."

"Yeah, it's a hurry-ass world," the clerk said. His fingers tripped over the keys of the NCR register with the dreamy slowness of the habitually stoned.

There was a rubber band lying on the counter beside a baseball-card display. Sam picked it up. "Could I have this?"

"Be my guest, dude—consider it a gift from me, the Prince of Piggly Wiggly, to you, the Lord of Licorice, on a rainy Monday evening."

As Sam slipped the rubber band over his wrist (it hung there like a loose bracelet), a gust of wind strong enough to rattle the windows shook the building. The lights overhead flickered.

"*Whoa,* dude," the Prince of Piggly Wiggly said, looking up. "That wasn't in the forecast. Just showers, they said." He looked back down at the register. "Fifteen forty-one."

Sam handed him a twenty with a small, bitter smile. "This stuff was a hell of a lot cheaper when I was a kid."

"Inflation sucks the big one, all right," the clerk agreed. He was slowly returning to that soft spot in the ozone where he had been when Sam came in. "You must really like that stuff, man. Me, I stick to good old Mars Bars."

"Like it?" Sam laughed as he pocketed his change. "I hate it. This is for someone else." He laughed again. "Call it a present."

The clerk saw something in Sam's eyes then, and suddenly took a big, hurried step away from him, almost knocking over a display of Skoal Bandits.

Sam looked at the clerk's face curiously and decided not to ask for a bag. He gathered up the packages, distributed them at random in the pockets of the sport-coat he had put on a thousand years ago, and left the store. Cellophane crackled busily in his pockets with every stride he took.

5

Naomi had slipped behind the wheel, and she drove the rest of the way to the Library. As she pulled out of the Piggly Wiggly's lot, Sam took the two books from the Pell's bag and looked at them ruefully for a moment. *All this trouble,* he thought. *All this trouble over an outdated book of poems and a self-help manual for fledgling public speakers.* Except, of course, that wasn't what it was about. It had never been about the books at all.

He stripped the rubber band from his wrist and put it around the books. Then he took out his wallet, removed a five-dollar bill from his dwindling supply of ready cash, and slipped it beneath the elastic.

"What's that for?"

"The fine. What I owe on these two, and one other from a long time ago—*The Black Arrow,* by Robert Louis Stevenson. This ends it."

He put the books on the console between the two bucket seats and took a package of red licorice out of his pocket. He tore it open and that old, sugary smell struck him at once, with the force of a hard slap. From his nose it seemed to go directly into his head, and from his head it plummeted into his stomach, which immediately cramped into a slick, hard fist. For one awful moment he thought he was going to vomit in his own lap. Apparently some things never changed.

Nonetheless, he continued opening packages of red licorice, making a bundle of limber, waxy-textured candy whips. Naomi slowed as the light at the next intersection turned red, then stopped, although Sam could not see another car moving in either direction. Rain and wind lashed at her little car. They were now only four blocks from the Library. "Sam, what on earth are you doing?"

And because he didn't really *know* what on earth he was doing, he said: "If fear is Ardelia's meat, Naomi, we have to find the other thing—the thing that's the opposite of fear. Because that, whatever it is, will be her poison. So . . . what do you think that thing might be?"

"Well, I doubt if it's red licorice."

He gestured impatiently. "How can you be so sure? Crosses are supposed to kill vampires—the blood-sucking kind—but a cross is only two sticks of wood or metal set at right angles to each other. Maybe a head of lettuce would work just as well . . . if it was turned on."

The light turned green. "If it was an *energized* head of lettuce," Naomi said thoughtfully, driving on.

"Right!" Sam held up half a dozen long red whips. "All I know is that this is what I have. Maybe it's ludicrous. Probably is. But I don't care. It's a by-God symbol of *all* the things my Library Policeman took away from me—the love, the friendship, the sense of belonging. I've felt like an outsider *all my life*, Naomi, and never knew why. Now I do. This is just another of the things he took away. I used to *love* this stuff. Now I can barely stand the smell of it. That's okay; I can deal with that. But I have to know how to turn it on."

Sam began to roll the licorice whips between his palms, gradually turning them into a sticky ball. He had thought the smell was the worst thing with which the red licorice could test him, but he had been wrong. The texture was worse . . . and the dye was coming off on his palms and fingers, turning them a sinister dark red. He went on nevertheless, stopping only to add the contents of another fresh package to the soft mass every thirty seconds or so.

"Maybe I'm looking too hard," he said. "Maybe it's plain old bravery that's the opposite of fear. Courage, if you want a fancier word. Is that it? Is that all? Is bravery the difference between Naomi and Sarah?"

She looked startled. "Are you asking me if quitting drinking was an act of bravery?"

"I don't know *what* I'm asking," he said, "but I think you're in the right neighborhood, at least. I don't need to ask about fear; I *know* what that is. Fear is an emotion which encloses and precludes change. *Was* it an act of bravery when you gave up drinking?"

"I never really gave it up," she said. "That isn't how alcoholics do it. They *can't* do it that way. You employ a lot of sideways thinking instead. One day at a time, easy does it, live and let live, all that. But the center of it is this: you give up believing you can *control* your drinking. That idea was a myth you told yourself, and *that's* what you give up. The myth. You tell me—is that bravery?"

"Of course. But it's sure not foxhole bravery."

"Foxhole bravery," she said, and laughed. "I like that. But you're right. What I do—what *we* do—to keep away from the first one . . . it's not that kind of bravery. In spite of movies like *The Lost Weekend*, I think what we do is pretty undramatic."

Sam was remembering the dreadful apathy which had settled over him after he had been raped in the bushes at the side of the Briggs Avenue Branch of the St. Louis Library. Raped by a man who had called himself a policeman. That had been pretty undramatic, too. Just a dirty trick, that was all it had been—a dirty, brainless trick played on a little kid by a man with serious mental problems. Sam supposed that, when you counted up the whole score, he ought to call himself lucky; the Library Cop might have killed him.

Ahead of them, the round white globes which marked the Junction City Public Library glimmered in the rain. Naomi said hesitantly, "I think the real opposite of fear might be honesty. Honesty and belief. How does that sound?"

"Honesty and belief," he said quietly, tasting the words. He squeezed the sticky ball of red licorice in his right hand. "Not bad, I guess. Anyway, they'll have to do. We're here."

6

The glimmering green numbers of the car's dashboard clock read 7:57. They had made it before eight after all.

"Maybe we better wait and make sure everybody's gone before we go around back," she said.

"I think that's a very good idea."

They cruised into an empty parking space across the street from the Library's entrance. The globes shimmered delicately in the rain. The rustle of the trees was a less delicate thing; the wind was still gaining strength. The oaks sounded as if they were dreaming, and all the dreams were bad.

At two minutes past eight, a van with a stuffed Garfield cat and a MOM'S TAXI sign in its rear window pulled up across from them. The horn honked, and the Library's door—looking less grim even in this light than it had on Sam's first visit to the Library, less like the mouth in the head of a vast granite robot—opened at once. Three kids, junior-high-schoolers by the look of them, came out and hurried down the steps. As they ran down the walk to MOM'S TAXI, two of them pulled their jackets up to shield their heads from the rain. The van's side door rumbled open on its track, and the kids piled into it. Sam could hear the faint sound of their laughter, and envied the sound. He thought about how good it must be to come out of a library with laughter in your mouth. He had missed that experience, thanks to the man in the round black glasses.

Honesty, he thought. *Honesty and belief.* And then he thought again: *The fine is paid. The fine is paid, goddammit.* He ripped open the last two packages of licorice and began kneading their contents into his sticky, nasty-smelling red ball. He glanced at the rear of MOM'S TAXI as he did so. He could see white exhaust drifting up and tattering in the windy air. Suddenly he began to realize what he was up to here.

"Once, when I was in high school," he said, "I watched a bunch of kids play a prank on this other kid they didn't like. In those days, watching was what I did best. They took a wad of modelling clay from the Art Room and stuffed it in the tailpipe of the kid's Pontiac. You know what happened?"

She glanced at him doubtfully. "No—what?"

"Blew the muffler off in two pieces," he said. "One on each side of the car. They flew like shrapnel. The muffler was the weak point, you see. I suppose if the gases had backflowed all the way to the engine, they might have blown the cylinders right out of the block."

"Sam, what are you talking about?"

"Hope," he said. "I'm talking about hope. I guess the honesty and belief have to come a little later."

MOM'S TAXI pulled away from the curb, its headlights spearing through the silvery lines of rain.

The green numbers on Naomi's dashboard clock read 8:06 when the Library's front door opened again. A man and a woman came out. The man, awkwardly buttoning his overcoat with an umbrella tucked under his arm, was unmistakably Richard Price; Sam knew him at once, even though he had only seen a single photo of the man in an old newspaper. The girl was Cynthia Berrigan, the Library assistant he had spoken to on Saturday night.

Price said something to the girl. Sam thought she laughed. He was suddenly aware that he was sitting bolt upright in the bucket seat of Naomi's Datsun, every muscle creaking with tension. He tried to make himself relax and discovered he couldn't do it.

Now why doesn't that surprise me? he thought.

Price raised his umbrella. The two of them hurried down the

walk beneath it, the Berrigan girl tying a plastic rain-kerchief over her hair as they came. They separated at the foot of the walk, Price going to an old Impala the size of a cabin cruiser, the Berrigan girl to a Yugo parked half a block down. Price U-turned in the street (Naomi ducked down a little, startled, as the headlights shone briefly into her own car) and blipped his horn at the Yugo as he passed it. Cynthia Berrigan blipped hers in return, then drove away in the opposite direction.

Now there was only them, the Library, and possibly Ardelia, waiting for them someplace inside.

Along with Sam's old friend the Library Policeman.

7

Naomi drove slowly around the block to Wegman Street. About halfway down on the left, a discreet sign marked a small break in the hedge. It read

LIBRARY DELIVERIES ONLY.

A gust of wind strong enough to rock the Datsun on its springs struck them, rattling rain against the windows so hard that it sounded like sand. Somewhere nearby there was a splintering crack as either a large branch or a small tree gave way. This was followed by a thud as whatever it was fell into the street.

"God!" Naomi said in a thin, distressed voice. "I don't like this!"

"I'm not crazy about it myself," Sam agreed, but he had barely heard her. He was thinking about how that modelling clay had looked. How it had looked bulging out of the tailpipe of the kid's car. It had looked like a blister.

Naomi turned in at the sign. They drove up a short lane into a small paved loading/unloading area. A single orange arc-sodium lamp hung over the little square of pavement. It cast a strong, penetrating light, and the moving branches of the oaks which ringed the loading zone danced crazy shadows onto the rear face of the building in its glow. For a moment two of these shadows seemed to coalesce at the foot of the platform, making a shape that was almost manlike: it looked as if someone had been waiting under there, someone who was now crawling out to greet them.

In just a second or two, Sam thought, *the orange glare from that overhead light will strike his glasses—his little round black glasses— and he will look through the windshield at me. Not at Naomi; just at me. He'll look at me and he'll say, "Hello, son; I've been waiting for you. All theeth yearth, I've been waiting for you. Come with me now. Come with me, because I'm a poleethman."*

There was another loud, splintering crack, and a tree-branch dropped to the pavement not three feet from the Datsun's trunk, exploding chunks of bark and rot-infested wood in every direction. If it had landed on top of the car, it would have smashed the roof in like a tomato-soup can.

Naomi screamed.

The wind, still rising, screamed back.

Sam was reaching for her, meaning to put a comforting arm around her, when the door at the rear of the loading platform opened partway and Dave Duncan stepped into the gap. He was holding onto the door to keep the wind from snatching it out of his grasp. To Sam, the old man's face looked far too white and almost grotesquely frightened. He made frantic beckoning gestures with his free hand.

"Naomi, there's Dave."

"Where—? Oh yes, I see him." Her eyes widened. "My God, he looks *horrible!*"

She began to open her door. The wind gusted, ripped it out of her grasp, and whooshed through the Datsun in a tight little tornado, lifting the licorice wrappers and dancing them around in dizzy circles.

Naomi managed to get one hand down just in time to keep from being struck—and perhaps injured—by the rebound of her own car door. Then she was out, her hair blowing in its own storm about her head, her skirt soaked and painted against her thighs in a moment.

Sam shoved his own door open—the wind was blowing the wrong way for him, and he did literally have to put his shoulder to it— and struggled out. He had time to wonder where in the hell this storm had come from; the Prince of Piggly Wiggly had said there had been no prediction for such a spectacular capful of wind and rain. Just showers, he'd said.

Ardelia. Maybe it was Ardelia's storm.

As if to confirm this, Dave's voice rose in a momentary lull. "Hurry up! *I can smell her goddam perfume everywhere!*"

Sam found the idea that the smell of Ardelia's perfume might somehow precede her materialization obscurely terrifying.

He was halfway to the loading-platform steps before he realized that, although he still had the snot-textured ball of red licorice, he had left the books in the car. He turned back, muscled the door open, and got them. As he did, the quality of the light changed— it went from a bright, penetrating orange to white. Sam saw the change on the skin of his hands, and for a moment his eyes seemed to freeze in their sockets. He backed out of the car in a hurry, the books in his hand, and whirled around.

The orange arc-sodium security lamp was gone. It had been re-placed by an old-fashioned mercury-vapor streetlight. The trees dancing and groaning around the loading platform in the wind were thicker now; stately old elms predominated, easily overtopping the oaks. The shape of the loading platform had changed, and now tangled runners of ivy climbed the rear wall of the Library—a wall which had been bare just a moment ago.

Welcome to 1960, Sam thought. *Welcome to the Ardelia Lortz edition of the Junction City Public Library.*

Naomi had gained the platform. She was saying something to Dave. Dave replied, then looked back over his shoulder. His body jerked. At the same moment, Naomi screamed. Sam ran for the steps to the platform, the tail of his coat billowing out behind him. As he climbed the steps, he saw a white hand float out of the darkness and settle on Dave's shoulder. It yanked him back into the Library.

"Grab the door!" Sam screamed. "Naomi, grab the door! *Don't let it lock!*"

But in this the wind helped them. It blew the door wide open, striking Naomi's shoulder and making her stagger backward. Sam reached it in time to catch it on the rebound.

Naomi turned horrified dark eyes on him. "It was the man who came to your house, Sam. The tall man with the silvery eyes. I saw him. He grabbed Dave!"

No time to think about it. "Come on." He slipped an arm around Naomi's waist and pulled her forward into the Library. Behind them, the wind dropped and the door slammed shut with a thud.

8

They were in a book-cataloguing area which was dim but not entirely dark. A small table-lamp with a red-fringed shade stood on the librarian's desk. Beyond this area, which was littered with boxes and packing materials (the latter consisted of crumpled newspapers, Sam saw; this was 1960, and those polyethylene popcorn balls hadn't been invented yet), the stacks began. Standing in one of the aisles, walled in with books on both sides, was the Library Policeman. He had Dave Duncan in a half-nelson, and was holding him with almost absent ease three inches off the floor.

He looked at Sam and Naomi. His silver eyes glinted, and a crescent grin rose on his white face. It looked like a chrome moon.

"Not a thtep closer," he said, "or I'll thnap his neck like a chicken bone. You'll hear it go."

Sam considered this, but only for a moment. He could smell lavender sachet, thick and cloying. Outside the building, the wind whined and boomed. The Library Policeman's shadow danced up the wall, as gaunt as a gantry. *He didn't have a shadow before,* Sam realized. *What does that mean?*

Maybe it meant the Library Policeman was more real now, more *here* . . . because Ardelia and the Library Policeman and the dark man in the old car were really the same person. There was only one, and these were simply the faces it wore, putting them on and taking them off again with the ease of a kid trying on Halloween masks.

"Am I supposed to think you'll let him live if we stand away from you?" he asked. "Bullshit."

He began to walk toward the Library Policeman.

An expression which sat oddly on the tall man's face now appeared. It was surprise. He took a step backward. His trenchcoat flapped around his shins and dragged against the folio volumes which formed the sides of the narrow aisle in which he stood.

"I'm warning you!"

"Warn and be damned," Sam said. "Your argument isn't with him. You've got a bone to pick with me, don't you? Okay—let's pick it."

"The *Librarian* has a score to thettle with the old man!" the Policeman said, and took another step backward. Something odd was happening to his face, and it took Sam an instant to see what it was. The silver light in the Library Policeman's eyes was fading.

"Then let her settle it," Sam said. "*My* score is with you, big boy, and it goes back thirty years."

He passed beyond the pool of radiance thrown by the table lamp.

"All right, then!" the Library Cop snarled. He made a half-turn and threw Dave Duncan down the aisle. Dave flew like a bag of laundry, a single croak of fear and surprise escaping him. He tried to raise one arm as he approached the wall, but it was only a dazed, half-hearted reflex. He collided with the fire-extinguisher mounted by the stairs, and Sam heard the dull crunch of a breaking bone. Dave fell, and the heavy red extinguisher fell off the wall on top of him.

"*Dave!*" Naomi shrieked, and darted toward him.

"*Naomi, no!*"

But she paid no attention. The Library Policeman's grin reappeared; he grabbed Naomi by the arm as she tried to go past and curled her to him. His face came down and was for a moment hidden by the chestnut-colored hair at the nape of her neck. He uttered a strange, muffled cough against her flesh and then began kissing her—or so it appeared. His long white hand dug into her upper arm. Naomi screamed again, and then seemed to slump a little in his grip.

Sam had reached the entrance to the stacks now. He seized the first book his hand touched, yanked it off the shelf, cocked his arm back, and threw it. It flew end over end, the boards spreading, the pages riffling, and struck the Library Policeman on the side of the head. He uttered a cry of rage and surprise and looked up. Naomi tore free of his grasp and staggered sideways into one of the high shelves, flagging her arms for balance. The shelf rocked backward as she rebounded, and then fell with a gigantic, echoing crash. Books flew off shelves where they might have stood undisturbed for years and struck the floor in a rain of slaps that sounded oddly like applause.

Naomi ignored this. She reached Dave and fell on her knees beside him, crying his name over and over. The Library Policeman turned in that direction.

"Your argument isn't with her, either," Sam said.

The Library Policeman turned back to him. His silver eyes had been replaced with small black glasses that gave his face a blind, molelike look.

"I should have killed you the firtht time," he said, and began to walk toward Sam. His walk was accompanied by a queer brushing sound. Sam looked down and saw the hem of the Library Cop's trenchcoat was now brushing the floor. He was growing shorter.

"The fine is paid," Sam said quietly. The Library Policeman stopped. Sam held up the books with the five-dollar bill beneath the elastic. "The fine is paid and the books are returned. It's all over, you bitch . . . or bastard . . . or whatever you are."

Outside, the wind rose in a long, hollow cry which ran beneath the eaves like glass. The Library Policeman's tongue crept out and slicked his lips. It was very red, very pointed. Blemishes had begun to appear on his cheeks and forehead. There was a greasy lens of sweat on his skin.

And the smell of lavender sachet was much stronger.

"Wrong!" the Library Policeman cried. "*Wrong!* Those aren't the bookth you borrowed! I know! That drunk old cockthucker took the bookth you borrowed! They were—"

"—destroyed," Sam finished. He began to walk again, closing in on the Library Policeman, and the lavender smell grew stronger with every step he took. His heart was racing in his chest. "I know whose idea that was, too. But these are perfectly acceptable replacements. Take them." His voice rose into a stern shout. "*Take them, damn you!*"

He held the books out, and the Library Policeman, looking confused and afraid, reached for them.

"No, not like that," Sam said, raising the books above the white, grasping hand. "Like *this.*"

He brought the books down in the Library Policeman's face—brought them down hard. He could not remember ever feeling such sublime satisfaction in his life as that which he felt when *Best Loved Poems of the American People* and *The Speaker's Companion* struck and broke the Library Policeman's nose. The round black glasses flew off his face and fell to the floor. Beneath them were black sockets lined with a bed of whitish fluid. Tiny threads floated up from this oozy stuff, and Sam thought about Dave's story—*looked like it was startin to grow its own skin,* he had said.

The Library Policeman screamed.

"*You can't!*" it screamed. "*You can't hurt me! You're afraid of me! Besides, you liked it! You LIKED it! YOU DIRTY LITTLE BOY, YOU LIKED IT!*"

"Wrong," Sam said. "I fucking *hated* it. Now take these books. Take them and get out of here. Because the fine is paid."

He slammed the books into the Library Policeman's chest. And, as the Library Policeman's hands closed on them, Sam hoicked one knee squarely into the Library Policeman's crotch.

"That's for all the other kids," he said. "The ones you fucked and the ones she ate."

The creature wailed with pain. His flailing hands dropped the books as he bent to cup his groin. His greasy black hair fell over his face, mercifully hiding those blank, thread-choked sockets.

Of course they are blank, Sam had time to think. *I never saw the eyes behind the glasses he wore that day . . . so SHE couldn't see them, either.*

"That doesn't pay *your* fine," Sam said, "but it's a step in the right direction, isn't it?"

The Library Policeman's trenchcoat began to writhe and ripple, as if some unimaginable transformation had begun beneath it. And when he—*it*—looked up, Sam saw something which drove him back a step in horror and revulsion.

The man who had come half from Dave's poster and half from Sam's own mind had become a misshapen dwarf. The dwarf was becoming something else, a dreadful hermaphroditic creature. A sexual storm was happening on its face and beneath the bunching, twitching trenchcoat. Half the hair was still black; the other half was ash-blonde. One socket was still empty; a savage blue eye glittered hate from the other.

"*I want you,*" the dwarfish creature hissed. "*I want you, and I'll have you.*"

"Try me, Ardelia," Sam said. "Let's rock and r—"

He reached for the thing before him, but screamed and withdrew his hand as soon as it snagged in the trenchcoat. It wasn't a coat at all; it was some sort of dreadful loose skin, and it was like trying to grip a mass of freshly used teabags.

It scuttered up the canted side of the fallen bookshelf and thumped into the shadows on the far side. The smell of lavender sachet was suddenly much stronger.

A brutal laugh drifted up from the shadows.

A woman's laugh.

"Too late, Sam," she said. "It's already too late. The deed is done."

Ardelia's back, Sam thought, and from outside there was a tremendous, rending crash. The building shuddered as a tree fell against it, and the lights went out.

9

They were in total darkness only for a second, but it seemed much longer. Ardelia laughed again, and this time her laughter had a strange, hooting quality, like laughter broadcast through a megaphone.

Then a single emergency bulb high up on one wall went on, throwing a pallid sheaf of light over this section of the stacks and flinging shadows everywhere like tangles of black yarn. Sam could hear the light's battery buzzing noisily. He made his way to where Naomi still knelt beside Dave, twice almost falling as his feet slid in piles of books which had spilled from the overturned case.

Naomi looked up at him. Her face was white and shocked and streaked with tears. "Sam, I think he's dying."

He knelt beside Dave. The old man's eyes were shut and he was breathing in harsh, almost random gasps. Thin trickles of blood spilled from both nostrils and from one ear. There was a deep, crushed dent in his forehead, just above the right eyebrow. Looking at it made Sam's stomach clench. One of Dave's cheekbones was clearly broken, and the fire-extinguisher's handle was printed on that side of his face in bright lines of blood and bruise. It looked like a tattoo.

"We've got to get him to a hospital, Sam!"

"Do you think she'd let us out of here now?" he asked, and, as if in answer to this question, a huge book—the T volume of *The Oxford English Dictionary*—came flying at them from beyond the rough circle of light thrown by the emergency unit mounted on the wall. Sam pulled Naomi backward and they both went sprawling in the dusty aisle. Seven pounds of *tabasco, tendril, tomcat,* and *trepan* slammed through the space where Naomi's head had been a moment before, hit the wall, and splashed to the floor in an untidy, tented heap.

From the shadows came shrill laughter. Sam rose to his knees in time to see a hunched shape flit down the aisle beyond the fallen bookcase. *It's still changing,* Sam thought. *Into what, God only knows.* It buttonhooked to the left and was gone.

"Get her, Sam," Naomi said hoarsely. She gripped one of his hands. "Get her, please get her."

"I'll try," he said. He stepped over Dave's sprawled legs and entered the deeper shadows beyond the overturned bookcase.

10

The smell freaked him out—the smell of lavender sachet mixed with the dusty aroma of books from all those latter years. That smell, mingled with the freight-train whoop of the wind outside, made him feel like H. G. Wells's Time Traveller . . . and the Library itself, bulking all around him, was his time machine.

He walked slowly down the aisle, squeezing the ball of red licorice nervously in his left hand. Books surrounded him, seemed to frown down at him. They climbed to a height that was twice his own. He could hear the click and squeak of his shoes on the old linoleum.

"Where are you?" he shouted. "If you want me, Ardelia, why don't you come on and get me? I'm right here!"

No answer. But she would have to come out soon, wouldn't she? If Dave was right, her change was upon her, and her time was short.

Midnight, he thought. *The Library Policeman gave me until midnight, so maybe that's how long she has. But that's over three and a half hours away . . . Dave can't possibly wait that long.*

Then another thought, even less pleasant, occurred: suppose that, while he was mucking around back here in these dark aisles, Ardelia was circling her way back to Naomi and Dave?

He came to the end of the aisle, listened, heard nothing, and slipped over into the next. It was empty. He heard a low whispering sound from above him and looked up just in time to see half a dozen heavy books sliding out from one of the shelves above his head. He lunged backward with a cry as the books fell, striking his thighs, and heard Ardelia's crazy laughter from the other side of the bookcase.

He could imagine her up there, clinging to the shelves like a spider bloated with poison, and his body seemed to act before his brain could think. He slewed around on his heels like a drunken soldier trying to do an about face and threw his back against the shelf. The laughter turned to a scream of fear and surprise as the stack tilted under Sam's weight. He heard a meaty thud as the thing hurled itself from its perch. A second later the stack went over.

What happened then was something Sam had not foreseen: the stack he had pushed toppled across the aisle, shedding its books in a waterfall as it went, and struck the next one. The second fell against a third, the third against a fourth, and then they were all falling like dominoes, all the way across this huge, shadowy storage area, crashing and clanging and spilling everything from Marryat's works to *The Complete Grimm's Fairy Tales.* He heard Ardelia scream again and then Sam launched himself at the tilted bookcase he had pushed over. He climbed it like a ladder, kicking books out of his way in search of toe-holds, yanking himself upward with one hand.

He threw himself down on the far side and saw a white, hellishly misshapen creature pulling itself from beneath a jackstraw tumble of atlases and travel volumes. It had blonde hair and blue eyes, but any resemblance to humanity ceased there. Its illusions were gone. The creature was a fat, naked thing with arms and legs that appeared to end in jointed claws. A sac of flesh hung below its neck like a deflated goiter. Thin white fibers stormed around its body. There was something horridly beetlelike about it, and Sam was suddenly screaming inside—silent, atavistic screams which seemed to radiate out along his bones. *This is it. God help me, this is it.* He felt revulsion, but suddenly his terror was gone; now that he could actually see the thing, it was not so bad.

Then it began to change again, and Sam's feeling of relief faded. It did not have a face, exactly, but below the bulging blue eyes, a horn shape began to extrude itself, pushing out of the horror-show face like a stubby elephant's trunk. The eyes stretched away to either side, becoming first Chinese and then insectile. Sam could hear it sniffing as it stretched toward him.

It was covered with wavering, dusty threads.

Part of him wanted to pull back—was screaming at him to pull back—but most of him wanted to stand his ground. And as the thing's fleshy proboscis touched him, Sam felt its deep power. A sense of lethargy filled him, a feeling that it would be better if he just stood still and let it happen. The wind had become a distant, dreamy howl. It was soothing, in a way, as the sound of the vacuum cleaner had been soothing when he was very small.

"Sam?" Naomi called, but her voice was distant, unimportant. "Sam, are you all right?"

Had he thought he loved her? That was silly. Quite ridiculous, when you thought about it . . . when you got right down to it, this was much better.

This creature had . . . stories to tell.

Very interesting stories.

The white thing's entire plastic body now yearned toward the proboscis; it fed itself into itself, and the proboscis elongated. The creature became a single tube-shaped thing, the rest of its body hanging as useless and forgotten as that sac below its neck had hung. All its vitality was invested in the horn of flesh, the conduit through which it would suck Sam's vitality and essence into itself.

And it was nice.

The proboscis slipped gently up Sam's legs, pressed briefly against his groin, then rose higher, caressing his belly.

Sam fell on his knees to give it access to his face. He felt his eyes sting briefly and pleasantly as some fluid—not tears, this was thicker than tears—began to ooze from them.

The proboscis closed in on his eyes; he could see a pink petal of flesh opening and closing hungrily inside there. Each time it opened, it revealed a deeper darkness beyond. Then it clenched, forming a hole in the petal, a tube within a tube, and it slipped with sensual slowness across his lips and cheek toward that sticky outflow. Misshapen dark-blue eyes gazed at him hungrily.

But the fine was paid.

Summoning every last bit of his strength, Sam clamped his right hand over the proboscis. It was hot and noxious. The tiny threads of flesh which covered it stung his palm.

It jerked and tried to draw back. For a moment Sam almost lost it and then he closed his hand in a fist, digging his fingernails into the meat of the thing.

"*Here!*" he shouted. "*Here, I've got something for you, bitch! I brought it all the way from East St. Louis!*"

He brought his left hand around and slammed the sticky ball of red licorice into the end of the proboscis, plugging it the way the kids in that long-ago parking lot had plugged the tailpipe of Tommy Reed's Pontiac. It tried to shriek and could produce only a blocked humming sound. Then it tried again to pull itself away from Sam. The ball of red licorice bulged from the end of its convulsing snout like a blood-blister.

Sam struggled to his knees, still holding the twitching, noisome flesh in his hand, and threw himself on top of the Ardelia-thing. It twisted and pulsed beneath him, trying to throw him off. They rolled over and over in the heaped pile of books. It was dreadfully strong. Once Sam was eye to eye with it, and he was nearly frozen by the hate and panic in that gaze.

Then he felt it begin to swell.

He let go and scrambled backward, gasping. The thing in the book-littered aisle now looked like a grotesque beachball with a trunk, a beachball covered with fine hair which wavered like tendrils of seaweed in a running tide. It rolled over in the aisle, its proboscis swelling like a firehose which has been tied in a knot. Sam watched, frozen with horror and fascination, as the thing which had called itself Ardelia Lortz strangled on its own fuming guts.

Bright red roadmap lines of blood popped out on its straining hide. Its eyes bulged, now staring at Sam in an expression of dazed surprise. It made one final effort to expel the soft blob of licorice, but its proboscis had been wide open in its anticipation of food, and the licorice stayed put.

Sam saw what was going to happen and threw an arm over his face an instant before it exploded.

Chunks of alien flesh flew in every direction. Ropes of thick blood splattered Sam's arms, chest, and legs. He cried out in mingled revulsion and relief.

An instant later the emergency light winked out, plunging them into darkness again.

11

Once more the interval of darkness was very brief, but it was long enough for Sam to sense the change. He felt it in his head—a clear sensation of things which had been out of joint snapping back into place. When the emergency lights came back on, there were four of them. Their batteries made a low, self-satisfied humming sound instead of a loud buzz, and they were very bright, banishing the shadows to the furthest corners of the room. He did not know if the world of 1960 they had entered when the arc-sodium light became a mercury-vapor lamp had been real or an illusion, but he knew it was gone.

The overturned bookcases were upright again. There was a litter of books in this aisle—a dozen or so—but he might have knocked those off himself in his struggle to get on his feet. And outside, the sound of the storm had fallen from a shout to a mutter. Sam could hear what sounded like a very sedate rain falling on the roof.

The Ardelia-thing was gone. There were no splatters of blood or chunks of flesh on the floor, on the books, or on him.

There was only one sign of her: a single golden earring, glinting up at him.

Sam got shakily to his feet and kicked it away. Then a grayness came over his sight and he swayed on his feet, eyes closed, waiting to see if he would faint or not.

"Sam!" It was Naomi, and she sounded as if she were crying. "Sam, *where are you?*"

"Here!" He reached up, grabbed a handful of his hair, and pulled it hard. Stupid, probably, but it worked. The wavery grayness didn't go away entirely, but it retreated. He began moving back toward the cataloguing area, walking in large, careful strides.

The same desk, a graceless block of wood on stubby legs, stood in the cataloguing area, but the lamp with its old-fashioned, tasselled shade had been replaced with a fluorescent bar. The battered typewriter and Rolodex had been replaced by an Apple computer. And, if he had not already been sure of what time he was now in, a glance at the cardboard cartons on the floor would have convinced him: they were full of poppers and plastic bubble-strips.

Naomi was still kneeling beside Dave at the end of the aisle, and when Sam reached her side he saw that the fire-extinguisher (although thirty years had passed, it appeared to be the same one) was firmly mounted on its post again . . . but the shape of its handle was still imprinted on Dave's cheek and forehead.

His eyes were open, and when he saw Sam, he smiled. "Not . . . bad," he whispered. "I bet you . . . didn't know you had it . . . in you."

Sam felt a tremendous, buoyant sense of relief. "No," he said. "I didn't." He bent down and held three fingers in front of Dave's eyes. "How many fingers do you see?"

"About . . . seventy-four," Dave whispered.

"I'll call the ambulance," Naomi said, and started to get up. Dave's left hand grasped her wrist before she could.

"No. Not yet." His eyes shifted to Sam. "Bend down. I need to whisper."

Sam bent over the old man. Dave put a trembling hand on the

back of his neck. His lips tickled the cup of Sam's ear and Sam had to force himself to hold steady—it tickled. "Sam," he whispered. "She waits. Remember . . . *she waits.*"

"What?" Sam asked. He felt almost totally unstrung. "Dave, what do you mean?"

But Dave's hand had fallen away. He stared up at Sam, through Sam, his chest rising shallowly and rapidly.

"I'm going," Naomi said, clearly upset. "There's a telephone down there on the cataloguing desk."

"No," Sam said.

She turned toward him, eyes glaring, mouth pulled back from neat white teeth in a fury. "What do you mean, no? Are you crazy? His skull is fractured, at the very least! He's—"

"*He's* going, Sarah," Sam said gently. "Very soon. Stay with him. Be his friend."

She looked down, and this time she saw what Sam had seen. The pupil of Dave's left eye had drawn down to a pinpoint; the pupil of his right was huge and fixed.

"Dave?" she whispered, frightened. "*Dave?*"

But Dave was looking at Sam again. "Remember," he whispered. "She w . . ."

His eyes grew still and fixed. His chest rose once more . . . dropped . . . and did not rise again.

Naomi began to sob. She put his hand against her cheek and closed his eyes. Sam knelt down painfully and put his arm around her waist.

CHAPTER FIFTEEN

ANGLE STREET (III)

1

That night and the next were sleepless ones for Sam Peebles. He lay awake in his bed, all the second-floor lights turned on, and thought about Dave Duncan's last words: *She waits.*

Toward dawn of the second night, he began to believe he understood what the old man had been trying to say.

2

Sam thought that Dave would be buried out of the Baptist Church in Proverbia, and was a little surprised to find that he had converted to Catholicism at some point between 1960 and 1990. The services were held at St. Martin's on April 11th, a blustery day that alternated between clouds and cold early-spring sunshine.

Following the graveside service, there was a reception at Angle Street. There were almost seventy people there, wandering through the downstairs rooms or clustered in little groups, by the time Sam arrived. They had all known Dave, and spoke of him with humor, respect, and unfailing love. They drank ginger ale from Styrofoam cups and ate small finger sandwiches. Sam moved from group to group, passing a word with someone he knew from time to time but not stopping to chat. He rarely took his hand from the pocket of his dark coat. He had made a stop at the Piggly Wiggly store on his way from the church, and now there were half a dozen cellophane packages in there, four of them long and thin, two of them rectangular.

Sarah was not here.

He was about to leave when he spotted Lukey and Rudolph sitting together in a corner. There was a cribbage board between them, but they didn't seem to be playing.

"Hello, you guys," Sam said, walking over. "I guess you probably don't remember me—"

"Sure we do," Rudolph said. "Whatcha think we are? Coupla feebs? You're Dave's friend. You came over the day we was making the posters."

"Right!" Lukey said.

"Did you find those books you were lookin for?" Rudolph asked.

"Yes," Sam said, smiling. "I did, eventually."

"Right!" Lukey exclaimed.

Sam brought out the four slender cellophane packages. "I brought you guys something," he said.

Lukey glanced down, and his eyes lit up. "Slim Jims, Dolph!" he said, grinning delightedly. "Look! Sarah's boyfriend brought us all fuckin Slim Jims! Beautiful!"

"Here, gimme those, you old rummy," Rudolph said, and snatched them. "Fuckhead'd eat em all at once and then shit the

bed tonight, you know," he told Sam. He stripped one of the Slim
Jims and gave it to Lukey. "Here you go, dinkweed. I'll hang onto
the rest of em for you."

"You can have one, Dolph. Go ahead."

"You know better, Lukey. Those things burn me at both ends."

Sam ignored this byplay. He was looking hard at Lukey. "Sarah's
boyfriend? Where did you hear that?"

Lukey snatched down half a Slim Jim in one bite, then looked
up. His expression was both good-humored and sly. He laid a finger
against the side of his nose and said, "Word gets around when you're
in the Program, Sunny Jim. Oh yes indeed, it do."

"He don't know nothing, mister," Rudolph said, draining his cup
of ginger ale. "He's just beating his gums cause he likes the sound."

"That ain't nothin but bullshit!" Lukey cried, taking another giant
bite of Slim Jim. "I know because Dave told me! Last night! I had
a dream, and Dave was in it, and he told me this fella was Sarah's
sweetie!"

"Where *is* Sarah?" Sam asked. "I thought she'd be here."

"She spoke to me after the benediction," Rudolph said. "Told
me you'd know where to find her later on, if you wanted to see
her. She said you'd seen her there once already."

"She liked Dave awful much," Lukey said. A sudden tear grew
on the rim of one eye and spilled down his cheek. He wiped it
away with the back of his hand. "We all did. Dave always tried so
goddam hard. It's too bad, you know. It's really too bad." And
Lukey suddenly burst into tears.

"Well, let me tell you something," Sam said. He hunkered beside
Lukey and handed him his handkerchief. He was near tears himself,
and terrified by what he now had to do . . . or try to do. "He made
it in the end. He died sober. Whatever talk you hear, you hold
onto that, because I know it's true. He died sober."

"Amen," Rudolph said reverently.

"Amen," Lukey agreed. He handed Sam his handkerchief.
"Thanks."

"Don't mention it, Lukey."

"Say—you don't have any more of those fuckin Slim Jims,
do you?"

"Nope," Sam said, and smiled. "You know what they say,
Lukey—one's too many and a thousand are never enough."

Rudolph laughed. Lukey smiled . . . then laid the tip of his finger against the side of his nose again.

"How about a quarter . . . wouldn't have an extra quarter, wouldja?"

3

Sam's first thought was that she might have gone back to the Library, but that didn't fit with what Dolph had said . . . he had been at the Library with Sarah once, on the terrible night that already seemed a decade ago, but they had been there together; he hadn't "seen" her there, the way you saw someone through a window, or—

Then he remembered when he *had* seen Sarah through a window, right here at Angle Street. She had been part of the group out on the back lawn, doing whatever it was they did to keep themselves sober. He now walked through the kitchen as he had done on that day, saying hello to a few more people. Burt Iverson and Elmer Baskin stood in one of the little groups, drinking ice-cream punch as they listened gravely to an elderly woman Sam didn't know.

He stepped through the kitchen door and out onto the rear porch. The day had turned gray and blustery again. The backyard was deserted, but Sam thought he saw a flash of pastel color beyond the bushes that marked the yard's rear boundary.

He walked down the steps and crossed the back lawn, aware that his heart had begun to thud very hard again. His hand stole back into his pocket, and this time came out with the remaining two cellophane packages. They contained Bull's Eye Red Licorice. He tore them open and began to knead them into a ball, much smaller than the one he'd made in the Datsun on Monday night. The sweet, sugary smell was just as sickening as ever. In the distance he could hear a train coming, and it made him think of his dream—the one where Naomi had turned into Ardelia.

Too late, Sam. It's already too late. The deed is done.

She waits. Remember, Sam—she waits.

There was a lot of truth in dreams, sometimes.

How had she survived the years between? All the years between? They had never asked themselves that question, had they? How did she make the transition from one person to another? They had never asked that one, either. Perhaps the thing which looked like a woman named Ardelia Lortz was, beneath its glamours and illusions, like one of those larvae that spin their cocoons in the fork of a tree, cover them with protective webbing, and then fly away to their place of dying. The larvae in the cocoons lie silent, waiting . . . changing . . .

She waits.

Sam walked on, still kneading his smelly little ball made of that stuff the Library Policeman—*his* Library Policeman—had stolen and turned into the stuff of nightmares. The stuff he had somehow changed again, with the help of Naomi and Dave, into the stuff of salvation.

The Library Policeman, curling Naomi against him. Placing his mouth on the nape of her neck, as if to kiss her. And coughing instead.

The bag hanging under the Ardelia-thing's neck. Limp. Spent. Empty.

Please don't let it be too late.

He walked into the thin stand of bushes. Naomi Sarah Higgins was standing on the other side of them, her arms clasped over her bosom. She glanced briefly at him and he was shocked by the pallor of her cheeks and the haggard look in her eyes. Then she looked back at the railroad tracks. The train was closer now. Soon they would see it.

"Hello, Sam."

"Hello, Sarah."

Sam put an arm around her waist. She let him, but the shape of her body against his was stiff, inflexible, ungiving. *Please don't let it be too late,* he thought again, and found himself thinking of Dave.

They had left him there, at the Library, after propping the door to the loading platform open with a rubber wedge. Sam had used a pay phone two blocks away to report the open door. He hung up when the dispatcher asked for his name. So Dave had been found, and of course the verdict had been accidental death, and those people in town who cared enough to assume anything at all would make the expected assumption: one more old sot had gone to that great ginmill in the sky. They would assume he had gone up the lane with a jug, had seen the open door, wandered in, and had fallen against the fire-extinguisher in the dark. End of story. The postmortem results, showing zero alcohol in Dave's blood, would not change the assumptions one bit—probably not even for the police. *People just expect a drunk to die like a drunk,* Sam thought, *even when he's not.*

"How have you been, Sarah?" he asked.

She looked at him tiredly. "Not so well, Sam. Not so well at all. I can't sleep . . . can't eat . . . my mind seems full of the most horrible thoughts . . . they don't feel like my thoughts at all . . . and I want to drink. That's the worst of it. I want to drink . . . and drink . . . and drink. The meetings don't help. For the first time in my life, the meetings don't help."

She closed her eyes and began to cry. The sound was strengthless and dreadfully lost.

"No," he agreed softly. "They wouldn't. They can't. And I imagine she'd like it if you started drinking again. She's waiting . . . but that doesn't mean she isn't hungry."

She opened her eyes and looked at him. "What . . . Sam, what are you talking about?"

"Persistence, I think," he said. "The persistence of evil. How it waits. How it can be so cunning and so baffling and so powerful."

He raised his hand slowly and opened it. "Do you recognize this, Sarah?"

She flinched away from the ball of red licorice which lay on his palm. For a moment her eyes were wide and fully awake. They glinted with hate and fear.

And the glints were silver.

"Throw that away!" she whispered. "Throw that damned thing away!" Her hand jerked protectively toward the back of her neck, where her brownish-red hair hung against her shoulders.

"I'm talking to you," he said steadily. "Not to her but to you. I love you, Sarah."

She looked at him again, and that look of terrible weariness was back. "Yes," she said. "Maybe you do. And maybe you should learn not to."

"I want you to do something for me, Sarah. I want you to turn your back to me. There's a train coming. I want you to watch that train and not look back at me until I tell you. Can you do that?"

Her upper lip lifted. That expression of hate and fear animated her haggard face again. "No! Leave me alone! Go away!"

"Is that what you want?" he asked. "Is it really? You told Dolph where I could find you, Sarah. Do you really want me to go?"

Her eyes closed again. Her mouth drew down in a trembling bow of anguish. When her eyes opened again, they were full of haunted terror and brimming with tears. "Oh, Sam, help me! Something is wrong and I don't know what it is or what to do!"

"I know what to do," he told her. "Trust in me, Sarah, and trust in what you said when we were on our way to the Library Monday night. Honesty and belief. Those things are the opposite of fear. Honesty and belief."

"It's hard, though," she whispered. "Hard to trust. Hard to believe."

He looked at her steadily.

Naomi's upper lip lifted suddenly, and her lower lip curled out, turning her mouth momentarily into a shape that was almost like a horn. "*Fuck* yourself!" she said. "Go on and fuck yourself, Sam Peebles!"

He looked at her steadily.

She raised her hands and pressed them against her temples. "I didn't mean it. I don't know why I said it. I . . . my head . . . Sam, my poor *head*! It feels like it's splitting in two."

The oncoming train whistled as it crossed the Proverbia River and rolled into Junction City. It was the mid-afternoon freight, the one that charged through without stopping on its way to the Omaha stockyards. Sam could see it now.

"There's not much time, Sarah. It has to be now. Turn around and look at the train. Watch it come."

"Yes," she said suddenly. "All right. Do what you want to do, Sam. And if you see . . . see it isn't going to work . . . then push me. Push me in front of the train. Then you can tell the others that I jumped . . . that it was suicide." She looked at him pleadingly— deathly-tired eyes staring into his from her exhausted face. "They know I haven't been feeling myself—the people in the Program. You can't keep how you feel from them. After awhile that's just not possible. They'll believe you if you say I jumped, and they'd be right, because I don't want to go on like this. But the thing is . . . Sam, the thing is, I think that before long I *will* want to go on."

"Be quiet," he said. "We're not going to talk about suicide. Look at the train, Sarah, and remember I love you."

She turned toward the train, less than a mile away now and coming fast. Her hands went to the nape of her neck and lifted her hair. Sam bent forward . . . and what he was looking for was there, crouched high on the clean white flesh of her neck. He knew that her brain-stem began less than half an inch below that place, and he felt his stomach twist with revulsion.

He bent forward toward the blistery growth. It was covered in a spiderweb skein of crisscrossing white threads, but he could see it beneath, a lump of pinkish jelly that throbbed and pulsed with the beat of her heart.

"Leave me alone!" Ardelia Lortz suddenly screamed from the mouth of the woman Sam had come to love. *"Leave me alone, you bastard!"* But Sarah's hands were steady, holding her hair up, giving him access.

"Can you see the numbers on the engine, Sarah?" he murmured. She moaned.

He drove his thumb into the soft glob of red licorice he held, making a well a little bigger than the parasite which lay on Sarah's neck. "Read them to me, Sarah. Read me the numbers."

"Two . . . six . . . oh Sam, oh my head hurts . . . it feels like big hands pulling my brain into two pieces . . ."

"Read the numbers, Sarah," he murmured, and brought the Bull's Eye licorice down toward that pulsing, obscene growth.

"Five . . . nine . . . five . . ."

He closed the licorice gently over it. He could feel it suddenly, wriggling and squirming under the sugary blanket. *What if it breaks? What if it just breaks open before I can pull it off her? It's all Ardelia's concentrated poison . . . what if it breaks before I get it off?*

The oncoming train whistled again. The sound buried Sarah's shriek of pain.

"Steady—"

He simultaneously pulled the licorice back and folded it over. He had it; it was caught in the candy, pulsing and throbbing like a tiny sick heart. On the back of Sarah's neck were three tiny dark holes, no bigger than pinpricks.

"It's gone!" she cried. *"Sam, it's gone!"*

"Not yet," Sam said grimly. The licorice lay on his palm again, and a bubble was pushing up its surface, straining to break through—

The train was roaring past the Junction City depot now, the depot where a man named Brian Kelly had once tossed Dave Duncan four bits and then told him to get in the wind. Less than three hundred yards away and coming fast.

Sam pushed past Sarah and knelt by the tracks.

"*Sam, what are you doing?*"

"Here you go, Ardelia," he murmured. "Try this." He slapped the pulsing, stretching blob of red licorice down on one of the gleaming steel rails.

In his mind he heard a shriek of unutterable fury and terror. He stood back, watching the thing trapped inside the licorice struggle and push. The candy split open . . . he saw a darker red inside trying to push itself out . . . and then the 2:20 to Omaha rushed over it in an organized storm of pounding rods and grinding wheels.

The licorice disappeared, and inside of Sam Peebles's mind, that drilling shriek was cut off as if with a knife.

He stepped back and turned to Sarah. She was swaying on her feet, her eyes wide and full of dazed joy. He slipped his arms around her waist and held her as the boxcars and flatcars and tankers thundered past them, blowing their hair back.

They stood like that until the caboose passed, trailing its small red lights off into the west. Then she drew away from him a little . . . but not out of the circle of his arms—and looked at him.

"Am I free, Sam? Am I really free of her? It *feels* like I am, but I can hardly believe it."

"You're free," Sam agreed. "Your fine is paid, too, Sarah. Forever and ever, your fine is paid."

She brought her face to his and began to cover his lips and cheeks and eyes with small kisses. Her own eyes did not close as she did this; she looked at him gravely all the while.

He took her hands at last and said, "Why don't we go back inside, and finish paying our respects? Your friends will be wondering where you are."

"They can be your friends, too, Sam . . . if you want them to be."

He nodded. "I do. I want that a lot."

"Honesty and belief," she said, and touched his cheek.

"Those are the words." He kissed her again, then offered his arm. "Will you walk with me, lady?"

She linked her arm through his. "Anywhere you want, sir. Anywhere at all."

They walked slowly back across the lawn to Angle Street together, arm in arm.

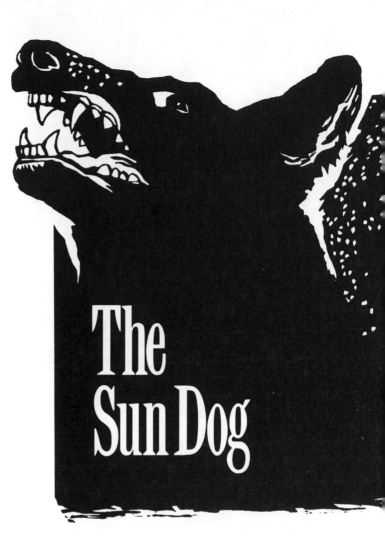

The
Sun Dog

THIS IS
IN MEMORY OF
JOHN D. MACDONALD.
I MISS YOU, OLD
FRIEND — AND YOU
WERE RIGHT ABOUT
THE TIGERS.

FOUR PAST MIDNIGHT

A NOTE ON
"THE SUN DOG"

Every now and then someone will ask me, "When are you going to get tired of this horror stuff, Steve, and write something serious?"

I used to believe the implied insult in this question was accidental, but as the years go by I have become more and more convinced that it is not. I watch the faces of the people who drop that particular dime, you see, and most of them look like bombardiers waiting to see if their last stick of bombs is going to fall wide or hit the targeted factory or munitions dump dead on.

The fact is, almost all of the stuff I have written—and that includes a lot of the funny stuff—was written in a serious frame of mind. I can remember very few occasions when I sat at the typewriter laughing uncontrollably over some wild and crazy bit of fluff I had just finished churning out. I'm never going to be Reynolds Price or Larry Woiwode—it isn't in me—but that doesn't mean I don't care as deeply about what I do. I have to do what I *can* do, however—as Nils Lofgren once put it, "I gotta be my dirty self . . . I won't play no jive."

If *real*—meaning !!SOMETHING THAT COULD ACTUALLY HAPPEN!!—is your definition of serious, you are in the wrong place and you should by all means leave the building. But please remember as you go that I'm not the only one doing business at this particular site; Franz Kafka had an office here, and George Orwell, and Shirley Jackson, and Jorge Luis Borges, and Jonathan Swift, and Lewis Carroll. A glance at the directory in the lobby shows the present tenants include Thomas Berger, Ray Bradbury, Jonathan Carroll, Thomas Pynchon, Thomas Disch, Kurt Vonnegut, Jr., Peter Straub, Joyce Carol Oates, Isaac Bashevis Singer, Katherine Dunn, and Mark Halpern.

I am doing what I do for the most serious reasons: love, money, and obsession. The tale of the irrational is the sanest way I know of expressing the world in which I live. These tales have served me as instruments of both metaphor and morality; they continue to offer the best window I know on the question of how we perceive things and the corollary question of how we do or do not behave on the basis of our perceptions. I have explored these questions as well as I can within the limits of my talent and intelligence. I am no one's National Book Award or Pulitzer Prize winner, but I'm serious, all right. If you don't believe anything else, believe this: when I take you by your hand and begin to talk, my friend, I believe every word I say.

A lot of the things I have to say—those Really Serious Things—have to do with the small-town world in which I was raised and where I still live. Stories and novels are scale models of what we laughingly call "real life," and I believe that lives as they are lived in small towns are scale models of what we laughingly call "society." This idea is certainly open to argument, and argument is perfectly fine (without it, a lot of literature teachers and critics would be looking for work); I'm just saying that a writer needs some sort of launching pad, and aside from the firm belief that story may exist with honor for its own self, the idea of the small town as social and psychological microcosm is mine. I began experimenting with this sort of thing in *Carrie,* and continued on a more ambitious level with *'Salem's Lot.* I never really hit my stride, however, until *The Dead Zone.*

That was, I think, the first of my Castle Rock stories (and Castle Rock is really just the town of Jerusalem's Lot without the vampires). In the years since it was written, Castle Rock has increasingly become "my town," in the sense that the mythical city of Isola is Ed McBain's town and the West Virginia village of Glory was Davis Grubb's town. I have been called back there time and time again to examine the lives of its residents and the geographies which seem to rule their lives—Castle Hill and Castle View, Castle Lake and the Town Roads which lie around it in a tangle at the western end of the town.

As the years passed, I became more and more interested in— almost entranced by—the secret life of this town, by the hidden relationships which seemed to come clearer and clearer to me. Much of this history remains either unwritten or unpublished: how the late Sheriff George Bannerman lost his virginity in the back seat of his dead father's car, how Ophelia Todd's husband was killed by a walking windmill, how Deputy Andy Clutterbuck lost the index finger on his left hand (it was cut off in a fan and the family dog ate it).

Following *The Dead Zone,* which is partly the story of the psychotic Frank Dodd, I wrote a novella called "The Body"; *Cujo,* the novel in which good old Sheriff Bannerman bit the dust; and a number of short stories and novelettes about the town (the best of them, at least in my mind, are "Mrs. Todd's Shortcut" and "Uncle Otto's Truck"). All of which is very well, but a state of entrancement with a fictional setting may not be the best thing in the world for a writer. It was for Faulkner and J. R. R. Tolkien, but sometimes a couple of exceptions just prove the rule, and besides, I don't play in that league.

So at some point I decided—first in my subconscious mind, I think, where all that Really Serious Work takes place—that the time had come to close the book on Castle Rock, Maine, where so many of my own favorite characters have lived and died. Enough, after all, is enough. Time to move on (maybe all the way next door to Harlow, ha-ha). But I didn't just want to walk away; I wanted to *finish* things, and do it with a bang.

Little by little I began to grasp how that could be done, and over the last four years or so I have been engaged in writing a Castle Rock Trilogy, if you please—the *last* Castle Rock stories. They were not written in order (I sometimes think "out of order" is the story of my life), but now they *are* written, and they are serious enough . . . but I hope that doesn't mean that they are sober-sided or boring.

The first of these stories, *The Dark Half,* was published in 1989. While it is primarily the story of Thad Beaumont and is in large part set in a town called Ludlow (the town where the Creeds lived in *Pet Sematary*), the town of Castle Rock figures in the tale, and the book serves to introduce Sheriff Bannerman's replacement, a fellow named Alan Pangborn. Sheriff Pangborn is at the center of the last story in this sequence, a long novel called *Needful Things,* which is scheduled to be published next year and will conclude my doings with what local people call The Rock.

The connective tissue between these longer works is the story which follows. You will meet few if any of Castle Rock's larger figures in "The Sun Dog," but it will serve to introduce you to Pop Merrill, whose nephew is town bad boy (and Gordie LaChance's *bête noire* in "The Body") Ace Merrill. "The Sun Dog" also sets the stage for the final fireworks display . . . and, I hope, exists as a satisfying story on its own, one that can be read with pleasure even if you don't give a hang about *The Dark Half* or *Needful Things.*

One other thing needs to be said: every story has its own secret life, quite separate from its setting, and "The Sun Dog" is a story about cameras and photographs. About five years ago, my wife, Tabitha, became interested in photography, discovered she was good at it, and began to pursue it in a serious way, through study, experiment, and practice-practice-practice. I myself take bad photos (I'm one of those guys who always manage to cut off my subjects' heads, get pictures of them with their mouths hanging open, or both), but I have a great deal of respect for those who take good ones . . . and the whole process fascinates me.

In the course of her experiments, my wife got a Polaroid camera, a simple one accessible even to a doofus like me. I became fascinated with this camera. I had seen and used Polaroids before, of course, but I had never really *thought* about them much, nor had I ever looked closely at the images these cameras produce. The more I thought about them, the stranger they seemed. They are, after all, not just images but moments of time . . . and there is something so *peculiar* about them.

This story came almost all at once one night in the summer of 1987, but the thinking which made it possible went on for almost a year. And that's enough out of me, I think. It's been great to be with all of you again, but that doesn't mean I'm letting you go home just yet.

I think we have a birthday party to attend in the little town of Castle Rock.

CHAPTER ONE

September 15th was Kevin's birthday, and he got exactly what he wanted: a Sun.

The Kevin in question was Kevin Delevan, the birthday was his fifteenth, and the Sun was a Sun 660, a Polaroid camera which does everything for the novice photographer except make bologna sandwiches.

There *were* other gifts, of course; his sister, Meg, gave him a pair of mittens she had knitted herself, there was ten dollars from his grandmother in Des Moines, and his Aunt Hilda sent—as she always did—a string tie with a horrible clasp. She had sent the first of

these when Kevin was three, which meant he already had twelve
unused string ties with horrible clasps in a drawer of his bureau, to
which this would be added—lucky thirteen. He had never worn
any of them but was not allowed to throw them away. Aunt Hilda
lived in Portland. She had never come to one of Kevin's or Meg's
birthday parties, but she might decide to do just that one of these
years. God knew she *could*; Portland was only fifty miles south of
Castle Rock. And suppose she *did* come . . . and asked to see Kevin
in one of his *other* ties (or Meg in one of her other scarves, for that
matter)? With some relatives, an excuse might do. Aunt Hilda,
however, was different. Aunt Hilda presented a certain golden possibility at a point where two essential facts about her crossed: she
was Rich, and she was Old.

Someday, Kevin's Mom was convinced, she might DO SOME-
THING for Kevin and Meg. It was understood that the SOMETHING
would probably come after Aunt Hilda finally kicked it, in the form
of a clause in her will. In the meantime, it was thought wise to keep
the horrible string ties and the equally horrible scarves. So this
thirteenth string tie (on the clasp of which was a bird Kevin thought
was a woodpecker) would join the others, and Kevin would write
Aunt Hilda a thank-you note, not because his mother would insist
on it and not because he thought or even cared that Aunt Hilda
might DO SOMETHING for him and his kid sister someday, but
because he was a generally thoughtful boy with good habits and no
real vices.

He thanked his family for all his gifts (his mother and father had,
of course, supplied a number of lesser ones, although the Polaroid
was clearly the centerpiece, and they were delighted with *his* delight), not forgetting to give Meg a kiss (she giggled and pretended
to rub it off but her own delight was equally clear) and to tell her
he was sure the mittens would come in handy on the ski team this
winter—but most of his attention was reserved for the Polaroid
box, and the extra film packs which had come with it.

He was a good sport about the birthday cake and the ice cream,
although it was clear he was itching to get at the camera and try it
out. And as soon as he decently could, he did.

That was when the trouble started.

He read the instruction booklet as thoroughly as his eagerness
to begin would allow, then loaded the camera while the family
watched with anticipation and unacknowledged dread (for some

reason, the gifts which seem the most wanted are the ones which
so often don't work). There was a little collective sigh—more puff
than gust—when the camera obediently spat out the cardboard
square on top of the film packet, just as the instruction booklet had
promised it would.

There were two small dots, one red and one green, separated by
a zig-zag lightning-bolt on the housing of the camera. When Kevin
loaded the camera, the red light came on. It stayed on for a couple
of seconds. The family watched in silent fascination as the Sun 660
sniffed for light. Then the red light went out and the green light
began to blink rapidly.

"It's ready," Kevin said, in the same straining-to-be-offhand-but-
not-quite-making-it tone with which Neil Armstrong had reported
his first step upon the surface of Luna. "Why don't all you guys
stand together?"

"I hate having my picture taken!" Meg cried, covering her face
with the theatrical anxiety and pleasure which only sub-teenage girls
and really bad actresses can manage.

"Come on, Meg," Mr. Delevan said.

"Don't be a goose, Meg," Mrs. Delevan said.

Meg dropped her hands (and her objections), and the three of
them stood at the end of the table with the diminished birthday
cake in the foreground.

Kevin looked through the viewfinder. "Squeeze a little closer to
Meg, Mom," he said, motioning with his left hand. "You too, Dad."
This time he motioned with his right.

"You're *squishing* me!" Meg said to her parents.

Kevin put his finger on the button which would fire the camera,
then remembered a briefly glimpsed note in the instructions about
how easy it was to cut off your subjects' heads in a photograph. *Off
with their heads,* he thought, and it should have been funny, but
for some reason he felt a little tingle at the base of his spine, gone
and forgotten almost before it was noticed. He raised the camera
a little. There. They were all in the frame. Good.

"Okay!" he sang. "Smile and say Intercourse!"

"*Kevin!*" his mother cried out.

His father burst out laughing, and Meg screeched the sort of mad
laughter not even bad actresses often essay; girls between the ages
of ten and twelve own sole title to that particular laugh.

Kevin pushed the button.

The flashbulb, powered by the battery in the film pack, washed the room in a moment of righteous white light.

It's mine, Kevin thought, and it should have been the surpassing moment of his fifteenth birthday. Instead, the thought brought back that odd little tingle. It was more noticeable this time.

The camera made a noise, something between a squeal and a whirr, a sound just a little beyond description but familiar enough to most people, just the same: the sound of a Polaroid camera squirting out what may not be art but what is often serviceable and almost always provides instant gratification.

"Lemme see it!" Meg cried.

"Hold your horses, muffin," Mr. Delevan said. "They take a little time to develop."

Meg was staring at the stiff gray surface of what was not yet a photograph with the rapt attention of a woman gazing into a crystal ball.

The rest of the family gathered around, and there was that same feeling of anxiety which had attended the ceremony of Loading the Camera: still life of the American Family waiting to let out its breath.

Kevin felt a terrible tenseness stealing into his muscles, and this time there was no question of ignoring it. He could not explain it . . . but it was there. He could not seem to take his eyes from that solid gray square within the white frame which would form the borders of the photograph.

"I think I see me!" Meg cried brightly. Then, a moment later: "No. I guess I don't. I think I see—"

They watched in utter silence as the gray cleared, as the mists are reputed to do in a seer's crystal when the vibrations or feelings or whatever they are are right, and the picture became visible to them.

Mr. Delevan was the first to break the silence.

"What is this?" he asked no one in particular. "Some kind of joke?"

Kevin had absently put the camera down rather too close to the edge of the table in order to watch the picture develop. Meg saw what the picture was and took a single step away. The expression on her face was neither fright nor awe but just ordinary surprise. One of her hands came up as she turned toward her father. The rising hand struck the camera and knocked it off the table and onto the floor. Mrs. Delevan had been looking at the emerging picture in a kind of trance, the expression on her face either that of a woman who is deeply puzzled or who is feeling the onset of a migraine headache. The sound of the camera hitting the floor startled her. She uttered a little scream and recoiled. In doing this, she tripped over Meg's foot and lost her balance. Mr. Delevan reached for her, propelling Meg, who was still between them, forward again, quite forcefully. Mr. Delevan not only caught his wife, but did so with some grace; for a moment they would have made a pretty picture indeed: Mom and Dad, showing they still know how to Cut A Rug, caught at the end of a spirited tango, she with one hand thrown up and her back deeply bowed, he bent over her in that ambiguous male posture which may be seen, when divorced from circumstance, as either solicitude or lust.

Meg was eleven, and less graceful. She went flying back toward the table and smacked into it with her stomach. The hit was hard enough to have injured her, but for the last year and a half she had been taking ballet lessons at the YWCA three afternoons a week. She did not dance with much grace, but she enjoyed ballet, and the dancing had fortunately toughened the muscles of her stomach enough for them to absorb the blow as efficiently as good shock absorbers absorb the pounding a road full of potholes can administer to a car. Still, there was a band of black and blue just above her hips the next day. These bruises took almost two weeks to first purple, then yellow, then fade . . . like a Polaroid picture in reverse.

At the moment this Rube Goldberg accident happened, she didn't even feel it; she simply banged into the table and cried out. The table tipped. The birthday cake, which should have been in the foreground of Kevin's first picture with his new camera, slid off the table. Mrs. Delevan didn't even have time to start her *Meg, are you all right?* before the remaining half of the cake fell on top of the Sun 660 with a juicy *splat!* that sent frosting all over their shoes and the baseboard of the wall.

The viewfinder, heavily smeared with Dutch chocolate, peered out like a periscope. That was all.

Happy birthday, Kevin.

Kevin and Mr. Delevan were sitting on the couch in the living room that evening when Mrs. Delevan came in, waving two dog-eared sheets of paper which had been stapled together. Kevin and Mr.

Delevan both had open books in their laps (*The Best and the Brightest* for the father; *Shoot-Out at Laredo* for the son), but what they were mostly doing was staring at the Sun camera, which sat in disgrace on the coffee table amid a litter of Polaroid pictures. All the pictures appeared to show exactly the same thing.

Meg was sitting on the floor in front of them, using the VCR to watch a rented movie. Kevin wasn't sure which one it was, but there were a lot of people running around and screaming, so he guessed it was a horror picture. Megan had a passion for them. Both parents considred this a low taste (Mr. Delevan in particular was often outraged by what he called "that useless junk"), but tonight neither of them had said a word. Kevin guessed they were just grateful she had quit complaining about her bruised stomach and wondering aloud what the exact symptoms of a ruptured spleen might be.

"Here they are," Mrs. Delevan said. "I found them at the bottom of my purse the second time through." She handed the papers— a sales slip from J. C. Penney's and a MasterCard receipt—to her husband. "I can never find anything like this the first time. I don't think anyone can. It's like a law of nature."

She surveyed her husband and son, hands on her hips.

"You two look like someone just killed the family cat."

"We don't *have* a cat," Kevin said.

"Well, you know what I mean. It's a shame, of course, but we'll get it sorted out in no time. Penney's will be happy to exchange it—"

"I'm not so sure of that," John Delevan said. He picked up the camera, looked at it with distaste (almost sneered at it, in fact), and then set it down again. "It got chipped when it hit the floor. See?"

Mrs. Delevan took only a cursory glance. "Well, if Penney's won't, I'm positive that the Polaroid company *will*. I mean, the fall obviously didn't cause whatever is wrong with it. The first picture looked just like all these, and Kevin took *that* one before Meg knocked it off the table."

"I didn't mean to," Meg said without turning around. On the screen, a pint-sized figure—a malevolent doll named Chucky, if Kevin had it right—was chasing a small boy. Chucky was dressed in blue overalls and waving a knife.

"I know, dear. How's your stomach?"

"Hurts," Meg said. "A little ice cream might help. Is there any left over?"

"Yes, I think so."

Meg gifted her mother with her most winning smile. "Would you get some for me?"

"Not at all," Mrs. Delevan said pleasantly. "Get it yourself. And what's that horrible thing you're watching?"

"*Child's Play*," Megan said. "There's this doll named Chucky that comes to life. It's neat."

Mrs. Delevan wrinkled her nose.

"Dolls don't come to life, Meg," her father said. He spoke heavily, as if knowing this was a lost cause.

"Chucky did," Meg said. "In movies, anything can happen." She used the remote control to freeze the movie and went to get her ice cream.

"Why does she want to watch that crap?" Mr. Delevan asked his wife, almost plaintively.

"I don't know, dear."

Kevin had picked up the camera in one hand and several of the exposed Polaroids in the other—they had taken almost a dozen in all. "I'm not so sure I *want* a refund," he said.

His father stared at him. "*What?* Jesus wept!"

"Well," Kevin said, a little defensively, "I'm just saying that maybe we ought to think about it. I mean, it's not exactly an ordinary defect, is it? I mean, if the pictures came out overexposed . . . or underexposed . . . or just plain blank . . . that would be one thing. But how do you get a thing like this? The same picture, over and over? I mean, look! And they're outdoors, even though we took every one of these pictures inside!"

"It's a practical joke," his father said. "It must be. The thing to do is just exchange the damned thing and forget about it."

"I don't think it's a practical joke," Kevin said. "First, it's too *complicated* to be a practical joke. How do you rig a camera to take the same picture over and over? Plus, the psychology is all wrong."

"Psychology, yet," Mr. Delevan said, rolling his eyes at his wife.

"Yes, psychology!" Kevin replied firmly. "When a guy loads your cigarette or hands you a stick of pepper gum, he hangs around to watch the fun, doesn't he? But unless you or Mom have been pulling my leg—"

"Your father isn't much of a leg-puller, dear," Mrs. Delevan said, stating the obvious gently.

Mr. Delevan was looking at Kevin with his lips pressed together.

It was the look he always got when he perceived his son drifting toward that area of the ballpark where Kevin seemed most at home: left field. *Far* left field. There was a hunchy, intuitive streak in Kevin that had always puzzled and confounded him. He didn't know where it had come from, but he was sure it hadn't been *his* side of the family.

He sighed and looked at the camera again. A piece of black plastic had been chipped from the left side of the housing, and there was a crack, surely no thicker than a human hair, down the center of the viewfinder lens. The crack was so thin it disappeared completely when you raised the camera to your eye to set the shot you would not get—what you *would* get was on the coffee table, and there were nearly a dozen other examples in the dining room.

What you got was something that looked like a refugee from the local animal shelter.

"All right, what in the devil are you going to do with it?" he asked. "I mean, let's think this over reasonably, Kevin. What practical good is a camera that takes the same picture over and over?"

But it was not practical good Kevin was thinking about. In fact, he was not thinking at all. He was feeling . . . and remembering. In the instant when he had pushed the shutter release, one clear idea

(*it's mine*)

had filled his mind as completely as the momentary white flash had filled his eyes. That idea, complete yet somehow inexplicable, had been accompanied by a powerful mixture of emotions which he could still not identify completely . . . but he thought fear and excitement had predominated.

And besides—his father *always* wanted to look at things reasonably. He would never be able to understand Kevin's intuitions or Meg's interest in killer dolls named Chucky.

Meg came back in with a huge dish of ice cream and started the movie again. Someone was now attempting to toast Chucky with a blowtorch, but he went right on waving his knife. "Are you two still arguing?"

"We're having a discussion," Mr. Delevan said. His lips were pressed more tightly together than ever.

"Yeah, right," Meg said, sitting down on the floor again and crossing her legs. "You always say that."

"Meg?" Kevin said kindly.

"What?"

"If you dump that much ice cream on top of a ruptured spleen, you'll die horribly in the night. Of course, your spleen might not actually be ruptured, but—"

Meg stuck her tongue out at him and turned back to the movie.

Mr. Delevan was looking at his son with an expression of mingled affection and exasperation. "Look, Kev—it's your camera. No argument about that. You can do whatever you want with it. But—"

"Dad, aren't you even the least bit interested in *why* it's doing what it's doing?"

"Nope," John Delevan said.

It was Kevin's turn to roll his eyes. Meanwhile, Mrs. Delevan was looking from one to the other like someone who is enjoying a pretty good tennis match. Nor was this far from the truth. She had spent years watching her son and her husband sharpen themselves on each other, and she was not bored with it yet. She sometimes wondered if they would ever discover how much alike they really were.

"Well, I want to think it over."

"Fine. I just want *you* to know that I can swing by Penney's tomorrow and exchange the thing—if you want me to and they agree to swap a piece of chipped merchandise, that is. If you want to keep it, that's fine, too. I wash my hands of it." He dusted his palms briskly together to illustrate.

"I suppose you don't want *my* opinion," Meg said.

"Right," Kevin said.

"Of course we do, Meg," Mrs. Delevan said.

"*I* think it's a supernatural camera," Meg said. She licked ice cream from her spoon. "I think it's a Manifestation."

"That's utterly ridiculous," Mr. Delevan said at once.

"No, it's not," Meg said. "It happens to be the only explanation that fits. You just don't think so because you don't believe in stuff like that. If a ghost ever floated up to you, Dad, you wouldn't even see it. What do you think, Kev?"

For a moment Kevin didn't—couldn't—answer. He felt as if another flashbulb had gone off, this one behind his eyes instead of in front of them.

"Kev? Earth to Kevin!"

"I think you might just have something there, squirt," he said slowly.

"Oh my dear God," John Delevan said, getting up. "It's the revenge of Freddy and Jason—my kid thinks his birthday camera's haunted. I'm going to bed, but before I do, I want to say just one more thing. A camera that takes photographs of the same thing over and over again—especially something as ordinary as what's in *these* pictures—is a *boring* manifestation of the supernatural."

"Still . . ." Kevin said. He held up the photos like a dubious poker hand.

"I think it's time we all went to bed," Mrs. Delevan said briskly. "Meg, if you absolutely need to finish that cinematic masterpiece, you can do it in the morning."

"But it's almost *over!*" Meg cried.

"I'll come up with her, Mom," Kevin said, and, fifteen minutes later, with the malevolent Chucky disposed of (at least until the sequel), he did. But sleep did not come easily for Kevin that night. He lay long awake in his bedroom, listening to a strong late-summer wind rustle the leaves outside into whispery conversation, thinking about what might make a camera take the same picture over and over and over again, and what such a thing might mean. He only began to slip toward sleep when he realized his decision had been made: he would keep the Polaroid Sun at least a little while longer.

It's mine, he thought again. He rolled over on his side, closed his eyes, and was sleeping deeply forty seconds later.

CHAPTER TWO

Amid the tickings and tockings of what sounded like at least fifty thousand clocks and totally undisturbed by them, Reginald "Pop" Merrill shone a pencil-beam of light from a gadget even more slender than a doctor's ophthalmoscope into Kevin's Polaroid 660 while Kevin stood by. Pop's eyeglasses, which he didn't need for close work, were propped on the bald dome of his head.

"Uh-huh," he said, and clicked the light off.

"Does that mean you know what's wrong with it?" Kevin asked.

"Nope," Pop Merrill said, and snapped the Sun's film compartment, now empty, closed. "Don't have a clue." And before Kevin could say anything else, the clocks began to strike four o'clock, and for a few moments conversation, although possible, seemed absurd.

I want to think it over, he had told his father on the evening he had turned fifteen—three days ago now—and it was a statement which had surprised both of them. As a child he had made a career of *not* thinking about things, and Mr. Delevan had in his heart of hearts come to believe Kevin never *would* think about things, whether he ought to or not. They had been seduced, as fathers and sons often are, by the idea that their behavior and very different modes of thinking would never change, thus fixing their relationship eternally . . . and childhood would thus go on forever. *I want to think it over:* there was a world of potential change implicit in that statement.

Further, as a human being who had gone through his life to that point making most decisions on instinct rather than reason (and he was one of those lucky ones whose instincts were almost always good—the sort of person, in other words, who drives reasonable people mad), Kevin was surprised and intrigued to find that he was actually On the Horns of a Dilemma.

Horn #1: he had wanted a Polaroid camera and he had gotten one for his birthday, but, dammit, he had wanted a Polaroid camera that *worked.*

Horn #2: he was deeply intrigued by Meg's use of the word *supernatural.*

His younger sister had a daffy streak a mile wide, but she wasn't stupid, and Kevin didn't think she had used the word lightly or thoughtlessly. His father, who was of the Reasonable rather than Instinctive tribe, had scoffed, but Kevin found he wasn't ready to go and do likewise . . . at least, not yet. That word. That fascinating, exotic word. It became a plinth which his mind couldn't help circling.

I think it's a Manifestation.

Kevin was amused (and a little chagrined) that only Meg had been smart enough—or brave enough—to actually say what should have occurred to all of them, given the oddity of the pictures the Sun produced, but in truth, it wasn't really that amazing. They were not a religious family; they went to church on the Christmas Day every third year when Aunt Hilda came to spend the holiday with them instead of her other remaining relatives, but except for the occasional wedding or funeral, that was about all. If any of them truly believed in the invisible world it was Megan, who couldn't get enough of walking corpses, living dolls, and cars that came to life and ran down people they didn't like.

Neither of Kevin's parents had much taste for the bizarre. They didn't read their horoscopes in the daily paper; they would never mistake comets or falling stars for signs from the Almighty; where one couple might see the face of Jesus on the bottom of an enchilada, John and Mary Delevan would see only an overcooked enchilada. It was not surprising that Kevin, who had never seen the man in the moon because neither mother nor father had bothered to point it out to him, had been likewise unable to see the possibility of *a supernatural Manifestation* in a camera which took the same picture over and over again, inside or outside, even in the dark of his bedroom closet, until it was suggested to him by his sister, who had once written a fan-letter to Jason and gotten an autographed glossy photo of a guy in a bloodstained hockey mask by return mail.

Once the possibility *had* been pointed out, it became difficult to unthink; as Dostoyevsky, that smart old Russian, once said to his little brother when the two of them were both smart *young* Russians, try to spend the next thirty seconds *not* thinking of a blue-eyed polar bear.

It was hard to do.

So he had spent two days circling that plinth in his mind, trying to read hieroglyphics that weren't even *there,* for pity's sake, and trying to decide which he wanted more: the camera or the possibility of a Manifestation. Or, put another way, whether he wanted the Sun . . . or the man in the moon.

By the end of the second day (even in fifteen-year-olds who are clearly destined for the Reasonable tribe, dilemmas rarely last longer than a week), he had decided to take the man in the moon . . . on a trial basis, at least.

He came to this decision in study hall period seven, and when the bell rang, signalling the end of both the study hall and the school-day, he had gone to the teacher he respected most, Mr. Baker, and had asked him if he knew of anyone who repaired cameras.

"Not like a regular camera-shop guy," he explained. "More like a . . . you know . . . a thoughtful guy."

"An F-stop philosopher?" Mr. Baker asked. His saying things like that was one of the reasons why Kevin respected him. It was just a cool thing to say. "A sage of the shutter? An alchemist of the aperture? A—"

"A guy who's seen a lot," Kevin said cagily.

"Pop Merrill," Mr. Baker said.

"Who?"

"He runs the Emporium Galorium."

"Oh. *That* place."

"Yeah," Mr. Baker said, grinning. "*That* place. If, that is, what you're looking for is a sort of homespun Mr. Fixit."

"I guess that's what I am looking for."

"He's got damn near everything in there," Mr. Baker said, and Kevin could agree with that. Even though he had never actually been inside, he passed the Emporium Galorium five, ten, maybe fifteen times a week (in a town the size of Castle Rock, you had to pass *everything* a lot, and it got amazingly boring in Kevin Delevan's humble opinion), and he had looked in the windows. It seemed crammed literally to the rafters with objects, most of them mechanical. But his mother called it "a junk-store" in a sniffing voice, and his father said Mr. Merrill made his money "rooking the summer people," and so Kevin had never gone in. If it had *only* been a "junk-store," he might have; almost certainly would have, in fact. But doing what the summer people did, or buying something where summer people "got rooked" was unthinkable. He would be as apt to wear a blouse and skirt to high school. Summer people could do what they wanted (and did). They were all mad, and conducted their affairs in a mad fashion. *Exist* with them, fine. But be *confused* with them? No. No. And no *sir.*

"Damn near everything," Mr. Baker repeated, "and most of what he's got, he fixed himself. He thinks that crackerbarrel-philosopher act he does—glasses up on top of the head, wise pronouncements, all of that—fools people. No one who knows him disabuses him. I'm not sure anyone would *dare* disabuse him."

"Why? What do you mean?"

Mr. Baker shrugged. An odd, tight little smile touched his mouth. "Pop—Mr. Merrill, I mean—has got his fingers in a lot of pies around here. You'd be surprised, Kevin."

Kevin didn't care about how many pies Pop Merrill was currently fingering, or what their fillings might be. He was left with only one more important question, since the summer people were gone and he could probably slink into the Emporium Galorium unseen tomorrow afternoon if he took advantage of the rule which allowed all students but freshmen to cut their last-period study hall twice a month.

"Do I call him Pop or Mr. Merrill?"

Solemnly, Mr. Baker replied, "I think the man kills anyone under the age of sixty who calls him Pop."

And the thing was, Kevin had an idea Mr. Baker wasn't exactly joking.

"You really don't know, huh?" Kevin said when the clocks began to wind down.

It has not been like in a movie, where they all start and finish striking at once; these were real clocks, and he guessed that most of them—along with the rest of the appliances in the Emporium Galorium—were not really running at all but sort of lurching along. They had begun at what his own Seiko quartz watch said was 3:58. They began to pick up speed and volume gradually (like an old truck fetching second gear with a tired groan and jerk). There were maybe four seconds when all of them really *did* seem to be striking, bonging, chiming, clanging, and cuckoo-ing at the same time, but four seconds was all the synchronicity they could manage. And "winding down" was not exactly what they did. What they did was sort of give up, like water finally consenting to gurgle its way down a drain which is almost but not quite completely plugged.

He didn't have any idea why he was so disappointed. Had he really expected anything else? For Pop Merrill, whom Mr. Baker had described as a crackerbarrel philosopher and homespun Mr. Fixit, to pull out a spring and say, "Here it is—this is the bastard causing that dog to show up every time you push the shutter release. It's a dog-spring, belongs in one of those toy dogs a kid winds up so it'll walk and bark a little, some joker on the Polaroid Sun 660 assembly line's *always* putting them in the damn cameras."

Had he expected that?

No. But he had expected . . . *something.*

"Don't have a friggin clue," Pop repeated cheerfully. He reached behind him and took a Douglas MacArthur corncob pipe from a holder shaped like a bucket seat. He began to tamp tobacco into it from an imitation-leather pouch with the words EVIL WEED stamped into it. "Can't even take these babies apart, you know."

"You can't?"

"Nope," Pop said. He was just as chipper as a bird. He paused long enough to hook a thumb over the wire ridge between the lenses of his rimless specs and give them a yank. They dropped off his bald dome and fell neatly into place, hiding the red spots on the sides of his nose, with a fleshy little thump. "You could take apart the old ones," he went on, now producing a Diamond Blue Tip match from a pocket of his vest (of course he was wearing a vest) and pressing the thick yellow thumbnail of his right hand on its head. Yes, this was a man who could rook the summer people with one hand tied behind his back (always assuming it wasn't the one he used to first fish out his matches and then light them)— even at fifteen years of age, Kevin could see that. Pop Merrill had *style*. "The Polaroid Land cameras, I mean. Ever seen one of those beauties?"

"No," Kevin said.

Pop snapped the match alight on the first try, which of course he would always do, and applied it to the corncob, his words sending out little smoke-signals which looked pretty and smelled absolutely foul.

"Oh yeah," he said. "They looked like those old-time cameras people like Mathew Brady used before the turn of the century— or before the Kodak people introduced the Brownie box camera, anyway. What I mean to say is" (Kevin was rapidly learning that this was Pop Merrill's favorite phrase; he used it the way some of the kids in school used "you know," as intensifier, modifier, qualifier, and most of all as a convenient thought-gathering pause) "they tricked it up some, put on chrome and real leather side-panels, but it still looked old-fashioned, like the sort of camera folks used to make daguerreotypes with. When you opened one of those old Polaroid Land cameras, it snapped out an accordion neck, because the lens needed half a foot, maybe even nine inches, to focus the image. It looked old-fashioned as hell when you put it next to one of the Kodaks in the late forties and early fifties, and it was like those old daguerreotype cameras in another way—it only took black-and-white photos."

"Is that so?" Kevin asked, interested in spite of himself.

"Oh, ayuh!" Pop said, chipper as a chickadee, blue eyes twinkling at Kevin through the smoke from his fuming stewpot of a pipe and from behind his round rimless glasses. It was the sort of twinkle which may indicate either good humor or avarice. "What I mean to say is that people laughed at those cameras the way they laughed at the Volkswagen Beetles when *they* first come out . . . but they bought the Polaroids just like they bought the VWs. Because the Beetles got good gas mileage and didn't go bust so often as American cars, and the Polaroids did one thing the Kodaks and even the Nikons and Minoltas and Leicas didn't."

"Took instant pictures."

Pop smiled. "Well . . . not exactly. When I mean to say is you took your pitcher, and then you yanked on this flap to pull it out. It didn't have no motor, didn't make that squidgy little whining noise like modern Polaroids."

So there *was* a perfect way to describe that sound after all, it was just that you had to find a Pop Merrill to tell it to you: the sound that Polaroid cameras made when they spat out their product was *a squidgy little whine.*

"Then you had to time her," Pop said.

"Time—?"

"Oh, ayuh!" Pop said with great relish, bright as the early bird who has found that fabled worm. "What I mean to say is they didn't have none of this happy automatic crappy back in those days. You yanked and out come this long strip which you put on the table or whatever and timed off sixty seconds on your watch. Had to be sixty, or right around there, anyway. Less and you'd have an under-exposed pitcher. More and it'd be overexposed."

"Wow," Kevin said respectfully. And this was not bogus respect, jollying the old man along in hopes he would get back to the point, which was not a bunch of long-dead cameras that had been wonders in their day but his *own* camera, the damned balky Sun 660 sitting on Pop's worktable with the guts of an old seven-day clock on its right and something which looked suspiciously like a dildo on its left. It wasn't bogus respect and Pop knew it, and it occurred to Pop (it wouldn't have to Kevin) how fleeting that great white god "state-of-the-art" really was; ten years, he thought, and the phrase itself would be gone. From the boy's fascinated expression, you would have thought he was hearing about something as antique as George Washington's wooden dentures instead of a camera every-one had thought was the ultimate only thirty-five years ago. But of course this boy had still been circling around in the unhatched void thirty-five years ago, part of a female who hadn't yet even met the male who would provide his other half.

"What I mean to say is it was a regular little darkroom goin on in there between the pitcher and the backing," Pop resumed, slow at first but speeding up as his own mostly genuine interest in the subject resurfaced (but the thoughts of who this kid's father was and what the kid might be worth to him and the strange thing the kid's camera was up to never completely left his mind). "And at the end of the minute, you peeled the pitcher off the back—had to be careful when you did it, too, because there was all this goo like jelly on the back, and if your skin was in the least bit sensitive, you could get a pretty good burn."

"Awesome," Kevin said. His eyes were wide, and now he looked like a kid hearing about the old two-holer outhouses which Pop and all his childhood colleagues (they were almost all colleagues; he had had few childhood friends in Castle Rock, perhaps preparing even then for his life's work of rooking the summer people and the other children somehow sensing it, like a faint smell of skunk) had taken for granted, doing your business as fast as you could in high summer because one of the wasps always circling around down there between the manna and the two holes which were the heaven from which the manna fell might at any time take a notion to plant its stinger in one of your tender little boycheeks, and also doing it as fast as you could in deep winter because your tender little boycheeks were apt to freeze solid if you didn't. *Well,* Pop thought, *so much for the Camera of the Future. Thirty-five years and to this kid it's interestin in the same way a backyard shithouse is interestin.*

"The negative was on the back," Pop said. "And your positive— well, it was black and white, but it was *fine* black and white. It was just as crisp and clear as you'd ever want even today. And you had this little pink thing, about as long as a school eraser, as I remember; it squeegeed out some kind of chemical, smelled like ether, and you had to rub it over the pitcher as fast as you could, or that pitcher'd roll right up, like the tube in the middle of a roll of bung-fodder."

Kevin burst out laughing, tickled by these pleasant antiquities.

Pops quit long enough to get his pipe going again. When he had, he resumed: "A camera like that, nobody but the Polaroid people really knew what it was doing—I mean to say those people were *close*—but it was *mechanical.* You could take it *apart.*"

He looked at Kevin's Sun with some distaste.

"And, lots of times when one went bust, that was as much as you needed. Fella'd come in with one of those and say it wouldn't work, moanin about how he'd have to send it back to the Polaroid people to get it fixed and that'd prob'ly take months and would I take a look. 'Well,' I'd say, 'prob'ly nothin I can do, what I mean to say is nobody really knows about these cameras but the Polaroid people and they're goddam close, but I'll take a look.' All the time knowin it was prob'ly just a loose screw inside that shutter-housin or maybe a fouled spring, or hell, maybe Junior slathered some peanut butter in the film compartment."

One of his bright bird-eyes dropped in a wink so quick and so marvellously sly that, Kevin thought, if you hadn't known he was talking about summer people, you would have thought it was your paranoid imagination, or, more likely, missed it entirely.

"What I mean to say is you had your perfect situation," Pop said. "If you could fix it, you were a goddam wonder-worker. Why, I have put eight dollars and fifty cents in my pocket for takin a couple of little pieces of potato-chip out from between the trigger and the shutter-spring, my son, and the woman who brought that camera in kissed me on the lips. Right . . . on . . . the lips."

Kevin observed Pop's eye drop momentarily closed again behind the semi-transparent mat of blue smoke.

"And of course, if it was somethin you couldn't fix, they didn't hold it against you because, what I mean to say, they never really expected you to be able to do nothin in the first place. You was only a last resort before they put her in a box and stuffed newspaper around her to keep her from bein broke even worse in the mail, and shipped her off to Schenectady.

"But—*this* camera." He spoke in the ritualistic tone of distaste all philosophers of the crackerbarrel, whether in Athens of the golden age or in a small-town junk-shop during this current one of brass, adopt to express their view of entropy without having to come right out and state it. "Wasn't put together, son. What I mean to say is it was *poured*. I could maybe pop the lens, and will if you want me to, and I *did* look in the film compartment, although I knew I wouldn't see a goddam thing wrong—that I recognized, at least—and I didn't. But beyond that I can't go. I could take a hammer and wind it right to her, could *break* it, what I mean to say, but fix it?" He spread his hands in pipe-smoke. "Nossir."

"Then I guess I'll just have to—" *return it after all,* he meant to finish, but Pop broke in.

"Anyway, son, I think you knew that. What I mean to say is you're a bright boy, you can see when a thing's all of a piece. I don't think you brought that camera in to be *fixed.* I think you know that even if it *wasn't* all of a piece, a man couldn't fix what *that* thing's doing, at least not with a screwdriver. I think you brought it in to ask me if I knew what it's *up* to."

"Do you?" Kevin asked. He was suddenly tense all over.

"I might," Pop Merrill said calmly. He bent over the pile of photographs—twenty-eight of them now, counting the one Kevin had snapped to demonstrate, and the one Pop had snapped to demonstrate to himself. "These in order?"

"Not really. Pretty close, though. Does it matter?"

"I think so," Pop said. "They're a little bit different, ain't they? Not much, but a little."

"Yeah," Kevin said. "I can see the difference in *some* of them, but . . ."

"Do you know which one is the first? I could prob'ly figure it out for myself, but time is money, son."

"That's easy," Kevin said, and picked one out of the untidy little pile. "See the frosting?" He pointed at a small brown spot on the picture's white edging.

"Ayup." Pop didn't spare the dab of frosting more than a glance. He looked closely at the photograph, and after a moment he opened the drawer of his worktable. Tools were littered untidily about inside. To one side, in its own space, was an object wrapped in jeweler's velvet. Pop took this out, folded the cloth back, and removed a large magnifying glass with a switch in its base. He bent over the Polaroid and pushed the switch. A bright circle of light fell on the picture's surface.

"That's neat!" Kevin said.

"Ayup," Pop said again. Kevin could tell that for Pop he was no longer there. Pop was studying the picture closely.

If one had not known the odd circumstances of its taking, the picture would hardly have seemed to warrant such close scrutiny. Like most photographs which are taken with a decent camera, good film, and by a photographer at least intelligent enough to keep his finger from blocking the lens, it was clear, understandable . . . and, like so many Polaroids, oddly undramatic. It was a picture in which you could identify and name each object, but its content was as flat as its surface. It was not well composed, but composition wasn't what was wrong with it—that undramatic flatness could hardly be called *wrong* at all, any more than a real day in a real life could be called wrong because nothing worthy of even a made-for-television movie happened during its course. As in so many Polaroids, the things in the picture were only *there,* like an empty chair on a porch or an unoccupied child's swing in a back yard or a passengerless car sitting at an unremarkable curb without even a flat tire to make it interesting or unique.

What was wrong with the picture was the *feeling* that it was wrong. Kevin had remembered the sense of unease he had felt while composing his subjects for the picture he *meant* to take, and the ripple of gooseflesh up his back when, with the glare of the flashbulb still lighting the room, he had thought, *It's mine.* That was what was wrong, and as with the man in the moon you can't unsee once you've seen it, so, he was discovering, you couldn't *unfeel* certain feelings . . . and when it came to these pictures, those feelings were bad.

Kevin thought: *It's like there was a wind—very soft, very cold— blowing out of that picture.*

For the first time, the idea that it might be something supernatural—that this was part of a Manifestation—did something more than just intrigue him. For the first time he found himself wishing he had simply let this thing go. *It's mine*—that was what he had thought when his finger had pushed the shutter-button for the first time. Now he found himself wondering if maybe he hadn't gotten that backward.

I'm scared of it. Of what it's doing.

That made him mad, and he bent over Pop Merrill's shoulder, hunting as grimly as a man who has lost a diamond in a sandpile, determined that, no matter what he saw (always supposing he *should* see something new, and he didn't think he would; he had studied all these photographs often enough now to believe he had seen all there was to see in them), he would *look* at it, *study* it, and under no circumstances allow himself to unsee it. Even if he could . . . and a dolorous voice inside suggested very strongly that the time for unseeing was now past, possibly forever.

———

What the picture showed was a large black dog in front of a white picket fence. The picket fence wasn't going to be white much longer, unless someone in that flat Polaroid world painted or at least whitewashed it. That didn't seem likely; the fence looked untended, forgotten. The tops of some pickets were broken off. Others sagged loosely outward.

The dog was on a sidewalk in front of the fence. His hindquarters were to the viewer. His tail, long and bushy, drooped. He appeared to be smelling one of the fence-pickets—probably, Kevin thought, because the fence was what his dad called a "letter-drop," a place where many dogs would lift their legs and leave mystic yellow squirts of message before moving on.

The dog looked like a stray to Kevin. Its coat was long and tangled and sown with burdocks. One of its ears had the crumpled look of an old battle-scar. Its shadow trailed long enough to finish outside the frame on the weedy, patchy lawn inside the picket fence. The shadow made Kevin think the picture had been taken not long after dawn or not long before sunset; with no idea of the direction the photographer (*what* photographer, ha-ha) had been facing, it was impossible to tell which, just that he (or she) must have been standing only a few degrees shy of due east or west.

There was something in the grass at the far left of the picture which looked like a child's red rubber ball. It was inside the fence, and enough behind one of the lackluster clumps of grass so it was hard to tell.

And that was all.

"Do you recognize anything?" Pop asked, cruising his magnifying glass slowly back and forth over the photo's surface. Now the dog's hindquarters swelled to the size of hillocks tangled with wild and ominously exotic black undergrowth; now three or four of the scaly pickets became the size of old telephone poles; now, suddenly, the object behind the clump of grass clearly became a child's ball (although under Pop's glass it was as big as a soccer ball): Kevin could even see the stars which girdled its middle in upraised rubber lines. So something new *was* revealed under Pop's glass, and in a few moments Kevin would see something else himself, without it. But that was later.

"Jeez, no," Kevin said. "How could I, Mr. Merrill?"

"Because there are *things* here," Pop said patiently. His glass went on cruising. Kevin thought of a movie he had seen once where the cops sent out a searchlight-equipped helicopter to look for escaped prisoners. "A dog, a sidewalk, a picket fence that needs paintin or takin down, a lawn that needs tendin. The sidewalk ain't much—you can't even see all of it—and the house, even the foundation, ain't in the frame, but what I mean to say is there's that dog. You recognize *it*?"

"No."

"The *fence*?"

"No."

"What about that red rubber ball? What about that, son?"

"No . . . but you look like you think I should."

"I look like I thought you *might*," Pop said. "You never had a ball like that when you were a tyke?"

"Not that I remember, no."

"You got a sister, you said."

"Megan."

"She never had a ball like that?"

"I don't think so. I never took that much interest in Meg's toys. She had a BoLo bouncer once, and the ball on the end of it was red, but a different shade. Darker."

"Ayuh. I know what a ball like that looks like. This ain't one. And that mightn't be your lawn?"

"Jes—I mean jeepers, no." Kevin felt a little offended. He and his dad took good care of the lawn around their house. It was a deep green and would stay that way, even under the fallen leaves, until at least mid-October. "We don't have a picket fence, anyway." *And if we did,* he thought, *it wouldn't look like that mess.*

Pop let go of the switch in the base of the magnifying glass, placed it on the square of jeweler's velvet, and with a care which approached reverence folded the sides over it. He returned it to its former place in the drawer and closed the drawer. He looked at Kevin closely. He had put his pipe aside, and there was now no smoke to obscure his eyes, which were still sharp but not twinkling anymore.

"What I mean to say is, could it have been your house before you owned it, do you think? Ten years ago—"

"We owned it ten years ago," Kevin replied, bewildered.

"Well, twenty? Thirty? What I mean to say, do you recognize how the land lies? Looks like it climbs a little."

"Our front lawn—" He thought deeply, then shook his head. "No, ours is flat. If it does anything, it goes down a little. Maybe that's why the cellar ships a little water in a wet spring."

"Ayuh, ayuh, could be. What about the back lawn?"

"There's no sidewalk back there," Kevin said. "And on the sides—" He broke off. "You're trying to find out if my camera's taking pictures of the past!" he said, and for the first time he was really, actively frightened. He rubbed his tongue on the roof of his mouth and seemed to taste metal.

"I was just askin." Pop rapped his fingers beside the photographs, and when he spoke, it seemed to be more to himself than to Kevin. "You know," he said, "some goddam funny things seem to happen from time to time with two gadgets we've come to take pretty much for granted. I ain't sayin they *do* happen; only if they don't, there are a lot of liars and out-n-out hoaxers in the world."

"What gadgets?"

"Tape recorders and Polaroid cameras," Pop said, still seeming to talk to the pictures, or himself, and there was no Kevin in this dusty clock-drumming space at the back of the Emporium Galorium at all. "Take tape recorders. Do you know how many people claim to have recorded the voices of dead folks on tape recorders?"

"No," Kevin said. He didn't particularly mean for his own voice to come out hushed, but it did; he didn't seem to have a whole lot of air in his lungs to speak with, for some reason or other.

"Me neither," Pop said, stirring the photographs with one finger. It was blunt and gnarled, a finger which looked made for rude and clumsy motions and operations, for poking people and knocking vases off endtables and causing nosebleeds if it tried to do so much as hook a humble chunk of dried snot from one of its owner's nostrils. Yet Kevin had watched the man's hands and thought there was probably more grace in that one finger than in his sister Meg's entire body (and maybe in his own; Clan Delevan was not known for its lightfootedness or -handedness, which was probably one reason why he thought that image of his father so nimbly catching his mother on the way down had stuck with him, and might forever). Pop Merrill's finger looked as if it would at any moment sweep all the photographs onto the floor—by mistake; this sort of clumsy finger would always poke and knock and tweak by mistake—but it did not. The Polaroids seemed to barely stir in response to its restless movements.

Supernatural, Kevin thought again, and shivered a little. An *actual* shiver, surprising and dismaying and a little embarrassing even if Pop had not seen it.

"But there's even a way they do it," Pop said, and then, as if Kevin had asked: "Who? Damn if I know. I guess some of them are 'psychic investigators,' or at least call themselves that or some such, but I guess it's more'n likely most of em are just playin around, like folks that use Ouija Boards at parties."

He looked up at Kevin grimly, as if rediscovering him.

"You got a Ouija, son?"

"No."

"Ever played with one?"

"No."

"Don't," Pop said more grimly than ever. "Fucking things are dangerous."

Kevin didn't dare tell the old man he hadn't the slightest idea what a weegee board was.

"Anyway, they set up a tape machine to record in an empty room. It's supposed to be an old house, is what I mean to say, one with a History, if they can find it. Do you know what I mean when I say a house with a History, son?"

"I guess . . . like a haunted house?" Kevin hazarded. He found he was sweating lightly, as he had done last year every time Mrs. Whittaker announced a pop quiz in Algebra I.

"Well, that'll do. These . . . people . . . like it best if it's a house with a *Violent* History, but they'll take what they can get. Anyhow, they set up the machine and record that empty room. Then, the next day—they always do it at night is what I mean to say, they ain't happy unless they can do it at night, and midnight if they can get it—the next day they play her back."

"An empty room?"

"Sometimes," Pop said in a musing voice that might or might not have disguised some deeper feeling, "there are voices."

Kevin shivered again. There were hieroglyphics on the plinth after all. Nothing you'd want to read, but . . . yeah. They were there.

"*Real* voices?"

"Usually imagination," Pop said dismissively. "But once or twice I've heard people I trust say they've heard real voices."

"But *you* never have?"

"Once," Pop said shortly, and said nothing else for so long Kevin was beginning to think he was done when he added, "It was one word. Clear as a bell. 'Twas recorded in the parlor of an empty house in Bath. Man killed his wife there in 1946."

"What was the word?" Kevin asked, knowing he would not be told just as surely as he knew no power on earth, certainly not his own willpower, could have kept him from asking.

But Pop *did* tell.

"Basin."

Kevin blinked. "Basin?"

"Ayuh."

"That doesn't mean anything."

"It might," Pop said calmly, "if you know he cut her throat and then held her head over a basin to catch the blood."

"Oh my God!"

"Ayuh."

"Oh my God, really?"

Pop didn't bother answering that.

"It couldn't have been a fake?"

Pop gestured with the stem of his pipe at the Polaroids. "Are those?"

"Oh my God."

"Polaroids, now," Pop said, like a narrator moving briskly to a new chapter in a novel and reading the words *Meanwhile, in another part of the forest,* "I've seen pitchers with people in em that the other people in the pitcher swear weren't there with em when the pitcher was taken. And there's one—this is a famous one—that a lady took over in England. What she did was snap a pitcher of some fox-hunters comin back home at the end of the day. You see em, about twenty in all, comin over a little wooden bridge. It's a tree-lined country road on both sides of that bridge. The ones in front are off the bridge already. And over on the right of the pitcher, standin by the road, there's a lady in a long dress and a hat with a veil on it so you can't see her face and she's got her pocketbook over her arm. Why, you can even see she's wearin a locket on her boosom, or maybe it's a watch.

"Well, when the lady that took the pitcher saw it, she got wicked upset, and wasn't nobody could blame her, son, because what I mean to say is she meant to take a pitcher of those fox-hunters comin home and no one else, because there wasn't nobody else *there*. Except in the pitcher there is. And when you look real close, it seems like you can see the trees right through that lady."

He's making all this up, putting me on, and when I leave he'll have a great big horselaugh, Kevin thought, knowing Pop Merrill was doing nothing of the sort.

"The lady that took that pitcher was stayin at one of those big English homes like they have on the education-TV shows, and when she showed that pitcher, I heard the man of the house fainted dead away. That part could be made up. Prob'ly is. *Sounds* made up, don't it? But I seen that pitcher in an article next to a painted portrait of that fella's great-grandmother, and it could be her, all right. Can't tell for certain because of the veil. But it *could* be."

"Could be a hoax, too," Kevin said faintly.

"Could be," Pop said indifferently. "People get up to all sorts of didos. Lookit my nephew, there, for instance, Ace." Pop's nose wrinkled. "Doin four years in Shawshank, and for what? Bustin into The Mellow Tiger. He got up to didos and Sheriff Pangborn slammed him in the jug for it. Little ringmeat got just what he deserved."

Kevin, displaying a wisdom far beyond his years, said nothing.

"But when ghosts show up in photographs, son—or, like you say, what people *claim* to be ghosts—it's almost always in *Polaroid* photographs. And it almost always seems to be by accident. Now your pitchers of flyin saucers and that Lock Nest Monster, they almost always show up in the other kind. The kind some smart fella can get up to didos with in a darkroom."

He dropped Kevin a third wink, expressing all the didos (whatever *they* were) an unscrupulous photographer might get up to in a well-equipped darkroom.

Kevin thought of asking Pop if it was possible someone could get up to didos with a weegee and decided to continue keeping his mouth shut. It still seemed by far the wisest course.

"All by way of sayin I thought I'd ask if you saw somethin you knew in *these* Polaroid pitchers."

"I don't, though," Kevin said so earnestly that he believed Pop would believe he was lying, as his mom always did when he made the tactical mistake of even controlled vehemence.

"Ayuh, ayuh," Pop said, believing him so dismissively Kevin was almost irritated.

"Well," Kevin said after a moment which was silent except for the fifty thousand ticking clocks, "I guess that's it, huh?"

"Maybe not," Pop said. "What I mean to say is I got me a little idear. You mind takin some more pitchers with that camera?"

"What good is it? They're all the same."

"That's the point. They ain't."

Kevin opened his mouth, then closed it.

"I'll even chip in for the film," Pop said, and when he saw the amazed look on Kevin's face he quickly qualified: "A little, anyway."

"How many pictures would you want?"

"Well, you got . . . what? Twenty-eight already, is that right?"

"Yes, I think so."

"Thirty more," Pop said after a moment's thought.

"Why?"

"Ain't gonna tell you. Not right now." He produced a heavy purse that was hooked to a belt-loop on a steel chain. He opened it and took out a ten-dollar bill, hesitated, and added two ones with obvious reluctance. "Guess that'd cover half of it."

Yeah, right, Kevin thought.

"If you really *are* int'rested in the trick that camera's doing, I guess you'd pony up the rest, wouldn't you?" Pop's eyes gleamed at him like the eyes of an old, curious cat.

Kevin understood the man did more than expect him to say yes; to Pop it was inconceivable that he could say no. Kevin thought, *If I said no he wouldn't hear it; he'd say "Good, that's agreed, then," and I'd end up back on the sidewalk with his money in my pocket whether I wanted it or not.*

And he *did* have his birthday money.

All the same, there was that chill wind to think about. That wind that seemed to blow not from the surface but right out of those photographs in spite of their deceptively flat, deceptively shiny surfaces. He felt that wind coming from them despite their mute declaration which averred *We are Polaroids, and for no reason we can tell or even understand, we show only the undramatic surfaces of things.* That wind was there. What about that wind?

Kevin hesitated a moment longer and the bright eyes behind the rimless spectacles measured him. *I ain't gonna ask you if you're a man or a mouse,* Pop Merrill's eyes said. *You're fifteen years old, and what I mean to say is at fifteen you may not be a man yet, not quite, but you are too goddam old to be a mouse and both of us know it. And besides you're not from Away; you're from town, just like me.*

"Sure," Kevin said with a hollow lightness in his voice. It fooled neither of them. "I can get the film tonight, I guess, and bring the pictures in tomorrow, after school."

"Nope," Pop said.

"You're closed tomorrow?"

"Nope," Pop said, and because he *was* from town, Kevin waited patiently. "You're thinkin about takin thirty pitchers all at once, aren't you?"

"I guess so."

"That ain't the way I want you to do it," Pop said. "It don't matter *where* you take them, but it *does* matter *when*. Here. Lemme figure."

Pop figured, and then even wrote down a list of times, which Kevin pocketed.

"So!" Pop said, rubbing his hands briskly together so that they made a dry sound that was like two pieces of used-up sandpaper rubbing together. "You'll see me in . . . oh, three days or so?"

"Yes . . . I guess so."

"I'll bet you'd just as lief wait until Monday after school, anyway," Pop said. He dropped Kevin a fourth wink, slow and sly and humiliating in the extreme. "So your friends don't see you coming in here and tax you with it, is what I mean to say."

Kevin flushed and dropped his eyes to the worktable and began to gather up the Polaroids so his hands would have something to do. When he was embarrassed and they didn't, he cracked his knuckles.

"I—" He began some sort of absurd protest that would convince neither of them and then stopped, staring down at one of the photos.

"What?" Pop asked. For the first time since Kevin had approached him, Pop sounded entirely human, but Kevin hardly heard his words, much less his tone of faint alarm. "Now you look like *you* seen a ghost, boy."

"No," Kevin said. "No ghost. I see who took the picture. Who *really* took the picture."

"What in glory are you talking about?"

Kevin pointed to a shadow. He, his father, his mother, Meg, and apparently Mr. Merrill himself had taken it for the shadow of a tree that wasn't itself in the frame. But it wasn't a tree. Kevin saw that now, and what you had seen could never be unseen.

More hieroglyphics on the plinth.

"I don't see what you're gettin at," Pop said. But Kevin knew the old man knew he was getting at *something,* which was why he sounded put out.

"Look at the shadow of the dog first," Kevin said. "Then look at this one here again." He tapped the left side of the photograph. "In the picture, the sun is either going down or coming up. That makes all the shadows long, and it's hard to tell what's throwing them. But looking at it, just now, it clicked home for me."

"*What* clicked home, son?" Pop reached for the drawer, probably meaning to get the magnifying glass with the light in it again . . . and then stopped. All at once he didn't need it. All at once it had clicked into place for him, too.

"It's the shadow of a man, ain't it?" Pop said. "I be go to hell if that one ain't the shadow of a man."

"Or a woman. You can't tell. Those are legs, I'm sure they are, but they could belong to a woman wearing pants. Or even a kid. With the shadow running so long—"

"Ayuh, you can't tell."

Kevin said, "It's the shadow of whoever took it, isn't it?"

"Ayuh."

"But it wasn't *me,*" Kevin said. "It came out of my camera—all of them did—but I didn't take it. So who did, Mr. Merrill? Who did?"

"Call me Pop," the old man said absently, looking at the shadow in the picture, and Kevin felt his chest swell with pleasure as those few clocks still capable of running a little fast began to signal the others that, weary as they might be, it was time to charge the half-hour.

CHAPTER THREE

When Kevin arrived back at the Emporium Galorium with the photographs on Monday after school, the leaves had begun to turn

color. He had been fifteen for almost two weeks and the novelty
had worn off.

The novelty of that plinth, *the supernatural,* had not, but this
wasn't anything he counted among his blessings. He had finished
taking the schedule of photographs Pop had given him, and by the
time he had, he had seen clearly—clearly enough, anyway—why
Pop had wanted him to take them at intervals: the first ten on the
hour, then let the camera rest, the second ten every two hours, and
the third at three-hour intervals. He'd taken the last few that day
at school. He had seen something else as well, something none of
them *could* have seen at first; it was not clearly visible until the final
three pictures. They had scared him so badly he had decided, even
before taking the pictures to the Emporium Galorium, that he
wanted to get rid of the Sun 660. Not exchange it; that was the
last thing he wanted to do, because it would mean the camera would
be out of his hands and hence out of his control. He couldn't have
that.

It's mine, he had thought, and the thought kept recurring, but it
wasn't a *true* thought. If it was—if the Sun only took pictures of
the black breedless dog by the white picket fence when he, Kevin,
was the one pushing the trigger—that would have been one thing.
But that wasn't the case. Whatever the nasty magic inside the Sun
might be, he was not its sole initiator. His father had taken the
same (well, *almost* the same) picture, and so had Pop Merrill, and
so had Meg when Kevin had let her take a couple of the pictures
on Pop's carefully timed schedule.

"Did you number em, like I asked?" Pop asked when Kevin
delivered them.

"Yes, one to fifty-eight," Kevin said. He thumbed through the
stack of photographs, showing Pop the small circled numbers in
the lower lefthand corner of each. "But I don't know if it matters.
I've decided to get rid of the camera."

"Get rid of it? That ain't what you mean."

"No. I guess not. I'm going to break it up with a sledgehammer."

Pop looked at him with those shrewd little eyes. "That so?"

"Yes," Kevin said, meeting the shrewd gaze steadfastly. "Last
week I would have laughed at the idea, but I'm not laughing now.
I think the thing is dangerous."

"Well, I guess you could be right, and I guess you could tape a
charge of dynamite to it and blow it to smithereens if you wanted.

It's yours, is what I mean to say. But why don't you hold off a little while? There's somethin I want to do with these pitchers. You might be interested."

"What?"

"I druther not say," Pop answered, "case it don't turn out. But I might have somethin by the end of the week that'd help you decide better, one way or the other."

"I *have* decided," Kevin said, and tapped something that had shown up in the last two photographs.

"What *is* it?" Pop asked. "I've looked at it with m'glass, and I feel like I *should* know what it is—it's like a name you can't quite remember but have right on the tip of your tongue, is what I mean to say—but I don't quite."

"I suppose I could hold off until Friday or so," Kevin said, choosing not to answer the old man's question. "I really don't want to hold off much longer."

"Scared?"

"Yes," Kevin said simply. "I'm scared."

"You told your folks?"

"Not all of it, no."

"Well, you might want to. Might want to tell your dad, anyway, is what I mean to say. You got time to think on it while I take care of what it is I want to take care of."

"No matter what you want to do, I'm going to put my dad's sledgehammer on it come Friday," Kevin said. "I don't even *want* a camera anymore. Not a Polaroid or any other kind."

"Where is it now?"

"In my bureau drawer. And that's where it's going to stay."

"Stop by the store here on Friday," Pop said. "Bring the camera with you. We'll take a look at this little idear of mine, and then, if you want to bust the goddam thing up, I'll provide the sledgehammer myself. No charge. Even got a chopping block out back you can set it on."

"That's a deal," Kevin said, and smiled.

"Just what *have* you told your folks about all this?"

"That I'm still deciding. I didn't want to worry them. My mom, especially." Kevin looked at him curiously. "Why did you say I might want to tell my dad?"

"You bust up that camera, your father is going to be mad at you," Pop said. "That ain't so bad, but he's maybe gonna think you're a little bit of a fool, too. Or an old maid, squallin burglar to the police on account of a creaky board is what I mean to say."

Kevin flushed a little, thinking of how angry his father had gotten when the idea of the supernatural had come up, then sighed. He hadn't thought of it in that light at all, but now that he did, he thought Pop was probably right. He didn't like the idea of his father being mad at him, but he could live with it. The idea that his father might think him a coward, a fool, or both, though . . . that was a different kettle of fish altogether.

Pop was watching him shrewdly, reading these thoughts as they crossed Kevin's face as easily as a man might read the headlines on the front page of a tabloid newspaper.

"You think he could meet you here around four in the afternoon on Friday?"

"No way," Kevin said. "He works in Portland. He hardly ever gets home before six."

"I'll give him a call, if you want," Pop said. "He'll come if I call."

Kevin gave him a wide-eyed stare.

Pop smiled thinly. "Oh, I know him," he said. "Know him of old. He don't like to let on about me any more than you do, and I understand that, but what I mean to say is I know him. I know a lot of people in this town. You'd be surprised, son."

"How?"

"Did him a favor one time," Pop said. He popped a match alight with his thumbnail, and veiled those eyes behind enough smoke so you couldn't tell if it was amusement, sentiment, or contempt in them.

"What kind of favor?"

"That," Pop said, "is between him and me. Just like this business here"—he gestured at the pile of photographs—"is between me and you. *That's* what I mean to say."

"Well . . . okay . . . I guess. Should I say anything to him?"

"Nope!" Pop said in his chipper way. "You let me take care of everything." And for a moment, in spite of the obfuscating pipe-smoke, there was something in Pop Merrill's eyes Kevin Delevan didn't care for. He went out, a sorely confused boy who knew only one thing for sure: he wanted this to be over.

———

When he was gone, Pop sat silent and moveless for nearly five minutes. He allowed his pipe to go out in his mouth and drummed his
fingers, which were nearly as knowing and talented as those of a
concert violinist but masqueraded as equipment which should more
properly have belonged to a digger of ditches or a pourer of cement,
next to the stack of photographs. As the smoke dissipated, his
eyes stood out clearly, and they were as cold as ice in a December
puddle.

Abruptly he put the pipe in its holder and called a camera-and-
video shop in Lewiston. He asked two questions. The answer to
both of them was yes. Pop hung up the phone and went back to
drumming his fingers on the table beside the Polaroids. What he
was planning wasn't really fair to the boy, but the boy had uncovered
the corner of something he not only didn't understand but didn't
want to understand.

Fair or not, Pop didn't believe he intended to let the boy do what
the boy wanted to do. He hadn't decided what he himself meant
to do, not yet, not entirely, but it was wise to be prepared.

That was *always* wise.

He sat and drummed his fingers and wondered what that thing
was the boy had seen. He had obviously felt Pop would know—
or might know—but Pop hadn't a clue. The boy might tell him on
Friday. Or not. But if the boy didn't, the father, to whom Pop had
once loaned four hundred dollars to cover a bet on a basketball
game, a bet he had lost and which his wife knew nothing about,
certainly would. If, that was, he could. Even the best of fathers
didn't know all about their sons anymore once those sons were
fifteen or so, but Pop thought Kevin was a very *young* fifteen, and
that his dad knew most things . . . or could find them out.

He smiled and drummed his fingers and all the clocks began to
charge wearily at the hour of five.

CHAPTER FOUR

Pop Merrill turned the sign which hung in his door from OPEN to
CLOSED at two o'clock on Friday afternoon, slipped himself behind

the wheel of his 1959 Chevrolet, which had been for years perfectly maintained at Sonny's Texaco at absolutely no cost at all (the fallout of another little loan, and Sonny Jackett another town fellow who would prefer hot coals pressed against the soles of his feet to admitting that he not only knew but was deeply indebted to Pop Merrill, who had gotten him out of a desperate scrape over in New Hampshire in '69), and took himself up to Lewiston, a city he hated because it seemed to him that there were only two streets in the whole town (maybe three) that weren't one-ways. He arrived as he always did when Lewiston and only Lewiston would do: not by driving to it but arriving somewhere near it and then spiraling slowly inward along those beshitted one-way streets until he reckoned he was as close as he could get and then walking the rest of the way, a tall thin man with a bald head, rimless specs, clean khaki pants with creases and cuffs, and a blue workman's shirt buttoned right up to the collar.

There was a sign in the window of Twin City Camera and Video that showed a cartoon man who appeared to be battling a huge tangle of movie-film and losing. The fellow looked just about ready to blow his stack. The words over and under the picture read: TIRED OF FIGHTING? WE TRANSFER YOUR 8 MM MOVIES (SNAPSHOTS TOO!) ONTO VIDEO TAPE!

Just another goddam gadget, Pop thought, opening the door and going in. World's dying of em.

But he was one of those people—world's dying of em—not at all above using what he disparaged if it proved expedient. He spoke briefly with the clerk. The clerk got the proprietor. They had known each other for many years (probably since Homer sailed the wine-dark sea, some wits might have said). The proprietor invited Pop into the back room, where they shared a nip.

"That's a goddam strange bunch of photos," the proprietor said.

"Ayuh."

"The videotape I made of them is even stranger."

"I bet so."

"That all you got to say?"

"Ayuh."

"Fuck ya, then," the proprietor said, and they both cackled their shrill old-man's cackles. Behind the counter, the clerk winced.

Pop left twenty minutes later with two items: a video cassette, and a brand-new Polaroid Sun 660, still in its box.

When he got back to the shop, he called Kevin's house. He was not surprised when it was John Delevan who answered.

"If you've been fucking my boy over, I'll kill you, you old snake," John Delevan said without preamble, and distantly Pop could hear the boy's wounded cry: *"Da-ad!"*

Pop's lips skinned back from his teeth—crooked, eroded, pipe-yellow, but his own, by the bald-headed Christ—and if Kevin had seen him in that moment he would have done more than *wonder* if maybe Pop Merrill was something other than the Castle Rock version of the Kindly Old Sage of the Crackerbarrel: he would have *known.*

"Now, John," he said. "I've been trying to *help* your boy with that camera. That's all in the world I've been trying to do." He paused. "Just like that one time I gave you a help when you got a little too proud of the Seventy-Sixers, is what I mean to say."

A thundering silence from John Delevan's end of the line which meant he had plenty to say on *that* subject, but the kiddo was in the room and that was as good as a gag.

"Now, your kid don't know nothing about *that,*" Pop said, that nasty grin broadening in the tick-tock shadows of the Emporium Galorium, where the dominant smells were old magazines and mouse-turds. "I told him it wasn't none of his business, just like I told him that this business here *was.* I wouldn't have even brought up that bet if I knew another way to get you here, is what I mean to say. And you ought to see what I've got, John, because if you don't you won't understand why the boy wants to smash that camera you bought him—"

"Smash it!"

"—and why I think it's a hell of a good idea. Now are you going to come down here with him, or not?"

"I'm not in Portland, am I, dammit?"

"Never mind the CLOSED sign on the door," Pop said in the serene tone of a man who has been getting his own way for many years and expects to go right on getting it for many more. "Just knock."

"Who in hell gave my boy your name, Merrill?"

"I didn't ask him," Pop said in that same infuriatingly serene tone of voice, and hung up the telephone. And, to the empty shop: "All I know is that he came. Just like they always do."

While he waited, he took the Sun 660 he had bought in Lewiston out of its box and buried the box deep in the trash-can beside his worktable. He looked at the camera thoughtfully, then loaded the four-picture starter-pack that came with the camera. With that done, he unfolded the body of the camera, exposing the lens. The red light to the left of the lightning-bolt shape came on briefly, and then the green one began to stutter. Pop was not very surprised to find he was filled with trepidation. *Well,* he thought, *God hates a coward,* and pushed the shutter-release. The clutter of the Emporium Galorium's barnlike interior was bathed in an instant of merciless and improbable white light. The camera made its squidgy little whine and spat out what would be a Polaroid picture—perfectly adequate but somehow lacking; a picture that was all surfaces depicting a world where ships undoubtedly *would* sail off the fuming and monster-raddled edge of the earth if they went far enough west.

Pop watched it with the same mesmerized expression Clan Delevan had worn as it waited for Kevin's first picture to develop. He told himself this camera would not do the same thing, of course not, but he was stiff and wiry with tension just the same and, tough old bird or not, if a random board had creaked in the place just then, he almost certainly would have cried out.

But no board *did* creak, and when the picture developed it showed only what it was supposed to show: clocks assembled, clocks in pieces, toasters, stacks of magazines tied with twine, lamps with shades so horrible only women of the British upper classes could truly love them, shelves of quarter paperbacks (six for a buck) with titles like *After Dark My Sweet* and *Fire in the Flesh* and *The Brass Cupcake,* and, in the distant background, the dusty front window. You could read the letters EMPOR backward before the bulky silhouette of a bureau blocked off the rest.

No hulking creature from beyond the grave; no knife-wielding doll in blue overalls. Just a camera. He supposed the whim which had caused him to take a picture in the first place, just to see, showed how deeply this thing had worked its way under his skin.

Pop sighed and buried the photograph in the trash-can. He opened the wide drawer of the worktable and took out a small hammer. He held the camera firmly in his left hand and then swung the hammer on a short arc through the dusty tick-tock air. He didn't use a great deal of force. There was no need. Nobody took any pride in workmanship anymore. They talked about the wonders of modern science, synthetics, new alloys, polymers, Christ knew what. It didn't matter. Snot. That was what everything was *really* made out of these days, and you didn't have to work very hard to bust a camera that was made of snot.

The lens shattered. Shards of plastic flew from around it, and that reminded Pop of something else. Had it been the left or right side? He frowned. Left. He thought. They wouldn't notice anyway, or remember which side themselves if they did, you could damn near take that to the bank, but Pop hadn't feathered his nest with damn-nears. It was wise to be prepared.

Always wise.

He replaced the hammer, used a small brush to sweep the broken chunks of glass and plastic off the table and onto the floor, then returned the brush and took out a grease-pencil with a fine tip and an X-Act-O knife. He drew what he thought was the approximate shape of the piece of plastic which had broken off Kevin Delevan's Sun when Meg knocked it on the floor, then used the X-Act-O to carve along the lines. When he thought he had dug deep enough into the plastic, he put the X-Act-O back in the drawer, and then knocked the Polaroid camera off the worktable. What had happened once ought to happen again, especially with the fault-lines he had pre-carved.

It worked pretty slick, too. He examined the camera, which now had a chunk of plastic gone from the side as well as a busted lens, nodded, and placed it in the deep shadow under the worktable. Then he found the piece of plastic that had split off from the camera, and buried it in the trash along with the box and the single exposure he had taken.

Now there was nothing to do but wait for the Delevans to arrive. Pop took the video cassette upstairs to the cramped little apartment where he lived. He put it on top of the VCR he had bought to watch the fuck-movies you could buy nowadays, then sat down to read the paper. He saw there had been a plane-crash in Pakistan.

A hundred and thirty people killed. Goddam fools were always getting themselves killed, Pop thought, but that was all right. A few less woggies in the world was a good thing all around. Then he turned to the sports to see how the Red Sox had done. They still had a good chance of winning the Eastern Division.

CHAPTER FIVE

"What was it?" Kevin asked as they prepared to go. They had the house to themselves. Meg was at her ballet class, and it was Mrs. Delevan's day to play bridge with her friends. She would come home at five with a large loaded pizza and news of who was getting divorced or at least thinking of it.

"None of your business," Mr. Delevan said in a rough voice which was both angry and embarrassed.

The day was chilly. Mr. Delevan had been looking for his light jacket. Now he stopped and turned around and looked at his son, who was standing behind him, wearing his own jacket and holding the Sun camera in one hand.

"All right," he said. "I never pulled that crap on you before and I guess I don't want to start now. You know what I mean."

"Yes," Kevin said, and thought: *I know exactly what you're talking about, is what I mean to say.*

"Your mother doesn't know anything about this."

"I won't tell her."

"Don't say that," his father told him sharply. "Don't start down that road or you'll never stop."

"But you said you never—"

"No, I never told her," his father said, finding the jacket at last and shrugging into it. "She never asked and I never told her. If she never asks you, you never have to tell her. That sound like a bullshit qualification to you?"

"Yeah," Kevin said. "To tell the truth, it does."

"Okay," Mr. Delevan said. "Okay . . . but that's the way we do it. If the subject ever comes up, you—*we*—have to tell. If it doesn't, we don't. That's just the way we do things in the grown-up world.

It sounds fucked up, I guess, and sometimes it *is* fucked up, but that's how we do it. Can you live with that?"

"Yes. I guess so."

"Good. Let's go."

They walked down the driveway side by side, zipping their jackets. The wind played with the hair at John Delevan's temples, and Kevin noted for the first time—with uneasy surprise—that his father was starting to go gray there.

"It was no big deal, anyway," Mr. Delevan said. He might almost have been talking to himself. "It never is with Pop Merrill. He isn't a big-deal kind of guy, if you know what I mean."

Kevin nodded.

"He's a fairly wealthy man, you know, but that junk-shop of his isn't the reason why. He's Castle Rock's version of Shylock."

"Of who?"

"Never mind. You'll read the play. sooner or later if education hasn't gone entirely to hell. He loans money at interest rates that are higher than the law allows."

"Why would people borrow from him?" Kevin asked as they walked toward downtown under trees from which leaves of red and purple and gold sifted slowly down.

"Because," Mr. Delevan said sourly, "they can't borrow anyplace else."

"You mean their credit's no good?"

"Something like that."

"But we . . . you . . . "

"Yeah. We're doing all right now. But we weren't *always* doing all right. When your mother and I were first married, how we were doing was all the way across town from all right."

He fell silent again for a time, and Kevin didn't interrupt him.

"Well, there was a guy who was awful proud of the Celtics one year," his father said. He was looking down at his feet, as if afraid to step on a crack and break his mother's back. "They were going into the play-offs against the Philadelphia Seventy-Sixers. They—the Celtics—were favored to win, but by a lot less than usual. I had a feeling the Seventy-Sixers were going to take them, that it was their year."

He looked quickly at his son, almost snatching the glance as a shoplifter might take a small but fairly valuable item and tuck it into his coat, and then went back to minding the cracks in the sidewalk again. They were now walking down Castle Hill and toward the town's single signal-light at the crossing of Lower Main Street and Watermill Lane. Beyond the intersection, what locals called the Tin Bridge crossed Castle Stream. Its overstructure cut the deep-blue autumn sky into neat geometrical shapes.

"I guess it's that feeling, that special *sureness,* that infects the poor souls who lose their bank accounts, their houses, their cars, even the clothes they stand up in at casinos and back-room poker games. That feeling that you got a telegram from God. I only got it that once, and I thank God for that.

"In those days I'd make a friendly bet on a football game or the World Series with somebody, five dollars was the most, I think, and usually it was a lot less than that, just a token thing, a quarter or maybe a pack of cigarettes."

This time it was Kevin who shoplifted a glance, only Mr. Delevan caught it, cracks in the sidewalk or no cracks.

"Yes, I smoked in those days, too. Now I don't smoke and I don't bet. Not since that last one. That last one cured me.

"Back then your mother and I had only been married two years. You weren't born yet. I was working as a surveyor's assistant, bringing home just about a hundred and sixteen dollars a week. Or that was what I cleared, anyway, when the government finally let go of it.

"This fellow who was so proud of the Celtics was one of the engineers. He even wore one of those green Celtics warm-up jackets to work, the kind that have the shamrock on the back. The week before the play-offs, he kept saying he'd like to find someone brave enough and stupid enough to bet on the Seventy-Sixers, because he had four hundred dollars just waiting to catch him a dividend.

"That voice inside me kept getting louder and louder, and the day before the championship series started, I went up to him on lunch-break. My heart felt like it was going to tear right out of my chest, I was so scared."

"Because you didn't have four hundred dollars," Kevin said. "The other guy did, but you didn't." He was looking at his father openly now, the camera completely forgotten for the first time since his first visit to Pop Merrill. The wonder of what the Sun 660 was doing was lost—temporarily, anyway—in this newer, brighter wonder: as a young man his father had done something spectacularly stupid, just as Kevin knew other men did, just as he might do himself someday, when he was on his own and there was no adult member of the Reasonable tribe to protect him from some terrible impulse, some misbegotten instinct. His father, it seemed, had briefly been a member of the Instinctive tribe himself. It was hard to believe, but wasn't this the proof?

"Right."

"But you bet him."

"Not right away," his father said. "I told him I thought the Seventy-Sixers would take the championship, but four hundred bucks was a lot to risk for a guy who was only a surveyor's assistant."

"But you never came right out and told him you didn't have the money."

"I'm afraid it went a little further than that, Kevin. I implied I *did* have it. I said I couldn't afford to *lose* four hundred dollars, and that was disingenuous, to say the least. I told him I couldn't risk that kind of money on an even bet—still not lying, you see, but skating right up to the edge of the lie. *Do* you see?"

"Yes."

"I don't know what would have happened—maybe nothing—if the foreman hadn't rung the back-to-work bell right then. But he did, and this engineer threw up his hands and said, 'I'll give you two-to-one, sonny, if that's what you want. It don't matter to me. It's still gonna be four hundred in my pocket.' And before I knew what was happening we'd shook on it with half a dozen men watching and I was in the soup, for better or worse. And going home that night I thought of your mother, and what she'd say if she knew, and I pulled over to the shoulder of the road in the old Ford I had back then and I puked out the door."

A police car came rolling slowly down Harrington Street. Norris Ridgewick was driving and Andy Clutterbuck was riding shotgun. Clut raised his hand as the cruiser turned left on Main Street. John and Kevin Delevan raised their hands in return, and autumn drowsed peacefully around them as if John Delevan had never sat in the open door of his old Ford and puked into the road-dust between his own feet.

They crossed Main Street.

"Well . . . you could say I got my money's worth, anyway. The Sixers took it right to the last few seconds of the seventh game,

and then one of those Irish bastards—I forget which one it was—
stole the ball from Hal Greer and went to the hole with it and there
went the four hundred dollars I didn't have. When I paid that
goddam engineer off the next day he said he 'got a little nervous
there near the end.' That was all. I could have popped his eyes out
with my thumbs."

"You paid him off the next *day*? How'd you do that?"

"I told you, it was like a fever. Once we shook hands on the bet,
the fever passed. I hoped like hell I'd win that bet, but I knew I'd
have to *think* like I was going to lose. There was a lot more at stake
than just four hundred dollars. There was the question of my job,
of course, and what might happen if I wasn't able to pay off the
guy I'd bet with. He was an engineer, after all, and technically my
boss. That fellow had just enough son of a bitch in him to have
fired my ass if I didn't pay the wager. It wouldn't have been the
bet, but he would have found something, and it would have been
something that would go on my work-record in big red letters, too.
But that wasn't the biggest thing. Not at all."

"What was?"

"Your mother. Our marriage. When you're young and don't have
either a pot to piss in or a window to throw it out of, a marriage
is under strain all the time. It doesn't matter how much you love
each other, that marriage is like an overloaded packhorse and you
know it can fall to its knees or even roll over dead if all the wrong
things happen at all the wrong times. I don't think she would have
divorced me over a four-hundred-dollar bet, but I'm glad I never
had to find out for sure. So when the fever passed, I saw that I
might have bet a little more than four hundred dollars. I might just
have bet my whole goddam future."

They were approaching the Emporium Galorium. There was a
bench on the verge of the grassy town common, and Mr. Delevan
gestured for Kevin to sit down.

"This won't take long," he said, and then laughed. It was a grating,
compressed sound, like an inexperienced driver working a transmission lever. "It hurts too much to stretch out, even after all these
years."

So they sat on the bench and Mr. Delevan finished the story of
how he happened to know Pop Merrill while they looked across
the grassy common with the bandstand in the middle.

"I went to him the same night I made the bet," he said. "I told your mother I was going out for cigarettes. I went after dark, so no one would see me. From town, I mean. They would have known I was in some kind of trouble, and I didn't want that. I went in and Pop said, 'What's a professional man like you doing in a place like this, Mr. John Delevan?' and I told him what I'd done and he said, 'You made a bet and already you have got your head set to the idea you've lost it.' 'If I do lose it,' I said, 'I want to make sure I don't lose anything else.'

"That made him laugh. 'I respect a wise man,' he said. 'I reckon I can trust you. If the Celtics win, you come see me. I'll take care of you. You got an honest face.' "

"And that was *all?*" Kevin asked. In eighth-grade math, they had done a unit on loans, and he still remembered most of it. "He didn't ask for any, uh, collateral?"

"People who go to Pop don't have collateral," his father said. "He's not a loan-shark like you see in the movies; he doesn't break any legs if you don't pay up. But he has ways of fixing people."

"What ways?"

"Never mind," John Delevan said. "After that last game ended, I went upstairs to tell your mother I was going to go out for cigarettes—again. She was asleep, though, so I was spared that lie. It was late, late for Castle Rock, anyway, going on eleven, but the lights were on in his place. I knew they would be. He gave me the money in tens. He took them out of an old Crisco can. All tens. I remember that. They were crumpled but he had made them straight. Forty ten-dollar bills, him counting them out like a bank-clerk with that pipe going and his glasses up on his head and for just a second there I felt like knocking his teeth out. Instead I thanked him. You don't know how hard it can be to say thank you sometimes. I hope you never do. He said, 'You understand the terms, now, don't you?' and I said I did, and he said, 'That's good. I ain't worried about you. What I mean to say is you got an honest face. You go on and take care of your business with that fella at work, and then take care of your business with me. And don't make any more bets. Man only has to look in your face to see you weren't cut out to be a gambler.' So I took the money and went home and put it under the floor-mat of the old Chevy and lay next to your mother and didn't sleep a wink all night long because I felt filthy. Next day I gave the tens to the engineer I bet with, and *he* counted them out, and then he just folded them over and tucked them into one of his shirt pockets and buttoned the flap like that cash didn't mean any more than a gas receipt he'd have to turn in to the chief contractor at the end of the day. Then he clapped me on the shoulder and said, 'Well, you're a good man, Johnny. Better than I thought. I won four hundred but I lost twenty to Bill Untermeyer. He bet you'd come up with the dough first thing this morning and I bet him I wouldn't see it till the end of the week. If I ever did.' 'I pay my debts,' I said. 'Easy, now,' he said, and clapped me on the shoulder again, and I think that time I really *did* come close to popping his eyeballs out with my thumbs."

"How much interest did Pop charge you, Dad?"

His father looked at him sharply. "Does he let you call him that?"

"Yeah, why?"

"Watch out for him, then," Mr. Delevan said. "He's a snake."

Then he sighed, as if admitting to both of them that he was begging the question, and knew it. "Ten per cent. That's what the interest was."

"That's not so m—"

"Compounded weekly," Mr. Delevan added.

Kevin sat struck dumb for a moment. Then: "But that's not *legal*!"

"How true," Mr. Delevan said dryly. He looked at the strained expression of incredulity on his son's face and his own strained look broke. He laughed and clapped his son on the shoulder. "It's only the world, Kev," he said. "It kills us all in the end, anyhow."

"But—"

"But nothing. That was the freight, and he knew I'd pay it. I knew they were hiring on the three-to-eleven shift at the mill over in Oxford. I told you I'd gotten myself ready to lose, and going to Pop wasn't the only thing I did. I'd talked to your mother, said I might take a shift over there for awhile. After all, she'd been wanting a newer car, and maybe to move to a better apartment, and get a little something into the bank in case we had some kind of financial setback."

He laughed.

"Well, the financial setback had happened, and she didn't know it, and I meant to do my damnedest to keep her from finding out. I didn't know if I could or not, but I meant to do my damnedest. She was dead set against it. She said I'd kill myself, working sixteen hours a day. She said those mills were dangerous, you were always reading about someone losing an arm or leg or even getting crushed to death under the rollers. I told her not to worry, I'd get a job in the sorting room, minimum wage but sit-down work, and if it really *was* too much, I'd give it up. She was still against it. She said she'd go to work herself, but I talked her out of *that*. That was the last thing I wanted, you know."

Kevin nodded.

"I told her I'd quit six months, eight at the outside, anyway. So I went up and they hired me on, but not in the sorting room. I got a job in the rolling shed, feeding raw stock into a machine that looked like the wringer on a giant's washing machine. It was dangerous work, all right; if you slipped or if your attention wandered— and it was hard to keep that from happening because it was so damned monotonous—you'd lose part of yourself or all of it. I saw a man lose his hand in a roller once and I never want to see anything like that again. It was like watching a charge of dynamite go off in a rubber glove stuffed with meat."

"God-*damn*," Kevin said. He had rarely said that in his father's presence, but his father did not seem to notice.

"Anyway, I got two dollars and eighty cents an hour, and after two months they bumped me to three ten," he said. "It was hell. I'd work on the road project all day long—at least it was early spring and not hot—and then race off to the mill, pushing that Chevy for all it was worth to keep from being late. I'd take off my khakis and just about jump into a pair of blue-jeans and a tee-shirt and work the rollers from three until eleven. I'd get home around midnight and the worst part was the nights when your mother waited up— which she did two or three nights a week—and I'd have to act cheery and full of pep when I could hardly walk a straight line, I was so tired. But if she'd seen that—"

"She would have made you stop."

"Yes. She would. So I'd act bright and chipper and tell her funny stories about the sorting room where I wasn't working and sometimes I'd wonder what would happen if she ever decided to drive up some night—to give me a hot dinner, or something like that. I did a pretty good job, but some of it must have showed, because she kept telling me I was silly to be knocking myself out for so little—and it really *did* seem like chicken-feed once the government dipped their beak and Pop dipped his. It seemed like just about what a fellow working in the sorting room for minimum wage would clear. They paid Wednesday afternoons, and I always made sure to cash my check in the office before the girls went home.

"Your mother never saw one of those checks.

"The first week I paid Pop fifty dollars—forty was interest, and ten was on the four hundred, which left three hundred and ninety owing. I was like a walking zombie. On the road I'd sit in my car at lunch, eat my sandwich, and then sleep until the foreman rang his goddamned bell. I *hated* that bell.

"I paid him fifty dollars the second week—thirty-nine was interest, eleven was on the principal—and I had it down to three hundred and seventy-nine dollars. I felt like a bird trying to eat a mountain one peck at a time.

"The third week I almost went into the roller myself, and it scared me so bad I woke up for a few minutes—enough to have an idea, anyway, so I guess it was a blessing in disguise. I had to give up smoking. I couldn't understand why I hadn't seen it before. In those days a pack of smokes cost forty cents. I smoked two packs a day. That was five dollars and sixty cents a week!

"We had a cigarette break every two hours and I looked at my pack of Tareytons and saw I had ten, maybe twelve. I made those cigarettes last a week and a half, and I never bought another pack.

"I spent a month not knowing if I could make it or not. There were days when the alarm went off at six o'clock and I knew I couldn't, that I'd just have to tell Mary and take whatever she wanted to dish out. But by the time the second month started, I knew I was probably going to be all right. I think to this day it was the extra five sixty a week—that, and all the returnable beer and soda bottles I could pick up along the sides of the road—that made the difference. I had the principal down to three hundred, and that meant I could knock off twenty-five, twenty-six dollars a week from it, more as time went on.

"Then, in late April, we finished the road project and got a week off, with pay. I told Mary I was getting ready to quit my job at the mill and she said thank God, and I spent that week off from my regular job working all the hours I could get at the mill, because it was time and a half. I never had an accident. I saw them, saw men fresher and more awake than I was have them, but I never did. I don't know why. At the end of that week I gave Pop Merrill a hundred dollars and gave my week's notice at the paper mill. After that last week I had whittled the nut down enough so I could chip the rest off my regular pay-check without your mother noticing."

He fetched a deep sigh.

"Now you know how I know Pop Merrill, and why I don't trust him. I spent ten weeks in hell and he reaped the sweat off my forehead and my ass, too, in ten-dollar bills that he undoubtedly took out of that Crisco can or another one and passed on to some other sad sack who had got himself in the same kind of mess I did."

"Boy, you must hate him."

"No," Mr. Delevan said, getting up. "I don't hate him and I don't hate myself. I got a fever, that's all. It could have been worse. My marriage could have died of it, and you and Meg never would have been born, Kevin. Or I might have died of it myself. Pop Merrill was the cure. He was a *hard* cure, but he worked. What's hard to forgive is *how* he worked. He took every damned cent and wrote it down in a book in a drawer under his cash register and looked at the circles under my eyes and the way my pants had gotten a way of hanging off my hip-bones and he said nothing."

They walked toward the Emporium Galorium, which was painted the dusty faded yellow of signs left too long in country store windows, its false front both obvious and unapologetic. Next to it, Polly Chalmers was sweeping her walk and talking to Alan Pangborn, the county sheriff. She looked young and fresh with her hair pulled back in a horsetail; he looked young and heroic in his neatly pressed uniform. But things were not always the way they looked; even Kevin, at fifteen, knew that. Sheriff Pangborn had lost his wife and youngest son in a car accident that spring, and Kevin had heard that Ms. Chalmers, young or not, had a bad case of arthritis and might be crippled up with it before too many more years passed. Things were not always the way they looked. This thought caused him to glance toward the Emporium Galorium again . . . and then to look down at his birthday camera, which he was carrying in his hand.

"He even did me a favor," Mr. Delevan mused. "He got me to quit smoking. But I don't trust him. Walk careful around him, Kevin. And no matter what, let me do the talking. I might know him a little better now."

So they went into the dusty ticking silence, where Pop Merrill waited for them by the door, with his glasses propped on the bald dome of his head and a trick or two still up his sleeve.

CHAPTER SIX

"Well, and here you are, father and son," Pop said, giving them an admiring, grandfatherly smile. His eyes twinkled behind a haze of pipe-smoke and for a moment, although he was clean-shaven, Kevin thought Pop looked like Father Christmas. "You've got a fine boy, Mr. Delevan. *Fine.*"

"I know," Mr. Delevan said. "I was upset when I heard he'd been dealing with you because I want him to stay that way."

"That's hard," Pop said, with the faintest touch of reproach. "That's hard comin from a man who when he had nowhere else to turn—"

"That's over," Mr. Delevan said.

"Ayuh, ayuh, that's just what I mean to say."

"But this isn't."

"It will be," Pop said. He held a hand out to Kevin and Kevin gave him the Sun camera. "It will be today." He held the camera up, turning it over in his hands. "This is a piece of work. What *kind* of piece I don't know, but your boy wants to smash it because he thinks it's dangerous. I think he's right. But I told him, 'You don't want your daddy to think you're a sissy, do you?' That's the only reason I had him ho you down here, John—"

"I liked 'Mr. Delevan' better."

"All right," Pop said, and sighed. "I can see you ain't gonna warm up none and let bygones be bygones."

"No."

Kevin looked from one man to the other, his face distressed.

"Well, it don't matter," Pop said; both his voice and face went cold with remarkable suddenness, and he didn't look like Father Christmas at all. "When I said the past is the past and what's done is done, I meant it . . . except when it affects what people do in the here and now. But I'm gonna say this, Mr. Delevan: I don't bottom deal, and you know it."

Pop delivered this magnificent lie with such flat coldness that both of them believed it; Mr. Delevan even felt a little ashamed of himself, as incredible as that was.

"Our business was our business. You told me what you wanted, I told you what I'd have to have in return, and you give it to me, and there was an end to it. This is another thing." And then Pop told a lie even more magnificent, a lie which was simply too towering to be disbelieved. "I got no stake in this, Mr. Delevan. There is nothing I want but to help your boy. I like him."

He smiled and Father Christmas was back so fast and strong that Kevin forgot he had ever been gone. Yet more than this: John Delevan, who had for months worked himself to the edge of exhaustion and perhaps even death between the rollers in order to pay the exorbitant price this man demanded to atone for a momentary lapse into insanity—John Delevan forgot that other expression, too.

Pop led them along the twisting aisles, through the smell of dead newsprint and past the tick-tock clocks, and he put the Sun 660 casually down on the worktable a little too near the edge (just as Kevin had done in his own house after taking that first picture) and then just went on toward the stairs at the back which led up to his little apartment. There was a dusty old mirror propped against the wall back there, and Pop looked into it, watching to see if the boy or his father would pick the camera up or move it further away from the edge. He didn't think either would, but it was possible.

They spared it not so much as a passing glance and as Pop led them up the narrow stairway with the ancient eroded rubber treads he grinned in a way it would have been bad business for anyone to see and thought, *Damn, I'm good!*

He opened the door and they went into the apartment.

Neither John nor Kevin Delevan had ever been in Pop's private quarters, and John knew of no one who had. In a way this was not surprising; no one was ever going to nominate Pop as the town's number-one citizen. John thought it was not *impossible* that the old fuck had a friend or two—the world never exhausted its oddities, it seemed—but if so, he didn't know who they were.

And Kevin spared a fleeting thought for Mr. Baker, his favorite teacher. He wondered if, perchance, Mr. Baker had ever gotten into the sort of crack he'd need a fellow like Pop to get him out of. This seemed as unlikely to him as the idea of Pop having friends seemed to his father . . . but then, an hour ago the idea that his own father—

Well. It was best let go, perhaps.

Pop *did* have a friend (or at least an acquaintance) or two, but he didn't bring them here. He didn't want to. It was his place, and it came closer to revealing his true nature than he wanted anyone to see. It struggled to be neat and couldn't get there. The wallpaper was marked with water-stains; they weren't glaring, but stealthy and brown, like the phantom thoughts that trouble anxious minds. There were crusty dishes in the old-fashioned deep sink, and although the table was clean and the lid on the plastic waste-can was shut, there was an odor of sardines and something else—unwashed feet, maybe—which was almost not there. An odor as stealthy as the water-stains on the wallpaper.

The living room was tiny. Here the smell was not of sardines and (maybe) feet but of old pipe-smoke. Two windows looked out on nothing more scenic than the alley that ran behind Mulberry Street, and while their panes showed some signs of having been washed— at least swiped at occasionally—the corners were bleared and greasy with years of condensed smoke. The whole place had an air of nasty things swept under the faded hooked rugs and hidden beneath the old-fashioned, overstuffed easy-chair and sofa. Both of these articles were light green, and your eye wanted to tell you they matched but couldn't, because they didn't. Not quite.

The only new things in the room were a large Mitsubishi television with a twenty-five-inch screen and a VCR on the endtable beside it. To the left of the endtable was a rack which caught Kevin's eye because it was totally empty. Pop had thought it best to put the better than seventy fuck-movies he owned in the closet for the time being.

One video cassette rested on top of the television in an unmarked case.

"Sit down," Pop said, gesturing at the lumpy couch. He went over to the TV and slipped the cassette out of its case.

Mr. Delevan looked at the couch with a momentary expression of doubt, as if he thought it might have bugs, and then sat down gingerly. Kevin sat beside him. The fear was back, stronger than ever.

Pop turned on the VCR, slid the cassette in, and then pushed the carriage down. "I know a fellow up the city," he began (to residents of Castle Rock and its neighboring towns, "up the city" always meant Lewiston), "who's run a camera store for twenty years or so. He got into this VCR business as soon as it started up, said it was going to be the wave of the future. He wanted me to go halves with him, but I thought he was nuts. Well, I was wrong on that one, is what I mean to say, but—"

"Get to the point," Kevin's father said.

"I'm tryin," Pop said, wide-eyed and injured. "If you'll let me."

Kevin pushed his elbow gently against his father's side, and Mr. Delevan said no more.

"Anyway, a couple of years ago he found out rentin tapes for folks to watch wasn't the only way to make money with these gadgets. If you was willin to lay out as little as eight hundred bucks, you could take people's movies and snapshots and put em on a tape for em. Lots easier to watch."

Kevin made a little involuntary noise and Pop smiled and nodded.

"Ayuh. You took fifty-eight pitchers with that camera of yours, and we all saw each one was a little different than the last one, and I guess we knew what it meant, but I wanted to see for myself. You don't have to be from Missouri to say show me, is what I mean to say."

"You tried to make a movie out of those snapshots?" Mr. Delevan asked.

"Didn't *try*," Pop said. "*Did*. Or rather, the fella I know up the city did. But it was my idea."

"*Is* it a movie?" Kevin asked. He understood what Pop had done, and part of him was even chagrined that he hadn't thought of it himself, but mostly he was awash in wonder (and delight) at the idea.

"Look for yourself," Pop said, and turned on the TV. "Fifty-eight pitchers. When this fella does snapshots for folks, he generally videotapes each one for five seconds—long enough to get a good look, he says, but not long enough to get bored before you go on to the next one. I told him I wanted each of these on for just a single second, and to run them right together with no fades."

Kevin remembered a game he used to play in grade school when he had finished some lesson and had free time before the next one began. He had a little dime pad of paper which was called a Rain-Bo Skool Pad because there would be thirty pages of little yellow sheets, then thirty pages of little pink sheets, then thirty pages of green, and so on. To play the game, you went to the very last page and at the bottom you drew a stick-man wearing baggy shorts and holding his arms out. On the next page you drew the same stick-man in the same place and wearing the same baggy shorts, only this time you drew his arms further up . . . but just a little bit. You did that on every page until the arms came together over the stick-man's head. Then, if you still had time, you went on drawing the stick-man, but now with the arms going down. And if you flipped the pages very fast when you were done, you had a crude sort of cartoon which showed a boxer celebrating a KO: he raised his hands over his head, clasped them, shook them, lowered them.

He shivered. His father looked at him. Kevin shook his head and murmured, "Nothing."

"So what I mean to say is the tape only runs about a minute," Pop said. "You got to look close. Ready?"

No, Kevin thought.

"I guess so," Mr. Delevan said. He was still trying to sound grumpy and put-out, but Kevin could tell he had gotten interested in spite of himself.

"Okay," Pop Merrill said, and pushed the PLAY button.

Kevin told himself over and over again that it was stupid to feel scared. He told himself this and it didn't do a single bit of good.

He knew what he was going to see, because he and Meg had both noticed the Sun was doing something besides simply reproducing the same image over and over, like a photocopier; it did not take long for them to realize that the photographs were expressing movement from one to the next.

"Look," Meg had said. "The dog's moving!"

Instead of responding with one of the friendly-but-irritating wise-cracks he usually reserved for his little sister, Kevin had said, "It *does* look like it . . . but you can't tell for sure, Meg."

"Yes, you can," she said. They were in his room, where he had been morosely looking at the camera. It sat on the middle of his desk with his new schoolbooks, which he had been meaning to cover, pushed to one side. Meg had bent the goose-neck of his study-lamp so it shone a bright circle of light on the middle of his desk blotter. She moved the camera aside and put the first picture— the one with the dab of cake-frosting on it—in the center of the light. "Count the fence-posts between the dog's behind and the righthand edge of the picture," she said.

"Those are pickets, not fence-posts," he told her. "Like what you do when your nose goes on strike."

"Ha-ha. Count them."

He did. He could see four, and part of a fifth, although the dog's scraggly hindquarters obscured most of that one.

"Now look at this one."

She put the fourth Polaroid in front of him. Now he could see *all* of the fifth picket, and part of the sixth.

So he knew—or believed—he was going to see a cross between a very old cartoon and one of those "flip-books" he used to make in grammar school when the time weighed heavy on his hands.

The last twenty-five seconds of the tape were indeed like that, although, Kevin thought, the flip-books he had drawn in the second grade were really better . . . the perceived action of the boxer raising and lowering his hands smoother. In the last twenty-five seconds of the videotape the action moved in rams and jerks which made the old Keystone Kops silent films look like marvels of modern filmmaking in comparison.

Still, the key word was *action,* and it held all of them—even Pop—spellbound. They watched the minute of footage three times without saying a word. There was no sound but breathing: Kevin's fast and smooth through his nose, his father's deeper, Pop's a phlegmy rattle in his narrow chest.

And the first thirty seconds or so . . .

He had expected action, he supposed; there was action in the flip-books, and there was action in the Saturday-morning cartoons, which were just a slightly more sophisticated version of the flip-books, but what he had not expected was that for the first thirty seconds of the tape it wasn't like watching notebook pages rapidly thumbed or even a primitive cartoon like *Possible Possum* on TV: for thirty seconds (twenty-eight, anyway), his single Polaroid photographs looked eerily like a real movie. Not a Hollywood movie, of course, not even a low-budget horror movie of the sort Megan sometimes pestered him to rent for their own VCR when their mother and father went out for the evening; it was more like a snippet of home movie made by someone who has just gotten an eight-millimeter camera and doesn't know how to use it very well yet.

In those first twenty-eight seconds, the black no-breed dog walked with barely perceptible jerks along the fence, exposing five, six, seven pickets; it even paused to sniff a second time at one of them, apparently reading another of those canine telegrams. Then it walked on, head down and toward the fence, hindquarters switched out toward the camera. And, halfway through this first part, Kevin noted something else he hadn't seen before: the photographer had apparently swung his camera to keep the dog in the frame. If he (or she) hadn't done so, the dog would have simply walked out of the picture, leaving nothing to look at but the fence. The pickets at the far right of the first two or three photographs disappeared beyond the righthand border of the picture and new pickets appeared at the left. You could tell, because the tip of one of those two rightmost pickets had been broken off. Now it was no longer in the frame.

The dog started to sniff again . . . and then its head came up. Its good ear stiffened; the one which had been slashed and laid limp in some long-ago fight tried to do the same. There was no sound, but Kevin felt with a certainty beyond repudiation that the dog had begun to growl. The dog had sensed something or someone. What or who?

Kevin looked at the shadow they had at first dismissed as the branch of a tree or maybe a phone-pole and knew.

Its head began to turn . . . and that was when the second half of this strange "film" began, thirty seconds of snap-jerk action that made your head ache and your eyeballs hot. Pop had had a hunch, Kevin thought, or maybe he had even read about something like this before. Either way, it had proved out and was too obvious to need stating. With the pictures taken quite closely together, if not exactly one after another, the action in the makeshift "movie" almost flowed. Not quite, but almost. But when the time between photographs was spaced, what they were watching became something that nauseated your eye because it wanted to see either a moving picture or a series of still photographs and instead it saw both and neither.

Time was passing in that flat Polaroid world. Not at the same speed it passed in this

(*real?*)

one, or the sun would have come up (or gone down) over there three times already and whatever the dog was going to do would be done (if it *had* something to do), and if it did not, it would just be gone and there would be only the moveless and seemingly eternal eroded picket fence guarding the listless patch of lawn, but it *was* passing.

The dog's head was coming around to face the photographer, owner of the shadow, like the head of a dog in the grip of a fit: at one moment the face and even the shape of the head was obscured by that floppy ear; then you saw one black-brown eye enclosed by a round and somehow mucky corona that made Kevin think of a spoiled egg-white; then you saw half the muzzle with the lips appearing slightly wrinkled, as if the dog were getting ready to bark or growl; and last of all you saw three-quarters of a face somehow more awful than the face of any mere dog had a right to be, even a mean one. The white spackles along its muzzle suggested it was no longer young. At the very end of the tape you saw the dog's lips were indeed pulling back. There was one blink of white Kevin thought was a tooth. He didn't see that until the third run-through. It was the eye that held him. It was homicidal. This breedless dog almost screamed rogue. And it was nameless; he knew that, as well. He knew beyond a shadow of a doubt that no Polaroid man or Polaroid woman or Polaroid child had ever named that Polaroid dog; it was a stray, born stray, raised stray, grown old and mean stray, the avatar of all the dogs who had ever wandered the world, unnamed and unhomed, killing chickens, eating garbage out of the cans they had long since learned to knock over, sleeping in culverts and beneath the porches of deserted houses. Its wits would be dim, but its instincts would be sharp and red. It—

When Pop Merrill spoke, Kevin was so deeply and fundamentally startled out of his thoughts that he nearly screamed.

"The man who took those pictures," he said. "If there *was* a person, is what I mean to say. What do you suppose happened to *him?*"

Pop had frozen the last frame with his remote control. A line of static ran through the picture. Kevin wished it ran through the dog's eye, but the line was below it. That eye stared out at them, baleful, stupidly murderous—no, not stupidly, not entirely, that was what made it not merely frightening but terrifying—and no one needed to answer Pop's question. You needed no more pictures to understand what was going to happen next. The dog had perhaps heard something: of course it had, and Kevin knew what. It had heard that squidgy little whine.

Further pictures would show it continuing to turn, and then beginning to fill more and more of each frame until there was nothing to see but dog—no listless patchy lawn, no fence, no sidewalk, no shadow. Just the dog.

Who meant to attack.

Who meant to kill, if it could.

Kevin's dry voice seemed to be coming from someone else. "I don't think it likes getting its picture taken," he said.

Pop's short laugh was like a bunch of dry twigs broken over a knee for kindling.

"Rewind it," Mr. Delevan said.

"You want to see the whole thing again?" Pop asked.

"No—just the last ten seconds or so."

Pop used the remote control to go back, then ran it again. The dog turned its head, as jerky as a robot which is old and running down but still dangerous, and Kevin wanted to tell them, *Stop now. Just stop. That's enough. Just stop and let's break the camera.* Because there was something else, wasn't there? Something he didn't want to think about but soon would, like it or not; he could feel it breaching in his mind like the broad back of a whale.

"Once more," Mr. Delevan said. "Frame by frame this time. Can you do that?"

"Ayuh," Pop said. "Goddam machine does everything but the laundry."

This time one frame, one picture, at a time. It was not like a robot now, or not exactly, but like some weird clock, something that belonged with Pop's other specimens downstairs. Jerk. Jerk. Jerk. The head coming around. Soon they would be faced by that merciless, not-quite-idiotic eye again.

"What's that?" Mr. Delevan asked.

"What's what?" Pop asked, as if he didn't know it was the thing the boy hadn't wanted to talk about the other day, the thing, he was convinced, that had made up the boy's mind about destroying the camera once and for all.

"Underneath its neck," Mr. Delevan said, and pointed. "It's not wearing a collar or a tag, but it's got something around its neck on a string or a thin rope."

"I dunno," Pop said imperturbably. "Maybe your boy does. Young folks have sharper eyes than us old fellas."

Mr. Delevan turned to look at Kevin. "Can you make it out?"

"I—" He fell silent. "It's really small."

His mind returned to what his father had said when they were leaving the house. *If she never asks you, you never have to tell her. . . . That's just the way we do things in the grown-up world.* Just now he had asked Kevin if he could make out what that thing under the dog's neck was. Kevin hadn't really answered that question; he had said something else altogether. *It's really small.* And it was. The fact that he knew what it was in spite of that . . . well . . .

What had his father called it? Skating up to the edge of a lie?

And he *couldn't* actually see it. Not *actually*. Just the same, he knew. The eye only suggested; the heart understood. Just as his heart understood that, if he was right, the camera must be destroyed. *Must* be.

At that moment, Pop Merrill was suddenly struck by an agreeable inspiration. He got up and snapped off the TV. "I've got the pitchers downstairs," he said. "Brought em back with the videotape. I seen that thing m'self, and ran my magnifying glass over it, but still couldn't tell . . . but it *does* look familiar, God cuss it. Just let me go get the pitchers and m'glass."

"We might as well go down with you," Kevin said, which was the last thing in the world Pop wanted, but then Delevan stepped in, God bless him, and said he might like to look at the tape again after they looked at the last couple of pictures under the magnifying glass.

"Won't take a minute," Pop said, and was gone, sprightly as a bird hopping from twig to twig on an apple tree, before either of them could have protested, if either had had a mind to.

Kevin did not. That thought had finally breached its monstrous back in his mind, and, like it or not, he was forced to contemplate it.

It was simple, as a whale's back is simple—at least to the eye of one who does not study whales for a living—and it was colossal in the same way.

It wasn't an idea but a simple certainty. It had to do with that odd flatness Polaroids always seemed to have, with the way they showed you things only in two dimensions, although all photographs did that; it was that other photographs seemed to at least *suggest* a third dimension, even those taken with a simple Kodak 110.

The things in *his* photographs, photographs which showed things he had never seen through the Sun's viewfinder or anywhere else, for that matter, were that same way: flatly, unapologetically two-dimensional.

Except for the dog.

The dog wasn't *flat*. The dog wasn't *meaningless,* a thing you could recognize but which had no emotional impact. The dog not only seemed to *suggest* three dimensions but to really *have* them, the way a hologram seems to really have them, or one of those 3-D movies where you had to wear special glasses to reconcile the double images.

It's not a Polaroid dog, Kevin thought, *and it doesn't belong in the world Polaroids take pictures of. That's crazy, I know it is, but I also know it's true. So what does it mean? Why is my camera taking pictures of it over and over . . . and what Polaroid man or Polaroid woman is snapping pictures of it? Does he or she even see it? If it IS a three-dimensional dog in a two-dimensional world, maybe he or she doesn't see it . . . can't see it. They say for us time is the fourth dimension, and we know it's there, but we can't see it. We can't even really feel it pass, although sometimes, especially when we're bored, I guess, it seems like we can.*

But when you got right down to it, all that might not even matter, and the questions were far too tough for him, anyway. There were other questions that seemed more important to him, vital questions, maybe even mortal ones.

Like why was the dog in *his* camera?

Did it want something of *him,* or just of anybody? At first he had thought the answer was anybody, anybody would do because anybody could take pictures of it and the movement always advanced. But the thing around its neck, that thing that wasn't a collar . . . that had to do with him, Kevin Delevan, and nobody else. Did it want to do something *to* him? If the answer to *that* question was yes, you could forget all the other ones, because it was pretty goddamned obvious what the dog wanted to do. It was in its murky eye, in the snarl you could just see beginning. He thought it wanted two things.

First to escape.

Then to kill.

There's a man or woman over there with a camera who maybe doesn't even see that dog, Kevin thought, *and if the photographer can't see the dog, maybe the dog can't see the photographer, and so the photographer is safe. But if the dog really* IS *three-dimensional, maybe he sees out—maybe he sees whoever is using my camera. Maybe it's still not me, or not specifically me; maybe whoever is using the camera is its target.*

Still—the thing it was wearing around its neck. What about that?

He thought of the cur's dark eyes, saved from stupidity by a single malevolent spark. God knew how the dog had gotten into that Polaroid world in the first place, but when its picture was taken, it could see *out,* and it wanted to *get* out, and Kevin believed in his heart that it wanted to kill him first, the thing it was wearing around its neck *said* it wanted to kill him first, *proclaimed* that it wanted to kill him first, but after that?

Why, after Kevin, anyone would do.

Anyone at all.

In a way it was like another game you played when you were a little kid, wasn't it? It was like Giant Step. The dog had been walking along the fence. The dog had heard the Polaroid, that squidgy little whine. It turned, and saw . . . what? Its own world or universe? A world or universe enough *like* its own so it saw or sensed it could or at least might be able to live and hunt here? It didn't matter. Now, every time someone took a picture of it, the dog would get closer. It would get closer and closer until . . . well, until what? Until it burst through, somehow?

"That's stupid," he muttered. "It'd never fit."

"What?" his father asked, roused from his own musings.

"Nothing," Kevin said. "I was just talking to myse—"

Then, from downstairs, muffled but audible, they heard Pop Merrill cry out in mingled dismay, irritation, and surprise: "Well shit fire and save matches! *Goddammit!*"

Kevin and his father looked at each other, startled.

"Let's go see what happened," his father said, and got up. "I hope he didn't fall down and break his arm, or something. I mean, part of me *does* hope it, but . . . you know."

Kevin thought: *What if he's been taking pictures? What if that dog's down there?*

It hadn't sounded like fear in the old man's voice, and of course there really was no way a dog that looked as big as a medium-sized German shepherd could come through either a camera the size of the Sun 660 or one of the prints it made. You might as well try to drag a washing machine through a knothole.

Still, he felt fear enough for both of them—for all three of them—

as he followed his father back down the stairs to the gloomy bazaar below.

Going down the stairs, Pop Merrill was as happy as a clam at high tide.

He had been prepared to make the switch right in front of them if he had to. Might have been a problem if it had just been the boy, who was still a year or so away from thinking he knew everything, but the boy's dad—ah, fooling *that* fine fellow would have been like stealing a bottle from a baby. Had he told the boy about the jam he'd gotten into that time? From the way the boy looked at him—a new, cautious way—Pop thought Delevan probably had. And what else had the father told the son? Well, let's see. *Does he let you call him Pop? That means he's planning to pull a fast one on you.* That was for starters. *He's a lowdown snake in the grass, son.* That was for seconds. And, of course, there was the prize of them all: *Let me do the talking, boy. I know him better than you do. You just let me handle everything.* Men like Delevan were to Pop Merrill what a nice platter of fried chicken was to some folks—tender, tasty, juicy, and all but falling off the bone. Once Delevan had been little more than a kid himself, and he would never fully understand that it wasn't Pop who had stuck his tit in the wringer but he himself. The man could have gone to his wife and she would have tapped that old biddy aunt of hers whose tight little ass was lined with hundred-dollar bills, and Delevan would have spent some time in the doghouse, but she would have let him out in time. He not only hadn't seen it that way; he hadn't seen it at all. And now, for no reason but idiot time, which came and went without any help from anyone, he thought he knew all there was to know about Reginald Marion Merrill.

Which was just the way Pop liked it.

Why, he could have swapped one camera for the other right in front of the man and Delevan never would have seen a goddamned thing—that was how sure he was he had old Pop figured out.

But this was better.

You never ever asked Lady Luck for a date; she had a way of standing men up just when they needed her the most. But if she showed up on her own . . . well, it was wise to drop whatever it was you were doing and take her out and wine her and dine her just as lavishly as you could. That was one bitch who always put out if you treated her right.

So he went quickly to the worktable, bent, and extracted the Polaroid 660 with the broken lens from the shadows underneath. He put it on the table, fished a key-ring from his pocket (with one quick glance over his shoulder to be sure neither of them had decided to come down after all), and selected the small key which opened the locked drawer that formed the entire left side of the table. In this deep drawer were a number of gold Krugerrands; a stamp album in which the least valuable stamp was worth six hundred dollars in the latest *Scott Stamp Catalogue*; a coin collection worth approximately nineteen thousand dollars; two dozen glossy photographs of a bleary-eyed woman having sexual congress with a Shetland pony; and an amount of cash totalling just over two thousand dollars.

The cash, which he stowed in a variety of tin cans, was Pop's loan-out money. John Delevan would have recognized the bills. They were all crumpled tens.

Pop deposited Kevin's Sun 660 in this drawer, locked it, and put his key-ring back in his pocket. Then he pushed the camera with the broken lens off the edge of the worktable (again) and cried out "Well shit fire and save matches! *Goddammit!*" loud enough for them to hear.

Then he arranged his face in the proper expression of dismay and chagrin and waited for them to come running to see what had happened.

"Pop?" Kevin cried. "Mr. Merrill? Are you okay?"

"Ayuh," he said. "Didn't hurt nothin but my goddam pride. That camera's just bad luck, I guess. I bent over to open the tool-drawer, is what I mean to say, and I knocked the fucking thing right off onto the floor. Only I guess it didn't come through s'well this time. I dunno if I should say I'm sorry or not. I mean, you was gonna—"

He held the camera apologetically out to Kevin, who took it, looked at the broken lens and shattered plastic of the housing around it. "No, it's okay," Kevin told him, turning the camera over in his hands—but he did not handle it in the same gingerly, tentative way he had before: as if it might really be constructed not of plastic and glass but some sort of explosive. "I meant to bust it up, anyhow."

"Guess I saved you the trouble."

"I'd feel better—" Kevin began.

"Ayuh, ayuh. I feel the same way about mice. Laugh if you want to, but when I catch one in a trap and it's dead, I beat it with a broom anyway. Just to be sure, is what I mean to say."

Kevin smiled faintly, then looked at his father. "He said he's got a chopping block out back, Dad—"

"Got a pretty good sledge in the shed, too, if ain't nobody took it."

"Do you mind, Dad?"

"It's your camera, Kev," Delevan said. He flicked a distrustful glance at Pop, but it was a glance that said he distrusted Pop on general principles, and not for any specific reason. "But if it will make you feel any better, I think it's the right decision."

"Good," Kevin said. He felt a tremendous weight go off his shoulders—no, it was from his *heart* that the weight was lifted. With the lens broken, the camera was surely useless . . . but he wouldn't feel really at ease until he saw it in fragments around Pop's chopping block. He turned it over in his hands, front to back and back to front, amused and amazed at how much he liked the broken way it looked and felt.

"I think I owe you the cost of that camera, Delevan," Pop said, knowing exactly how the man would respond.

"No," Delevan said. "Let's smash it and forget this whole crazy thing ever hap—" He paused. "I almost forgot—we were going to look at those last few photos under your magnifying glass. I wanted to see if I could make out the thing the dog's wearing. I keep thinking it looks familiar."

"We can do that after we get rid of the camera, can't we?" Kevin asked. "Okay, Dad?"

"Sure."

"And then," Pop said, "it might not be such a bad idear to burn the pitchers themselves. You could do it right in my stove."

"I think that's a *great* idea," Kevin said. "What do you think, Dad?"

"I think Mrs. Merrill never raised any fools," his father said.

"Well," Pop said, smiling enigmatically from behind folds of rising blue smoke, "there was five of us, you know."

———

The day had been bright blue when Kevin and his father walked down to the Emporium Galorium; a perfect autumn day. Now it was four-thirty, the sky had mostly clouded over, and it looked like it might rain before dark. The first real chill of the fall touched Kevin's hands. It would chap them red if he stayed out long enough, but he had no plans to. His mom would be home in half an hour, and already he wondered what she would say when she saw Dad was with him, and what his dad would say.

But that was for later.

Kevin set the Sun 660 on the chopping block in the little back-yard, and Pop Merrill handed him a sledgehammer. The haft was worn smooth with usage. The head was rusty, as if someone had left it carelessly out in the rain not once or twice but many times. Yet it would do the job, all right. Kevin had no doubt of that. The Polaroid, its lens broken and most of the housing around it shattered as well, looked fragile and defenseless sitting there on the block's chipped, chunked, and splintered surface, where you expected to see a length of ash or maple waiting to be split in two.

Kevin set his hands on the sledgehammer's smooth handle and tightened them.

"You're sure, son?" Mr. Delevan asked.

"Yes."

"Okay." Kevin's father glanced at his own watch. "Do it, then."

Pop stood to one side with his pipe clamped between his wretched teeth, hands in his back pockets. He looked shrewdly from the boy to the man and then back to the boy, but said nothing.

Kevin lifted the sledgehammer and, suddenly surprised by an anger at the camera he hadn't even known he felt, he brought it down with all the force he could muster.

Too hard, he thought. *You're going to miss it, be lucky not to mash your own foot, and there it will sit, not much more than a piece of hollow plastic a little kid could stomp flat without half trying, and even if you're lucky enough to miss your foot, Pop will look at you. He won't say anything: he won't have to. It'll all be in the way he looks at you.*

And thought also: *It doesn't matter if I hit it or not. It's magic, some kind of magic camera, and you CAN'T break it. Even if you hit it dead on the money the sledge will just bounce off it, like bullets off Superman's chest.*

But then there was no more time to think anything, because the sledge connected squarely with the camera. Kevin really *had* swung much too hard to maintain anything resembling control, but he got lucky. And the sledgehammer didn't just bounce back up, maybe hitting Kevin square between the eyes and killing him, like the final twist in a horror story.

The Sun didn't so much shatter as detonate. Black plastic flew everywhere. A long rectangle with a shiny black square at one end—a picture which would never be taken, Kevin supposed—fluttered to the bare ground beside the chopping block and lay there, face down.

There was a moment of silence so complete they could hear not only the cars on Lower Main Street but kids playing tag half a block away in the parking lot behind Wardell's Country Store, which had gone bankrupt two years before and had stood vacant ever since.

"Well, that's *that*," Pop said. "You swung that sledge just like Paul Bunyan, Kevin! I should smile n kiss a pig if you didn't.

"No need to do that," he said, now addressing Mr. Delevan, who was picking up broken chunks of plastic as prissily as a man picking up the pieces of a glass he has accidentally knocked to the floor and shattered. "I have a boy comes in and cleans up the yard every week or two. I know it don't look like much as it is, but if I didn't have that kid . . . Glory!"

"Then maybe we ought to use your magnifying glass and take a look at those pictures," Mr. Delevan said, standing up. He dropped the few pieces of plastic he had picked up into a rusty incinerator that stood nearby and then brushed off his hands.

"Fine by me," Pop said.

"Then burn them," Kevin reminded. "Don't forget that."

"I didn't," Pop said. "I'll feel better when they're gone, too."

"Jesus!" John Delevan said. He was bending over Pop Merrill's worktable, looking through the lighted magnifying glass at the second-to-last photograph. It was the one in which the object around the dog's neck showed most clearly; in the last photo, the object had swung back in the other direction again. "Kevin, look at that and tell me if it's what I think it is."

Kevin took the magnifying glass and looked. He had known, of course, but even so it still wasn't a look just for form's sake. Clyde

Tombaugh must have looked at an actual photograph of the planet Pluto for the first time with the same fascination. Tombaugh had known it was there; calculations showing similar distortions in the orbital paths of Neptune and Uranus had made Pluto not just a possibility but a necessity. Still, to *know* a thing was there, even to know what it *was* . . . that did not detract from the fascination of actually *seeing* it for the first time.

He let go of the switch and handed the glass back to Pop. "Yeah," he said to his father. "It's what you think it is." His voice was as flat as . . . as flat as the things in that Polaroid world, he supposed, and he felt an urge to laugh. He kept the sound inside, not because it would have been inappropriate to laugh (although he supposed it would have been) but because the sound would have come out sounding . . . well . . . flat.

Pop waited and when it became clear to him they were going to need a nudge, he said: "Well, don't keep me hoppin from one foot to the other! What the hell is it?"

Kevin had felt reluctant to tell him before, and he felt reluctant now. There was no reason for it, but—

Stop being so goddamned dumb! He helped you when you needed help-ing, no matter how he earns his dough. Tell him and burn the pictures and let's get out of here before all those clocks start striking five.

Yes. If he was around when *that* happened, he thought it would be the final touch; he would just go completely bananas and they could cart him away to Juniper Hill, raving about real dogs in Polaroid worlds and cameras that took the same picture over and over again except not quite.

"The Polaroid camera was a birthday present," he heard himself saying in that same dry voice. "What it's wearing around its neck was another one."

Pop slowly pushed his glasses up onto his bald head and squinted at Kevin. "I don't guess I'm followin you, son."

"I have an aunt," Kevin said. "Actually she's my great-aunt, but we're not supposed to call her that, because she says it makes her feel old. Aunt Hilda. Anyway, Aunt Hilda's husband left her a lot of money—my mom says she's worth over a million dollars—but she's a tightwad."

He stopped, leaving his father space to protest, but his father only smiled sourly and nodded. Pop Merrill, who knew all about *that* situation (there was not, in truth, much in Castle Rock and the surrounding areas Pop didn't know at least something about), simply held his peace and waited for the boy to get around to spilling it.

"She comes and spends Christmas with us once every three years, and that's about the only time we go to church, because *she* goes to church. We have lots of broccoli when Aunt Hilda comes. None of us like it, and it just about makes my sister puke, but Aunt Hilda likes broccoli a *lot,* so we have it. There was a book on our summer reading list, *Great Expectations,* and there was a lady in it who was just like Aunt Hilda. She got her kicks dangling her money in front of her relatives. Her name was Miss Havisham, and when Miss Havisham said frog, people jumped. We jump, and I guess the rest of our family does, too."

"Oh, your Uncle Randy makes your mother look like a piker," Mr. Delevan said unexpectedly. Kevin thought his dad meant it to sound amused in a cynical sort of way, but what came through was a deep, acidic bitterness. "When Aunt Hilda says frog in Randy's house, they all just about turn cartwheels over the roofbeams."

"Anyway," Kevin told Pop, "she sends me the same thing for my birthday every year. I mean, each one is different, but each one's really the same."

"What is it she sends you, boy?"

"A string tie," Kevin said. "Like the kind you see guys wearing in old-time country-music bands. It has something different on the clasp every year, but it's always a string tie."

Pop snatched the magnifying glass and bent over the picture with it. "Stone the crows!" he said, straightening up. "A string tie! That's just what it is! Now how come I didn't see that?"

"Because it isn't the sort of thing a dog would wear around his neck, I guess," Kevin said in that same wooden voice. They had been here for only forty-five minutes or so, but he felt as if he had aged another fifteen years. *The thing to remember,* his mind told him over and over, *is that the camera is gone. It's nothing but splinters. Never mind all the King's horses and all the King's men; not even all the guys who work making cameras at the Polaroid factory in Schenectady could put* that *baby back together again.*

Yes, and thank God. Because this was the end of the line. As far as Kevin was concerned, if he never encountered *the supernatural* again until he was eighty, never so much as brushed up against it, it would still be too soon.

"Also, it's very small," Mr. Delevan pointed out. "I was there when Kevin took it out of the box, and we all knew what it was going to be. The only mystery was what would be on the clasp this year. We joked about it."

"What *is* on the clasp?" Pop asked, peering into the photograph again . . . or peering *at* it, anyway: Kevin would testify in any court in the land that peering *into* a Polaroid was simply impossible.

"A bird," Kevin said. "I'm pretty sure it's a woodpecker. And that's what the dog in the picture is wearing around its neck. A string tie with a woodpecker on the clasp."

"Jesus!" Pop said. He was in his own quiet way one of the world's finer actors, but there was no need to simulate the surprise he felt now.

Mr. Delevan abruptly swept all the Polaroids together. "Let's put these goddam things in the woodstove," he said.

When Kevin and his father got home, it was ten minutes past five and starting to drizzle. Mrs. Delevan's two-year-old Toyota was not in the driveway, but she had been and gone. There was a note from her on the kitchen table, held down by the salt and pepper shakers. When Kevin unfolded the note, a ten-dollar bill fell out.

> Dear Kevin,
>   At the bridge game Jane Doyon asked if Meg and I would like to have dinner with her at Bonanza as her husband is off to Pittsburgh on business and she's knocking around the house alone. I said we'd be delighted. Meg especially. You know how much she likes to be "one of the girls"! Hope you don't mind eating in "solitary splendor." Why not order a pizza & some soda for yourself, and your father can order for himself when he gets home. He doesn't like reheated pizza & you know he'll want a couple of beers.
>
> Luv you,
Mom

They looked at each other, both saying *Well, there's one thing we don't have to worry about* without having to say it out loud. Apparently neither she nor Meg had noticed that Mr. Delevan's car was still in the garage.

"Do you want me to—" Kevin began, but there was no need to

finish because his father cut across him: "Yes. Check. Right now."

Kevin went up the stairs by twos and into his room. He had a bureau and a desk. The bottom desk drawer was full of what Kevin simply thought of as "stuff": things it would have seemed somehow criminal to throw away, although he had no real use for any of them. There was his grandfather's pocket-watch, heavy, scrolled, magnificent . . . and so badly rusted that the jeweler in Lewiston he and his mother had brought it to only took one look, shook his head, and pushed it back across the counter. There were two sets of matching cufflinks and two orphans, a *Penthouse* gatefold, a paperback book called *Gross Jokes*, and a Sony Walkman which had for some reason developed a habit of eating the tapes it was supposed to play. It was just stuff, that was all. There was no other word that fit.

Part of the stuff, of course, was the thirteen string ties Aunt Hilda had sent him for his last thirteen birthdays.

He took them out one by one, counted, came up with twelve instead of thirteen, rooted through the stuff-drawer again, then counted again. Still twelve.

"Not there?"

Kevin, who had been squatting, cried out and leaped to his feet.

"I'm sorry," Mr. Delevan said from the doorway. "That was dumb."

"That's okay," Kevin said. He wondered briefly how fast a person's heart could beat before the person in question simply blew his engine. "I'm just . . . on edge. Stupid."

"It's not." His father looked at him soberly. "When I saw that tape, I got so scared I felt like maybe I'd have to reach into my mouth and push my stomach back down with my fingers."

Kevin looked at his father gratefully.

"It's not there, is it?" Mr. Delevan asked. "The one with the woodpecker or whatever in hell it was supposed to be?"

"No. It's not."

"Did you keep the camera in that drawer?"

Kevin nodded his head slowly. "Pop—Mr. Merrill—said to let it rest every so often. That was part of the schedule he made out."

Something tugged briefly at his mind, was gone.

"So I stuck it in there."

"Boy," Mr. Delevan said softly.

"Yeah."

They looked at each other in the gloom, and then suddenly Kevin smiled. It was like watching the sun burst through a raft of clouds.

"What?"

"I was remembering how it felt," Kevin said. "I swung that sledge-hammer so hard—"

Mr. Delevan began to smile, too. "I thought you were going to take off your own damned—"

"—and when it hit it made this CRUNCH! sound—"

"—flew every damn whichway—"

"BOOM!" Kevin finished. "Gone!"

They began to laugh together in Kevin's room, and Kevin found he was almost—*almost*—glad all this had happened. The sense of relief was as inexpressible and yet as perfect as the sensation one feels when, either by happy accident or by some psychic guidance, another person manages to scratch that one itchy place on one's back that one cannot scratch oneself, hitting it exactly, bang on the money, making it wonderfully worse for a single second by the simple touch, pressure, arrival, of those fingers . . . and then, oh blessed relief.

It was like that with the camera and with his father's knowing.

"It's gone," Kevin said. "Isn't it?"

"As gone as Hiroshima after the *Enola Gay* dropped the A-bomb on it," Mr. Delevan replied, and then added: "Smashed to shit, is what I mean to say."

Kevin gawped at his father and then burst into helpless peals—screams, almost—of laughter. His father joined him. They orderd a loaded pizza shortly after. When Mary and Meg Delevan arrived home at twenty past seven, they both still had the giggles.

"Well, you two look like you've been up to no good," Mrs. Delevan said, a little puzzled. There was something in their hilarity that struck the woman center of her—that deep part which the sex seems to tap into fully only in times of childbirth and disaster—as a little unhealthy. They looked and sounded like men who may have just missed having a car accident. "Want to let the ladies in on it?"

"Just two bachelors having a good time," Mr. Delevan said.

"*Smashing* good time," Kevin amplified, to which his father added, "Is what we mean to say," and they looked at each other and were howling again.

Meg, honestly bewildered, looked at her mother and said: "Why are they doing that, Mom?"

Mrs. Delevan said, "Because they have penises, dear. Go hang up your coat."

Pop Merrill let the Delevans, *père et fils*, out, and then locked the door behind them. He turned off all the lights save for the one over the worktable, produced his keys, and opened his own stuff-drawer. From it he took Kevin Delevan's Polaroid Sun 660, chipped but otherwise undamaged, and looked at it fixedly. It had scared both the father and the son. That was clear enough to Pop; it had scared him as well, and still did. But to put a thing like this on a block and smash it to smithereens? That was crazy.

There was a way to turn a buck on this goddam thing.

There always was.

Pop locked it away in the drawer. He would sleep on it, and by the morning he would know how to proceed. In truth, he already had a pretty goddam good idea.

He got up, snapped off the work-light, and wove his way through the gloom toward the steps leading up to his apartment. He moved with the unthinking surefooted grace of long practice.

Halfway there, he stopped.

He felt an urge, an amazingly strong urge, to go back and look at the camera again. What in God's name for? He didn't even have any *film* for the Christless thing . . . not that *he* had any intentions of taking any pictures with it. If someone *else* wanted to take some snapshots, watch that dog's progress, the buyer was welcome. Caveet emperor, as he always said. Let the goddam emperor caveet or not as it suited him. As for him, he'd as soon go into a cage filled with lions without even a goddam whip and chair.

Still . . .

"Leave it," he said roughly in the darkness, and the sound of his own voice startled him and got him moving and he went upstairs without another look back.

CHAPTER SEVEN

Very early the next morning, Kevin Delevan had a nightmare so horrible he could only remember parts of it, like isolated phrases of music heard on a radio with a defective speaker.

He was walking into a grungy little mill-town. Apparently he was on the bum, because he had a pack on his back. The name of the town was Oatley, and Kevin had the idea it was either in Vermont or upstate New York. *You know anyone hiring here in Oatley?* he asked an old man pushing a shopping-cart along a cracked sidewalk. There were no groceries in the cart; it was full of indeterminate junk, and Kevin realized the man was a wino. *Get away!* the wino screamed. *Get away! Feef! Fushing feef! Fushing FEEF!*

Kevin ran, darted across the street, more frightened of the man's madness than he was of the idea anyone might believe that he, Kevin, was a thief. The wino called after him: *This ain't Oatley! This is Hildasville! Get out of town, you fushing feef!*

It was then that he realized that this town wasn't Oatley or Hildasville or any other town with a normal name. How could an utterly abnormal town have a normal name?

Everything—streets, buildings, cars, signs, the few pedestrians— was two-dimensional. Things had height, they had width . . . but they had no thickness. He passed a woman who looked the way Meg's ballet teacher might look if the ballet teacher put on a hundred and fifty pounds. She was wearing slacks the color of Bazooka bubble gum. Like the wino, she was pushing a shopping-cart. It had a squeaky wheel. It was full of Polaroid Sun 660 cameras. She looked at Kevin with narrow suspicion as they drew closer together. At the moment when they passed each other on the sidewalk, she disappeared. Her *shadow* was still there and he could still hear that rhythmic squeaking, but she was no longer there. Then she reappeared, looking back at him from her fat flat suspicious face, and Kevin understood the reason why she had disappeared for a moment. It was because the concept of "a side view" didn't exist, *couldn't* exist, in a world where everything was perfectly flat.

This is Polaroidsville, he thought with a relief which was strangely mingled with horror. *And that means this is only a dream.*

Then he saw the white picket fence, and the dog, and the photographer standing in the gutter. There were rimless spectacles propped up on his head. It was Pop Merrill.

Well, son, you found him, the two-dimensional Polaroid Pop said to Kevin without removing his eye from the shutter. *That's the dog, right there. The one tore up that kid out in Schenectady.* YOUR *dog, is what I mean to say.*

Then Kevin woke up in his own bed, afraid he had screamed but more concerned at first not about the dream but to make sure he was *all there,* all three dimensions of him.

He was. But something was wrong.

Stupid dream, he thought. *Let it go, why can't you? It's over. Photos are burned, all fifty-eight of them. And the camera's bus—*

His thought broke off like ice as that something, that something *wrong,* teased at his mind again.

It's not over, he thought. *It's n—*

But before the thought could finish itself, Kevin Delevan fell deeply, dreamlessly asleep. The next morning, he barely remembered the nightmare at all.

CHAPTER EIGHT

The two weeks following his acquisition of Kevin Delevan's Polaroid Sun were the most aggravating, infuriating, *humiliating* two weeks of Pop Merrill's life. There were quite a few people in Castle Rock who would have said it couldn't have happened to a more deserving guy. Not that anyone in Castle Rock did know . . . and that was just about all the consolation Pop could take. He found it cold comfort. Very cold indeed, thank you very much.

But who would have ever believed the Mad Hatters would have, *could* have, let him down so badly?

It was almost enough to make a man wonder if he was starting to slip a little.

God forbid.

CHAPTER NINE

Back in September, he hadn't even bothered to wonder if he would sell the Polaroid; the only questions were how soon and how much. The Delevans had bandied the word *supernatural* about, and Pop hadn't corrected them, although he knew that what the Sun was doing would be more properly classed by psychic investigators as a paranormal rather than supernatural phenomenon. He *could* have told them that, but if he *had,* they might both have wondered how come the owner of a small-town used-goods store (and part-time usurer) knew so much about the subject. The fact was this: he knew a lot because it was *profitable* to know a lot, and it was profitable to know a lot because of the people he thought of as "my Mad Hatters."

Mad Hatters were people who recorded empty rooms on expensive audio equipment not for a lark or a drunken party stunt, but either because they believed passionately in an unseen world and wanted to prove its existence, or because they wanted passionately to get in touch with friends and/or relatives who had "passed on" ("passed on": that's what they always called it; Mad Hatters never had relatives who did something so simple as die).

Mad Hatters not only owned and used Ouija Boards, they had regular conversations with "spirit guides" in the "other world" (never "heaven," "hell," or even "the rest area of the dead" but the "other world") who put them in touch with friends, relatives, queens, dead rock-and-roll singers, even arch-villains. Pop knew of a Mad Hatter in Vermont who had twice-weekly conversations with Hitler. Hitler had told him it was all a bum rap, he had sued for peace in January of 1943 and that son of a bitch Churchill had turned him down. Hitler had also told him Paul Newman was a space alien who had been born in a cave on the moon.

Mad Hatters went to séances as regularly (and as compulsively) as drug addicts visited their pushers. They bought crystal balls and amulets guaranteed to bring good luck; they organized their own little societies and investigated reputedly haunted houses for all the usual phenomena: teleplasm, table-rappings, floating tables and beds, cold spots, and, of course, ghosts. They noted all of these, real or imagined, with the enthusiasm of dedicated bird-watchers.

Most of them had a ripping good time. Some did not. There was that fellow from Wolfeboro, for instance. He hanged himself in the notorious Tecumseh House, where a gentleman farmer had, in the 1880s and '90s, helped his fellow men by day and helped himself to them by night, dining on them at a formal table in his cellar. The table stood upon a floor of sour packed dirt which had yielded the bones and decomposed bodies of at least twelve and perhaps as many as thirty-five young men, all vagabonds. The fellow from Wolfeboro had left this brief note on a pad of paper beside his Ouija Board: *Can't leave the house. Doors all locked. I hear him eating. Tried cotton. Does no good.*

And the poor deluded asshole probably thought he really did, Pop had mused after hearing this story from a source he trusted.

Then there was a fellow in Dunwich, Massachusetts, to whom Pop had once sold a so-called spirit trumpet for ninety dollars; the fellow had taken the trumpet to the Dunwich Cemetery and must have heard something exceedingly unpleasant, because he had been raving in a padded cell in Arkham for almost six years now, totally insane. When he had gone into the boneyard, his hair had been black; when his screams awoke the few neighbors who lived close enough to the cemetery to hear them and the police were summoned, it was as white as his howling face.

And there was the woman in Portland who lost an eye when a session with the Ouija Board went cataclysmically wrong . . . the man in Kingston, Rhode Island, who lost three fingers on his right hand when the rear door of a car in which two teenagers had committed suicide closed on it . . . the old lady who landed in Massachusetts Memorial Hospital short most of one ear when her equally elderly cat, Claudette, supposedly went on a rampage during a séance . . .

Pop believed some of these things, disbelieved others, and mostly held no opinion—not because he didn't have enough hard evidence one way or the other, but because he didn't give a fart in a high wind about ghosts, séances, crystal balls, spirit trumpets, rampaging cats, or the fabled John the Conquerer Root. As far as Reginald Marion "Pop" Merrill was concerned, the Mad Hatters could all take a flying fuck at the moon.

As long, of course, as one of them handed over some mighty tall tickets for Kevin Delevan's camera before taking passage on the next shuttle.

Pop didn't call these enthusiasts Mad Hatters because of their

spectral interests; he called them that because the great majority—
he was sometimes tempted to say *all* of them—seemed to be rich,
retired, and just begging to be plucked. If you were willing to spend
fifteen minutes with them nodding and agreeing while they assured
you they could pick a fake medium from a real one just by walking
into the *room*, let alone sitting down at the séance table, or if you
spent an equal amount of time listening to garbled noises which
might or might not be words on a tape player with the proper
expression of awe on your face, you could sell them a four-dollar
paperweight for a hundred by telling them a man had once glimpsed
his dead mother in it. You gave them a smile and they wrote you
a check for two hundred dollars. You gave them an encouraging
word and they wrote you a check for two *thousand* dollars. If you
gave them both things at the same time, they just kind of passed
the checkbook over to you and asked you to fill in an amount.

It had always been as easy as taking candy from a baby.

Until now.

Pop didn't keep a file in his cabinet marked MAD HATTERS any more
than he kept one marked COIN COLLECTORS or STAMP COLLEC-
TORS. He didn't even *have* a file-cabinet. The closest thing to it was
a battered old book of phone numbers he carried around in his
back pocket (which, like his purse, had over the years taken on the
shallow ungenerous curve of the spindly buttock it lay against every
day). Pop kept his files where a man in his line of work should
always keep them: in his head. There were eight full-blown Mad
Hatters that he had done business with over the years, people who
didn't just dabble in the occult but who got right down and rolled
around in it. The richest was a retired industrialist named McCarty
who lived on his own island about twelve miles off the coast. This
fellow disdained boats and employed a full-time pilot who flew him
back and forth to the mainland when he needed to go.

Pop went to see him on September 28th, the day after he obtained
the camera from Kevin (he didn't, couldn't, exactly think of it as
robbery; the boy, after all, had been planning to smash it to shit
anyway, and what he didn't know surely couldn't hurt him). He
drove to a private airstrip just north of Boothbay Harbor in his old
but perfectly maintained car, then gritted his teeth and slitted his
eyes and held onto the steel lockbox with the Polaroid Sun 660 in

it for dear life as the Mad Hatter's Beechcraft plunged down the dirt runway like a rogue horse, rose into the air just as Pop was sure they were going to fall off the edge and be smashed to jelly on the rocks below, and flew away into the autumn empyrean. He had made this trip twice before, and had sworn each time that he would never get into that goddam flying coffin again.

They bumped and jounced along with the hungry Atlantic less than five hundred feet below, the pilot talking cheerfully the whole way. Pop nodded and said ayuh in what seemed like the right places, although he was more concerned with his imminent demise than with anything the pilot was saying.

Then the island was ahead with its horribly, dismally, suicidally short landing strip and its sprawling house of redwood and field-stone, and the pilot swooped down, leaving Pop's poor old acid-shrivelled stomach somewhere in the air above them, and they hit with a thud and then, somehow, miraculously, they were taxiing to a stop, still alive and whole, and Pop could safely go back to believing God was just another invention of the Mad Hatters . . . at least until he had to get back in that damned plane for the return journey.

"Great day for flying, huh, Mr. Merrill?" the pilot asked, un-folding the steps for him.

"Finest kind," Pop grunted, then strode up the walk to the house where the Thanksgiving turkey stood in the doorway, smiling in eager anticipation. Pop had promised to show him "the god-damnedest thing I ever come across," and Cedric McCarty looked like he couldn't wait. He'd take one quick look for form's sake, Pop thought, and then fork over the lettuce. He went back to the mainland forty-five minutes later, barely noticing the thumps and jounces and gut-goozling drops as the Beech hit the occasional air-pocket. He was a chastened, thoughtful man.

He had aimed the Polaroid at the Mad Hatter and took his pic-ture. While they waited for it to develop, the Mad Hatter took a picture of Pop . . . and when the flashbulb went off, had he heard something? Had he heard the low, ugly snarl of that black dog, or had it been his imagination? Imagination, most likely. Pop had made some magnificent deals in his time, and you couldn't do that without imagination.

Still—

Cedric McCarty, retired industrialist *par excellence* and Mad Hatter *extraordinaire,* watched the photographs develop with that same childlike eagerness, but when they finally came clear, he looked amused and even perhaps a little contemptuous and Pop knew with the infallible intuition which had developed over almost fifty years that arguing, cajolery, even vague hints that he had another customer just *slavering* for a chance to buy this camera—none of those usually reliable techniques would work. A big orange NO SALE card had gone up in Cedric McCarty's mind.

By why?

Goddammit, *why?*

In the picture Pop took, that glint Kevin had spotted amid the wrinkles of the black dog's muzzle had clearly become a tooth—except *tooth* wasn't the right word, not by any stretch of the imagination. That was a *fang.* In the one McCarty took, you could see the beginnings of the neighboring teeth.

Fucking dog's got a mouth like a bear-trap, Pop thought. Unbidden, an image of his arm in that dog's mouth rose in his mind. He saw the dog not *biting* it, not *eating* it, but *shredding* it, the way the many teeth of a wood-chipper shred bark, leaves, and small branches. *How long would it take?* he wondered, and looked at those dirty eyes staring out at him from the overgrown face and knew it wouldn't take long. Or suppose the dog seized him by the crotch, instead? Suppose—

But McCarty had said something and was waiting for a response. Pop turned his attention to the man, and any lingering hope he might have held of making a sale evaporated. The Mad Hatter *extraordinaire,* who would cheerfully spend an afternoon with you trying to call up the ghost of your dear departed Uncle Ned, was gone. In his place was McCarty's other side: the hardheaded realist who had made *Fortune* magazine's listing of the richest men in America for twelve straight years—not because he was an airhead who had had the good fortune to inherit both a lot of money and an honest, capable staff to husband and expand it, but because he had been a genius in the field of aerodynamic design and development. He was not as rich as Howard Hughes but not quite as crazy as Hughes had been at the end, either. When it came to psychic phenomena, the man was a Mad Hatter. Outside that one area, however, he was a shark that made the likes of Pop Merrill look like a tadpole swimming in a mud-puddle.

"Sorry," Pop said. "I was woolgatherin a little, Mr. McCarty."

"I said it's fascinating," McCarty said. "Especially the subtle indications of passing time from one photo to the next. How does it work? Camera in camera?"

"I don't understand what you're gettin at."

"No, not a camera," McCarty said, speaking to himself. He picked the camera up and shook it next to his ear. "More likely some sort of roller device."

Pop stared at the man with no idea what he was talking about . . . except it spelled NO SALE, whatever it was. That goddam Christless ride in the little plane (and soon to do over again), all for nothing. But why? *Why?* He had been so *sure* of this fellow, who would probably believe the Brooklyn Bridge was a spectral illusion from the "other side" if you *told* him it was. So *why?*

"Slots, of course!" McCarty said, as delighted as a child. "*Slots!* There's a circular belt on pulleys inside this housing with a number of slots built into it. Each slot contains an exposed Polaroid picture of this dog. Continuity suggests"—he looked carefully at the pictures again—"yes, that the dog might have been *filmed,* with the Polaroids made from individual frames. When the shutter is released, a picture drops from its slot and emerges. The battery turns the belt enough to position the next photo, and—*voilà!*"

His pleasant expression was suddenly gone, and Pop saw a man who looked like he might have made his way to fame and fortune over the broken, bleeding bodies of his competitors . . . and enjoyed it.

"Joe will fly you back," he said. His voice had gone chill and impersonal. "You're good, Mr. Merrill"—this man, Pop realized glumly, would never call him Pop again—"I'll admit that. You've finally overstepped yourself, but for a long time you had me fooled. How much did you take me for? Was it all claptrap?"

"I didn't take you for one red cent," Pop said, lying stoutly. "I never sold you one single thing I didn't b'lieve was the genuine article, and what I mean to say is that goes for that camera as well."

"You make me sick," McCarty said. "Not because I trusted you; I've trusted others who were fakes and shams. Not because you took my money; it wasn't enough to matter. You make me sick because it's men like you that have kept the scientific investigation of psychic phenomena in the dark ages, something to be laughed at, something to be dismissed as the sole province of crackpots and dimwits. The one consolation is that sooner or later you fellows always overstep yourselves. You get greedy and try to palm off something ridiculous like *this*. I want you out of here, Mr. Merrill."

Pop had his pipe in his mouth and a Diamond Blue Tip in one shaking hand. McCarty pointed at him, and the chilly eyes above that finger made it look like the barrel of a gun.

"And if you light that stinking thing in here," he said, "I'll have Joe yank it out of your mouth and dump the coals down the back of your pants. So unless you want to leave my house with your skinny ass in flames, I suggest—"

"What's the *matter* with you, Mr. McCarty?" Pop bleated. "These pitchers didn't come out all developed! *You watched em develop with your own eyes!*"

"An emulsion any kid with a twelve-dollar chemistry set could whip up," McCarty said coldly. "It's not the catalyst-fixative the Polaroid people use, but it's close. You expose your Polaroids— or create them from movie-film, if that's what you did—and then you take them in a standard darkroom and paint them with goop. When they're dry, you load them. When they pop out, they look like any Polaroid that hasn't started to develop yet. Solid gray in a white border. Then the light hits your home-made emulsion, creating a chemical change, and it evaporates, showing a picture you yourself took hours or days or weeks before. Joe?"

Before Pop could say anything else, his arms were seized and he was not so much walked as propelled from the spacious, glass-walled living room. He wouldn't have said anything, anyway. Another of the many things a good businessman had to know was when he was licked. And yet he wanted to shout over his shoulder: *Some dumb cunt with dyed hair and a crystal ball she ordered from* Fate *magazine floats a book or a lamp or a page of goddam sheet-music through a dark room and you bout shit yourself, but when I show you a camera that takes pitchers of some other world, you have me thrown out by the seat of m'pants! You're mad as a hatter, all right! Well, fuck ya! There's other fish in the sea!*

So there were.

On October 5th, Pop got into his perfectly maintained car and drove to Portland to pay a visit on the Pus Sisters.

The Pus Sisters were identical twins who lived in Portland. They were eighty or so but looked older than Stonehenge. They chain-smoked Camel cigarettes, and had done so since they were seventeen, they were happy to tell you. They never coughed in spite of the six packs they smoked between them each and every day. They were driven about—on those rare occasions when they left their red brick Colonial mansion—in a 1958 Lincoln Continental which had the somber glow of a hearse. This vehicle was piloted by a black woman only a little younger than the Pus Sisters themselves. This female chauffeur was probably a mute, but might just be something a bit more special: one of the few truly taciturn human beings God ever made. Pop did not know and had never asked. He had dealt with the two old ladies for nearly thirty years, the black woman had been with them all that time, mostly driving the car, sometimes washing it, sometimes mowing the lawn or clipping the hedges around the house, sometimes stalking down to the mailbox on the corner with letters from the Pus Sisters to God alone knew who (he didn't know if the black woman ever went or was allowed inside the house, either, only that he had never seen her there), and during all that time he had never heard this marvellous creature speak.

The Colonial mansion was in Portland's Bramhall district, which is to Portland what the Beacon Hill area is to Boston. In that latter city, in the land of the bean and the cod, it's said the Cabots speak only to Lowells and the Lowells speak only to God, but the Pus Sisters and their few remaining contemporaries in Portland would and did calmly assert that the Lowells had turned a private connection into a party line some years after the Deeres and their Portland contemporaries had set up the original wire.

And of course no one in his right mind would have called them the Pus Sisters to their identical faces any more than anyone in his right mind would have stuck his nose in a bandsaw to take care of a troublesome itch. They were the Pus Sisters when they weren't around (and when one was fairly sure one was in company which didn't contain a tale-bearer or two), but their real names were Miss Eleusippus Deere and Mrs. Meleusippus Verrill. Their father, in his determination to combine devout Christianity with an exhibition of his own erudition, had named them for two of three triplets who had all became saints . . . but who, unfortunately, had been *male* saints.

Meleusippus's husband had died a great many years before, during the Battle of Leyte Gulf in 1944, as a matter of fact, but she had resolutely kept his name ever since, which made it impossible to take the easy way out and simply call them the Misses Deere.

No; you had to practice those goddamned tongue-twister names until they came out as smooth as shit from a waxed asshole. If you fucked up once, they held it against you, and you might lose their custom for as long as six months or a year. Fuck up twice, and don't even bother to call. Ever again.

Pop drove with the steel box containing the Polaroid camera on the seat beside him, saying their names over and over again in a low voice: "Eleusippus. *Mel*eusippus. Eleusippus and Meleusippus. Ayuh. *That's* all right."

But, as it turned out, that was the only thing that *was* all right. They wanted the Polaroid no more than McCarty had wanted it . . . although Pop had been so shaken by *that* encounter he went in fully prepared to take ten thousand dollars less, or fifty per cent of his original confident estimate of what the camera might fetch.

The elderly black woman was raking leaves, revealing a lawn which, October or not, was still as green as the felt on a billiard table. Pop nodded to her. She looked at him, looked *through* him, and continued raking leaves. Pop rang the bell and, somewhere in the depths of the house, a bell bonged. *Mansion* seemed the perfectly proper word for the Pus Sisters' domicile. Although it was nowhere near as big as some of the old homes in the Bramhall district, the perpetual dimness which reigned inside made it seem much bigger. The sound of the bell really *did* seem to come floating through a depth of rooms and corridors, and the sound of that bell always stirred a specific image in Pop's mind: the dead-cart passing through the streets of London during the plague year, the driver ceaselessly tolling his bell and crying, "Bring outcher dead! Bring outcher dead! For the luvva Jaysus, bring outcher dead!"

The Pus Sister who opened the door some thirty seconds later looked not only dead but embalmed; a mummy between whose lips someone had poked the smouldering butt of a cigarette for a joke.

"Merrill," the lady said. Her dress was a deep blue, her hair colored to match. She tried to speak to him as a great lady would speak to a tradesman who had come to the wrong door by mistake, but Pop could see she was, in her way, every bit as excited as that son of a bitch McCarty had been; it was just that the Pus Sisters had been born in Maine, raised in Maine, and would die in Maine, while McCarty hailed from someplace in the Midwest, where the art and craft of taciturnity were apparently not considered an important part of a child's upbringing.

A shadow flitted somewhere near the parlor end of the hallway, just visible over the bony shoulder of the sister who had opened the door. The other one. Oh, they were eager, all right. Pop began to wonder if he couldn't squeeze twelve grand out of them after all. Maybe even fourteen.

Pop knew he *could* say, "Do I have the honor of addressing Miss Deere or Mrs. Verrill?" and be completely correct and completely polite, but he had dealt with this pair of eccentric old bags before and he knew that, while the Pus Sister who had opened the door wouldn't raise an eyebrow or flare a nostril, would simply tell him which one he was speaking to, he would lose at least a thousand by doing so. They took great pride in their odd masculine names, and were apt to look more kindly on a person who tried and failed than one who took the coward's way out.

So, saying a quick mental prayer that his tongue wouldn't fail him now that the moment had come, he gave it his best and was pleased to hear the names slip as smoothly from his tongue as a pitch from a snake-oil salesman: "Is it Eleusippus or Meleusippus?" he asked, his face suggesting he was no more concerned about getting the names right than if they had been Joan and Kate.

"Meleusippus, Mr. Merrill," she said, ah, good, now he was *Mister* Merrill, and he was sure everything was going to go just as slick as ever a man could want, and he was just as wrong as ever a man could be. "Won't you step in?"

"Thank you kindly," Pop said, and entered the gloomy depths of the Deere Mansion.

"Oh *dear,*" Eleusippus Deere said as the Polaroid began to develop.

"What a *brute* he looks!" Meleusippus Verrill said, speaking in tones of genuine dismay and fear.

The dog *was* getting uglier, Pop had to admit that, and there was something else that worried him even more: the time-sequence of the pictures seemed to be speeding up.

He had posed the Pus Sisters on their Queen Anne sofa for the demonstration picture. The camera flashed its bright white light, turning the room for one single instant from the purgatorial zone between the land of the living and that of the dead where these two old relics somehow existed into something flat and tawdry, like a police photo of a museum in which a crime had been committed.

Except the picture which emerged did not show the Pus Sisters sitting together on their parlor sofa like identical bookends. The picture showed the black dog, now turned so that it was full-face to the camera and whatever photographer it was who was nuts enough to stand there and keep snapping pictures of it. Now all of its teeth were exposed in a crazy, homicidal snarl, and its head had taken on a slight, predatory tilt to the left. That head, Pop thought, would continue to tilt as it sprang at its victim, accomplishing two purposes: concealing the vulnerable area of its neck from possible attack and putting the head in a position where, once the teeth were clamped solidly in flesh, it could revolve upright again, ripping a large chunk of living tissue from its target.

"It's so *awful!*" Eleusippus said, putting one mummified hand to the scaly flesh of her neck.

"So *terrible!*" Meleusippus nearly moaned, lighting a fresh Camel from the butt of an old one with a hand shaking so badly she came close to branding the cracked and fissured left corner of her mouth.

"It's totally in-ex-*PLICK*-able!" Pop said triumphantly, thinking: *I wish you was here, McCarty, you happy asshole. I just wish you was. Here's two ladies been round the Horn and back a few times that don't think this goddam camera's just some kind of a carny magic-show trick!*

"Does it show something which *has* happened?" Meleusippus whispered.

"Or something which *will* happen?" Eleusippus added in an equally awed whisper.

"I dunno," Pop said. "All I know for sure is that I have seen some goldarn strange things in my time, but I've never seen the beat of these pitchers."

"I'm not surprised!" Eleusippus.

"Nor I!" Meleusippus.

Pop was all set to start the conversation going in the direction of price—a delicate business when you were dealing with *anyone,* but never more so than when you were dealing with the Pus Sisters: when it got down to hard trading, they were as delicate as a pair of virgins—which, for all Pop knew, at least one of them was. He was just deciding on the *To start with, it never crossed my mind to sell something like this, but . . .* approach (it was older than the Pus Sisters themselves—although probably not by much, you would have said after a good close look at them—but when you were dealing with Mad Hatters, that didn't matter a bit; in fact, they *liked* to hear it, the way small children like to hear the same fairy tales over and over) when Eleusippus absolutely floored him by saying, "I don't know about my sister, Mr. Merrill, but I wouldn't feel comfortable looking at anything you might have to"—here a slight, pained pause—"offer us in a business way until you put that . . . that camera, or whatever God-awful thing it is . . . back in your car."

"I couldn't agree more," Meleusippus said, stubbing out her half-smoked Camel in a fish-shaped ashtray which was doing everything but *shitting* Camel cigarette butts.

"*Ghost* photographs," Eleusippus said, "are one thing. They have a certain—"

"*Dignity*," Meleusippus suggested.

"Yes! Dignity! But that *dog*—" The old woman actually shivered. "It looks as if it's ready to jump right out of that photograph and *bite* one of us."

"*All* of us!" Meleusippus elaborated.

Up until this last exchange, Pop had been convinced—perhaps because he *had* to be—that the sisters had merely begun their own part of the dickering, and in admirable style. But the tone of their voices, as identical as their faces and figures (if they could have been said to *have* such things as figures), was beyond his power to disbelieve. They had no doubt that the Sun 660 was exhibiting some sort of paranormal behavior . . . *too* paranormal to suit them. They weren't dickering; they weren't pretending; they weren't playing games with him in an effort to knock the price down. When they said they wanted no part of the camera and the weird thing it was doing, that was exactly what they meant—nor had they done him the discourtesy (and that's just what it would have been, in their minds) of supposing or even *dreaming* that selling it had been his purpose in coming.

Pop looked around the parlor. It was like the old lady's room in a horror movie he'd watched once on his VCR—a piece of claptrap called *Burnt Offerings,* where this big old beefy fella tried to drown his son in the swimming pool but nobody even took their clothes off. That lady's room had been filled, overfilled, actually *stuffed* with old and new photographs. They sat on the tables and the mantel in every sort of frame; they covered so much of the walls you couldn't even tell what the pattern on the frigging paper was supposed to be.

The Pus Sisters' parlor wasn't quite that bad, but there were still plenty of photographs; maybe as many as a hundred and fifty, which seemed like three times that many in a room as small and dim as this one. Pop had been here often enough to notice most of them at least in passing, and he knew others even better than that, for he had been the one to sell them to Eleusippus and Meleusippus.

They had a great many more "ghost photographs," as Eleusippus Deere called them, perhaps as many as a thousand in all, but apparently even they had realized a room the size of their parlor was limited in terms of display-space, if not in those of taste. The rest of the ghost photographs were distributed among the mansion's other fourteen rooms. Pop had seen them all. He was one of the fortunate few who had been granted what the Pus Sisters called, with simple grandiosity, The Tour. But it was here in the parlor that they kept their *prize* "ghost photographs," with the prize of prizes attracting the eye by the simple fact that it stood in solitary splendor atop the closed Steinway baby grand by the bow windows. In it, a corpse was levitating from its coffin before fifty or sixty horrified mourners. It was a fake, of course. A child of ten—hell, a child of *eight*—would have known it was a fake. It made the photographs of the dancing elves which had so bewitched poor Arthur Conan Doyle near the end of his life look accomplished by comparison. In fact, as Pop ranged his eye about the room, he saw only two photographs that weren't obvious fakes. It would take closer study to see how the trickery had been worked in those. Yet these two ancient pussies, who had collected "ghost photographs" all their lives and claimed to be great experts in the field, acted like a couple of teenage girls at a horror movie when he showed them not just a paranormal *photograph* but a goddam Jesus-jumping paranormal *camera* that didn't just do its trick once and then quit, like the one that had taken the picture of the ghost-lady watching the fox-hunters come home, but one that did it *again* and *again* and *again,* and how much had they spent on this stuff that was nothing but *claptrap?* Thousands? Tens of thousands? *Hundreds* of—

"—show us?" Meleusippus was asking him.

Pop Merrill forced his lips to turn up in what must have been at least a reasonable imitation of his Folksy Crackerbarrel Smile, because they registered no surprise or distrust.

"Pardon me, dear lady," Pop said. "M'mind went woolgatherin all on its own for a minute or two there. I guess it happens to all of us as we get on."

"We're eighty-three, and *our* minds are as clear as window-glass," Eleusippus said with clear disapproval.

"*Freshly washed* window-glass," Meleusippus added. "I asked if you have some new photographs you would care to show us . . . once you've put that wretched thing away, of course."

"It's been *ages* since we saw any really *good* new ones," Eleusippus said, lighting a fresh Camel.

"We went to The New England Psychic and Tarot Convention in Providence last month," Meleusippus said, "and while the lectures were enlightening—"

"—and uplifting—"

"—so many of the photographs were *arrant* fakes! Even a child of ten—"

"—of *seven!*—"

"—could have seen through them. So . . ." Meleusippus paused. Her face assumed an expression of perplexity which looked as if it might hurt (the muscles of her face having long since atrophied into expressions of mild pleasure and serene knowledge). "I am puzzled. Mr. Merrill, I must admit to being a bit puzzled."

"I was about to say the same thing," Eleusippus said.

"Why *did* you bring that awful thing?" Meleusippus and Eleusippus asked in perfect two-part harmony, spoiled only by the nicotine rasp of their voices.

The urge Pop felt to say *Because I didn't know what a pair of chickenshit old cunts you two were* was so strong that for one horrified second he believed he *had* said it, and he quailed, waiting for the twin screams of outrage to rise in the dim and hallowed confines of the parlor, screams which would rise like the squeal of rusty bandsaws biting into tough pine-knots, and go on rising until the glass in the frame of every bogus picture in the room shattered in an agony of vibration.

The idea that he had spoken such a terrible thought aloud lasted only a split-second, but when he relived it on later wakeful nights while the clocks rustled sleepily below (and while Kevin Delevan's Polaroid crouched sleeplessly in the locked drawer of the worktable), it seemed much longer. In those sleepless hours, he sometimes found himself wishing he *had* said it, and wondered if he was maybe losing his mind.

What he *did* do was react with a speed and a canny instinct for self-preservation that were nearly noble. To blow up at the Pus Sisters would give him immense gratification, but it would, unfortunately, be *short-lived* gratification. If he buttered them up—which was exactly what they expected, since they had been basted in butter all their lives (although it hadn't done a goddam thing for their skins)—he could perhaps sell them another three or four thousand dollars' worth of claptrap "ghost photographs," if they continued to elude the lung cancer which should surely have claimed one or both at least a dozen years ago.

And there were, after all, other Mad Hatters in Pop's mental file, although not quite so many as he'd thought on the day he'd set off to see Cedric McCarty. A little checking had revealed that two had died and one was currently learning how to weave baskets in a posh northern California retreat which catered to the incredibly rich who also happened to have gone hopelessly insane.

"Actually," he said, "I brought the camera out so you ladies could look at it. What I mean to say," he hastened on, observing their expressions of consternation, "is I know how much experience you ladies have in this field."

Consternation turned to gratification; the sisters exchanged smug, comfy looks, and Pop found himself wishing he could douse a couple of their goddam packs of Camels with barbecue lighter fluid and jam them up their tight little old-maid asses and then strike a match. They'd smoke then, all right. They'd smoke just like plugged chimneys, was what he meant to say.

"I thought you might have some advice on what I should do with the camera, is what I mean to say," he finished.

"Destroy it," Eleusippus said immediately.

"I'd use dynamite," Meleusippus said.

"Acid first, *then* dynamite," Eleusippus said.

"Right," Meleusippus finished. "It's dangerous. You don't have to look at that devil-dog to know that." She did look though; they both did, and identical expressions of revulsion and fear crossed their faces.

"You can feel *eee*vil coming out of it," Eleusippus said in a voice of such portentousness that it should have been laughable, like a high-school girl playing a witch in *Macbeth*, but which somehow wasn't. "Destroy it, Mr. Merrill. Before something awful happens. Before—perhaps, you'll notice I only say *perhaps*—it destroys *you*."

"Now, now," Pop said, annoyed to find he felt just a little uneasy in spite of himself, "that's drawing it a little strong. It's just a camera is what I mean to say."

Eleusippus Deere said quietly: "And the planchette that put out poor Colette Simineaux's eye a few years ago—that was nothing but a piece of fiberboard."

"At least until those foolish, foolish, *foolish* people put their fingers on it and woke it up," Meleusippus said, more quietly still.

There seemed nothing left to say. Pop picked up the camera—careful to do so by the strap, not touching the actual camera itself, although he told himself this was just for the benefit of these two old pussies—and stood.

"Well, you're the experts," he said. The two old women looked at each other and preened.

Yes; retreat. Retreat was the answer . . . for now, at least. But he wasn't done yet. Every dog had its day, and you could take *that* to the bank. "I don't want to take up any more of y'time, and I surely don't want to discommode you."

"Oh, you haven't!" Eleusippus said, also rising.

"We have so very few guests these days!" Meleusippus said, also rising.

"Put it in your car, Mr. Merrill," Eleusippus said, "and then—"

"—come in and have tea."

"*High* tea!"

And although Pop wanted nothing more in his life than to be *out* of there (and to tell them exactly that: *Thanks but no thanks, I want to get the fuck OUT of here*), he made a courtly little half-bow and an excuse of the same sort. "It would be my pleasure," he said, "but I'm afraid I have another appointment. I don't get to the city as often as I'd like." If you're going to tell one lie, you might as well tell a pack, Pop's own Pop had often told him, and it was advice he had taken to heart. He made a business of looking at his watch. "I've stayed too long already. You girls have made me late, I'm afraid, but I suppose I'm not the first man you've done *that* to."

They giggled and actually raised identical blushes, like the glow of very old roses. "Why, Mr. *Merrill!*" Eleusippus trilled.

"Ask me next time," he said, smiling until his face felt as if it would break. "Ask me next time, by the Lord Harry! You just ask and see if I don't say yes faster'n a hoss can trot!"

He went out, and as one of them quickly closed the door behind him (maybe they think the sun'll fade their goddam fake ghost photographs, Pop thought sourly), he turned and snapped the Polaroid at the old black woman, who was still raking leaves. He did it on impulse, as a man with a mean streak may on impulse swerve across a country road to kill a skunk or raccoon.

The black woman's upper lip rose in a snarl, and Pop was stunned to see she was actually forking the sign of the evil eye at him.

He got into his car and backed hurriedly down the driveway.

The rear end of his car was halfway into the street and he was turning to check for traffic when his eye happened upon the Polaroid he had just taken. It wasn't fully developed; it had the listless, milky look of all Polaroid photographs which are still developing.

Yet it had come up enough so that Pop only stared at it, the breath he had begun to unthinkingly draw into his lungs suddenly ceasing like a breeze that unaccountably drops away to nothing for a moment. His very heart seemed to cease in mid-beat.

What Kevin had imagined was now happening. The dog had finished its pivot, and had now begun its relentless ordained irrefutable approach toward the camera and whoever held it . . . ah, but *he* had held it this time, hadn't he? *He,* Reginald Marion "Pop" Merrill, had raised it and snapped it at the old black woman in a moment's pique like a spanked child that shoots a pop bottle off the top of a fence-post with his BB gun because he can't very well shoot his father, although in that humiliating, bottom-throbbing time directly after the paddling he would be more than happy to.

The dog was coming. Kevin had known that would happen next, and Pop would have known it, too, if he'd had occasion to think on it, which he hadn't—although from this moment on he would find it hard to think of anything else when he thought of the camera, and he would find those thoughts filling more and more of his time, both waking and dreaming.

It's coming, Pop thought with the sort of frozen horror a man might feel standing in the dark as some Thing, some unspeakable and unbearable Thing, approaches with its razor-sharp claws and teeth. *Oh my God, it's coming, that dog is coming.*

But it wasn't just *coming;* it was *changing.*

It was impossible to say how. His eyes hurt, caught between what they should be seeing and what they *were* seeing, and in the end the only handle he could find was a very small one: it was as if someone had changed the lens on the camera, from the normal one to a fish-eye, so that the dog's forehead with its clots of tangled fur seemed somehow to bulge and recede at the same time, and the dog's murderous eyes seemed to have taken on filthy, barely visible glimmers of red, like the sparks a Polaroid flash sometimes puts in people's eyes.

The dog's *body* seemed to have elongated but not thinned; if anything, it seemed thicker—not fatter, but more heavily muscled.

And its teeth were bigger. Longer. Sharper.

Pop suddenly found himself remembering Joe Camber's Saint Bernard, Cujo—the one who had killed Joe and that old tosspot Gary Pervier and Big George Bannerman. The dog had gone rabid. It had trapped a woman and a young boy in their car up there at Camber's place and after two or three days the kid had died. And now Pop found himself wondering if *this* was what they had been looking at during those long days and nights trapped in the steaming oven of their car; this or something like this, the muddy red eyes, the long sharp teeth—

A horn blared impatiently.

Pop screamed, his heart not only starting again but *gunning,* like the engine of a Formula One racing-car.

A van swerved around his sedan, still half in the driveway and half in the narrow residential street. The van's driver stuck his fist out his open window and his middle finger popped up.

"Eat my dick, you son of a whore!" Pop screamed. He backed the rest of the way out, but so jerkily that he bumped up over the curb on the far side of the street. He twisted the wheel viciously (inadvertently honking his horn in the process) and then drove off. But three blocks south he had to pull over and just sit there behind the wheel for ten minutes, waiting for the shakes to subside enough so he could drive.

So much for the Pus Sisters.

During the next five days, Pop ran through the remaining names on his mental list. His asking price, which had begun at twenty thousand dollars with McCarty and dropped to ten with the Pus Sisters (not that he had gotten far enough into the business to mention price in either case), dropped steadily as he ran out the string. He was finally left with Emory Chaffee, and the possibility of realizing perhaps twenty-five hundred.

Chaffee presented a fascinating paradox: in all Pop's experience with the Mad Hatters—an experience that was long and amazingly varied—Emory Chaffee was the only believer in the "other world" who had absolutely no imagination whatsoever. That he had ever spared a single thought for the "other world" with such a mind was surprising; that he *believed* in it was amazing; that he paid good money to collect objects connected with it was something Pop found absolutely astounding. Yet it was so, and Pop would have put Chaffee much higher on his list save for the annoying fact that Chaffee was by far the least well off of what Pop thought of as his "rich" Mad Hatters. He was doing a game but poor job of holding onto the last unravelling threads of what had once been a great family fortune. Hence, another large drop in Pop's asking price for Kevin's Polaroid.

But, he had thought, pulling his car into the overgrown driveway of what had in the '20s been one of Sebago Lake's finest summer homes and which was now only a step or two away from becoming one of Sebago Lake's shabbiest year-round homes (the Chaffee house in Portland's Bramhall district had been sold for taxes fifteen years before), *if anyone'll buy this beshitted thing, I reckon Emory will.*

The only thing that really distressed him—and it had done so more and more as he worked his way fruitlessly down the list— was the demonstration part. He could *describe* what the camera did until he was black in the face, but not even an odd duck like Emory Chaffee would lay out good money on the basis of a description alone.

Sometimes Pop thought it had been stupid to have Kevin take all those pictures so he could make that videotape. But when you got right down to where the bear shit in the buckwheat, he wasn't sure it would have made any difference. Time passed over there in that world (for, like Kevin, he had come to think of it as that: an actual world), and it passed much more slowly than it did in this one . . . but wasn't it speeding up as the dog approached the camera? Pop thought it was. The movement of the dog along the fence had been barely visible at first; now only a blind man could fail to see that the dog was closer each time the shutter was pressed. You could see the difference in distance even if you snapped two photographs one right after the other. It was almost as if time over there were trying to . . . well, trying to *catch up* somehow, and get in sync with time over here.

If that had been all, it would have been bad enough. But it *wasn't* all.

That was no *dog,* goddammit.

Pop didn't know what it *was,* but he knew as well as he knew his mother was buried in Homeland Cemetery that it was no *dog.*

He thought it *had* been a dog, when it had been snuffling its way along that picket fence which it had now left a good ten feet behind; it had *looked* like one, albeit an exceptionally mean one once it got its head turned enough so you could get a good look at its phiz.

But to Pop it now looked like no creature that had ever existed on God's earth, and probably not in Lucifer's hell, either. What troubled him even more was this: the few people for whom he had taken demonstration photographs did not seem to see this. They inevitably recoiled, inevitably said it was the ugliest, meanest-looking junkyard mongrel they had ever seen, but that was all. Not a single one of them suggested that the dog in Kevin's Sun 660 was turning into some kind of monster as it approached the photographer. As it approached the lens which might be some sort of portal between that world and this one.

Pop thought again (as Kevin had), *But it could never get through. Never. If something is going to happen, I'll tell you what that something will be, because that thing is an* ANIMAL, *maybe a goddam ugly one, a scary one, even, like the kind of thing a little kid imagines in his closet after his momma turns off the lights, but it's still an* ANIMAL, *and if anything happens it'll be this: there'll be one last pitcher where you can't see nothing but blur because that devil-dog will have jumped, you can see that's what it means to do, and after that the camera either won't work, or if it does, it won't take pitchers that develop into anything but black squares, because you can't take pitchers with a camera that has a busted lens or with one that's broke right in two for that matter, and if whoever owns that shadow drops the camera when the devil-dog hits it and him, and I imagine he will, it's apt to fall on the sidewalk and it probably* WILL *break. Goddam thing's nothing but plastic, after all, and plastic and cement don't get along hardly at all.*

But Emory Chaffee had come out on his splintery porch now, where the paint on the boards was flaking off and the boards themselves were warping out of true and the screens were turning the rusty color of dried blood and gaping holes in some of them; Emory Chaffee wearing a blazer which had once been a natty blue but had now been cleaned so many times it was the nondescript gray of an elevator operator's uniform; Emory Chaffee with his high forehead sloping back and back until it finally disappeared beneath what little hair he had left and grinning his *Pip-pip, jolly good, old boy, jolly good, wot, wot?* grin that showed his gigantic buck teeth and made him look the way Pop imagined Bugs Bunny would look if Bugs had suffered some cataclysmic mental retardation.

Pop took hold of the camera's strap—God, how he had come to hate the thing!—got out of his car, and forced himself to return the man's wave and grin.

Business, after all, was business.

"That's one ugly pup, wouldn't you say?"

Chaffee was studying the Polaroid which was now almost completely developed. Pop had explained what the camera did, and had been encouraged by Chaffee's frank interest and curiosity. Then he had given the Sun to the man, inviting him to take a picture of anything he liked.

Emory Chaffee, grinning that repulsive buck-toothed grin, swung the Polaroid Pop's way.

"Except me," Pop said hastily. "I'd ruther you pointed a shotgun at my head instead of that camera."

"When you sell a thing, you really sell it," Chaffee said admiringly, but he had obliged just the same, turning the Sun 660 toward the wide picture window with its view of the lake, a magnificent view that remained as rich now as the Chaffee family itself had been in those years which began after World War I, golden years which had somehow begun to turn to brass around 1970.

He pressed the shutter.

The camera whined.

Pop winced. He found that now he winced every time he heard that sound—that squidgy little whine. He had tried to control the wince and had found to his dismay that he could not.

"Yes, sir, one goddamned ugly brute!" Chaffee repeated after examining the developed picture, and Pop was sourly pleased to see that the repulsive buck-toothed wot-ho, bit-of-a-sticky-wicket grin had disappeared at last. The camera had been able to do that much, at least.

Yet it was equally clear to him that the man wasn't seeing what he, Pop, was seeing. Pop had had some preparation for this eventuality; he was, all the same, badly shaken behind his impassive Yankee mask. He believed that if Chaffee *had* been granted the power (for that was what it seemed to be) to see what Pop was seeing, the stupid fuck would have been headed for the nearest door, and at top speed.

The dog—well, it wasn't a dog, not anymore, but you had to call it *something*—hadn't begun its leap at the photographer yet, but it was getting ready; its hindquarters were simultaneously bunching and lowering toward the cracked anonymous sidewalk in a way that somehow reminded Pop of a kid's souped-up car, trembling, barely leashed by the clutch during the last few seconds of a red light; the needle on the rpm dial already standing straight up at 60 x 10, the engine screaming through chrome pipes, fat deep-tread tires ready to smoke the macadam in a hot soul-kiss.

The dog's face was no longer a recognizable thing at all. It had twisted and distorted into a carny freak-show thing that seemed to have but a single dark and malevolent eye, neither round nor oval but somehow *runny,* like the yolk of an egg that has been stabbed with the tines of a fork. Its nose was a black beak with deep flared holes drilled into either side. And was there *smoke* coming from those holes—like steam from the vents of a volcano? Maybe—or maybe that part was just imagination.

Don't matter, Pop thought. *You just keep workin that shutter, or lettin people like this fool work it, and you are gonna find out, aren't you?*

But he didn't *want* to find out. He looked at the black, murdering thing whose matted coat had caught perhaps two dozen wayward burdocks, the thing which no longer had fur, exactly, but stuff like living spikes, and a tail like a medieval weapon. He observed the shadow it had taken a damned snot-nosed kid to extract meaning from, and saw it had changed. One of the shadow-legs appeared to have moved a stride backward—a very *long* stride, even taking the effect of the lowering or rising sun (but it was going down; Pop had somehow become very sure it was going down, that it was night coming in that world over there, not day) into account.

The photographer over there in that world had finally discovered that his subject did not mean to sit for its portrait; that had never been a part of its plan. It intended to *eat,* not *sit. That* was the plan.

Eat, and, maybe, in some way he didn't understand, escape.

Find out! he thought ironically. *Go ahead! Just keep taking pitchers! You'll find out! You'll find out* PLENTY!

"And you, sir," Emory Chaffee was saying, for he had only been stopped for a moment; creatures of little imagination are rarely stopped for long by such trivial things as consideration, "are one hell of a salesman!"

The memory of McCarty was still very close to the surface of Pop's mind, and it still rankled.

"If you think it's a fake—" he began.

"A fake? Not at all! Not . . . at *all*!" Chaffee's buck-toothed smile spread wide in all its repulsive splendor. He spread his hands in a surely-you-jest motion. "But I'm afraid, you see, that we can't do business on this particular item, Mr. Merrill. I'm sorry to say so, but—"

"Why?" Pop bit off. "If you don't think the goddam thing's a fake, why in the hell don't you want it?" And he was astonished to hear his voice rising in a kind of plaintive, balked fury. There had never been anything like this, never in the history of the *world,* Pop was sure of it, nor ever would be again. Yet it seemed he couldn't *give* the goddam thing away.

"But . . ." Chaffee looked puzzled, as if not sure how to state it, because whatever it was he had to say seemed so obvious to him. In that moment he looked like a pleasant but not very capable pre-school teacher trying to teach a backward child how to tie his shoes. "But it doesn't *do* anything, does it?"

"Doesn't *do* anything?" Pop nearly screamed. He couldn't believe he had lost control of himself to such a degree as this, and was losing more all the time. What was happening to him? Or, cutting closer to the bone, what was the son-of-a-bitching *camera* doing to him? "Doesn't *do* anything? What are you, blind? It takes pitchers of *another world*! It takes pitchers that move in time from one to the next, no matter *where* you take em or *when* you take em in *this* world! And that . . . that thing . . . that *monster*—"

Oh. Oh dear. He had finally done it. He had finally gone too far. He could see it in the way Chaffee was looking at him.

"But it's just a dog, isn't it?" Chaffee said in a low, comforting voice. It was the sort of voice you'd use to try and soothe a madman while the nurses ran for the cabinet where they kept the hypos and the knock-out stuff.

"Ayuh," Pop said slowly and tiredly. "Just a dog is all it is. But you said yourself it was a hell of an ugly brute."

"That's right, that's right, I did," Chaffee said, agreeing much too quickly. Pop thought if the man's grin got any wider and broader he might just be treated to the sight of the top three-quarters of the idiot's head toppling off into his lap. "But . . . surely you see, Mr. Merrill . . . what a problem this presents for the collector. The *serious* collector."

"No, I guess I don't," Pop said, but after running through the entire list of Mad Hatters, a list which had seemed so promising at first, he was beginning to. In fact, he was beginning to see a whole *host* of problems the Polaroid Sun presented for the serious collector. As for Emory Chaffee . . . God knew what Emory thought, exactly.

"There are most certainly such things as ghost photographs," Chaffee said in a rich, pedantic voice that made Pop want to strangle him. "But these are not ghost photographs. They—"

"They're sure as hell not *normal* photographs!"

"My point exactly," Chaffee said, frowning slightly. "But what sort of photographs *are* they? One can hardly say, can one? One can only display a perfectly normal camera that photographs a dog which is apparently preparing to leap. And once it leaps, it will be gone from the frame of the picture. At that point, one of three things may happen. The camera may start taking normal pictures, which is to say, pictures of the things it is aimed at; it may take no more pictures at all, its one purpose, to photograph—to *document*, one might even say—that dog, completed; or it may simply go on taking pictures of that white fence and the ill-tended lawn behind it." He paused and added, "I suppose someone might walk by at some point, forty photographs down the line—or four hundred— but unless the photographer raised his angle, which he doesn't seem to have done in any of these, one would only see the passerby from the waist down. More or less." And, echoing Kevin's father without even knowing who Kevin's father was, he added: "Pardon me for saying so, Mr. Merrill, but you've shown me something I thought I'd never see: an inexplicable and almost irrefutable paranormal occurrence that is really quite boring."

This amazing but apparently sincere remark forced Pop to disregard whatever Chaffee might think about his sanity and ask again: "It really *is* only a dog, as far as you can see?"

"Of course," Chaffee said, looking mildly surprised. "A stray mongrel that looks exceedingly bad-tempered."

He sighed.

"And it wouldn't be taken seriously, of course. What I mean is it wouldn't be taken seriously by people who don't know you personally, Mr. Merrill. People who aren't familiar with your honesty and reliability in these matters. It looks like a trick, you see? And not even a very good one. Something on the order of a child's Magic Eight-Ball."

Two weeks ago, Pop would have argued strenuously against such an idea. But that was before he had been not walked but actually *propelled* from that bastard McCarty's house.

"Well, if that's your final word," Pop said, getting up and taking the camera by the strap.

"I'm very sorry you made a trip to such little purpose," Chaffee said . . . and then his horrid grin burst forth again, all rubbery lips and huge teeth shining with spit. "I was about to make myself a Spam sandwich when you drove in. Would you care to join me, Mr. Merrill? I make quite a nice one, if I do say so myself. I add a little horseradish and Bermuda onion—that's my secret—and then I—"

"I'll pass," Pop said heavily. As in the Pus Sisters' parlor, all he really wanted right now was to get out of here and put miles between himself and this grinning idiot. Pop had a definite allergy to places where he had gambled and lost. Just lately there seemed to be a lot of those. Too goddam many. "I already had m'dinner, is what I mean to say. Got to be gettin back."

Chaffee laughed fruitily. "The lot of the toiler in the vineyards is busy but yields great bounty," he said.

Not just lately, Pop thought. *Just lately it ain't yielded no fuckin bounty at all.*

"It's a livin, anyway," Pop replied, and was eventually allowed out of the house, which was damp and chill (what it must be like to live in such a place come February, Pop couldn't imagine) and had that mousy, mildewed smell that might be rotting curtains and sofa-covers and such . . . or just the smell money leaves behind when it has spent a longish period of time in a place and then departed. He thought the fresh October air, tinged with just a small taste of the lake and a stronger tang of pine-needles, had never smelled so good.

He got into his car and started it up. Emory Chaffee, unlike the Pus Sister who had shown him as far as the door and then closed it quickly behind him, as if afraid the sun might strike her and turn her to dust like a vampire, was standing on the front porch, grinning his idiot grin and actually *waving,* as if he were seeing Pop off on a goddam ocean cruise.

And, without thinking, just as he had taken the picture of (or *at,* anyway) the old black woman without thinking, he had snapped Chaffee and the just-starting-to-moulder house which was all that remained of the Chaffee family holdings. He didn't remember picking the camera up off the seat where he had tossed it in disgust before closing his door, was not even aware that the camera was in his hands or the shutter fired until he heard the whine of the mechanism shoving the photograph out like a tongue coated with some bland gray fluid—Milk of Magnesia, perhaps. That sound seemed to vibrate along his nerve-endings now, making them scream; it was like the feeling you got when something too cold or hot hit a new filling.

He was peripherally aware that Chaffee was laughing as if it was the best goddam joke in the world before snatching the picture from the slot in a kind of furious horror, telling himself he had imagined the momentary, blurred sound of a snarl, a sound like you might hear if a power-boat was approaching while you had your head ducked under water; telling himself he had imagined the momentary feeling that the camera had *bulged* in his hands, as if some huge pressure inside had pushed the sides out momentarily. He punched the glove-compartment button and threw the picture inside and then closed it so hard and fast that he tore his thumbnail all the way down to the tender quick.

He pulled out jerkily, almost stalling, then almost hitting one of the hoary old spruces which flanked the house end of the long Chaffee driveway, and all the way up that driveway he thought he could hear Emory Chaffee laughing in loud mindless cheery bellows of sound: *Haw! Haw! Haw! Haw!*

His heart slammed in his chest, and his head felt as if someone was using a sledgehammer inside there. The small cluster of veins which nestled in the hollows of each temple pulsed steadily.

He got himself under control little by little. Five miles, and the little man inside his head quit using the sledgehammer. Ten miles (by now he was almost halfway back to Castle Rock), and his heartbeat was back to normal. And he told himself: *You ain't gonna look at it. You AIN'T. Let the goddam thing rot in there. You don't need to look at it, and you don't need to take no more of em, either. Time to mark the thing off as a dead loss. Time to do what you should have let the boy do in the first place.*

So of course when he got to the Castle View rest area, a turn-out from which you could, it seemed, see all of western Maine and half of New Hampshire, he swung in and turned off his motor and opened the glove compartment and brought out the picture which he had taken with no more intent or knowledge than a man might have if he did a thing while walking in his sleep. The photograph had developed in there, of course; the chemicals inside that deceptively flat square had come to life and done their usual efficient job. Dark or light, it didn't make any difference to a Polaroid picture.

The dog-thing was crouched all the way down now. It was as fully coiled as it was going to get, a trigger pulled back to full cock. Its teeth had outgrown its mouth so that the thing's snarl seemed now to be not only an expression of rage but a simple necessity; how could its lips ever fully close over those teeth? How could those jaws ever chew? It looked more like a weird species of wild boar than a dog now, but what it really looked like was nothing Pop had ever seen before. It did more than hurt his eyes to look at it; it hurt his *mind.* It made him feel as if he was going crazy.

Why not get rid of that camera right here? he thought suddenly. *You can. Just get out, walk to the guardrail there, and toss her over. All gone. Goodbye.*

But that would have been an impulsive act, and Pop Merrill belonged to the Reasonable tribe—belonged to it body and soul, is what I mean to say. He didn't want to do anything on the spur of the moment that he might regret later, and—

If you don't *do this, you'll regret it later.*

But no. And no. And no. A man couldn't run against his nature. It was unnatural. He needed time to think. To be sure.

He compromised by throwing the print out instead and then drove on quickly. For a minute or two he felt as if he might throw up, but the urge passed. When it did, he felt a little more himself. Safely back in his shop, he unlocked the steel box, took out the Sun, rummaged through his keys once more, and located the one for the drawer where he kept his "special" items. He started to put

the camera inside . . . and paused, brow furrowed. The image of
the chopping block out back entered his mind with such clarity,
every detail crisply limned, that it was like a photograph itself.

He thought: *Never mind all that about how a man can't run against
his nature. That's crap, and you know it. It ain't in a man's nature to
eat dirt, but you could eat a whole bowl of it, by the bald-headed Christ,
if someone with a gun pointed at your head told you to do it. You know
what time it is, chummy—time to do what you should have let the boy
do in the first place. After all, it ain't like you got any investment in
this.*

But at this, another part of his mind rose in angry, fist-waving
protest. *Yes I do! I do have an investment, goddammit! That kid
smashed a perfectly good Polaroid camera! He may not know it, but that
don't change the fact that I'm out a hundred and thirty-nine bucks!*

"Oh, shit on toast!" he muttered agitatedly. "It ain't that! It ain't
the fuckin *money!*"

No—it wasn't the fucking money. He could at least admit that
it wasn't the money. He could afford it; Pop could indeed have
afforded a great deal, including his own mansion in Portland's Bramhall district and a brand-new Mercedes-Benz to go in the carport.
He never would have bought those things—he pinched his pennies
and chose to regard almost pathological miserliness as nothing more
than good old Yankee thrift—but that didn't mean he couldn't have
had them if he so chose.

It wasn't about money; it was about something more important
than money ever could be. It was about *not getting skinned.* Pop
had made a life's work out of *not getting skinned,* and on the few
occasions when he had been, he had felt like a man with red ants
crawling around inside his skull.

Take the business of the goddam Kraut record-player, for instance. When Pop found out that antique dealer from Boston—
Donahue, his name had been—had gotten fifty bucks more than
he'd ought to have gotten for a 1915 Victor-Graff gramophone
(which had actually turned out to be a much more common 1919
model), Pop had lost three hundred dollars' worth of sleep over it,
sometimes plotting various forms of revenge (each more wild-eyed
and ridiculous than the last), sometimes just damning himself for
a fool, telling himself he must really be slipping if a city man like
that Donahue could skin Pop Merrill. And sometimes he imagined
the fucker telling his poker-buddies about how easy it had been,

hell, they were all just a bunch of rubes up there, he believed that if you tried to sell the Brooklyn Bridge to a fellow like that country mouse Merrill in Castle Rock, the damned fool would ask "How much?" Then him and his cronies rocking back in their chairs around that poker-table (why he always saw them around such a table in this morbid daydream Pop didn't know, but he did), smoking dollar cigars and roaring with laughter like a bunch of trolls.

The business of the Polaroid was eating into him like acid, but he still wasn't ready to let go of the thing yet.

Not quite yet.

You're crazy! a voice shouted at him. *You're crazy to go on with it!*

"Damned if I'll eat it," he muttered sulkily to that voice and to his empty shadowed store, which ticked softly to itself like a bomb in a suitcase. "*Damned* if I will."

But that didn't mean he had to go haring off on any more stupid goddam trips trying to sell the sonofawhore, and he *certainly* didn't mean to take any more pictures with it. He judged there were at least three more "safe" ones left in it, and there were *probably* as many as seven, but he wasn't going to be the one to find out. Not at all.

Still, something might come up. You never knew. And it could hardly do him or anyone else any harm locked up in a drawer, could it?

"Nope," Pop agreed briskly to himself. He dropped the camera inside, locked the drawer, repocketed his keys, and then went to the door and turned CLOSED over to OPEN with the air of a man who has finally put some nagging problem behind him for good.

CHAPTER TEN

Pop woke up at three the next morning, bathed with sweat and peering fearfully into the dark. The clocks had just begun another weary run at the hour.

It was not this sound which awakened him, although it could have done, since he was not upstairs in his bed but down below, in the shop itself. The Emporium Galorium was a cave of darkness crowded with hulking shadows created by the streetlamp outside, which managed to send just enough light through the dirty plate-glass windows to create the unpleasant feeling of things hiding beyond the borders of vision.

It wasn't the *clocks* that woke him; it was the *flash*.

He was horrified to find himself standing in his pajamas beside his worktable with the Polaroid Sun 660 in his hands. The "special" drawer was open. He was aware that, although he had taken only a single picture, his finger had been pushing the button which triggered the shutter again and again and again. He would have taken a great many more than the one that protruded from the slot at the bottom of the camera but for simple good luck. There had only been a single picture left in the film pack currently in the camera.

Pop started to lower his arms—he had been holding the camera pointed toward the front of the shop, the viewfinder with its minute hairline crack held up to one open, sleeping eye—and when he got them down as far as his ribcage, they began to tremble and the muscles holding the hinges of his elbows just seemed to give way. His arms fell, his fingers opened, and the camera tumbled back into the "special" drawer with a clatter. The picture he had taken slipped from the slot and fluttered. It struck one edge of the open drawer, teetered first one way as if it would follow the camera in, and then the other. It fell on the floor.

Heart attack, Pop thought incoherently. *I'm gonna have a goddam Christing heart attack.*

He tried to raise his right arm, wanting to massage the left side of his chest with the hand on the end of it, but the arm wouldn't come. The hand on the end of it dangled as limp as a dead man at the end of a hangrope. The world wavered in and out of focus. The sound of the clocks (the tardy ones were just finishing up) faded away to distant echoes. Then the pain in his chest diminished, the light seemed to come back a little, and he realized all he was doing was trying to faint.

He made to sit down in the wheeled chair behind the worktable, and the business of lowering himself into the seat, like the business of lowering the camera, began all right, but before he had gotten even halfway down, *those* hinges, the ones that strapped his thighs and calves together by way of his knees, also gave way and he didn't so much sit in the chair as cave into it. It rolled a foot backward, struck a crate filled with old *Life* and *Look* magazines, and stopped.

Pop put his head down, the way you were supposed to do when

you felt lightheaded, and time passed. He had no idea at all, then or later, how much. He might even have gone back to sleep for a little while. But when he raised his head, he was more or less all right again. There was a steady dull throbbing at his temples and behind his forehead, probably because he had stuffed his goddam noodle with blood, hanging it over so long that way, but he found he could stand up and he knew what he had to do. When the thing had gotten hold of him so badly it could make him walk in his sleep, then make him (his mind tried to revolt at that verb, that *make,* but he wouldn't let it) take pictures with it, that was enough. He had no idea what the goddam thing was, but one thing was clear: you couldn't compromise with it.

Time to do what you should have let the boy do in the first place.

Yes. But not tonight. He was exhausted, drenched with sweat, and shivering. He thought he would have his work cut out for him just climbing the stairs to his apartment again, let alone swinging that sledge. He supposed he could do the job in here, simply pick it out of the drawer and dash it against the floor again and again, but there was a deeper truth, and he'd better own up to it: he couldn't have any more truck with that camera tonight. The morning would be time enough . . . and the camera couldn't do any damage between now and then, could it? There was no film in it.

Pop shut the drawer and locked it. Then he got up slowly, looking more like a man pushing eighty than seventy, and tottered slowly to the stairs. He climbed them one at a time, resting on each, clinging to the bannister (which was none too solid itself) with one hand while he held his heavy bunch of keys on their steel ring in the other. At last he made the top. With the door shut behind him, he seemed to feel a little stronger. He went back into his bedroom and got into bed, unaware as always of the strong yellow smell of sweat and old man that puffed up when he lay down—he changed the sheets on the first of every month and called it good.

I won't sleep now, he thought, and then: *Yes you will. You will because you can, and you can because tomorrow morning you're going to take the sledge and pound that fucking thing to pieces and there's an end to it.*

This thought and sleep came simultaneously, and Pop slept without dreaming, almost without moving, all the rest of that night. When he woke he was astonished to hear the clocks downstairs seeming to chime an extra stroke, all of them: eight instead of seven.

It wasn't until he looked at the light falling across the floor and wall in a slightly slanted oblong that he realized it really *was* eight; he had overslept for the first time in ten years. Then he remembered the night before. Now, in daylight, the whole episode seemed less weird; had he nearly *fainted*? Or was that maybe just a natural sort of weakness that came to a sleepwalker when he was unexpectedly wakened?

But of course, that was it, wasn't it? A little bright morning sunshine wasn't going to change that central fact: he *had* walked in his sleep, he *had* taken at least one picture and would have taken a whole slew of them if there had been more film in the pack.

He got up, got dressed, and went downstairs, meaning to see the thing in pieces before he even had his morning's coffee.

CHAPTER ELEVEN

Kevin wished his *first* visit to the two-dimensional town of Polaroidsville had also been his *last* visit there, but that was not the case. During the thirteen nights since the first one, he'd had the dream more and more often. If the dumb dream happened to take the night off—*little vacation, Kev, but seeya soon, okay?*—he was apt to have it twice the next night. Now he always *knew* it was a dream, and as soon as it started he would tell himself that all he had to do was wake himself up, *dammit, just wake yourself up!* Sometimes he *did* wake up, and sometimes the dream just faded back into deeper sleep, but he never succeeded in waking *himself* up.

It was always Polaroidsville now—never Oatley or Hildasville, those first two efforts of his fumbling mind to identify the place. And like the photograph, each dream took the action just a little bit further. First the man with the shopping-cart, which was never empty now even to start with but filled with a jumble of objects . . . mostly clocks, but all from the Emporium Galorium, and all with the eerie look not of real things but rather of *photographs* of real things which had been cut out of magazines and then somehow, impossibly, paradoxically, stuffed into a shopping-cart, which, since it was as two-dimensional as the objects themselves, had no breadth in which to store them. Yet there they were, and the old man hunched protectively over them and told Kevin to get out, that he was a fushing feef . . . only now he also told Kevin that if he *didn't* get out, "I'll sic Pop's dawg on you! Fee if I don't!"

The fat woman who couldn't be fat since she was perfectly flat but who was fat anyway came next. She appeared pushing her own shopping-cart filled with Polaroid Sun cameras. She also spoke to him before he passed her. "Be careful, boy," she'd say in the loud but toneless voice of one who is utterly deaf, "Pop's dog broke his leash and he's a mean un. He tore up three or four people at the Trenton Farm in Camberville before he came here. It's hard to take his pitcher, but you can't do it at all, 'less you have a cam'ra."

She would bend to get one, would sometimes get as far as holding it out, and he would reach for the camera, not knowing why the woman would think he should take the dog's picture or why he'd want to . . . or maybe he was just trying to be polite?

Either way, it made no difference. They both moved with the stately slowness of underwater swimmers, as dream-people so often do, and they always just missed making connections; when Kevin thought of this part of the dream, he often thought of the famous picture of God and Adam which Michelangelo had painted on the ceiling of the Sistine Chapel: each of them with an arm outstretched, and each with the hand at the end of the arm also outstretched, and the forefingers almost—not quite, but *almost*—touching.

Then she would disappear for a moment because she had no width, and when she reappeared again she was out of reach. *Well just go back to her, then,* Kevin would think each time the dream reached this point, but he couldn't. His feet carried him heedlessly and serenely onward to the peeling white picket fence and Pop and the dog . . . only the dog was no longer a dog but some horrible mixed thing that gave off heat and smoke like a dragon and had the teeth and twisted, scarred snout of a wild pig. Pop and the Sun dog would turn toward him at the same time, and Pop would have the camera—*his* camera, Kevin knew, because there was a piece chipped out of the side—up to his right eye. His left eye was squinted shut. His rimless spectacles glinted on top of his head in hazy sunlight. Pop and the Sun dog had all three dimensions. They were the only things in this seedy, creepy little dreamtown that did.

"He's the one!" Pop cried in a shrill, fearful voice. "He's the thief! Sic em, boy! *Pull his fuckin guts out is what I mean to say!*"

And as he screamed out this last, heatless lightning flashed in the day as Pop triggered the shutter and the flash, and Kevin turned to run. The dream had stopped here the second time he had had it. Now, on each subsequent occasion, things went a little further. Again he was moving with the aquatic slowness of a performer in an underwater ballet. He felt that, if he had been outside himself, he would even have *looked* like a dancer, his arms turning like the blades of a propeller just starting up, his shirt twisting with his body, pulling taut across his chest and his belly at the same time he heard the shirt's tail pulling free of his pants at the small of his back with a magnified rasp like sandpaper.

Then he was running back the way he came, each foot rising slowly and then floating dreamily (of *course* dreamily, what else, you fool? he would think at this point every time) back down until it hit the cracked and listless cement of the sidewalk, the soles of his tennis shoes flattening as they took his weight and spanking up small clouds of grit moving so slowly that he could see the individual particles revolving like atoms.

He ran slowly, yes, of course, and the Sun dog, nameless stray Grendel of a thing that came from nowhere and signified nothing and had all the sense of a cyclone but existed nevertheless, chased him slowly . . . but not *quite* as slowly.

On the third night, the dream faded into normal sleep just as Kevin began to turn his head in that dragging, maddening slow motion to see how much of a lead he had on the dog. It then skipped a night. On the following night it returned—twice. In the first dream he got his head halfway around so he could see the street on his left disappearing into limbo behind him as he ran along it; in the second (and from this one his alarm-clock woke him, sweating lightly in a crouched fetal position on the far side of the bed) he got his head turned enough to see the dog just as its forepaws came down in his own tracks, and he saw the paws were digging crumbly little craters in the cement because they had sprouted claws . . . and from the back of each lower leg-joint there protruded a long thorn of bone that looked like a spur. The thing's muddy reddish eye was locked on Kevin. Dim fire blew and dripped from its nostrils. *Jesus, Jesus Christ, its SNOT'S on fire,* Kevin thought, and when he woke he was horrified to hear himself whispering it over and over, very rapidly: ". . . snot's on fire, snot's on fire, snot's on fire."

Night by night the dog gained on him as he fled down the side-

walk. Even when he wasn't turning to look he could *hear* the Sun
dog gaining. He was aware of a spread of warmth from his crotch
and knew he was in enough fear to have wet himself, although the
emotion came through in the same diluted, numbed way he seemed
to have to move in this world. He could hear the Sun dog's paws
striking the cement, could hear the dry crack and squall of the
cement breaking. He could hear the hot blurts of its breath, the
suck of air flowing in past those outrageous teeth.

And on the night Pop woke up to find he had not only walked
in his sleep but taken at least one picture in it, Kevin *felt* as well
as heard the Sun dog's breath for the first time: a warm rush of air
on his buttocks like the sultry suck of wind a subway on an express
run pulls through a station where it needn't stop. He knew the dog
was close enough to spring on his back now, and that would come
next; he would feel one more breath, this one not just warm but
hot, as hot as acute indigestion in your throat, and then that crooked
living bear-trap of a mouth would sink deep into the flesh of his
back, between the shoulderblades, ripping the skin and meat off
his spine, and did he think this was really just a dream? *Did* he?

He awoke from this last one just as Pop was gaining the top of
the stairs to his apartment and resting one final time before going
inside back to bed. This time Kevin woke sitting bolt upright, the
sheet and blanket which had been over him puddled around his
waist, his skin covered with sweat and yet *freezing,* a million stiff
little white goose-pimples standing out all over his belly, chest,
back, and arms like stigmata. Even his cheeks seemed to crawl with
them.

And what he thought about was not the dream, or at least not
directly; he thought instead: *It's wrong, the number is wrong, it says
three but it can't—*

Then he flopped back and, in the way of children (for even at
fifteen most of him was still a child and would be until later that
day), he fell into a deep sleep again.

The alarm woke him at seven-thirty, as it always did on school
mornings, and he found himself sitting up in bed again, wide-eyed,
every piece suddenly in place. The Sun he had smashed hadn't been
his Sun, and that was why he kept having this same crazy dream
over and over and over again. Pop Merrill, that kindly old crackerbarrel philosopher and repairer of cameras and clocks and small
appliances, had euchered him and his father as neatly and compe-

tently as a riverboat gambler does the tenderfeet in an old Western movie.

His father—!

He heard the door downstairs slam shut and leaped out of bed. He took two running strides toward the door in his underwear, thought better of it, turned, yanked the window up, and hollered "*Dad!*" just as his father was folding himself into the car to go to work.

CHAPTER TWELVE

Pop dredged his key-ring up from his pocket, unlocked the "special" drawer, and took out the camera, once again being careful to hold it by the strap only. He looked with some hope at the front of the Polaroid, thinking he might see that the lens had been smashed in its latest tumble, hoping that the goddam thing's eye had been poked out, you might say, but his father had been fond of saying that the devil's luck is always in, and that seemed to be the case with Kevin Delevan's goddamned camera. The chipped place on the thing's side had chipped away a little more, but that was all.

He closed the drawer and, as he turned the key, saw the one picture he'd taken in his sleep lying face-down on the floor. As unable not to look at it as Lot's wife had been unable not to turn back and look at the destruction of Sodom, he picked it up with those blunt fingers that hid their dexterity from the world so well and turned it over.

The dog-creature had begun its spring. Its forepaws had barely left the ground, but along its misshapen backbone and in the bunches of muscle under the hide with its hair like the stiff filaments sticking out of black steel brushes he could see all that kinetic energy beginning to release itself. Its face and head were actually a little blurred in this photograph as its mouth yawned wider, and drifting up from the picture, like a sound heard under glass, he seemed to hear a low and throaty snarl beginning to rise toward a roar. The shadow-photographer looked as if he were trying to stumble back another pace, but what did it matter? That was smoke jetting from the holes in the dog-thing's muzzle, all right, *smoke,* and more smoke drifting back from the hinges of its open jaws in the little space where the croggled and ugly stake-wall of its teeth ended, and any man would stumble back from a horror like *that,* any man would try to turn and run, but all Pop had to do was look to tell you that the man (of *course* it was a man, maybe once it had been a boy, a teenage boy, but who had the camera now?) who had taken that picture in mere startled reflex, with a kind of wince of the finger . . . that man didn't have a nickel's worth of chances. That man could keep his feet or trip over them, and all the difference it would make would be as to how he died: while he was on his feet or while he was on his ass.

Pop crumpled the picture between his fingers and then stuck his key-ring back into his pocket. He turned, holding what had been Kevin Delevan's Polaroid Sun 660 and was now *his* Polaroid Sun 660 by the strap and started toward the back of the store; he would pause on the way just long enough to get the sledge. And as he neared the door to the back shed, a shutterflash, huge and white and soundless, went off not in front of his eyes but behind them, in his brain.

He turned back, and now his eyes were as empty as the eyes of a man who has been temporarily blinded by some bright light. He walked past the worktable with the camera now held in his hands at chest level, as one might carry a votive urn or some other sort of religious offering or relic. Halfway between the worktable and the front of the store was a bureau covered with clocks. To its left was one of the barnlike structure's support beams, and from a hook planted in this there hung another clock, an imitation German cuckoo clock. Pop grasped it by the roof and pulled it off its hook, indifferent to the counterweights, which immediately became entangled in one another's chains, and to the pendulum, which snapped off when one of the disturbed chains tried to twine around it. The little door below the roofpeak of the clock sprang ajar; the wooden bird poked out its beak and one startled eye. It gave a single choked sound—*kook!*—as if in protest of this rough treatment before creeping back inside again.

Pop hung the Sun by its strap on the hook where the clock had been, then turned and moved toward the back of the store for the second time, his eyes still blank and dazzled. He clutched the clock by its roof, swinging it back and forth indifferently, not hearing the cluds and clunks from inside it, or the occasional strangled sound

that might have been the bird trying to escape, not noticing when
one of the counterweights smacked the end of an old bed, snapped
off, and went rolling beneath, leaving a deep trail in the undisturbed
dust of years. He moved with the blank mindless purpose of a
robot. In the shed, he paused just long enough to pick up the
sledgehammer by its smooth shaft. With both hands thus filled, he
had to use the elbow of his left arm to knock the hook out of the
eyebolt so he could push open the shed door and walk into the
backyard.

He crossed to the chopping block and set the imitation German
cuckoo clock on it. He stood for a moment with his head inclined
down toward it, both of his hands now on the handle of the sledge.
His face remained blank, his eyes dim and dazzled, but there was
a part of his mind which not only thought clearly but thought *all*
of him was thinking—and acting—clearly. This part of him saw not
a cuckoo clock which hadn't been worth much to begin with and
was now broken in the bargain; it saw Kevin's Polaroid. This part
of his mind really believed he had come downstairs, gotten the
Polaroid from the drawer, and proceeded directly out back, pausing
only to get the sledge.

And it was this part that would do his remembering later . . .
unless it became convenient for him to remember some other truth.
Or any other truth, for that matter.

Pop Merrill raised the sledgehammer over his right shoulder and
brought it down hard—not as hard as Kevin had done, but hard
enough to do the job. It struck squarely on the roof of the imitation
German cuckoo clock. The clock did not so much break or shatter
as *splatter;* pieces of plastic wood and little gears and springs flew
everywhere. And what that little piece of Pop which saw would
remember (unless, of course, it became convenient to remember
otherwise) were pieces of *camera* splattering everywhere.

He pulled the sledge off the block and stood for a moment with
his meditating, unseeing eyes on the shambles. The bird, which to
Pop looked exactly like a film-case, a Polaroid Sun film-case, was
lying on its back with its little wooden feet sticking straight up in
the air, looking both deader than any bird outside of a cartoon ever
looked and yet somehow miraculously unhurt at the same time. He
had his look, then turned and headed back toward the shed door.

"There," he muttered under his breath. "Good 'nuff."

Someone standing even very close to him might have been unable to pick up the words themselves, but it would have been hard to miss the unmistakable tone of relief with which they were spoken.

"*That's* done. Don't have to worry about *that* anymore. Now what's next? Pipe-tobacco, isn't it?"

But when he got to the drugstore on the other side of the block fifteen minutes later, it was not pipe-tobacco he asked for (although that was what he would *remember* asking for). He asked for film.

Polaroid film.

CHAPTER THIRTEEN

"Kevin, I'm going to be late for work if I don't—"

"Will you call in? Can you? Call in and say you'll be late, or that you might not get there at all? If it was something really, really, *really* important?"

Warily, Mr. Delevan asked, "What's the something?"

"*Could* you?"

Mrs. Delevan was standing in the doorway of Kevin's bedroom now. Meg was behind her. Both of them were eyeing the man in his business suit and the tall boy, still wearing only his Jockey shorts, curiously.

"I suppose I—yes, say I could. But I won't until I know what it *is*."

Kevin lowered his voice, and, cutting his eyes toward the door, he said: "It's about Pop Merrill. And the camera."

Mr. Delevan, who had at first only looked puzzled at what Kevin's eyes were doing, now went to the door. He murmured something to his wife, who nodded. Then he closed the door, paying no more attention to Meg's protesting whine than he would have to a bird singing a bundle of notes on a telephone wire outside the bedroom window.

"What did you tell Mom?" Kevin asked.

"That it was man-to-man stuff." Mr. Delevan smiled a little. "I think *she* thinks you want to talk about masturbating."

Kevin flushed.

Mr. Delevan looked concerned. "You don't, do you? I mean, you know about—"

"I know, I know," Kevin said hastily; he was not about to tell his father (and wasn't sure he would have been able to put the right string of words together, even if he had wanted to) that what had thrown him momentarily off-track was finding out that not only did his *father* know about whacking off—which of course shouldn't have surprised him at all but somehow did, leaving him with feelings of surprise at his own surprise—but that his *mother* somehow did, too.

Never mind. All this had nothing to do with the nightmares, or with the new certainty which had locked into place in his head.

"It's about Pop, I told you. And some bad dreams I've been having. But mostly it's about the camera. Because Pop stole it somehow, Dad."

"Kevin—"

"I beat it to pieces on his chopping block, I know. But it wasn't *my* camera. It was *another* camera. And that isn't even the worst thing. The worst thing is that *he's still using mine to take pictures*! And that dog is going to get out! When it does, I think it's going to kill me. In that other world it's already started to j-j-j—"

He couldn't finish. Kevin surprised himself again—this time by bursting into tears.

By the time John Delevan got his son calmed down it was ten minutes of eight, and he had resigned himself to at least being late for work. He held the boy in his arms—whatever it was, it really had the kid shook, and if it really *was* nothing but a bunch of dreams, Mr. Delevan supposed he would find sex at the root of the matter someplace.

When Kevin was shivering and only sucking breath deep into his lungs in an occasional dry-sob, Mr. Delevan went to the door and opened it cautiously, hoping Kate had taken Meg downstairs. She had; the hallway was empty. *That's one for our side, anyway,* he thought, and went back to Kevin.

"Can you talk now?" he asked.

"Pop's got my camera," Kevin said hoarsely. His red eyes, still watery, peered at his father almost myopically. "He got it somehow, and he's using it."

"And this is something you *dreamed?*"

"Yes . . . and I remembered something."

"Kevin . . . that *was* your camera. I'm sorry, son, but it *was*. I even saw the little chip in the side."

"He must have rigged that somehow—"

"Kevin, that seems pretty farf—"

"Listen," Kevin said urgently, "will you just *listen?*"

"All right. Yes. I'm listening."

"What I remembered was that when he handed me the camera—when we went out back to crunch it, remember?"

"Yes—"

"I looked in the little window where the camera keeps count of how many shots there are left. And it said three, Dad! It said *three!*"

"Well? What about it?"

"It had film in it, too! *Film!* I know, because I remember one of those shiny black things jumping up when I squashed the camera. It jumped up and then it fluttered back down."

"I repeat: so what?"

"*There wasn't any film in my camera when I gave it to Pop!* That's so-what. I had twenty-eight pictures. He wanted me to take thirty more, for a total of fifty-eight. I might have bought more film if I'd known what he was up to, but probably not. By then I was scared of the thing—"

"Yeah. I was, a little, too."

Kevin looked at him respectfully. "Were you?"

"Yeah. Go on. I think I see where you're heading."

"I was just going to say, he chipped in for the film, but not enough—not even half. He's a *wicked* skinflint, Dad."

John Delevan smiled thinly. "He is that, my boy. One of the world's greatest, is what I mean to say. Go on and finish up. *Tempus* is *fugiting* away like mad."

Kevin glanced at the clock. It was almost eight. Although neither of them knew it, Pop would wake up in just under two minutes and start about his morning's business, very little of which he would remember correctly.

"All right," Kevin said. "All I'm trying to say is I couldn't have bought any more film even if I'd wanted to. I used up all the money I had buying the three film packs. I even borrowed a buck from Megan, so I let her shoot a couple, too."

"Between the two of you, you used up *all* the exposures? Every single one?"

"Yes! *Yes!* He even *said* it was fifty-eight! And between the time when I finished shooting all the pictures he wanted and when we went to look at the tape he made, I never bought any more film. It was *dead empty* when I brought it in, Dad! The number in the little window was a *zero!* I saw it, I remember! So if it was my camera, how come it said *three* in the window when we went back downstairs?"

"He *couldn't* have—" Then his father stopped, and a queer look of uncharacteristic gloom came over his face as he realized that Pop *could* have, and that the truth of it was this: he, John Delevan, didn't want to believe that Pop *had;* that even bitter experience had not been sufficient vaccination against foolishness, and Pop might have pulled the wool over his own eyes as well as those of his son.

"Couldn't have *what?* What are you thinking about, Dad? Something just hit you!"

Something had hit him, all right. How eager Pop had been to go downstairs and get the original Polaroids so they could all get a closer look at the thing around the dog's neck, the thing that turned out to be Kevin's latest string tie from Aunt Hilda, the one with the bird on it that was probably a woodpecker.

We might as well go down with you, Kevin had said when Pop had offered to get the photos, but hadn't Pop jumped up himself, chipper as a chickadee? *Won't take a minute,* the old man had said, or some such thing, and the truth was, Mr. Delevan told himself, I hardly noticed *what* he was saying or doing, because I wanted to watch that goddamned tape again. And the truth *also* was this: Pop hadn't even had to pull the old switcheroo right in front of them— although, with his eyes unwooled, Mr. Delevan was reluctantly willing to believe the old son of a bitch had probably been prepared to do just that, if he had to, and probably *could* have done it, too, pushing seventy or not. With them upstairs and him downstairs, presumably doing no more than getting Kevin's photographs, he could have swapped *twenty* cameras, at his leisure.

"*Dad?*"

"I suppose he could have," Mr. Delevan said. "But why?"

Kevin could only shake his head. He didn't know why. But that was all right; Mr. Delevan thought *he* did, and it was something of a relief. Maybe honest men *didn't* have to learn the world's simplest truths over and over again; maybe some of those truths eventually stuck fast. He'd only had to articulate the question aloud in order to find the answer. Why did the Pop Merrills of this world do anything? To make a profit. That was the reason, the whole reason, and nothing but the reason. Kevin had wanted to destroy it. After looking at Pop's videotape, Mr. Delevan had found himself in accord with that. Of the three of them, who had been the only one capable of taking a longer view?

Why, Pop, or course. Reginald Marion "Pop" Merrill.

John Delevan had been sitting on the edge of Kevin's bed with an arm about his son's shoulders. Now he stood up. "Get dressed. I'll go downstairs and call in. I'll tell Brandon I'll probably just be late, but to assume I won't be in at all."

He was preoccupied with this, already talking to Brandon Reed in his mind, but not so preoccupied he didn't see the gratitude which lighted his son's worried face. Mr. Delevan smiled a little and felt that uncharacteristic gloom first ease and then let go entirely. There was this much, at least: his son was as yet not too old to take comfort from him, or accept him as a higher power to whom appeals could sometimes be directed in the knowledge that they would be acted upon; nor was he himself too old to take comfort from his son's comfort.

"I think," he said, moving toward the door, "that we ought to pay a call on Pop Merrill." He glanced at the clock on Kevin's night-table. It was ten minutes after eight, and in back of the Emporium Galorium, a sledgehammer was coming down on an imitation German cuckoo clock. "He usually opens around eight-thirty. Just about the time we'll get there, I think. If you get a wiggle on, that is."

He paused on his way out and a brief, cold smile flickered on his mouth. He was not smiling at his son. "I think he's got some explaining to do, is what I mean to say."

Mr. Delevan went out, closing the door behind him. Kevin quickly began to dress.

CHAPTER FOURTEEN

The Castle Rock LaVerdiere's Super Drug Store was a lot more than just a drugstore. Put another way, it was really only a drugstore as an afterthought. It was as if someone had noticed at the last moment—just before the grand opening, say—that one of the words in the sign was still "Drug." That someone might have made a mental note to tell someone else, someone in the company's management, that here they were, opening yet another LaVerdiere's, and they had by simple oversight neglected yet again to correct the sign so it read, more simply and accurately, LaVerdiere's Super Store . . . and, after making the mental note, the someone in charge of noticing such things had delayed the grand opening a day or two so they could shoe-horn in a prescription counter about the size of a telephone booth in the long building's furthest, darkest, and most neglected corner.

The LaVerdiere's Super Drug Store was really more of a jumped-up five-and-dime than anything else. The town's last *real* five-and-dime, a long dim room with feeble, fly-specked overhead globes hung on chains and reflected murkily in the creaking but often-waxed wooden floor, had been The Ben Franklin Store. It had given up the ghost in 1978 to make way for a video-games arcade called Galaxia and E-Z Video Rentals, where Tuesday was Toofers Day and no one under the age of twenty could go in the back room.

LaVerdiere's carried everything the old Ben Franklin had carried, but the goods were bathed in the pitiless light of Maxi-Glo fluorescent bars which gave every bit of stock its own hectic, feverish shimmer. *Buy me!* each item seemed to shriek. *Buy me or you may die! Or your wife may die! Or your kids! Or your best friend! Possibly all of them at once! Why? How should I know? I'm just a brainless item sitting on a pre-fab LaVerdiere's shelf! But doesn't it feel true? You know it does! So buy me and buy me RIGHT . . . NOW!*

There was an aisle of notions, two aisles of first-aid supplies and nostrums, an aisle of video and audio tapes (both blank and pre-recorded). There was a long rack of magazines giving way to paperback books, a display of lighters under one digital cash-register and a display of watches under another (a third register was hidden in the dark corner where the pharmacist lurked in his lonely shadows). Halloween candy had taken over most of the toy aisle (the toys would not only come back after Halloween but eventually take over two whole aisles as the days slid remorselessly down toward Christmas). And, like something too neat to exist in reality except as a kind of dumb admission that there *was* such a thing as Fate with a capital F, and that Fate might, in its own way, indicate the existence of that whole "other world" about which Pop had never before cared (except in terms of how it might fatten his pocketbook, that was) and about which Kevin Delevan had never before even thought, at the front of the store, in the main display area, was a carefully arranged work of salesmanship which was billed as the FALL FOTO FESTIVAL.

This display consisted of a basket of colorful autumn leaves spilling out on the floor in a bright flood (a flood too large to actually have come from that one basket alone, a careful observer might have concluded). Amid the leaves were a number of Kodak and Polaroid cameras—several Sun 660s among the latter—and all sorts of other equipment: cases, albums, film, flashbars. In the midst of this odd cornucopia, an old-fashioned tripod rose like one of H. G. Wells's Martian death-machines towering over the crispy wreck of London. It bore a sign which told all patrons interested enough to look that this week one could obtain SUPER REDUCTIONS ON ALL POLAROID CAMERAS & ACCESSORIES!

At eight-thirty that morning, half an hour after LaVerdiere's opened for the day, "all patrons" consisted of Pop Merrill and Pop alone. He took no notice of the display but marched straight to the only open counter, where Molly Durham had just finished laying out the watches on their imitation-velvet display-cloth.

Oh no, here comes old Eyeballs, she thought, and grimaced. Pop's idea of a really keen way to kill a stretch of time about as long as Molly's coffee-break was to kind of *ooze* up to the counter where she was working (he always picked hers, even if he had to stand in line; in fact, she thought he liked it better when there *was* a line) and buy a pouch of Prince Albert tobacco. This was a purchase an ordinary fellow could transact in maybe thirty seconds, but if she got Eyeballs out of her face in under three minutes, she thought she was doing very well indeed. He kept all of his money in a cracked leather purse on a chain, and he'd haul it out of his pocket— giving his doorbells a good feel on the way, it always looked to Molly—and then open it. It always gave out a little *screee-eek!* noise, and honest to God if you didn't expect to see a moth flutter out of it, just like in those cartoons people draw of tightwads. On top of the purse's contents there would be a whole mess of paper money, bills that looked somehow as if you shouldn't handle them, as if they might be coated with disease germs of some kind, and jingling silver underneath. Pop would fish out a dollar bill and then kind of hook the other bills to one side with one of those thick fingers of his to get to the change underneath—he'd never give you a couple of bucks, hunh-uh, that would make everything too quick to suit him—and then he'd work *that* out, too. And all the time his eyes would be busy, flicking down to the purse for a second or two but mostly letting the fingers sort out the proper coins by touch while his eyes crawled over her boobs, her belly, her hips, and then back up to her boobs again. Never once her face; not even so far as her mouth, which *was* a part of a girl in which most men seemed to be interested; no, Pop Merrill was strictly interested in the lower portions of the female anatomy. When he finally finished—and no matter how quick that was, it always seemed like three times as long to Molly—and got the hell out of the store again, she always felt like going somewhere and taking a long shower.

So she braced herself, put on her best it's-only-eight-thirty-and-I've-got-seven-and-a-half-hours-to-go smile, and stood at the counter as Pop approached. She told herself, *He's only looking at you, guys have been doing that since you sprouted,* and that was true, but this wasn't the same. Because Pop Merrill wasn't like most of the guys who had run their eyes over her trim and eminently watchable superstructure since that time ten years ago. Part of it was that Pop was *old,* but that wasn't all of it. The truth was that some guys looked at you and some—a very few—seemed to actually be feeling you up with their eyes, and Merrill was one of *those.* His gaze actually seemed to have weight; when he fumbled in his creaky old-maid's purse on its length of incongruously masculine chain, she seemed to actually *feel* his eyes squirming up and down her front, lashing their way up her hills on their optic nerves like tadpoles and then sliding bonelessly down into her valleys, making her wish she had worn a nun's habit to work that day. Or maybe a suit of armor.

But her mother had been fond of saying *What can't be cured must be endured, sweet Molly,* and until someone discovered a method of weighing gazes so those of dirty men both young and old could be outlawed, or, more likely, until Pop Merrill did everyone in Castle Rock a favor by dying so that eyesore of a tourist trap he kept could be torn down, she would just have to deal with it as best she could.

But today she was in for a pleasant surprise—or so it seemed at first. Pop's usual hungry appraisal was not even an ordinary patron's look; it seemed utterly blank. It wasn't that he looked through her, or that his gaze struck her and bounced off. It seemed to Molly that he was so deep in his thoughts that his usually penetrating look did not even reach her, but made it about halfway and then petered out—like a man trying to locate and observe a star on the far side of the galaxy with just the naked eye.

"May I help you, Mr. Merrill?" she asked, and her feet were already cocking so she could turn quickly and reach up for where the pouches of tobacco were kept. With Pop, this was a task she always did as quickly as possible, because when she turned and reached, she could feel his eyes crawling busily over her ass, dropping for a quick check of her legs, then rising again to her butt for a final ocular squeeze and perhaps a pinch before she turned back.

"Yes," he said calmly and serenely, and he might as well have been talking to one of those automated bank machines for all the interest in her he showed. That was fine by Molly. "I'd like some" and then either a word she didn't hear right or one that was utter gibberish. If it was gobbledegook, she thought with some hope, maybe the first few parts of the complicated network of dikes, levees, and spillways the old crock had constructed against the rising sea of senility were finally giving way.

It *sounded* as if he had said *toefilmacco,* which wasn't a product they stocked . . . unless it was a prescription drug of some sort.

"I beg pardon, Mr. Merrill?"

"Film," he said, so clearly and firmly that Molly was more than disappointed; she was convinced he must have said it just that way the first time and her ears had picked it up wrong. Maybe *she* was the one who was beginning to lose her dikes and levees.

"What kind would you like?"

"Polaroid," he said. "Two packs." She didn't know exactly what was going on here, but it was beyond doubt that Castle Rock's premier dirty old man was not himself today. His eyes would still not focus, and the words . . . they reminded her of something, something she associated with her five-year-old niece, Ellen, but she couldn't catch hold of it.

"For what model, Mr. Merrill?"

She sounded brittle and actressy to herself, but Pop Merrill didn't even come close to noticing. Pop was lost in the ozone.

After a moment's consideration in which he did not look at her at all but seemed instead to study the racks of cigarettes behind her left shoulder, he jerked out: "For a Polaroid Sun camera. Model 660." And then it came to her, even as she told him she'd have to get it from the display. Her niece owned a big soft panda toy, which she had, for reasons which would probably make sense only to another little girl, named Paulette. Somewhere inside of Paulette was an electronic circuit-board and a memory chip on which were stored about four hundred short, simple sentences such as "I like to hug, don't you?" and "I wish you'd *never* go away." Whenever you poked Paulette above her fuzzy little navel, there was a brief pause and then one of those lovesome little remarks would come out, almost *jerk* out, in a somehow remote and emotionless voice that seemed by its tone to deny the content of the words. Ellen thought Paulette was the nuts. Molly thought there was something creepy about it; she kept expecting Ellen to poke the panda-doll in the guts someday and it would surprise them all (except for Aunt Molly from Castle Rock) by saying what was *really* on its mind. "I think tonight after you're asleep I'll strangle you dead," perhaps, or maybe just "I have a knife."

Pop Merrill sounded like Paulette the stuffed panda this morning. His blank gaze was uncannily like Paulette's. Molly had thought any change from the old man's usual leer would be a welcome one. She had been wrong.

Molly bent over the display, for once totally unconscious of the way her rump was poking out, and tried to find what the old man wanted as quickly as she could. She was sure that when she turned around, Pop would be looking at anything but her. This time she was right. When she had the film and started back (brushing a couple of errant fall leaves from one of the boxes), Pop was still staring at the cigarette racks, at first glance appearing to look so closely he might have been inventorying the stock. It took a second or two to see that that expression was no expression at all, really, but a gaze of almost divine blankness.

Please get out of here, Molly prayed. *Please, just take your film and go. And whatever else you do, don't touch me. Please.*

If he touched her while he was looking like that, Molly thought she would scream. Why did the place have to be empty? Why couldn't at least one other customer be in here, preferably Sheriff Pangborn, but since he seemed to be otherwise engaged, anyone at all? She supposed Mr. Constantine, the pharmacist, was in the store someplace, but the drug counter looked easily a quarter of a mile away, and while she knew it *couldn't* be that far, not really, it was still too far for him to reach her in a hurry if old man Merrill decided to touch her. And suppose Mr. Constantine had gone out to Nan's for coffee with Mr. Keeton from the selectmen's office? The more she thought about that possibility, the more likely it seemed. When something genuinely weird like this happened, wasn't it an almost foregone conclusion that it should happen while one was alone?

He's having a mental breakdown of some kind.

She heard herself saying with glassy cheerfulness: "Here you are, Mr. Merrill." She put the film on the counter and scooted to her left and behind the register at once, wanting it between her and him.

The ancient leather purse came out of Pop Merrill's pants, and her stuttering fingers miskeyed the purchase so she had to clear the register and start again.

He was holding two ten-dollar bills out to her.

She told herself they were only *rumpled* from being squashed up with the other bills in that little pocketbook, probably not even old, although they *looked* old. That didn't stop her galloping mind, however. Her mind insisted that they weren't just *rumpled,* they were rumpled and *slimy.* It further insisted that *old* wasn't the right word, that *old* wasn't even in the ballpark. For those particular items of currency, not even the word *ancient* would do. Those were *prehistoric* tens, somehow printed before Christ was born and Stonehenge was built, before the first low-browed, no-neck Neanderthal had crawled out of his cave. They belonged to a time when even God had been a baby.

She didn't want to touch them.

She *had* to touch them.

The man would want his change.

Steeling herself, she took the bills and shoved them into the cash register as fast as she could, banging a finger so hard she ripped most of the nail clear off, an ordinarily exquisite pain she would not notice, in her extreme state of distress, until sometime later . . . when, that was, she had chivvied her willing mind around enough to scold herself for acting like a whoopsy little girl on the edge of her first menstrual period.

At the moment, however, she only concentrated on getting the bills into the register as fast as she could and getting her hand *off* them, but even later she would remember what the surfaces of those tens had felt like. It felt as if they were actually crawling and moving under the pads of her fingers; as if billions of germs, *huge* germs almost big enough to be seen with the naked eye, were sliding along them toward her, eager to infect her with whatever *he* had.

But the man would want his change.

She concentrated on that, lips pressed together so tightly they were dead white; four singles that did not, absolutely did *not* want to come out from beneath the roller that held them down in the cash drawer. Then a dime, but oh Jesus-please-us, there *were* no dimes, and what the hell was *wrong* with her, what had she done to be saddled for so long with this weird old man on the one morning in recorded history when he actually seemed to want to get out of here in a hurry?

She fished out a nickel, feeling the silent, stinky loom of him so close to her (and she felt that when she was finally forced to look up she would see he was even closer, that he was leaning over the counter toward her), then three pennies, four, five . . . but the last one dropped back into the drawer among the quarters and she had to fish for it with one of her cold, numb fingers. It almost squirted away from her again; she could feel sweat popping out on the nape of her neck and on the little strip of skin between her nose and her upper lip. Then, clutching the coins tightly in her fist and praying he wouldn't have his hand outstretched to receive them so she would have to touch his dry, reptilian skin, but knowing, somehow *knowing* that he would, she looked up, feeling her bright and cheery LaVerdiere's smile stretching the muscles of her face in a kind of frozen scream, trying to steel herself for even *that,* telling herself it would be the last, and never mind the image her stupid, insisting mind kept trying to make her see, an image of that dry hand suddenly snapping shut over hers like the talon of some old and horrid bird, a bird not of prey, no, not even that, but one of carrion; she told herself she did not see those images, absolutely did *NOT*, and, seeing them all the same, she looked up with that smile screaming off her face as brightly as a cry of murder on a hot still night, and the store was empty.

Pop was gone.

He had left while she was making change.

Molly began to shudder all over. If she had needed concrete proof that the old geezer was not right, this was it. This was proof positive, proof indubitable, proof of the purest ray serene: for the first time in her memory (and in the living memory of the town, she would have bet, and she would have won her bet), Pop Merrill, who refused to tip even on those rare occasions when he was forced to eat in a restaurant that had no take-out service, had left a place of business without waiting for his change.

Molly tried to open her hand and let go of the four ones, the nickel, and the five pennies. She was stunned to find she couldn't do it. She had to reach over with her other hand and pry the fingers loose. Pop's change dropped to the glass top of the counter and she swept it off to one side, not wanting to touch it.

And she never wanted to see Pop Merrill again.

CHAPTER FIFTEEN

Pop's vacant gaze held as he left LaVerdiere's. It held as he crossed the sidewalk with the boxes of film in his hand. It broke and became an expression of somehow unsettling alertness as he stepped off into the gutter . . . and stopped there, with one foot on the sidewalk and one planted amid the litter of squashed cigarette butts and empty potato-chip bags. Here was another Pop Molly would not have recognized, although there were those who had been sharp-traded by the old man who would have known it quite well. This was neither Merrill the lecher nor Merrill the robot, but Merrill the animal with its wind up. All at once he was *there,* in a way he seldom allowed himself to be *there* in public. Showing so much of one's true self in public was not, in Pop's estimation, a good idea. This morning, however, he was far from being in command of himself, and there was no one out to observe him, anyway. If there had been, that person would not have seen Pop the folksy cracker-barrel philosopher or even Pop the sharp trader, but something like the *spirit* of the man. In that moment of being totally *there,* Pop looked like a rogue dog himself, a stray who has gone feral and now pauses amid a midnight henhouse slaughter, raggedy ears up, head cocked, bloodstreaked teeth showing a little as he hears some sound from the farmer's house and thinks of the shotgun with its wide black holes like a figure eight rolled onto its side. The dog knows nothing of figure eights, but even a dog may recognize the dim shape of eternity if its instincts are honed sharp enough.

Across the town square he could see the urine-yellow front of the Emporium Galorium, standing slightly apart from its nearest neighbors: the vacant building which had housed The Village Wash-tub until earlier that year, Nan's Luncheonette, and You Sew and Sew, the dress-and-notions shop run by Evvie Chalmers's great-granddaughter, Polly—a woman of whom we must speak at another time.

There were slant-parking spaces in front of all the shops on Lower Main Street, and all of them were empty . . . except for one, which was just now being filled with a Ford station-wagon Pop recognized. The light throb of its engine was clearly audible in the morning-still air. Then it cut off, the brakelights went out, and Pop pulled back the foot which had been in the gutter and prudently withdrew himself to the corner of LaVerdiere's. Here he stood as still as that dog who has been alerted in the henhouse by some small sound, the sort of sound which might be disregarded in the killing frenzy of dogs neither so old nor so wise as this one.

John Delevan got out from behind the wheel of the station-wagon. The boy got out on the passenger side. They went to the door of the Emporium Galorium. The man began to knock impa-tiently, loud enough so the sound of it came as clearly to Pop as the sound of the engine had done. Delevan paused, they both listened, and then Delevan started in again, not knocking now but *hammering* at the door, and you didn't have to be a goddam mind-reader to know the man was steamed up.

They know, Pop thought. *Somehow they know. Damned good thing I smashed the fucking camera.*

He stood a moment longer, nothing moving except his hooded eyes, and then he slipped around the corner of the drugstore and into the alley between it and the neighboring bank. He did it so smoothly that a man fifty years younger might have envied the almost effortless agility of the movement.

This morning, Pop figured, it might be a little wiser to go back home by backyard express.

CHAPTER SIXTEEN

When there was still no answer, John Delevan went at the door a third time, hammering so hard he made the glass rattle loosely in its rotting putty gums and hurt his hand. It was hurting his hand that made him realize how angry he was. Not that he felt the anger was in any way unjustified if Merrill had done what Kevin thought he had done—and yes, the more he thought about it, the more John Delevan was sure that Kevin was right. But he was surprised that he hadn't recognized the anger for what it was until just now.

This seems to be a morning for learning about myself, he thought, and there was something schoolmarmish in that. It allowed him to smile and relax a little.

Kevin was not smiling, nor did he look relaxed.

"It seems like one of three things has happened," Mr. Delevan said to his son. "Merrill's either not up, not answering the door, or he figured we were getting warm and he's absconded with your camera." He paused, then actually laughed. "I guess there's a fourth, too. Maybe he died in his sleep."

"He didn't die." Kevin now stood with his head against the dirty glass of the door he mightily wished he had never gone through in the first place. He had his hands cupped around his eyes to make blinders, because the sun rising over the east side of the town square ran a harsh glare across the glass. "Look."

Mr. Delevan cupped his own hands to the sides of his face and pressed his nose to the glass. They stood there side by side, backs to the square, looking into the dimness of the Emporium Galorium like the world's most dedicated window-shoppers. "Well," he said after a few seconds, "it looks like if he absconded he left his shit behind."

"Yeah—but that's not what I mean. Do you see it?"

"See what?"

"Hanging on that post. The one by the bureau with all the clocks on it."

And after a moment, Mr. Delevan did see it: a Polaroid camera, hanging by its strap from a hook on the post. He thought he could even see the chipped place, although that might have been his imagination.

It's not your imagination.

The smile faded off his lips as he realized he was starting to feel what Kevin was feeling: the weird and distressing certainty that some simple yet terribly dangerous piece of machinery was running . . . and unlike most of Pop's clocks, it was running right on time.

"Do you think he's just sitting upstairs and waiting for us to go away?" Mr. Delevan spoke aloud, but he was really talking to himself. The lock on the door looked both new and expensive . . . but he was willing to bet that if one of them—probably Kevin was in better shape—hit the door hard enough, it would rip right through the old wood. He mused randomly: *A lock is only as good as the door you put it in. People never think.*

Kevin turned his strained face to look at his father. In that moment, John Delevan was as struck by Kevin's face as Kevin had been by his not long ago. He thought: *I wonder how many fathers get a chance to see what their sons will look like as men? He won't always look this strained, this tightly drawn—God, I hope not—but this is what he will look like. And, Jesus, he's going to be handsome!*

He, like Kevin, had that one moment in the midst of whatever it was that was going on here, and the moment was a short one, but he also never forgot; it was always within his mind's reach.

"What?" Kevin asked hoarsely. "What, Dad?"

"You want to bust it? Because I'd go along."

"Not yet. I don't think we'll have to. I don't think he's here . . . but he's close."

You can't know any such thing. Can't even think it.

But his son *did* think it, and he believed Kevin was right. Some sort of link had been formed between Pop and his son. "Some sort" of link? Get serious. He knew perfectly well what the link was. It was that fucking camera hanging on the wall in there, and the longer this went on, the longer he felt that machinery running, its gears grinding and its vicious unthinking cogs turning, the less he liked it.

Break the camera, break the link, he thought, and said: "Are you sure, Kev?"

"Let's go around to the back. Try the door there."

"There's a gate. He'll keep it locked."

"Maybe we can climb over."

"Okay," Mr. Delevan said, and followed his son down the steps of the Emporium Galorium and around to the alley, wondering as he went if he had lost his mind.

But the gate wasn't locked. Somewhere along the line Pop had forgotten to lock it, and although Mr. Delevan hadn't liked the idea of climbing over the fence, or maybe *falling* over the fence, quite likely tearing the hell out of his balls in the process, he somehow liked the open gate even less. All the same, he and Kevin went through it and into Pop's littered backyard, which not even the drifts of fallen October leaves could improve.

Kevin wove his way through the piles of junk Pop had thrown out but not bothered to take to the dump, and Mr. Delevan followed him. They arrived at the chopping block at about the same time Pop was coming out of Mrs. Althea Linden's backyard and onto Mulberry Street, a block west. He would follow Mulberry Street until he reached the offices of the Wolf Jaw Lumber Company. Although the company's pulp trucks would already be coursing the roads of western Maine and the yowl and yark of the cutters' chain-saws would have been rising from the area's diminishing stands of hardwood since six-thirty or so, no one would come in to man the office until nine, which was still a good fifteen minutes away. At the rear of the lumber company's tiny backyard was a high board fence. It was gated, and this gate *was* locked, but Pop had the key. He would unlock the gate and step through into his own backyard.

Kevin reached the chopping block. Mr. Delevan caught up, followed his son's gaze, and blinked. He opened his mouth to ask what in the hell *this* was all about, then shut it again. He was starting to have an idea of what in the hell it was all about without any aid from Kevin. It wasn't *right* to have such ideas, wasn't *natural,* and he knew from bitter experience (in which Reginald Marion "Pop" Merrill himself had played a part at one point, as he had told his son not so long ago) that doing things on impulse was a good way to reach the wrong decision and go flying off half-cocked, but it didn't matter. Although he did not think it in such terms, it would be fair to say Mr. Delevan just hoped he could apply for readmittance to the Reasonable tribe when this was over.

At first he thought he was looking at the smashed remains of a Polaroid camera. Of course that was just his mind, trying to find a little rationality in repetition; what lay on and around the chopping block didn't look anything at all like a camera, Polaroid or otherwise. All those gears and flywheels could only belong to a clock. Then he saw the dead cartoon-bird and even knew what kind of clock. He opened his mouth to ask Kevin why in God's name Pop would bring a cuckoo clock out back and then sledgehammer it to death. He thought it over again and decided he didn't have to ask, after all. The answer to that was also beginning to come. He didn't *want* it to come, because it pointed to madness on what seemed to Mr. Delevan a grand scale, but that didn't matter; it came anyway.

You had to hang a cuckoo clock on something. You had to hang it because of the pendulum weights. And what did you hang it on? Why, a hook, of course.

Maybe a hook sticking out of a beam.

Like the beam Kevin's Polaroid had been hanging on.

Now he spoke, and his words seemed to come from some long distance away: "What in the hell is wrong with him, Kevin? Has he gone nuts?"

"Not *gone*," Kevin answered, and his voice also seemed to come from some long distance away as they stood above the chopping block, looking down on the busted timepiece. "*Driven* there. By the camera."

"We've got to smash it," Mr. Delevan said. His voice seemed to float to his ears long after he had felt the words coming out of his mouth.

"Not yet," Kevin said. "We have to go to the drugstore first. They're having a special sale on them."

"Having a special sale on wh—"

Kevin touched his arm. John Delevan looked at him. Kevin's head was up, and he looked like a deer scenting fire. In that moment the boy was more than handsome; he was almost divine, like a young poet at the hour of his death.

"*What?*" Mr. Delevan asked urgently.

"Did you hear something?" Alertness slowly changing to doubt.

"A car on the street," Mr. Delevan said. How much older was he than his son? he wondered suddenly. Twenty-five years? Jesus, wasn't it time he started acting it?

He pushed the strangeness away from him, trying to get it at arm's length. He groped desperately for his maturity and found a little of it. Putting it on was like putting on a badly tattered overcoat.

"You sure that's all it was, Dad?"

"Yes. Kevin, you're wound up too tight. Get hold of yourself or . . ." Or what? But he knew, and laughed shakily. "Or you'll have us both running like a pair of rabbits."

Kevin looked at him thoughtfully for a moment, like someone coming out of a deep sleep, perhaps even a trance, and then nodded. "Come on."

"Kevin, why? What do you want? He could be upstairs, just not answering—"

"I'll tell you when we get there, Dad. Come *on*." And almost dragged his father out of the littered backyard and into the narrow alleyway.

"Kevin, do you want to take my arm off, or what?" Mr. Delevan asked when they got back to the sidewalk.

"He was back there," Kevin said. "Hiding. Waiting for us to go. I felt him."

"He was—" Mr. Delevan stopped, then started again. "Well . . . let's say he was. Just for argument, let's say he was. Shouldn't we go back there and collar him?" And, belatedly: "*Where* was he?"

"On the other side of the fence," Kevin said. His eyes seemed to be floating. Mr. Delevan liked this less all the time. "He's already been. He's already got what *he* needs. We'll have to hurry."

Kevin was already starting for the edge of the sidewalk, meaning to cut across the town square to LaVerdiere's. Mr. Delevan reached out and grabbed him like a conductor grabbing a fellow he's caught trying to sneak aboard a train without a ticket. "*Kevin, what are you talking about?*"

And then Kevin actually said it: looked at him and *said* it. "It's coming, Dad. Please. It's my life." He looked at his father, pleading with his pallid face and his fey, floating eyes. "The dog is coming. It won't do any good to just break in and take the camera. It's gone way past that now. Please don't stop me. Please don't wake me up. It's my *life*."

Mr. Delevan made one last great effort not to give in to this creeping craziness . . . and then succumbed.

"Come on," he said, hooking his hand around his son's elbow and almost dragging him into the square. "Whatever it is, let's get it done." He paused. "Do we have enough time?"

"I'm not sure," Kevin said, and then, reluctantly: "I don't think so."

CHAPTER SEVENTEEN

Pop waited behind the board fence, looking at the Delevans through a knothole. He had put his tobacco in his back pocket so that his hands would be free to clench and unclench, clench and unclench.

You're on my property, his mind whispered at them, and if his mind had had the power to kill, he would have reached out with it and struck them both dead. *You're on my property, goddammit, you're on my property!*

What he ought to do was go get old John Law and bring him down on their fancy Castle View heads. That was what he *ought* to do. And he would have done it, too, right then, if they hadn't been standing over the wreckage of the camera the boy himself had supposedly destroyed with Pop's blessing two weeks ago. He thought maybe he would have tried to bullshit his way through anyway, but he knew how they felt about him in this town. Pangborn, Keeton, all the rest of them. Trash. That's what they thought of him. Trash.

Until they got their asses in a crack and needed a fast loan and the sun was down, that was.

Clench, unclench. Clench, unclench.

They were talking, but Pop didn't bother listening to what they were saying. His mind was a fuming forge. Now the litany had become: *They're on my goddam property and I can't do a thing about it! They're on my goddam property and I can't do a thing about it! Goddam them! Goddam them!*

At last they left. When he heard the rusty screech of the gate in the alley, Pop used his key on the one in the board fence. He slipped through and ran across the yard to his back door—ran with an unsettling fleetness for a man of seventy, with one hand clapped firmly against his upper right leg, as if, fleet or not, he was fighting a bad rheumatism pain there. In fact, Pop was feeling no pain at all. He didn't want either his keys or the change in his purse jingling, that was all. In case the Delevans were still there, lurking just beyond where he could see. Pop wouldn't have been surprised if they were doing just that. When you were dealing with skunks, you expected them to get up to stinking didos.

He slipped his keys out of his pocket. *Now* they rattled, and although the sound was muted, it seemed very loud to him. He cut his eyes to the left for a moment, sure he would see the brat's staring sheep's face. Pop's mouth was set in a hard, strained grin of fear. There was no one there.

Yet, anyway.

He found the right key, slipped it into the lock, and went in. He was careful not to open the door to the shed too wide, because the hinges picked up a squeal when you exercised them too much.

Inside, he turned the thumb-bolt with a savage twist and then went into the Emporium Galorium. He was more than at home in these shadows. He could have negotiated the narrow, junk-lined corridors in his sleep . . . *had,* in fact, although that, like a good many other things, had slipped his mind for the time being.

There was a dirty little side window near the front of the store that looked out upon the narrow alleyway the Delevans had used to trespass their way into his backyard. It also gave a sharply angled view on the sidewalk and part of the town common.

Pop slipped up to this window between piles of useless, valueless magazines that breathed their dusty yellow museum scent into the dark air. He looked out into the alley and saw it was empty. He looked to the right and saw the Delevans, wavery as fish in an aquarium through this dirty, flawed glass, crossing the common just below the bandstand. He didn't watch them out of sight in this window or go to the front windows to get a better angle on them. He guessed they were going over to LaVerdiere's, and since they had already been here, they would be asking about him. What could the little counter-slut tell them? That he had been and gone. Anything else?

Only that he had bought two pouches of tobacco.

Pop smiled.

That wasn't likely to hang him.

He found a brown bag, went out back, started for the chopping block, considered, then went to the gate in the alleyway instead. Careless once didn't mean a body had to be careless again.

After the gate was locked, he took his bag to the chopping block and picked up the pieces of shattered Polaroid camera. He worked as fast as he could, but he took time to be thorough.

He picked up everything but little shards and splinters that could be seen as no more than anonymous litter. A Police Lab investigating unit would probably be able to ID some of the stuff left around; Pop had seen TV crime shows (when he wasn't watching X-rated movies on his VCR, that was) where those scientific fellows went over the scene of a crime with little brushes and vacuums and even pairs of tweezers, putting things in little plastic bags, but the Castle Rock Sheriff's Department didn't have one of those units. And Pop doubted if Sheriff Pangborn could talk the State Police into sending their crime wagon, even if Pangborn himself could be persuaded to make the effort—not for what was no more than a case of camera theft, and that was all the Delevans could accuse him of without sounding crazy. Once he had policed the area, he went back inside, unlocked his "special" drawer, and deposited the brown bag inside. He relocked the drawer and put his keys back in his pocket. *That* was all right, then. He knew all about search warrants, too. It would be a snowy day in hell before the Delevans could get Pangborn into district court to ask for one of those. Even if he was crazy enough to try, the remains of the goddamned camera would be gone—*permanently*—long before they could turn the trick. To try and dispose of the pieces for good right now would be more dangerous than leaving them in the locked drawer. The Delevans would come back and catch him right in the middle of it. Best to wait.

Because they *would* be back.

Pop Merrill knew that as well as he knew his own name.

Later, perhaps, after all this hooraw and foolishment died down, he would be able to go to the boy and say *Yes. That's right. Everything you think I did, I did. Now why don't we just leave her alone and go back to not knowin each other . . . all right? We can afford to do that. You might not think so, at least not at first, but we can. Because look—you wanted to bust it up because you thought it was dangerous, and I wanted to sell it because I thought it was valuable. Turned out you was right and I was wrong, and that's all the revenge you're ever gonna need. If you knew me better, you'd know why—there ain't many men in this town that have ever heard me say such a thing. It sticks in my gut, is what I mean to say, but that don't matter; when I'm wrong, I like to think I'm big enough to own up to it, no matter how bad it hurts. In the end, boy, I did what you meant to do in the first place. We all came out on the same street, is what I mean to say, and I think we ought to let bygones be bygones. I know what you think of me, and I know what I think of you, and neither of us would ever vote for the other one to be Grand Marshal in the annual Fourth of July parade, but that's all right; we can live with that, can't we? What I mean to say is just this: we're both glad that goddam camera is gone, so let's call it quits and walk away.*

But that was for later, and even then it was only perhaps. It wouldn't do for right now, that was for sure. They would need time to cool down. Right now both of them would be raring to tear a chunk out of his ass, like

(*the dog in that pitcher*)

like . . . well, never mind what they'd be like. The important thing was to be down here, business as usual and as innocent as a goddam baby when they got back.

Because they *would* be back.

But that was all right. It was all right because—

"B'cause things are under control," Pop whispered. "*That's* what I mean to say."

Now he did go to the front door, and switched the CLOSED sign over to OPEN (he then turned it promptly back to CLOSED again, but this Pop did not observe himself doing, nor would he remember it later). All right; that was a start. What was next? Make it look like just another normal day, no more and no less. He had to be all surprise and what-in-the-tarnation-are-you-talking-about when they came back with steam coming out of their collars, all ready to do or die for what had already been killed just as dead as sheepdip.

So . . . what was the most normal thing they could find him doing when they came back, with Sheriff Pangborn or without him?

Pop's eye fixed on the cuckoo clock hanging from the beam beside that nice bureau he'd gotten at an estate sale in Sebago a month or six weeks ago. Not a very nice cuckoo clock, probably one originally purchased with trading stamps by some soul trying to be thrifty (people who could only *try* to be thrifty were, in Pop's estimation, poor puzzled souls who drifted through life in a vague and constant state of disappointment). Still, if he could put it right so it would run a little, he could maybe sell it to one of the skiers who would be up in another month or two, somebody who needed a clock at their cottage or ski-lodge because the last bargain had up and died and who didn't understand yet (and probably never would) that another bargain wasn't the solution but the problem.

Pop would feel sorry for that person, and would dicker with him or her as fairly as he thought he could, but he wouldn't disappoint the buyer. *Caveet emperor* was not only what he *meant* to say but often *did* say, and he had a living to make, didn't he?

Yes. So he would just sit back there at his worktable and fuss around with that clock, see if he could get it running, and when the Delevans got back, that was what they would find him doing. Maybe there'd even be a few prospective customers browsing around by then; he could hope, although this was always a slack time of year. Customers would be icing on the cake, anyway. The important thing was how it would look: just a fellow with nothing to hide, going through the ordinary motions and ordinary rhythms of his ordinary day.

Pop went over to the beam and took the cuckoo clock down, being careful not to tangle up the counterweights. He carried it back to his worktable, humming a little. He set it down, then felt his back pocket. Fresh tobacco. That was good, too.

Pop thought he would have himself a little pipe while he worked.

CHAPTER EIGHTEEN

"You can't *know* he was in here, Kevin!" Mr. Delevan was still protesting feebly as they went into LaVerdiere's.

Ignoring him, Kevin went straight to the counter where Molly Durham stood. Her urge to vomit had passed off, and she felt much better. The whole thing seemed a little silly now, like a nightmare you have and then wake up from and after the initial relief you think: *I was afraid of* THAT? *How could I ever have thought* THAT *was really happening to me, even in a dream?*

But when the Delevan boy presented his drawn white face at the counter, she *knew* how you could be afraid, yes, oh yes, even of things as ridiculous as the things which happened in dreams, because she was tumbled back into her own waking dreamscape again.

The thing was, Kevin Delevan had almost the same *look* on his face: as though he were so deep inside somewhere that when his voice and his gaze finally reached her, they seemed almost expended.

"Pop Merrill was in here," he said. "What did he buy?"

"Please excuse my son," Mr. Delevan said. "He's not feeling w—"

Then *he* saw *Molly's* face and stopped. She looked like she had just seen a man lose his arm to a factory machine.

"Oh!" she said. "Oh my God!"

"Was it film?" Kevin asked her.

"What's wrong with him?" Molly asked faintly. "I *knew* something was the minute he walked in. What is it? Has he . . . done something?"

Jesus, John Delevan thought. *He DOES know. It's all true, then.*

At that moment, Mr. Delevan made a quietly heroic decision: he gave up entirely. He gave up entirely and put himself and what he believed could and could not be true entirely in his son's hands.

"It was, wasn't it?" Kevin pressed her. His urgent face rebuked her for her flutters and tremors. "Polaroid film. From *that*." He pointed at the display.

"Yes." Her complexion was as pale as china; the bit of rouge she had put on that morning stood out in hectic, flaring patches. "He was so . . . strange. Like a talking doll. What's wrong with him? What—"

But Kevin had whirled away, back to his father.

"I need a camera," he rapped. "I need it right now. A Polaroid Sun 660. They have them. They're even on special. See?"

And in spite of his decision, Mr. Delevan's mouth would not quite let go of the last clinging shreds of rationality. "Why—" he began, and that was as far as Kevin let him get.

"*I don't KNOW why!*" he shouted, and Molly Durham moaned. She didn't want to throw up now; Kevin Delevan was scary, but not *that* scary. What she wanted to do right now was simply go home and creep up to her bedroom and draw the covers over her head. "*But we have to have it, and time's almost up, Dad!*"

"Give me one of those cameras," Mr. Delevan said, drawing his wallet out with shaking hands, unaware that Kevin had already darted to the display.

"Just take one," she heard a trembling voice entirely unlike her own say. "Just take one and go."

CHAPTER NINETEEN

Across the square, Pop Merrill, who believed he was peacefully repairing a cheap cuckoo clock, innocent as a babe in arms, finished loading Kevin's camera with one of the film packs. He snapped it shut. It made its squidgy little whine.

Damn cuckoo sounds like he's got a bad case of laryngitis. Slipped a gear, I guess. Well, I got the cure for that.

"I'll fix you," Pop said, and raised the camera. He applied one blank eye to the viewfinder with the hairline crack which was so tiny you didn't even see it when you got your eye up to it. The camera was aimed at the front of the store, but *that* didn't matter; wherever you pointed it, it was aimed at a certain black dog that wasn't any dog God had ever made in a little town called for the want of a better word Polaroidsville, which He also hadn't ever made.

FLASH!

That squidgy little whine as Kevin's camera pushed out a new picture.

"There," Pop said with quiet satisfaction. "Maybe I'll do more than get you talking, bird. What I mean to say is I might just get you *singing*. I don't promise, but I'll give her a try."

Pop grinned a dry, leathery grin and pushed the button again.

FLASH!

They were halfway across the square when John Delevan saw a silent white light fill the dirty windows of the Emporium Galorium. The *light* was silent, but following it, like an aftershock, he heard a low, dark rumble that seemed to come to his ears from the old man's junk-store . . . but only because the old man's junk-store was the only place it could find a way to get out. Where it seemed to be *emanating* from was under the earth . . . or was it just that the earth itself seemed the only place large enough to cradle the owner of that voice?

"Run, Dad!" Kevin cried. *"He's started doing it!"*

That flash recurred, lighting the windows like a heatless stroke of electricity. It was followed by that subaural growl again, the sound of a sonic boom in a wind-tunnel, the sound of some animal which was horrible beyond comprehension being kicked out of its sleep.

Mr. Delevan, helpless to stop himself and almost unaware of what he was doing, opened his mouth to tell his son that a light that big and bright could not possibly be coming from the built-in flash of a Polaroid camera, but Kevin had already started to run.

Mr. Delevan began to run himself, knowing perfectly well what he meant to do: catch up to his son and collar him and drag him away before something dreadful beyond his grasp of all dreadful things could happen.

CHAPTER TWENTY

The second Polaroid Pop took forced the first one out of the slot. It fluttered down to the top of the desk, where it landed with a thud heavier than such a square of chemically treated cardboard could possibly make. The Sun dog filled almost the entire frame now; the foreground was its impossible head, the black pits of the eyes, the smoking, teeth-filled jaws. The skull seemed to be elongating into a shape like a bullet or a teardrop as the dog-thing's speed and the shortening distance between it and the lens combined to drive it further out of focus. Only the tops of the pickets in the fence behind it were visible now; the bulk of the thing's flexed shoulders ate up the rest of the frame.

Kevin's birthday string tie, which had rested next to the Sun camera in his drawer, showed at the bottom of the frame, winking back a shaft of hazy sunlight.

"Almost got you, you son of a whore," Pop said in a high, cracked voice. His eyes were blinded by the light. He saw neither dog nor camera. He saw only the voiceless cuckoo which had become his life's mission. "You'll sing, damn you! I'll *make* you sing!"

FLASH!

The third picture pushed the second from the slot. It fell too fast, more like a chunk of stone than a square of cardboard, and when it hit the desk, it dug through the ancient frayed blotter there and sent startled splinters flying up from the wood beneath.

In this picture, the dog's head was torn even further out of focus; it had become a long column of flesh that gave it a strange, almost three-dimensional aspect.

In the third one, still poking out of the slot in the bottom of the camera, the Sun dog's snout seemed, impossibly, to be coming back into focus again. It was impossible because it was as close to the lens as it could get; so close it seemed to be the snout of some sea-monster just below that fragile meniscus we call the surface.

"Damn thing still ain't quite right," Pop said.

His finger pushed the Polaroid's trigger again.

CHAPTER TWENTY-ONE

Kevin ran up the steps of the Emporium Galorium. His father reached for him, caught nothing but the air an inch from the fluttering tail of Kevin's shirt, stumbled, and landed on the heels of his hands. They slid across the second step from the top, sending a quiver of small splinters into his skin.

"Kevin!"

He looked up and for a moment the world was almost lost in another of those dazzling white flashes. This time the roar was much louder. It was the sound of a crazed animal on the verge of making its weakening cage give it up. He saw Kevin with his head down, one hand shielding his eyes from the white glare, frozen in that stroboscopic light as if he himself had turned into a photograph. He saw cracks like quicksilver jig-jag their way down the show windows.

"*Kevin, look ou—*"

The glass burst outward in a glittery spray and Mr. Delevan ducked his own head. Glass flew around him in a squall. He felt it patter into his hair and both cheeks were scratched, but none of the glass dug deeply into either the boy or the man; most of it had been pulverized to crumbs.

There was a splintering crunch. He looked up again and saw that Kevin had gained entry just as Mr. Delevan had thought they might earlier: by ramming the now-glassless door with his shoulder and tearing the new locking bolt right through the old, rotted wood.

"*KEVIN, GODDAMMIT!*" he bawled. He got up, almost stumbled to one knee again as his feet tangled together, then lurched upright and plunged after his son.

———

Something had happened to the goddam cuckoo clock. Something *bad*.

It was striking again and again—bad enough, but that wasn't all. It had also gained weight in Pop's hands . . . and it seemed to be growing uncomfortably hot, as well.

Pop looked down at it, and suddenly tried to scream in horror through jaws which felt as if they had been wired together somehow.

He realized he had been struck blind, and he *also* suddenly realized that what he held was not a cuckoo clock at all.

He tried to make his hands relax their death-grip on the camera and was horrified to find he could not open his fingers. The field of gravity around the camera seemed to have increased. And the horrid thing was growing steadily hotter. Between Pop's splayed, white-nailed fingers, the gray plastic of the camera's housing had begun to smoke.

His right index finger began to crawl upward toward the red shutter-button like a crippled fly.

"No," he muttered, and then, in a plea: *"Please . . ."*

His finger paid no attention. It reached the red button and settled upon it just as Kevin slammed his shoulder into the door and burst in. Glass from the door's panes crunched and sprayed.

Pop didn't push the button. Even blind, even feeling the flesh of his fingers begin to smoulder and scorch, he knew he didn't push the button. But as his finger settled upon it, that gravitational field first seemed to double, then treble. He tried to hold his finger up and off the button. It was like trying to hold the push-up position on the planet Jupiter.

"Drop it!" the kid screamed from somewhere out on the rim of his darkness. "Drop it, *drop it!*"

"NO!" Pop screamed back. *"What I mean to say is I CAN'T!"*

The red button began to slide in toward its contact point.

Kevin was standing with his legs spread, bent over the camera they had just taken from LaVerdiere's, the box it had come in lying at his feet. He had managed to hit the button that released the front of the camera on its hinge, revealing the wide loading slot. He was trying to jam one of the film packs into it, and it stubbornly refused to go—it was as if this camera had turned traitor, too, possibly in sympathy to its brother.

Pop screamed again, but this time there were no words, only an inarticulate cry of pain and fear. Kevin smelled hot plastic and roasting flesh. He looked up and saw the Polaroid was melting, actually *melting,* in the old man's frozen hands. Its square, boxy silhouette was rearranging itself into an odd, hunched shape. Somehow the glass of both the viewfinder and the lens had also become plastic. Instead of breaking or popping out of the camera's increasingly shapeless shell, they were elongating and drooping like taffy, becoming a pair of grotesque eyes like those in a mask of tragedy.

Dark plastic, heated to a sludge like warm wax, ran over Pop's fingers and the backs of his hands in thick runnels, carving troughs in his flesh. The plastic cauterized what it burned, but Kevin saw blood squeezing from the sides of these runnels and dripping down Pop's flesh to strike the table in smoking droplets which sizzled like hot fat.

"*Your film's still wrapped up!*" his father bawled from behind him, breaking Kevin's paralysis. "*Unwrap it! Give it to me!*"

His father reached around him, bumping Kevin so hard he almost knocked him over. He snatched the film pack, with its heavy paper-foil wrapping still on it, and ripped the end. He stripped it off.

"*HELP ME!*" Pop screeched, the last coherent words either of them heard him say.

"Quick!" his father yelled, putting the fresh film pack back in his hands. "Quick!"

The sizzle of hot flesh. The patter of hot blood on the desk, what had been a shower now becoming a storm as the bigger veins and arteries in Pop's fingers and the backs of his hands began to let go. A brook of hot, running plastic braceleted his left wrist and the bundle of veins so close to the surface there let go, spraying out blood as if through a rotten gasket which has first begun to leak in several places and now begins to simply disintegrate under the insistent, beating pressure.

Pop howled like an animal.

Kevin tried to jam the film pack in again and cried out "*Fuck!*" as it still refused to go.

"*It's backwards!*" Mr. Delevan hollered. He tried to snatch the camera from Kevin, and Kevin tore away, leaving his father with a scrap of shirt and no more. He pulled the film pack out and for a moment it jittered on the ends of his fingers, almost dropping to the floor—which, he felt, longed to actually hump itself up into a fist and smash it when it came down.

Then he had it, turned it around, socked it home, and slammed the front of the camera, which was hanging limply downward like a creature with a broken neck, shut on its hinge.

Pop howled again, and—

FLASH!

CHAPTER TWENTY-TWO

This time it was like standing in the center of a sun which goes supernova in one sudden, heatless gust of light. Kevin felt as if his shadow had actually been hammered off his heels and driven into the wall. Perhaps this was at least partly true, for all of the wall behind him was instantly flash-baked and threaded with a thousand crazy cracks except for one sunken area where his shadow fell. His outline, as clear and unmistakable as a silhouette cut-out, was tattooed there with one elbow stuck out in a flying wedge, caught and frozen even as the arm which cast the shadow left its frozen image behind, rising to bring the new camera up to his face.

The top of the camera in Pop's hands tore free of the rest with a thick sound like a very fat man clearing his throat. The Sun dog growled, and this time that bass thunder was loud enough, clear enough, *near* enough, to shatter the glass in the fronts of the clocks and to send the glass in the mirrors and in the frames of pictures belching across the floor in momentary crystal arcs of amazing and improbable beauty.

The camera did not moan or whine this time; the sound of its mechanism was a scream, high and drilling, like a woman who is dying in the throes of a breech delivery. The square of paper which shoved and bulled its way out of that slitted opening smoked and fumed. Then the dark delivery-slot itself began to melt, one side drooping downward, the other wrinkling upward, all of it beginning to yawn like a toothless mouth. A bubble was forming upon the shiny surface of the last picture, which still hung in the widening mouth of the channel from which the Polaroid Sun gave birth to its photographs.

As Kevin watched, frozen, looking through a curtain of flashing, zinging dots that last white explosion had put in front of his eyes, the Sun dog roared again. The sound was smaller now, with less of that sense that it was coming from beneath and from everywhere, but it was also more deadly because it was more *real,* more *here.*

Part of the dissolving camera blew backward in a great gray gobbet, striking Pop Merrill's neck and expanding into a necklace. Suddenly both Pop's jugular vein and carotid artery gave way in spraying gouts of blood that jetted upward and outward in bright-red spirals. Pop's head whipped bonelessly backward.

The bubble on the surface of the picture grew. The picture itself began to jitter in the yawning slot at the bottom of the now-decapitated camera. Its sides began to spread, as if the picture was no longer on cardboard at all but some flexible substance like knitted nylon. It wiggled back and forth in the slot, and Kevin thought of the cowboy boots he had gotten for his birthday two years ago, and how he had had to wiggle his feet into them, because they were a little too tight.

The edges of the picture struck the edges of the camera delivery-slot, where they should have stuck firmly. But the camera was no longer a solid; was, in fact, losing all resemblance to what it had been. The edges of the picture sliced through its sides as cleanly as the razor-sharp sides of a good double-edged knife slide through tender meat. They poked through what had been the Polaroid's housing, sending gray drops of smoking plastic flying into the dim air. One landed on a dry, crumbling stack of old *Popular Mechanics* magazines and burrowed a fuming, charred hole into them.

The dog roared again, an angry, ugly sound—the cry of something with nothing but rending and killing on its mind. Those things, and nothing else.

The picture teetered on the edge of the sagging, dissolving slit, which now looked more like the bell of some misshapen wind instrument than anything else, and then fell forward to the desk with the speed of a stone tumbling into a well.

Kevin felt a hand claw at his shoulder.

"What's it doing?" his father asked hoarsely. "Jesus Christ almighty, Kevin, *what's it doing?*"

Kevin heard himself answer in a remote, almost disinterested voice: "Being born."

CHAPTER TWENTY-THREE

Pop Merrill died leaning back in the chair behind his worktable, where he had spent so many hours sitting: sitting and smoking; sitting and fixing things up so they would run for at least awhile and he could sell the worthless to the thoughtless; sitting and loaning money to the impulsive and the improvident after the sun went down. He died staring up at the ceiling, from which his own blood dripped back down to splatter on his cheeks and into his open eyes.

His chair overbalanced and spilled his lolling body onto the floor. His purse and his key-ring clattered.

On his desk, the final Polaroid continued to jiggle about restlessly. Its sides spread apart, and Kevin seemed to sense some unknown thing, both alive and not alive, groaning in horrid, unknowable labor pains.

"We've got to get out of here," his father panted, pulling at him. John Delevan's eyes were large and frenzied, riveted on that spreading, moving photograph which now covered half of Merrill's worktable. It no longer resembled a photograph at all. Its sides bulged out like the cheeks of someone trying frantically to whistle. The shiny bubble, now a foot high, humped and shuddered. Strange, unnameable colors raced aimlessly back and forth across a surface which seemed to have broken some oily sort of sweat. That roar, full of frustration and purpose and frantic hunger, ripped through his brain again and again, threatening to split it and let in madness.

Kevin pulled away from him, ripping his shirt along the shoulder. His voice was full of a deep, strange calm. "No—it would just come after us. I think it wants me, because if it wanted Pop it's already got him and I was the one who owned the camera first, anyway. But it wouldn't stop there. It'd take you, too. And it might not stop there, either."

"*You can't do anything!*" his father screamed.

"Yes," Kevin said. "I've got one chance."

And raised the camera.

The edges of the picture reached the edges of the worktable. Instead of lolling over, they curled up and continued to twist and spread. Now they resembled odd wings which were somehow equipped with lungs and were trying to breathe in some tortured fashion.

The entire surface of the amorphous, pulsing thing continued to puff up; what should have been flat surface had become a horrid tumor, its lumped and cratered sides trickling with vile liquid. It gave off the bland smell of head cheese.

The dog's roars had become continuous, the trapped and furious belling of a hell-hound bent on escape, and some of the late Pop Merrill's clocks began to strike again and again, as if in protest.

Mr. Delevan's frantic urge to escape had deserted him; he felt overcome by a deep and dangerous lassitude, a kind of lethal sleepiness.

Kevin held the camera's viewfinder to his eye. He had only been deer-hunting a few times, but he remembered how it was when it was your turn to wait, hidden, with your rifle as your hunting partners walked through the woods toward you, deliberately making as much noise as they could, hoping to drive something out of the trees and into the clearing where you were waiting, your field of fire a safe angle that would cross in front of the men. You didn't have to worry about hitting them; you only had to worry about hitting the deer.

There was time to wonder if you *could* hit it, when and if it showed itself. There was also time to wonder if you could bring yourself to fire at all. Time to hope that the deer would remain hypothetical, so the test did not have to be made . . . and so it had always turned out to be. The one time there *had* been a deer, his father's friend Bill Roberson had been lying up in the blind. Mr. Roberson had put the bullet just where you were supposed to put it, at the juncture of neck and shoulder, and they had gotten the game-warden to take their pictures around it, a twelve-point buck any man would be happy to brag on.

Bet you wish it'd been your turn in the puckies, don't you, son? the game-warden had asked, ruffling Kevin's hair (he had been twelve then, the growth spurt which had begun about seventeen months ago and which had so far taken him to just an inch under six feet still a year away . . . which meant he had not been big enough to be resentful of a man who wanted to ruffle his hair). Kevin had nodded, keeping his secret to himself: he was *glad* it hadn't been his turn in the puckies, his the rifle which must be responsible for throwing the slug or not throwing it . . . and, if he had turned out to have the courage to do the shooting, his reward would have been only another troublesome responsibility: to shoot the buck clean. He didn't know if he could have mustered the courage to put another bullet in the thing if the kill *wasn't* clean, or the strength to chase the trail of its blood and steaming, startled droppings and finish what he had started if it ran.

He had smiled up at the game-warden and nodded and his dad had snapped a picture of *that,* and there had never been any need to tell his dad that the thought going on behind that upturned brow and under the game-warden's ruffling hand had been *No. I don't wish it. The world is full of tests, but twelve's too young to go hunting them. I'm glad it was Mr. Roberson. I'm not ready yet to try a man's tests.*

But now he was the one in the blind, wasn't he? And the animal was coming, wasn't it? And it was no harmless eater of grasses this time, was it? This was a killing engine big enough and mean enough to swallow a tiger whole, and it meant to kill *him,* and that was only for starters, and he was the only one that could stop it.

The thought of turning the Polaroid over to his father crossed his mind, but only momentarily. Something deep inside himself knew the truth: to pass the camera would be tantamount to murdering his father and committing suicide himself. His father believed *something,* but that wasn't specific enough. The camera wouldn't work for his father even if his father managed to break out of his current stunned condition and press the shutter.

It would only work for him.

So he waited on the test, peering through the viewfinder of the camera as if it were the gunsight of a rifle, peering at the photograph as it continued to spread and force that shiny, liquescent bubble wider and wider and higher and higher.

Then the actual birthing of the Sun dog into this world began to happen. The camera seemed to gain weight and turn to lead as the thing roared again with a sound like a whiplash loaded with steel shot. The camera trembled in his hands and he could feel his wet, slippery fingers simply wanting to uncurl and let go. He held on, his lips pulling back from his teeth in a sick and desperate grin.

Sweat ran into one eye, momentarily doubling his vision. He threw his head back, snapping his hair off his forehead and out of his eyebrows, and then nestled his staring eye back into the viewfinder as a great ripping sound, like heavy cloth being torn in half by strong, slow hands, filled the Emporium Galorium.

The shiny surface of the bubble tore open. Red smoke, like the blast from a tea-kettle set in front of red neon, billowed out.

The thing roared again, an angry, homicidal sound. A gigantic jaw, filled with croggled teeth, burst up through the shrivelling membrane of the now-collapsing bubble like the jaw of a breaching pilot whale. It ripped and chewed and gnawed at the membrane, which gave way with gummy splattering sounds.

The clocks struck wildly, crazily.

His father grabbed him again, so hard that Kevin's teeth rapped against the plastic body of the camera and it came within a hair of spilling out of his hands and shattering on the floor.

"*Shoot it!*" his father screamed over the thing's bellowing din. "*Shoot it, Kevin, if you can shoot it, SHOOT IT NOW, Christ Jesus, it's going to—*"

Kevin yanked away from his father's hand. "Not yet," he said. "Not just y—"

The thing *screamed* at the sound of Kevin's voice. The Sun dog lunged up from wherever it was, driving the picture still wider. It gave and stretched with a groaning sound. This was replaced by the thick cough of ripping fabric again.

And suddenly the Sun dog was up, its head rising black and rough and tangled through the hole in reality like some weird periscope which was all tangled metal and glittering, glaring lenses . . . except it wasn't metal but that twisted, spiky fur Kevin was looking at, and those were not lenses but the thing's insane, raging eyes.

It caught at the neck, the spines of its pelt shredding the edges of the hole it had made into a strange sunburst pattern. It roared again, and sickly yellow-red fire licked out of its mouth.

John Delevan took a step backward and struck a table overloaded with thick copies of *Weird Tales* and *Fantastic Universe*. The table tilted and Mr. Delevan flailed helplessly against it, his heels first rocking back and then shooting out from under him. Man and table went over with a crash. The Sun dog roared again, then dipped its head with an unsuspected delicacy and tore at the membrane which held it. The membrane ripped. The thing barked out a thin stream of fire which ignited the membrane and turned it to ash. The beast lunged upward again and Kevin saw that the thing on the tie around its neck was no longer a tie-clasp but the spoon-shaped tool which Pop Merrill had used to clean his pipe.

In that moment a clean calmness fell over the boy. His father bellowed in surprise and fear as he tried to untangle himself from the table he had fallen over, but Kevin took no notice. The cry seemed to come from a great distance away.

It's all right, Dad, he thought, fixing the struggling, emerging beast more firmly in the viewfinder. *It's all right, don't you see? It* can *be all right, anyway . . . because the charm it wears has changed.*

He thought that perhaps the Sun dog had its master, too . . . and its master had realized that Kevin was no longer sure prey.

And perhaps there was a dog-catcher in that strange nowhere town of Polaroidsville; there must be, else why had the fat woman been in his dream? It was the fat woman who had told him what he must do, either on her own or because that dog-catcher had put her there for him to see and notice: the two-dimensional fat woman with her two-dimensional shopping-cart full of two-dimensional cameras. *Be careful, boy. Pop's dog broke his leash and he's a mean un. . . . It's hard to take his pitcher, but you can't do it at all, 'less you have a cam'ra.*

And now he had his camera, didn't he? It was not sure, not by any means, but at least he had it.

The dog paused, head turning almost aimlessly . . . until its muddy, burning gaze settled on Kevin Delevan. Its black lips peeled back from its corkscrewed boar's fangs, its muzzle opened to reveal the smoking channel of its throat, and it gave a high, drilling howl of fury. The ancient hanging globes that lit Pop's place at night shattered one after another in rows, sending down spinning shards of frosted fly-beshitted glass. It lunged, its broad, panting chest bursting through the membrane between the worlds.

Kevin's finger settled on the Polaroid's trigger.

It lunged again, and now its front legs popped free, and those cruel spurs of bone, so like gigantic thorns, scraped and scrabbled for purchase on the desk. They dug long vertical scars in the heavy rock-maple. Kevin could hear the dusky thud-and-scratch of its pistoning rear legs digging for a grip down there (wherever *down there* was), and he knew that this was the final short stretch of seconds in which it would be trapped and at his mercy; the next convulsive lunge would send it flying over the desk, and once free of the hole through which it was squirming, it would move as fast as liquid death, charging across the space between them, setting his pants ablaze with its fiery breath split-seconds before it tore into his warm innards.

Very clearly, Kevin instructed: "Say *cheese,* you motherfucker."

And triggered the Polaroid.

CHAPTER TWENTY-FOUR

The flash was so bright that Kevin could not conceive of it later; could, in fact, barely remember it at all. The camera he was holding did not grow hot and melt; instead there were three or four quick, decisive breaking sounds from inside it as its ground-glass lenses burst and its springs either snapped or simply disintegrated.

In the white afterglare he saw the Sun dog *frozen,* a perfect black-and-white Polaroid photograph, its head thrown back, every twisting fold and crevasse in its wildly bushed-out fur caught like the complicated topography of a dry river-valley. Its teeth shone, no longer subtly shaded yellow but as white and nasty as old bones in that sterile emptiness where water had quit running millennia ago. Its single swollen eye, robbed of the dark and bloody porthole of iris by the merciless flash, was as white as an eye in the head of a Greek bust. Smoking snot drizzled from its flared nostrils and ran like hot lava in the narrow gutters between its rolled-back muzzle and its gums.

It was like a negative of all the Polaroids Kevin had ever seen: black-and-white instead of color, and in three dimensions instead of two. And it was like watching a living creature turned instantly to stone by a careless look at the head of Medusa.

"You're *done,* you son of a bitch!" Kevin screamed in a cracked, hysterical voice, and as if in agreement, the thing's frozen forelegs lost their hold on the desk and it began to disappear, first slowly and then rapidly, into the hole from which it had come. It went with a rocky coughing sound, like a landslide.

What would I see if I ran over now and looked into that hole? he wondered incoherently. *Would I see that house, that fence, the old man with his shopping-cart, staring with wide-eyed wonder at the face of a giant, not a boy but a Boy, staring back at him from a torn and charred hole in the hazy sky? Would it suck me in? What?*

Instead, he dropped the Polaroid and raised his hands to his face.

Only John Delevan, lying on the floor, saw the final act: the twisted, dead membrane shrivelling in on itself, pulling into a complicated but unimportant node around the hole, crumpling there, and then falling (or being *inhaled*) into itself.

There was a whooping sound of air, which rose from a broad gasp to a thin tea-kettle whistle.

Then it turned inside-out and was gone. Simply gone, as if it had never been.

Getting slowly and shakily to his feet, Mr. Delevan saw that the final inrush (or outrush, he supposed, depending on which side of that hole you were on) of air had pulled the desk-blotter and the other Polaroids the old man had taken in with it.

His son was standing in the middle of the floor with his hands over his face, weeping.

"Kevin," he said quietly, and put his arms around his boy.

"I had to take its picture," Kevin said through his tears and through his hands. "It was the only way to get rid of it. I had to take the rotten whoredog's picture. *That's* what I mean to say."

"Yes." He hugged him tighter. "Yes, and you did it."

Kevin looked at his father with naked, streaming eyes. "*That's* how I had to shoot it, Dad. Do you see?"

"Yes," his father said. "Yes, I see that." He kissed Kevin's hot cheek again. "Let's go home, son."

He tightened his grip around Kevin's shoulders, wanting to lead him toward the door and away from the smoking, bloody body of the old man (Kevin hadn't really noticed yet, Mr. Delevan thought, but if they spent much longer here, he would), and for a moment Kevin resisted him.

"What are people going to *say*?" Kevin asked, and his tone was so prim and spinsterish that Mr. Delevan laughed in spite of his own sizzling nerves.

"Let them say whatever they want," he told Kevin. "They'll never get within shouting distance of the truth, and I don't think anyone will try very hard, anyway." He paused. "No one really liked him much, you know."

"I never *want* to be in shouting distance of the truth," Kevin whispered. "Let's go home."

"Yes. I love you, Kevin."

"I love you, too," Kevin said hoarsely, and they went out of the smoke and the stink of old things best left forgotten and into the bright light of day. Behind them, a pile of old magazines burst into flame . . . and the fire was quick to stretch out its hungry orange fingers.

EPILOGUE

It was Kevin Delevan's sixteenth birthday, and he got exactly what he wanted: a WordStar 70 PC and word processor. It was a could, in fact, barely remember it at all. The camera he was holding afforded it in the old days, but in January, about three months after that final confrontation in the Emporium Galorium, Aunt Hilda had died quietly in her sleep. She had indeed Done Something for Kevin and Meg; had, in fact, Done Quite a Lot for the Whole Family. When the will cleared probate in early June, the Delevans found themselves richer by nearly seventy thousand dollars . . . and that was after taxes, not before.

"Jeez, it's neat! Thank you!" Kevin cried, and kissed his mother, his father, and even his sister, Meg (who giggled but, being a year older, made no attempt to rub it off; Kevin couldn't decide if this change was a step in the right direction or not). He spent much of the afternoon in his room, fussing over it and trying out the test program.

Around four o'clock, he came downstairs and into his father's den. "Where's Mom and Meg?" he asked.

"They've gone out to the crafts fair at . . . Kevin? Kevin, what's wrong?"

"You better come upstairs," Kevin said hollowly.

At the door to his room, he turned his pale face toward his father's equally pale face. There was something more to pay, Mr. Delevan had been thinking as he followed his son up the stairs. Of course there was. And hadn't he also learned that from Reginald Marion "Pop" Merrill? The debt you incurred was what hurt you.

It was the *interest* that broke your back.

"Can we get another one of these?" Kevin asked, pointing to the laptop computer which stood open on his desk, glowing a mystic yellow oblong of light onto the blotter.

"I don't know," Mr. Delevan said, approaching the desk. Kevin stood behind him, a pallid watcher. "I guess, if we *had* to—"

He stopped, looking down at the screen.

"I booted up the word-processing program and typed 'The quick brown fox jumped over the lazy sleeping dog,'" Kevin said. "Only *that* was what came out of the printer."

Mr. Delevan stood, silently reading the hard copy. His hands and forehead felt very cold. The words there read:

```
The dog is loose again.
  It is not sleeping.
    It is not lazy.
  It's coming for you, Kevin.
```

The original debt was what hurt you, he thought again; it was the interest that broke your back. The last two lines read:

```
    It's very hungry.
  And it's VERY angry.
```